No one combines the thrill of attraction with jolting suspense the way Linda Howard has in her acclaimed bestsellers. Now, two of her classic novels are brought together to savor all over again—or discover for the first time—in a collection that burns with the heat of desire . . . and the mysteries of the night.

"Small towns are the perfect background for mysterious secrets, and Ms. Howard pens a tale loaded with them. Her sensuous style of writing makes the reader aware of the all-consuming desire between the hero and the heroine. Add to this the dramatic climax, and you get extraordinary pleasure from this novel."

—*Rendezvous*

LINDA HOWARD

NIGHT MOVES

Dream Man

After the Night

AFTER THE NIGHT

A poor, outcast child in Prescott, Louisiana, Faith Devlin had always adored the town's golden boy from afar. But he called her white trash that sultry Southern night when his rich, respected father disappeared, along with her pretty mom. Now Faith wanted to hate Gray Rouillard . . . not to feel a powerful surge of desire. But she couldn't quench her passion, any more than she could hide the truth about the past she had waited so long to unravel.

Even when he raised hell, Gray Rouillard did it with style. Reckless, charming, and backed by Rouillard money, Gray controlled the town of Prescott—and Devlin was a name he never wanted to hear again. But when he gazed at Faith Devlin, all he saw was a swirl of tangled sheets and her silken flesh beneath him. To care for her was impossible, unthinkable . . . because Gray Rouillard planned to use all his power to ruin her.

After the Night

❧ One ❧

It was a good day for dreaming. It was late in the afternoon, the sun throwing long shadows when it could manage to break through the thick woods, but for the most part the translucent golden light was tangled in the tops of the trees, leaving the forest floor mysteriously shadowed. The hot, humid summer air was redolent with the pink sweetness of honeysuckle nectar, all mingled with the rich, brown odor of the earth and rotting vegetation as well as the crisp green scent of the leaves. Odors had color for Faith Devlin, and since she'd been a little girl she had entertained herself by coloring the smells around her.

Most of the colors were obvious, drawn from the way something looked. Of course the earth smelled brown; of course that fresh, tangy scent of leaves would be green in her mind. Grapefruit smelled bright yellow; she'd never eaten one, but once had picked up one in the grocery store and hesitantly sniffed its skin, and the scent had exploded on her taste buds, sour and sweet all at the same time.

The smell of things was easy to color in her mind; the color scent of people was more difficult, because people were never just one thing, but different colors mixed together. Colors didn't mean the same in people smells that they did in thing smells. Her mother, Renee, had a dark, spicy red

1

scent, with a few sworls of black and yellow, but the spicy red almost crowded out all the other colors. Yellow was good in things, but not in people; neither was green, or at least some shades of it. Her father, Amos, was a sickening mixture of green, purple, yellow, and black. That one was real easy, because from a very early age she had associated him with vomit. Drink and puke, drink and puke, that's all Pa did. Well, and pee. He peed a lot.

The best smell in the world, Faith thought as she meandered through the woods, staring up at the captured sunlight and holding her secret happiness cradled deep in her chest, was Gray Rouillard. Faith lived for the glimpses of him she got in town, and if she was close enough to hear the deep, dark rumble of his voice, she trembled with joy. Today she'd gotten close enough to *smell* him, and he had actually touched her! She was still giddy from the experience.

She had gone into the drugstore in Prescott with Jodie, her older sister, because Jodie had stolen a couple of bucks from Renee's purse and wanted to buy some fingernail polish. Jodie's smell was orange and yellow, a pale imitation of Renee's scent. They had been coming out of the drugstore, the precious hot pink polish carefully tucked into Jodie's bra so Renee wouldn't see it. Jodie had been wearing a bra for almost three years now, and she was only thirteen, a fact she used to taunt Faith whenever she thought about it, because Faith was eleven and still didn't have any boobs. Lately Faith's flat, childish little nipples had begun to swell, though, and she was in an agony of embarrassment that someone would notice them. She had been intensely conscious of them poking out under the thin, purple LSU T-shirt she wore, but when they almost collided with Gray on the sidewalk as he was going into the drugstore and they were coming out, Faith forgot about the flimsiness of her shirt.

"Nice shirt," Gray had said, amusement dancing in his dark eyes, and patted her on the shoulder. Gray was home for the summer from college. He played football for LSU, a starting linebacker in his freshman year. He was nineteen, six foot three and still growing, and weighed a hard-packed two hundred thirty pounds. Faith knew because she'd read all that in the sports page of the local newspaper. She knew he ran a 4.6 forty, and had great lateral speed, whatever that was. She also knew that he was beautiful, not in a pretty way, but in the same wild, powerful way that his father's prize stallion, Maximillian, was beautiful. His French Creole ancestry was obvious in his dark coloring, and in the clear, strong bones of his face. His thick black hair hung down to his shoulders, making him look like a medieval warrior accidentally set down in the present time. Faith read every romance about medieval knights and their fair ladies that she could get her hands on, so she knew a knight when she saw one.

Her shoulder had tingled where Gray touched it, and her swelling nipples throbbed, making her blush and duck her head. Her senses were whirling dizzily with his scent, a rich, indefinable blend that she couldn't describe, warm and musky, with an even deeper red than Renee's, full of tantalizing colors in deep, luxurious hues.

Jodie thrust out her round breasts, covered by a sleeveless, hot pink blouse. She had left the top two buttons undone. "What about *my* shirt?" she asked, pouting a little to make her lips stick out more too, as she had seen Renee do thousands of times.

"Wrong color," Gray had said, his voice going hard and contempt leaking into the tone. Faith knew why. It was because Renee was sleeping with his father, Guy. She'd heard the way others talked about Renee, knew what "whore" meant.

He had brushed past them then, pushing open the door and disappearing into the drugstore. Jodie stared after him for a few seconds, then turned her greedy eyes on Faith. "Let me have your shirt," she said.

"It's too little for you," Faith replied, and was fiercely glad that it was. Gray had liked her shirt, had touched it, and she wasn't about to give it up.

Jodie had scowled at the obvious truth. Faith was small and skinny, but even her narrow shoulders strained at the seams of the two-year-old T-shirt.

"I'll get my own," she'd declared.

She would, too, Faith thought now as she gazed dreamily

3

up at the flickering patterns made by the sun in the trees. But Jodie wouldn't have the one Gray had touched; Faith had taken it off as soon as she'd gotten home, carefully folded it, and hidden it under her mattress. The only way anyone would find it there would be if they stripped the bed to wash the sheets, and since Faith was the only one who did that, the shirt would be safe, and she could sleep on it every night.

Gray. The violence of her emotions scared her, but she couldn't control them. All she had to do was see him and her heart would begin pounding so hard in her skinny chest that it hurt her ribs, and she felt hot and shivery all at the same time. Gray was like a god in the small town of Prescott, Louisiana; he was wild as a buck, she'd heard people say, but he was backed by the Rouillard money, and even as a young boy he'd had a hard, reckless charm that made feminine hearts flutter. The Rouillards had spawned their share of rascals and renegades, and Gray had early shown the potential to be the wildest of the lot. But he was a Rouillard, and even when he raised hell, he did it with style.

For all that, he'd never been unkind to Faith, the way some of the people in town had. His sister, Monica, had once spat in their direction when Faith and Jodie had met her on the sidewalk. Faith was glad that Monica was in New Orleans at some fancy private girls' school, and wasn't home very often even during the summer, because she was visiting with friends. On the other hand, Faith's heart had bled for months when Gray had gone off to LSU; Baton Rouge wasn't that far away, but during football season he didn't get much time off, and came home only on the holidays. Whenever she knew he was home, Faith tried to hang around town where she might catch a glimpse of him, strolling with the indolent grace of a big cat, so tall and strong and dangerously exciting.

Now that it was summer, he spent a lot of time at the lake, which was one of the reasons for Faith's afternoon expedition through the woods. The lake was a private one, over two thousand acres, and totally contained by Rouillard land. It was long and irregularly shaped, with several curves in it; broad and fairly shallow in some places, narrow and deep in others. The big, white Rouillard mansion was to the east of it, the Devlin shack on the west, but neither was actually on the lakeshore. The only house on the lake was the Rouillard summerhouse, a white, one-story house with two bedrooms, a kitchen, a living room, and a screened-in porch that totally encircled it. Down from the summerhouse was a boathouse and a pier, and a brick barbecue pit had been built there. Sometimes, during the summer, Gray and his friends would gather there for a rowdy afternoon of swimming and boating, and Faith would slip along the edge of the woods so she could watch him to her heart's content.

Maybe he'd be there today, she thought, aching with the sweet yearning that filled her every time she thought about him. It would be wonderful to see him twice in one day.

She was barefoot, and her threadbare shorts left her skinny legs unprotected from scratches and snakes, but Faith was as at home in the woods as the other shy creatures; she wasn't worried about the snakes, and disregarded the scratches. Her long, dark red hair tended to hang untidily in her eyes and annoy her, so she had pulled it back and secured it with a rubber band. She slipped like a wraith through the trees, her big cat eyes dreamy as she pictured Gray in her mind. Maybe he'd be there; maybe one day he'd see her hiding in the bushes, or peeking out from behind a tree, and he'd hold his hand out to her and say, "Why don't you come out from there and have some fun with us?" She lost herself in the delicious daydream of being part of that group of laughing, roughhousing, suntanned kids, of being one of those curvy girls in a brief bikini.

Even before she got to the edge of the clearing where the summerhouse was, she could see the silver gleam of Gray's Corvette parked in front of it, and her heart began the familiar violent pounding. He was here! She slid cautiously behind the shelter of a big tree trunk, but after a moment she realized that she couldn't hear anything. There were no splashing sounds, no yells or shrieks or giggles.

Maybe he was fishing from the pier, or maybe he'd taken the boat out. Faith moved closer, angling for a view of the pier, but the wooden length was empty. He wasn't there. Disappointment filled her. If he'd taken the boat out, there

5

was no telling how long he'd be gone, and she couldn't stay there waiting for him. She had stolen this time for herself, but she had to get back soon and start cooking supper, and take care of Scottie.

She was turning to go when a muted sound reached her ears and she stopped, head cocked to try to locate it. She left the edge of the woods and took a few steps into the clearing, closer to the house, and now she could hear a murmur of voices, too low and indistinct for her to understand. Instantly her heart swelled again; he *was* here, after all. But he was inside the house; it would be difficult to catch a glimpse of him from the woods. If she went closer, though, she could hear him, and that was all she required.

Faith had the knack of small, wild things for silence. Her bare feet didn't make a sound as she crept closer to the house, trying to stay out of a direct line to any of the windows. The murmur of voices seemed to be coming from the back of the house, where the bedrooms were located.

She reached the porch and squatted by the steps, her head cocked again as she tried to catch the words, but she couldn't quite understand them. It was Gray's voice, though; the deep tones were unmistakable, at least to her. Then she heard a gasp, and a kind of moan, in a much lighter voice.

Irresistibly drawn by curiosity and the lodestone of Gray's voice, Faith eased out of her squatting position and cautiously tugged at the handle of the screen door. It was unlatched. She eased it open barely enough for a cat to slip through, and wriggled her own lithe, skinny body inside, then just as silently let the door close. Going down on hands and knees, she crawled across the plank porch to the open window of one of the bedrooms, from which the voices seemed to be coming.

She heard another gasp. "Gray," said the other voice, a girl's voice, strained and shaking.

"Shhh, shhh," Gray murmured, the sound low and barely reaching Faith. He said something else, but the words didn't make any sense to her. They slid past her ears without triggering any understanding. Then he said, *"Mon chère,"* and the tumblers clicked into place. He was speaking

6

French, she realized, and as soon as she did so, the words became clear, as if it had taken that small understanding for the sounds to find the needed rhythm in her brain. Though the Devlins were neither Cajun nor Creole, Faith understood most of what he was saying. The majority of the people in the parish spoke and understood French, in varying degrees.

It sounded as if he were trying to coax a scared dog to him, Faith thought. His voice was warm and crooning, the words scattered with reassurances and endearments. When the girl spoke again, her voice was still strained, but now there was a drugged undertone to it.

Curious, Faith eased to the side and carefully moved her head so that one eye peeked around the frame of the open window. What she saw froze her to the spot.

Gray and the girl were both naked on the bed, which was positioned with the headboard under the window on the adjoining wall. Neither of them was likely to see her, which was a stroke of fortune, because Faith couldn't have moved then even if they had both looked straight at her.

Gray was lying with his back to her, his left arm positioned under the girl's tousled blond head. He was leaning over her in a way that made Faith catch her breath, for there was something both protective and predatory in him. He was kissing her, long kisses that left the room in silence except for their deep sighs, and his right arm—it looked as if—he *was*—he shifted his position, and Faith could clearly see that his right hand was between the girl's naked thighs, right there on her kitty cat.

Faith felt dizzy, and she realized that her chest hurt from holding her breath. Carefully she let it out, and rested her cheek against the white wood. She knew what they were doing. She was eleven, and she wasn't a little girl anymore even if her breasts hadn't started to grow yet. Several years ago she had heard Renee and Pa carrying on in their bedroom, and her oldest brother, Russ, had leeringly and graphically explained what was going on. She had seen dogs doing it, too, and heard cats screeching while they did it.

The girl cried out, and Faith peeked again. Gray was on top of her now, still gently murmuring in French, cajoling, soothing. He told her how pretty she was, how much he wanted her, how hot and delicious she was. And as he talked, he was adjusting his position, reaching between their bodies with his right hand while he remained propped on his left arm. Because of the angle, Faith couldn't see what he was doing, but she knew anyway. With a shock, she recognized the girl. Lindsey Partain; her father was a lawyer in Prescott.

"Gray!" Lindsey cried, her voice tight with strain. "My God! I can't—"

Gray's muscular buttocks tightened, and the girl arched beneath him, crying out again. But she was clinging to him, and the cry was one of intense pleasure. Her long legs lifted, one twining around his hip, the other hooking around his leg.

He began moving slowly, his muscled young body rippling with power. The scene was raw and disturbing, but there was also a beauty to it that kept Faith riveted. Gray was so big and strong, his darkly tanned body graceful and intensely masculine, while Lindsey was slim and shapely, delicately feminine in his grasp. He seemed to be taking such care of her, and she was enjoying it so much, her slim hands clinging to his back, her head arched back and her hips lifting in time with his slow rhythm.

Faith stared at them, her eyes burning. She wasn't jealous. Gray was so far above her, and she was so young, that she had never thought of him in a romantic, possessive sense. Gray was the shining center of her universe, to be worshiped from afar, and she was giddily happy with the occasional glimpse of him. Today, when he had actually spoken to her, and touched her shirt, had been paradise. She couldn't imagine herself in Lindsey's place, lying naked in his arms, or even imagine what it felt like.

Gray's movements were getting faster, and the girl was crying out again as she strained up to him, her teeth clenched as if she were in pain, but instinctively Faith knew that she wasn't. Gray was hammering at her now, his own head thrown back, long black hair damp at the temples and the ends sticking to his sweaty shoulders. He tensed and shuddered, and a raw, deep sound burst from his throat.

Faith's heart was hammering, and her greenish cat eyes were huge as she ducked away from the window, slipping through the screen door and off the porch as silently as she had arrived. So that was what *it* was like. She had actually seen Gray doing *it*. Without his clothes, he was even more beautiful than she had imagined. He hadn't made disgusting snorting pig noises the way Pa did, whenever he was sober enough to talk Renee into the bedroom, which wasn't very often for the past couple of years.

If Gray's father, Guy, was as beautiful doing it as Gray was, Faith thought fiercely, she didn't blame Renee for choosing him over Pa.

She gained the safety of the woods and slipped silently through the trees. It was late, and she'd likely get a belting from Pa when she got home, for not being there to start his supper and look after Scottie, the way she was supposed to do, but it would be worth it. She had seen Gray.

Exhausted, elated, shaking and breathing hard in the aftermath of orgasm, Gray lifted his head from the curve of Lindsey's neck and shoulder. She was still gasping herself, her eyes closed. He had spent the better part of the after-noon seducing her, but it had been worth the effort. That long, slow buildup had made the sex even better than he'd expected.

A flash of color, a tiny movement in his peripheral vision, caught his attention and he turned his head toward the open window and the woods beyond the porch. He caught only a glimpse of a small, frail figure topped by dark red hair, but that was enough for him to identify the youngest Devlin girl.

What was the kid doing wandering around the woods this far from their shack? Gray didn't say anything to Lindsey, because she would panic if she thought someone might have seen her sneaking into the summerhouse with him, even if that someone was just one of the trashy Devlins. She was engaged to Dewayne Mouton, and she wouldn't take kindly to anything screwing that up, even her own screwing. The Moutons weren't as rich as the Rouillards—no one in this part of Louisiana was—but Lindsey knew she could handle Dewayne in a way she could never hope to do with Gray.

9

Gray was the bigger catch, but he wouldn't be a very comfortable husband, and Lindsey was shrewd enough to know she didn't have a chance with him anyway.

"What is it?" she murmured now, stroking his shoulder.

"Nothing." He turned his head and kissed her, hard, then disengaged their bodies and sat up on the edge of the bed. "I just noticed how late it is."

Lindsey took a look out the window at the lengthening shadows, and sat up with a squeal. "My God, I'm supposed to have dinner with the Moutons tonight! I'll never be able to get ready on time!" She scrambled from the bed and began grabbing up her scattered articles of clothing.

Gray dressed in a more leisurely fashion, but his mind was still on the Devlin kid. Had she seen them, and if she had, would she say anything? She was a strange little kid, shyer than her older sister, who was already showing signs of being as big a slut as their mother. But the younger one had wise old eyes in that thin kid's face, eyes that reminded him of a cat's eyes, hazel green with flecks of gold in them so that sometimes they were green and sometimes looked yellowish. He got the feeling that she didn't miss much. She would know that her mother was his father's piece on the side, that the Devlins lived rent-free in that shack so Renee would be handy whenever Guy Rouillard wanted her. The kid wouldn't risk getting on the bad side of any Rouillard.

Poor little skinny kid, with the fey eyes. She'd been born into trash and wouldn't have the chance to ever get out of it, assuming she even wanted to. Amos Devlin was a mean drunk, and the two older boys, Russ and Nicky, were lazy, thieving bullies, as mean as their father and showing signs of turning into drunks as well. Her mother, Renee, liked the booze too, but she hadn't let it get the upper hand on her the way it had on Amos. She was lush and beautiful, despite having borne five children, with the dark red hair that only her youngest daughter had inherited, as well as the green eyes and creamy, delicate skin. Renee wasn't mean, like Amos, but she wasn't much of a mother to those kids, either. All Renee cared about was getting screwed. The joke in the parish was that her heels were so round, she had been used as the pattern for Weebles. Unlike Weebles, however, Renee would stay down, as long as there was a man ready to crawl on top of her. She exuded sex, raunchy sex, drawing men to her like dogs to a bitch in heat.

Jodie, the oldest girl, was pure jailbait, already on the lookout for any hard cock she could get. She had Renee's single-mindedness when it came to sex, and he very much doubted that she was still a virgin, though she was only in junior high. She kept offering it to him, but Gray wasn't the least bit tempted. He'd rather screw a snake than Jodie Devlin.

The youngest Devlin boy was retarded. Gray had only seen him once or twice, and each time he had been clinging to the youngest girl's legs—what was her name, damn it? Something he'd thought a minute ago had reminded him of it. Fay? Fay with the fey eyes? No, it was something else, but like that—Faith. That was it. Funny name for a Devlin, since neither Amos nor Renee was the least bit religious.

With a family like that, the kid was doomed. In another couple of years, she'd be following in her mother's and sister's footsteps, because she wouldn't know any better. And even if she did know better, all the boys would come sniffing around her anyway, just because her name was Devlin, and she wouldn't hold out for long.

The whole parish knew that his father was screwing Renee, had been for years. As much as Gray loved his mother, he figured he couldn't blame Guy for going else-where; God knows, his mother didn't. Noelle was the least physical person Gray had ever seen. At thirty-nine, she was still as cool and lovely as a Madonna, unfailingly composed and remote. She didn't like to be touched, even by her children. The wonder was that she'd even *had* children. Of course Guy wasn't faithful, had never been, much to Noelle's relief. Guy Rouillard was hot-blooded and lusty, and he'd found his way into a lot of beds before settling, more or less, on Renee Devlin. But Guy was always gently courteous and protective with Noelle, and Gray knew he would never leave her, especially not for a cheap slut like Renee.

The only person upset by the arrangement, apparently, was his sister, Monica. Starved by Noelle's emotional distance, Monica doted on her father, and was fiercely jealous of Renee, both on behalf of her mother and because Guy spent so much time with Renee. It was a lot calmer around the house now that Monica had gone away to school and become involved with her friends there.

"Gray, *hurry,*" Lindsey begged frantically.

He shoved his arms into his shirtsleeves, but disdained to button the garment, leaving it hanging open. "I'm ready." He kissed her, and patted her butt. "Don't get your feathers ruffled, *chérie.* All you have to do is change clothes. The rest of you looks beautiful just as you are."

She smiled, pleased by the compliment, and calmed down. "When can we do this again?" she asked as they left the summerhouse.

Gray laughed aloud. It had taken him most of the summer to get into her pants, but now she didn't want to waste any more time. Perversely, now that he'd had her, much of his ruthless determination had faded. "I don't know," he said lazily. "I have to report back to school soon, for football practice."

To her credit, she didn't pout. Instead she tossed her head so the wind lifted her hair as the Corvette streaked down the private road toward the highway, and smiled at him. "Any time." She was a year older than he was, and had her own share of confidence.

The Corvette skidded into the highway, the tires grabbing asphalt. Lindsey laughed as Gray handled the powerful car with ease. "I'll have you home in five minutes," he promised. He didn't want anything to interfere with her engagement to Dewayne, either.

He thought of skinny little Faith Devlin, and wondered if she'd made it safely home. She shouldn't be wandering around alone in the woods like that. She could get hurt, or lost. Worse, though this was private land, the lake drew the local high school boys like a magnet, and Gray had no illusions about teenage boys when they were in a pack. If they ran across Faith, they might not stop to think about how young she was, only that she was a Devlin. Little Red wouldn't have a chance against the wolves.

Someone needed to keep a closer eye on the kid.

∼ Two ∼

Three Years Later

"Faith," Renee said fretfully, "make Scottie stop. He's driving me crazy with that whining."

Faith put aside the potatoes she was peeling, wiped her hands, and went to the screen door, where Scottie was slapping at the screen and making the little snuffling sounds that meant he wanted to go outside. He was never allowed to go out by himself, because he didn't understand what "stay in the yard" meant, and he would wander off and get lost. There was a latch high on the screen, where he couldn't reach it, that was always kept fastened to prevent him from going out by himself. Faith was busy with supper, though likely only she and Scottie would be here to eat it, and couldn't go out with him right now.

She pulled his hands away from the screen and said, "Do you want to play ball, Scottie? Where's the ball?" Easily distracted, he trotted off in search of his dog-chewed red ball, but Faith knew that wouldn't occupy him for long. With a sigh, she went back to the potatoes.

Renee drifted out of her bedroom. She was dressed fit to kill tonight, Faith noted, in a tight, short red dress that showed off her long, shapely legs and somehow didn't clash with her hair. Renee had great legs; she had great everything,

13

and she knew it. Her thick red hair was brushed into a cloud, and her musky perfume clung to her in a deep, rich red scent. "How do I look?" she asked, whirling on her red high heels as she attached cheap rhinestone earrings to her earlobes.

"Beautiful," Faith said, knowing it was what Renee expected, and it was nothing less than the truth. Renee was as amoral as a cat, but she was also a startlingly beautiful woman, with a perfectly formed, slightly exotic face.

"Well, I'm off." She bent to brush a careless kiss over the top of Faith's head.

"Have fun, Mama."

"I will." She gave a husky laugh. "Oh, I will." She unlatched the screen and left the shack, long legs flashing.

Faith got up to latch the door again, and stood watching Renee get into her flashy little sports car and drive off. Her mother loved that car. She had driven up in it one day without a word of explanation about how she had gotten it, not that there was much doubt in anyone's mind. Guy Rouillard had bought it for her.

Seeing her at the door, Scottie returned and began making his "go outside" noise again. "I can't take you outside," Faith explained, endlessly patient though he didn't understand much. "I have to cook supper. Would you rather have fried potatoes or mashed ones?" It was a rhetorical question, because mashed potatoes were much easier for him to eat. She smoothed his dark hair and returned once again to the table and the bowl of potatoes.

Lately, Scottie wasn't as energetic as usual, and more and more his lips took on a blue tinge when he played. His heart was failing, just like the doctors had said would likely happen. There wouldn't be a miracle heart transplant for Scottie, even had the Devlins been able to afford it. The few available children's hearts were too precious to be wasted on a little boy who would never be able to dress himself, or read, or manage more than a few garbled words no matter how long he lived. "Severely retarded" was how he was categorized. Though a hard little lump formed in Faith's chest at the thought of Scottie dying, she wasn't bitter that nothing would be done about his failing health. A new heart wouldn't help Scottie, not in any way that mattered. The doctors hadn't expected him to live this long, and she would just take care of him for whatever time he had left.

For a while, she had wondered if he was Guy Rouillard's son, and felt furious on his behalf that he wasn't taken to live in the big white house, where he would have the best of care, and his few years would be happy. Because Scottie was retarded, she thought, Guy was happy to keep him out of sight.

The truth was, Scottie could just as easily be Pa's son, and it was impossible to tell. Scottie didn't look like either man; he simply looked like himself. He was six years old now, a placid little boy who was pleased by the smallest things, and whose security was rooted in his fourteen-year-old sister. Faith had taken care of him from the day Renee had brought him home from the hospital, protected him from Pa's drunken rages, kept Russ and Nicky from teasing him unmercifully. Renee and Jodie mostly ignored him, which was okay with Scottie.

Jodie had asked Faith to "double date" with her that night, and shrugged when Faith refused because someone had to stay home and take care of Scottie. She wouldn't have gone out with Jodie anyway; their ideas of fun were radically different. Jodie thought having fun was sneaking some illegal booze, since she was only sixteen, getting drunk, and having sex with the boy or group of boys who were hanging around her that night.

Everything in Faith shuddered in revulsion at the thought. She had seen Jodie come in, stinking of beer and sex, her clothes torn and stained, giggling at how much "fun" she had had. It never seemed to bother her that those same boys wouldn't speak to her if they met her in public.

It bothered Faith. Her soul burned with humiliation at the contempt in people's eyes whenever they looked at her, at anyone in her family. The trashy Devlins, that's what they were called. Drunks and whores, the whole bunch.

But I'm not like that! The silent cry sometimes welled up in Faith, but she always held it in. Why couldn't folks see beneath the name? She didn't paint herself up and wear too short, too tight clothes like Renee and Jodie. She didn't drink, didn't hang around rough joints trying to pick up anything in pants. Her clothes were cheap and ill made, but she kept them clean. She never missed a day of school, if she could help it, and she had good grades. She hungered for respectability, wanted to be able to walk into a store and not have the clerks watch her like a hawk, because she was one of those trashy Devlins and everyone knew they'd steal you blind. She didn't want people to make comments behind their hands whenever they saw her.

It didn't help that she resembled Renee far more than did Jodie. Faith had the same thick, dark red hair, as vibrant as a flame, the same porcelain-grained skin, the same high cheekbones and exotic green eyes. Her face wasn't perfectly proportioned like Renee's; her face was thinner, her jaw more square, her mouth as wide but not as full. Renee was voluptuous; Faith was both taller and leaner, her body more delicately made. Her breasts had finally grown, firm and pert, but Jodie, at the same age, had been wearing a bra cup two sizes bigger.

Because she looked like Renee, people seemed to expect Faith to act like her, too, and then never looked beyond their own expectations. She was tarred with the same brush that had painted the rest of the family.

"But I'll get out someday, Scottie," she said softly. "See if I don't."

He didn't react to the words, just kept patting the screen.

As always, when she needed to cheer herself, she thought of Gray. Her painful feelings for him hadn't lessened in the three years since she had seen him making love to Lindsey Partain, but rather had intensified as she had matured. The awestruck joy with which she had watched him at eleven had grown and changed, as she had grown and changed. When she dreamed of him now, physical feelings mingled sharply with the romantic ones, and with her upbringing the details were far sharper and more explicit than other fourteen-year-old girls could have been expected to know.

Her dreams weren't colored just by her own surroundings; that day at the summerhouse when she had seen Gray with Lindsey Partain—Lindsey Mouton now—had given her a great deal of knowledge about his body. She hadn't actually seen his genitals, because at first his back had been turned to her, and then when he had gotten on top, their legs had blocked her view. It didn't much matter, though, because she knew what one looked like. Not only had she taken care of Scottie all of his life, but Pa and Russ and Nicky, when they were drunk, were just as likely as not to pull it out of their pants and take a pee off the front step as they were to use the toilet.

But Faith knew enough details about Gray's body to heat her dreams. She knew how muscled those long legs were, and that black hair grew on them. She knew that his buttocks were small and round and tight, and that he had adorable twin dimples just above them. She knew that his shoulders were broad and powerful, that his back was long, with the groove of his spine deeply indented between the thick layers of muscle. There had been a light dusting of black hair on his wide chest.

She knew that he made love in French, his deep voice soft and dark and crooning.

She had followed his career at LSU with secret pride. He had just been graduated with a double major in finance and business administration, with an eye toward taking over the Rouillard holdings someday. As good as he had been at football, he hadn't wanted a career in the pros, and instead had come home to begin helping Guy. She would be able to catch glimpses of him year round now, rather than just during the summer and holidays.

Unfortunately, Monica was home for good, too, and was as spiteful as ever. Everyone else was merely contemptuous; Monica actively *hated* anyone with the name of Devlin. Faith couldn't blame her, though, and sometimes even sympathized with her. No one had ever said that Guy Rouillard wasn't a good father; he loved both of his children, and they loved him. How did Monica feel, hearing people talk about Guy's long-standing arrangement with Renee, knowing that he was openly unfaithful to her mother?

When she was younger, Faith had daydreamed that Guy was her father too; Amos was nowhere in the picture. Guy was tall and dark and exciting, his lean face so much like

Gray's that, no matter what, she couldn't hate him. He had always been kind to her, to all Renee's kids, but he had sometimes gone out of his way to speak to Faith and had once or twice bought her a small treat. It was probably because she looked like Renee, Faith thought. If Guy had been her father, then Gray would be her brother, and she would be able to worship him up close, live in the same house with him. Those daydreams had always made her feel guilty about Pa, and then she would try to be extra nice to him to make up for it. Lately, however, she was fiercely glad that Guy wasn't her father, because now she didn't want Gray to be her brother.

She wanted to marry him.

This most private of her daydreams was so shocking that sometimes it startled her, that she would dare to even dream so high. A Rouillard, marry a Devlin? A Devlin set foot in that hundred-year-old mansion? All the Rouillard ancestors would rise up from their graves to drive out the intruder. The parish would be aghast.

But still she dreamed. She dreamed of being dressed in white, of walking down the wide aisle of the church with Gray waiting for her at the altar, turning to watch her with those heavy-lidded dark eyes, the expression in them hot and wanting, and just for her. She dreamed of him sweeping her up in his arms and carrying her over the threshold—not at Rouillard House, she couldn't imagine that, but somewhere else that was theirs alone, maybe a honeymoon cottage—to a big bed that awaited them. She imagined lying under him, her legs around him as she had seen Lindsey's, imagined him moving, heard his seductive voice whispering French love words in her ear. She knew what men and women did together, knew where he would put his thing, even though she couldn't imagine how it would feel. Jodie said that it felt wonderful, the best thing in the world . . .

Scottie gave a sharp cry, jerking Faith from her daydream. She dropped the potato she had been dicing and jumped to her feet, because Scottie didn't cry unless he was hurt. He was still standing at the screen, holding his finger. Faith picked him up and carried him to the table, where she sat down with him on her lap and examined his hand. There was a small, deep scratch on the tip of his index finger; probably he had raked his hand across a hole in the screen, and the torn wire had dug into his skin. A single drop of blood had welled in the tiny wound.

"There, there, it's all right," she soothed, hugging him and wiping away his tears. "I'll put a Band-Aid on it and it'll get well. You like Band-Aids."

He did. Whenever he had a scrape that needed bandaging, she ended up plastering the things over his arms and legs, because he would keep nudging her until all the Band-Aids in the box had been used. She had learned to take most of the bandage strips out of the box and hide them, so that only two or three were there for him to see.

She washed his finger and got the box down from the top shelf, where it was kept to keep him out of it. His round little face was glowing with delight and anticipation as he held out his stubby finger. Making a big production out of it, Faith applied the bandage to the wound.

He leaned forward and peered into the open box, then grunted as he held out his other hand.

"Is that one hurt, too? Poor hand!" She kissed the grubby little paw and applied a bandage to the back of it.

He leaned over and looked into the box again, and grinned as he held up his right leg.

"My goodness! You're hurt all over!" she exclaimed, and bandaged his knee.

He checked the box again, but it was now empty. Satisfied, he trotted back to the door, and Faith returned to fixing supper.

With the long summer days, it was just twilight at eight-thirty, but by eight that evening Scottie was already tired and nodding off. Faith gave him a bath and put him to bed, her heart squeezing painfully as she stroked his hair. He was such a sweet little boy, oblivious to the health problems that would keep him from living to adulthood.

At nine-thirty she heard Amos driving up, his old truck clanking and backfiring. She went to unlatch the screen and let him in. The stink of whiskey came in with him, a purulent, greenish yellow stench.

He stumbled over the threshold, and righted himself.

19

"Where's your ma?" he growled, in the ugly mean tone he always used when he was drinking, which was most of the time.

"She went out a couple of hours ago."

He lurched toward the table, the uneven floor making his steps that much more perilous. "Damn bitch," he muttered. "Ain't never here. Always out shakin' her ass at her fancy rich boyfriend. Ain't never here to fix my supper. How's a man supposed to eat?" he suddenly roared, hitting the table with his fist.

"Supper's ready, Pa," Faith said quietly, hoping the uproar didn't wake Scottie. "I'll fix you a plate."

"Don't want anything to eat," he said, as she had expected. When he was drinking, he never wanted food, just more booze.

"Is there anythin' in this damn house to drink?" He staggered to his feet and began opening cabinet doors, slamming them when they didn't reveal what he wanted.

Faith moved quickly. "There's a bottle in the boys' bedroom. I'll get it." She didn't want Amos stumbling around in there, cussing and probably puking, and waking Scottie. She darted into the dark little room and blindly searched under Nick's cot until her hand brushed against cool glass. Dragging the bottle out, she carried it back into the kitchen. It was only about one quarter full, but anything would pacify Pa. She twisted the cap off and handed the bottle to Amos.

"Here, Pa."

"Good girl," he said, brightening as he tipped the bottle to his mouth. "You're a good girl, Faith, not a whore like your ma and sister."

"Don't talk like that about them," she protested, unable to listen. Knowing it was one thing, but talking about it was another. It wasn't as if Pa had any room to throw stones.

"I'll say what I damn well please!" Amos flared. "Don't sass me, girl, or I'll belt you one."

"I wasn't sassing you, Pa." She kept her voice calm, but prudently moved out of reach. If he couldn't reach her, he couldn't hit her. He was likely to throw something, but she was quick and his missiles seldom struck her.

"Fine kids she gave me," he sneered. "Russ and Nick are the only two I can stomach. Jodie's a whore like her ma, you're a prissy smart-ass, and the last one's a goddamn idiot."

Keeping her head turned away so he couldn't see the tears that burned her eyes, Faith sat down on the ragged, sagging couch and began folding the laundry she'd done that day. It would never do to let Amos see that he'd hurt her. If he ever scented blood, he moved in for the kill, and the drunker he was, the more vicious he became. The best thing to do was ignore him. Like all drunks, he was easily distracted, and she figured he'd soon be passed out anyway.

She didn't know why it hurt. She had long since ceased to have any feelings for Amos, not even fear. There was certainly nothing there to love, the man he had been long since destroyed in countless bottles of whiskey. If he had ever shown any promise, it had been gone by the time she'd been born, but somehow she thought he had always been pretty much as he was now. He was simply the type of person who always blamed others for his problems rather than doing something to correct them.

Sometimes, when he was sober, Faith thought she could see why Renee had once been attracted to him. Amos was a little over average height, with a wiry body that had never gone to fat. His hair was still dark, if thinning on top, and he could even be called a good-looking man—when he was sober. Drunk, as he was now, unshaven and with his hair mussed and hanging in dirty strings, his eyes red and rheumy with alcohol, his face bloated, there was nothing the least attractive about him. His clothes were dirty and stained, and he stank to high heaven. Judging by the sourness of his smell, he had already puked at least once, and the stains on the front of his pants meant that he hadn't been as careful as he should have been when he'd peed.

He finished off the bottle in silence, then belched loudly. "Gotta piss," he announced, staggering to his feet and heading toward the front door.

Faith's movements were measured, her hands never faltering as she listened to the stream of urine spattering in front of the step, for everyone else who came in that night to tramp into the house. She would mop the floor first thing in the morning.

Amos weaved back into the house. He hadn't zipped his pants, she noticed, but at least his sex wasn't exposed.

"Goin' to bed," he said, making his way toward the back room. Faith watched him stumble and right himself by bracing his hand on the doorframe. He didn't undress, but fell across the bed as he was. When Renee came home and found Amos lying across the bed in his filthy clothes, she would raise hell and wake everyone in the house.

Within minutes, Amos's heavy snoring was echoing through the cramped shack.

Faith immediately got up and went into the lean-to that had been built onto the back of the shack, which she shared with Jodie. Only Amos and Renee had an honest-to-goodness bed; all the rest of them had cots. She turned on the light, the single bare bulb glaring, and quickly changed into her nightgown. Then she pulled her book out from under the mattress. Now that Scottie was in bed and Amos passed out drunk, she would likely have a couple of peaceful hours before anyone else came home. Amos was always the first one home, but then he always got started first.

She had learned not to hesitate when an opportunity for enjoyment presented itself, but to seize each moment. There were too few of them in her life for her to allow any to pass untasted. She loved books, and read anything that came to hand. There was something magical in the way words could be strung together and a whole new world fashioned by the arrangement. While reading she could leave this crowded shack far behind, and go to worlds filled with excitement and beauty and love. When she was reading, she was someone else in her mind, someone worthwhile, rather than one of the trashy Devlins.

She had learned not to read in front of Pa or the boys, though. The least they did was make fun of her. Any one of them, in one of their meaner moods, was likely to snatch the book from her and throw it in the fire, or into the toilet, and laugh uproariously as if her frantic efforts to save it were the funniest thing they'd ever seen. Renee would grumble about her wasting her time reading instead of doing her chores, but she wouldn't do anything to the book. Jodie made fun of her sometimes, but in a careless, impatient way. She couldn't understand for the life of her why Faith would rather stick her nose in a book than go out to have some fun.

These precious moments alone, when she could read in peace, were the highlight of Faith's day, unless she had happened to see Gray. Sometimes she thought that if she couldn't read, just for a few minutes, she would go crazy and start screaming, and not be able to stop. But no matter what Pa did, no matter what she overheard someone say about her family, no matter what Russ and Nicky had been up to or how weak Scottie seemed, if she could open a book, she would lose herself in the pages.

Tonight she had more than a few minutes free for reading, for losing herself in the pages of *Rebecca*. She settled on her cot and pulled out the candle that she kept under her bed. She lit the candle, positioned it just so, balanced on a crate to the right of the cot, and scooted so that her back was braced against the wall. The light from the candle, small as it was, was enough to offset the back glare of the light bulb and allow her to read without straining her eyes too much. One of these days, she promised herself, she would get a lamp. She imagined it, a real reading lamp that gave off soft, bright light. And she would have one of those wedge-shaped pillows to lean against.

One of these days.

It was almost midnight when she gave up the battle against her heavy eyelids. She hated to stop reading, not wanting to waste any of this time to herself, but she was so sleepy, she couldn't make sense of the words any longer, and wasting the words seemed a lot worse than wasting the time. Sighing, she got up and returned the book to its hiding place, then turned out the light. She crawled between the threadbare sheets, the frame of the cot squeaking under her weight, and blew out the candle.

Perversely, in the sudden darkness, sleep wouldn't come. She shifted restlessly on the thin cot, drifting in a half daydream, half doze, reliving the strained, shadowed romance in the book she'd been reading. She knew instantly when Russ and Nicky drove up, close to one o'clock. They staggered into the house, making no effort to be quiet, laughing uproariously at something their drinking buddies had done that night. Both of them were still underage, but a little thing like a law had never gotten in the way whenever a Devlin wanted to do something. The boys couldn't go to roadhouses, but there were plenty of other ways they could get booze, and they knew them all. Sometimes they stole it, sometimes they paid other people to buy it for them, in which case they had stolen the money. Neither of them had a job, part-time or otherwise, because no one would hire them. It was well known the Devlin boys would steal you blind.

"Ol' Poss," Nicky was giggling. "Boooooom!"

It was enough to send Russ into drunken whoops. From the incoherent fragments she heard, evidently "Ol' Poss," whoever that was, had been scared by something that had made a loud booming noise. The boys seemed to think it was hilarious, but they probably wouldn't remember it in the morning.

They woke Scottie, and she heard him grunting, but he didn't cry, so she remained in bed. She wouldn't have liked traipsing into the boys' bedroom in her nightgown—in fact, she would have gone cold with dread—but she would have done it if they'd scared Scottie and made him cry. But Nicky said, "Shaddup and go back to sleep," and Scottie was quiet again. After a few minutes, they were all asleep, the chorus of snores rising and falling in the darkness.

Half an hour later, Jodie came home. She was quiet, or at least tried to be, tiptoeing through the shack with her shoes in hand. The stench of beer and sex came with her, all yellow and red and brown in a noxious swirl. She didn't bother to undress but flopped down on her cot and heaved a deep sigh, almost like a purr.

"You awake, Faithie?" she asked after a moment, her voice slurred.

"Yeah."

"Thought you were. You should've come with me. Had fun, lots of fun." The last sentence was deep with sensuality. "You don't know what you're missin', Faithie."

24

"Then I don't miss it, do I?" Faith whispered, and Jodie giggled.

Faith dozed lightly, listening for Renee's car so she would know everyone was safely home. Twice she came awake with a start, wondering if Renee had managed to come in without waking her, and got up to look out the window to see if her car was there. It wasn't.

Renee didn't come home at all that night.

❦ Three ❦

"Daddy didn't come home last night."

Monica's face was tight with misery as she stood at the window of the dining room. Gray continued eating his breakfast; there wasn't much that could curb his appetite. So that was why Monica was up so early, since she usually didn't crawl out of bed until ten or later. What did she do, wait up until Guy came home? He wondered with a sigh what Monica thought he could do about their father's hours; send him to bed without supper? He couldn't remember when Guy hadn't had women on the side, though Renee Devlin had certainly had a lot more staying power than the rest of them.

His mother, Noelle, didn't care where Guy spent his nights, so long as it wasn't with her, and simply pretended that her husband's affairs didn't exist. Because Noelle didn't care, Gray didn't either. It would have been different if Noelle had been distressed, but that was far from the case. It wasn't that she didn't love Guy; Gray supposed she did, in her fashion. But Noelle intensely disliked sex, disliked being touched, even casually. For Guy to have a mistress was the best solution all around. He didn't mistreat Noelle, and though he never bothered to hide his affairs, her position as his wife was safe. It was a very Old World arrangement that

26

his parents had, and one that Gray knew he wouldn't like at all when he finally decided to get married, but it suited both of them fine.

Monica hadn't ever been able to see that, however. She was painfully protective of Noelle, relating to her in a way that Gray never could, imagining that Noelle was humiliated and hurt by Guy's affairs. At the same time, Monica adored Guy, and was never happier than when he was paying attention to her. She had a picture in her mind of how families should be, close-knit and loving, always supporting each other, with the parents devoted to each other, and she had been trying her entire life to make her own family match that picture.

"Does Mother know?" he asked calmly, and refrained from asking if Monica really thought Noelle would care even if she did know. He sometimes felt sorry for Monica, but he also loved her, and didn't deliberately try to hurt her.

Monica shook her head. "She isn't up yet."

"Then why worry about it? By the time she gets up, when he comes in she'll just think he's already gone somewhere this morning."

"But he's been out with *her!*" Monica whirled to face him, her dark eyes swimming with tears. "That Devlin woman."

"You don't know that. He could have gotten into an all-night poker game." Guy did love to play poker, but Gray doubted that cards had anything to do with his absence. If he knew his father, and he knew him very well, Guy had far more likely spent the night with Renee Devlin, or some other woman who caught his eye. Renee was a fool if she thought Guy was any more faithful to her than he was to his wife.

"You think so?" Monica asked, eager to believe any excuse other than the most likely one.

Gray shrugged. "It's possible." It was also possible a meteor would strike the house that day, but not very likely. He drank the last of his coffee and pushed back his chair. "When he comes in, tell him I've gone to Baton Rouge to look over that property we were talking about. I'll be back by three, at the latest." Because she still looked so forlorn, he put an arm around her shoulders and hugged her. Somehow

Monica had been born without the decisiveness and arrogant self-assurance of the rest of the family. Even Noelle, as remote as she was, always knew exactly what she wanted and how to go about getting it. Monica always seemed so helpless against the forceful personalities of everyone else in the family.

She buried her dark head in his shoulder for a moment, just as she had when she'd been a little girl and gone running to her big brother whenever something had gone wrong and Guy hadn't been available to put things to rights again. Though he was only two years older, he had always been protective of her, knowing even as a child that she lacked his own inner toughness.

"What do I do if he *has* been out with that slut?" she asked, her voice muffled against his shoulder.

Gray tried to stifle his impatience, but some of it leaked through in his voice. "You don't do anything. It's none of your business."

She drew back, stung, and stared reproachfully at him. "How can you say that? I'm worried about him!"

"I know you are." He managed to soften his tone. "But it's a waste of time, and he wouldn't thank you for it."

"You always take his side, because you're just like him!" The tears were slowly dripping down her cheeks now, and she turned away. "I bet the property in Baton Rouge happens to have two legs and big boobs. Well, have fun!"

"I will," he said ironically. He really was going to see some property; afterwards was a different story. He was a strong, healthy young man, with a sex drive that had shown no signs of slacking off since his middle teens. It was a persistent burning in his guts, a hungry ache in his balls. He was lucky enough to be able to get women to ease that hunger, and cynical enough to realize that his family's money added to his sexual success.

He didn't care what the woman's reason was, whether she came to him because she liked him and enjoyed his body, or whether she had her eye on the Rouillard bank account. Reasons didn't matter, because all he wanted was a soft, warm body beneath him, taking his surging lust and giving him temporary ease. He'd never loved a woman yet, but he definitely loved sex, loved everything about it: the smells, the sensations, the sounds. He was particularly entranced by his favorite moment, the instant of penetration when he felt the small resistance of the woman's body to his pressure, then the acceptance, the sensation of being taken in and enveloped with hot, tight, wet flesh. God, that was wonderful! He was always extremely careful to protect against unwanted pregnancies, wearing a rubber even if the woman said she was on birth control pills, because women had been known to lie about things like that and a smart man didn't take chances.

He didn't know for certain, but he suspected Monica was still virgin. Though she was far more emotional than Noelle, there was still something of their mother in her, some deep remoteness that so far hadn't let any man get too close. She was an awkward mix of their parents' natures, receiving some of Noelle's cool distance without any of her self-assurance, and some of Guy's emotionalism without his intense sexuality. Gray, on the other hand, had his father's sexuality tempered with Noelle's control. As much as he wanted sex, he wasn't a slave to his cock the way Guy was. He knew when, and how, to say no. Thank God, he seemed to have better sense picking his women than Guy did, too.

He tugged on a strand of Monica's dark hair. "I'll call Alex and see if he knows where Dad is." Alexander Chelette, a lawyer in Prescott, was Guy's best friend.

Her lips trembled, but she smiled through her tears. "He'll go find Daddy and tell him to come home."

Gray snorted. It was a wonder how Monica had reached the age of twenty and learned absolutely nothing about men. "I wouldn't bet on that, but maybe he can ease your mind." He intended to tell Monica that Guy was in a poker game, even if Alex knew the number of the motel room in which Guy was screwing the morning away.

He went into the study from which Guy handled the myriad Rouillard financial interests, and where Gray was learning how to handle them. Gray was fascinated by the intricacies of business and finance, so much so that he had willingly bypassed a chance to play pro football in favor of plunging headlong into the business world. It hadn't been that much of a sacrifice for him; he knew he was good enough to play pro, because he had been scouted, but he knew he wasn't star material. Had he given his life to football, he would have played eight years or so, if he'd been lucky enough to escape injury, and made a good but not spectacular salary. What it came down to, in the end, was that, as much as he loved football, he loved business more. This was a game that he could play much longer than he could football, make a hell of a lot more money, and was just as dog-eat-dog.

Though Guy would have burst his buttons with pride if his son had gone into pro football, Gray thought he'd been somehow relieved when Gray had chosen to come home instead. In the few months since Gray had gotten his degree, Guy had been happily cramming his head full of business knowledge, stuff that couldn't be gotten from a textbook.

Gray ran his fingers over the polished wood of the big desk. An eight-by-ten photograph of Noelle was positioned on one corner, surrounded by smaller photos of himself and Monica at various stages of growth, like a queen with her subjects gathered around her. Most people would have thought of a mother with her children gathered about her knee, but Noelle wasn't in the least motherly. The morning sunlight was falling across the photograph, picking up details that usually went unnoticed, and Gray paused to look at the still image of his mother's face.

She was a beautiful woman, in a totally different way from Renee Devlin's beauty. Renee was the sun, bold and hot and bright, while Noelle was the moon, cool and remote. She had thick, sleek, dark hair which she wore in a sophisticated twist, and lovely blue eyes which neither of her children had inherited. She wasn't French Creole, but plain old American; some folks in the parish had wondered if Guy Rouillard wasn't marrying beneath himself. But she had turned out to be more queenly than any Creole born to the role could have been, and those old doubts had long since been forgotten. The only reminder was his own name, Grayson, which was her family name, but as it had long since been shortened to Gray, most people thought it had been chosen because of its similarity to his father's name.

Guy's appointment book was open on the desk. As Gray hitched one hip onto the desk and reached for the telephone, he ran his eye down the appointments listed for that day. Guy had an appointment with William Grady, the banker, at ten. For the first time, Gray felt a twinge of uneasiness. No matter what, Guy had never let his women get in the way of business, and he would never go to a business meeting unshaven, and without a fresh change of clothes.

Quickly he dialed Alex Chelette's number, and his secretary answered on the first ring. "Chelette and Anderson, Attorneys at Law."

"Good morning, Andrea. Is Alex in yet?"

"Of course," she replied with good humor, having immediately recognized Gray's distinctive deep voice, like smoky velvet. "You know how he is. It would take an earthquake to keep him from coming through the door on the dot of nine. Hold on and I'll get him."

He heard the click as he was put on hold, but he knew Andrea too well to think that she was buzzing Alex on the intercom. He'd been in the office often enough, as both child and man, to know that the only time she used the intercom was when a stranger was in the office. Most of the time, she simply turned around in her chair and raised her voice, since the open door of Alex's office was right behind her.

Gray smiled as he remembered Guy roaring with laughter as he told how Alex had once tried to get Andrea to behave more formally, as was proper for a law office. Poor easygoing Alex hadn't stood a chance against his secretary. Affronted, she had turned so cold, the office had frosted over. Instead of the usual "Alex," she had started calling him "Mr. Chelette" whenever she had to address him, the intercom was always used, and their easy camaraderie had gone out the window. When he stopped by her desk to try to chat, she got up and went to the rest room. All of the small details that she had once handled as a matter of course, taking a good deal of work off his shoulders, were now dumped on Alex's desk for him to do. He found himself coming in earlier and staying later, while Andrea suddenly developed a very precise time schedule. There was no question of replacing her; legal secretaries weren't easy to come by in Prescott.

Within two weeks, Alex had abjectly surrendered, and Andrea had been yelling through his office door ever since.

The line clicked again as Alex picked up. His lazy, good-natured drawl came over the line. "Good mornin', Gray. You're out and about early today."

"Not so early." He had always kept earlier hours than Guy, but most people assumed like father, like son. "I'm going to Baton Rouge to look at some property. Alex, do you know where Dad is?"

There was a small silence on the other end of the line. "No, I don't." Another cautious little pause. "Is something wrong?"

"He didn't come home last night, and he has an appointment with Bill Grady at ten."

"Damn," Alex said softly, but Gray could hear the alarm in the word. "Oh, God. I didn't think he'd—god*damn* it!"

"Alex." Gray's voice was as hard and sharp as polished steel, slicing through the wire. "What's going on?"

"I swear, Gray, I didn't think he'd do it," Alex said miserably. "Maybe he didn't. Maybe he just overslept."

"Do what?"

"He mentioned it a couple of times, but only when he'd been drinking. I swear, I never thought he was serious. God, how could he be?"

The plastic of the receiver cracked under Gray's grip. "Serious about what?"

"About leaving your mother." Alex audibly swallowed, the gulping sound plain. "And running away with Renee Devlin."

Very gently, Gray replaced the receiver in its cradle. He stood motionless for several seconds, staring down at the instrument. It couldn't—Guy wouldn't have done that. Why should he? Why run away with Renee when he could and did screw her whenever he wanted? Alex had to be wrong. Guy would never have left his children or the business—but he had been relieved when Gray had chosen to turn down pro football, and had given Gray a crash course in running everything.

For a blessed little while Gray was numb with disbelief, but he was too much of a realist for it to last long. The numbness began to fade, and pure rage rushed in to fill the void. He moved like a snake striking, snatching the phone from the desk and hurling it through the window, shattering glass and bringing several sets of footsteps rushing down the hall to the study.

Everyone slept late except Faith and Scottie, and she left the shack as soon as she had fed Scottie his breakfast, taking him down to the creek so he could splash in the shallow water and try to catch the darting crawfish. He never did, but he loved to try. It was a gorgeous morning, with the sunlight slanting bright and golden through the trees, dappling the water. The smells were fresh and sharp, full of good, clean colors that wiped out the sour miasma of alcohol lingering in her nostrils, exuded from the four people she had left sleeping off the effects of the night.

Expecting Scottie to keep his clothes dry was like expecting the sun to rise in the west. When they reached the creek, she pulled off his shorts and shirt, and let him plunge into the water wearing only his diaper. She had brought a dry one to put on him when they left. She carefully hung the discarded garments on limbs, then stepped into the creek to wade and keep an eye on him. If a snake slithered toward him, he wouldn't know to be alarmed. She wasn't afraid of them either, but she was definitely cautious.

She let him play for a couple of hours, then had to pick him up and carry him out of the water, with him kicking and protesting every inch of the way. "You can't stay in the water," she explained. "Look, your toes are wrinkled like a prune." She sat down on the ground and changed his diaper, then dressed him. It was a difficult job, with him still squirming and trying to escape back into the water.

"Let's look for squirrels," she said. "Can you see any squirrels?"

Distracted, he immediately looked upward, his eyes rounded with excitement as he searched the trees for a squirrel. Faith took his stubby hand in hers and slowly led him through the woods, taking a meandering path back to the shack. Maybe by the time they got back, Renee would be home.

Though her mother had stayed out all night before, it always made Faith uneasy. She kept it in the back of her mind, but she lived with the constant fear that Renee would leave one night and never come home. Faith knew, with bitter realism, that if Renee met some man who had a bit of money and promised her pretty things, she would be gone like a shot. Probably the only thing that kept her in Prescott anyway was Guy Rouillard, and what he could give her. If Guy ever dumped her, Renee wouldn't hang around any longer than it took her to pack her clothes.

Scottie managed to spot two squirrels, one jumping along a tree limb and another climbing a tree, so he was happy to go where Faith led him. When they came in sight of the shack, however, he realized that they were going home and began to make grunting noises of disapproval as he pulled back, trying to tug his hand from her grip.

"Scottie, stop it," Faith said, as she dragged him out of the woods into the rutted dirt road leading up to the shack. "I can't play with you anymore right now, I've got to do the wash. But I promise I'll play cars with you when I get—"

She heard the low, rumbling sound of a car engine behind her, getting louder as it got closer, and her first, relieved thought as she turned was *Mama's home.* But it wasn't Renee's flashy red car that came into sight around the curve. It was a black Corvette convertible, one bought to replace the silver one Gray had driven since high school. Faith stopped in her tracks, forgetting all about Scottie and Renee as her heart stopped, then began pounding against her rib cage with a force that almost made her sick. Gray was coming here!

She was so stunned with joy that she barely remembered to pull Scottie out of the road to stand in the weeds on the side. *Gray,* her heart sang. A fine trembling began in her knees and worked its way up her slender body at the thought of actually speaking to him again, even if it was just to mumble a hello.

Her gaze locked on him, drinking in the details as he drove closer. Though he was sitting behind the wheel and she couldn't see that much of him, she thought that he seemed leaner than he'd been while he was playing football, and his hair was a little longer. His eyes were the same, though, dark as sin and just as tempting. They flashed over her as the Corvette bumped past where she and Scottie were standing, and he curtly nodded his head.

Scottie squirmed and tugged at his hand, fascinated by the pretty car. He loved Renee's car, and Faith had to watch to keep him away from it, because it made Renee mad if he patted it and left his dirty little handprints behind.

"All right," Faith whispered, still dazed. "We'll go see the pretty car." They stepped back into the road and followed the Corvette, which had now stopped in front of the shack. Gray slid up from behind the wheel and swung one long leg over the door, then the other, stepping out of the low-slung car as if it were a child's vehicle. Going up the two rickety steps, he jerked open the screen door and went inside.

He didn't knock, Faith thought. Something's wrong. He didn't knock.

She speeded up, hurrying Scottie so that his short legs pumped and he gave a squawk of protest. She thought of his heart, and terror squeezed her insides. She skidded to a stop, and swiftly stooped down to pick him up. "I'm sorry, honey. I didn't mean to make you run." Her back arched from the strain of carrying him, but she ignored it and hurried her steps again. Small rocks rolled unnoticed under her bare feet, and little clouds of dust flew up with every thud of her heels. Scottie's weight seemed to drag at her, keeping her from reaching the shack. Blood roared in her ears, and a sense of dread swelled in her chest until she almost choked.

She heard some dim, faraway roar that she recognized as Pa's voice, underlaid by Gray's deeper, more thunderous tones. Panting, she pumped her thin legs even harder, and finally reached the shack. The screen door squeaked as she jerked it open and hurled herself inside, only to skid to a stop, blinking in an effort to adjust her eyes to the dimness. Unintelligible shouts and curses swirled around her, making her feel as if she were caught in some nightmare tunnel.

She gulped in air as she let Scottie slip to the floor. Scared by the shouting, he latched on to her legs and buried his face against her.

As her vision adjusted and the roaring in her ears subsided, the shouts began to make sense, and she wished they hadn't.

Gray had hauled Amos out of bed and was dragging him into the kitchen. Amos was yelling and swearing, grabbing at the doorframe in an effort to halt Gray's momentum. He was no match for the young man's enraged strength, however, and could only scramble for balance as Gray shoved him toward the center of the room.

"Where's Renee?" Gray barked, looming threateningly over Amos, who shrank back.

Amos's rheumy eyes darted around the room, as if looking for his wife. "Not here," he mumbled.

"I can see she isn't here, you stupid bastard! I want to know where in hell she *is!*"

Amos weaved back and forth on his bare feet, and suddenly belched. He was bare-chested, his pants still gaping open. His uncombed hair stood out in all directions, he was unshaven, his eyes bloodshot, and his breath foul with sleep and drink. In contrast, Gray towered over him, six feet four of lean, steely muscle, his black hair neatly brushed back, his white shirt spotless and his slacks hand-tailored to fit him.

"You ain't got no call to be shovin' me around, I don't care who your daddy is," Amos complained. Despite his bluster, he cowered back every time Gray moved.

Russ and Nicky had crowded out of their bedroom, but they made no move to back their father. Facing down a raging Gray Rouillard wasn't their style; attacking anyone who could cause them trouble wasn't their style.

"Do you know where Renee is?" Gray asked again, his voice icy.

Amos hitched one shoulder. "Must've gone out," he mumbled sullenly.

"When?"

"Whaddaya mean, when? I was in bed. How in hell would I know what time she left?"

"Did she come home last night?"

"Course she did! Gawddammit, what're you sayin'?"

Amos yelled, the slur in his words testimony to the alcohol still in his blood.

"I'm saying your whore of a wife has left!" Gray yelled back, his dark face twisted with rage, his neck corded.

Pure terror sliced through Faith, and her vision blurred again. "No," she gasped.

Gray heard her, and his head snapped around. His dark eyes were glittering with fury as they raked over her. "You look sober, at least. Do you know where Renee is? Did she come home last night?"

Numbly Faith shook her head. Black disaster loomed in front of her, and her nostrils were filled with the sharp, yellow, acrid smell of fear . . . her own.

His upper lip curled, showing strong white teeth in a snarl. "I didn't think so. She's run away with my father."

Faith shook her head again, and then couldn't seem to stop it from wagging. *No.* The word reverberated through her brain. *God, please, no.*

"You're lyin'!" Amos yelled, tottering toward the rickety table and sagging into one of the chairs. "Renee wouldn't leave me and our kids. She loves me. Your whore-hoppin' pa's out with some new piece he's found—"

Gray lunged forward like a snake striking. His fist connected with Amos's jaw, knuckles smashing against bone, and both Amos and the chair crashed to the floor. The chair splintered into kindling beneath him.

With a terrified wail, Scottie burrowed his face harder against Faith's hip. She was too frozen to even put a comforting arm around his shoulders, and he began to cry.

Amos groggily scrambled up from the floor, and staggered to put the table between him and Gray. "Why'd you hit me?" he whined, holding his jaw. "I ain't done nothin' to you. Whatever Renee and your pa done, it ain't my fault!"

"What's all the yellin' about?" came Jodie's deliberately sultry voice, the one she put on whenever she was trying to entice a man. Faith looked toward the entrance to the lean-to, and her eyes widened with horror. Jodie posed against the doorframe, her uncombed reddish blond hair tossed back over her bare shoulders. She wore only a pair of red lace panties, and demurely held the matching lace camisole so that it barely covered her breasts. She blinked at Gray with wide-eyed innocence so blatantly false that Faith cringed inside.

Gray's expression tightened with disgust as he glanced at her; his mouth curled and he deliberately turned his back. "I want you gone by nightfall," he said to Amos, his voice steely. "You stink up our land, and I'm tired of smelling you."

"Leave?" Amos croaked. "You high-and-mighty bastard, you can't make us leave. There're laws—"

"You don't pay rent," Gray said, a cold, deadly smile twisting his lips. "Eviction laws don't apply to trespassers. Get out." He turned and started toward the door.

"Wait!" Amos cried. His panicked gaze darted around the room as if looking for inspiration. He licked his lips. "Don't be so hasty. Maybe . . . maybe they just took a little trip. They'll come back. Yeah, that's right. Renee'll be back, she didn't have no reason to leave."

Gray gave a harsh bark of laughter, his contemptuous gaze moving around the room, taking in the mean interior of the shack. Someone, probably the youngest girl, had made an effort to keep it clean, but it was like trying to hold back the tide. Amos and the two boys, who were younger editions of their father, sullenly watched him. The older girl still lounged in the doorway trying to show him as much of her tits as she could without actually dropping that scrap of cloth. The little boy with Down's syndrome was clinging to the younger girl's legs and bawling. The girl was standing as if turned to stone, staring at him with huge, blank green eyes. Her dark red hair hung untidily around her shoulders, and her bare feet were dirty.

Standing so close to him, Faith could read his expression, and she cringed inside as his gaze swept over the shack and its inhabitants, finally settling on her. He catalogued her life, her family, herself, and found it all worthless.

"No reason to leave?" he sneered. "My God, as far as I can tell, she doesn't have a reason to come back!"

In the silence that followed, he stepped around Faith and shoved the screen door open. It banged against the side of the shack, then slammed shut. The Corvette's engine roared to life, and a moment later Gray was gone. Faith stood frozen in the middle of the floor, with Scottie still clinging to her legs and crying. Her mind felt numb. She knew she needed to do something, but what? Gray had said they had to leave, and the enormity of it stunned her. Leave? Where would they go? She couldn't make her mind start working. All she could do was lift her hand, which felt as heavy as lead, and smooth Scottie's hair while saying, "It's all right, it's all right," even though she knew it was a lie. Mama was gone, and it would never be all right again.

✑ Four ✑

Gray managed to make it almost half a mile before the shaking became so hard that he had to stop the car. He leaned his head on the steering wheel and closed his eyes, trying to fight off the waves of panic. God, what was he going to do? He had never before been as scared as he was now.

Bewildered pain filled him, and he felt like a child who runs to hide his face in his mother's lap, much as that Devlin kid had tried to hide against his sister's skinny legs. But he couldn't go to Noelle; even when he had *been* a child, she'd pulled away from clinging little hands, and he'd learned to go to his father for reassurance. Even had Noelle been more affectionate, he couldn't look to her for support, because she would be looking to him for the same thing. Taking care of his mother and sister was his responsibility now.

Why had Guy done it? How could he have left? His father's absence, his betrayal, made Gray feel as if his heart had been torn out. Guy had had Renee anyway; what had she offered that tempted him into turning his back on his children, his business, his heritage? Gray had always been close to his father, had grown up surrounded by his love, had always felt his support like a solid rock at his back, but now that loving, reassuring presence was gone, and with it the foundation of his life.

He was terrified. He was only twenty-two, and the problems looming over him looked like unscalable mountains. Noelle and Monica still didn't know; somehow he had to find the strength to tell them. He had to be a rock for them, and he had to put aside his own pain and concentrate on holding the family finances together, or they stood to lose everything. This wasn't the same situation it would have been if Guy had died, for Gray would have inherited the shares, the money, and the control. As it was now, Guy still owned everything, and he was gone. The Rouillard fortune could come tumbling down around their ears, with wary investors jumping ship and various boards of directors seizing power. Gray would have to fight like a son of a bitch to keep even half of what they now had.

He, Monica, and Noelle had some assets in their own names, but it wouldn't be enough. Guy had been giving Gray a crash course in managing it all, but hadn't given him the power to do so, unless he'd left a letter giving Gray his proxy. Desperate hope reared its head. Any such letter, if it existed, would be in the desk in the study.

Failing that, he'd have to call Alex and get his help in laying out a strategy. Alex was a damn smart man and a good corporate lawyer; he could have had a much more lucrative practice somewhere else, but he was backed by his own family money and hadn't felt the need to leave Prescott. He had handled all of Guy's business, as well as being his best friend, so he knew as much or more about the legal situation as did Gray.

God knows, Gray thought bleakly, he'd need all the help he could get. If there wasn't a letter of proxy, he'd be lucky to keep a roof over them.

When he raised his head from the steering wheel, he had regained his self-control, the pain pushed to the background and steely determination taking its place. By God, his mother and sister would have a hard enough time dealing with this as it was; he'd be damned if he let them lose their home, too.

He put the car into gear and drove away, leaving the last remnants of his boyhood behind on the rutted dirt track.

* * *

He went first into Prescott, to Alex's office. He would have to move fast to salvage anything. Andrea broke into a smile when he came in, something women often did at the sight of him. Color heightened a little on her round, pleasant face. She was forty-five, old enough to be his mother, but age had nothing to do with her instinctive female reaction to his tall, muscular presence.

Gray automatically returned the smile, but his mind was racing with plans. "Is anyone with Alex? I need to see him."

"No, he's alone. Go on in, hon."

Gray walked past her desk and into Alex's office, firmly closing the door behind him. Alex looked up from the well-ordered mountain of files on his desk, and got to his feet. His good-looking face was taut with worry. "Did you find him?"

Gray shook his head. "Renee Devlin's gone, too."

"Oh, God." Alex collapsed back into his chair and shut his eyes, pinching the bridge of his nose. "I can't believe it. I didn't think he was serious. My God, why would he be? He was—" He stopped and opened his eyes, flushing a little.

"Fucking her anyway," Gray finished bluntly. He walked over to the window and stood with his hands in his pockets, looking down on the main street. Prescott was a small town, only about fifteen thousand citizens, but today traffic hummed around the courthouse square. Soon everyone down there would know that Guy Rouillard had left his wife and children and run off with the Devlin whore.

"Does your mama know?" Alex's voice was strained.

Gray shook his head. "Not yet. I'll tell her and Monica when I go home." The original shock and pain had gone, leaving behind a ruthless willpower and a certain remoteness, as if he were standing at a distance watching himself go through the motions. Some of that distance leaked into his tone, making him sound cool and steady. "Did Dad leave a letter of proxy with you?"

Until then, evidently, Alex had thought only of the personal ramifications of Guy's defection. Now the legal aspects dawned on him, and his eyes widened with horror. "Shit," he said, lapsing into unusual vulgarity. "No, he

42

didn't. If he had, I'd have known he was serious about leaving and tried to stop him."

"There may be a letter in the desk at home. He may call in a day or so. If so, there's no problem with the financial side of things. But if there isn't a letter, and he doesn't call . . . I can't afford to wait. I'll have to liquidate as much as I can, before news of this gets around and stock prices drop like a rock."

"He'll call," Alex said feebly. "He has to. He can't just walk away from this kind of financial obligation. A fortune is involved!"

Gray shrugged, his face a careful blank. "He walked away from his family. I can't afford to assume that the business means more to him." He paused. "I don't think he'll come back or call. I think he meant to walk away from everything and never come back. He's been teaching me as much as he could, and now I know why. If he had meant to stay in charge of everything, he wouldn't have done that."

"Then there should be a letter of proxy," Alex said insistently. "Guy was too sharp of a businessman not to have taken care of that."

"Maybe, but I have Mother and Monica to think about. I can't wait. I have to liquidate now, and get as much money as I can, so I'll have something to work with and rebuild. If I don't, and he doesn't make arrangements, we won't have a pot to piss in."

Alex swallowed, but he nodded. "Okay. I'll start doing what I can to shore up your legal position, but I have to tell you, unless Guy gets back in touch or left a letter of proxy, it's a mess. Everything is tied up unless Noelle divorces him and the court awards her half of his assets, but that will take time."

"I have to plan for the worst," Gray said. "I'll go home and look for a letter, but don't wait until you hear from me to get started. If there isn't a letter, I'll call the broker immediately and start selling. Either way, I'll let you know. Keep it quiet until I call."

Alex got to his feet. "I won't even let Andrea know." He shoved his hands through his dark hair, an indication of his worry, because Alex wasn't given to nervous gestures. His gray eyes were dark with misery. "I'm sorry, Gray. I feel like this is my fault. I should have done something."

Gray shook his head. "Don't blame yourself. Like you said, who would have thought he was serious? No, the only people I blame are Dad and Renee Devlin." He gave a wintry smile. "I can't imagine anything she had being good enough to make him walk out on his family, but evidently it was." He paused, lost for a moment in the grimness of his thoughts, then shook himself and headed toward the door. "I'll call you when I find out something."

After he had gone, Alex sank back into his chair, his movements stiff and feeble. He barely managed to control his expression when Andrea popped into the office, alive with curiosity. "What's going on with Gray?"

"Nothing much. A personal matter he wanted to talk over with me."

She was disappointed that he didn't confide in her. "Is there anything I can do to help?"

"No, everything will be all right." He sighed, and rubbed his eyes. "Why don't you go on to lunch, and bring me back a sandwich or something. I'm waiting for a call, so I can't leave."

"Okay. What do you want?"

He waved his hand. "Anything. You know what I like. Surprise me."

She rambled around in the outer office for a few minutes, cutting off the computer he'd bought the year before, storing the disks, collecting her purse. After she'd gone, Alex waited a few minutes before going into the other room and locking the door. Then he sat down in her chair and turned on the computer, and swiftly began typing. "Damn you, Guy," he whispered. "You son of a bitch."

Gray parked the Corvette in front of the five wide steps leading up to the covered porch and double front doors, though Noelle frowned on that and preferred that the family's cars be properly protected and out of sight in the attached garage behind. The front drive was for visitors, who shouldn't be able to tell which family members were at home by the vehicles parked in front. That way, one felt no obligation to admit to being there, and thus forced to receive unwanted guests. Some of Noelle's notions were positively Victorian; usually he indulged her, but today he had more important things on his mind, and was in a hurry.

He leaped up the steps with two strides, and pushed open the door. Monica had probably been watching from her bedroom window, because she was hurrying down the stairs, anxiety twisting her face. "Daddy *still* hasn't come home!" she hissed, glancing toward the breakfast parlor, where Noelle was evidently lingering over a late breakfast. "Why did you break the window in his study, then light out of here like a cat with its tail on fire? And why did you park in front? Mother won't like that."

Guy didn't answer, but strode rapidly down the hall to the study, his bootheels thudding on the parquet floor. Monica rushed after him, and slipped into the study as he began examining, one by one, the papers on Guy's desk.

"I don't believe Alex told the truth about the poker game," she said, her lips trembling a little. "Call him again, Gray. Make him tell you where Daddy is."

"In a minute," Gray murmured, not sparing her a glance. None of the papers on top of the desk was a letter of proxy. He began opening drawers.

"Gray!" Her voice rose sharply. "Surely finding Daddy's more important than looking through his desk!"

He stopped, took a deep breath, and straightened. "Monica, honey, sit down over there and hush," he said in a kind tone that nevertheless was underlaid with steel. "I have to look for a very important paper that Dad may have left here. I'll be with you in a minute."

She opened her mouth to say something else, but he gave her a look that changed her mind. Silently, vague surprise on her face, she sat down, and Gray returned to his search.

Five minutes later, he sat back with the taste of defeat bitter in his mouth. There was no letter. It didn't make sense. Why would Guy have gone to so much trouble to teach him everything, then leave without providing the proxies? As Alex had said, Guy was too smart not to have thought of it. If he intended to stay in charge himself, why had he bothered to give Gray such intense instruction? Maybe he had intended to turn over the reins to Gray, then changed his mind. That was the only other explanation there could be. In that case, they would be hearing from him again, within a few days at the most, because his financial dealings were too complicated to leave for longer than that.

But, as he'd told Alex, he couldn't afford to assume things would be taken care of. He couldn't imagine Guy *not* taking care of business, but until this morning he hadn't been able to imagine Guy leaving them for Renee Devlin, either. The impossible had happened, so how could he blindly trust in anything else he had always assumed to be true of his father? Responsibility for his mother and sister weighed heavily on his shoulders. He couldn't risk their welfare.

He reached for the telephone, but it wasn't there. Dimly he remembered throwing it earlier, and glanced at the window that was now boarded over, awaiting new panes. He got up and walked out into the hallway, to the phone on the table at the foot of the stairs. Monica trailed after him, still silent but plainly resenting the restriction.

He called Alex first. Alex answered the phone on the first ring. "No letter," Gray said briefly. "See what you can do about getting power of attorney for me, or anything else that will shore up my position." Power of attorney was a long shot, but maybe a few strings could be pulled.

"I've already started," Alex said quietly.

Next Gray called his broker. His instructions were brief, and explicit. If worst came to worst, he would need every bit of ready cash he could scrape together.

Now for the hardest part. Monica was staring at him, her big, dark eyes filled with alarm. "Something's wrong, isn't it?" she asked.

He mentally braced himself, then took Monica's hand in his. "Let's go talk to Mother," he said.

She started to ask something else, but he shook his head. "I can only say it once," he said, his voice rough.

Noelle was enjoying her last cup of tea as she read the society section of the New Orleans newspaper. Prescott had its own small weekly paper, in which she was regularly mentioned, but being in the New Orleans paper was what really counted. Her name was listed there often enough to make her the envy of the rest of the parish society. She was dressed in her favorite white, with her sleek dark hair pulled back into a French twist. Her makeup was minimal but perfect, her jewelry expensive but understated. There was nothing gaudy or frivolous about Noelle, not one bow or ruffle or jarring bit of color, just clean, classic lines. Even her nails never wore anything but clear polish.

She looked up as Gray and Monica entered the breakfast parlor, and her gaze flicked briefly to their clasped hands. She didn't comment on it, though, for that would express personal interest, and perhaps invite the same. "Good morning, Gray," she greeted him, her voice perfectly composed as always. Noelle could violently hate someone, but the person would never be able to tell by her voice; it never revealed warmth, affection, anger, or any other emotion. Such a display would be common, and Noelle allowed nothing about herself to sink to that low standard. "Shall I call for another pot of tea?"

"No, thank you, Mother. I need to talk to you and Monica; something serious has happened." He felt Monica's hand tremble in his, and squeezed it reassuringly.

Noelle put aside the newspaper. "Should we be more private?" she asked, concerned that one of the servants would overhear them discussing a personal matter.

"There's no need." Gray pulled out a chair for Monica, then stood behind her with one hand on her shoulder. Noelle would be upset because of the social nuances, the embarrassment of it, but Monica's pain would be worse. "I don't know of any way to make this easier. He didn't leave a note or anything like that, but Dad seems to have left town with Renee Devlin. They're both gone."

Noelle's slender hand fluttered toward her throat. Monica was motionless, not even breathing.

"I'm sure he wouldn't take a woman like that on a business trip," Noelle said with calm certainty. "Think how it would look."

"Mother—" Gray cut himself off, stifling his impatience. "He isn't on a business trip. Dad and Renee Devlin have run away together. He won't be coming back."

47

Monica gave a thin cry, and pressed both hands to her mouth to cut off the sound. Noelle's face lost its color, but her movements were precise as she placed her teacup in the center of the saucer. "I'm sure you're mistaken, dear. Your father wouldn't risk his social position for—"

"For God's sake, Mother!" Gray snapped, his tenuous control on his patience snapping like a thread. "Dad doesn't give a rat's ass about his social position. You're the one it's important to, not him!"

"Grayson, it isn't necessary to be vulgar."

He ground his teeth together. It was typical of her to ignore something she found unpleasant and focus on the trivial. "Dad's gone," he said, deliberately emphasizing the words. "He's left you for Renee. They've run away together, and he won't be coming back. No one else knows it yet, but it'll probably be all over the parish by tomorrow morning."

Her eyes widened at that last sentence, and horror filled them as she realized the humiliation of her position. "No," she whispered. "He couldn't do that to me."

"He did. It's done."

Blindly she got to her feet, shaking her head. "He—he's really gone?" she asked in a faint murmur. "He left *me* for that . . . that—" Unable to finish, she walked quickly from the room, almost as if she were fleeing.

As soon as Noelle was gone, as soon as she was no longer there to frown at unseemly displays, Monica wilted onto the table, falling forward to bury her face against her arm. Harsh sobs tore up from her throat and shook her slim body. Almost as angry at Noelle as he was at Guy, Gray knelt beside his sister and put his arms around her.

"It's going to be tough," he said, "but we'll get through this. I'm going to be really busy the next few days, getting our finances under control, but I'll be here if you need me." He couldn't bring himself to tell her that financial disaster was looming. "I know it hurts now, but we'll make it all right."

"I hate him," Monica sobbed, her voice muffled. "He left us for that . . . that *whore!* I hope he doesn't come back. I *hate* him, I never want to see him again!" Abruptly she tore away from him, overturning her chair as she shoved it back

48

from the table. She was still sobbing as she ran from the parlor, and he heard the harsh, gulping sounds continue all the way up the stairs. A moment later the slam of her bedroom door echoed through the house.

Gray wanted to bury his own face in his hands. He wanted to punch something, preferably his father's nose. He wanted to roar his rage to the heavens. The situation was bad enough as it was; why did Noelle have to make it worse by being concerned only with what her friends would say? For once, why couldn't she give some support to her daughter? Couldn't she see how much Monica needed her now? But she had never been there for them, so why should that change now? Unlike Guy, Noelle was at least constant.

He needed a drink, a stiff one. He left the breakfast parlor and went back to the study, to the bottle of Scotch that Guy always kept in the liquor cabinet behind his desk. Oriane, their longtime housekeeper, was going up the stairs with an armload of towels, and she gave him a curious look. Not being deaf, of course, she had heard some of the uproar. The speculation between Oriane, her husband, Garron, who took care of the grounds, and Delfina, the cook, would be rampant. They would have to be told, of course, but he couldn't bring himself to do it right then. Maybe after he had that drink of Scotch.

He opened the cabinet and took out the bottle, and splashed a couple of inches of the amber liquid into a glass. The smoky, biting flavor was sharp on his tongue as he took the first sip, then threw the rest of it back with a neat, stiff motion of his wrist. He needed the sedative effect, not the taste. He had just poured himself a second drink when a shrill scream from upstairs pierced the air, followed by Oriane shrieking his name, over and over.

Monica. As soon as he heard Oriane scream, Gray knew. Dread congealed in his chest as he bolted from the study and took the stairs three at a time, his long, powerful legs propelling him upward. Oriane rushed down the hall toward him, her eyes wide with panic. "She's cut herself, bad! Ohmigod, ohmigod, there's blood all over the place—"

Gray pushed past her and ran into Monica's bedroom. She wasn't there, but the door to her bathroom was open, and he threw himself toward it, only to stop, frozen, in the doorway.

Monica had decorated her bedroom and bath herself, in delicate pinks and pearly whites that looked absurdly little-girlish. Normally Gray was reminded of cotton candy, but now the pink ceramic tile on the bathroom floor was covered with dark red splotches. Monica sat calmly on the fuzzy pink toilet lid, her big, dark eyes empty as she stared out the window. Her hands were neatly folded on her lap. Blood pulsed from the deep gashes she had made in both wrists, soaking her lap, running down her legs to pool on the floor.

"I'm sorry for the commotion," she said in an eerily remote little voice. "I didn't expect Oriane to bring up clean towels."

"Jesus," he groaned, and snatched up the towels Oriane had dropped. He went down on one knee beside Monica and grabbed her left wrist. "Damn it, Monica, I ought to tan your ass!" He wrapped one towel around her wrist, then tied another one around it as tightly as he could.

"Just leave me alone," she whispered, trying to tug her arm away from him, but she was already frighteningly weak.

"Shut up!" he barked, taking her right wrist and repeating the procedure. "Goddamn it, how could you do something this stupid?" This, on top of everything else he had gone through that day, was almost more than he could bear. Fear and rage mingled in his chest and swelled until he thought he would choke. "Did you stop to think about anyone but yourself? Did you think that maybe I could use your help, that this is as hard on everyone else as it is on you?" He ground the words out between clenched teeth as he snatched her up against his chest and ran, past Noelle, who was simply standing in the hallway with a dazed expression on her bloodless face, down the stairs, and past Oriane and Delfina clutching each other in the foyer.

"Call the clinic and let Dr. Bogarde know we're on the way," he ordered as he carried Monica out the front door and down the steps, to the Corvette parked there.

"I'll get blood in your car," Monica protested feebly.

"I told you to shut up," he snapped. "Don't talk unless

you have something sensible to say." Probably he was supposed to be more sensitive with someone who had just attempted suicide, but this was his sister, and he was damned if he would let her take her own life. He was in a towering rage, the fury just barely controlled. It seemed as if his life had gone to hell in just the past few hours, and he was fed up with the people he loved doing stupid things.

He didn't bother opening the door of the Corvette, but simply leaned over and deposited her in the seat, then vaulted over her into the driver's seat. He started the engine, let out the clutch, and left rubber on the driveway as he pushed the powerful motor to the limit. Monica slumped weakly against the passenger door, her eyes closed. He shot her a panicked glance, but didn't risk taking the time to stop. She was deathly white, and there was a faint bluish tinge forming around her mouth. Blood was already seeping through the towels, the bright red garish against the white fabric. He had seen the cuts; they hadn't been shallow slices, gestures made more to frighten and gain attention than seriously threaten a life. No, Monica had been very serious about the attempt. His sister might die because his father couldn't resist chasing after that redheaded Devlin whore.

He made the fifteen-mile trip to the clinic in just under ten minutes. The parking lot was full, but he pulled around to the back door of the one-story brick building and blew the horn, then leaped out to lift Monica into his arms again. She was totally limp, her head lolling against his shoulder, and hot tears seared his eyelids.

The back door opened and Dr. Bogarde rushed out, followed by both his nurses. "Put her in the first room on the right," he said, and Gray turned sideways to get her through the doorway. Sadie Lee Fanchier, the senior nurse, held the door to the examining room open and he carried Monica inside, then gently deposited her on the narrow table, the sheet-covered vinyl creaking as it took her weight.

Sadie Lee was wrapping a blood pressure cuff around Monica's arm even as Dr. Bogarde was untying Gray's first-aid efforts. Quickly she pumped it up, then listened through the stethoscope pressed to the inside of Monica's elbow. "Seventy-five over forty."

"Start an IV," Dr. Bogarde ordered. "Glucose." The other nurse, Kitty, moved to follow his instructions.

Dr. Bogarde kept his eyes on Monica's wrists as he worked. "She needs blood," he said. "Fast. We have to get her to the hospital in Baton Rouge, because I can't do it here. She'll need a vascular specialist to repair her veins, too. I can stabilize her, Gray, but I can't do any more than that."

Kitty hung the clear bag of glucose on the metal rack and deftly inserted the IV needle in Monica's arm. "We don't have time to get an ambulance here," the doctor continued. "We'll take her ourselves, in my car. You okay to drive?" he asked Gray, shooting him a sharp glance.

"Yes." The answer was flat, unequivocal.

Dr. Bogarde tightly taped Monica's wrists. "Okay, that's got the bleeding stopped. Kitty, I need a couple of blankets. Put one over the backseat of my car, and tuck the other one over Monica. Gray, pick her up again, and be careful of that IV line. Sadie Lee, call the hospital and let 'em know we're on the way, and then give a call to the sheriff's department so they can clear the roads a mite."

Gently Gray lifted his sister. Dr. Bogarde took the glucose bag in one hand and his medical bag in the other, and trotted at Gray's side as he carried Monica out to the doctor's four-door Chrysler. The doctor climbed in first, then helped Gray carefully maneuver Monica onto the backseat. Dr. Bogarde hooked the glucose bag on the garment hanger over the side window, and took up a position on his knees on the floorboard.

"Don't go slamming us around," he instructed as Gray squeezed his long frame under the steering wheel. Dr. Bogarde was barely five foot five, so the seat was so close to the steering wheel that Gray's chest was brushing it. He couldn't let the seat back, though, with Dr. Bogarde on the back floorboard. "Keep it at a steady speed and we'll make better time. And put on the emergency lights."

Gray had a violent thought about backseat drivers, but he kept it to himself. Following orders, he left the clinic more sedately than he had arrived, though his instincts were screaming at him to push the gas pedal to the floorboard and keep it there. Only the knowledge that the roomy sedan, built more for comfort than road handling, would likely straighten out a curve if he pushed it the way he did the Corvette kept him at a reasonable speed.

"How'd this happen?" Dr. Bogarde asked.

Gray glanced at him in the rearview mirror. The doctor was a small, dapper man with shrewd blue eyes. Despite his name, he was neither Creole nor Cajun; he had to be in his mid-fifties, with graying, sandy blond hair. Gray had known him all of his life. Noelle had never gone to him, preferring an urbane physician in New Orleans, but everyone else in the family had been to see him with everything from childhood cuts to influenza to the broken arm Gray had received in spring practice when he was fifteen.

Gray didn't want to tell him everything, preferring to keep the details quiet for a while longer until his broker had had time to sell and Alex had done his legal maneuvers, but it wouldn't be possible to completely stifle the news. He gave Dr. Bogarde the central fact, the only one that mattered. "Dad and Mother have separated. Monica . . . ." He hesitated.

Dr. Bogarde sighed. "I see." Everyone in the parish knew how Monica doted on Guy.

Gray concentrated on his driving. The Chrysler's suspension evened out the bumpy roads, and the tires sang on the pavement. The sense of unreality he'd experienced earlier returned. The sun poured hotly through the window, burning his jean-clad leg, and the tall pines flashed by. The sky overhead was a deep, pure blue. It was high summer, and everything was as familiar as his own face. That was what was strange. How could it all be so unchanged, when his world had crashed around him today?

Behind him, Dr. Bogarde checked Monica's pulse and blood pressure again. "Gray," he said quietly. "You'd better go faster."

∽ Five ∽

It was ten-thirty that night when Gray and Dr. Bogarde left the hospital in Baton Rouge. Gray's eyes burned with fatigue, and he was numb from the emotional roller coaster he'd been on all day long. Monica had finally been stabilized and undergone surgery, and was sleeping peacefully, under sedation. She had gone into cardiac arrest soon after arriving at the hospital, but the emergency room team had gotten her heartbeat back almost immediately. She had been given four units of blood prior to surgery, and another two units in surgery. The doctor who had done the repair work thought there was no permanent damage in her right wrist, but she had severed a couple of tendons in her left wrist and might not regain full mobility there.

All that mattered to Gray was that she was going to live. She had awakened briefly when she was transferred from recovery to the private room he'd gotten for her, and had groggily murmured, "I'm sorry, Gray," when she had seen him. He didn't know if she'd meant she was sorry she'd tried to kill herself, sorry that she hadn't succeeded, or sorry that she had caused him so much worry. He chose to believe she meant the first possibility, because he couldn't handle the thought that she might try again.

"I'll drive," Dr. Bogarde said, reaching up to slap him on the shoulder. "You look like hell."

"I feel like hell," Gray rumbled. "I need a cup of coffee." He was just as glad to let Doc drive. His brain felt like a wasteland; it probably wouldn't be safe for him to do the driving, and it *was* the doc's car. His knees would still be sticking up under his chin, but at least he'd have room to breathe.

"I can manage that. There's a McDonald's a few blocks from here."

Gray folded and inserted himself, and thanked God that the Chrysler had a padded dashboard. If it hadn't, his shins would have been black and blue.

Fifteen minutes later, with a large polystyrene cup of coffee gently steaming in his hand, he watched the street-lights of Baton Rouge slide past. Some of the happiest years of his life had been spent here, at LSU. He had prowled all over this city, a wild, energetic, perpetually horny kid on the hunt for action, and there was plenty of it. No one knew how to have more fun than a Cajun, and Baton Rouge was full of coon-asses. His four years here had been a ball.

It hadn't been that long ago that he'd come home for good, only a couple of months, but it felt like a lifetime. This nightmarish, unending day had forever sealed away that high-spirited kid, leaving a definite line of demarcation between the two parts of his life. Gray had been growing up gradually, like most people, but today the full weight of adult responsibility had been dumped on his shoulders. They were broad enough to carry the load, so he'd braced himself and done what had to be done. If the man who emerged from the wreckage was grimmer and more ruthless than he'd been when he'd gotten out of bed that morning— well, if that was the price of survival, he'd gladly pay it.

More problems awaited him at home. Under these circumstances, most mothers would have had to be pried from their child's bedside with a crowbar, but not Noelle. He hadn't even been able to get her to the telephone. He'd talked instead to Oriane, who told him that Miss Noelle had locked herself in her bedroom and wouldn't come out. At his instruction, Oriane had relayed the information that Monica would be all right, shouting it through the locked door.

At least he had no fears that Noelle would try the same stunt Monica had pulled. He knew his mother too well; she was too self-centered to harm herself.

Despite the coffee, he dozed on the way home, and woke only when Dr. Bogarde stopped the car at the rear of the clinic. He'd left the top down on the Corvette, having more important things on his mind, so dew had collected on the seats. He'd have a wet ass on the drive home, and he was almost grateful. Maybe it would keep him awake.

"Will you be able to sleep tonight?" Dr. Bogarde asked. "I can give you something if you think you'll need it."

Gray gave a short bark of laughter. "My problem will be staying awake until I get home."

"In that case, maybe you'd better sleep here at the clinic."

"Thanks, Doc, but if the hospital needs me, they'll call me at home."

"All right. Be careful, then."

"I will." Gray swung his leg over the door of the 'Vette and slid into the seat. Yep. A definite wet ass. The cool moisture made him shiver.

He left the top down, letting the air slap him in the face. The night smells were clear and sweet, fresher than when heated by the sun. As he left Prescott behind, the rural darkness closed in around him, soothing and protective.

One oasis of light disturbed the darkness, though. Jimmy Jo's, the local roadhouse, was still booming. The gravel parking lot was crowded with cars and pickup trucks, the neon sign blinked in endless welcome, and the walls were thudding with the force of the music. As Gray neared, the black Corvette slicing through the night, a battered pickup shot out of the parking lot into his path, tires screeching as they grabbed for traction.

Gray stomped the brake pedal, bringing the 'Vette to a sliding halt. The truck skidded sideways, almost overturned, then righted itself. His headlights caught the faces of the occupants, roaring with laughter as the one on the passenger side, waving a bottle of beer in his hand, leaned out and shouted something at Gray.

Gray froze. He couldn't understand what had been shouted, but that didn't matter. What mattered was that the occupants were Russ and Nicky Devlin, and that they were headed in the same direction he'd been going, toward Rouillard land.

The bastards hadn't left. They were still on his property. The rage built slowly. It was cold, but it was powerful. Oddly detached, he felt it come, starting at his feet and working up, as if transmuting the very cells of his body. It reached his abdomen and tightened the muscles, then filled his chest before spreading upward to explode in his brain. It was almost a relief, banishing the fatigue and mental fog, leaving his thought processes cool and precise even as all systems kicked into overdrive.

He turned the Corvette around and headed back toward Prescott. Sheriff Deese wouldn't like being woken up this time of night, but Gray was a Rouillard, and the sheriff would do as he asked. Hell, he'd even enjoy it. Getting rid of the Devlins would cut the crime rate of the parish in half.

Faith hadn't been able to relax all day. She had been almost sick with a sense of disaster and loss, unable to eat. Scottie, sensing her mood, had been whiny and fearful, continually clutching at her legs and getting in her way as she mechanically tried to do her chores.

After Gray had left that morning, Faith had numbly started packing, but Amos had slapped her on the side of the head and yelled at her not to be stupid. Renee might've gone off for a couple of days, but she'd be back, and old man Rouillard wouldn't let that young son of a bitch run them out of their home.

Even in her misery, Faith wondered why Pa called Guy an old man, when he was a year younger than Pa.

After a while, Amos had gotten into his truck and gone in search of a drink. As soon as he was out of sight, Jodie darted into the bedroom and began going through Renee's closet.

Faith followed her sister, and watched in bewilderment as she began tossing garments onto the bed. "What are you doing?"

"Mama won't need these anymore," Jodie blithely replied. "Guy will buy her all new stuff. Why do you think she didn't carry this with her? I can sure use it, though. She never would let me borrow any of her clothes." This last was said with a tinge of bitterness. She held up a tight yellow dress with sequins around the neckline. It had been oddly striking on Renee, with her dark red hair, but clashed horribly with Jodie's carroty locks. "I had a hot date with Lane Foster last week and wanted to wear this, but she wouldn't let me," she said resentfully. "I had to wear my old blue dress, and he'd seen it before."

"Don't take Mama's clothes," Faith protested, her eyes filling with tears.

Jodie gave her an exasperated look. "Why not? She won't be needin' them."

"Pa said she'll come back."

Jodie hooted with laughter. "Pa don't know his ass from a hole in the ground. Gray was right. Why on earth would she come back? Nah, even if Guy chickens out and goes running home to that ice cube he's married to, Mama will get enough from him to keep herself real pretty for a long time."

"Then we'll have to leave," Faith said, and a salty tear trickled down her cheek to puddle at the corner of her mouth. "We should be packing."

Jodie patted her on the shoulder. "Baby sister, you're too innocent for your own good. Gray was mad as hell, but like as not, he won't do anything. He was just shootin' off his mouth. I think I'll go see him, and maybe get the same kind of arrangement his pa had with Mama." She licked her lips, and a hungry look came over her face. "I've always wanted to find out if what he has in his britches is as big as I've heard it is."

Faith jerked away, jealousy slicing through her misery. Jodie didn't have the sense to see that a snowball would have a better chance at surviving a Fourth of July picnic on the equator than she had of attracting Gray, but oh, how Faith envied her the gumption to try. She tried to imagine how powerful it would feel, to have the self-confidence to walk up to a man and be certain he found her attractive. Even when Gray turned Jodie down, it wouldn't put a dent in her ego, because there were too many other boys and men panting after her. It would just make Gray more of a challenge to her.

But Faith had seen the cold contempt in his eyes that morning when he had surveyed the shack and its inhabitants, and shame had shriveled her soul. She had wanted to say, "I'm not like that," wanted him to look at her with admiration. But she *was* like that, as far as he was concerned, because she lived in this squalor.

Humming happily, Jodie took Renee's gaudy rainbow of clothes into the back room, to try them on and put darts in the bodice, because Renee's breasts were larger.

Barely choking back sobs, Faith grabbed Scottie by the hand and took him outside to play. She sat on a stump with her face buried in her hands while he pushed his little cars around in the dirt. Normally he would be happy doing that all day, but after about an hour he came over to her and curled up by her legs, and was soon asleep. She smoothed his hair, terrified by the faint blue tinge of his lips.

She rocked back and forth on the stump, her eyes stark with misery as she stared at nothing. Mama was gone, and Scottie was dying. There was no telling how much longer he could last, but she didn't think it would be more than a year. As bad as things had been, at least there had been a kind of security, because things were the same day after day and she knew what to expect. Now everything had come apart, and she was terrified. She had learned how to get along, how to manage Pa and the boys, but nothing was going according to plan now and she was helpless. She hated the feeling, hated it with a ferocity that made her stomach knot.

Damn Mama, she thought rebelliously. *And damn Guy Rouillard.* All they had thought about was themselves, not their families, nor about the turmoil they would leave behind.

She hadn't felt like a child in a long time. Responsibility had been pushed onto her frail shoulders at an early age, giving her eyes a solemn maturity that jarred with her youth, but now she acutely felt her lack of years. She was too young to *do* anything. She couldn't take Scottie and leave, because she was too young to work and support them. She was too young even to live by herself, according to law. She was helpless, her life controlled totally by the whim of the adults around her.

She couldn't even run away, because she couldn't leave Scottie. No one else would look after him, and he was almost as helpless as an infant. She had to stay.

So she sat on the stump as the afternoon hours slid away, too miserable to go inside and do any of her regular chores. She felt as if she were on a guillotine, waiting for the blade to fall, and as evening approached the tension grew and stretched until every nerve ending felt raw and exposed, until she felt like screaming to shatter the waiting stillness. Scottie had awakened from his nap and played close by her legs, as if afraid to get too far from her.

But evening came, and the blade didn't fall. Scottie was hungry, pulling at her, wanting to go in. Reluctantly Faith got up from the stump and took him inside just as Russ and Nicky left to go about their nightly carousing. Jodie dressed in the yellow dress she had coveted, and left too.

Maybe Jodie was right, Faith thought. Maybe Gray had just been blowing off steam, and hadn't meant what he'd said. Maybe Guy had gotten in touch with his family sometime during the day, and somehow defused the situation. He could have changed his mind about leaving, and denied having Renee with him. Anything was possible.

No matter what, though, she didn't expect Renee to come back. And without Renee, even if Guy did return to his family, there wouldn't be any reason for him to let them stay on in the shack. It wasn't much, but it was a roof over their heads, and it was free. No, it was no use hoping; she had to use her common sense. One way or another, maybe not right away but pretty soon, they were going to have to leave. If she knew Pa, though, he wouldn't make a move to get out until he was forced. He would milk every free hour he could from the Rouillards.

She fed Scottie and bathed him, then put him to bed. For the second night in a row she had blessed privacy, and she hurried to take her own bath and put on her nightgown. But when she pulled out her precious book, she couldn't concentrate enough to read. The scene that morning with

Gray continually replayed itself in her mind, like film on a mental tape that just kept running. Every time she thought of that look of contempt in his eyes, pain expanded in her chest until she could barely breathe. She rolled over and buried her face in her pillow, fighting the hot tears. She loved him so, and he despised her, because she was a Devlin.

She dozed, exhausted by the restless night before and the trauma of the day. Always a light sleeper, as alert as a cat, she awakened and mentally checked the roll every time a member of the family came home. Pa came home first. He was drunk, of course, having gotten such an early start on the process, but for once he didn't bellow for a supper that he wouldn't eat anyway. Faith listened to his progress as he stumbled and lurched toward his bedroom. Moments later came the familiar, labored snoring.

Jodie came home about eleven, sullen and pouting. Her evening must not have gone as she had planned, Faith thought, but she lay quietly on her cot and didn't ask. Jodie took off the yellow dress, wadded it up, and threw it into a corner. Then she flounced onto her own cot and turned her back.

It was an early night for everyone. The boys rolled in not long after, laughing and raising a ruckus, waking Scottie as usual. Faith didn't get up, and soon things quieted down again.

They were all home, all except for Mama. Faith cried silently, wiping her tears with the thin sheet, and soon dozed again.

A huge crash brought her upright in the cot, confused and terrified. A bright light flashed in her eyes, blinding her, and a rough hand hauled her out of the cot. Faith screamed and tried to tear away from the painful grip on her arm, tried to dig in her heels and brace herself, but whoever it was jerked her off her feet as if she weighed no more than a child, and literally dragged her through the shack. Over her own terrified screams she could hear Scottie's shrieks, hear Pa and the boys cussing and yelling, hear Jodie sobbing.

There was a semicircle of piercingly bright lights arranged out on the dirt yard, and Faith had a blurred impression of a lot of people, moving back and forth. The man holding her

61

kicked open the screen door and shoved her outside. She tripped over the rickety steps and sprawled on her face in the dirt, her nightgown riding high on her legs. Rocks and grit skinned the hide from her knees and palms, and scraped a raw place on her forehead.

"Here," someone said. "Take the kid." Scottie was roughly deposited beside her. He was screaming hysterically, his round blue eyes blank and terrified. Faith scrambled to a sitting position, shoving her nightgown down over her legs, and gathered him into her arms.

Things were flying through the air, crashing and thudding all around her. She saw Amos, clinging to the doorframe as two men in brown uniforms bodily hauled him out of the house. Deputies, she thought, dazed. What were deputies doing out here, unless Pa or the boys had been caught stealing something? As she watched, one of the deputies cracked Amos's fingers with his flashlight. Amos cried out and released the frame, and they tossed him into the yard.

A chair came sailing out the door, and Faith ducked to the side. It hit the ground right where she had been, and splintered. Half crawling, with Scottie's arms locked around her neck and dragging her down, she struggled toward the shelter of Pa's old truck, where she huddled against the front tire.

Stunned, she stared at the nightmare scene, trying to make sense of it. Things were being tossed out windows, clothes and pots and dishes flying. The dishes were plastic, and made a huge clatter as they landed. A drawer of flatware was emptied out a window, the cheap stainless steel flashing in the lights of the patrol cars.

"Clean it out," she heard a deep voice growl. "I don't want anything left inside."

Gray! The recognition of that beloved voice froze her, crouched there on the ground with Scottie clutched protectively to her. She found him almost immediately, his tall, powerful form standing with arms crossed over his chest, next to the sheriff.

"You ain't got no call to do this to us!" Amos was bawling, trying to grab Gray by the arm. Gray shook him off with no more effort than if he'd been a pesky little dog. "You can't throw us out in the middle of the night! What about my children, my poor little retarded boy? Ain't you got no feelin' at all, treatin' a helpless child like that?"

"I told you to be out by nightfall, and I meant it," Gray snapped. "Gather up what you want to take with you, because in half an hour I'm setting fire to whatever is left."

"My clothes!" Jodie yelped, leaping out from between the safety of two cars. She began darting around the wreckage, grabbing up garments and discarding them when they proved to be someone else's, draping her own over one shoulder.

Faith struggled to her feet with Scottie still clinging to her, desperation giving her strength. Their possessions were probably trash to Gray, but it was all they had. She managed to pry Scottie's hands loose long enough for her to bend down and scoop up an armful of tangled clothes, which she tossed into the back of Amos's truck. She didn't know what belonged to whom, but it didn't matter. She had to save as much as she could.

Scottie latched around her leg like a tick, determined to hang on. Hampered by him, Faith grabbed Amos's arm and shook him. "Don't just stand there!" she yelled urgently. "Help me get our things in the truck!"

He shoved her away, sending her sprawling. "Don't tell me what to do, you stupid little bitch!"

She bounced up, not even feeling the extra bruises and scrapes, anesthetized by urgency. The boys were even drunker than Amos, staggering around and cussing. The deputies had finished emptying the shack now and were standing around, watching the show.

"Jodie, help me!" She clutched at Jodie as her sister stormed past, crying because she couldn't find her clothes. "Grab what you can, as fast as you can. We'll sort it out later. Gather all the clothes, and that way you know yours will be there." It was the only argument she could think of to gain Jodie's cooperation.

The two girls began darting swiftly around the yard, gathering up every item they came to. Faith worked harder than she ever had in her life, her slender body bending and weaving, moving so fast that Scottie couldn't keep up with her. He followed in her path, sobbing hoarsely, his pudgy little hands clutching at her whenever she came within reach.

Her mind was numb. She didn't let herself think, couldn't think. She moved automatically, cutting her hand on a broken bowl and not even noticing. One of the deputies did, though, and gruffly said, "Here, girl, you're bleeding," and tied his handkerchief around her hand. She thanked him without knowing what she said.

She was too innocent, and too dazed, to realize how the lights of the cars shone through the thin fabric of her nightgown, silhouetting her youthful body, her slim thighs and high, graceful breasts. She bent and lifted, each change of position outlining a different part of her body, pulling the fabric tight across her breast and showing the small peak of her nipple, the next time revealing the round curve of her buttock. She was only fourteen, but in the stark, artificial light, with her long, thick hair flowing over her shoulders like dark flame, with the shadows catching the angle of her high cheekbones and darkening her eyes, her age wasn't apparent.

What was apparent was her uncanny resemblance to Renee Devlin, a woman who had only to walk across a room to bring most men to some degree of arousal. Renee's sensuality was sultry and vibrant, beckoning like a neon sign to male instincts. When the men looked at Faith, it wasn't her whom they were seeing, but her mother.

Gray stood silently, watching the proceedings. The rage was still there, still cold and consuming, undiluted. Disgust filled him as the Devlins, father and sons, staggered around, cussing and making wild threats. With the sheriff and his deputies there, though, they weren't going to do anything more than shoot off their mouths, so Gray ignored them. Amos had had a close call when he'd pushed the youngest girl down; Gray's fists balled, but she had jumped up, apparently unhurt, and he had restrained himself.

The two girls were rushing around, valiantly trying to gather up the most necessary items. The male Devlins took out their vicious, stupid frustrations on the girls, snatching things from their arms and throwing the items to the ground, loudly proclaiming that no goddamn body was going to throw *them* out of their house, not to waste time picking things up because they weren't goin' nowhere, goddamn it. The oldest girl, Jodie, pleaded with them to help, but their drunken boasting drowned out her useless efforts.

The younger girl didn't waste her time trying to reason with them, just moved silently back and forth, trying to bring order to chaos despite the clinging hands of the little boy. Despite himself, Gray found his gaze continually seeking her out, and himself unwillingly fascinated by the graceful, feminine outline of her body beneath that almost transparent nightgown. Her very silence drew attention to her, and when he glanced sharply around, he noticed that most of the deputies were watching her, too.

There was an odd maturity to her, and a trick of the lights gave him the strange feeling that he was looking at Renee rather than her daughter. The whore had taken his father from him, driven his mother into mental withdrawal, and nearly cost his sister her life, and here she was again, tempting men in her daughter's flesh.

Jodie was more voluptuous, but she was noisy and cheap. Faith's long, dark red hair swirled over the pearly sheen of her shoulders, bared by the straps of that nightgown. She looked older than he knew she was, not quite real, an incarnation of her mother drifting silently through the night, every move like a carnal dance.

Unwillingly, Gray felt his shaft stir and thicken, and he was disgusted with himself. He looked around at the deputies and saw his response mirrored in their eyes, an animal heat that they should be ashamed of having for a girl that young.

God, he was no better than his father. Give him a whiff of a Devlin woman and he was like a wild buck in rut, hard and ready. Monica had nearly died today because of Renee Devlin, and here he was watching Renee's daughter with his cock twitching in his britches.

She walked toward him, carrying a pile of clothes. No, not toward him, but toward the truck behind him. Her green cat eyes flickered at him, the expression in them hooded and mysterious. His pulse leaped, and the look of her broke his tenuous hold on his temper. The events of the day piled up on him and he lashed out with devastating fierceness, wanting the Devlins to suffer as he had suffered.

"You're trash," he said in a deep, harsh voice as the girl drew even with him. She halted, frozen to the spot, with the kid still clinging to her legs. She didn't look at Gray, just stared straight ahead, and the stark, pure outline of her face enraged him even more. "Your whole family is trash. Your mother is a whore and your father is a thieving drunk. Get out of this parish and don't ever come back."

∽ Six ∽

Twelve years later, Faith Devlin Hardy returned to Prescott, Louisiana.

Curiosity had been her companion on the drive up from Baton Rouge, and she hadn't thought much beyond her reason for going back. Nothing about the road was familiar, because when she had lived in Prescott she'd seldom ventured farther than the small town, so no memories rose to link the past with the present, the girl with the woman.

But when she passed the Prescott city limit sign, when houses became closer together, forming actual streets and neighborhoods, when the tall pine and hardwood forests gave way to service stations and convenience stores, she felt an aching tension begin to grow in her. It increased when she reached the town square, with the redbrick courthouse looking exactly as it had in her memory. Cars still parked at angles all around the square, and park benches were still situated one to each side, for the old men to gather there on hot summer days, sheltering beneath the dense shade of the immense oak trees that grew on the square.

Some things had changed, of course. Some of the buildings were newer, while a few of the older ones were no longer there. Flower beds had been added to each corner of the courthouse square, no doubt by the enterprising Ladies'

67

Club, and pansies nodded their purple funny faces to passersby.

For the most part, though, things were the same, and the small differences only made the familiar stand out. The ache in her chest swelled until she could barely breathe, and her hands shook on the steering wheel. A piercing sense of sweetness went through her. *Home.*

It was so sharp that she had to stop the car, easing it into a parking slot in front of the courthouse. Her heart was pounding wildly, and she took deep breaths to steady herself. She hadn't expected this, hadn't expected the tug of roots she thought had been severed a dozen years before. It shook her, it exhilarated her. She had been led here by nothing more than puzzlement, wanting to know for certain what had happened after the Devlins had been forcibly escorted out of the parish, but this burgeoning sense of belonging pushed curiosity aside.

But she didn't belong here, she told herself. Even when she had lived here, she had never really *belonged,* only been tolerated. Whenever she had gone into any store in town, she had been watched like a hawk, because everyone knew a Devlin would steal anything that wasn't nailed down. That wasn't acceptance.

Knowing that, however, had no effect on her heart. Her instincts, her senses, recognized this as home. The rich, colorful scents that were like nowhere else on earth, the sights that had been imprinted on her brain from birth, the subtle influences of latitude and longitude that were recognized by every cell in her body, said that this was home. She had been born here, grown up here. Her memories of Prescott were bitter, but still it pulled at her with invisible strings she hadn't even known existed. She hadn't wanted this. She had wanted only to satisfy her curiosity, gain a sense of closure, so she could completely let go of the past and build her future.

It hadn't been easy, coming back. Gray Rouillard's words still burned in her memory as if it had been yesterday he'd said them rather than twelve years before. Sometimes she went for days without thinking of him, but the pain was always there—under control, but there, a permanent companion. Coming back made the memories more immediate, and she heard his voice echoing in her mind: *You're trash.*

She drew in a deep, shaking breath, and inhaled the sweet green scent so bound up in memories of her childhood. Steadying herself, she made a more leisurely examination of the square, familiarizing herself once again with what had once been as well known as her own hand.

Some of the old businesses lining the square had been spruced up; the hardware store had a rock and cedar front now, and rustic double doors. A McDonald's occupied the space where the Dairy Dip had been. A new bank had been built, and she'd bet money that it belonged to the Rouillards.

People walked by, glancing curiously at her as small-town people did at strangers, but no one recognized her. She hadn't expected them to; twelve years had changed her from child into woman, and she had changed herself from helpless to capable, from poor to prosperous. In her tailored creamy business suit, with her heavy red hair tucked into a sophisticated twist and her eyes protected by sunglasses, there was nothing about her to remind people of Renee Devlin.

It was ironic, Faith supposed; Renee had been guilty as sin of most of the charges laid at her door, but she had been innocent of the one that had finally gotten the Devlins run out of town. She hadn't run away with Guy Rouillard.

It was curiosity about exactly what Guy had done that had brought Faith back to Prescott after all these years. Had he been shacked up with a new girlfriend, and turned up a day or so later astonished at the uproar he'd caused? Had he been on a drinking spree, or maybe even a marathon poker game? Faith wanted to know. She wanted to come face-to-face with him, look him in the eye, and tell him what his irresponsibility had cost her.

She stared sightlessly at the courthouse square, memories washing over her. Her family had splintered after that dreadful night. They had driven as far as Baton Rouge before stopping for the night, sleeping in their vehicles. Amos had been alone in his truck, Russ and Nicky in their truck, with Jodie following in her old rattletrap of a car.

Faith and Scottie had been in the car with Jodie, Scottie asleep on Faith's lap.

Looking back, most of what she remembered was terror and shame. Certain memories were frozen, crystal-clear in her mind: the blinding lights of the patrol cars, that moment of sheer terror when she had been dragged out of bed and pushed through the door onto the ground, Scottie's shrieks. Sometimes she could even feel the way his hands had clung to her, feel the terrified pressure of his little body against her legs. The most acute memory, though, the one that echoed in her mind with painful clarity, was Gray looking at her with that paralyzing contempt.

She remembered desperately trying to gather their pitiful possessions. She remembered the long drive through the darkness; it hadn't been that long, but had seemed to take forever, each second expanded so that a minute took an hour to pass. She didn't remember sleeping, even after they got to Baton Rouge; she had sat stiffly, staring with burning eyes into nothing, cradling Scottie's warm weight on her lap.

Barely after dawn, a cop had run them off from the city park where they had stopped, and the shabby little caravan had started out again. They made it to Beaumont, Texas, before stopping again. Amos rented a motel room in the worst part of town, and the six of them crowded into it. At least it was a roof over their heads.

A week later, they got up one morning to find Amos gone, just as Renee had left, though Amos did at least take his clothes. Nicky and Russ handled the crisis by spending the meager remains of their cash on beer, and getting roaring drunk. Not long after that, Russ left, too.

Nicky tried. To his credit, he tried. He was only eighteen, but when suddenly faced with the care of his three younger siblings, he took what odd jobs he could. Jodie helped out by working at fast-food restaurants, but even with her help, it wasn't enough. It wasn't long before the social workers came around, and Jodie, Faith, and Scottie were taken into the custody of the state. Nicky made a few noises of protest, but Faith could tell that he was mostly relieved. She never saw him again.

Adoption wasn't an option; Jodie and Faith were too old,

and no one wanted Scottie. The best they could hope for was to be in the same foster home, where Faith could take care of Scottie. The best wasn't what they got, but the alternative was workable, at least for Faith. Jodie went to one foster home, while Faith and Scottie went to another. All of Scottie's care fell on her shoulders, but since she had been taking care of him since his birth anyway, that wasn't a burden to her. That had been the condition under which they had been able to stay together, so she worked hard to fulfill her promise.

Jodie didn't stay long at any one foster home, but was moved twice. Faith counted herself lucky in her foster home; the Greshams hadn't had much, but they had been willing to share what they did have with foster kids. For the first time in her life, Faith saw how respectable people lived, and she soaked up the life like a sponge. It was an unfailing delight to her to come home from school to a clean house, to the smells of supper cooking. Her clothes, though inexpensive, were neat and as stylish as the Greshams could afford on the money they were given for her upkeep. At school, no one called her "a trashy Devlin." She learned what it was like to live in a house where the adults loved and respected each other, and her hungry heart reveled in the wonder of it.

Scottie was petted, and they bought new toys for him, though it wasn't long before he began failing drastically. For Faith, the kindness that surrounded Scottie for the short time left of his life had been worth everything. For a little while, he had been happy. That first Christmas after Renee left had made him delirious with joy. He had sat for hours, too tired to play but content to stare at the twinkling lights on the Christmas tree. He had died in January, easing away in his sleep. Faith had known that the time was near and had started spending the nights in a chair by his bed. Something, perhaps the change in his breathing, had awakened her. So she took his stubby little hand in hers, and held it while his indrawn breaths came further and further apart, and finally, gently, ceased altogether. She had continued to hold his hand until she felt the growing coolness of his flesh, and only then did she wake the Greshams.

She had spent almost four full years with the kindly

Greshams. Jodie finished high school, got married right away, and left for the bright lights of Houston. Faith was totally alone, all of her real family gone. She concentrated on school, ignoring the boys who continually pestered her for dates. She had been too numb, too traumatized by the upheaval in her life, to throw herself into the giddy teenage social whirl. The Greshams had shown her how good stability and respectability could be, how sweet, and that was what she wanted for herself. To that end, she focused all of her energy on building something out of the ashes to which her life had been reduced. After endless hours of study, she made valedictorian, and won a scholarship to a small college. Leaving the Greshams wasn't easy, but with the state no longer paying for her upkeep, she had to move on. She worked two part-time jobs to support herself while going to school, but Faith didn't mind hard work, having known little else for most of her life.

Her senior year in college, she fell in love with a graduate student, Kyle Hardy. They dated for six months, and got married the week after Faith was graduated. For a short while she had been almost dizzy with happiness, certain that dreams did come true, after all. The dream hadn't lasted long, not even as long as her brief marriage. Faith had envisioned settling down, furnishing a cute little apartment, and saving for the future, which included kids, a nice house, and two cars. It hadn't worked out that way. Despite the responsibilities of his new job, Kyle had continued to enjoy the heavy-drinking, freewheeling life he had enjoyed as a student. It had gotten the best of him one night, coming home from a bar, when his car went off a bridge. No other cars were involved, which was a blessing; when an autopsy was performed, it was found that his blood alcohol level was twice what was legal.

At twenty-two, Faith was alone again. She grieved, then doggedly rebuilt her life. She had a degree in business administration and money from the small life insurance policy Kyle had had, as well as that provided by his job. She moved to Dallas and got a job in a small travel agency; two years later, the agency belonged to her. It had already expanded to a branch in Houston; Faith took a leap of faith and spent her capital to open another branch, this time in New Orleans. To her joy, the business grew steadily.

She had achieved financial stability, and it was as wonderful as she had always imagined it would be, but she was aware of an aching emptiness in her life. She needed emotional solid ground, too. She didn't want to become romantically involved with anyone; the two men she had dared to love, Gray Rouillard and Kyle Hardy, had both taught her how dangerous that was. But she still had family out there, somewhere, and she wanted to find them.

Vaguely she had recalled that her grandmother on Renee's side had lived around Shreveport; Faith could remember seeing her only once in her life, and when the social services in Texas had tried to contact her grandmother, they hadn't been able to find her. But the social services were overworked and understaffed, and had given up after a desultory search. Faith had more time, and more determination. She began calling around, and thankfully there weren't that many Armsteads in the Shreveport area. She finally reached someone, a cousin on her grandfather Armstead's side, who knew that Jeanette Armstead had moved to Jackson, Mississippi, about ten or twelve years ago, right after that oldest daughter of hers had turned up again.

Faith had been stunned. Her mother, Renee, had been the oldest daughter. But Renee had run away with Guy Rouillard; what had happened that she had sought out her mother? Was Guy still with her, or had he returned to the bosom of his family? A lot of years lay between the present and that horrible night in Prescott. For all she knew, Guy might have spent them very happily with his family, while her own family had been torn apart, destroyed.

Faith had called Information, gotten her grandmother's number, and called. To her surprise, Renee had answered the phone. Even after all those years, she still remembered her mother's voice. Startled, excited, she had identified herself. Their conversation had been awkward at first, but finally Faith got up the nerve to ask Renee what had happened with Guy Rouillard.

"What about him?" Renee had said, sounding bored. "Jodie told me that wild tale about me and him runnin' off, but it was news to me. I got fed up with bein' Amos's punching bag and living like dirt, and God knows Guy Rouillard wasn't goin' to do nothing about it, so I just left, went up to Shreveport and moved in with Mama. Your aunt Wilma lives here in Jackson, so about a month after that, we moved here, too. I ain't seen Guy Rouillard."

Faith had had trouble absorbing everything at once, there were so many thoughts flying in her head. Jodie had obviously found their mother, but neither of them had made any effort to get in touch with Faith. Renee could have gotten her two youngest children out of foster care, but she had been content to leave them where they were. She hadn't even asked about Scottie, Faith noticed.

Then there was the mystery of Guy Rouillard. Maybe he hadn't left with Renee, but he *had* left, at least temporarily, and by his leaving had set in motion the events that had shaped her life. Puzzled and intrigued, Faith decided to find out for certain what had happened. At the age of fourteen, she had literally been thrown out into the night like a piece of trash, and she had lived with that pain ever since. She needed to know the end of the story. She wanted to close out her past, so she could get on with her future.

So here she sat, parked on the courthouse square in Prescott, swamped by memories and wasting time. It shouldn't be very difficult to find out where Guy Rouillard had been for what was probably only that one day, that one crucial day that had totally altered her life.

Her first order of business, she supposed, was to find somewhere to stay for the night. She had flown into Baton Rouge that morning, conducted the business she had, then rented a car and driven to Prescott. It was late afternoon, and she was tired. It wouldn't take long to find out what she wanted to know, but she didn't want to make the drive back to Baton Rouge if she could get a motel room in Prescott.

There had been a motel twelve years ago, but it had been slightly seedy even then and might not still be there. It had been on the east side of town, on the road leading to I-55.

She rolled down the car window and called to a woman walking down the sidewalk. "Excuse me. Is there a motel in town?"

The woman stopped, and came over to the side of the car. She was in her mid-forties and looked vaguely familiar, but Faith couldn't place her. "Yes, there is," the woman replied, and turned to point. "Go to the corner of the square and turn right. It's about a mile and a half that way."

It sounded like the same motel. Faith smiled. "Thank you."

"You're welcome." The woman smiled and nodded, and returned to the sidewalk.

Faith reversed out of the parking space and maneuvered the small rental car into the leisurely traffic. Prescott didn't bustle now any more than it had twelve years ago. In two minutes she reached the motel. It was in the same place, but it wasn't the same motel. This one looked new, no more than a couple of years old, and much more substantial. It was still only one story, though this one was built in a U around a center courtyard where a fountain bubbled and flowers grew. It lacked a pool, which she didn't mind. The fountain was much more charming.

The desk clerk was a man in his fifties, and his name tag read "Reuben." Memory stirred, and a last name surfaced to go with the first. Reuben Odell. One of his daughters had been in Faith's class. He chatted as he took her credit card imprint, glancing curiously at the name, but nothing about "Faith D. Hardy" rang a bell in his memory. Faith wasn't a common name, but probably he hadn't even known her first name back then, so of course, he wouldn't recognize it now.

"I'll give you number twelve," he said, taking the key from its compartment. "It's at the back of the courtyard, farther away from the road so the traffic won't bother you."

"Thank you." Faith smiled, and removed her sunglasses to sign the credit card slip. He blinked at her smile, his own expression growing fractionally warmer.

She parked the car at the rear of the courtyard, in front of number twelve. When she unlocked the door, she was pleasantly surprised. The room was larger than most motel rooms, with a love seat and coffee table close to the door, and a king-size bed beyond that. The dresser was long, with the television on one end, and a desk area on the end closest to the bathroom. The clothes rack was adequate, the vanity in the dressing area boasted two basins and was large enough for two people to get ready without continually bumping into each other. She looked into the bathroom, expecting the standard tub, but instead there was a sizeable shower stall with sliding doors. Since she never took a tub bath, she was pleased by the extra room to bathe. All in all, the little motel was a cut above the norm.

She unpacked her toiletries and the single change of clothes she'd brought, then plotted her course of action. There shouldn't be much problem in finding out what she wanted to know, as long as no one recognized her as a Devlin. Small towns could have notoriously long memories, and the town of Prescott had belonged to the Rouillards heart and soul, as well as most of its brick.

The easiest and most anonymous way, probably, was to go to the library and look through the old newspapers. The Rouillards had constantly been in the news, so if Guy Rouillard had returned from his little jaunt and resumed business as usual, she wouldn't have to check many editions before his name would crop up.

She checked her watch and saw that she probably wouldn't have more than an hour to do what she'd come to do; from what she remembered about the small library, it closed about six P.M. during the summer, and in a town the size of Prescott, that wasn't likely to change. She was hungry, but first things first; food could wait, the library wouldn't.

It was odd how selective memory could be; she had never been to the motel when she had lived here, and had often gone to the library, whenever she'd gotten the chance, but she had remembered the motel's location while she drew a blank on the library. She fished the small phone book out of the dresser and looked up the address, and after a moment remembered the library's location. Grabbing her purse and keys, she went out to the car and drove back to downtown Prescott. Before, the library had been located behind the post office, but when she got there she was dismayed to find the building gone.

She looked around, and heaved a sigh of relief. A prominent sign in front of the new building next door to the post office proclaimed it the Prescott Library. The builders had disdained the sleekness of modern architecture and instead used an antebellum style, a redbrick two-story with four white columns out front, and shutters on the six-foot windows. There were plenty of parking spaces, probably more than needed, for only three cars were parked in the lot. Faith brought the total to four, parking in front and hurrying to the double doors. The sign posted on the left-hand door told her that she'd been right about the hours the library was open: nine A.M. to six P.M.

The librarian was a small, plump, chatty woman who wasn't in the least familiar to Faith. She went up to the desk and asked where the old newspaper files were.

"Right over here," the woman said, coming out from behind the counter. "Everything's on microfiche now, of course. Are you looking for any particular dates? I'll show you how the microfiches are filed, and how to work the scanner."

"I'd appreciate that, thanks," said Faith. "I want to start about ten years ago, but I may have to go a little further back."

"That's no problem. It would have been until a couple of years ago, but Mr. Rouillard insisted that everything be put on microfiche when we moved into this building. I declare, the system here was positively antiquated; it's so much easier now."

"Mr. Rouillard?" asked Faith, keeping her tone casual despite the way her heart jumped. So Guy *had* come back.

"Gray Rouillard," said the librarian. "The family practically owns this town—the whole parish, come to that—but he's just as nice as he can be." She paused. "Are you from around here?"

"A long time ago," Faith replied. "My family moved away when I was a child. I thought I'd check the old obituaries for some of my parents' cousins. We lost track of them through the years, but I've started working on a family tree and got curious about what happened to them." For a spur-of-the-moment explanation, it wasn't bad. People trying to trace their family trees always made up the bulk of those using the microfiche machines, at least in her experience. From what she had gathered, listening to them talk and exchange tales of extended detective work that finally unearthed the whereabouts of Great-great-aunt Ruby on Mother's side of the family, the quest could become addictive.

She had hit the right tone, for the librarian beamed. "Good luck, dear, I hope you find them. I'm Carlene DuBois. Call me if you need any help. We do close at six, though, and that's less than an hour."

"It shouldn't take long," said Faith, while searching her memory for a DuBois family in the parish. None came to mind, so perhaps they had moved to the area after the Devlin family had left so ignominiously.

Once she was alone, she quickly began scrolling through the files, scanning page after page of the *Prescott Weekly,* beginning from the date they had been escorted from the parish. She found several mentions of Gray, and though she tried to ignore them, she found that she couldn't. Though that long-ago night had cured her of her infatuation for him, she had never been able to forget him; his image had lingered in her memory like a sore tooth, to be worried occasionally.

Helplessly giving in to the probing of that mental tongue, she scrolled back to the places where she had seen Gray's name. The *Weekly* would never print anything derogatory or scandalous about the Rouillards—that was left to the Baton Rouge and New Orleans newspapers—but the normal comings and goings of the family were all duly reported to the inquiring minds that wanted to know, which was most of the parish. The first two tiny articles were mere mentions that Gray had attended such and such function. The third article was in the business section, and, stunned, Faith read it through twice before the words really sank in.

No one else would have seen anything alarming or even unusual in the sentence. ". . . Grayson Rouillard, who has taken financial control of the family enterprises, voted against the measure to . . ."

Taken control of the family enterprises. Why would he have done that? Guy would still have been in charge, for after all, everything had belonged to him. Faith glanced at the date of the newspaper. August fifth, not quite three weeks after Renee had left. What had happened?

She switched off the microfiche machine and sat back in the chair, staring at the blank screen. She had come back to Prescott only to tie off some loose ends in her life, to see that things had gone on as before. No one would have missed the Devlins; their absence would have been noted with relief, and then forgotten, but Faith had never been able to forget. She had thought that, once she had seen Prescott again, seen how no one had missed them, or even remembered them, she would be able to forget about the town in return. If she ran into Guy Rouillard, so much the better. She had never blamed Gray for what he'd done; she'd seen the pain in his face, heard it in his voice. But Guy . . . yes, she blamed him, and Renee. Even if they hadn't run away together, Renee had walked out on her children, and Guy's irresponsibility had caused a lot of suffering.

But Gray had taken over the family business. Instead of tying up all the old loose ends, she had found another one: Why had Gray taken charge?

She got up and went in search of Carlene DuBois. The front desk was empty, and the rest of the library appeared to be, too. "Mrs. DuBois?" she called, the sound absorbed and flattened by the rows of books. Carlene heard her, however, for there was the squeak of rubber-soled shoes on the tile.

"Right here," said Carlene cheerfully, emerging from the back of the reference book section. "Did you find what you needed?"

"Yes, I did, thank you. I noticed something else that puzzled me, though. It was just a little article, but it said that Gray Rouillard had taken over control of the family businesses. This was twelve years ago, and it seemed strange, because Gray had to have been only in his early twenties—"

"My, yes. You must have left before the big scandal, or maybe you were too young to pay much attention to that sort of thing. We moved to town, oh, eleven years ago, and it was still a hot topic of conversation then, I can tell you."

"What scandal?" Faith tensed, her puzzlement turning into alarm. Something wasn't right.

"Why, when Guy Rouillard ran off with his mistress. I don't know who she was, but everyone says she was nothing but trash. He must have absolutely lost his mind, is all I can say, to walk off from his family and fortune the way he did."

"He never came back?" Faith couldn't hide her shock, but Carlene saw nothing wrong with that reaction.

"No one's seen hide nor hair of him since then. When he left, he stayed gone. Some say his wife was enough to drive any man away, but I can't say for sure myself, because I've never met her. Folks say she hasn't left the house since the day he walked out. He never even bothered to get in touch with his own children again."

Faith was staggered. Guy Rouillard had adored his kids; regardless of his feelings for his wife, there had never been any doubt about how much he had loved Gray and Monica.

"I suppose Mrs. Rouillard divorced him?" she asked, but Carlene shook her head.

"Never has. Reckon she didn't want him to be able to marry again, if he was so inclined. Anyway, as young as Mr. Gray was, he stepped into his father's shoes and things carried on just as if Mr. Rouillard was still here. Probably better, from what folks say."

"I was too young to remember much about him," Faith lied. "I do remember that he was a sort of local hero, playing football at LSU, things like that."

"Well, honey, let me tell you, things haven't changed much," Carlene said, and fanned herself with her hand. "Lordy, that man rates a ten on my scale, I can tell you. He makes my heart flutter, and me ten years older than he is and about to be a grandmother besides!" She blushed, but gave a surprisingly bawdy laugh. "It might be those bedroom eyes, or maybe it's the hair. Or it *could* be that tight little butt!" She sighed dreamily. "He's a scoundrel, all right, but who cares?"

"Does he know you're sweet on him?" Faith teased.

"Honey, every woman in town is sweet on him, and yes, he knows it, the devil." Carlene gave her lusty laugh again. "My husband teases me about getting *his* ear pierced so he can compete."

Gray had a pierced ear? Faith found herself caught in

imagination, and shook herself free. What she had learned was startling, and she needed to be alone so she could think things through.

She glanced at her watch. "It's almost closing time, so I'd better clear out. Thanks for your help, Mrs. DuBois. It was nice meeting you."

"You, too." Carlene paused. "I'm sorry, I don't believe I caught your name."

Because it hadn't been thrown, but Faith saw no reason not to tell her. "I'm Faith Hardy," she said.

"Well, nice to meet you, Faith. That's such a pretty, old-fashioned name. You don't hear it much anymore."

"No, I suppose you don't." Faith glanced at her watch again. "Good-bye. Thanks again for your help."

"Any time."

Faith drove back to the motel, stopping by McDonald's for a sandwich. She didn't particularly like fast food, but didn't want to go to a restaurant where she might be recognized, so she made do. She ate half the sandwich and tossed the rest of it in the trash, too disturbed to have much of an appetite.

Guy Rouillard had disappeared. But if he hadn't run away with Renee, what *had* happened to him?

Faith lay down on the bed and stared up at the ceiling, trying to sort things out. Guy wouldn't have walked away from his home, his family, his wealth, without a reason. Everyone had thought Renee was that reason, but Faith knew it wasn't so. And even if he had simply gotten fed up with his marriage, why hadn't he just gotten a divorce? The Rouillards were Catholic, but divorce wasn't a problem unless he wanted to remarry. But he had never seemed to be an unhappy man; why should he be? His world had been the way he wanted it. She couldn't think of any reason why he would have left so abruptly, without word, and never tried to contact his family.

Unless he was dead.

The possibility—no, the *probability*—was stunning. Faith felt almost sick at the idea as she considered and rejected scenarios. He might have simply gone away for a couple of days and suddenly gotten sick, or maybe had an accident, but if either of those possibilities had been the case, he would have been found, identified, his family notified. That hadn't happened. Guy Rouillard had disappeared, on the same night her mother had run away.

Dear God, had Renee killed him? Faith sat up and distractedly ran her hands through her hair. She couldn't dismiss the thought, even though she couldn't see her mother doing such a thing. Renee had the morals of an alley cat, but she wasn't, never had been, a violent person.

Amos, then? Faith could better envision that. If he'd thought he could get away with it, Amos had been capable of anything. But she remembered that night well; Amos had staggered home around nine, already falling down drunk and swearing at her because Renee wasn't at home. Both Russ and Nicky, also drunk, had come home after that. Could one of them have killed Guy Rouillard, or perhaps even both of them? But nothing had seemed out of the ordinary, and Faith would have sworn they had been as surprised as she when Renee didn't come home. More than that, they simply hadn't *cared* that their mother was sleeping with Guy; neither had Amos, for that matter.

Who else was possible? Maybe Mrs. Rouillard. Maybe Noelle had killed her husband because she was tired of his unfaithfulness, though from all reports he had been sleeping around since the beginning of their marriage, and she had never seemed to care, had even been grateful. His affair with Renee had been going on for years; why should she suddenly object to it? No, Faith doubted Noelle had cared enough even to scold him, much less go to the trouble of murder.

That left one person: Gray.

Forcefully she rejected that thought. No, not Gray. She remembered his face as it had been when he had come to the shack that morning, and as he had been that awful night. She remembered his fury, his implacable hatred. Gray had thought his father had run away with her mother, and he'd been in a rage.

But Gray had had the most to gain from his father's death. With Guy gone, he had taken over the reins to the Rouillard fortune, and made himself even wealthier, from what the librarian had said. He had been groomed from the day of his

82

birth to one day step into his father's shoes; had he gotten tired of waiting, and put Guy out of the way?

Faith's thoughts darted around like a squirrel in a cage, banging against the bars. The door rattled under the force of several heavy blows and she jumped, startled and not a little alarmed. Why would anyone be at her door? No one knew where she was, so there couldn't be a message from her office. She got up and went to the door, but didn't open it. There wasn't a peephole, either, she noticed. "Who is it?"

"Gray Rouillard."

Her heart almost stopped beating. It had been twelve years since she had heard that deep, smoky voice, but she went weak at the sound of it, excitement mingled with fear. He had hurt her worse than anyone else in her life, but still he had the power to electrify every cell in her body with nothing but his voice. Just hearing him again made her feel like the child she had been at fourteen, all shivery and agitated at his nearness. And always, always, was that ugly counterweight pulling her in the opposite direction, the stark memory of him saying, *You're trash*. She had never been able to find any balance where Gray was concerned, had never been able to forget him, dream and nightmare combined.

The timing of his arrival made her skin prickle. Had she conjured him up with her thoughts? She stood there for so long that the door rattled again under the impact of his fist.

"Open up." In his tone was the iron authority of someone who expected to be obeyed, immediately, and intended to see that he was.

Cautiously she unchained the door and opened it, and looked up at the man she hadn't seen for a dozen years. It didn't matter. No matter how long it had been, she would have recognized him. He stood there in the doorway, disdaining to come in, and the impact of his physical presence took her breath.

He was bigger than she remembered, but then six four always seemed taller when you were looking up at it. His waist and hips were still lean, but he was heavier through the chest and shoulders, having achieved the hard solidity of manhood. And he was definitely a man, all hint of boyhood long gone. His face was leaner, stronger, more harsh, with grooves bracketing his mouth and lines of maturity at the corners of his eyes. She stared up into the face of a pirate, and knew why Carlene DuBois had gotten the shivers at the mere mention of his name. His black hair was longer than she had ever seen it before, pulled back from his face and secured at the nape of his neck. A tiny diamond winked in his left earlobe. At twenty-two, he had been impressive. At thirty-four, he was dangerous, a pirate in nature as well as appearance. Looking at him made her feel hot and shivery all at once, her heart suddenly pounding so hard, she wondered that he couldn't hear it. She recognized the symptoms, and hated her sickness. God, was she doomed to spend her entire life going weak at the sight or sound of Gray Rouillard? Why couldn't she get beyond that leftover childhood reaction?

Above the thin blade of his nose, his sinfully dark eyes were still cold and implacable.

The sensual line of his mouth twisted as he looked down at her. "Faith Devlin," he said. "Reuben was right; you look just like your mother."

But if he had changed, so had she. Faith had won her confidence the hard way. She gave him a cool little smile and said, "Thank you."

"It wasn't a compliment. I don't know why you're here, and it doesn't matter. This motel belongs to me. You aren't welcome. You have half an hour to get packed and get out." He gave her a wolfish smile that wasn't really a smile. "Or do I have to call the sheriff again to get rid of you?"

The memory of that night lay between them, so strong that it was almost tangible. For a moment she saw again the lights, felt the confused terror, but she refused to let him throw her into a state of panic. Instead she gave a graceful shrug and turned away from him, strolling into the small dressing area, where she efficiently swept her few toiletries into her overnight case and took her single change of clothes from the rack. Acutely aware of those dark eyes boring a hole through her, Faith folded the clothes over her arm, slipped on her shoes, picked up her purse, and sauntered past him without ever changing her calm expression.

As she drove away from the motel, on her way back to Baton Rouge, he was still standing in the open door staring after her.

Faith Devlin! How about that for a blast from the past? Gray stood watching her taillights until they disappeared from view. When Reuben had called to tell him that a woman who was the spitting image of Renee Devlin had checked into the motel, and that she had registered as Faith D. Hardy, he'd had no doubt about her identity. So one of the Devlin spawn had finally worked up the nerve to come back to Prescott! He wasn't surprised that it was Faith. She had always had more backbone than the rest of the bunch put together. Which didn't mean he'd been inclined to let her stay.

He turned back into the lighted room that she had abandoned with so little fuss. Without any fuss, damn it. If he'd wanted a fight, she hadn't obliged him. She hadn't even asked for a refund on her credit card. Without so much as a flicker of an eyelash, she had gathered up her stuff and left. It hadn't taken a minute; hell, he doubted it had taken her thirty seconds.

She was gone, and except for the wrinkled bedspread, the room was as pristine as if she'd never been there, but her presence still lingered. There was a sweet, faintly spicy scent in the air that overrode the staleness endemic to all motel rooms, and his blood stirred in instinctive reaction to it. It was the smell of woman, universal in some ways, exclusive to her in others. He stepped farther into the room, drawn by that elusive scent, his nostrils flaring like a stallion's.

Faith Devlin. Just hearing her name had brought back that night and he had seen her again in his mind, silent and willowy, with that dark-fire hair tumbling over her shoulders and her slender body silhouetted inside her thin nightgown, weaving a sensual spell over the deputies and himself. She had been only a kid then, for God's sake, but she had had her mother's sultry aura even then.

When she had opened the door to this room and he had seen her again, he had been stunned. She looked so much like Renee that he'd wanted to throttle her, but at the same time there was no mistaking her for her mother. Faith was a little taller, still more slender than voluptuous, though she had filled out nicely in the twelve years since he'd last seen her. Her coloring was the same as Renee's: the dark red mane, the slumberous gold-flecked green eyes, the translucent skin. What had infuriated him, though, was her effortless sensuality, and his own unwilling reaction to it. It wasn't anything she had said or done, or even what she'd been wearing, which had been a stylish business suit. A Devlin wearing a suit, by God! No, it had been something intrinsic in her nature, something Renee had also possessed. The older daughter—he couldn't remember her name—hadn't had that potent allure. She had been easy and cheap, not sexy. Faith was sexy. Not overtly so, as Renee had been, but just as potent. He had looked into those cat eyes and thought of the bed just behind her, thought of tangled sheets and hot flesh, of having her naked beneath him and feeling her thighs clasp his hips just as he found the soft opening between her legs and pushed deep inside . . .

Gray broke out in a sweat and swore aloud in the empty room. Damn, he was as bad as his father! Give him a whiff, and he was ready to forget everything else in his rush to screw a Devlin woman. No, not every Devlin woman, he mentally amended. Thank God for that, at least. He had seen Renee's potent appeal but found it resistible, and the idea of sharing a woman with his father repellent. Nothing about the older girl had been attractive to him. Faith, though . . . If she were anyone but a Devlin, he wouldn't rest until he had her in bed and settled down to a long, hard ride.

But she was a Devlin, and just the mention of that name made him furious. His family had been wrecked because of Renee, and he could never forgive or forget that. Forgetting was impossible, when he lived every day with the results of Guy's desertion. His mother had withdrawn until she was just a shell of her former self. She hadn't left her bedroom for over two years, and even now refused to venture from the house except for doctors' appointments in New Orleans, on those rare occasions when she was ill. Gray had lost his father, and to all intents and purposes had also lost his mother.

Noelle was a silent, sad ghost of a woman who spent most of her time in her room. Only Alex Chelette could coax her into a little smile and bring a hint of life to her blue eyes. Gray had realized some time ago that Alex had fallen in love with his mother, but it was a hopeless cause. Not only was Noelle oblivious to his devotion, she wouldn't have done anything about it if she had been aware of it. She was married to Guy Rouillard, and that was that. Divorce was unthinkable. Gray sometimes wondered if Noelle was still clinging to the hope that Guy would come back. He himself had long ago accepted that he would never see his father again. If Guy had intended to come back, he wouldn't have sent that letter of proxy which Gray had received two days after his disappearence. It had been mailed in Baton Rouge the day he left; the language had been terse and to the point, with nothing personal included. He hadn't even signed it "Love, Dad," but limited himself to a businesslike "Sincerely, Guy A. Rouillard." When he had read that, Gray had known that Guy was gone from his life forever, and his eyes had burned with tears for the first and only time.

He didn't know what he would have done without Alex those first desperate months when he had been scrambling to solidify his position with the stockholders and various boards of directors. Alex had guided him through the rocky shoals, fought with him for every advantage, done whatever he could to help with Noelle and Monica. Alex had grieved, too, for the loss of his best friend. Guy and Alex had grown up together, been as close as brothers. He had been stunned that Guy would actually turn his back on his family for the sake of Renee Devlin, and had left without even saying good-bye.

In some ways, Monica was stronger now than she had been before. She wasn't as emotionally needy, so dependent on others. She had quietly apologized to Gray for her suicide attempt, and assured him that she would never do something that stupid again. But if she was stronger, she was also more remote, as if that paroxysm of pain and grief had burned out her excess of emotion, leaving her calm but also distant. She had interested herself in his work and gradually became an excellent assistant, one on whom he could rely with every faith in her judgment and ability, but she was almost as reclusive as Noelle. Monica did go out into the community; she was particular about her appearance and got her hair styled regularly, and made an effort to dress well. She hadn't dated for years, though. At first Gray thought she was embarrassed by her suicide attempt, and would relax as the scars faded. She hadn't, though, and eventually he had realized that it wasn't embarrassment that had kept her at home. Monica simply wasn't interested in socializing with anyone. She would do it at a business function, but on a personal level she refused all invitations, and steadfastly turned aside his suggestions that she reenter the dating scene. All he could do to bolster her confidence was show her how he trusted her in their work, and pay her a good salary so she would have a tangible proof of her worth, and a sense of independence.

Last year, though, the new sheriff, Michael McFane, had somehow talked her into going out with him. Monica had been seeing him fairly regularly since then. Gray had been so relieved, he could have cried. Maybe, just maybe, Monica had a shot at a normal life, after all.

No, he would never forget what the Devlins had done to his family. And with luck, he would never see Faith Devlin again.

Thank you. Those had been the only words she'd uttered, other than to ask who was at the door. She had been cool and enigmatic, watching him as if faintly amused, her poise unshaken by his threat. It hadn't been a threat, though, but a promise. He would have had her escorted out of the parish for a second time if she hadn't left on her own. And he would have had to call the sheriff, because if he had touched her himself, he would have lost control, and he had known it.

She was a woman now, not the kid he remembered. She had always been different from the rest of the Devlins, a fey woodland creature who had grown up to be as much of a temptation as her mother. Some poor fool had evidently thought so, because the fact that her last name was now Hardy meant that she was married, though she hadn't been wearing a wedding ring. He had noticed her hands, slim, elegant, well kept, and been cynically amused by the absence of a wedding band. Renee hadn't worn one, either; it had cramped her style. Evidently her daughter felt the same way, at least when she was traveling sans the unknown Mr. Hardy.

She had looked prosperous, so, like a cat, she had landed on her feet. Gray wasn't surprised. It had always been a particular talent of the Devlin women that they could always find someone to support them. Her husband must be a good provider, the poor sap. He wondered how often she left her husband at home while she rambled.

And he wondered why she had come back to Prescott. There was nothing for her here, no family, no friends. The Devlins hadn't had friends, only victims. She had to have known she wouldn't be welcomed back with open arms. Probably she had thought she could slip in without anyone being the wiser, but folks around here had long memories, and her resemblance to her mother was too marked. Reuben had recognized her as soon as she'd taken off her sunglasses.

Well, it didn't make any difference. He had rid the parish of the Devlin vermin for the second time, and with a hell of a lot less trouble than it had been twelve years ago. He just wished she hadn't come back at all, hadn't revived the potent memory of his unwilling response to her, hadn't replaced his image of her as a young girl with the image of her as she was now, a woman. He wished he had never heard her soft, cool voice saying, "Thank you."

Faith drove steadily along the dark road, not letting herself stop even though her insides were shaking like jelly. She refused to let her reaction get the best of her. She had learned the hard way what Gray Rouillard thought of her, dealt with the shock and pain years ago. She would *not* let him hurt her again, or get the best of her. She hadn't had any choice but to leave the motel, because she had seen the ruthless determination in his eyes and known he hadn't been bluffing about having her thrown out. Why should he balk at that, when he hadn't balked at having her entire family removed? Her calm acquiescence didn't mean, however, that he had won.

The threat of the sheriff hadn't frightened her. What had her both scared and angry was the intensity of her reaction to Gray. Even after all those years, after what he had done to her family, she was as helpless as a Pavlovian dog to stop her response to him. It was infuriating. She hadn't rebuilt her life just to let him reduce her to the status of trash, to be gotten rid of as soon as possible.

The day had long passed when she could be intimidated. The quiet, vulnerable child she had been had died one hot summer night twelve years ago. Faith was still a fairly quiet person, but she had learned how to survive, how to use her own steely will and determination to get what she wanted out of life. She had even become confident enough to indulge in her redheaded temper from time to time. If he had wanted to get rid of her, Gray had made a mistake in forcing the issue. He would soon learn that what looked like a retreat just meant she was adjusting her position for attack from another angle.

She couldn't let him run her off again. Not only was it a matter of honor, she still hadn't found out what had happened to Guy. She couldn't forget about it, couldn't let it go.

A plan began to form in her agile mind, and a smile touched her lips as she drove. Gray would find himself outflanked before he knew it. She was going to move to Prescott, and there wasn't a thing he could do to stop it, because she would be ensconced before he knew it. It was past time she faced all of her old ghosts, cemented her own self-respect. She would prove herself to the town that had looked down on her, and then she could forget about the past.

And she wanted to prove to Gray that he had been wrong about her from the beginning. She wanted that so fiercely that she could taste it, the victory sweet in her mouth. Because she had loved him so intensely as a child, because he had been the stern, ruthless judge and executioner, so to speak, on the night when he had run them out of the parish, he had assumed far too much importance in her mind. It shouldn't be that way, she should have been able to forget him, but the fact was there: She wouldn't *feel* like anything other than trash until Gray was forced to admit that she was a decent, moral, successful person.

She didn't just want to find out what had happened to Guy. Maybe it had begun as that, or maybe she had hidden the truth from herself, but now she knew.

She wanted to go home.

❧ Seven ❧

"Yes, that's right. I want everything handled in the agency's name. Thank you, Mr. Bible. I knew I could count on you." Faith's smile was warm in her voice, something Mr. Bible must have heard, because his reply made her laugh aloud. "You'd better be careful," she teased. "Remember, I know your wife."

She hung up the phone and her assistant, Margot Stanley, gave her a rueful look. "Was that old goat flirting with you?" Margot asked.

"Of course," Faith said good-naturedly. "He always does. It gives him a thrill if he thinks he's being wicked, but he's actually a sweet old guy."

Margot snorted. "Sweet? Harley Bible's as sweet as a rattlesnake. Let's face it, you have a way with men."

Faith restrained herself from an unladylike snort. If Margot had seen Gray run her out of town—again—she wouldn't think Faith had such a "way" with men. "I'm just nice to him, is all. It's nothing special. And he can't be as bad as you say he is, or he wouldn't still be in business."

"He's still in business because the old fart is a smart businessman," Margot said. "He has an evil genius for sniffing out prime property right before it becomes prime, and buying it up for a song. Damn him, people only go to him because he has the land they want."

Faith grinned. "Like you said, a smart businessman. He's always been as nice as he can be to me."

She might have restrained herself from snorting, but Margot had no such inhibition. "I've never seen a man who *wasn't* nice to you. How many times have you been stopped for speeding?"

"All total?"

"Just this past year will do."

"Ummm . . . four times, I think. But that's unusual; it's just that I've been traveling so much this past year."

"Uh-huh. And how many times have you gotten a ticket?"

"None," Faith admitted, rolling her eyes. "That's just coincidence. Not once have I tried to talk my way out of it."

"You don't have to, and that's my point. The cop walks up to your car, you hand him your license and say, 'I'm sorry, I know I was flying,' and he ends up handing your license back and telling you to slow down, because he'd hate to see your pretty face all cut up in an accident."

Faith burst out laughing, because Margot had been in the car with her when she had been stopped that time. The Texas state trooper in question had been a burly gentleman of the old school, with a thick gray mustache and a drawl as slow as molasses. "That's the only time a cop has said anything about my 'pretty face,' quote and unquote."

"But they were all thinking it. Admit it. Have you *ever* gotten a speeding ticket?"

"Well, no." She controlled her amusement. Margot had gotten two speeding tickets within the past six months, and now was having to stick strictly to the speed limit, to her great resentment, because a third ticket would result in the temporary loss of her driver's license.

"You can bet neither one of the cops who stopped me said anything about slowing down before I got my pretty face all cut up," Margot muttered. "No sirree, they were pure business. 'Let me see your license, ma'am. You were doing sixty-five in a fifty-five zone, ma'am. Your court date will be such and such, or you can mail in your fine by such and such date and waive your right to a court appearance.'" She sounded so disgusted that Faith had to turn away to keep from laughing in her face. Margot didn't see anything funny about her two speeding tickets.

"I'd never had a ticket before in my life," Margot continued, scowling. Faith had heard it many times before, so that she could almost say the words in unison with her friend. "I've been driving for half my life without so much as a parking ticket, and then all of a sudden the damn things seem to be coming out of the woodwork."

"You make it sound as if you could paper your walls with them."

"Don't laugh. Two tickets are pretty damn serious, and a third one is a catastrophe. I'll be poking along at fifty-five for two years. Do you know how much this throws off a schedule? I have to get up earlier and leave earlier, everywhere I go, because it takes me so long to get there!" She sounded so aggrieved that Faith gave up the struggle and began giggling helplessly.

Margot was a joy. She was thirty-six, divorced, and had absolutely no intention of staying that way. Faith didn't know what she would have done without her. When she had finally scraped up enough money to buy the agency, she had known how to handle the customer part of the business, but despite her college degree in administration, there was a great deal of difference between textbooks and real life. Margot had been assistant to J. B. Holladay, the previous owner of Holladay Travel, and had been glad to handle the same duties for Faith. Her experience had been invaluable. She had kept Faith from making some serious mistakes in financial matters.

More than that, Margot had become a friend. She was a tall, lean woman with bleached blond hair and a dramatic flair for clothes. She made no bones about being in search of a new husband—"Men are a lot of trouble, honey, but they do have their good points, one big one in particular"—and was so good-natured about it that she had no trouble getting dates. Her social life would have exhausted the strongest debutante. For her to claim that Faith had a way with men, when Faith seldom went out with anyone and she herself was seldom at home, was pushing it a bit, in Faith's opinion.

"Don't laugh," Margot warned. "You're going to be stopped by a female cop one of these days, and that's when your luck will run out."

"That's all it is, luck."

"Sure it is." Margot abandoned that subject and gave her a curious look. "Now, what's this about a house in Godforsaken Louisiana?"

"Prescott," Faith corrected, smiling. "It's a little town north of Baton Rouge, almost at the Mississippi state line."

Margot snorted again. "That's what I said. Godforsaken."

"It's my hometown. I was born there."

"You don't say. And you actually admit that out loud?" Margot asked with all the incredulity of a true Dallas native.

"I'm going home," Faith said softly. "I want to live there." It wasn't a step she took lightly; she was going back with the full knowledge that the Rouillards would do everything they could to cause trouble for her. She was deliberately placing herself once more in proximity with Gray, and the danger of it made her lie awake at nights. Besides trying to find out what had happened to his father, all those years ago, she had a lot of ghosts to face, and Gray was the biggest one. He had tormented her, in one way or another, for most of her life, and she was still caught in the helpless childhood whirl of emotions where he was concerned. In her mind he was omnipotent, bigger than life, with the power to either destroy her or exalt her, and her last meeting with him had done nothing to dilute that impression. She needed to see him as a normal man, meet him on equal footing as an adult, rather than a vulnerable, terrified young girl. She didn't want him to have this power over her; she wanted to get over him, once and for all.

"It was that trip to Baton Rouge that did it, wasn't it? You got that close and just couldn't stand it." Margot didn't know about what had happened twelve years ago, didn't know anything about Faith's childhood other than she'd been in foster care and was very fond of her foster parents. Faith had never talked about her past or her family.

"I guess it's true about roots."

Margot leaned back in her chair. "Are you going to sell the agency, or what?"

Startled, Faith stared at her. "Of course not!"

There was a subtle relaxation of Margot's expression, and abruptly Faith realized how alarming her decision could be for her employees. "Everything will go on just like before, with two minor exceptions," she said.

"How minor?" Margot asked suspiciously.

"Well, for starters, I'm going to be living in Prescott. When Mr. Bible finds a house for me, I'm going to put in a fax machine, a computer, and a photocopier, so I'll be as in touch, electronically speaking, as I am now."

"Okay, that's one. What's the other?"

"You're going to be in charge of all the offices. A district manager, you might say, except there's only one district and you're the only manager. You don't mind traveling, do you?" Faith asked, suddenly anxious. She had forgotten to consider that when making her plans.

Margot's eyebrows arched in disbelief. "Me, mind traveling? Honey, are you out of your ever-lovin' mind? I *love* to travel. You might say it expands my hunting area, and God knows I've already given most of the prime bucks around here their chance for a life of excitement. It's their hard luck if some lucky guy somewhere else takes me out of circulation. Besides, it's never a hardship to go to New Orleans."

"And Houston and Baton Rouge."

"Cowboys in Houston, Cajuns in Baton Rouge. Yum, yum," said Margot, licking her lips. "I'll have to come back to Dallas to *rest.*"

Her plan fell smoothly into place, but then Faith went to a lot of trouble to make certain it did. She took a great deal of satisfaction in her efforts; she had been helpless at fourteen, but now she had resources of her own, and four years in the business community had given her a lot of contacts.

With Mr. Bible's help, she quickly located and settled on a small house for sale. It wasn't in Prescott, but was situated a couple of miles outside the town limits, on the edge of Rouillard land. Buying it put a sizable dent in her savings, but she paid for it in full, so Gray wouldn't be able to pull any strings with a mortgage holder and cause her any trouble. She knew enough now to foresee what steps he might take to make things rough for her, and counteract them. It gave her great pleasure to know she was outflanking him, and he wouldn't know anything about it until it was too late to stop her.

Very quietly, handling everything through the agency so her name didn't appear anywhere that it might cause an alert, she got the utilities turned on, the house cleaned, and gleefully shipped her furniture to her new home. Only a month after Gray had run her out of town for the second time, Faith pulled her car into the driveway of her house and looked at it with extreme satisfaction.

She hadn't bought a pig in a poke. Mr. Bible had arranged for her to look at photos of the house, both inside and out. The house was small, only five rooms, and had been built back in the fifties, but it had been remodeled and modernized with an eye toward selling it. The previous owner had done a good job; the new front porch went all the way across the front, and there was a porch swing at one end to lure the new inhabitants out to enjoy the good weather. Ceiling fans at each end of the porch guaranteed that the heat would seldom become too uncomfortable. Each room inside also had a ceiling fan.

Both bedrooms were the same size, so she had chosen the back one for herself and converted the front one into a home office. There was only one bath, but she was only one person, so she didn't expect to have a problem with that. The living room and dining room were pleasant, but the best thing about the house was the kitchen. Evidently it had been remodeled several years before, because she couldn't imagine anyone spending the money to customize a kitchen when a more standard approach would have made the house just as saleable and cost a lot less. Someone had loved to cook. There was a six-eye cooktop, and built-in microwave and conventional ovens. Floor-to-ceiling cupboards all along one wall provided enough storage space for a year's worth of food, if she so chose. Instead of a work island, a six-foot butcher-block table occupied the middle of the room, providing plenty of work space for any culinary adventures. Faith wasn't that enthralled with cooking herself, but she liked the room. She was, in fact, thrilled with the entire house. It was the first place she had ever lived that belonged to her; apartments didn't count, because she had rented those. This house was hers. She had a real home.

She was fizzing with internal delight when she drove into Prescott to stock up on groceries, and take care of two necessary errands. Her first stop was the courthouse, where she bought a Louisiana tag for her car and applied for her Louisiana driver's license. Next was the grocery store. It was a subtle pleasure to shop without thought of cost in the same store where the owner had once followed her around every time she came in, eyeing every move she made to make certain she didn't slip something into her pocket and walk out without paying for it. Morgan had been his name, she remembered, Ed Morgan. His youngest son had been in Jodie's class.

Leisurely she selected fruit and produce, putting each selection in a plastic bag and twisting a green tie around the bag to close it. A gray-haired man in a stained apron came out of the stockroom carrying a crate of bananas, which he began arranging on an almost empty display shelf. He glanced at her, then looked back, his eyes widening in disbelief.

Though his hair was a great deal thinner and what was left had changed color, Faith had no trouble recognizing the man about whom she had just been thinking. "Hello, Mr. Morgan," she said pleasantly as she wheeled her buggy past him. "How are you?"

"R-Renee," he sputtered, and something in the way he said her mother's name made Faith freeze inside, and look at him with new eyes. God, not him, too! Well, why not? Guy Rouillard hadn't always been available, and Renee wasn't the type of woman to deny herself.

Her smile faded, and her voice cooled. "No, not Renee. I'm Faith, the youngest daughter." She was incensed on behalf of her childhood self, constantly humiliated by being treated like a thief, when all the while the man who had made such a production of following her around in the store had been part of the pack of hounds baying after her mother.

She pushed the buggy on down the aisle. It wasn't a large store, so she heard the flurry of voices as he hurried to tell his wife who she was. Not long afterward, she became aware that she had picked up a shadow. She didn't recognize the teenage boy, also wearing a long, stained apron, who blushed uncomfortably when she glanced at him, but it was obvious he'd been told to make certain everything went into the buggy and not her purse.

Her temper flared, but she held it in tight control and didn't allow herself to be hurried. When she had gotten everything on her list, she wheeled the buggy to the checkout counter and began unloading it.

Mrs. Morgan had been operating the cash register when Faith had entered the store, but Mr. Morgan had taken over the duty and his wife was watching intently from the small office cubicle. He eyed the groceries she was unloading. "You'd better have the money to pay for all this," he said unpleasantly. "I'm real careful who I take a check from."

"I always pay cash," Faith retorted coolly. "I'm careful who I let see the number of my checking account."

It was a moment before he realized he had been insulted in kind, and he flushed darkly. "Watch your mouth. I don't have to take that kind of lip in my own store, especially from the likes of you."

"Really." She gave him a smile and kept her voice low. "You weren't that particular when it came to my mother, were you?"

The flush faded as abruptly as it had come, leaving him pale and sweating, and he cast a swift glance toward his wife. "I don't know what you're talking about."

"Fine. See that the subject never comes up again." She pulled out her wallet and stood waiting. He began pulling the items down the counter, punching in prices as he went. Faith watched each price as he rang it up, and stopped him once. "Those apples are a dollar twenty-nine a pound, not a dollar sixty-nine."

He flushed again, furious that she had caught him in an

error. At least, she assumed it was an error, rather than deliberate cheating. She would make certain she checked every item on the sales receipt before leaving the store. Let him get a taste of what it was like to be automatically assumed dishonest. Once she would have backed down, humiliated to the core, but those days were long past.

When he rang up the total, she opened her wallet and pulled out six twenty-dollar bills. Normally her grocery bill was less than half that, but she had let herself run out of a lot of things rather than going to the trouble of moving them, so she had to restock. She saw him eyeing the cash left in her wallet, and knew the story would fly around town that Faith Devlin had come back, and was flashing a roll that would choke a horse. No one would think she had come by it honestly.

She couldn't tell herself that she didn't care what the townspeople thought; she always had. That was one of the reasons she'd come back, to prove to them, and herself, that not all Devlins were trash. She knew in her mind that she was respectable, but she didn't know it in her heart yet, and wouldn't until the folks in her hometown accepted her. She couldn't divorce herself from Prescott; this town had helped shape who she was as a person, and her roots went deep. But wanting acceptance from the people here didn't mean she would let anyone insult her and get away with it. As a child she had been quietly obstinate about going her own way, but in the twelve years since she had lived here, she had grown up and learned how to stand up for herself.

The same boy who had followed her in the store carried the bags out to her car. He was about sixteen, she guessed; his joints still had the looseness of childhood, and his feet and hands were too big for the rest of him. "Are you related to the Morgans?" she asked as they walked across the parking lot, with him pushing the buggy.

He blushed at being personally addressed. "Uh, yeah. They're my grandparents."

"What's your name?"

"Jason."

"I'm Faith Hardy. I used to live here, and I've just moved back." She stopped at her car and unlocked the trunk. Like most teenage boys, he was interested in anything with four wheels on it, and gave it a good look. She had bought a solid, reliable sedan rather than a sports car; the sedan was better for business, and it took a certain type of attitude to drive around in a sports car anyway, an attitude Faith had never had. She had always been older than her years, and stability, dependability, were far more important to her than speed and flashy looks. But the car, a dark, sophisticated European green, was less than a year old and had a certain style to it, for all its reliability.

"Nice car," Jason felt moved to comment as he transferred the groceries from the buggy to the trunk.

"Thanks." She tipped him, and he looked at the dollar in surprise. By that, she could deduce that either tipping wasn't the norm in Prescott, or people usually carried out their own groceries and he had been pressed into duty so he could see if she kept the inside of her car clean, or something like that. She suspected the latter; the nosiness of small-town people knew no bounds.

A small, white Cadillac wheeled into the parking lot as Faith was unlocking her car door, and abruptly braked as it came even with her. She glanced up and saw a woman staring at her, dumbstruck. It took a moment before she recognized Monica Rouillard, or whatever her name was now. The two women faced each other, and Faith remembered how Monica had always gone out of her way to be nasty to the Devlins, unlike Gray, who had pretty much treated them normally until Guy had disappeared. Despite herself, Faith felt a flash of pity; if her suspicions were right, their father was dead, and they had gone all these years without knowing what had happened to him. The Devlins had suffered because of Guy's actions, but the Rouillards had suffered, too.

Even in the shadows of the car, Faith could see how pale and strained Monica looked as she stared at her. This was one confrontation that would be best postponed; though she intended to stand her ground, there was no need to flaunt her presence in the Rouillards' faces. Turning away, she got into her car and started the engine. Monica was blocking her so she couldn't back out, but the space in front of her was empty, so there was no need. She simply drove out through the empty parking slot, leaving Monica still sitting there staring after her.

When she got home, she found several faxes waiting for her, all from Margot. She put up the groceries before settling down in the office to take care of whatever problems had cropped up. She enjoyed the travel industry; it wasn't without its share of headaches and crises, but for the most part, by the very nature of the business, the customers were upbeat and excited. The agency's job was to make sure their vacation tours were properly booked, with reliable accommodations. They gently steered vacationers away from inappropriate tour packages; for instance, a family with small children probably wouldn't be all that pleased with a cruise on a party ship geared more toward adult pleasures. Her employees knew how to handle things like that; most of the problems that came Faith's way were of a different nature. There was a payroll to meet, tax forms to complete, an unending parade of paper. Faith had decided that she would still handle the payroll, with the pertinent information faxed to her from the four office locations every Monday morning. She would do the paperwork, prepare the checks, and Express Mail them on Wednesday morning. It was a workable solution, and the convenience of working at home delighted her.

The biggest inconvenience was still doing her banking in Dallas, both business and personal, but she had decided against transferring her funds to Prescott or even Baton Rouge; the Rouillard influence had long arms. She hadn't checked to see if the family owned the new bank in town, because it hadn't really mattered; whether they owned it or not, Gray would have a lot of pull. There were rules and laws in banking, but in this part of the state the Rouillards were a law unto themselves. The balance in her accounts, even copies of her canceled checks, would be easy for Gray to get. She had no doubt that he could also cause trouble for her by delaying credit for checks deposited until the last possible minute, and bouncing her own checks if he could. No, it was best to keep her account in Dallas.

Gravel crunched in the driveway and she looked out the

window to see a sleek, gunmetal gray Jaguar come to a stop. Resigned, she let the curtain fall back into place and pushed her chair away from the desk. She didn't have to see who got out of the car to know who had come calling, just as she knew this wasn't the Welcome Wagon.

Going into the living room, she opened the door as she heard footsteps on the porch. "Hello, Gray. Please come in. I see you've given up your 'Vettes."

Surprise flickered in his eyes as he stepped over the threshold, immediately overwhelming her with his size. He hadn't expected her to calmly invite him inside, the rabbit offering the hospitality of its burrow to the wolf. "I'm slower in a lot of things than I used to be," he drawled.

It was on the tip of her tongue to say, "Better, too, I suppose," but she bit the words back. She doubted that Gray Rouillard would be making suggestive remarks to her, of all people, and if she took it as such, he would think it was just what he might have expected from a Devlin. There was no room for normal flirtatious byplay between the two of them.

The weather was hot this late spring day, and Gray was dressed in a loose, white cotton shirt that was open at the throat, and khaki linen trousers. Curly black chest hair was visible in the open vee of the shirt, and Faith forced herself to look away, conscious of a sudden difficulty in breathing. He brought with him the fresh, earthy scent of clean sweat and the animal muskiness of man. She never had been able to decide what color his scent was, she thought dazedly, inhaling his rich, subtle odor. His physical impact made her senses reel, just as it always had. Nothing had changed. It hadn't been the unexpectedness of seeing him the last time that had so shaken her; the old reactions were still there, still potent, undimmed by time and maturity. She looked at him with hidden, helpless rage. God, this man had all but ground her into the dirt, and wouldn't hesitate to do it again; what was *wrong* with her that she couldn't see him without feeling that hot, automatic tingle of excitement?

He stood too close to her, just inside the door, staring down at her with narrowed dark eyes. She moved away to give herself breathing space. He was physically too imposing, ten inches taller and with that lean, hard athlete's body.

She would have to go on tiptoe to kiss even the hollow of his tanned, muscular throat. The aberrant thought shocked her, shook her, and instinctively she guarded her expression. She could never let him know that she was even remotely attracted to him; it would give him a weapon of devastating power to use against her.

"This is a surprise," she said lightly, though it wasn't. "Have a seat. Would you like a cup of coffee, or maybe iced tea?"

"Skip the pleasantries," he said, moving toward her, and she heard the cold anger in his smoky voice. "What are you doing here?"

"I live here," she replied, arching her brows in mock surprise. She hadn't expected the confrontation to come quite so soon; he was more efficient than she had expected. She moved away from him again, desperate to keep a safe distance between them. His gaze sharpened, then gleamed with satisfaction, and with a chill she knew he had realized that his closeness made her nervous. She halted, determined not to let him know that he could intimidate her that way, and turned to squarely face him. She lifted her chin, the expression in her green eyes cool and unruffled. It took a lot of effort, but she managed it.

"You won't for long. You've wasted your time and effort in coming back."

With gentle amusement she said, "Even you could have problems throwing me out of my own house."

His gaze sharpened as he glanced around the neat, cozy living room. "I bought it," she enlarged. "It isn't financed, it's mine free and clear."

He gave a harsh crack of laughter, startling her. "You must have divorced Mr. Hardy and taken him to the cleaners. Did you get everything he had?"

Faith stiffened. "As a matter of fact, I did. But I didn't divorce him."

"What did you do, snare yourself an old geezer who kicked off after a year or two? Did he have heirs you gypped out of their inheritance?"

Color fled her cheeks, leaving her as pale as a statue. "No,

I snared myself a healthy young man of twenty-three, who died in a car accident before we'd been married a year."

His mouth tightened. "I'm sorry," he said gruffly. "I shouldn't have said that."

"No, you shouldn't have, but I've never noticed that concern for other's feelings has ever worried a Rouillard."

He gave a snort of derision. "A Devlin should be careful about throwing rocks in that particular glass house."

"I've never harmed anyone," she said with a bitter little smile. "I just got caught between the lines when the battle started."

"All innocence, hmmm? You were pretty young when all that happened, but I have a real good memory, and you were sashaying around in front of me and all those deputies, wearing your little thin nightgown that we could see through. Like mother, like daughter, I'd say."

Faith's eyes widened, full of outrage and horrified embarrassment, and color flooded back into her face. She took two quick steps forward and jabbed him in the chest with her forefinger. "Don't you *dare* throw that in my face!" she said, choking with rage. "I was dragged out of my bed in the middle of the night, and tossed into the yard like a piece of trash. Don't say it," she warned sharply, when he opened his mouth to retort that trash was exactly what she'd been, and jabbed him in the chest again. "Everything we owned was dumped out, my little brother was hysterical and wouldn't turn loose of me. What was I supposed to do, take time out to find some of my own clothes and retire into the woods to change? Why didn't you so-called *decent* men turn your backs, if you were seeing a little too much?"

He looked down into her furious face, his expression strangely arrested, then his eyes became more heavy-lidded and intent. He took hold of her hand, moving it away from his chest. He didn't release her, but kept her fingers folded against his hard, calloused palm. "You've got a little redheaded temper there, haven't you?" he asked with amusement.

His touch shocked her with a hot twinge of electricity. She tried to jerk her hand free, but he merely tightened his grip, effortlessly restraining her. "Now, don't get all in a pucker," he said lazily. "Maybe you thought I'd stand here and let you poke holes in me with your fingernail, but I have to be in a different mood to enjoy that."

Faith glared up at him. She could humiliate herself by giving in to the useless urge to struggle, or she could wait until he decided to release her. Her instincts were to struggle away from the disturbing heat of his touch, the surprising roughness of his palm, but she forced herself to stand still, sensing that he would enjoy watching her try to free herself. Then the sensual undertone of his comment registered, and her eyes widened as shock rippled through her. There was no mistaking his meaning this time.

"Smart girl," he said, his gaze sliding down to her breasts. He took his time, examining the shape of them beneath her silk, mint green shirt. She caught her breath, his gaze like an actual touch that made her breasts tingle. "You don't want to start a tussle with me that you can't win—or do you? Your mama probably taught you that a man gets hard real quick when a woman starts wiggling against him. Did you come back thinking you might step into your mother's shoes? Do you want to be my whore, the way she was my dad's?"

Swift fury glittered in her eyes, and she swung her free hand with all her strength. Quick as a rattlesnake his other hand lashed out, blocking the blow and capturing that hand, too. He gave a low whistle at the force she had put into the swing. "Temper, temper," he chided, looking as if he were enjoying her anger. "Were you trying to knock my teeth out?"

"Yes!" she flared, gritting her teeth together and forgetting her determination to deny him the pleasure of a struggle. She jerked her hands, trying to twist free, and succeeded only in bruising her wrists. "Get out! Get out of my house."

He laughed down at her, easily reducing her to a standstill as he brought her hard against him. "What are you going to do, throw me out?"

She froze, alarmed to find that his reaction to a struggle was exactly what he'd said it would be. There was no mistaking the ridge pressed against her belly. She struck out with the only weapon left to her, her tongue. "If you'll let *go* of me, you Neanderthal, what I'll do is put ice on my wrists to stop them from turning black and blue!" she hotly retorted.

He looked down at his long fingers encircling her slender wrists, loosening his grip and scowling at the dark red marks that quickly formed. "I didn't mean to hurt you," he said, surprising her. He immediately released her. "You have skin like a baby."

She drew back, massaging her wrists and steadfastly refusing to look at the front of his trousers. That, too, could be ignored. "My guess is you didn't care if you hurt me. Now, get out."

"In a minute. I have a few things to say."

She gave him a cold look. "Then for God's sake, say them and leave."

Danger glittered in those dark eyes, and before she knew it, he was right in front of her again, almost playfully pinching her chin. "You're a ballsy little babe, aren't you? Maybe too ballsy for your own good. Don't take me on in a fight, sweet thing, because you'll get hurt. The best thing you can do is pack up your stuff and get out of here, just as fast as you moved in; I'll buy the house from you, for what you gave for it, so you won't be out anything. You aren't welcome here, and I don't want my mother and sister hurt by seeing you parading around as if nothing ever happened, bringing up that old scandal again and getting everybody upset. If you stay, if you force my hand, I can make things rough for you here, and you'll wind up getting hurt. You won't be able to get a job, and you'll find out damn fast that you don't have any friends here."

She jerked her chin away from him. "What will you do, burn me out?" she goaded. "I'm not a helpless fourteen-year-old anymore, and you'll find that it isn't as easy to bully me now. I'm here, and I'm staying."

"We'll see about that, won't we?" His hooded gaze dropped to her breasts again, and suddenly he grinned. "You're right about one thing: You're not fourteen anymore."

He walked out then, leaving Faith staring after him, her

fists clenched with impotent anger, and panic clenching her stomach. She didn't want him to notice her as a woman, didn't want him to turn that hot, hooded gaze on her, because she wasn't certain of her ability to resist him. She felt sick at the thought of being like her mother, of being what he had taunted her with being, a whore for a Rouillard.

"Was it Renee?" Monica asked quietly, though she was drawn so tight that the tension was almost visible. She had called Gray from Morgan's grocery store, more upset than he had heard her in years, since the day he'd had to tell her that their father had left them for Renee Devlin, in fact. Monica had come a long way since then, but the haunted look in her eyes told Gray that the pain was still too close to the surface for her to be objective about it.

"No, but it was definitely a Devlin." He poured himself a finger of Scotch and tossed it back, then poured another finger, feeling that he needed it after another encounter with Faith Devlin. Faith Devlin *Hardy,* that is. A widow. A young, lovely, red-haired widow with so much fire in her that he'd wanted to check his hands for singe marks after touching her. He had disconcerted her a couple of times, but for the most part she exhibited a maddeningly cool confidence. She hadn't been the least bit worried by his threats, though she had to know he wasn't bluffing.

They were in the study, enjoying a before-dinner drink, at least Gray was. Alex was coming to dinner, and Noelle would be down soon, so Gray and Monica had gone into the study to have a few minutes of privacy for their discussion.

Monica looked blank. "It wasn't Renee? It looked just like her, as if she hadn't aged at all. She even looked younger. Oh—I see." Comprehension dawned. "It was one of the girls, wasn't it?"

"The youngest one. Faith. She always looked more like Renee than any of the others."

"What's she doing here?"

"She says she's come back to stay."

Horror filled Monica's dark eyes. "She can't! Mother couldn't bear it! Alex has gotten her to come out of her shell a little, but if she hears any of the Devlins are back in town, there's no telling how far it will set her back. You'll have to get rid of her again, Gray."

Wryly he considered his Scotch, and finished it with one gulp. The whole town knew the story about him running the Devlin family out of the parish. It wasn't something he was particularly proud of, but neither did he regret it, and the incident had become enshrined as a sort of local legend. Monica hadn't been there, hadn't seen the ugliness; she knew only the results, not the process. She didn't have the memory seared into her brain. It was always with him: Faith's terror, the little boy's hysterical shrieks and pitiful attempts to cling to her, her desperate struggle to gather up their belongings . . . and the potent, uncomfortable lust with which the men had watched her, the night shadows concealing her youth and revealing only her resemblance to her mother.

With a sharp little pang he realized that that night was a link between them, him and Faith, a bond forged by a common memory that couldn't be broken short of death. He had never really known her, and twelve years lay between then and now, and yet . . . he hadn't thought of her or treated her as a stranger. It was as if they had resumed an acquaintance of long standing. They weren't strangers; there was that night between them.

"Getting rid of her may be harder this time," he said abruptly. "She's bought the Cleburne place, and as she pointed out to me, I can't kick her off her own property."

"If she's buying it, there has to be some way to interfere with the mortgage—"

"I didn't say she's buying it, I said she's bought it. There's a difference."

Monica frowned. "Where would a Devlin get that kind of money?"

"Probably life insurance. She's a widow. Her last name is Hardy now."

"How convenient for her," Monica said sarcastically.

"No, from what I gather, it wasn't," Gray said, seeing in his mind how pale Faith had gone when he had said much the same thing. He heard the doorbell ring, and Alex's voice as Oriane opened the door to him. Discussion time was over. He patted Monica's shoulder as they moved to the door. "I'll do what I can to make her leave, but it isn't a foregone conclusion. She isn't a typical Devlin."

No, not typical in any way. Even when she'd been a teenager, looking at her had been enough to get him hard. That hadn't changed. But she was also a more capable opponent than any of the rest of her family ever could have been. She was poised and intelligent, and seemed to have pulled herself, by whatever means, out of the gutters where her family had always lived. He respected her for that, but it didn't make any difference; she had to go. Monica was worried about what her presence would do to Noelle, but he was worried about what it would do to Monica as well.

They went out into the foyer as Noelle came gracefully down the stairs to greet Alex, offering her cheek for his kiss, allowing him to tuck her hand into the crook of his arm, small touches that she had seldom allowed her husband. Alex's devotion had been good for Noelle, soothing a bit the pain of her shattered self-confidence, but Gray wasn't so sure it had been good for Alex. His wife had died fifteen years before and he should have remarried; he'd been only forty-one at the time of her death. Perhaps he would have, in time, but then Guy had left, and Alex, good friend that he was, had devoted himself to helping the Rouillards through the crisis. Even after receiving the letter of proxy, it had taken Gray a good two years to consolidate his position, and Alex had been right there, sitting up through all-night strategy sessions, becoming a sort of surrogate father to Monica, gradually cajoling Noelle out of her total depression. He had fallen painfully in love with Noelle, a fact to which she seemed oblivious.

He should have seen it coming, Gray thought, watching his mother. She was still incredibly lovely, in a cool, classic way that would appeal to Alex's romanticism. Her dark hair was only lightly grayed, and it was remarkably becoming. Her skin was still smooth and unwrinkled, though somehow there was no mistaking her age. There was no youth in her, no lightness of spirit, and sadness always lurked in the depths of her blue eyes. Looking at his mother, at Monica, at

Alex, Gray savagely damned his father for what he had done.

As Alex seated Noelle, he said to Gray, "I heard a curious rumor today, about one of the Devlins." Monica froze, her anxious gaze darting to Noelle, who had gone still and pale. Alex didn't see Gray's sharp, warning motion. "I ran into Ed Morgan, and it seems one of the girls has moved back to town."

Alex straightened, his eyes levelly meeting Gray's, and Gray realized that Alex had chosen not to see his warning. He had deliberately brought up the subject, forcing Noelle to confront it. He had done that a few times before, talking about Guy when Noelle recoiled from any mention of her husband. Perhaps it was the right thing to do; God knows, Alex had been able to get more response from Noelle than either Gray or Monica had ever managed.

Noelle's hand fluttered toward her throat. "Moved . . . back?"

"It's the youngest daughter, Faith," Gray said, keeping his voice calm. "She's bought the old Cleburne place and moved into it."

"No." Noelle turned her agonized gaze on her son. "I can't—I can't bear it."

"Of course you can," Alex said comfortably, taking his seat. "You don't go out or talk to any of the townspeople, so you'll never see her or know anything about her. There's no reason for you to be upset."

Gray leaned back in his chair, controlling a slight smile. He and Monica tended to handle Noelle with kid gloves; he couldn't help it, even when she frustrated the hell out of him. Alex had no such compunction. He was relentless in his efforts to completely pry her out of her shell and back into society. Probably he was right to bring the subject into the open, and Gray's and Monica's inclinations were too protective.

Noelle shook her head, still looking at Gray. "I don't want her here," she said, openly pleading. "People will talk . . . it will all be rehashed again, and I can't bear it."

"You won't know anything about it," Alex said.

She shuddered. "I don't have to hear it to know it's going on."

No, she probably didn't. Anyone who had ever lived in a small town would know all too well how gossip was recycled, and nothing was ever forgotten.

"Please," she said to Gray, blue eyes haunted. "Make her leave."

Gray sipped his wine, carefully expressionless. He was getting damn tired of the way people thought he could wave a magic wand and make people disappear. Short of kidnapping or murder, all he could do was make things as uncomfortable for Faith as possible. He had no legal ground this time, no charge of trespass, no family of drunks and thieves the sheriff had been glad to escort out of his parish. What he had was one young woman, stubbornly determined to stand her ground.

"It won't be easy," he said.

"But you have so much influence . . . with the sheriff, the bank—"

"She hasn't opened an account at the bank, and the sheriff can't do anything unless she breaks a law. So far, she hasn't." She wouldn't be opening an account at his bank, either, he realized. She was too smart. She had known exactly what she would be facing when she moved back to Prescott, otherwise she wouldn't have bought the Cleburne place outright. She had taken steps to limit what moves he could make against her. He had to respect her as an opponent, for her foresight. She had definitely made things more difficult for him. He would check around, use his sources to try to verify that she had indeed paid for the house rather than financing it, but he suspected she had been telling the truth.

"There must be something," Noelle said desperately.

Gray arched his brows. "I draw the line at murder," he drawled.

"Gray!" Shocked, she stared at him. "I wasn't suggesting anything of the sort!"

"Then we may have to get used to the idea of her living here. I can make things damned inconvenient for her, but that's about it. And I don't want anyone getting any bright ideas about having her physically harassed," he said, giving both Monica and Noelle a hard look, just in case the thought had occurred to either of them. It wasn't likely, but he didn't intend to take the chance. "If we can get rid of her my way, fine, but I won't have her hurt." He didn't question this odd protectiveness on behalf of a Devlin. Faith had had enough pain and fear in her life, he thought, remembering the terrified girl caught in the glare of a semicircle of headlights.

"As if we'd do anything like that," Monica said, insulted.

"I didn't think you would, but I didn't want to leave the matter open to question."

Delfina brought in the first course, a creamy cucumber soup, and by mutual consent the subject was dropped, to Gray's amusement. There wasn't anything going on in the house that Oriane and Delfina didn't know almost as soon as it happened, but Noelle and Monica both adhered to the old stricture against personal conversation in front of the servants. He doubted that anyone who worked for them considered him or herself a "servant," especially Delfina. She had worked there for as long as he could remember, and had whacked his hands with a wooden spoon whenever she'd caught him trying to sneak one of the petit fours she baked for Noelle's luncheons.

Monica began telling Alex about an interesting documentary she'd seen on television. Gray glanced at Noelle to make a comment, and stilled when he saw the tears gliding silently down her cheeks. She was calmly eating her soup, the spoon dipping and lifting in graceful rhythm, and all the while she was crying.

Alex joined Gray in the study after dinner, and they discussed business for half an hour before Gray said wryly, "Monica and I had decided not to tell Mother about Faith."

Alex grimaced. "I figured as much. I know it isn't my place to butt in—" Gray snorted, bringing a quick grin to Alex's face before he resumed. "But she can't keep hiding from the world forever."

"Can't she? She's been giving it a damn good try for the past twelve years."

"If she won't go to the world, I've decided to bring the world to her. Maybe she'll see that, if she can't escape it, she might as well join it."

"Good luck," Gray said, and meant it.

Alex gave him a curious look. "Are you really going to make Faith leave?"

Gray leaned back in his chair and propped his feet on the desk, lounging like a sleepy panther, relaxed but still danger-ous. "I'm damn sure going to try, but I told Mother the truth. Legally, there isn't a lot I can do."

"Why not leave the girl alone?" Alex asked, and sighed. "I'd say she's had a rough enough life as it is, without folks deliberately trying to make trouble for her."

"Have you seen her?"

"No, why?"

"She looks enough like Renee to be her twin," Gray said. "Just being a Devlin is bad enough, but looking the way she does . . ." He shook his head. "She's going to stir up a lot of memories, and not just in my family. Renee Devlin got around."

"I still say give her a chance," Alex argued. "If she's trying to make something of herself, it would be a shame to stand in her way."

Gray shook his head. "I have to think of Mother and Monica. They're more important to me than a little piece of white trash trying to make good."

Alex regarded him with disappointment. Gray was a hard man and a dangerous enemy, but he'd always been fair. Guy's disappearance had thrust him headlong into a situa-tion wherein responsibility for the family's financial, as well as emotional, well-being had been dumped on his young shoulders. Gray had been a cheerful, happy-go-lucky hell-raiser until then, but overnight he had changed into a much harder, more ruthless man. His sense of humor still bor-dered on the bawdy and outrageous, when he indulged in humor, but for the most part he was far more serious. Gray was a man who knew the extent of his power, and didn't shrink from using it. If Guy had been respected in the financial community, Gray was regarded with the awe and caution one would afford a marauder.

"You're too protective," Alex finally said. "Noelle and Monica won't collapse if Faith Devlin lives in Prescott. They won't like it, but they'll learn to live with it."

Gray shrugged. Maybe—hell, probably—he was too protective, but Alex wasn't the one who had watched Monica nearly bleed to death, or seen how total Noelle's emotional collapse had been. By the time Alex had become involved in cajoling Noelle out of her room, at least she'd been talking again, and feeding herself.

"I give up," Alex said, shaking his head. "You'll do whatever you want, anyway. But think about it, and maybe cut the girl some slack."

Later that night, sitting alone in the study with his feet still propped on the desk in his usual position, while he read a financial report on some stocks he'd bought, Gray found it difficult to concentrate. It wasn't the Scotch; he had poured himself a drink when he had begun doing paperwork, over two hours before, and most of the liquor was still in the glass. The fact was, he couldn't get the problem of Faith Devlin out of his mind. Noelle's silent tears had reached him in a way nothing she could have said would have. If Faith didn't deserve to be hurt again, neither did his mother or sister. They had been innocent victims too, and Monica had almost died. He couldn't forget that, and he couldn't see them upset without trying to do something about it.

And it was a fact that if Faith Hardy stayed in Prescott, Noelle and Monica would be even more hurt and upset than they were now.

Gray stared broodingly at the level of Scotch in the glass. Maybe if he drank it, he could forget how warm and vital Faith had felt under his hands, how that sweet, spicy scent of hers had gone straight to his head and made him dizzy with lust. Maybe if he drank the whole goddamn bottle, he could forget about the urge to plunge his hands into the fire of her hair to see if it burned him, or the hunger to taste the wide, full bloom of her lips. He thought of her skin, so fine-grained and translucent that he marked her with the lightest touch; her breasts, high and round, the peaks of her nipples discernible even beneath her bra. She had *it,* the same indefinable quality Renee had possessed, an effortless sensuality that drew men to her like a lodestone. Faith wasn't as blatant about it as Renee had been; she had toned it down with better clothes, but the quality had merely been refined, not diluted. What Faith Hardy looked like was a classy lady who loved a long, hard ride in bed, and damn if he didn't want to give it to her.

If she didn't leave, it was likely that the residents of Prescott were going to be shocked out of their small-town minds, and Noelle ten times more upset than she was now, by the spectacle of another Rouillard man having a hot and heavy affair with a Devlin woman.

❧ Eight ❧

Ed Morgan made a point of meeting Faith at the door as she entered the grocery store. "Sorry," he said, not looking the least bit regretful. "I don't have anything you need."

Faith stopped, and gave him a cool look. "You don't know what I need," she pointed out.

"Doesn't matter." He folded his arms and smirked at her. "Guess you'll have to shop somewhere else."

Faith controlled her temper. She detected the fine hand of Gray Rouillard in this, and getting into an argument with Mr. Morgan wouldn't accomplish anything except possibly getting her arrested for causing a public disturbance, which would suit Gray just fine.

He had kept his word about making it difficult for her to live in the parish. Not ten minutes earlier, the attendant at the service station where she stopped had gleefully told her that they were out of gas, and she'd have to go elsewhere. At the time, the man at the next pump had been filling his car.

If Gray thought this would send her packing, he had seriously underestimated his opponent. She could sue these people for refusing service, but that wouldn't make her very popular in town. She intended to live here, so she discarded that option. Besides, the real battle was between her and Gray; everyone else was secondary.

She shrugged as she turned to leave. "Fine. If you can do without my money, I can do without your groceries."

"All the other stores in town are in the same predicament," he called after her, gloating. "Fresh out of whatever it is you want."

Faith contemplated giving him the finger, but resisted the urge; he might take it as an invitation. She walked calmly back to her car. Obviously she'd have to do her shopping and buy her gasoline somewhere else, but it was only an inconvenience, not an insurmountable problem.

Inconvenient in the short term, that is; long term, she would have to do something about it. And in the *very* short term, she was mad as hell.

There was a pay phone on the corner. Faith stalked past her car and down to the open kiosk. This one had a phone book in it, swinging from a stiff metal cord. It would be just like the Rouillards to have an unlisted number, she silently fumed as she opened the thin little book and flipped through the pages until she reached the *R*s. But no, there it was. She dug a quarter out of her purse and fed it into the slot, then punched in the number.

A woman's voice answered on the second ring. "Rouillard residence."

"Gray Rouillard, please," Faith said in her most business-like tone.

"May I say who is calling?"

"Mrs. Hardy," she replied.

"Just a moment."

No more than ten seconds later, the line clicked and Gray's velvety dark voice purred, "Is this *the* Mrs. Hardy?"

She could hear the mocking amusement in his voice, and her hand clenched around the receiver so hard, it was a wonder the plastic didn't crack. "It is."

"Well, well. I'll bet you didn't think you'd be asking for favors so soon, did you, sweetheart? What can I do for you today?" He didn't even try to disguise the satisfaction in his tone.

"Not a damn thing," she said coldly. "I just wanted you to know your childish little tricks won't work. I'll have my

118

groceries shipped in from Dallas before I'll give you the satisfaction of seeing me leave!" She slammed down the receiver before he could reply, and marched to her car. She hadn't really accomplished anything, other than blowing off some steam and letting him know that she realized who was behind this latest development, and that it wasn't going to work. It was satisfying anyway.

At Rouillard House, Gray chuckled as he sat back in his chair. He'd been right about her redheaded temper. He'd have liked to see her just now, with those green eyes snapping fire. Maybe his maneuver had made her dig in her heels rather than prompting her to go to a friendlier locale, but one thing for certain, it had gotten a reaction! Then his eyes sharpened. Dallas, huh? Maybe he should do some checking there.

Faith allowed herself to stew for a minute, then put her anger aside as a waste of energy. She refused to let this town, and Gray Rouillard, get the best of her. She would change their opinions of her if it took twenty years! The key to changing their minds, she realized, was proving that Guy Rouillard hadn't run off with her mother. For whatever reason he had left, it couldn't be blamed on her family. Taking that into consideration, she had far more reason to hold a grudge than did the Rouillards or anyone else in the parish.

Knowing that Guy hadn't been with Renee and proving it, however, were two different things. Perhaps if she could get Renee to talk to Gray, he would at least be curious enough to start searching for his father. Maybe he already had, and Mrs. DuBois at the library simply didn't know the result of the search. If Guy was alive, though, there would be a traceable paper record somewhere.

She drove to New Roads, where she filled up the car and bought the few groceries she had needed. So much for Gray's effort to starve her out, she thought with satisfaction when she returned home and carried in the bag. She hadn't even had to go that much farther afield.

After she had put up the groceries, she went into her office and called her grandmother Armstead in Jackson. As before, Renee answered the phone.

"Mama, this is Faith."

"Faith! Hi, honey," Renee said in her lazy, sultry voice. "How're you doin', baby? I didn't expect to hear from you again so soon."

"I'm fine, Mama. I've moved back to Prescott."

There was a moment of silence on the line. "Why'd you do that? From what Jodie told me, them folks didn't treat you right."

"It was home," Faith said simply, knowing Renee wouldn't understand. "But that isn't why I called. Mama, everyone here still thinks you ran off with Guy Rouillard."

"Well, I told you that isn't so, didn't I? It's no skin off my nose what they think."

"It's causing me a little bit of trouble, though. Mama, if I can get Gray Rouillard to call you, would you talk to him and tell him that you didn't run away with his father?"

Renee gave an uneasy laugh. "Gray wouldn't believe a word I said. Guy was easy to get along with, but Gray . . . No, I don't want to talk to him."

"Please, Mama. If he doesn't believe you, that's up to him, but—"

"I said no," Renee interrupted sharply. "I'm not going to talk to him, and you're just wastin' your breath. I don't give a shit what those bastards in Prescott think." She slammed down the receiver, and Faith winced at the crash in her ear.

She hung up the phone, frowning in thought. For whatever reason, Renee was nervous about talking to Gray, and that meant Faith didn't have much chance of changing her mind. Renee had never been one to go out of her way for anyone, even in a matter as simple as a telephone call.

Well, if Renee wouldn't talk to Gray, then Faith had to find some other way to convince him, and the best way to do that was find out what had really happened to Guy.

How did you go about finding out if someone who had disappeared twelve years ago was alive or dead? Faith wondered. She wasn't a detective, didn't know the procedures to follow to gain access to the records that would normally be examined if you were looking for someone. The thing to do, she supposed, was to hire a real private detective, one who would know those things. It would be expensive, though, and she didn't have much extra money after spending her ready cash on the house.

Where to find a detective? There wasn't any such animal in Prescott, but she supposed they could be found in any moderate-sized town; Baton Rouge was a city of almost a quarter million people, but it was also a little too close to Gray's sphere of influence. New Orleans would probably be safer. Maybe she was being paranoid about Gray's power, but she would rather be paranoid than caught unawares. A man who would try to stop a woman from buying groceries was diabolical! Her mouth quirked at the thought, and she allowed herself a tiny smile. On a more serious note, she had a healthy respect for the lengths to which he would go to follow through on his promises, and his warnings.

She would find a good detective and hire him to search credit card and bank records, things like that. If Guy was alive, surely he would have used some of his vast financial assets to support himself; she couldn't see him washing dishes at minimum wage. Perhaps it would be possible to find out if he had filed an income tax return. Surely any decent detective would be able to do that in a short amount of time, maybe a week, so the cost should be manageable.

What if the detective did find a paper trail? If Guy had used a credit card, Gray would have known about it, seen the charge on the monthly statement. Had Gray known where his father was all these years, and not said anything? The possibility was intriguing . . . and infuriating. If Gray *had* found Guy, wouldn't he have contacted him? And if he had done that, then he would know that Guy hadn't left with Renee. It followed, then, that for whatever reason, Gray had never tried to find his father, otherwise he would know there was no reason for this vendetta against her.

She couldn't forget what she considered the most likely scenario: Guy was dead. She could see him leaving, though divorce would have been a more logical step, but she couldn't see him never contacting his kids again, or walking away from the Rouillard money. That just wasn't human nature. She had to give the private detective a chance to find Guy, but she didn't think he'd succeed. After that, she would start asking questions around town; she didn't know what she could discover, but the answer to the puzzle was there, if she could just figure out how to put the pieces together. Someone had to know what had happened that night. The truth was there, waiting for someone to find it.

She pulled out a sheet of paper, paused for a moment, and unwillingly wrote her mother's name at the top. It was asking too much of coincidence for Renee to have left the same night Guy had disappeared and not know anything about it. Maybe they really *had* run away together, and something had happened to Guy afterward, something that Renee didn't want known. Though the only circumstances under which Faith could imagine Renee stirring herself to violence would be to protect herself, she had to put Renee's name at the top of the list.

Beside Renee's name, because he had the motive, she wrote "Gray" in block letters. She looked at the two names. One of them, possibly both of them, knew what had happened to Guy. She would bet her socks on it. Nausea roiled in her stomach. Between murder suspects, which did she choose as the most likely: her mother, or the man she had always loved?

Stricken, Faith stared bitterly at the paper. Self-knowledge was seldom sweet. She must be the biggest fool alive, for no matter how Gray had wrecked her life or tried to make things impossible for her, no matter that she thought he might be involved in his father's death, she couldn't run from, destroy, or even ignore that bone-deep, compelling attraction to him, like metal shavings to a magnet. Just the sight of him made her go weak inside, and when he touched her she felt the electricity of it in every cell of her body. He had never touched her except in anger; what would it be like if he came to her as a lover, with pleasure his intention? She couldn't imagine it. Her blood would boil, her heart stop.

What would she do if she found that Gray had indeed killed his father, or had him killed? The thought caused a sharp pain in her chest, and she barely stifled a moan. She would have to do the same thing she would do if it were anyone else. She couldn't live with herself otherwise. And she would grieve for the rest of her life.

There were other suspects, though less likely. She listed them under the two top names. Noelle. Amos. Perhaps Monica. Thinking laterally, the list widened to the other men Renee had slipped around and slept with, as well as Guy's other women. For two people infatuated with each other, they had been remarkably unfaithful. Ed Morgan had to go on that list, and Faith wrote his name down with pleasure. She racked her brain, trying to think of more names, but twelve years was a long time and most of the men had been eminently forgettable. Maybe town gossip could supply them, as well as some of Guy's conquests. From his reputation, he had cut quite a swath through southeastern Louisiana. Probably she could list quite a few of Prescott's society ladies, which would also make their husbands legitimate candidates for the list. Wryly she tossed down the pen. The way this list was going, she might as well take a phone book and start at the *A*'s.

"You don't look like a private detective."

Francis P. Pleasant looked like a prosperous, conservative businessman. There were no ashtrays in his office; it was neat, and his light gray suit fit well. He had sad, dark eyes, but the expression in them lightened and warmed as he smiled at her. "Did you think I would have a bottle of bourbon on my desktop, and a cigarette with an inch-long ash dangling from my mouth?"

"Something like that." She returned his smile. "Or that you'd be wearing a Hawaiian shirt."

He laughed aloud at that. "Not my style. My wife always picked out my clothes—" He stopped, and the sadness returned to his eyes as he glanced at a photograph on his desk.

Faith followed his gaze. The frame was set at an angle to her, but she could still see that it was a picture of a pretty middle-aged woman, her expression so cheerful that it invited smiles. She must have died, for that sadness to be in his eyes. "Is that your wife?" she asked gently.

He managed another smile, but it was strained. "Yes, it is. I lost her a few months ago."

"I'm so sorry." She had just met him, but her sympathy was genuine.

"It was a sudden illness," he said, his voice a little jerky. "I have a bad heart; we both thought I would be the first to go. We were prepared for that. We were saving as much money as we could, for the time when I wouldn't be able to work. Then she got sick, just a cold, we thought, but forty-eight hours later she was dead from viral pneumonia. By the time she realized she was really sick, that it wasn't just a cold, it was too late."

Tears swam in his eyes, and Faith reached across the desk to put her hand on his. He turned his hand to squeeze her fingers, then blinked in bewilderment.

"I'm sorry," he apologized, blushing. He took out his handkerchief and blotted his eyes. "I don't know what came over me. You're a client, we've just met, and here I am crying on your shoulder."

"I've lost people I loved, too," she said, thinking of Scottie and Kyle. "Sometimes it helps to talk about it."

"Yes, it does, but that was still inappropriate of me. My only excuse is that there's something very warm about you, my dear." He realized that he had added an endearment, and blushed again. "Well! Perhaps I'd better ask what has brought you here."

"A man disappeared twelve years ago," she said. "I'd like you to find out if he's still alive."

He picked up a pen and rapidly scrawled something on a legal pad. "Your father? An old boyfriend?"

"Nothing like that. He was my mother's lover."

Mr. Pleasant glanced up at her, but didn't appear startled. Probably in his business he had received requests far more bizarre than hers. Thinking that he would have a better chance of finding something if he knew all the details and circumstances, rather than just the bare facts of Guy's name, age, and description, she related everything that had happened twelve years ago, and why she wanted to find out if Guy was still alive.

"I have to tell you," she said, "I think he's dead. Maybe

my imagination is running away with me, but I think someone killed him."

Mr. Pleasant carefully placed the pen on the legal pad, positioning it between the blue lines. "You do realize, Mrs. Hardy, that, considering what you've told me, your mother is likely involved. For her to have left the same night . . . well, you understand how that looks."

"Yes, I understand. I can't think, though, that she would have killed him herself. My mother," Faith said with a faint smile, "would never kill the goose that laid the golden egg."

"But you do think that she knows what happened."

Faith nodded. "I've tried to get her to talk about it, but she won't."

"I assume there's no evidence to bring to the attention of the sheriff?"

"None. I don't want you to find out if Guy was murdered, Mr. Pleasant, I just want you to find out, if you can, whether or not he's alive. There *is* a remote possibility that he simply walked away from everything."

"Very remote," he said dryly. "Though I have to admit that stranger things have happened. If there's a paper trail, though, I'll find it. If he had been running from the law, he would have changed his name, but there was no reason for him to disguise his identity. It should be fairly easy to find out if he's ever surfaced."

"Thank you, Mr. Pleasant." She took out a business card and gave it to him. "Here's my number. Call me when you know something."

She left his office feeling pleased with her selection. She had contacted him first by phone, discussed his fee, and made an appointment. Then she had checked his references, and been well satisfied with the answers. Mr. Pleasant had been highly recommended by her business contacts, described as both honest and competent, the kind of person one instinctively trusted. If Guy was alive, Mr. Pleasant would find him.

She glanced at her watch. She had left Prescott early that morning and driven down to New Orleans for her appointment with Mr. Pleasant, which hadn't taken as long as she had anticipated. Margot was in town, and Faith had made a lunch date with her at the Court of Two Sisters. She had plenty of time to get there, so she drove back to her hotel and left the car, then set out on foot to do some window-shopping along the way.

It was steaming hot as she walked along the narrow streets of the French Quarter, and she crossed over to the shady side. She visited New Orleans frequently, because of the agency office here, but she had never really taken the time to explore this old district. Horse-drawn carriages moved slowly through the streets, with the driver and guide pointing out attractions to the tourists in the carriage. Most people, though, depended on their own feet to take them through the Quarter. Later, the main attraction would be the bars and clubs; this early in the day, shopping was the goal, and the myriad of boutiques, antiques shops, and specialty stores gave plenty of choice and opportunity to people who wanted to spend their money.

She went into a lingerie shop and bought a peach silk nightgown that looked like something one of the Hollywood movie queens would have worn back in the forties and fifties. After wearing almost nothing but hand-me-downs for the first fourteen years of her life, she felt sinfully self-indulgent about new clothes now. She could never bring herself to go on shopping binges now that she had a bit of cash, but every so often she allowed herself a luxury purchase: lace underwear, a sumptuous nightgown, a really good pair of shoes. Those small indulgences made her feel as if the bad times were truly in the past.

When she reached the restaurant, Margot was waiting for her inside. The tall blonde jumped up and hugged her enthusiastically, though it had been only a little over a week since Faith had left Dallas. "It's so good to see you! Well, are you settling down okay in your little burg? *I* don't think I'll ever settle down again! My first business trip, and it's to New Orleans. Isn't this a great place? I hope you don't mind sitting in the courtyard rather than inside. I know it's hot, but how often do you get to eat lunch in a courtyard in New Orleans?"

Faith smiled at the barrage of words. Yes, Margot was definitely excited by her new job. "Well, let's see. I'm twenty-six, and this is the first time I've eaten lunch or anything else in a courtyard, so I'd say it doesn't happen too often."

"Honey, I can give you ten years, so it's even rarer than you think, and I intend to enjoy every minute." They took their seats at one of the tables in the courtyard. Actually, it wasn't uncomfortably hot; there were umbrellas, and trees to give shade. Margot eyed the bag in Faith's hand. "I see you've been shopping. What did you buy?"

"A nightgown. I would show it to you, but I don't want to drag it out here in the middle of the restaurant."

Margot's eyes twinkled. "That kind of nightgown, huh?"

"Let's just say it isn't a Mother Hubbard," Faith replied delicately, and they laughed. A smiling waiter poured water for them, the light tinkle of the ice cubes making her suddenly aware of her thirst, and how hot she had become on the walk to the restaurant. She glanced around at the other diners as she sipped the cold water, and looked straight at Gray Rouillard.

Her heart gave that immediate, betraying little jump. He was sitting, with another man whose back was to her, two tables over from her and Margot. His dark eyes gleamed as he lifted his glass of wine to her in a silent toast. She lifted the water glass in a return salute, inclining her head in a mock gracious nod.

"Do you know someone here?" Margot asked, turning in her seat. Gray smiled at her. Margot smiled in return, a rather weak effort, then turned back to Faith with a poleaxed expression on her face. "Holy cow," she said in a dazed voice.

Faith understood perfectly. The flamboyance of New Orleans suited Gray. He was wearing a lightweight, Italian-cut suit, and a pale blue shirt that flattered the olive tones of his skin. His thick black hair was brushed back from his face and secured with a bronze clasp at the nape of his neck. The tiny diamond stud glittered in his left earlobe. With the breadth of his linebacker's shoulders and the feline grace with which he lounged at the small table, he drew the eye of every woman in the courtyard. He wasn't pretty-boy hand-some; his French ancestors had bequeathed him a thin, high-bridged Gallic nose, slightly too long, and a heavy beard that left him with a five-o'clock shadow even at lunchtime. His jaw looked as solid as a rock. No, there was nothing pretty about Gray. What he was, was striking, and dangerously exciting, with his bold, dark eyes and the lazy, sensual curve of his mouth. He looked like a man who was adventurous and confident, both in bed and out.

"Who is he?" Margot breathed. "And do you know him, or are you flirting with a stranger?"

"I'm not flirting," Faith said, startled, and deliberately turned her gaze to the other side of the courtyard, away from Gray.

Margot laughed. "Honey, that little toast you gave him said, 'Come and get me, big boy, if you think you're man enough.' Do you think a pirate like that is going to ignore the challenge?"

Faith's eyes widened. "It did not! He raised his wineglass to me, so I did the same with my water glass. Why would he think anything about it when he started it?"

"Have you looked in the mirror lately?" Margot asked, sneaking another look over her shoulder at Gray, and a smile spread across her face.

Faith made a dismissive gesture. "That has nothing to do with it. He wouldn't—"

"He is," Margot said with satisfaction, and Faith couldn't control a little jump as she looked around and saw Gray almost upon them.

"Ladies," he drawled, lifting Faith's hand from the table and bowing over it with an Old World gesture that seemed entirely natural to him. Her startled eyes met his, and she saw deviltry, as well as something hot and dangerous, in those dark depths before he shielded them as he touched his lips to her fingers. His lips were soft and warm, very warm. Her heart banged painfully against her ribs and she tried to withdraw her hand, but his grip tightened and she felt the tip of his tongue probe delicately into the sensitive hollow between her last two fingers. Startled, she jumped again, and his awareness of that betraying little movement was in his eyes as he straightened and finally released her hand.

He turned to Margot, bending low over the hand she had

extended with a dazed expression, but Faith noticed that he didn't kiss Margot's fingers. It didn't matter. Margot couldn't have looked more bedazzled if he had presented her with diamonds. Wondering if that same weak, yielding expression was on her face, Faith quickly looked down to disguise it, though of course it was too late. Gray was too experienced to miss any of the nuances. Her fingers tingled, and the skin between her fingers throbbed where his tongue had touched. The tiny damp spot felt both hot and cold, and she clenched her hand to dispel the sensation. Her face was burning. His action had been a subtle parody of sex, a mock penetration that her body recognized, and responded to with a pooling of heat in her lower body, a growing moistness. She could feel her nipples tighten and thrust against the lace of her bra. *Damn* him!

"Gray Rouillard," he was murmuring to Margot. "Faith and I are old acquaintances."

At least he hadn't lied and said they were friends, Faith thought, watching tautly as Margot introduced herself, and, to her horror, asked Gray to join them. Too late, she gave Margot a warning nudge with her foot.

"Thank you," Gray said, smiling down at Margot with such charm that she didn't react at all to Faith's kick. "But I'm here on business, and I have to get back to my own table. I just wanted to come over and speak to Faith for a moment. Have you known each other long?"

"Four years," Margot replied, and proudly added, "I'm her district manager."

Faith nudged her ankle again, harder this time, and when Margot gave her a surprised look, she glared a warning.

"Really," Gray said, sounding interested. His gaze was sharper. "What business are you in?"

Finally having gotten the message, Margot gave Faith a swift, questioning glance.

"Nothing on your scale," Faith said, smiling at him so coolly that he shrugged, realizing he wasn't going to gain any more information.

She exhaled with relief, but tensed again when he squatted by the table, a gracefully masculine action that brought his face more on a level with hers. It was more difficult to hide her expression now than when he had been standing. This close, she could see the bottomless black pupils of his eyes, the glitter in them as he looked at her. "I wish I'd known you were coming to New Orleans, sweetheart. We could have driven down together."

If he thought she would dissemble in front of Margot, he had sadly mistaken her. If he thought his charm had turned her brain into mush, he was wrong there, too. How she would like to rub his nose in the fact that she was a successful businesswoman, but the past week had made her wary of giving him any information about herself. Respectability wouldn't make any difference to either him or the town of Prescott, until—and if—she could prove that her mother hadn't run away with his father, nothing would change his attitude. Lifting her chin, a sure sign of temper, she said, "I'd rather have walked all the way than get in a car with you."

Margot made a choking sound, but Faith didn't spare a look for her; she kept her gaze locked with Gray's, the battle visually joined. He grinned with a buccaneer's reckless enjoyment of a fight.

"But we could have had a lot of fun, and shared . . . expenses."

"I'm sorry you're having money problems," she said sweetly. "Perhaps your business associate will put you up if you can't afford your own hotel room."

"I don't have to worry about hotel expenses." The grin broadened. "I own the hotel."

Damn, she thought. She'd have to find out which one he owned, and make sure she didn't book any tour groups into it.

"Why don't we have dinner together tonight?" he suggested. "We have a lot to talk about."

"I can't imagine what. Thank you, but no." She was driving back to Prescott this afternoon, but she would much rather he think she was refusing the invitation purely because she didn't want his company.

"It would be to your advantage," he said, and the dangerous look was back in his eyes.

"I doubt that anything a Rouillard suggested would be to my advantage."

"You haven't listened to my . . . suggestions yet."

"I don't intend to, either. Go back to your table and leave me alone."

"I'd planned on doing the first." He stood and trailed a long forefinger down her cheek. "There's no way in hell I'll do the last." He nodded to Margot and strolled back to his own table.

Margot blinked, her eyes owlish. "Shouldn't I check him for wounds? You really had the knife out for him. What on earth has that dark-eyed piece of work done to make you so mad at him?"

Faith took refuge in her water glass again, sipping from it until she had her expression under control. When she lowered it, she said, "It goes back a long way. He's a Hatfield and I'm a McCoy."

"A family feud? C'mon."

"He's trying to run me out of Prescott," Faith said baldly. "If he found out about the travel agency, it's possible he could cause trouble by ruining some of the tours we arrange. That would hurt our reputation, and we'd lose money. You heard him: He owns a hotel here. Not only is he filthy rich, so he has the money to bribe people to do what he wants, but he has contacts in the business. I wouldn't put anything past him."

"Wow. This sounds serious. What started this feud, and has there ever been actual bloodshed?"

"I don't know." Faith fiddled with her silverware, not wanting to mention her suspicion that Guy had been killed. "My mother used to be his father's mistress. Needless to say, his family hates anyone with the name of Devlin." That would do for an explanation; she couldn't go into the full tale, couldn't trot out her memories of that night even for a sympathetic audience.

"What did you say is the name of this town?" Margot demanded. "Prescott? Are you sure it isn't Peyton Place?"

They both laughed, and the waiter approached then to ask their preference for lunch. They both chose the buffet, and went inside to make their selections. Faith was acutely aware of a dark gaze following her every move, and wished Margot hadn't been so set on eating in the courtyard. She would much rather have been shielded from his view. Who could have guessed that he would be in New Orleans today, though, or that in a city of this size they would immediately run into each other? True, the Court of Two Sisters was a popular restaurant, but New Orleans was larded with popular restaurants.

Gray and his business associate left the restaurant not long after Faith and Margot returned to the table with their loaded plates. He paused beside Faith. "I do want to talk to you," he said. "Come to my suite tonight at six. I'm at the Beauville Courtyard."

She hid her dismay. The Beauville was a lovely, mid-size hotel with a great atmosphere, built around an open courtyard. She had booked tour groups and vacationers in there many times. If Gray owned it, she would have to find another lovely, mid-size hotel with a great atmosphere, because she didn't dare use his again. In answer to his command, for that was what it was, she shook her head. "No. I won't be there."

His eyes gleamed. "Then take your chances," he said, and walked away.

"Take your chances?" Margot echoed indignantly, staring at his broad back. "What the hell did he mean by that? Was he *threatening* you?"

"Probably," Faith said, lifting a bite of pasta salad to her mouth. She closed her eyes in delight. "Mmmm, taste this. It's wonderful."

"Are you out of your mind? How can you eat when Mr. Macho just threatened to . . . do something, I guess." Frustrated, Margot picked up her fork and tasted the pasta salad. She paused. "This *is* good. You're right, worrying about him can wait until after we eat."

Faith chuckled. "I'm used to his threats."

"Does he ever carry through with them?"

"Always. One thing about Gray, he means what he says, and he isn't shy about throwing his weight around."

Margot's fork clattered to the table. "Then what are you going to do?"

"Nothing. After all, he didn't actually threaten anything specific."

"That means you have to be on your guard against everything."

"I am anyway, where he's concerned." Pain pierced her at her own words, and she looked down at her plate to hide it. How wonderful it would be to feel safe and relaxed with Gray, to feel she could trust that all his ruthless determination, his vital intensity, would be used in defense of her rather than against her. Did Noelle and Monica know how lucky they were, to have someone like him standing ready to go to battle on their behalf? She loved him, but he was her enemy. She could never let herself forget that, not let wishful thinking cloud her common sense.

Deliberately she steered the conversation into safer waters, namely the few problems that had developed with her in Prescott rather than on the scene in Dallas. She was relieved that the problems *were* few, and relatively minor. Some difficulties had been expected, but Margot was a good business manager and got on well with the travel agents in the other offices. The only real difference was that now Margot was the one traveling around, instead of Faith, though there would be times when Faith's presence was required. For the most part, everything had worked out. They decided that, since Faith was so close to Baton Rouge and New Orleans anyway, she would continue overseeing those offices, because it would be foolish for Margot to fly or drive all that way. Margot was a little disappointed, because she was entranced with New Orleans, but she was also extremely practical, and the change was her suggestion. There would be times when it wouldn't be convenient for Faith to get to either city, so she would content herself with the occasional visit.

After lunch, they parted company outside the restaurant, for Margot's hotel was in the opposite direction from where Faith had left her car. It was even hotter now than it had been before, the mugginess making the air feel thick, hard to breathe. The smell of the river was stronger, and black clouds were looming on the horizon, promising a spring thunderstorm that would temporarily relieve the heat, then turn the streets into a steam bath. Faith speeded up her steps, wanting to be on her way home before the storm broke.

As she drew even with a recessed doorway that led into a darkened, deserted shop, a strong hand seized her arm from behind and dragged her into the doorway. *Mugged!* she thought, and anger flashed through her, red-hot and reckless. She had struggled too hard for what she had to give it up without protest, the way the police advised. Instead she jabbed her elbow backward, slamming it into a hard belly and eliciting a very satisfactory grunt from her assailant. She turned, her fist drawn back, and belatedly opened her mouth to yell for help. She had a blurred impression of height and wide shoulders, then she was jerked hard against him and her voice was muffled against an expensive, oatmeal-colored Italian suit.

"God Almighty," Gray said, amusement rich in his deep voice. "You little redheaded wildcat, if you're as wild as this in bed, it must be a hell of a ride."

Shock at his comment mingled with relief at his identity, and neither diluted her anger. Breathing hard, she shoved at his chest, freeing herself. "Damn you! I thought I was being mugged!"

His eyebrows drew together. "And you started slinging that sharp little elbow?" he asked in disbelief, rubbing his stomach. "What if I *had* been a mugger, and had a knife or a gun? Don't you know you're supposed to give up your purse rather than chance getting hurt?"

"Like hell," she snapped, pushing her hair out of her face.

His face cleared, and he laughed. "No, I guess you wouldn't." He reached out and tucked a fiery strand behind her ear. "Attack first and think about it later, hm?"

She jerked her head away from his touch. "Why did you grab me like that?"

"I've been following you since you left the restaurant, and thought this would be as good a place as any for our little chat. You really should pay more attention to who's behind you."

"Skip the lecture, if you don't mind." She glanced at the sky. "I want to get to my car before that storm gets here."

"We can go to my hotel—or yours—if you don't want to talk here."

"No. I'm not going anywhere with you." Especially to a hotel room. He kept making those sexually loaded remarks, alarming her. She didn't trust his motives, and she didn't trust herself to resist him. All in all, it was best to stay as far away from him as she could.

"Then here it is." Gray looked down at her, standing so close to her in the narrow space of the doorway that her breasts were almost brushing his suit. When he had jerked her against him to muffle her scream, he had felt them, firm and round and luscious. He wanted to see them, wanted to touch them, taste them. He was so physically aware of her that he felt as if he were standing in the middle of an electrical field, with the air snapping and sizzling around them, sparks flying. Fighting with her was more exhilarating than making love to other women. Maybe as a young girl she had been as shy as a fawn, but she had grown into a woman who wasn't afraid of anger, hers or anyone else's.

"I'll buy the house from you," he said abruptly, reminding himself why he had wanted to talk to her. "I'll give you double what you paid for it."

Her green eyes narrowed, making them look even more catlike. "That isn't a good business decision," she said, her tone light, but with temper still seething just below the surface.

He shrugged. "I can afford it. Can you afford to turn it down?"

"Yes," she said, and smiled.

The satisfaction in that smile almost made him laugh again. So she had made something of herself, had she? More than had been obvious at first; if she had a district manager, then obviously she had other employees, in several locations. He felt unwilling pride at what she had accomplished swell in his chest. He knew in intimate detail how little she had possessed when he'd had the Devlins thrown out, because he had watched her frantically picking her things up out of the dirt. Most people had a backup system of friends and relatives, pooled resources; Faith had had nothing, making her accomplishments all the more remarkable. If she'd had *his* assets, Gray thought, she might own the whole state by now. It wouldn't be easy to get rid of a woman with that kind of grit.

Lust coiled and tightened in his guts. He'd never been attracted to weak, helpless women who needed protecting; he had enough of that with his family. There was nothing weak about Faith.

He studied her face, seeing both the resemblance to Renee and the differences. Her mouth was wider, more mobile, her lips red and lush and as velvety as rose petals. Her skin was perfect, with a porcelain texture that would show the imprint of a touch, a kiss. He thought of marking her with his mouth, kissing his way down her body until he reached the soft folds between her legs, folds that protected places even more tender. The image brought him to full, painful erection. Standing this close to her, he could smell the sweet, delicious scent of her skin, and he wondered if that sweetness would be more intense between her legs. He had always loved the way women smelled, but Faith's scent was so enticing that every muscle in his body tightened with need, making it difficult for him to think of anything clsc.

He knew he shouldn't do it, even as he reached for her. The last thing he wanted was to follow his father's example; he still couldn't think of his father's leaving without feeling the hurt and anger, the betrayal, as fresh as if it had just happened. He didn't want to hurt Noelle and Monica, didn't want to revive that old scandal.

There were a hundred reasons, all of them good, why he shouldn't want Faith Devlin in his arms, but in that instant none of them mattered a rat's ass. His hands closed on her waist, and the feel of her, warm and soft, so vibrant that his palms tingled where he touched her, went to his head like a potent wine. He saw her eyes widen, the black pupils expanding until only a thin rim of green remained. Her hands lifted and flattened against his chest, the placement covering his own nipples, and a shiver of response rippled his skin. Inexorably, his gaze fastened on her mouth, he drew her closer until her slim body rested against him. He felt her legs tangle with his, her firm breasts push against his stomach, saw those soft, full lips part as she drew in a startled breath. Then he lifted her on tiptoe and bent his head, and fed that particular hunger.

Her lips felt like rose petals, too, soft and velvety. He slanted his head and increased the pressure of his mouth, forcing them to open, a flower blooming at his command. Blood thundered through his veins and he pulled her tighter, sliding his arms around her and holding her welded to his body, letting her feel the swollen ridge of his erection against the softness of her belly. He felt her shudder, felt the convulsive movement of her hips, arching into him, and fierce male triumph flooded him. Her arms slid upward over his shoulders, to twine around his neck, and her teeth parted to allow him deeper access. A low growl sounded deep in his throat, and he took it, plundering her mouth with his tongue. Her taste was sweet and hot, flavored with the strong coffee she had drunk with her dessert. Her tongue curled around his in heated welcome, then she sucked daintily, holding him within her mouth.

He drove her backward, forcing her against the locked and boarded door. Dimly he could hear the voices of the people passing on the sidewalk behind them, hear the sullen rumble of thunder, but they meant nothing. She was live fire in his arms, not struggling against his kiss, not just accepting it, but responding wildly to his touch. Her lips trembled and clung and caressed. He wanted more, wanted everything. Deliberately he cupped her buttocks and lifted her, drawing her hips inward so that his erection was nestled in the soft notch of her legs. He rubbed her back and forth against him, groaning aloud at the exquisite pressure.

Rain pattered on the street, signaling the arrival of the storm, and there was a scurry of movement as people darted for cover. A clap of thunder made him lift his head and look around, a little irritated by this intrusion into the sensual haze that clouded his mind.

Whether it was the thunder or his own reaction to it that

broke the spell on Faith, she suddenly stiffened in his arms and began shoving against him. He caught a glimpse of her furious face and quickly set her on her feet, releasing her and stepping back before she began screaming bloody murder.

She wriggled past him, onto the sidewalk, where the rain immediately soaked her, and turned to face him. Her eyes were yellowish with turbulence. "Don't touch me again," she said, her voice rough and low. Then she turned and began walking as fast as she could, her head lowered against the rain that swept down the narrow street like a gray curtain. He started after her, intending to drag her to shelter, but forced himself to stop and step back into the doorway. She would fight him like a wildcat if he went after her now. He watched her until she turned the corner two blocks down, and disappeared from sight. She was almost running by then . . . escaping. From him.

For now.

❧ Nine ❧

Faith was dripping wet and shaking with both cold and reaction when she reached her car. Her hands trembled as she tried to fit the key into the lock, and it took her several tries before she succeeded. Crawling in, she collapsed against the steering wheel, pressing her forehead hard against the cold vinyl. *Idiot!* she thought violently. *Fool!*

She had to have been insane to give in to the craving to kiss him. Now he knew; she couldn't hide it from him any longer. For the sake of a few moments of pleasure, she had let him see her weakness, and now he knew that she wanted him. Humiliation burned in her face, ate like acid at her insides. She knew his nature very well, having firsthand experience of his ruthlessness. He was a predator, and the first hint of weakness would draw him straight in for the kill.

He wouldn't rest now until he'd had her; the occasional suggestive remark would become full-fledged attempts at seduction, and what had just happened proved that she couldn't trust her common sense to resist him. Where he was concerned, she didn't have any common sense. Horror filled her at the thought of being casually used and discarded, as if she were a sexual Kleenex. He thought of her as her mother's clone, a slut willing to spread her legs for anyone who had the equipment—and from what she'd felt, he had more than his share—while she ached for him, her childhood infatuation having changed into a very adult yearning. She wanted nothing more than to be loved by him, to be free to open the floodgates on her own dammed-up reservoir of love; he would turn that dream into a bitter nightmare, using her weakness for him as a means to hurt her, reduce her to being, after all, another Devlin whore for a Rouillard to use.

As much as she wanted to stay in Prescott, she would rather leave than live with that humiliation, to see contempt in his eyes when he looked at her, as she had seen it once before. His words echoed in her mind, a refrain that she had heard many times over the years: *You're trash.* The phrase was branded on her subconscious, surfacing every so often to taunt her.

No. She couldn't live through that again.

But for a few minutes, she had been in heaven. His arms had been around her and she had been free to touch him, to stroke his shoulders, thrust her fingers into the thick, silky tail of hair gathered at the nape of his neck. What would he look like with his hair loose, hanging to his shoulders? Or damp with sweat, and swinging forward as he bent over her, his face tight with passion—

She moaned, aching with a sweet pain that only he could ease. She had never been promiscuous; she had been a virgin when she'd married Kyle, and he was the only man with whom she'd ever made love. Her chastity, however, reflected her horror of being like Renee, with all the ugly association of being the town whore, rather than a lack of interest in the act itself. She loved making love, loved the feel of a man inside her, loved the scents and sounds, the tangled sweatiness. As her grief at Kyle's death had eased, her hunger for sexual contact had grown, intensified by her own restraint. She simply couldn't bring herself to have sex purely for the physical release, and after Kyle's death she hadn't wanted emotional involvement, either. She had gone four years without being held, without being kissed, until Gray had taken her in his arms and briefly opened the door to paradise.

There was a hot earthiness in him that fanned the banked coals of her own sexual fire. He had been as hard as a rock, and blatant about it. He had wanted her to feel him, had deliberately pulled her into him, lifted her to push the hard ridge of his erection against her mound. They had been on a public street, in daylight, but that hadn't stopped him. Even though this *was* New Orleans, where such things might not be all that unusual, *she* had never before done anything like that. She had always gone out of her way to avoid even the appearance of impropriety. Respectability, responsibility, were too important to her for her to allow herself to be publicly fondled, yet that was exactly what she had done.

When he touched her, she forgot everything else but the hot joy of being in his arms. Despairing, she wondered if she would have stopped him even if he had done more, or if she would have let herself be taken there in the street like the lowest of whores, oblivious to decency, modesty, even legality. Her face burned at the thought of being arrested for public lewdness, or whatever it was called. Acute stupidity would be a better term.

It would never have happened with anyone but Gray. With no one else would she have lost herself so completely.

She sat motionless in the car, watching the rain beat down in sheets beyond the concrete pillars of the public parking garage, and let appalled realization seep into her mind. Perhaps she had always sensed the truth, but pushed it away. She couldn't hide from the full reach of reality any longer.

She had loved Kyle, enjoyed sleeping with him, but it was as if only half of her had been involved. There had always been this other part of herself that was set aside, and belonged, irrevocably, to Gray. She had cheated Kyle; perhaps he had never known, and granted, their marriage had been in trouble because of his drinking, but still she should never have married him without loving him whole-heartedly. In the back of her mind had always been the thought that she would remarry someday, but now she knew that she couldn't; she couldn't cheat another man. There was only one man whom she could love completely, heart and soul and body, nothing held back, and that was Gray

Rouillard. And he was the one man to whom she didn't dare give herself, because he would destroy her.

When the rain stopped, Gray walked back to his hotel and went up to his suite, where he made one phone call, to Dallas. "Truman, look something up for me. You have a city directory, don't you? See if there's a Faith Hardy listed in it."

He crossed his legs at the ankle, his feet propped on the coffee table, and waited while his friend and business associate thumbed through the massive volume. A moment later the Texas accent twanged in his ear. "I got two Faith Hardys, and about ten other Hardys with the first initial F."

"Any of them F. D. Hardy?"

"Ah . . . no. There's an F. C. and an F. G., but not an F. D."

"Occupations?"

"Let's see. One's a schoolteacher, one's retired . . ." Truman ran down the list of occupations. None fit the meager facts Gray had on Faith. Dallas might not be the right city, after all, but it was more likely that Faith had declined to be listed in the city directory.

"Okay, that's a dead end, I think. Look up Margot Stanley, M-a-r-g-o-t."

Truman snorted. "Are you sure it isn't M-a-r-g-a-u-x? Isn't that the way the 'in' people spell it these days?"

"Look up both spellings."

There was the sound of more pages being turned, and Truman humming. He paused. "There's a shit pot full of Stanleys."

"Any Margots, of either the American or 'in' variety?"

"Yeah, here's an American-variety Margot."

"Where does she work?"

"Holladay Travel. Spelled with two *l*'s and an *a.*"

"Cross-reference that, and see if it lists the owner."

More humming. "Bingo," Truman said. "The owner is F. D. Hardy."

"Thanks," Gray said, amused at how easy it had been, after all.

"Any time."

Gray hung up the phone and considered what he had just discovered. Faith owned a travel agency. Good for her, he thought, inexplicably pleased. On a hunch, he dragged the New Orleans phone directory out of the desk and looked through the yellow pages. There it was, in a discreet, tasteful ad: "Holladay Travel—Put the Holiday Back in Your Vacation, and Leave the Worry to Us."

So she had at least two offices, and probably more, which explained how she had been able to pay cash for her house. He grinned as he remembered the satisfied little smile on her face when she had thrown his offer to buy the house back in his face. But if she was this prosperous, why did she want to keep it such a secret? Why wasn't she broadcasting it all over Prescott, to show everyone that a Devlin could crawl out of the trash heap, after all? Why had she so obviously interrupted Margot and kept her from giving out any more information than she had already let slip?

It didn't take a rocket scientist to figure it out. Faith was afraid he would do something to sabotage her business. Not only did he carry a lot of weight in Louisiana and beyond, but he had just told her that he owned a hotel, in a city that made its living from tourists. It would be easy for him to cause trouble for her agency, and she evidently expected him to do exactly that. Her opinion of him wasn't very high, he thought wryly.

Hell, why should it be? On a steamy summer night, twelve years ago, he had ground her into the dirt. After that night, she probably thought of him as the devil incarnate.

Only an hour before, he had scared her by unceremoniously grabbing her from behind, though Little Red had seemed more furious than frightened; she had come out swinging, those green eyes narrowed and determined. Then he had all but mauled her on a public street, gripping her ass, lifting her up and grinding his cock against her mound. No wonder she had run from him, when he had finally turned her loose.

Except . . . she hadn't protested. Instead she had been so hot and sweet that he felt dizzy remembering her in his arms, plastered against his body. She had been taut and trembling with desire, vibrating with it. Her response had broadsided him, knocked him so crazy that he still hadn't recovered. For a moment he had been blind with lust, insensible to everything else but the driving need to be inside her. If that clap of thunder hadn't startled him, he might have tried to take her right there, standing in the doorway, with people walking past no more than two feet away. He couldn't remember ever before being so wild for a woman that nothing else mattered, but Faith had reduced him to that level with only a kiss.

Just a kiss, sweet and spicy at the same time, so hot it had seared him. Her tongue, curling against his in love play. The unreserved sensuality in the way she had sucked on his tongue. The press of her body, eager and instinctive. She wanted him, as fiercely as he wanted her.

Memory re-created the resilient fullness of her buttocks in his hands, and he clenched them into fists to contain the tingling of his palms. It was worse than he had thought, this gnawing lust to have her. He wasn't accustomed to denying himself any of his sexual appetites, but the barriers between them were both solid and maddening. There was his mother, who had so totally withdrawn when faced with the humiliation of her husband leaving her for the town whore. Monica, her wrists slashed and her blood pooling at her feet; her white face was another image that never left him. There were his own feelings, the rage and pain at being abandoned by his father. The barriers weren't all on his side, either; the memory of that night lay between him and Faith, a mental Berlin Wall, stark and shattering. Too much pain, too many reasons.

Their bodies didn't give a damn.

That was it in a nutshell. He wasn't a Don Juan, but it was a fact that getting sex had always been easy for him. Nothing in his considerable experience, however, had prepared him for this . . . fever. They couldn't look at each other without feeling its heat. And when they touched, it was like an inferno.

Restlessly he paced the floor, trying to find some way around the barriers. She couldn't stay in Prescott; that was asking too much of his family. No, he couldn't let up on making life as miserable as possible for her there, not that he had been able, or willing, to do much anyway. He had inconvenienced her, period. He couldn't bring himself to really persecute her. She didn't deserve it; she had been a victim, too. She had worked hard to make something of her life, and had succeeded. If it weren't for his family, hell, he'd welcome her with open arms. An open fly, too, he thought wryly, and felt the twinge of arousal in his groin.

But he couldn't make his family go away, couldn't change the way they felt, so Faith had to go. Maybe not far. Maybe he could convince her to move to Baton Rouge, or even any of the small towns around Prescott. Just somewhere out of the parish, but close enough that they could see each other. She had made a strategic mistake in letting him see how much she wanted him, because he could use that as a means of convincing her to move. *We can't be together here. Move, and we'll see each other as often as possible.* She wouldn't like it; she'd probably tell him to go to hell, at first. But the fever was there, burning in her the same way it was burning in him. If he used every opportunity to fan the flames, she would eventually see things his way, assuming they didn't both go up in smoke in the meantime.

She could keep the house in Prescott, if selling it made her feel as if she was giving up too much. He'd buy her another house, anywhere she wanted.

He was faced with two facts. She had to leave Prescott, and he had to have her. Whatever it took, he had to have her.

"I agree with you," Mr. Pleasant said, sipping from the glass of iced tea Faith had given him. "I think Guy Rouillard is dead, and has been for twelve years."

He was dressed today in a pale blue seersucker suit; it would have been tacky if it hadn't fit so well, if his white shirt hadn't been so pristine, his tie so impeccable. On Mr. Pleasant, a seersucker suit looked natty. Some of the sadness was gone from his dark eyes, replaced by the sparkle of interest.

They sat in the air conditioned coolness of her living room. Faith had been surprised when he'd called her; it had been only two days since she had hired him. But here he was, with a notepad balanced on his knee.

"There's been no trace of him since the night he vanished," he said. "No credit card purchases, no bank withdrawals, no Social Security taxes paid in or tax return filed. Mr. Rouillard wasn't a criminal, so there was no need for him to change his name or disappear so completely. Logically, then, he's dead."

Faith drew a deep breath. "That's what I thought. I wanted to make certain, though, before I begin asking questions."

"You do realize that, if he was murdered, your questions could make someone very anxious." He took another sip of his tea. "The situation could be dangerous for you, my dear. Perhaps it would be better to let sleeping dogs lie."

"I've thought of the possibility of danger," she admitted. "But considering my mother's involvement with him and the fact that everyone thinks they ran away together, no one would be surprised at my interest. My gall, maybe, but not my interest."

He chuckled. "It depends on the nature of the questions, I suppose. If you came right out and said you thought Mr. Rouillard had been killed, that would attract a lot of attention." He sobered, and his tone softened. "My advice is to forget about it. The murder, if there was one, is twelve years old. Time covers a lot of tracks, and you have no evidence to tell you where to begin looking. You aren't likely to find anything, but you may put yourself in danger."

"Not even try to find out what happened?" she asked softly. "Let a murderer go unpunished?"

"Ah. You're thinking about justice. It's a wonderful concept, if you have the means to accomplish it. Sometimes, though, justice has to be weighed against other considerations, and reality gets in the way. Probably Mr. Rouillard was murdered. Probably your mother is involved, in knowledge if not in deed. Could you handle that? What if his death was an accident, but she was brought up on murder charges? Gray Rouillard is a powerful man; do you think he'd let his father's death go unpunished? The worst scenario, of course, is if his death wasn't an accident. In that case, my dear, you would definitely be in danger yourself."

She sighed. "My reasons for wanting to find out what

happened to him aren't entirely altruistic. In fact, they're mostly selfish. I want to live here; this is home, this is where I grew up. But I won't be accepted here as long as everyone thinks Guy ran away with my mother. The Rouillards don't want me here; Gray is making things difficult for me. I can't buy my groceries in Prescott, I can't fill up my car. Unless I can prove Mama didn't have anything to do with Guy's disappearance, I'll never have a friend here."

"And what if you prove she killed him?" Mr. Pleasant softly asked.

Faith bit her lip, and rolled the cold, damp glass between her hands. "That's a chance I'll have to take." The words were low, almost inaudible. "I know that, if she's guilty, I won't be able to live here. But knowing what really happened, no matter how bad, won't be as bad as *not* knowing. Maybe I won't find out anything, but I'm going to try."

He sighed. "I thought you'd say that. If you don't mind, I'd like to ask a few questions around town, just out of curiosity. Folks might tell me things that they wouldn't tell you."

That was true. Now that her identity was known, most people would clam up around her rather than defy Gray. Still, Mr. Pleasant had already completed the job for which she'd hired him. "I can't afford any further investigation," she said honestly.

He waved his hand in dismissal. "This is for my own curiosity. I've always loved a good mystery."

She eyed him doubtfully. "Has that ever kept you from charging your regular fees?"

"Well, no," he admitted, and laughed. "But I don't need the money, and I'd like to know what happened to Mr. Rouillard. I don't know how much longer I'll be able to work with my heart the way it is. Probably not long, so I'm only going to spend my time on cases that interest me. As for money . . . well, let's just say I don't have much need for it now."

With his wife dead, he meant. He suddenly busied himself with flipping through his notes, and she knew he was once again fighting tears. She allowed him the dignity of pretense and asked if he would like more iced tea.

"No, thank you. It was delicious, just the thing on a hot day." He stood, smoothing the crisp seersucker into place. "I'll let you know if I get any interesting answers. Is there a motel in town?"

She gave him the directions to the motel as she walked out on the porch with him. "Have supper with me tonight," she invited on impulse, disliking the thought of him eating alone, making do with a fast-food sandwich.

He blushed, the color extending all the way into his thinning hair. "I'd be delighted."

"Would you mind if we ate at six? I prefer eating early."

"So do I, Mrs. Hardy. Six o'clock, then."

He was smiling as he walked jauntily to his car. Faith watched him drive away, then returned to the paperwork she had abandoned at his arrival. She looked forward to supper; she had developed a definite soft spot for Mr. Pleasant.

He arrived promptly at six, as she had known he would, and they sat down to a light meal of tender grilled pork chops, saffron rice, and fresh green beans. He kept looking around, absorbing the little details—the starched linen napkins, the fragrant centerpiece of tiny wild roses, the aromas of home-cooked food—and she knew that he had missed this since his wife had died. They lingered over dessert, a lemon sorbet with just the right amount of tartness. Talking with him was easy; he was very old-fashioned, and she found that comforting. Consideration of any sort had been in such short supply during her formative years that she doubly appreciated it now.

It was almost eight when a single hard knock rattled her front door. Faith stiffened; she didn't have to open the door to know who was standing on her porch.

"Is something wrong?" Mr. Pleasant asked, too astute to miss her change of expression.

"I think you're about to meet Gray Rouillard," she said, getting to her feet and crossing to the door. As usual, her heart was beating too fast and too hard at the prospect of seeing him, talking to him. In over fifteen years, that hadn't changed; she might as well be eleven again, big-eyed with hero worship.

It was twilight, the long spring days reluctant to give up

their glow. He was silhouetted against the pale opal of the sky, a tall, broad-shouldered, faceless figure. "I hope I'm not interrupting you," he said, but there was a hard undertone to his rumbling voice that told her he didn't give a damn if he was or not.

"If you were, I wouldn't have answered the door," she replied as she let him in. She couldn't erase the challenge of her own tone, though she tried to moderate it for Mr. Pleasant's sake.

Gray's smile was nothing more than a baring of teeth as he turned to Mr. Pleasant, who had politely risen from his seat at Gray's entrance. The room suddenly seemed too small, filled and dominated by Gray's vital masculine presence, all six feet four of it. He was wearing a white shirt, black jeans, and low-heeled boots, and looked more like a pirate than ever. His teeth flashed as white as the tiny diamond in his ear.

"We've already finished dinner," Faith said smoothly, recovering her control. "Mr. Pleasant, this is Gray Rouillard, a neighbor. Gray, Francis Pleasant, from New Orleans."

Gray held out his hand, and Mr. Pleasant's smaller hand was swallowed by his grip. "A friend or a business associate?" he asked, as if he had a right to the information.

Mr. Pleasant's eyes twinkled, and he thoughtfully pursed his mouth as he retrieved his hand. "Why, both, I believe. And you? A friend as well as a neighbor?"

"No," Faith said.

Gray shot her a hard, quick look. "Not exactly," he said.

Mr. Pleasant's eyes twinkled even more. "I see." He took Faith's hand in his and lifted it to his mouth for a courtly kiss, then bestowed another one on her cheek. "I must be going, my dear; my old bones want to rest. My hours resemble an infant's these days. It was a lovely dinner. Thank you for inviting me."

"It was my pleasure," she said, patting his hand and kissing his cheek, too.

"I'll call," he promised as he went out the door. As she had that morning, Faith waited in the doorway until he was in his car, and waved as he reversed out of the driveway.

Fighting down her dread, she closed the door and turned to face Gray, who had silently approached until he stood only a foot behind her. His eyes were black with temper. "Who the hell is he?" he growled. "Your sugar daddy? Did you mix business with pleasure in New Orleans, or is it all business to you?"

"None of your business," she said flatly, mocking him with her repetition of the word. She glared up at him, fighting the tiny red flare of rage and not completely succeeding. Mr. Pleasant was forty years older than she, but of course, Gray's first thought was that she was sleeping with him.

He moved one step closer, erasing the small distance between them. "By God, it is my business, and has been for the past two days."

Hot color ran into Faith's cheeks at the reference to what had happened between them in New Orleans. "That didn't mean anything," she began, her voice gruff with embarrassment, but he gripped her shoulders and gave her a single shake.

"The hell it didn't. Maybe you need to refresh your memory." He bent his head and, too late, she put up her hands to try to hold him away. Her palms flattened against his chest as his mouth covered hers, and immediately she was engulfed in heat. His heat. Her own. Dizziness roared in her ears. She swayed against him, her lips parting to mold more precisely to the demanding pressure of his, to admit the hot probe of his tongue. All the rich blues and golds and burgundies of his scent swirled around her, inside her, possessing her. His heartbeat thudded, strong and heavy, beneath her right palm. She felt the hard, immediate swell of his erection against her belly, and her hips moved automatically, seeking.

He lifted his head and moved back, putting a few inches between them. He was breathing hard, his eyes fierce with arousal, his lips red and moist and a little swollen from that hard kiss. His fingers moved on her shoulders, massaging, caressing. "Don't deny what happened."

"Nothing happened." She uttered the lie with a defiance that hid her desperation. He knew it was a lie, she saw the anger in his face, but she said it anyway. She knew what he was doing. In New Orleans she had made the mistake of giving him an inch, and now he was trying to take full advantage of it and gain a mile. Perhaps he had come here tonight thinking she would be easy for him; he could take her to bed, then cajole her into leaving town. For him, he would say. So they could be together without upsetting his mother. Her blatant lie served notice that she didn't intend to let him have his way. She wrenched away from him, sliding sideways to prevent him from pinning her against the door. "It was just a kiss—"

"Yeah, and King Kong was just a monkey. Goddammit, stand still," he said irritably, reaching out to grab her, this time holding her arms. "You make me dizzy with that damn two-step. I'm not going to throw you down and crawl on top of you—not just yet, anyway."

Her eyes flared with panic. "You can bet your sweet bottom dollar, you're not!" she shouted, once again trying to jerk away. "Tonight, or any other time!"

"Would you stop that?" he snapped. "You're going to bruise yourself." With a quick movement he whirled her around and folded his arms about her, crossing them under her breasts and holding her wrists manacled. Just that quickly, that easily, she was subdued and surrounded, his muscled body hard and warm against her back. Temptation rose, strong and immediate, urging her to relax her neck and let her head fall backward onto his chest, let her body soften and mold itself against his, let herself inhale the rich, musky scent of his skin and grow intoxicated on it. She shuddered as hunger surged within her, and knew that if she gave him the smallest response now, she would be lost. It wouldn't take five minutes for him to have her flat on the bed.

"You see?" he asked, his voice softening to a velvety purr as he felt her tremble. His warm breath stirred her hair. "All I have to do is touch you. It's the same for me, Faith. I don't like this worth a damn, but by God, I want you, and we're going to do something about it."

She closed her eyes, still shaking with the effort of resisting him, and gave a sharp little shake of her head. "No."

"No, what?" He nuzzled his cheek against the top of her head. "No, you don't want me, or no, we aren't going to do something about it? Which one are you lying about now?"

"I won't let you," she said, not letting him distract her. She opened her eyes and stared straight ahead, focusing on one of the lamps in an effort to ignore the feel of his arms around her. ".I won't let you treat me like dirt again."

He stilled, even his breath halting for a moment. Then he let it out with a quiet sigh. "It's always between us, isn't it?" There was no need to be more specific; the memory of that night was almost tangible. He paused. "Baby, I know about Holladay Travel, that you've worked for everything you have. I know you're not like your mother."

Oh, God. He knew about her agency. She fought a lurch of panic, and instead concentrated on his last statement. "Sure you do," she said bitterly. "You think so highly of my character that you just accused me of having a sugar daddy. My God, I invited a lonely old man to have dinner with me, so of course I'm crawling into bed with him!" Infuriated, she tried once again to wrench free.

His arms tightened until she could barely breathe. "I told you to stop that," he warned. "You'll be black and blue."

"If I am, it'll be your fault, not mine! You're the one doing the manhandling!" She kicked backward, catching his shin with her heel, but she was wearing soft-soled slippers and he was wearing boots; he grunted, but she knew she hadn't hurt him. She twisted her body, trying to turn around so she could do more damage.

"You . . . little . . . wildcat," he said, panting with the effort of controlling her. "Damn it, would you be still! I was jealous," he admitted baldly.

For a moment, she was too stunned to react. She stood motionless in the circle of his arms, wariness at battle with a dizzying spurt of elation. Jealous! He couldn't be jealous unless he cared—no. She couldn't let herself fall into that trap. She didn't dare believe him. She had witnessed his seduction technique before; she remembered how he had soothed Lindsey Partain, complimenting her, telling her how much he wanted her, needed her. He was adept at getting what he wanted. While she had no doubt that he wanted her physically, with the evidence so prominent, she knew that nothing else had changed. He still wanted her to leave, and would use her weakness for him to convince her to go.

"Do you honestly expect me to believe you?" she finally asked, weariness in every word.

He nudged his hips forward. "Do you deny this?"

She forced herself to shrug. "What's there to deny? You have a hard-on. Big deal. That doesn't mean anything."

A chuckle vibrated in his chest. "It's a good thing I have a healthy ego, or you'd give me an inferiority complex."

She wished he wouldn't laugh. She didn't want him to have a sense of humor. She wanted him to be mean-spirited and small-minded, so she could despise him. Instead he was bold and audacious, with a disarming laugh. He was ruthless, but he wasn't mean.

He bent his head to nuzzle her ear, his warm breath tickling the sensitive whorls. "There doesn't have to be a problem," he murmured. "We can be together—not here, but there's a workable solution."

Faith stiffened again. "I'll just bet there is. And it involves my leaving town, doesn't it?"

His tongue flicked out, lazily playing with her earlobe before he caught it between his teeth and sensuously nipped at it. "You wouldn't have to go far," he cajoled. "You don't even have to sell this house. I'll buy another house for you, a bigger one, if you want—"

Rage engulfed her, red-hot and seething. She wrenched free of his slackened embrace and spun to face him, her face white and her eyes burning. "Shut up! You can't stop thinking that I'm for sale, can you? The only change is that you've moved me up into a higher price bracket! I don't want your damn house, but I do want you out of mine. Right now!"

His eyes narrowed, and he didn't move an inch. "I wasn't thinking about buying you. I was trying to make things as easy as possible for you."

"Nice try, but I know too much about you. I've seen you in action, remember?" The memory of that night was bitter in her tone, and flashed starkly between them. She had that other memory, too, one he didn't know about: the time she had watched him with Lindsey Partain. She'd seen him in action, all right.

He was silent a moment, his dark gaze moving over her. "That won't happen again," he said gently.

"No, it won't," she agreed, lifting her chin. "I won't let you ever treat me that way again."

"You wouldn't have much choice, if I decided to do it," he said, that dangerous glitter coming into his eyes. He chucked her under the chin. "Remember that, baby. I can play a lot rougher than I have so far."

She jerked her head away. "So can I."

His gaze slid down her body, the expression in his eyes changing into something slow and heated. "I'll bet you can. You almost tempt me to find out how rough you can be, just for the fun of it. But this discussion has gone way off course. We aren't in a war, baby. We can have a nice arrangement, and enjoy ourselves without hurting my family, if you'll only agree to it."

"No," she said.

"That must be your favorite word. I'm getting damn tired of hearing it."

"Then stay away." She sighed, weary of the battle, and shook her head. "I don't want to hurt your family. That isn't why I came back. This is my home; I don't want to cause any trouble, I just want to live here. If I have to fight you to do that, then I will."

"The battle lines are drawn, then." He shrugged. "It's up to you, how much trouble you want to put up with to live here. I won't back down; you're still going to be unwelcome in town. If you change your mind, though, all you have to do is call me. I'll take care of you, no questions asked, and no gloating."

"I won't call."

"Maybe you won't, but maybe you will. Think about what we could have together."

"What? A couple of quickies every week? Lying about where you are, because you don't want your family to know? Thanks, but no thanks."

He reached out and cupped her cheek, and this time she

didn't pull away. His touch was gentle as his thumb rubbed her lower lip, probing the inner softness. "There's more to it than just the fucking," he said softly. "Though God knows I want that so much I hurt."

Because she wanted so desperately to believe him, she didn't dare. She had to fight tears as she shook her head. "Please leave."

"All right, I'll go. But think about it." He turned toward the door, then stopped. "About your company—"

Instantly she was alarmed, and tensed for another battle. "If you dare do anything to hurt my business—"

He gave her an impatient look. "Hush. I'm not going to do a thing. I just wanted you to know how proud I am of you. I'm glad you've accomplished as much as you have. In fact, I told my manager at the hotel to give special consideration to any groups booked by your agency."

Proud of her? Faith stood silently as he left, and the tears she had successfully held back began to trickle down her cheeks. Did she dare believe him in this? She couldn't, she realized. She would keep to her original decision not to book any more groups into his hotel.

But the tears still fell. He'd said he was *proud* of her.

~ Ten ~

Monica took her time in the bathroom, needing the privacy to get herself back. It was always slightly alarming, that loss of self, of personhood. Michael didn't seem to feel it; he was always content, a little drowsy, when he moved off of her. She could hear the squeak of the bed now as he moved, probably to put out his cigarette. He didn't smoke much, he was trying to quit, but after sex was one of the times when he found cigarettes harder to resist. Today his hand had been shaking a little as he flicked his lighter, making the tiny flame dance.

That telltale reaction made her feel soft inside, and she stayed in the bathroom longer than usual so he wouldn't see. It was bad enough that he knew how wild she went when he was inside her, moaning, clutching at him with wet hands, her hips moving. No matter how she tried, she couldn't make them stay still. And she was wet down there, too; she heard the embarrassing slurping sounds when he moved in and out of her. She wasn't embarrassed *then,* all she could think of was the fever building inside her, but afterward she felt the shame.

It wasn't that way with Alex. With Alex she could restrain herself; he seemed to prefer it that way, and she knew why. He was pretending she was Mama.

She didn't want to do it with Alex, but at the same time, she did. She couldn't say that he forced her, not even to make herself feel better about what she did. She loved Alex, but—he was almost like a father to her. He couldn't take Daddy's place, no one could do that, but Alex had been Daddy's best friend, and he had been so hurt when Daddy had left like that. Quietly he had given them all a shoulder to lean on, or to cry on, as the case may be. Sometimes, in those first awful days, she had been able to pretend a little bit that he *was* her father, that nothing had changed.

But the pretense hadn't held up for long. The horrible shock of that day had forever changed something inside her, and she had accepted that things would never be perfect. Daddy wasn't coming back; he'd preferred living with that slut rather than living with his own family. He didn't love Mama and never had.

Alex loved Mama, though. Poor Alex. She couldn't remember when she had first realized how he felt, when she had seen the devotion and sadness in his eyes; it had been several years after Daddy had left, though. It was about the time he had first coaxed Mama to eat dinner with them. He could do more with Mama than either she or Gray could; maybe it was the gentle, devoted courtesy with which he treated her. God knows Daddy had never been like that with her. He had been polite, and gentle, but you could tell he was just going through the motions and didn't really care. Alex cared.

She remembered the night it had first happened. Gray had been in New Orleans on business. Mama had come down for dinner, but despite Alex's cajoling, had been more depressed than usual and had really made an effort just to eat with them. She had gone back to her room almost immediately, despite his pleas. When he had turned back to face Monica, she had seen the desolation in his eyes, and impulsively reached out to put her hand on his arm, wanting to comfort him.

It had been a chilly winter night. There was a fire in the parlor, so they had gone in there, and she had set herself to easing that look from his eyes. They had sat on the sofa in front of the fire, talking quietly of many things while he sipped an after-dinner brandy, his favorite. The house was quiet, the room dim, with only one lamp on. The fire had softly snapped. And in the firelight, she must have looked like Mama. She had worn her dark hair in a twist that night, and she always dressed in the conservative, classic style Mama preferred. For all those reasons, the brandy, the solitude, the darkened room, his own disappointment, her resemblance to Mama—it had happened.

A kiss had become two, then more. His hands were in her hair, and he was groaning. Monica remembered how her heart had pounded, in fear and an almost painful sympathy. He had touched her breasts, almost reverentially, but only through her clothes. And he had pushed up her skirt only enough to bare the essential part, as if he didn't want to violate her modesty more than was necessary. She had a confused memory of naked flesh, unseen but felt, as he pressed himself to her, then a sharp sting of pain and the quick pumps into her. Unfaded by time, however, was the memory of how his voice had broken as he murmured, "Noelle," in her ear.

He didn't seem to know he'd been the first. In his mind, she'd been Mama.

And in her mind, God help her, he'd been Daddy.

It was so sick that she was still disgusted at herself. She'd never had any sexual feelings for Daddy; hadn't had any at all, until Michael. But in the tumult of emotion that night, she'd thought, Maybe he won't leave, if I give him what Mama won't. So she had taken her mother's place, offering herself sexually as a bribe to keep Daddy at home. Poor Alex . . . poor *her*. Both of them surrogates for something neither one could ever have. Freud would have had a field day with her.

But that night had been the first of many, over the past seven years. Though not that many, come to think of it. Michael had probably had her more often in just a year than Alex had in seven. Alex had been so ashamed, so apologetic. But he had come to her again, helplessly needing the pretense that Noelle would ever lie in his arms, and Monica had let him have the ease that he needed. He never approached her when Gray was home, only when he was out of town on business.

The last time had been just two days ago, when Gray had been in New Orleans. She had gone to Alex's office that night, as she usually did, and he had done it to her on the sofa there. It never took long. He never undressed her, or himself. Seven years he'd been doing it to her, and she'd never seen him naked, had actually only seen his thing a few times. He was still apologetic about his need, as if she really were Mama, and thought the process was nasty. So he finished as fast as he could, and Monica cleaned herself and went home.

It wasn't like that with Michael. She still didn't know what had attracted him to her, or how she had actually allowed things to progress so far. He'd grown up in Prescott, so she'd known him, to put a name to his face, to speak to, all of her life. He was five years older than Gray, and already a deputy with the sheriff's department when she had finished high school. He'd married his high school sweetheart and had two little boys. They'd been like Ward and June Cleaver, and then she'd up and left him, right out of the blue. She had moved to Bogalusa and remarried a couple of years later. His sons were seventeen and eighteen now, and he had a good relationship with them.

Michael had a good relationship with everyone, she thought, a smile curving her mouth. That was why he'd been elected sheriff when Sheriff Deese had finally retired three years ago. He was a true good old boy, disdaining suits in favor of a uniform, and wing tips in favor of boots. He was a lanky six feet, with sandy hair and friendly blue eyes, and a smattering of freckles across his nose. Opie, all grown up.

One day, a year ago, she'd been in town and decided to eat lunch at the courthouse grill, which made the best hamburgers in town. Mama would have been horrified at such a plebeian taste, but Monica loved hamburgers and treated herself occasionally. She'd been sitting at the little table when Michael had come in, gotten his own hamburger, and was on his way back to a booth when he suddenly paused by her table and asked if he could join her. Startled, she'd said yes.

At first she'd been stiff, but Michael could tease the starch out of a shirt. Soon they'd been laughing and talking as easily as if they were best friends. She'd had another moment of stunned awkwardness when he'd asked her to have dinner with him; she was acutely aware that Mama wouldn't approve. There was nothing upper-crust about Michael McFane. But she had agreed, and to her surprise, he had cooked dinner himself, grilling steaks in his backyard. He lived now on the small farm where he'd grown up, with the closest neighbor a mile down the road, and Monica had felt relaxed by the quiet solitude of his rural home.

Relaxed enough, after they'd eaten and danced to country tunes on the radio, moving slowly around his small living room, to let him take her into his bedroom. She hadn't planned to let him, hadn't even considered that he'd try. But he'd started kissing her, and his kisses were warm and slow, and for the first time in her life she felt the curl of desire deep in her body. Alarmed by what was happening, and the speed of it, she had nevertheless stood in his bedroom and let him unzip her dress, then unhook her bra and remove it. No one had ever seen her bare breasts, but all of a sudden Michael had not only seen them, but was busy sucking on them. The drawing pressure of his mouth had made her go wild, and they had tumbled to the bed. Not for him a discreet pumping, with trousers barely lowered. Soon they were both naked, locked together on the cotton sheets, and that curl of desire had exploded into a wantonness that still alarmed her.

No *lady* would act in such a manner, but then Monica had always known she wasn't a lady. Mama was a lady; Monica had been trying all her life to be like Mama, so Mama would love her, but she'd always fallen short. Mama would be horrified and disgusted if she knew her daughter spent several hours a week in bed with Michael McFane—the *sheriff,* of all people!—screwing like a rabbit.

Sometimes Monica felt resentful of the strictures that had been drummed into her from the cradle. *Gray* hadn't been subjected to, and confined by, all the things that ladies didn't do. It was as if Mama had written Gray off as a lost cause from the moment of his birth; he was a male, therefore

160

she expected him to act like an animal. Because she was a lady, she had ignored the sexual escapades of both father and son; such things were of no interest to her, and she expected her daughter not to be interested in them, either.

It hadn't worked that way, though Monica had tried. She had tried really hard, for the first twenty-five years of her life. Even after Mama had withdrawn from them, after Daddy left, Monica had kept trying, hoping that, if she was good enough, Mama wouldn't feel so bad about Daddy being gone.

But she had always hungered for more. Mama had always been so reserved and cool, perfect, untouchable. Daddy had been warm and loving; he had hugged her, tussled with her despite Mama's disapproval of such rowdiness with her daughter. Gray was even more physical than Daddy; he had always burned with an inner fire that Monica had recognized at an early age.

She remembered once, when Gray had been home from college, they had lingered around the dinner table, talking. Gray had been lounging in his chair with that big-cat grace of his, laughing as he described a prank some of the football players had pulled on one of the coaches, and there had been . . . she couldn't quite describe it . . . a sort of sensual wildness in the tilt of his head, the motion of his hand as he picked up his glass. She had glanced at Mama and found her staring at Gray with an expression of revulsion on her face, as if he were a disgusting animal. He *had* been an animal, of course, a healthy, rambunctious teenage boy, blazing with the testosterone pumping into his body. But there was nothing repulsive about him, and Monica had felt resentful of that disapproval, on his behalf.

Gray was a wonderful brother; she didn't know what she would have done without him, in those awful days after Daddy left. She had been so ashamed of her own attempted suicide that she had sworn then she would never again be that weak, that much of a burden to Gray. It had been a struggle, but she'd kept that promise to herself. She had only to look at the thin, silvery lines on her wrists to forcibly remind herself of the price of weakness.

Seeing Faith Devlin in the parking lot at the grocery store

had shocked her so much that, for the first time in a long while, she'd fallen into the old habit of running to Gray, expecting him to take care of her problems. She was disgusted with herself for falling to pieces the way she had, but when she had seen that dark red hair, such a rich color that it was almost wine-colored, her heart had almost stopped. For a wild, dizzying moment, she had thought, *Daddy's back!* because if Renee was here, then surely Daddy was, too.

But Daddy was nowhere in sight. There was only Renee, looking even younger than when she had left, which was pure injustice. Someone as wicked and trashy as Renee Devlin should wear her sins on her face, so everyone would know. But the face staring back at Monica had been as exquisitely complexioned as ever, without a wrinkle in sight. The same slumberous green eyes, the wide, soft, sensual mouth—nothing had changed. And for a moment, Monica had been again the hurt, helpless girl she'd been before, and she had gone running to Gray.

Only it hadn't been Renee; the woman in the parking lot was Faith Devlin, and Gray had been oddly reluctant to use all his influence against her. Monica couldn't recall much about Faith, just a vague memory of a skinny little girl with her mother's hair, but that didn't matter. What wasn't vague was the twist of pain at seeing her, the rush of memories, the old sense of betrayal and abandonment. She had been afraid to go to town since then, afraid she would see Faith again and feel the sting of salt in the reopened wound.

"Monica?" came Michael's lazy voice. "You go to sleep in there, honey?"

"No, I was just primping," Monica called, and ran the water in the basin to give credence to her lie. Her reflection looked back at her. Not bad, for thirty-two. Sleek dark hair, not as black as Gray's, but not a silver strand in sight. Her face was fine-boned, like Mama's, but she had the Rouillard dark eyes. Not overweight, and her breasts were firm.

Michael was still sprawled naked on the bed when she left the bathroom, and a slow smile lit his face as he held out his hand to her. "Come snuggle," he invited, and her heart turned over. She crawled back into bed, and into the warmth of his encircling arm. He sighed with contentment as he settled her against him, and his big hand moved to squeeze one resilient breast. "I think we should get married," he said.

Her heart didn't just turn over this time, it almost stopped. She stared up at him, eyes round with both panic and astonishment. "M-Marry?" she stuttered, then crammed both hands against her mouth to hold back the hysterical giggle that bubbled up. "Michael and Monica McFane?" The giggle erupted anyway.

He grinned. "So it sounds like we're twins. I can live with it if you can." He thumbed her nipple, enjoying the way it peaked at his touch. "But if we have a kid, its name will start with anything but an *M.*"

Marriage. Kids. Oh, God. Somehow she had never envisioned that he might want to marry her. She had never even thought of marriage in connection with herself. Her life had gone into deep freeze twelve years ago, and she had never expected it to change.

But nothing is static. Even rock changed, ground down by time and the elements. Alex hadn't disrupted the even rhythm of her life, but Michael had blazed through like a comet.

Alex. Oh, God.

"I know I don't have much to offer you," Michael was saying. "This house sure ain't nothing like what you're used to, but I'll fix it up any way you want; you just tell me what to do and I'll do it."

Another shock. She had lived her entire thirty-two years at Rouillard House. She tried to imagine living anywhere else, and couldn't. Twelve years ago the entire foundation of her life had crumbled, and since then she hadn't dealt well with any change, even a relatively minor one such as getting a new car. Gray had finally forced her to give up the one she had been driving since she was nineteen, just as, five years ago, he had forced her to redo her bedroom. She had been heartily sick of the little-girl decor for years, but the thought of changing it had made her feel even worse. It had been a relief when Gray had brought a decorator in one day while she had a dentist appointment, and returned to find the wallpaper already stripped off and the carpet removed. Still, she had cried for three days. So little of her former life had remained the way it was before Daddy left, and it hurt to give up anything else. After she stopped crying, and the decorator was finished, she loved the room; it was the transition that was so wrenching.

"Honey?" Michael said now, hesitation creeping into his voice. "I'm sorry, I guess I thought—"

Fiercely she put her hand against his mouth. "Don't you dare put yourself down to me," she said, low and violent, aching inside that he would think for a minute that she would consider herself too good for him. The reverse was true; Michael was too good for her. Only two days ago she had lain on the leather sofa in Alex's office and let him screw her. Ugly word. Ugly process. It had nothing in common with Michael's lovemaking. She had felt nothing, except pity, and relief when it was over.

If Michael knew about Alex, he wouldn't want her any longer. How could he? For the past year he had thought she was his alone, and all the while she had been letting an old family friend screw her, just as she had for the six years before.

She hadn't felt any guilt at all, on Alex's behalf, when Michael had become her lover. She didn't feel any connection with Alex; how could she? It wasn't even her he was doing it to, but her mother. But she was eaten alive with guilt when she went to Alex, because it was such a betrayal of Michael. She would have to tell Alex that it had to stop, but the old terror was still there, buried deep. If she stopped letting him do it, would he leave? Would it matter if he did? She wasn't a hurt, confused girl any longer; she didn't need Daddy—or his stand-in.

But what would happen to Mama if Alex stopped coming to the house? He loved Mama, but could he bear to see her, so lost to him, if he didn't have the release of pretending that he was making love to her?

"I love you," she said now to Michael, and tears trickled

from her eyes. "I just—I never thought you'd want to marry me."

"Silly." He wiped the wetness from her cheeks, and a crooked smile lit his grown-up Opie face. "It took me a year to work up the nerve, is all."

She managed a smile of her own. "I hope it doesn't take me that long to work up the nerve to say yes."

"That scary, huh?" he asked, and laughed.

"Any . . . any change is hard for me." She swallowed, terrified at the prospect, and of telling Mama about Michael. Gray knew about him, of course; it was no secret that they were seeing each other, but no one suspected they'd been sleeping together for a year. But since Mama never went to town anymore, and didn't have any friends over to visit, she knew nothing about what went on these days. She wouldn't like it on two counts. One, she wouldn't like the idea of Monica marrying anyone, because that would mean her pristine daughter would be subjected to a man's disgusting touch. Two, she especially wouldn't like it if that man were Michael McFane. The McFanes had never been anything but poor farmers, certainly not in the same social stratum as the Graysons and the Rouillards. The fact that Michael was the sheriff wouldn't raise him any in her estimation; he was just a public servant earning a nice but unspectacular salary.

And she would have to tell Alex.

"It'll be all right," Michael said comfortingly. "I'll get started on fixing up the house. It should be finished in, say, six months. That'll give you enough time to get used to the idea, won't it?"

She looked up into his beloved face and said, "Yes." Yes to it all. Her heart was pounding wildly. She would manage. She would tell Mama, and face that chilly disapproval. She would tell Alex that she couldn't meet him again. It would hurt him, but he would understand. He wouldn't abandon Mama; it was silly of her even to think it. She had to look at things as an adult, not a scared girl. Alex hadn't remained a friend because she'd allowed him to stick his thing in her; he was Gray's legal representative, and a friend even before she'd been born. Probably he had just gotten into the habit of using her. Maybe he'd be glad of an excuse to stop, maybe he felt as guilty about it as she did.

She had to make things as right as possible. Not even one little thing could be wrong, or it would all unravel. A normal, happy life loomed before her like the golden ring on a carousel, and she could grab it if she could just manage to do everything right. The last time, Renee Devlin had wrecked her dream—

Her thoughts jolted. Even as Michael was hugging her exuberantly, a face swam before her eyes: sleepy green eyes, a sensuous mouth that drove men wild. Renee was still there, in the form of her daughter.

Faith had to go. Mama would be much happier if Faith left town. She might even approve of Monica, if she were the one to make Faith leave. And if Michael were involved, too . . .

Her hands pushed at his bare shoulders. "There's a problem."

He released her, sighing with disappointment. The reason for his disappointment twitched in his lap. "What?"

"It's Mama."

He sighed again. "You don't think she'll like the idea of you marryin' me?"

"She won't like the idea of me marrying anyone," Monica said bluntly. "You don't know—she'll be so upset."

He looked startled. "For God's sake, why?"

Monica bit her lip, uncomfortable with airing their family laundry. "Because that means I'd be sleeping with you."

"Of course you'd—oh." Now he looked uncomfortable. He was probably recalling all the old gossip about the arrangement Mama and Daddy had had. "I guess she doesn't like things like that."

"She hates the very idea. And with Faith Devlin back in town, she's already upset." Cautiously Monica nudged him in the direction she wanted him to go. "If Faith left again, it would put Mama in a lot better mood, but I don't know how to manage that. Gray is trying to make her leave, but he says there isn't much he can do, not like before."

To her surprise, Michael went still, and a grim look darkened his face.

"I know how he feels. I wouldn't want to do anything to put that girl out of another home, either."

Monica drew back, uneasy that he had responded directly opposite to the way she had wanted. She had expected him to understand immediately. "She's a Devlin! I can't look at her without feeling sick—"

"She didn't do anything," Michael pointed out in a reasonable tone that set her teeth on edge. "We had trouble with all the other Devlins, but not her."

"She looks just like her mother. Mama nearly went to pieces when she found out one of the Devlins had come back here to live."

"There's no law that says she can't live where she wants."

Because he seemed to have trouble grasping the point, Monica decided to be blunt. "You could do something about it, though, couldn't you? Gray isn't doing much, but you could think of some way to make her leave."

But Michael shook his head, and disappointment knotted her stomach. "I was there the last time," he said soberly, a distant and somber look darkening the blue of his eyes. "When we ran them out of that shack they lived in. For the rest of the Devlins, I didn't care, it was nice to get rid of them, but Faith and that little boy—well, they suffered. I'll never forget the look that was on her face, and I bet Gray still thinks about it, too. That's probably why he's taking it easy on her this time. God knows I couldn't do something like that to her again."

"But if Mama—" Monica stopped herself. He wasn't going to do it. He couldn't understand, not really, because he didn't live with Mama, didn't know how that cold disapproval could slice to the bone. She controlled her dismay, and smiled at him. "Never mind. I'll handle Mama, somehow."

But how? She had never yet managed to handle Mama, to shrug off those hurtful things she said the way Gray did. Gray loved Mama, she knew, but he ignored her a lot of the time. Monica still felt like an anxious little girl, trying so desperately to live up to the standards Mama set, and always falling short.

She would have to do it. She couldn't lose Michael. She would tell Alex she couldn't meet him anymore, and somehow—somehow—she would get rid of Faith Devlin, and make Mama so happy, she wouldn't mind if Monica got married.

❧ Eleven ❧

Faith hung up the phone, a puzzled frown on her face. That was the sixth time she'd called Mr. Pleasant and not gotten an answer. He didn't have a secretary; Mrs. Pleasant had filled that role, and he hadn't had the heart to replace her when she had died. Mr. Pleasant had checked out of the motel; rather, the key had been left on the nightstand in the room, and his things were gone. The room had been paid for in advance, so there was nothing unusual in that. She had done it herself, more than once.

What was unusual was that he hadn't called her, and he'd said that he would. She couldn't believe he had forgotten. He would have called if something wasn't wrong. Given the state of his health, she was afraid he was in a hospital somewhere and was too ill to call. He could even be dying, and she wouldn't know about it. The thought of dying alone made her chest hurt. Someone should at least be there to hold his hand, as she had held Scottie's.

Other than being worried about him, she didn't know what, if anything, he had found or whom he had questioned. She would have to continue on her own, without the benefit of whatever answers he had gotten.

She didn't have a clear idea of how to go about it, what

clues to look for, even what questions to ask—assuming anyone would talk to her. The only ones who were likely to answer her questions would be any newcomers, and they wouldn't be in a position to know anything. The old-timers would know, but they would heed Gray's edict against having anything to do with her.

A thought came to her, and she grinned with anticipation. There was one person, at least, who would talk to her—unwillingly, but he would talk.

She dragged a brush through her hair and twisted the heavy mass into a top-knot, securing it with a few pins and leaving tendrils loose around her face and at the nape of her neck. That was the limit of her grooming; a few minutes after having made up her mind, she was on her way to Prescott, to Morgan's Grocery.

As she had expected, Mrs. Morgan spotted her the moment she entered the door. Faith ignored her and wandered toward the dairy section, which was at the back of the store, safely away from Mrs. Morgan's sharp ears. It wasn't long before Ed came hot-footing it down the aisles, his beefy face florid with both indignation and exertion. "Maybe you didn't understand too good," he said, huffing to a stop in front of her. "Get on out of my store. You can't buy your groceries here."

Faith stood her ground and gave him a cool smile. "I didn't come here to buy anything. I want to ask you a few questions."

"If you don't leave, I'm goin' to call the sheriff," he said, but an uneasy expression crossed his face.

His mention of the sheriff made her stomach clench, probably the reaction he had hoped to get. Her spine stiffened, and she forced herself to ignore the threat. "If you answer my questions," she said quietly, "I'll be gone in a few minutes. If you don't, your wife may learn more than you want her to know." When it came to threats, she could make a few of her own.

He paled, and cast an anxious look toward the front of the store. "I don't know what you're talking about."

"Fine. My questions don't concern my mother. I want to know about Guy Rouillard."

He blinked, surprised by the turn. "About Guy?" he repeated.

"Who else was he seeing that summer?" she asked. "I know my mother wasn't the only one. Do you remember any of the gossip?"

"Why do you want to know about all that? It don't matter who else he was seeing, because it was Renee he ran away with, not any of the others."

She glanced at her watch. "I figure you have about two minutes before your wife comes back here to see what's going on."

He glared at her, but said reluctantly, "I heard he was seeing Andrea Wallice, Alex Chelette's secretary. Alex was Guy's best friend. Don't know that it's true, though, because she didn't seem tore up when Guy left. There was a waitress out at Jimmy Jo's, I can't remember her name, but Guy saw her a few times. She's not there anymore. Heard tell he had a thing going with Yolanda Foster, too. Guy got around. I can't remember who all he was messin' around with, or when, exactly."

Yolanda Foster. That must be the ex-mayor's wife. Their son, Lane, had been one of that group of boys who hung around Jodie when they wanted a good time, but wouldn't speak to her if they met her in public.

"Was that common knowledge?" she asked. "Were there any jealous husbands around?"

He shrugged, and glanced again toward the front of the store. "Maybe the mayor knew, but Guy donated a lot of money to his campaigns, so I doubt Lowell Foster would have kicked up very much if he'd known Yolanda was . . . uh, collecting donations." He smirked, and Faith thought how much she disliked him.

"Thanks for the information," she said, and turned to go.

"You won't come here again?" he asked anxiously.

She paused and gave him a considering look. "Maybe not," she said. "Call me if you think of any more names." Then she walked briskly from the store, not even glancing at Mrs. Morgan on the way out.

Two names, plus the possibility of the unknown waitress. It was a beginning. What intrigued her, though, was the mention of Guy's best friend, Alex Chelette. *He* would likely have the answers to most of her questions.

The Chelettes were one of the old, monied families in the parish—not on a level with the Rouillards, but then neither was anyone else. She knew the name, but couldn't dredge up any memories of them as people. She had been only fourteen when she'd left, and more withdrawn than most, keeping to herself as much as possible. She had paid attention only to those who had direct contact with her family, and as far as she could remember, she had never met any of the Chelettes. Alex was still likely to be around, though; the case of Guy Rouillard aside, old money tended to remain in one place.

She walked down to the pay phone at the end of the parking lot and looked up the Chelettes. The residence was listed as "Alexander Chelette, atty." Below it was the number for "Chelette and Anderson, Attorneys at Law."

Thinking that now was as good a time as any, she fed in a quarter and dialed the law office. A musical voice answered on the second ring.

Faith said, "My name is Faith Hardy. Could Mr. Chelette see me today?"

There was a tiny pause that told Faith her name had been recognized, then the musical voice said, "He's in court all morning, but he can see you this afternoon at one-thirty, if that's convenient."

"It is. Thank you." As she hung up, Faith wondered if the musical voice belonged to Andrea Wallice, who had been Mr. Chelette's secretary when it had all happened, or if this was a different one.

She had almost three hours to kill, unless she wanted to drive home and come back later. Her stomach rumbled, reminding her that the slice of toast she'd eaten at six-thirty had long since vanished. She wondered if she would be served in any of the restaurants in town, or if Gray's influence had extended there, too. She shrugged. No time like the present for finding out.

There was a small café on the square. She had never been in it, she thought as she parked almost directly in front of the door. She had never eaten out until she had gone to live with the Greshams, and they had introduced her to the wonders of restaurants. The thought of them made her smile as she entered the cool, darkened café, and she made a mental note to call them that night. She tried to stay in touch, calling them at least once a month, and it had been almost that long since they last spoke.

Customers seated themselves, so Faith chose the booth at the rear of the café. A pleasant-faced young woman, short and round, bustled up with a menu. "What will you have to drink?"

"Sweet tea." That the tea would be iced was a given, unless hot tea was specifically requested. The usual choices were merely between sweet and unsweetened.

The waitress darted off to get the tea, and Faith glanced down the selections on the plastic menu. She had just decided on the chicken salad when someone paused beside the booth. "Aren't you Faith Devlin?"

Faith tensed, wondering if she would be asked to leave. She looked up at the woman standing there. "Yes, I am." The woman looked vaguely familiar, brown eyes, brown hair, and a square-jawed, dimple-cheeked face. She was smallish, about five foot three, and had the perkiness of a cheerleader.

"I thought so. It's been a while, but it's hard to forget hair that color." The woman smiled. "I'm Halley Bruce—Johnson, now. I was in your class at school."

"Of course!" As soon as she heard the name, the face clicked in her memory. "I remember you. How are you?" Halley had never been her friend—she hadn't had any friends—but neither had Halley taken part in any of the cruel teasing Faith had endured. She had been civil, at least.

The expression in her eyes now, however, was downright friendly. "Will you join me?" Faith invited.

"Just for a minute," Halley said, slipping into the booth opposite Faith. The waitress returned with Faith's tea, and took the order for her chicken salad. When they were alone again, Halley smiled wryly. "My husband's folks own this place, and I run it for them. I'm expecting a delivery any minute now, and I'll have to check it in."

Since Gray already knew about the agency, there was no

point in not talking about it, so Faith said, "I'm playing hooky. I have a travel agency in Dallas, and I really should have told my manager where I'd be, but I forgot to call before I left the house."

Social and financial positions established, they smiled at each other as equals. Faith felt a warm rush of pleasure. Even after she had gone to live with the Greshams and attended high school, she hadn't had any girlfriends; she had still been too wary and withdrawn, too traumatized, to form any friendships. It wasn't until she had started college that she had made any friends at all, and the casual acceptance of her dorm mates had been a revelation to her. Shy at first, she had quickly bloomed, joyfully participating in the female rituals that had been closed to her as a girl: the all-night gab sessions, the teasing and laughter, the swapping of clothes and makeup, the frenzy of getting ready in the mornings, sharing the bathroom mirror with her roommate. For the first time she had participated in the endless analysis of the murky mystery of men—rather, she had listened, smiling a little at their naïveté. Though at that point many of her dorm mates had already had sex and Faith had still been virgin, she had felt infinitely older, more experienced. They still viewed men through the rosy lenses of romance, while she had no such illusion.

But female friendship had remained a special joy to her, and she looked at Halley Johnson with the hope of finding that trembling within her.

"Where did you move to, when you left?" Halley asked, with a casual note that glossed over the circumstances under which Faith had left Prescott.

"Beaumont, Texas. Then I moved to Austin when I started college, and Dallas afterward."

Halley sighed. "I've never lived anywhere but here, don't guess I ever will. I used to think about traveling, but then Joel and I got married, and the kids came. We have two," she said, brightening. "A boy and a girl. With one of each, it seemed like a good time to stop. How about you?"

"I'm a widow," Faith said, her eyes darkening with the shadow of sadness that she always felt when she thought about Kyle, dying so young and so needlessly. "I married right out of college, and he died in a car wreck within the year. No kids."

"That's rough." There was genuine sympathy in Halley's voice. "I'm so sorry. I can only imagine what it would be like to lose Joel. He drives me crazy sometimes, but he's my rock, always there when I need him." She was silent a moment, then the smile came back to her face. "What brings you back to Prescott? I can imagine someone leaving Prescott to move to Dallas, but not vice versa."

"It's home. I wanted to come back."

"Well, I don't want to be nosy or rude, but I would have thought Prescott would be the last place you'd want to live. After what happened, I mean."

Faith gave her a quick look, but couldn't see any malice in Halley's expression, only a certain watchfulness, as if she hadn't quite made up her mind about Faith.

"It hasn't been a bowl of cherries," she replied, and decided she could be as frank as the other woman. "I don't know if you've heard or not, but Gray Rouillard won't like it if he finds out you've served me. I gather he's put out the word to all the merchants that he doesn't want them doing business with me."

"Oh, I've heard," Halley said, and grinned, some of the watchfulness fading. "But I like to make up my own mind about people."

"I don't want to cause trouble for you."

"You won't. Gray isn't vindictive." She paused. "I can see where you might not agree with me. Granted, I wouldn't want him for an enemy, but he won't turn mean just because you ate some chicken salad in here."

"Everyone else in town seems to take him seriously."

"He has a lot of influence," Halley agreed.

"But not with you?"

"I didn't say that. It's just that I remember you from school. You weren't like the others. If it had been Jodie, now—she wouldn't be sitting here waiting for her chicken salad. You're welcome any time, though."

"Thanks, but let me know if there's a problem."

"I'm not worried about it." Halley smiled as the waitress set the plate of chicken salad on the table. "If he'd meant to be a hard-ass about it, he'd have said so. One thing about Gray, you don't have to second-guess him. He says what he means, and means what he says."

Alex Chelette's secretary was still Andrea Wallice, according to the nameplate on her desk. The woman sitting behind the desk was comfortably fiftyish, her face wearing every one of the years, her gray hair styled in a short, neat bob. Looking at her, trying to subtract a dozen years, Faith still couldn't imagine her as the type of woman Guy Rouillard would pursue. His taste had run toward the flamboyant, not this tidy woman with the openly curious gaze.

"You look like your mother," Andrea finally said, her head tilting a bit to one side as she studied Faith's face. "A few differences, but for the most part you could be her, especially in your coloring."

"Did you know her?" Faith asked.

"Only by sight." She gestured to the sofa. "Have a seat. Alex hasn't come back from lunch yet."

Just as Faith sat down, the door opened and a slim, good-looking man entered. He was wearing a suit, an oddity in Prescott, unless one happened to be an attorney who had been at the courthouse all morning. He glanced toward Faith and visibly started, then relaxed, and a smile touched his mouth. "You must be Faith. God knows, you couldn't be anyone else, unless Renee discovered the Fountain of Youth."

"That's what I thought," Andrea said, turning to him, and for a moment the expression in her eyes was unguarded. Faith quickly looked down. From what she had just seen, she very much doubted that Andrea had ever been involved with Guy, because she was very much in love with her boss. She wondered if Mr. Chelette knew, and just as quickly decided that he didn't. There was no hint of awareness on his part.

"Come in," he invited, ushering Faith into his office ahead of him, and closing the door. "I know we must seem rude, discussing you that way. I'm sorry. It's just that the resemblance is so pronounced, and yet, on second glance, the differences are obvious."

"Everyone seems to have that reaction when they see me for the first time," she admitted, and smiled at him. It was very easy to smile at Alex Chelette. He was the type of man whom age refined; always slim, he would pare down even more with the passing years. His dark hair had grayed at the sides, and there were lines at the corners of his gray eyes, but he easily looked to be in his mid-forties, rather than his fifties. His scent was light green, as fresh as newly cut grass.

"Sit down, please," he said, and settled into his own chair. "What can I do for you today?"

Faith seated herself on the leather sofa. "Actually, I came on personal reasons, and I realize now I shouldn't have taken up your work time—"

He shook his head, smiling. "It's my pleasure. Now, tell me what's bothering you. Is it Gray? I tried to get him to leave you alone, but he's very protective of his mother and sister, and he doesn't want them upset."

"I understand Gray's position very well," Faith said dryly. "That isn't why I'm here."

"Oh?"

"I wanted to ask you some questions about Guy Rouillard. You were his best friend, weren't you?"

He gave her a faint smile. "I thought so. We grew up together."

Should she tell him that Guy hadn't, after all, left with Renee? She toyed with the idea, then discarded it. As friendly as he seemed, she couldn't forget that he was an old family friend of the Rouillards. She had to assume that anything she told him would go straight to Gray.

"I'm curious about him," she finally said. "That night wrecked my family, just as it did Gray's. What was he like? I know he wasn't faithful to my mother any more than he was to his wife, so why would he all of a sudden walk away from everything, his family, his business, to be with her?"

"I don't think you really want me to answer that," he replied wryly. "To put it as politely as I can, Renee was a fascinating woman, at least to men. Physically she was . . . well, Guy was very responsive to Renee's sensuality."

"But he was already having an affair with her. There wasn't any reason for them to leave."

Alex shrugged, a very Gallic gesture. "I've never understood it myself."

"Why didn't he just get a divorce?"

"Again, I don't have an answer for that. Perhaps because of his religion; Guy wasn't a regular at mass, but he felt more strongly about religion than you might have expected. Perhaps he thought it would be easier on Noelle if he didn't divorce her, if he just handed everything over to Gray and left. I simply don't know."

"Hand everything over to Gray?" Faith repeated. "What do you mean?"

"I'm sorry," he said gently. "I can't divulge details of my clients' business dealings."

"No, of course not." Quickly she backtracked. "Do you remember anything else about that summer? Who else Guy was seeing?"

He looked startled. "Why would you want to know?"

"Like I said, I have an interest in the man. Because of him, I haven't seen my mother since that day. Was he likeable? Did he have any honor, or was he just a tomcat?"

He stared at her for a moment, and pain crept into his eyes. "Guy was the most likeable man in the world," he finally said. "I loved him like a brother. He was always laughing, teasing, but if I needed him for anything, he was there like a shot. His marriage to Noelle was a disappointment to him, but still I was surprised when he left, because he was so close to Gray and Monica. He was a terrible husband, but a wonderful father." He looked down at his hands. "It's been twelve years," he said softly. "And I still miss him."

"Did he ever call?" she asked. "Or get in touch with his family in any way?"

He shook his head. "Not to my knowledge."

"Who else was he seeing that summer, besides Yolanda Foster?"

Once again, her question startled him. His eyebrows rose, and rebuke was in his voice when he spoke. "None of that matters. As I keep telling Gray, it's in the past; let it go. There was a lot of pain that summer, and keeping it alive doesn't do anyone any good."

"I can't let it go, when no one else in the parish will. No matter how successful I am, or respectable, some people here still think of me as trash." Her voice trembled a little on the last word. She hadn't meant to let her control waver, and she was both embarrassed and irritated that it had. Sometimes, though, the pain leaked through.

Alex must have heard it, because his expression changed, and suddenly he left his chair to come sit beside her and take one of her hands in both of his. "I know it's been difficult for you," he said gently. "They'll change their minds, when they get to know you better. And Gray will eventually relent. As I said, he reacted the way he did because he's so protective of his family, but basically he's a very fair man."

"And ruthless," Faith added.

A rueful smile touched his face. "That, too. But not unkind. Take my word for it. If there's anything I can do to change his mind, I promise you I'll do it."

"Thank you," Faith said. That wasn't why she'd come to see him, but he was too conscientious to divulge personal details about his clients and friends. The visit wasn't a total waste, however, she felt she could safely mark Andrea Wallice off her list.

She took her leave, and drove home pondering the scraps of information she'd gotten that day. If Guy had been murdered, Lowell or Yolanda Foster seemed to be the most likely suspects. She wondered how she could contrive a meeting with either of them. And she wondered where Mr. Pleasant was, and if he was all right.

"I met Faith today," Alex said that night as he and Gray were going over some papers. He picked up his brandy and keenly eyed the younger man over the rim of the glass. "The resemblance is eerie, at first glance, but by the second look there's no way of mistaking her for Renee. Odd, isn't it, the way Renee was more beautiful, but Faith is more attractive?"

Gray glanced up, wry awareness in his dark eyes as he caught the expression in Alex's gray ones. "Yes, I've noticed how attractive she is, if that's what you're asking. Where did you meet her?" He picked up his own glass, filled with his favorite Scotch, and savored the smoky bite of it on his tongue.

"At my office. She came to ask me about Guy."

Gray almost choked. He set his glass down with a force that made the whisky slosh dangerously close to the rim. "She *what?* What in hell did she want to know about Dad?" The thought of Faith asking anything about his father made him bitterly angry. It was a knee-jerk reaction; for a moment she wasn't *Faith,* the person, but a *Devlin,* with all the connotations elicited by the name. He himself wanted her with a fierce need that both alarmed and disgusted him, even though he knew he was going to ease that need if possible, but he didn't want anything about her touching his family. He didn't want Monica or Noelle exposed to her, and he sure as hell didn't want her asking about his father. Guy was gone. His absence, his betrayal, was a wound that remained perilously close to the surface, and bled at the slightest scratch.

"She wanted to know what he was like, had he ever gotten in touch, if he'd been seeing anyone else that summer."

Furious, Gray half rose from his chair, intending to go to her house right now and have it out with her. Alex stopped him with a hand on his arm. "She has a right to know," he said mildly. "Or at least to be curious."

"I'll be goddamned if she does!" Gray snapped.

"She hasn't seen her mother since then, either."

Gray froze, then sank back into the chair. Alex was right, damn it. It rankled, but he had to admit the truth. At least he'd been a grown man, if inexperienced in business, when his father had left; Faith had been only fourteen, as helpless and vulnerable as a child. He didn't know anything about her life between then and now, except that she was a widow and now owned a successful travel agency, but he'd bet his last red cent it hadn't been pleasant. Living with Amos Devlin and those two hoodlum boys, as well as her slut of a sister, couldn't have been easy. It wouldn't have been easy before, but at least Renee had been there.

"Let up on her, Gray," Alex said softly. "She deserves better than the reception she's getting from some people, and part of it's your fault."

Gray picked up the glass and swirled the whiskey, looking down into the amber depths. "I can't," he said gruffly. He got up and carried his drink to the window, where he stood staring at his reflection in the glass, and the darkness beyond. He took another sip of fortification. "She has to go, before I do something that really hurts Monica and Mother."

"Such as?" Alex asked, puzzled.

"Let's just say that, where Faith is concerned, I'm caught between a rock and a hard place. The rock is my family, and the hard place—" he looked around with a sort of angry amusement in his eyes "—is in my pants."

Appalled, Alex stared at him. "My God."

"It must be genetic." That was the only explanation for it, he thought grimly. He had inherited his father's cock. Put a Devlin woman in front of it, and it got hard. No, not just any Devlin woman; two of them had left him cold. But Faith . . . Nothing about him was cold if she was anywhere within a country mile.

"You can't do that to your mother," Alex whispered. "The humiliation would kill her."

"Hell, I know that! That's why I want Faith to leave, before I do something stupid." He turned to face Alex, that angry amusement still burning in his eyes. "The attraction isn't all on my side, damn it. It'd be easier if it was. I went to her house the other night to put a proposition to her: If she didn't want to leave the area, I'd buy a house for her in any town close by, as long as it wasn't in this parish. That way we could see each other without hurting anyone. There was an old man there, having dinner with her, and I was so jealous, I accused her of having a sugar daddy." He shook his head, and laughed softly at himself. "Can you believe it? The old guy looked as frail as a toothpick, but he was all dressed up like something out of the fifties, and all I could think was that he was trying to get her in bed."

"What old guy?" Alex asked, plainly curious. "Anyone I know?"

"He was from New Orleans. His last name was Pleasant. I was so mad, I don't remember if she told me his first name. He said he was a business associate."

181

"Was he?"

Gray shrugged. "Probably. Faith owns a travel agency, and she has a branch in New Orleans."

"She *owns* it?"

"She's done pretty good for herself, hasn't she?" There it was again, that damn little twinge of pride. "She started out in Dallas. I don't know how many branch offices she has, but I have someone gathering information on her. I expect to have a report any day."

"Are you going to try to ruin her business if she doesn't leave?" Alex asked, but less sharply than Gray had expected.

"No. For one thing, I'm not that big of a bastard. For another, if I did, I could kiss my chances with her good-bye." His mouth twisted in a wry smile. "Decide for yourself which reason is the most important."

Alex didn't smile in return. "This is a hell of a situation. If you're bound and determined to have her—"

"I am," Gray said, and tossed back the last of the whiskey.

"—then she can't live here. Noelle would be devastated."

"I'm worried more about Monica than I am Mother."

Alex blinked, as if he hadn't considered Monica. He probably hadn't; all of his attention was focused on Noelle. He knew about Monica's suicide attempt, of course; it hadn't been possible to keep it quiet, not with all the commotion at Dr. Bogarde's office. Monica didn't try to hide the scars, anyway. She was too proud to let herself take the cowardly route of long sleeves or wide bracelets.

"Monica is a lot stronger than she was then," Alex finally said. "But Noelle doesn't have anything to fall back on. I thought at the beginning, and still do, that she should face up to facts and get on with her life, but if she found out you were having an affair with Faith—no. She couldn't stand it. She might try suicide herself."

Gray shook his head, amazed that Alex could have known Noelle all these years and still not realized that she was too self-centered to harm herself. The myopia of love allowed him to see only her cool, perfect, unattainable beauty. It was that romantic streak in him, a strange characteristic for a lawyer.

"She has to go," Alex said regretfully.

❦ Twelve ❦

The fax machine was humming, so Faith didn't hear the car turn in to the driveway. When the knock rattled the front door, she leaned over to look out the window. She couldn't see who was standing on the porch, but she could see the gray Jaguar parked behind her car, and she sighed as she went, coffee cup in hand, into the living room to answer the door. It was barely eight-thirty, too early to have to deal with Gray Rouillard.

The first thing she noticed when she opened the door was that he was in a towering rage.

The only other time she had seen him like this was the day he'd come to the shack to tell them Renee had left, and again that night, when he'd had them thrown out. As she looked up into the cold ruthlessness of those dark eyes, the memory of that night flashed in her mind, the stark images reducing her in an instant to the terrified girl she'd been then. Her blood chilled, and she fell back a step as he came inside, letting the screen door slam behind him.

She jumped at the sound. Her eyes, green and unblinking, were fastened on his face as if she didn't dare look away.

"What the hell do you think you're doing?" he asked very softly, the velvety sound as chilling as a sword sliding against another blade. He advanced another step, so that he loomed over her, and Faith retreated again. The coffee cup shook in her hand.

For every step he took forward, she took one back, a slow dance that ended when she bumped into the wall, her shoulder blades pressing hard against the Sheetrock as if she could force her way through it. His arms shot out before she could slide sideways, his palms flattening against the wall on either side of her shoulders, imprisoning her within the cage of his arms and body. He leaned down slightly; the top two buttons of his white shirt were open, revealing a wedge of warm olive skin decorated with curly black hair. His pulse throbbed visibly in the hollow at the base of his strong throat, right in front of her eyes. Faith fastened her gaze on that rhythmic movement, desperately seeking to steady herself. She was *not* fourteen. He could *not* throw her out of her own house.

"Well?" he asked, still in that dangerous, purring tone.

His thick wrists were squeezing her shoulders, bared by her sleeveless blouse; his skin was hot against hers. His wide shoulders and broad chest were like a wall in front of her, and his rich, musky male scent made her nostrils flare in automatic delight. Still clasping the coffee cup, holding it like a shield between them, she swallowed and managed to say, "What are you talking about?"

He leaned closer, so close that his stomach brushed against her fingers. "I'm talking about all those questions you've been asking. Alex told me last night you'd been to his office. Talking to Alex is one thing, he'll keep his mouth shut, but guess who I saw this morning. Ed Morgan." Despite the calmness of his tone, she could see the cold fury flickering in his eyes. If he'd been having a roaring fit, she wouldn't have been half as nervous. In this mood, he was capable of anything, but oddly enough, she didn't fear him physically. No, if Gray harmed her, the damage would be to her emotions.

"I'm only going to tell you once." He said the words very precisely, leaning down even closer, until his nose was almost touching hers. "Don't ask any more questions about my father. Your nosiness will only stir up gossip, and hurt my family again. If that happens, Faith, I *will* run you out of the parish again, by any means necessary. You can take that to the bank. So keep it in mind: I don't want your pretty mouth even shaping my father's name."

Wide green eyes stared into chilly dark ones, only a couple of inches apart. Her chin tilted upward, and her mouth, which he thought was pretty, parted as she deliberately tugged on the tiger's tail, and uttered two words: "Guy Rouillard."

She saw his pupils widen in disbelief, then the chill in his eyes was swallowed by pure fire. Maybe it hadn't been prudent to provoke him, but watching the result was fascinating. He seemed to expand with fury, dark color running into his face, and if his long hair hadn't been pulled back and secured, she rather thought it would have lifted from his head.

She had a split second in which to enjoy the entertainment. Then he moved with the blurring speed she had seen before, his hands leaving the wall to clasp hard around her upper arms, and he gave her a teeth-rattling shake. Her grip loosened on the forgotten cup in her hands, and she felt it slip. With a cry she tried to juggle it, but he was too close, and all she could do was knock the falling cup toward herself, rather than let the steaming liquid burn him. The coffee soaked into her thin skirt, plastering it to her right thigh, and splattered over their feet. She cried out again, this time in pain. The cup hit the floor with a crash, breaking off the handle but otherwise remaining intact. Gray jumped back, automatically releasing her, and frantically she pulled the wet fabric away from her stinging thigh.

His dark gaze swept down her, and he said, "Shit," in a rough tone. He grabbed her, pulling her against him, and his hands worked briefly at the back of her waist. Her skirt loosened and dropped to her feet. He lifted her out of the circle of fabric, swinging her up in his arms, and dizzily she clutched his shoulders as the room whirled around her.

"What are you doing?" she cried in alarm as he rapidly carried her into the kitchen. She was confused by the shock of pain, and he was moving too fast for her to get her bearings. Beneath all that, she was acutely aware of her bare legs draped over his arm, and that she was dressed in only her panties and blouse.

He hooked his foot around a chair leg and pulled the chair away from the table, then carefully set her in it. Turning to the sink, he pulled off several paper towels, folded them into a pad, and wet them under the cold water. The pad was still dripping when he plopped it over her reddened, stinging thigh. She jumped at the chill. Trickles of water ran down her thigh, into the seat of the chair, and soaked into her panties.

"I forgot about the coffee," he muttered. Truth to tell, he hadn't even noticed it until he'd seen it spilling down her leg. "I'm sorry, Faith. Do you have any tea?" Before she could answer, he was already opening the refrigerator door, and taking out the pitcher of tea that was almost de rigueur in southern kitchens.

He opened and closed cabinet drawers until he found her clean towels. Taking one out, he dropped it into the pitcher of tea, then removed it and carefully squeezed out most of the excess liquid. She watched in bemusement as he took away the pad of paper towels, tossing it into the sink with a sodden plop, and replaced it with the tea-soaked towel. If the water had been cold, the tea was icy. Faith drew in a hissing breath as it, too, ran down her leg to pool beneath her bottom.

"Does it hurt?" Gray asked, going down on his knee beside the chair to smooth the towel over her thigh. His voice was tight with anxiety.

"No," she said bluntly. "It's cold, and you're soaking my rear end."

His face was level with hers. At her words, she saw the worry leave his eyes, and the tension ease from his shoulders. He grasped the back of the chair with his left hand, and with wry, faint humor asked, "Did I overreact?"

She pursed her lips. "A tad."

"Your thigh is red. I know you're burned."

"Only a little. It stings a bit, is all. I doubt it'll blister." She narrowed her eyes at him, trying to hide the laughter she could feel bubbling in her chest. "I appreciate your concern, but it certainly didn't warrant having half my clothes stripped off."

He looked down at her bare legs, and the white cotton underwear barely visible beneath the hem of her blouse. A tremor ran through him. He put his right hand on her uninjured thigh, smoothing his palm over the firm, cool resilience of her flesh, entranced by the silky texture. "I've wanted to get your panties wet for a long time," he murmured. "But not with tea."

Her laughter disappeared as if it had never existed. Tension stretched between them, almost palpable in its thickness. Her insides clenched at his words, heat pooling in her loins, her breasts tightening. She felt the dampening of desire, and the admission *You have* trembled on her lips. She bit it back, knowing that voicing the telltale response would cross a boundary over which she didn't dare pass. Sexual tension emanated from him like a force field, hot and urgent. It would take only that confession, and he would be on her.

She ached with the need to touch him, to press herself against that big, steely body and open her own body to him. Only the instinct for self-preservation kept her silent, and still.

He leaned imperceptibly closer, inhaling her spicy sweet scent. His blood throbbed through his veins, pulsing, swelling. Silently they watched each other, like two adversaries coming face-to-face in a dusty street. He wanted to pull down her panties and bury his face in her lap, the impulse so strong that he shuddered with the effort of resisting it, and wondered what she would do if he gave in. Would she be frightened, would she push him away . . . or would her legs fall open, and her hands clench in his hair?

His hand flexed on her thigh, his fingers pressing into the silky flesh that had warmed beneath his touch. He saw her pupils dilate, then her lashes droop heavily as she drew in a deep, slow breath that made him acutely aware of her breasts. He shifted his hand a little, and rubbed his thumb back and forth, each sweep moving higher, probing deeper into the cleft of her clenched thighs. He wanted to touch her.

He forgot about Monica, about Guy, about everything but the slow, hot movement of his thumb, closer and closer to the exquisitely tender flesh between her legs, so flimsily protected by the thin layer of cotton. He would slide his thumb under the elastic of the leg opening, and find the furrow of her tightly closed folds. Then he would drag his thumb upward, opening her as he went, until he found the tiny bud at the top of her sex.

If she let him touch her, she'd be his. He'd have her then.

His thumb brushed elastic. And she moved, her hand clamping down over his and tugging it away from her thigh. "No," she whispered.

Frustration roared through him like a brush fire. A sound very much like a growl rumbled in his throat as physical instincts fought for supremacy over thought. His brain won, but barely. He was sweating, shaking with the need to have her. His erection strained painfully against the restriction of his pants.

"No," she said again, as if the original refusal needed reinforcing, and perhaps it did.

Slowly he turned his hand, so that his fingers meshed with hers. "Then hold my hand for a minute."

She did, clinging tightly to him, feeling his fingers twitch and flex as if reaching for something. His other hand was clamped around the slat of the chairback, his knuckles white from the pressure.

After a moment of unknown duration, time suspended as their gazes locked and lust shimmered between them, the terrible tension in him began to fade. He winced and shifted position, stretching his leg out. He freed his hand to reach down and make an adjustment, the furrow between his brows smoothing out as he made himself more comfortable.

She cleared her throat, uncertain what to say, if anything.

He rose stiffly to his feet. The thick ridge in his pants was unmistakable, but he was in control now. He plucked the hand towel from its rack and draped it over her thighs, removing temptation from sight, if not proximity.

After a minute he said in a quiet voice, "Are you certain you're not hurt?"

"Yes." She too spoke quietly, as if a too loud noise would

shatter their control and send them tumbling over the precipice she had barely managed to avoid. The hunger hadn't been one-sided. "It's a minor burn. I probably won't even feel it tomorrow." The stinging had completely vanished, soothed away by the cold, wet tea.

"All right." He looked down at her, and lifted his hand as if he would smooth her hair, but then let it fall back to his side. He couldn't safely allow himself to touch her just yet. "Now, tell me why you've been asking all those questions about Dad."

She looked up at him, the dark fire of her hair spilling down her back. She wanted to tell him what she suspected, that his father was dead, but found that the words stuck in her throat. She couldn't do it. She had to believe he knew nothing about it, that he had nothing to do with his father's death, because she loved him and it would break her heart otherwise. And because she loved him, she couldn't bring herself to hurt him. She had deliberately tilted the falling coffee cup towards herself to keep him from suffering a minor scald; how could she now tell him that the father he loved was probably dead, murdered?

So instead she told him what was both the truth in substance and a lie in intent, murmuring, "He was my past, too. I can barely remember when he wasn't there, but I never really knew him. He was always kind when he saw me, which wasn't often, but then I lost my mother because of him. Do you think I'm not curious about the kind of person he was? That I shouldn't try to fill in the gaps, to make sense of what happened?"

"Good luck," he growled. "I thought I knew him better than anyone else on earth, and I still can't make sense of it." He paused. "If you have any more questions about him, ask *me,* because I meant what I said. I don't want to get rough with you, Faith, but I'll do what's necessary to protect my family. Remember that."

Since he'd offered . . . But, no, it was hardly the time to prolong this encounter by firing questions at him, with her sitting there half-naked, and Gray a sexual powder keg, primed and ready to explode. So she merely looked at him in silence, and after a moment his mouth quirked with a smile. "I'm not hearing any promises, am I? Think about it, baby. Don't make it any tougher on yourself than it has to be. Just keep quiet, and behave yourself."

"Like a good little girl?"

"Like a smart woman," he corrected. Again his hand moved toward her, and again the movement was aborted. She could sense that he wanted to stay, wanted to continue what he had begun, but she had refused him and he was forcing himself to accept her decision—for now. Every time they met, the battle would be joined again, and the temptation to give in would be just that much stronger for having been denied.

"I'm going to go," he said.

"All right."

He didn't move. Then: "I don't want to."

"Do it anyway."

He chuckled. "You're a hard woman, Faith Devlin."

"Hardy."

"I didn't know him. He isn't real to me. Did you love him?"

"Yes." *But not the way I love you. Never like that.*

His dark eyes glittered, and this time he did touch her, his hand cupping her cheek. "You'll always be a Devlin to me, with that red hair and your witch's eyes." He bent, and moved his mouth warmly against hers in a brief kiss. Then he was gone, and when the door closed behind him, Faith sagged back in the chair with relief.

She felt as if a storm had entered the room and tossed her around. Her heart was still pounding, and her muscles felt like spaghetti noodles. Those few moments had been among the most erotic of her life, and all he had done was touch her leg. If he had actually made love to her, she would have totally lost control of herself. She was frightened by the intensity of the desire he could arouse with a look, a brief touch, even the delicious muskiness of his male scent.

You'll always be a Devlin to me.

Not the greatest of recommendations. She could only suppose that he meant he'd never be able to forget her background, her heritage, that nothing she did would ever change his mind about her.

And I'll always love you, she whispered to him in her mind. *Always.*

Just a touch on her leg, and he'd been almost ready to come, Gray thought wryly. God, if he ever actually got inside her, his heart would probably explode from the strain.

His hands were shaking as he drove, a common reaction if he spent more than a minute in Faith's company. It would be easier if she didn't respond to him the way she did; she might hold herself still, she might be able to say no, but that hot, languorous look was still in her eyes. He knew all the signs. Her breathing deepened, her breasts rising round and full, her nipples peaking. Though he hadn't kissed her until that light peck on the lips as he was leaving, because he couldn't resist the urge any longer, her mouth had been red and swollen. A delicate flush had glowed under her translucent skin.

He wanted her. He had to make her leave. He wanted her. The opposing needs were driving him crazy.

She hadn't agreed to stop asking questions. She hadn't argued with him, but he was beginning to realize that her silence masked a streak of stubbornness as wide as the Grand Canyon. She might not fight, but she definitely resisted. As a girl, Faith had too often been beaten down by life, when she had been helpless to make her own decisions. Now that she could decide her own course, she let very little sway her from it. That single-mindedness was probably the main reason why, at the young age of twenty-six, she owned her own business.

Given that, it wasn't likely he would be able to convince her to leave. And since he sure as hell couldn't trust his own good sense to keep him away from her, he foresaw some rocky days ahead.

Monica's hands were shaking as she opened the door to Alex's office and smiled at Andrea. She managed to keep her voice steady and cheerful, though, as she said, "I hope he's in. I was in town, and thought of something I wanted to ask him."

"It's your lucky day," Andrea said, smiling. She had known Monica since babyhood. "He came in about five minutes ago. He's washing up, but he'll be out in a minute. Go on in and have a seat."

Washing up, of course, was a polite way of saying he was in the bathroom. It was what Mama would say, Monica thought, if she alluded to a bathroom at all. In thirty-two years, she couldn't remember her mother in any way acknowledging the real function of a toilet. Physical reality had to be hidden if possible, and ignored if not. Try as she might, Monica couldn't imagine her mother having sex, though she and Gray were proof that it had happened at least twice. And as for visiting an obstetrician, and the indignity of having a baby—the wonder was that Mama hadn't locked Daddy out of the bedroom after Gray was born, rather than go through that again.

Monica avoided the leather sofa and walked over to the window, to look out at the courthouse square. The fresh blooms of spring were rapidly giving way to the lush, heavy foliage of full summer. Time moved relentlessly onward, the earth and plants going through their cycles oblivious to the puny humans who were so caught up in their own grandeur that they thought they affected everything.

Alex entered the room, smiling as he saw her. "What brings you here today?" He'd had dinner with them the night before, so any business would have been discussed then.

Monica looked at that lean, good-looking face, the kind gray eyes, and her throat went dry. She had been trying for a week to work up enough courage to talk to him. She had actually made it as far as his office, but now her voice had failed her.

He frowned at the misery in her dark eyes. "What is it, dear?" he asked softly, closing the door and coming over to take her hand.

She sucked in a deep breath. Sometimes she thought she was crazy, that those times with Alex existed only in her imagination. There was never any hint of it in his eyes, or his manner, when they were together during normal times. He was just Alex, as he had always been, a sturdy shoulder to lean on, quietly stepping in to take on as much of the weight as he could, until she and Gray had been able to manage. It really was as if those furtive moments existed between two other people, between Daddy and Mama, coming together in borrowed flesh.

This was *Alex,* she reminded herself. He wouldn't leave. His love and support didn't depend on whether or not she slept with him. She had been a convenience for him, that was all, an outlet for his pent-up emotions.

That was what logic told her. Emotionally, however, she was terrified. One father had already left her, his love for her not strong enough to hold him against the lure of screwing Renee Devlin. She couldn't bear it if she lost Alex, too.

But then there was Michael. Sweet, sexy Michael. If she didn't seize her chance now, she might lose *him* forever, and of the choice between the two men, there was no choice at all. Michael was her heart, the very blood moving through her body.

"Monica?" Alex prodded, gray eyes darkening with worry.

She gulped. She had to tell him. She closed her eyes and blurted it out. "I'm going to marry Michael McFane."

There was silence for a moment, and she squeezed her eyes tighter, waiting with dread. But the seconds ticked past, and still Alex didn't say anything, and finally the stress became so acute that she couldn't stand it any longer and opened her eyes.

He was smiling at her, fond exasperation on his face. "Congratulations," he said, then chuckled. "What did you expect me to say?"

Stunned, she stared at him. "I—I don't know."

"I'm happy for you, dear. Neither you nor Gray have shown any inclination to get married, and I've worried about that. The sheriff is a good, steady man."

She wet her lips. "Mama won't like it."

He paused, considering that for a moment. "Probably not, but don't let that stop you. You deserve happiness, Monica."

"I don't want to upset her."

"There are some things she needs to face, and some things

she shouldn't have to. In this case, marry Michael, and be as happy as possible. Believe me, this won't upset her half as much as hearing about Faith Devlin."

Faith Devlin? Monica blinked. "What about her?" Since Mama already knew the woman had moved back to Prescott, Alex's statement didn't make sense.

"Gray hasn't told you?" He seemed surprised.

"Evidently not. Told me what?"

He sighed. "She's been asking questions around town— about Guy. Personal questions. If she isn't stopped, she'll stir everything up again, and that will hurt Noelle far more than your marriage."

Monica felt as if she'd been slapped. Faith Devlin was asking around town about her father? The very thought outraged her. Wasn't it enough that her slut of a mother had taken her daddy away, and she'd never seen him again? Her face flushed with anger. "What sort of questions has she been asking? My God, what business is it of hers?"

"Personal questions, what sort of person he was, things like that. She came here yesterday, because she'd heard I was Guy's best friend. Talking to me is one thing, but Gray found out this morning that she'd been pestering Ed Morgan with questions, too."

"She's been asking *Ed Morgan* about Daddy?" Monica cried. "The man's the biggest gossip in town!"

"Gray took care of it," Alex said soothingly, and patted her hand. "You know Gray. He had Ed stuttering and back-stepping within ten seconds."

Gray in a temper *was* a fearsome sight, with those dark eyes turning so cold and deadly. She couldn't imagine Ed Morgan withstanding him for even ten seconds. The notion entertained her for a brief moment, but then was pushed aside by her indignation at Faith Devlin's gall.

"I understand her curiosity," Alex said, "but as I told Gray, it could be disastrous for your mother to find out."

"Well, *I* don't understand her curiosity!" Monica cried. God, it took so little to bring it all back, the sense of loss, and of being lost, and the suffocating pain. Hatred swelled within her. She pulled her hand free, and turned away. "Gray shut up Ed Morgan, but what's he doing about *her?*"

"I don't know." He shook his head. "I know you don't agree, but when she first moved back, I was all for leaving her alone. What happened wasn't her fault, and she deserves the right to live where she wants. That was something Noelle should have faced, and made the best of. This is different. This is deliberate, and it's something that *is* her fault."

"Gray will take care of it," Monica said. "He has to."

"I don't know if he can."

"Of course he can! There are a lot of things he could do."

"Then let me put it another way. I don't think he can be that drastic with Faith, considering how he feels about her. Wake up, Monica!" he admonished. "Pay attention to your brother. He's attracted to her. Nothing about this is easy for him."

Monica felt the blood drain out of her face, leaving it stiff. Gray was . . . *attracted* to that woman? No. God couldn't be that cruel. He wouldn't make her live through that nightmare again.

Unable to say anything else, she warded off Alex with an outstretched hand, unable to cope with the sympathy she could see in his eyes. Hurriedly she left his office, and it wasn't until she reached the street that she realized she hadn't told him she couldn't be with him anymore.

It would kill Mama if Gray took up with Renee Devlin's daughter. The gossip would be so vicious, she would never be able to lift her head again. Monica gave a bitter little laugh. And to think she'd been worried what Mama would think about Michael McFane!

✌ Thirteen ✌

Mr. Pleasant's office was located on the top floor of a two-story building. Faith climbed the stairs, hoping against hope that she would find him there, that his telephone had been out of service, that he would be all right. A malfunctioning telephone wasn't much of a possibility, because if he hadn't been able to call out, he would have known about it and simply gone to another phone. Surely, too, he would have noticed if there were no incoming calls. Maybe he'd taken another case, and forgotten about her.

She doubted Francis P. Pleasant ever forgot anything.

His office was the first door on the left. The upper half of the door was glass, but the interior blinds had been closed, preventing her from seeing inside. The day she had met him, the blinds had been open. She tried to open the door and found it locked. Not really expecting a response, she knocked, and put her ear against the glass. The room beyond was silent.

There was a mail slot in the door. Faith pushed the little flap open, and angled her head to look inside. Her view was extremely limited, but she could see the mail, quite a lot of it, scattered across the floor.

He wasn't here, and the amount of his mail indicated that he hadn't been here in several days.

Growing more worried by the minute, Faith walked down the hall to the next door. According to the lettering on the door, she was at the law office of Houston H. Manges. She could hear the clatter of a typewriter and voices, so she opened the door and entered.

Houston H. Manges's environs were small and cramped, with file cabinets crammed into every available space. She was in the reception area, populated by a tiny white-haired woman and three rubber plants, one of which had reached gargantuan size. The room beyond, which she could see through the open door, was about the same size, with floor-to-ceiling books. A heavyset man lounged behind a battered desk, and he was talking to a client who sat in one of the two cracked imitation leather chairs positioned in front of the desk. All that was visible of the client was the back of his head.

The tiny woman looked up and smiled in question, but made no move to close the door and give her employer and his client any privacy. Faith gave a mental shrug and approached.

"I'm a client of Mr. Pleasant, next door," she said. "I've been trying to reach him for several days and can't seem to locate him. Do you happen to have any idea where he is?"

"Why, no," the tiny woman said. "He left about a week ago to go to this little town up close to Mississippi, I don't remember the name. Perkins, something like that. I assumed he was still there."

"No, he left there the next day. He has a bad heart, and I'm worried about him."

"Oh, dear." The small face took on a distressed look. "I never thought about his heart. I knew, of course. His wife, Virginia—we used to have lunch together, it was so sad when she died—told me about his trouble. It was really bad, she said. I never thought to check on him." She reached immediately for the phone index, and flipped through it until she came to the *P*s. "I'll try his home phone. It's unlisted, you know. He didn't like business intruding on his private life."

Faith knew. She had called information, trying to get the

number. It was her lack of success that had spurred her to drive down and try to find him.

After a minute the little lady hung up the phone. "There's no answer. Oh, dear. I *am* worried now. It isn't like Francis not to let someone know where he is."

"I'm going to call all the hospitals," Faith said decisively. "May I borrow your telephone?"

"Of course, honey. We have two lines, so people will still be able to get through. If a call comes in, though, I'll need you to hang up so I can answer it."

Thanking God for southern hospitality, Faith accepted the New Orleans directory and flipped to the listing of hospitals. There were more than she had expected. Starting at the top, she began dialing.

Thirty minutes and three interruptions for incoming calls later, she hung up in defeat. Mr. Pleasant wasn't a patient in any of the local hospitals. If he had taken ill while driving back from Prescott, he could be in a hospital somewhere else, but where?

Or something could have happened to him. It was a possibility she didn't want to consider, but one she had to accept. If Guy Rouillard had been murdered, and Mr. Pleasant had been asking questions that made someone uncomfortable . . . She felt sick at the thought. If anything had happened to that sweet old man, it would be her fault for involving him. It wasn't as if she'd had anything to go on, other than Renee's statement that Guy hadn't been with her at all, that she hadn't seen him since that night twelve years ago.

Most people wouldn't have suspected murder. Most people wouldn't now be afraid that poor Mr. Pleasant had somehow run afoul of the same person who had killed Guy. But neither had most people been dragged out of their home in the middle of the night and thrown into the dirt; until Renee and Guy had disappeared, Faith's life had been predictable, if a bit grim. But that night her trust in the comforting ordinariness of life had been shattered, and she had never regained that sense of security, of obliviousness to things that just didn't happen to normal people. It was as if a curtain had been torn aside, and after that night she was acutely aware of all the dangers and what-ifs. Bad things were not only possible; in her experience, there was a damn good chance they would happen. She had held Scottie's hand as he died, she had identified Kyle's body in a morgue . . . Yes, bad things happened.

"What are you going to do?" the little secretary asked, automatically accepting that Faith would do *something*.

"File a missing person's report," Faith said, because it was the only thing she could think to do. Mr. Pleasant had disappeared as suddenly and thoroughly as Guy Rouillard had; he had been asking questions about Guy. Coincidence? Not likely, but neither did she have any evidence that would warrant a criminal investigation. The best she could do was file a missing person's report. At least that would trigger an investigation of some sort.

She asked directions to police headquarters, and managed to find it with only two wrong turns. A desk sergeant directed her to the proper office, and soon she was seated in a straight-back chair reciting what information she had to a tired detective in a tired suit, who nevertheless managed to seem interested.

"You called the motel where he'd been staying, and he'd checked out?" Detective Ambrose asked, his world-weary eyes warming a bit when he looked at her.

"The clerk didn't actually see Mr. Pleasant. He said the key was left on the nightstand, and Mr. Pleasant's things were gone."

"Had the room been paid for in advance?"

Faith nodded.

"Nothing unusual in that, then. Let's see. No one has seen him since he left Prescott, the mail is piling up at his office, there's no answer at his home, and he has a bum ticker." The detective shook his head. "I'll go by his house and see what I can find, but . . ." He hesitated, sympathy in his expression.

But probably the old guy's heart failed, was what he was thinking. Faith hunched her shoulders in misery. She would hate it if Mr. Pleasant had died, and she hadn't been there to hold his hand or even attend his funeral. She had checked only the current admissions at the hospitals, not whether he'd been a patient any time in the past week. But he'd known about his heart, had been prepared, had even been waiting to join his wife; she would grieve, but there would be a sense of rightness if he'd gone that way. The real nightmare would be if the detective couldn't find him. Then she would fear the worst, and have no way of knowing for certain.

She extracted a business card from her purse and handed it across the desk. "Please call me if you find anything," she said. "I didn't know him very well, but I liked him a lot. He was a sweet old man." To her horror, she realized she was referring to him in the past tense, and flinched.

The detective took the card, and rubbed his fingers along the thin edges. "There's something I'd like to know, Mrs. Hardy. What was he investigating for you?"

She'd known he would ask, and told him the truth. "Twelve years ago, my mother ran away with her lover. I wanted Mr. Pleasant to find them, if he could."

"And did he?"

She shook her head. "He hadn't the last time I talked to him."

"Which was . . . ?"

"I had dinner with him, the night before he left the motel."

"Did anyone see him after that?"

"I don't know." It was easy to see the direction of this line of questioning. At least the detective was taking her seriously.

"Did he seem all right when he left?"

"He seemed fine. I had some unexpected company, and Mr. Pleasant left right after dinner."

"So you weren't the only one to see him?"

She gave him a faint smile. "No."

"Who was your visitor?"

"A neighbor, Gray Rouillard. He came to see about buying my house." It was amazing how far the bare facts could be from what had really happened. She was becoming an expert at exposing the tip while keeping the rest of the iceberg of truth submerged.

"Gray Rouillard," Detective Ambrose repeated, tired

eyes lighting with recognition. "Would that be the same Rouillard who played football for LSU, oh, ten or so years ago?"

"Almost thirteen years," she said. "Yes, he's the same man."

"The Rouillards are big stuff in this part of the state. Well, well. So you're selling your house to him?"

"No. He asked to buy it, but I don't want to sell."

"Are you on good terms with him?"

"Not exactly."

"Oh." He seemed disappointed. Faith stared at him a moment, then her mouth curved in a tiny smile. This was the South, after all. Pro football had made some inroads, but college football still reigned supreme.

"No, I don't have any influence with him to get tickets to the games," she said.

He shrugged, and a responding smile twitched his lips. "It was worth a try." He clicked his pen and rose to his feet, indicating that he had no more questions to ask. "I'll see what I can find out about Mr. Pleasant. Will you be in town awhile longer, or are you going home now?"

"I'm going home. My only reason for driving down was to see if I could find him." Gratefully she stood up from the straight-back chair, and refrained from stretching.

He put his hand on her arm, the touch light. "You know my first check will be of the obituaries," he said gently.

Faith bit her lip, and nodded.

His hand made two brief pats. "I'll let you know."

She cried during most of the drive back to Prescott. She had cried very little in the past twelve years, some tears shed for Kyle and more for Scottie, but the thought of losing Mr. Pleasant made her ache inside. She hadn't had much room for optimism in her life, and she expected the worst.

Detective Ambrose was on the ball. When she checked the answering machine immediately on arriving home, there was a message from him: "I've checked Mr. Pleasant's residence, and there's no sign of him. The mail has piled up there, too, and the neighbors haven't seen him." A pause. "He hasn't been listed in the obits, either. I'll keep checking, and get back to you."

He wasn't there. The thought echoed around and around in her mind. No one had seen him since he'd left Prescott. Assuming he had ever left.

Pure rage began to build, and push aside the grief. Her mother and Guy had created a tangle, twelve years ago, that was still wreaking destruction. Faith had to absolve Renee of any involvement in Mr. Pleasant's disappearance, since her mother hadn't known the man existed, but she was still part and parcel of the root cause.

For Faith, deed followed closely on the heels of thought. Furiously she picked up the telephone and dialed her grandmother's number.

She was thwarted, however, by the endless ringing on the other end. No one was home.

She called four more times before she got an answer, and her grandmother's cracked voice called Renee to the phone.

"Who is it?" she heard Renee ask in the background.

"That girl of yourn, the youngest one."

"I don't want to talk to her. Tell her I'm not here."

Faith's hand tightened on the receiver, and her eyes narrowed. She heard her grandmother fumbling with the phone again. She didn't wait for the parroted excuse. "Tell Mama that if she doesn't talk to me, I'm going to the sheriff." It was a bluff, at least at this point, but a calculated one. Renee's response to it would tell her a lot. If her mother didn't have anything to hide, the bluff wouldn't work. If she did—

There was a pause as the message was relayed, then more fumbling with the telephone. "What on earth are you talkin' about, Faithie? What's the sheriff got to do with anything?" The tone was too bright, too cheerful.

"I'm talking about Guy Rouillard. Mama—"

"Would you quit harping about Guy Rouillard? I told you, I ain't seen him."

Faith suppressed the nausea roiling in her stomach, and made her voice more soothing. "I know, Mama. I believe you. But I think something happened to him that night, after you left." Don't let Mama think she was suspected of anything, or she'd close up tighter than a miser's purse.

"I don't know nothing about that, and if you're as smart

as you think you are, missy, you'll stop pokin' your nose into other folks' business."

"Where did you meet him that night, Mama?" Faith asked, ignoring the motherly advice.

"I don't know why you're so worried about him," Renee said sullenly. "If he'd done what he should, I'd've been taken care of. You kids, too," she added as an afterthought. "But he kept puttin' it off, waiting until Gray was out of school—well, it don't make no difference now."

"Did you go to the motel? Or did you meet him somewhere else?"

Renee drew in a seething breath. "You're like a bulldog when you get something on your mind, did you know that? You always were the most stubborn of my kids, so bound and determined to have your way that you'd do what you wanted, even knowin' your Pa would slap you for it. We met at the summerhouse, where we usually went, if you just have to know! Go nosing around there, and you'll find out in a hurry that Gray ain't nearly as easygoin' as Guy was!"

Faith winced as Renee slammed down the phone, then drew a deep, shaky breath as she replaced her own receiver. Whatever had happened that night, Renee knew about it. Only her own self-interest could stir her to do something she didn't want to do, so she had a reason for not wanting Faith to talk to the sheriff. Getting her to admit it, however, would take some doing.

It had to be the summerhouse, of course, Faith thought with resignation. Why couldn't Guy and Renee have rendezvoused at a motel, in keeping with the American tradition? Faith's memories of the summerhouse were bittersweet, like everything else connected with Gray Rouillard. She didn't want to see it again, for doing so would remind her too vividly of the child she had been, of the long hours she had spent lurking at the edge of the woods, hoping for a glimpse of Gray. She had lain on her belly in the pine needles and contentedly watched him and his friends swimming in the lake, listened to their boisterous shouts of laughter, and woven fancy daydreams of one day joining in their fun. Silly dreams. Silly child.

There, too, she had watched Gray making love to Lindsey

Partain. Her stomach tightened now as she thought of it, and her hands curled with an impotent mixture of anger and jealousy. At the time, she had merely thought how beautiful he was. Now, however, she was a woman, with a woman's needs and desires, and she didn't want even to think of him making love to another woman, much less see it.

That had been fifteen long years ago, but she could still call up his image in her mind as if it had been yesterday. She could hear his deep, smoky voice murmuring French love words and husky reassurances, see his powerful young body moving between Lindsey's spread legs.

Damn him. Why had he kissed her, that day in New Orleans? It was one thing to dream of his kisses, and another to know exactly how he tasted, how soft his lips were, how it felt to be in his arms and feel his erection thrusting insistently against her stomach. It was unfair of him to feed her hunger, and then try to use it against her. But then, everything about Gray was unfair. Why couldn't his hair have thinned over the years, rather than remaining that thick, vibrant mane? Why couldn't he have put on weight, developed a beer belly and worn his pants slung low under it, rather than honing down to such lean muscularity, even more finely tuned than during his football days? And even if he hadn't changed, why couldn't *she* have, altering enough so that he no longer affected her so violently, or her heart would beat normally in his presence?

Instead, in that respect, she was still the adoring girl who had spent hours, weeks, *months* of her childhood lying on her belly in the woods, her eyes straining for a glimpse of her hero. Not even finding out that her hero could be a ruthless bastard when he wanted had been able to shake that painful fixation.

She didn't want to go back to the summerhouse, to the scene of her youthful foolishness. What could she possibly find there, after twelve years? Nothing.

But no one else had looked at it with her eyes. No one had suspected that Guy Rouillard might have spent the last hours of his life there.

Faith growled at herself. She was tired and hungry, after the long drive to New Orleans and back, as well as exhausted by worry over Mr. Pleasant. She didn't want to go to the summerhouse, but she had just given herself a convincing argument on why it was necessary. And if she was going, she should do it now, while the afternoon sun was still strong.

She grabbed her keys and stalked out of the house.

The best way to get there, she supposed, was the way she had gone when she'd been eleven. There was a road from the Rouillard house to the lake, but she could hardly take that route. From her younger days of roaming and spying, however, she knew the Rouillard land as well as she knew her own face. She drove to a secluded spot close to the old shack where she had grown up, but when she reached the last curve before the shack would come into view, she stopped the car and sat for a moment, hands gripping the steering wheel. She couldn't bring herself to drive around the curve. The shack had probably fallen in by now, but that wouldn't ease her memories. She didn't want to see it, didn't want to relive the memories of that night.

Pain was a lump in the middle of her chest, obstructing her breathing, making her eyes burn. She didn't cry. She had cried for Mr. Pleasant, for Scottie, for Kyle. She hadn't cried for herself since the night Renee had left.

Well, delaying wouldn't accomplish anything except putting off dinner, and she was already starving. She got out of the car and locked the doors, and dropped the keys into her skirt pocket. Brush grew thickly along the sides of the road, now little more than a track as the vegetation gradually reclaimed the land. She had to pick her way around some briar bushes, but once into the woods, it was fairly easy to walk. She picked up a stick, in case she came across a snake, but she wasn't at all afraid. She had grown up in these woods, played in them, hidden in them when Amos had been drunk and slinging his fists at anyone who got in his way.

The familiar scents washed over her, fresh and powerful with spring, and she stopped for a moment to absorb them. Her eyes closed so she could concentrate. There was the rich brown scent of the earth, the fresh verdant of leaves, the spicy golden scent of pine sap. She inhaled that last with a little shiver of recognition. Gray's scent contained a hint of that golden spice. She would love to have him naked and at her disposal, so she could explore all the shadings of his scent. She would absolutely wallow on him, drunk with delight—

Her eyes popped open. The telltale warming of her body told her where that particular fantasy had been going. It was coming back here that had done it; in her mind, the smells of the forest were inextricably linked with Gray: the hope of seeing him, the fizzing joy of seeing him.

Resolutely she walked on. If she didn't get him out of her mind, she'd find herself lying on her stomach in the pine needles at the edge of the woods, completely reverted to childhood.

The walk to the lake wasn't a long one, about twenty minutes. The forest had changed, of course; time didn't stand still with trees any more than it did with people. She had to pick her way around obstacles that hadn't been there before, and old landmarks were missing, but still she knew her way with the accuracy of a homing pigeon.

She approached the summerhouse from the angle she always had, from the back and right side. From there she could see the dock, and a corner of the boathouse. Once she had prayed to see a Corvette parked in front, but now she was just as glad not to see a Jaguar there. It would have been too ironic for Gray to appear. Thank God he had business concerns now, and didn't have the luxury of spending long, lazy days swimming and fishing.

Time had laid its hand on the summerhouse, too. It wasn't dilapidated, Gray had kept it up, but an air of disuse had fallen over it. Things that had regular human use wore a certain sheen of accomplishment, a sheen that the summerhouse no longer possessed. There was a subtle reverse of order. Before, the grass had always been neatly manicured, and though the yard wasn't overgrown with weeds now, it still showed a certain roughness that said it had been over a week since the grass had been cut. On the other hand, the summerhouse had always been littered with the flotsam of human habitation, and now it was *too* neat, without the activity that had kept it cluttered and alive.

She went up the back steps, the same steps where she had crouched to listen to Gray making love to Lindsey Partain. The screen door to the porch wasn't latched, and creaked a little as she opened it. The sound made her smile, so woven was it into the days of her childhood.

For all the difficulties, she hadn't had a horrible childhood. Much of it had been downright enjoyable, rich with fantasy, especially the long hours spent exploring the woods. She had waded in creeks, caught crawdads with her bare hands, marveled at the delicate tracery of a leaf held up to the sun. She had never had a bicycle, but she'd had fresh air and blue skies, the anticipation of turning over a rotting log to see how many insects and worms it hid. She had eaten wild berries straight off the bush, found the occasional arrowhead, and painstakingly constructed her own bow and arrow from a green limb, old fishing line, and sharpened sticks. The joys of all those things had created a reserve of strength for her to draw on when times were bad.

The boards of the porch creaked beneath her feet as she crossed to the back door. In the old days, there had been several rocking chairs scattered about the porch, for the enjoyment of fine summer nights. All swimming and fishing paraphernalia was supposed to have been kept in the boathouse, but somehow bits of it had always been lying about on the porch: an inner tube that needed patching, a fishing rod, an assortment of lures, hooks, and floats. Now, however, the porch was empty, no longer a place for rowdy teenagers and rendezvousing adults.

She walked to the window where she had watched Gray and Lindsey making love; the room was empty now, the hardwood floors bare and coated with a light layer of dust. She stood for a moment, remembering that long-ago summer day, gilded with the magic of childhood.

Turning away, she tried the back door, and was surprised when the knob twisted easily in her hand. She had never been inside the summerhouse. The closest she had ever been was on the porch, that one time. She stepped into the kitchen, looking around with interest. Once there had been a refrigerator and stove, for empty spaces and the electrical connections marked where they had stood. She opened the cabinet doors and drawers, but they were all empty. Each sound echoed through the bare rooms.

Everything was clean enough, without the smell of mice, though it had obviously been a couple of weeks since the last cleaning. As she wandered into the other rooms, she saw that none of the light fixtures sported so much as a single light bulb. There was a small closet in each of the two bedrooms, and she looked in both of them. Nothing, not even a single clothes hanger. The summerhouse was completely empty.

Which one of the bedrooms had Renee and Guy used? It didn't matter; there was nothing to be found here, no interesting nooks or crannies where a body could have been hidden. There was absolutely nothing suspicious about the house. Any evidence had long since been swept away, mopped up, or painted over. She wondered that there wasn't any sign of vagrants, considering the house was unlocked, but since it was in the middle of Rouillard land, she supposed there weren't many passersby.

There was still the boathouse to check, though she didn't really expect to find anything. She had come only to satisfy herself that she had done everything possible to find out what had happened to Guy, and Mr. Pleasant. Leaving by the front door, she walked down to the dock. Both the dock and boathouse were set at an angle to the house, slightly to the left, positioned on the curve of a small slough. Since she had been here last, twelve years ago, vegetation had been allowed to grow over the banks. Young willow trees, growing in clumps along the lake's edge, had matured to provide much more shade and cover than she remembered. Once there had been an almost unobstructed view of the lake, except for the boathouse, but now saplings and bushes had taken advantage of the subtle neglect to sink their roots into the rich soil.

The dock had been kept in good repair, though, and she walked out to the end. It was a calm day, with an almost imperceptible breeze making faint ripples in the water, which lapped against the dock pilings with wet, rhythmic slaps. It was one of those hot, lazy days that made her want to lie on her back on the dock, and stare up at the fat white clouds floating across a deep blue sky. Birds were calling in the trees, and somewhere a fish jumped, a quiet splash that didn't disturb the peace. Over to the left, a red and white float bobbed happily on the little ripples—

She stiffened, her eyes widening with dread as she slowly turned. A fishing float meant someone was fishing, someone who had been hidden from her view by the angle of the boathouse. Like a felon approaching the gallows, her gaze followed the fishing line as it arced gracefully up from the float, across the water, to where it was threaded through the eyes of a fishing rod. A fishing rod that was held by Gray Rouillard, standing shirtless on the bank on the other side of the boathouse, watching her with narrowed dark eyes.

For an instant they stared at each other across the small expanse of water. Faith's thoughts darted about in panic, trying to think of a good reason for her presence, but her normally nimble mind was blank with shock. She had thought herself totally alone, and then to turn and see Gray, of all people—a shirtless Gray, at that. It wasn't fair. She needed all her wits about her when dealing with him; she couldn't afford to be distracted by that bare expanse of chest, and his long hair hanging loose to his shoulders.

He began reeling in the float with quick, deliberate movements. Choosing caution over valor, Faith bolted up the dock, her feet thudding on the planks. He threw down the fishing rod and sprinted around the boathouse. Panting, she reached for more speed; if she could just get to the edge of the woods ahead of him, he wouldn't be able to catch her. She was smaller, slimmer, and would be able to dodge between trees he would have to go around. But as fast as she was, he still had the speed of a linebacker. She saw him out of the corner of her eye, too close, and gaining ground with each long stride. He beat her by a split second, his big body suddenly blocking her way off the dock. She tried to stop, but she was already on him, and her shoes weren't made for traction. She slammed into his chest, the impact knocking her breath out with a *whoof!* He grunted and staggered back a few steps, his arms coming up just in time to catch her against his chest and prevent her from falling on her face.

He caught his balance, and gave a muffled laugh as his arms tightened around her, holding her off the ground. "That's a pretty good hit, for a lightweight. Nice speed, too. Where're you going in such a hurry, Red? And what the hell are you doing here in the first place?"

She fought for her breath, sucking in desperate drafts to fill her aching lungs. God, he was as hard as a rock! She had probably bruised herself, barreling into him that way. After a short while she managed to say, "Reminiscing," and pushed against his bare shoulders in a hint that he should set her on her feet.

He snorted, and ignored the hint. "You're trespassing. You'll have to think of a better reason than that."

"Nosy," she offered breathlessly, still finding oxygen in somewhat short supply. The tightness of his arms was interfering with her efforts to take deep breaths. She squirmed against him, then immediately stopped. The friction of his bare skin against her was too distracting, too dangerous.

"That I can believe," he muttered. "What are you up to now?" He decided to let her down, loosening his grip so that she slid against his body. Faith's cheeks flushed as she stepped away from him, and the color wasn't just from the deep breaths she was taking. He was wearing only a pair of glove-soft jeans and scuffed boots, and she stared in helpless fascination at his naked torso. His shoulders were a good two feet wide, and heavy with muscle, a powerful layering that continued in plates across his chest. Curly black hair grew there, almost completely hiding his tiny, flat nipples, and arrowing down the middle of his abdomen to where it grew straight and downy around his shallow navel, which was exposed by sinfully low-riding jeans. A light sheen of sweat gleamed on his skin, making him glisten like a warm-toned statue with carved muscle and sinew.

"How did you get here?" she blurted, not answering his question. "I didn't see a car."

"Horseback." He jerked his head toward the field on the other side of the slough. "He's over there, eating his head off."

"Maximillian?" she asked, remembering the name of the prize stallion Guy had owned.

"One of his sons." Gray frowned down at her. "How do you know about Maximillian? And how did *you* get here?"

"I imagine most of the people in the parish know you have horses." As she spoke, she edged sideways.

He reached out and clamped one hand on her arm. "Hold it. Yeah, a lot of people know we have horses, but not many would know the name of our breeding stallion. You've been asking questions about us again, haven't you?" His hand tightened. "Who have you been talking to now? Tell me, damn it!" He emphasized the demand with a slight shake.

"No one," she flared. "I remembered the name from before."

"How would you have known it back then? Renee didn't balk at much, but I doubt she went home and regaled her family with details of her lover's life."

Faith closed her lips tightly together. She had known the stallion's name because she had been like a sponge, absorbing every little snippet of conversation she overhead, if it pertained to Gray. She wasn't about to admit such a thing to him, though. "I remembered it from before," she finally repeated.

He didn't believe her, and his face darkened.

"I haven't been talking to anyone!" she cried, trying to tug away from him. "I remembered the horse's name, that's all." Why did every encounter with him seem to involve playing tug-of-war with one or both of her arms?

He surveyed her upturned face with narrowed eyes. "All right, I'll give you that one. Now tell me why you're poking around my summerhouse, and how you got here. I know damn good and well *you* don't have a horse."

That, at least, seemed safe enough to tell him. "I walked," she said. "Through the woods."

Pointedly he looked down at her feet. "You're not dressed for hiking through the woods."

That was true enough. She hadn't taken the time to change clothes, so she was still wearing the midcalf skirt, hosiery, and dress flats that she'd worn to New Orleans. She had grown up roaming barefoot through those woods, so she certainly hadn't worried about wearing flats. Shrugging to show her indifference, she said, "I didn't think about it." Quickly she added, "I'm sorry I trespassed. I'll leave—"

"Whoa." He drew her to a standstill again. "You'll leave when I say you can leave, and not before. I'm still waiting for an answer to my other question."

Thankfully her brain was working again. "I was just curious," she said. "They used to meet here, so . . . I wanted to see it." There was no need to elaborate on who "they" were.

To her dismay, his eyes grew cold. "Don't give me that. You've been here before, because I've seen you."

Shocked, she stared at him. "When?"

"When you were a kid. You slipped around through the woods like a little ghost, but you forgot to cover your head." He tugged on a strand of hair, then smoothed it behind her ear. "It was like watching a flame bob through the trees."

He had known she was there. For an appalled, heart-stopping moment she wondered if he had guessed he was the attraction that had drawn her like a moth. Bitterly she remembered all her childish fantasies, that one day he would look up and see her, and ask her to join their fun. He'd seen her, all right, but no invitation had been issued. The surprise would have been if he *had* asked her to join them. The eight-year age difference between twenty-six and thirty-four was almost nonexistent, but an enormous gulf between eleven and nineteen. Even if she hadn't been too young, she was a Devlin, forever locked outside his circle.

"I'm going to ask you one more time," he said softly, when she remained silent. A chill ran down her spine at the steel in his tone. "What are you doing here?"

"I told you." She lifted her chin and met his gaze. "Nosing around."

"The next question is: Why? You've been doing a lot of nosing around since you moved back here. What are you up to, Faith? I warned you about stirring up old gossip and upsetting my family, and I meant every word of it."

She had already given him the only answer she could, and he hadn't believed it. She could tell him the entire truth, or

212

she could lie. In the end, she chose to do neither, but stood silently in his grasp.

His jaw flexed with anger, and his hand tightened on her arm. Faith winced, and his gaze dropped to the livid marks where his fingers bit into her soft skin. He cursed and relaxed his grip, and like a shot she tore away from him, sprinting for the safety of the woods. Within two steps she knew it was a mistake, but emotion rather than logic had the upper hand. He reacted like the predator he was, springing after her. She was barely halfway across the grass when the impact of his heavy body knocked her off her feet, a tiger bringing down a gazelle. He fell with her, holding her tight against his chest and twisting his body so that he took the brunt of the fall, with her on top of him. Her vision was filled with a confusing tumble of grass, trees, and sky as he rolled, deftly placing her beneath him.

Oh, God. The surge of primal recognition shocked her body into stillness, as if she didn't dare move in that first shattering moment of delight. Being in his arms was one thing; lying sprawled beneath him was quite another. His considerable weight pressed her into the grass, releasing the sweet green fragrance of the crushed blades to mingle with the heady masculine scent of his sweaty skin. The fall had rucked her skirt up to midthigh, and one of his legs rode high between hers, so that her thighs clasped the muscular column. Instinctively she had clung to him as they were falling, and now her fingers were digging hard into his bare back, feeling the slick heat of his flesh. Their position was that of lovemaking, and her body responded with mindless intensity. Her senses blurred, overloaded in that first explosion of sexual signals.

"Are you all right?" he muttered, raising his head.

Faith swallowed, words sticking in her throat. Her insides were clenching, urging her to lift against him in blind, searing need. She resisted the urge, turning her head to the side so she couldn't see if it was mirrored in his dark eyes.

"Faith?" His tone was more insistent, demanding an answer.

"Yes," she whispered.

"Look at me." He lifted himself to his elbows, removing

213

most of his weight so that she breathed easier, but he was still far too close, his face mere inches from hers.

Temptation shimmered between them, made all the more potent by the times she had resisted it. It took so little to bring desire into full flame, a kiss, a touch, like a spark to dry straw. Each time it was more difficult to resist him, and only the strength of her aversion to casual sex, to being a moral replica of her mother, had enabled her to hold him at bay. But each contact with him eroded her willpower, wearing it down bit by bit so that each refusal took more effort.

His breath wafted over her lips, the subtle touch making them part as if she would inhale his essence. His head lowered, his mouth moving toward hers.

Desperately she wedged her arms between them, bracing her hands against his chest. The curls of hair tickled her palms, and she felt the hard nubs of his nipples against the heels of her hands. Hidden beneath blouse and bra, her own nipples had peaked.

He paused, hovering over her. A trickle of sweat ran down his temple and curved along his jaw. His nipples felt like tiny spikes, burning into her hands. She wanted to touch them, to put her mouth over them and feel them with her tongue, taste the saltiness of his skin, feel him stiffen and shudder from excitement.

Temptation gnawed at her, sharp and insistent. He inhaled, his chest expanding beneath her palms, and the sand castle of her resistance crumbled beneath the wave of pleasure. Letting out her breath on a soft sigh, she turned her hands, moving them so that her thumbs brushed over his nipples, once, twice, again. The delight of it made her feel dizzy.

His pupils dilated, the black centers flaring until they all but eclipsed the dark irises. His head fell forward between his arms, his long black hair curtaining their faces, and his breath hissed between his teeth. Having given in, she couldn't make herself stop touching him. She explored the hard planes of his chest, returning time and again to the hard little peaks that had lured her so far into dangerous territory. She couldn't touch him enough, couldn't sate her hunger for the feel of him.

Then he drew her hands away from his body, and his eyes were fierce as he looked down at her. "Turnabout's fair play," he said, and put his hand on her breast.

She arched beneath him, crying out at the hot lash of pleasure. Her breasts strained into his touch, so taut and sensitive that the hot weight of his hand was almost unbearable, and yet the cessation of contact would be torture. Even through her clothes, the rasp of his thumbs made her nipples burn and throb.

He lowered his head and kissed her, the pressure hard and ravaging, while he tugged her blouse loose from the waistband of her skirt. When it was free, he thrust his hand beneath the cloth, burrowing under her bra to close his fingers on the satiny mound of her bare breast. "You know what I want," he said roughly, moving more fully onto her and pushing his muscular legs between hers to make a place for himself.

She knew. She wanted it too, so fiercely that the need almost obliterated all other considerations. His callused fingers plucked at her nipple, rolling it between finger and thumb. She wanted his mouth there, sucking strongly. She wanted him to take her, here on the grass with the hot sun burning down on their bare bodies. She wanted *him,* forever.

"Tell me," he said. "Tell me why." The words were muffled against her throat as he trailed kisses down to her collarbone.

She blinked, staring up at the clouds in confusion. Then the meaning of the words washed over her like a dash of ice water. He wanted her—the thick ridge of proof pushed against her loins—but while she had been lost in the fog of desire, his brain had been clear, still working, still trying to get answers.

With a hiss of rage she erupted, shoving against him, kicking. He rolled off of her and sat up, looking like a half-naked savage with his hair tangled around his face and his dark eyes narrowed with dangerous lust.

"You bastard!" she spat, so angry she was quivering. She surged to her knees, hands clenched into fists as she fought the urge to hurl herself at him. Now wasn't the time to challenge him physically, not with his entire big body taut with the need to mate. Control, his and hers, was stretched to a hairsbreadth; the least pressure would snap it. He waited, poised to meet her attack, and she saw the sexual anticipation hot in his eyes. For a long moment they faced each other, until gradually she forced herself to relax. There was nothing to be gained in this confrontation.

There was nothing to be said, either. Perhaps she hadn't exactly started the fire, but she had certainly fanned the flames by caressing his nipples the way she had. If things had gone beyond what she wanted, she had only herself to blame.

At last she got to her feet, moving stiffly. Her skirt was torn, her panty hose shredded down one leg. She turned away, only to find herself caught again, this time by a handful of skirt. "I'll take you back," he said. "Let me get the horse."

"Thank you, but I'd rather walk," she replied, the words as stiff as her body.

"I didn't ask what you wanted. I said I'll take you back. You shouldn't be wandering around in the woods by yourself." Not trusting her to remain there if he released her, he began dragging her along in his wake.

"I wandered around them by myself for over half my life," she growled.

"Maybe so, but you aren't doing it now." He slanted a brief, hard glance her way. "It's my land, and I make the rules."

He kept his fist twisted in her skirt, so she was obliged to keep step with him or have her clothes torn off. They walked past the boathouse and around the slough, a distance of about a hundred yards, to where Gray had hobbled the stallion so he could graze. At his whistle, the big, dark brown animal began moving toward him. To her dismay, there was no saddle anywhere in evidence.

"You rode him bareback?" she asked uneasily.

His dark eyes glinted. "I won't let you fall."

She didn't know a lot about horses, having never been on one, but she did know that stallions were fractious animals, difficult to control. She tried to back away as the horse ambled closer, but Gray's grip on her skirt kept her at his side.

"Don't be afraid. He's the sweetest-tempered stallion I've ever seen, or I wouldn't be riding him without a saddle." The horse came within reach and he caught the halter, crooning praise into the pricked ears.

"I've never been on a horse," she admitted, staring up at the big head as it lowered. Velvety lips whuffled at her arm, scooped-out nostrils flaring as he caught her scent. Hesitantly she put out her hand and stroked above his nose.

"Then your first ride will be on a Thoroughbred," Gray said, and lifted her onto the broad back. She clutched at the thick mane, alarmed by the height at which she found herself, while the living platform beneath her moved restlessly.

Gray gathered the reins, then caught two handfuls of mane and swung up behind her. The stallion skittered beneath the extra weight, making Faith catch her breath, but Gray's touch, and the sound of his voice, soothed him immediately.

"Where did you leave your car?" he asked.

"On the last curve before you get to the shack," she replied, and those were the only words spoken during the ride. Gray guided the horse through the trees, avoiding low-hanging limbs, walking him around obstacles. Faith held on, acutely aware of Gray's bare chest against her back, and of the way her buttocks were nestled against his crotch. His muscular thighs hugged her hips, and she felt them clenching and relaxing as he guided the horse. They reached the road far too quickly, but in another sense the journey had taken a small eternity.

He reined in beside her car and swung to the ground, then reached up to catch her under the arms and lift her down. Suddenly alarmed that she might have lost her keys in the scuffle, she patted her skirt pocket, and heard the reassuring rattle. She didn't want to look at him, so she took out the keys and turned to unlock the car.

"Faith."

She hesitated, then turned the key in the lock and opened the door. He stepped forward, and the expression in his eyes made her grateful for the car door between them.

"Stay off my property," he said evenly. "If I catch you on Rouillard land again, I'm going to give you the fucking you've been asking for."

~ Fourteen ~

The next day, Faith found the note inside her car, lying on the driver's seat. She saw the folded piece of paper and picked it up, wondering what she had dropped. She unfolded it, and saw the block letters:

DON'T ASK ANY MORE QUESTIONS ABOUT GUY ROUILLARD SHUT UP IF YOU KNOW WHAT'S GOOD FOR YOU

She leaned against the car, a light breeze fluttering the paper in her hands. She didn't lock her car at home, so she didn't have to wonder how the note had gotten in there. She stared at the paper, reading it again and wondering if she had been threatened, or if the writer had simply used a familiar phrase. *Shut up if you know what's good for you.* She had heard variations of it a hundred times, with only the command changing. The note might or might not be a threat; likely it was more of a warning. Someone didn't like her asking questions about Guy.

Gray hadn't left the note. It wasn't his style, for one thing; he had delivered his threats in person, and spelled them out. The last one still had her rattled. Who else would have been disturbed by her questions? There were two possibilities: someone with something to hide, or someone who thought to curry Gray's favor.

She had been on her way to town for yet another fact-finding mission, this time to try having a word with Yolanda Foster, so there was a certain irony to the timing of the note's appearance. After a moment's consideration, she decided that she was still going to try. If the writer wanted her to take the threat seriously, he or she would have to be more specific.

First, though, she carried the note inside and locked it in the desk, being careful not to handle the paper more than necessary. In itself, this wasn't something that warranted calling the sheriff, but if she received another, she wanted to be able to present both of them to him for evidence. She wasn't eager to see the sheriff in any case. She had a stark memory of him standing beside his patrol car, beefy arms folded as he approvingly watched his deputies empty the shack of the Devlins' belongings. Sheriff Deese was thoroughly in Gray's hip pocket; the question was whether or not he would do anything even if she received a death threat.

The note properly stored, she drove to town. Lying in bed last night, unable to sleep, she had planned her strategy. She wouldn't call Mrs. Foster; that would give her a chance to refuse a meeting. It would be best to take her by surprise, face-to-face, and slip in a few questions before Yolanda got over being startled. She didn't know where the Fosters lived, however, and the address in the phone book had been unfamiliar to her.

Her first stop was the library. To her disappointment, the chatty Carlene DuBois wasn't behind the desk; instead it was manned—or girled—by a frothy little blonde who barely looked old enough to be out of high school. She was chewing gum as she leafed through a rock music fanzine. What had happened to the stereotypical librarian with her hair pulled back in a bun and reading glasses perched on a thin nose? The gum-chewing rock fan wasn't an improvement.

Realistically, Faith knew, she herself was probably no more than four or five years older than the little librarian. Mentally and emotionally, however, she wasn't even in the same generation. She had never been young in the way this girl still was, and she didn't think it was a bad thing. She'd had responsibilities from an early age; she could remember cooking when the iron frying pan had been too heavy for her to lift, and she'd had to stand on a chair to stir a pot of beans. She had swept with a broom that was almost twice as tall as herself. Then she'd had Scottie to care for, the greatest responsibility of all. But when she had finished high school, she'd been prepared for life, unlike kids who had never taken care of anything and had no idea how to cope. Those "kids" were still running back to their parents for help when they were twenty-five.

The girl looked up from her magazine to pull her bubble-gum pink lips into what passed for a professional smile. Her eyes were so heavily lined with black that they looked like almonds in a pit of coal dust. "May I help you?"

The tone was competent, Faith thought with relief. Maybe the girl was just stuck in makeup limbo. "Do you have maps of both the town and parish?"

"Sure." She led Faith to a table on which a large globe stood. "Here are all the maps and atlases. They're updated yearly, so if it's an older map you need, you'll have to go to the archives."

"No, I need a current map."

"Here you go, then." The girl pulled out an enormous book, easily three by two feet, but she handled it easily as she placed it on the table. "We have to seal the maps in plastic and put them in the book," she explained. "If we don't, they get stolen."

Faith smiled as the girl left her. The solution made sense to her. It was one thing to fold a map and put it in your pocket; spiriting out a huge, plastic-encased sheet would take some ingenuity.

She didn't know if the Fosters lived in town or out in the parish, but she looked first in the town map, running her finger down the list of streets printed on the back. Bingo. Noting the coordinates, she flipped the page and quickly located Meadowlark Drive, in a subdivision that hadn't existed when she had lived here before. With a name like Meadowlark Drive, she should have known. Land developers were an unimaginative bunch. After memorizing how to get there, she replaced the map book and left. The librarian was engrossed in her magazine again, and didn't look up as Faith passed the desk.

Prescott being the size it was, finding Meadowlark Drive took less than five minutes. The subdivision included acreage, rather than just lots, so the houses were fewer and farther apart than normal. There probably weren't many people in Prescott who could afford to build there, either, as the houses looked to be in the two-hundred-thousand range. In the Northeast and along the West Coast, they would have been worth a cool million, easy.

The Foster house was designed to look like a Mediterranean villa, nestled comfortably amid huge oaks draped with Spanish moss. Faith parked in the driveway and walked up the brown brick pathway to the double front doors. The button for the door bell was disguised amid some scrolls, then discreetly lit so people could find it. She pressed it, and heard the chimes echo through the house.

After a moment there was the rapid tapping of heels on a tiled floor, and the right half of the door was pulled open to reveal a very pretty middle-aged woman, stylishly clad in slim taupe pants and a white tunic. Her short, ash brown hair was a tumble of curls, swept to one side, and she wore gold hoop earrings. Startled recognition flashed in the dark blue eyes.

"Hello, I'm Faith Hardy," Faith said, hurrying to correct the woman's horrified assumption that she was Renee. "Are you Mrs. Foster?"

Yolanda Foster nodded, evidently struck speechless. She continued to stare.

"I'd like to talk to you, if it's convenient." To tilt the answer in her favor, Faith took a step forward. Yolanda fell back, in an involuntary gesture of admittance.

"I really don't have much time," Yolanda said, her tone apologetic rather than impatient. "I'm having lunch with a friend."

That was believable, unless Yolanda always dressed at home as if she were the nineties version of June Cleaver. "Ten minutes," Faith promised.

Looking puzzled, Yolanda led her into a spacious living room, and they sat down. "I don't mean to stare, but you *are*

Renee Devlin's daughter, aren't you? I heard you were in town, and the resemblance—well, I'm sure you've been told it's startling."

Unlike a lot of people, there was no censure in Yolanda's tone, and Faith found herself unexpectedly liking the woman. "Several people have mentioned it," she said dryly, earning a chuckle from her hostess that made her like her even more. Liking her, however, didn't deflect Faith from her course. "I want to ask you some questions about Guy Rouillard, if I may."

The blusher-pinkened cheeks paled a bit. "About *Guy?*" Her hands fluttered a bit, then she clasped them in her lap. "Why ask me?"

Faith paused. "Are you alone?" she finally asked, not wanting to cause the woman any trouble if someone should overhear their conversation.

"Why, yes. Lowell is in New York this week."

That was fortuitous in one way, and not in another, because depending on her conversation with Yolanda, she might want to talk to Lowell, too. She took a deep breath and went right to the heart of the matter. "Were you having an affair with Guy that summer before he left?"

The blue eyes darkened with distress, and the cheeks paled even more. Yolanda stared at her, the seconds ticking away in silence. Faith waited for a denial, but instead Yolanda gave a curiously gentle sigh. "How did you find out?"

"I asked questions." She didn't say that it had evidently been common knowledge, for Ed Morgan to know about it. If Yolanda wanted to think she had been discreet, let her have that dubious comfort.

"That was the only time I was ever unfaithful to Lowell." The older woman looked away, and her fingers plucked nervously at her slacks.

"I'm sure it was," Faith said, because Yolanda seemed to need to be believed. "From what I've heard about Guy Rouillard, he was an expert at seduction."

An unwilling, rueful little smile touched Yolanda's lips. "He was, but I can't blame it on him. I was determined to sleep with him before I ever approached him." Her fingers continued their nervous little movements, now smoothing the upholstered arm of the chair. "I found out Lowell was carrying on with his secretary, and had been for years. I pitched a fit, let me tell you. I threatened him with all sorts of things if he didn't stop, immediately, and divorce was the only one of them that wasn't physically damaging. He begged me not to leave him, swore that she didn't mean anything to him, it was just the sex, and he'd never do it again—you know, that kind of bull. But I caught him, not three weeks later. It's so silly, the little things that give them away. When he undressed one night, his shorts were on wrong side out, the label visible in the back. The only way he could have gotten them turned wrong would be if he'd had them off."

She shook her head, as if she couldn't understand why he hadn't been more careful. The words were spilling out of her now, as if she had held them inside for twelve years. "I didn't say anything to him. But the next day I called Guy and asked him to meet me at the summerhouse on their lake. Lowell and I, and some other friends, had been there for barbecues and picnics, so I knew the place."

The summerhouse again! Faith thought wryly. Between father and son, the sheets in those two bedrooms must have stayed hot. "Why did you pick Guy?" she asked.

Yolanda gave her a surprised look. "Well, I'd hardly have picked anyone repulsive, would I?" she asked reasonably. "If I was going to have an affair, I at least wanted it to be with someone who knew what he was doing, and from Guy's reputation, I thought he likely filled the bill. Then, too, Guy was safe. I intended to tell Lowell what I'd done, because what good is revenge if no one knows about it, and Guy was powerful enough that Lowell couldn't do anything to him, if Lowell found out his identity. I intended to keep *that* secret, at least.

"So I met Guy at the summerhouse, and told him what I wanted. He was very sweet, very reasonable. He tried to talk me out of it, if you can imagine! Talk about a wound to the ego!" Yolanda smiled, her eyes misty with memory as they met Faith's. "Here was a man who tomcatted all over the state, and he turned me down. I had always considered myself attractive, but evidently he didn't. I almost cried. I did tear up a little bit, and Guy was frantic. He was so sweet, a real woman's man. Tears turned him to mush. He started patting my shoulder, explaining that he really thought I was pretty and he'd love to take me to bed, but I had asked for all the wrong reasons, and Lowell was his friend—he went on and on."

"But you finally convinced him?"

"What I said was, 'If it isn't you, it'll be someone else.' He just looked at me with those dark eyes that made you feel like you could drown in them, and I could tell he was wondering who I would pick next. He was *worried* about me, thinking I'd be down at Jimmy Jo's, looking that crowd over for candidates. Then he took my hand, put it on his crotch, and he was ready. He said, 'I'm it,' and took me to the bedroom." She shivered a little, her gaze unfocused as she looked back in time. She fell silent, and Faith waited patiently for her to sort through her memories.

"Can you imagine," Yolanda finally said, her voice soft, "what it's like to be married for twenty years, to love your husband and be perfectly satisfied in bed—and then find out that you had no idea what passion could be? Guy was . . . God, I can't tell you what Guy was like as a lover. He made me scream, he made me feel and do things I didn't—I only meant it to be that one time. But we stayed there the whole afternoon, making love.

"I didn't tell Lowell. Telling him would have ended my revenge, and I couldn't do it, I couldn't stop seeing Guy. We met at least once a week, if I could manage it. Then he left." She glanced at Faith, as if gauging the effect of her next sentence. "With your mother. When I heard, I cried for a week. And then I told Lowell.

"He was furious, of course. He ranted and raved, and threatened to divorce me. I sat there and watched him, not arguing or anything, and that made him even madder. Then I said, 'You should always make sure your shorts are right side out before you put them back on,' and he stopped dead, staring at me with his mouth open. He knew that I'd caught him again. I got up and left the room. He followed me about half an hour later, and he was crying. We made up," she said, briskly now. "And as far as I know, he's never been unfaithful again."

"Did you ever hear from Guy?"

Slowly Yolanda shook her head. "I hoped, at first, but . . . no, he never wrote, or called." Her lips trembled, and she looked at Faith with anguish stark on her face. "My God," she whispered, "I loved him so."

Another dead end, Faith thought as she drove home. According to Yolanda, her husband hadn't known about her affair with Guy until after Guy had already disappeared, which put Lowell in the clear. Yolanda had been too open, too oblivious to even the possibility that Guy had been killed, or that there was the slightest reason why she shouldn't unburden herself to Faith. Instead she had wound up clinging to Faith's hands while she wept for a man whom she hadn't seen in twelve years, but with whom she had shared a summer of passion.

She had finally recovered her poise, flustered and embarrassed. "My goodness, look at the time—I'm going to be late. I can't imagine—I mean, you're a *stranger*—crying all over you this way, carrying on—oh, my." This last as she fully realized just what she had been saying to this stranger. She had stared at Faith with horrified dismay.

Feeling compelled to comfort Yolanda, Faith had touched her shoulder and said, "You needed to talk about it. I understand, and I swear I'll keep your confidence."

After a few strained seconds, Yolanda had relaxed. "I believe you. I don't know why, but I do."

So now Faith was left with no suspects or leads, not that she'd had anything concrete to begin with. All she had was questions, and her questions were annoying someone. The proof of that was in the note she'd found that morning. Whether the note was indicative of a guilty conscience, she didn't know.

Nor did she know what else to do, except keep asking questions. Sooner or later, someone would be stung to respond.

If she could keep busy enough, maybe she wouldn't think about Gray.

The theory was proving difficult to put into practice. She had avoided thinking about him, purposefully pushing him from her mind after she had left him the afternoon before. She had ignored the unfulfilled ache in her body, and refused to think about what had almost happened between them. But for all her will, her subconscious had betrayed her, admitting him into her dreams so that she had awakened in the early morning to find herself reaching for him. The dream had been so vivid that she had cried out, in longing and disappointment.

She had no more resistance to him; she might as well admit it. If he hadn't said what he had, she'd have given in to him there on the grass. Her morals and standards were useless when he took her in his arms, paper tigers that were vanquished by his first kiss.

As she eliminated each person from her list of suspects, the tower of motive leaned more and more toward Gray. Logically, she could see it. Emotionally, the idea met with total rejection. Not Gray. *Not Gray!* She couldn't believe it; she wouldn't believe it. The man she knew was capable of going to extraordinary lengths to protect those he loved, but cold-blooded murder wasn't one of them.

Her mother knew who the killer was. Faith was as certain of that as she'd ever been of anything. Getting Renee to admit it, however, would take some doing, for that would mean trouble for herself. Renee wasn't likely to act against her own self-interest, certainly not for such an abstract notion as justice. Faith knew her mother well; if she pushed too hard, Renee would run, partly from fear, but the biggest reason would be to avoid trouble for herself. After wringing the information about the summerhouse from her, Faith knew she would have to wait awhile before calling again.

The box was delivered the next day.

She returned home from a grocery-shopping expedition to the neighboring parish, and after carrying the groceries in and putting them away, went out to the mailbox to collect the day's mail. When she opened the lid of the oversized box, there was the usual assortment of bills, magazines, and sales papers lying there, with a box deposited on top of them. Curiously she picked it up; she hadn't ordered anything, but the weight of the box was intriguing. The flaps had been sealed with shipping tape, and her name and address were scrawled across the top.

She carried everything in and placed it on the kitchen table. Taking a knife from the cabinet drawer, she slit the tape down the seam of the flap and opened the two halves, then parted the froth of tissue paper that had been used for packing.

After one horrified glance, she turned and vomited into the sink.

The cat wasn't just dead, it had been mutilated. It was wrapped in plastic, probably to keep the smell from alerting anyone before the box was opened.

Faith didn't think, she reacted instinctively. When the violent retching had stopped, she reached out blindly for the telephone.

She closed her eyes as the deep, smoky voice spoke in her ear, and she held on to the receiver as if it were a lifeline. "G-Gray," she stammered, then fell silent as her mind went blank. What could she say to him? *Help, I'm scared, and I need you?* She had no claim on him. Their relationship was a volatile mixture of enmity and desire, and any weakness on her part would only give him another weapon. But she was both sickened and abruptly terrified, and he was the only person she could think of to call for help.

"Faith?" Something of her terror must have been evident in the one word she'd spoken, because his voice became very calm. "What is it?"

Turning her back on the obscenity on the table, she fought to regain control of her voice, but still it emerged as only a whisper. "There's a . . . cat here," she managed to say.

"A cat? Are you afraid of cats?"

She shook her head, then realized he couldn't see her over the phone. Her silence must have made him think the answer was yes, though, because he said soothingly, "Just throw something at it; it'll scat."

She shook her head again, more violently this time. "No." She took a deep breath. "Help."

"All right." Evidently deciding she was too terrified of cats to deal with it on her own, he assumed a brisk and reassuring tone. "I'll be right there. Just sit someplace where you can't see it, and I'll take care of it when I get there."

He hung up, and Faith took his advice. She couldn't bear to be in the house with the thing, so she went outside on the porch and sat motionless in the swing, waiting numbly for him to arrive.

He was there in less than fifteen minutes, but those fifteen minutes seemed like an eternity. His tall form unfolded from the Jaguar, and he strolled up to the porch with his graceful, loose-hipped gait and a faint smile of masculine condescension on his lips, the hero arrived to save the helpless little woman from the ferocious beast. Faith didn't take umbrage; he could think what he liked, if he would just get rid of that thing in her kitchen. She stared up at him, her face so bloodless that his smile faded.

"You're really frightened, aren't you?" he asked gently, hunkering down in front of her and taking one of her hands in his. Her fingers were icy, despite the steamy heat of the day. "Where is it?"

"In the kitchen," she said, through stiff lips. "On the table."

With a comforting pat to her hand, he stood and opened the screen door. Faith listened to his footsteps moving through the living room and into the kitchen.

"Goddamn fucking son of a bitch!" She heard the vicious curse, followed by a string of others. Then the back door slammed. She put her hands over her face. Oh, God, she should have warned him, she shouldn't have given him the same shock she had received, but she simply hadn't been able to say the right words.

A few minutes later he came around to the front of the house, and remounted the steps to the porch. His jaw was set, and his dark eyes were colder than she had ever seen them before, but this time his rage wasn't turned on her.

"It's all right," he said, still in that gentle tone. "I got rid of it. Come inside, baby." Putting his arm around her, he urged her up from the swing and into the house. He directed her toward the kitchen; she stiffened and tried to pull back, but he was having none of it. "It's okay," he reassured her, and forced her into a chair. "You look a little shocky. What do you have to drink around here?"

"There's tea and orange juice in the refrigerator," she said, her voice faint.

"I meant the alcoholic variety. Do you have any wine?"

She shook her head. "I don't drink alcohol."

Despite the fury in his eyes, he gave her a little grin. "Puritan," he said mildly. "Okay, orange juice it is." He took a glass from the cabinet and filled it with orange juice, then thrust it into her hand. "Drink it. All of it, while I make a call."

She sipped obediently, more because it gave her something to concentrate on than because she wanted it. Gray opened the phone book, ran his finger down the first page, then punched in the number. "Sheriff McFane, please."

Faith lifted her head, suddenly more alert. Gray stared down at her, his expression daring her to protest. "Mike, this is Gray. Could you come out to Faith Hardy's house? Yeah, it's the old Cleburne place. She just got a real ugly surprise in her mail. A dead cat . . . Yeah, there's one of those, too."

He hung up, and Faith cleared her throat. "One of what, too?"

"A threatening letter. Didn't you see it?"

She shook her head. "No. All I saw was the cat." A shudder rippled through her body, making the glass tremble in her hand.

He began opening and closing doors. "What are you looking for?" she asked.

"The coffee. After the sugar to counteract shock, you need a shot of caffeine."

"I keep it in the refrigerator. Top shelf."

He got out the canister, and she directed him to the filters. He made coffee rather competently, for a rich man who probably never did it at home, she thought, and felt a ghost of amusement flicker inside.

Once the coffee was in the process of making, he drew up

another chair and sat facing her, so close that their legs touched, his on the outside of hers, warmly clasping. He didn't ask her what had happened, knowing she would soon be going through that with the sheriff, and she was grateful for his tact. He just sat there, lending her his heat and the comfort of his nearness, those dark eyes sharp on her face as if he were debating pouring the orange juice down her, if she didn't drink it as fast as he thought she should.

To forestall just such an action, she took a healthy swallow of juice, and actually felt a slight lessening of tension in his muscles. "Don't you dare," she muttered. "I'm trying my best not to throw up again."

The grimness of his expression was lightened briefly by amusement. "How did you know what I was thinking?"

"The way you were staring at the glass, and then at me." She took another swallow. "I thought Deese was the sheriff."

"He retired." Gray had the fleeting thought that her memory of Sheriff Deese wouldn't be a pleasant one, and wondered if that was why she had looked at him with such alarm when he'd asked for the sheriff. "You'll like Michael McFane. How's that for a good Irish name? He's young for the job, still interested in keeping up with new techniques." Mike had also been at the shack that night, Gray remembered, but Faith wouldn't know that, probably wouldn't recognize him. In her shock, the deputies would have been faceless uniformed figures. Only he and the sheriff, standing off to the side, would have been locked in her memory.

The puzzling contradiction formed in his mind. She had been obviously reluctant to meet Sheriff Deese, but she had never revealed any such uneasiness in her dealings with himself. She'd been bold, provoking, maddening, *frustrating,* but she'd never shown the least hesitation about being in his company.

Nor was hesitation something that had troubled him. Why else, when he'd gotten her call, he thought to remove a pesky cat from the premises, had he promptly canceled a business meeting and driven here as fast as possible, with Monica's enraged protests still ringing in his ears? Faith had

called him for help, and no matter how minor he thought
the problem, he would help her if he could. As it turned out,
the problem hadn't been minor at all, and all his protective
instincts had been outraged. He intended to find out who
had done such a disgusting thing, and someone would catch
hell. His fists ached with the need to pound them into the
culprit's face.

"Why didn't you think I'd done it?" he asked softly, his
attention locked on her face to catch every flicker of
expression. "I've been trying to get you to leave town, so
logically I should have been the person you'd suspect first."

She was shaking her head before he'd finished speaking,
the movement making the sleek bell of her hair swing about
her face. "You wouldn't do something like that," she said
with absolute conviction. "Any more than you would have
left me the first note."

He paused, distracted from the pleasure of her trust in
him. "Note?" Sternness laced that one word.

"Yesterday. When I went out, there was a note in the front
seat of the car."

"Did you report it?"

She shook her head again. "It wasn't a specific threat."

"What did it say?"

The look she gave him now was slightly uneasy, and he
wondered why. "To quote: Shut up if you know what's good
for you."

The coffee was ready. He got up and poured a cup for both
of them. "How do you drink yours?" he asked absently, his
thoughts still on the note and the package, which this time
had been accompanied by a more specific threat. The wings
of cold, black fury beat upward within him, barely controlled.

"Black."

He gave her the cup, and sat down again in his original
position, close enough to touch. She was more adept than
anyone else at reading his face, and something in his
expression must have alarmed her, because she launched
into one of those deflecting maneuvers of hers. "I used to
drink coffee with loads of sugar, but Mr. Gresham is

diabetic. He said that it was easier to give up everything sweet than to fool with artificial sweeteners, so there wasn't anything in the house to use. They would have bought it for me if I'd asked, but I didn't want to impose—"

If she'd meant to distract him, he thought irritably, she'd succeeded. Even recognizing the maneuver didn't blunt its effectiveness, because she used such interesting bait. "Who's Mr. Gresham?" he asked, breaking into the flow of words. He felt the burn of jealousy, wondering if she was telling him about some guy she'd lived with before moving back to Prescott.

The slumberous green eyes blinked at him. "The Greshams were my foster parents."

A foster home. God. A cold fist clenched his stomach. He had imagined her life as continuing in much the same vein as before. Realistically, a good foster home would have been far preferable to the way she'd been living, but it was never easy for kids to lose their families, no matter how rotten, and be deposited with strangers. Finding a good home was a crapshoot, at best. A lot of kids were abused in foster homes, and for a young girl who looked like Faith . . .

The crunch of gravel signaled Mike's arrival. "Stay here," Gray growled, and went out the back door. He beckoned to Mike as the other man's lanky form unfolded from the patrol car, and walked around to the back of the house where he had left the box.

Mike joined him, his freckled face tightening with disgust as he looked down at the carcass. "I see a lot of sick things in this job," he said conversationally, squatting by the box, "but some things still turn my stomach. Why in hell would someone do this to a helpless animal? Have you handled the box much?"

"Just to carry it out. I was careful to touch only the front left corner, and the back right. I don't know how much Faith handled it before she opened it. I used a pen to open the flaps wider," he added. "There's a message on one of them."

Mike used the same technique, taking a ballpoint from his pocket. He pursed his lips as he read the message, printed in block letters, with a felt-tip marker, on the cardboard:

GET OUT OF PRESCOTT OR YOU'LL BE JUST LIKE
THE CAT

"I'll carry it in, see if we can get any fingerprints. The
plastic would be our best bet, since it hasn't been disturbed." He glanced toward the house. "Is she okay?"

"She was pretty shaky when I got here, but she's settled
down now."

"Okay." Still using the pen, Mike closed the flaps and
stared down at the box for a few seconds, then grunted.

Gray looked down, too, and saw what he had missed the
first time. "Shit. There's no postage mark. It was on top of
her other mail, so I thought it had been mailed, too."

"Nope. Someone hand-delivered it. Let's go see if she
heard anything, or saw a car."

They entered the kitchen, and Gray saw that Faith was
still sitting where he had left her, sipping her coffee. She
glanced up, outwardly calm now, but he suspected her
control was hanging by no more than a few thin threads.

She immediately got to her feet, looking at Mike.
"Ma'am." He touched his fingers to his hat. "I'm Michael
McFane, the sheriff here. Do you feel like answering a few
questions?"

"Of course," she said. "Would you like some coffee?"

"Please."

"Sugar or cream?"

"Sugar."

That social nicety taken care of, Faith returned to her
chair. Gray stood beside her, propped against the enormous
table. Mike took up his position by the sink, his feet crossed
at the ankles.

"Where did you find the box?" Mike asked.

"In the mailbox."

"There's no postage mark on it. It wasn't mailed, so I'm
assuming someone put it in the box after your mail was
delivered. No one's supposed to use the box except the
postal service, so the carrier probably would have taken it
out. Did you hear the mail run, or see another car pass by?"

She shook her head. "I wasn't here. I'd been grocery
shopping. I came home, put up the groceries, then went out
to get the mail."

"Is anyone mad at you? Someone who might give you a dead cat to get even?"

Another shake of the head.

"She found a note in her car yesterday," Gray interjected.

"What kind of note? What did it say?"

"To shut up if I knew what was good for me," Faith replied.

"Did you keep it?"

She sighed, gave Gray a wary glance, and went to get the note. She came back holding the sheet of paper by one corner. "Put it on the counter," Mike said. "I don't want to handle it."

She obeyed, and Gray moved beside Mike to read it. It was printed in the same block letters than adorned the cardboard box. *Don't ask any more questions about Guy Rouillard shut up if you know what's good for you.* Gray flashed her an irritated glance, understanding now that wary look she'd given him.

"All right," he growled. "What have you been up to now?"

"You know as much about it as I do," she replied, with a smoothness that he was beginning to think hid as much as it revealed.

"Well, now." Mike scratched his jaw. "What does your daddy have to do with this, Gray?"

"Little Miss Nosy has been asking questions about him all over town." He scowled at her.

"Why would that aggravate someone so much that they'd send her a note like this, and leave a dead cat in the mailbox?"

"It aggravated the hell out of me," Gray said frankly. "I don't want Monica or Mother upset by having all the old gossip stirred up again. I don't know who it would piss off this much."

The sheriff was silent, blue eyes hooded as he thought. "On the surface," he finally drawled, "you're the most likely suspect, Gray." Faith started an immediate protest, but he waved her to silence. "Guess you knew that, too, what with the note and all," he said to her. "So that makes me wonder why you called him, rather than the sheriff's department."

"I knew he didn't leave the note, or the box."

"It's no secret that you weren't happy when she moved back," Michael said, looking at Gray.

"No, I wasn't. I'm still not." Gray's hard mouth curved into a humorless smile. "But threatening notes and dead cats aren't my style. I fight my battles out in the open."

"Hell, I know that. I just wondered why Mrs. Hardy called you for help."

Gray snorted. "Figure it out."

"Reckon I already have."

"Then stop being an asshole."

The sheriff didn't take umbrage, just grinned. An instant later, he was all business again. "I need for both of you to come down to the courthouse so we can get your finger-prints, and check the box and note for any sets that don't match. You'll need to give us a statement, too, Mrs. Hardy."

"All right. I'll get my keys." Faith stood, and Gray caught her arm.

"I'll drive you."

"There's no need in your coming all the way back here—"

"I said I'll drive you." Implacably he looked down at her, forcing his will on her. She looked irritated, but made no further protest, and the sheriff grinned again.

Gray hustled her out and deposited her in the luxurious leather seat of the Jaguar. "You don't have to drive me," she said grumpily, as she buckled the seat belt.

"Sure I do, if I want to talk to you."

"What's there to say?"

He started the car and reversed out of the driveway, following Sheriff McFane's patrol car down the road. "Obviously some nutcase has it in for you. You'll be a lot safer somewhere away from Prescott."

She averted her head, staring stonily out the window. "It didn't take long for you to come up with that angle," she retorted.

"You stubborn little witch, can't you get it through that red head of yours that you might be in danger?"

❧ Fifteen ❧

Faith was boiling mad by the time she left the courthouse, though she had kept her temper mostly under control. Gray had badgered her all the way to town about moving out of Prescott, and to her fury, Sheriff McFane had agreed that she might not be entirely safe, living alone as she did, and with no close neighbors. Faith had pointed out that if she left, the harassment would stop, they'd never find who did it, and the guilty party would be pleased as punch that his tactics had worked. She wasn't inclined to give him the satisfaction.

Sheriff McFane had allowed that her logic was impeccable, and her bravery was commendable, but her common sense was a mite off. She could get *hurt*.

She had agreed with him in that assessment, and stubbornly refused to budge an inch. Now that she had gotten over the shakes, she was seeing cause and effect. The dead cat meant that, somehow, she had gotten close to finding out what had really happened to Guy, and if she left now, she would never know for certain. The sheriff and Gray thought someone was harassing her; she knew that it was far more serious than that. She had to fight the temptation to tell them what she thought was behind the cat and the notes; if word got out that she was suggesting Guy had been murdered, it would warn the guilty party, making him or her even more difficult to catch. So she kept silent, and the frustration of it made her irritable.

She could ignore Sheriff McFane's arguments that she leave; Gray's went straight to her heart. His cajoling suggestions had long since deteriorated to forceful demands by the time they left the courthouse for the drive back to her house.

"For the last time, no!" she shouted, for at least the fifth time, as they got into the car. Heads swiveled in their direction.

"Shit," Gray muttered. For a man who wanted to avoid gossip, he'd been pretty blatant today. His Jaguar wasn't a car that was easily overlooked, and Faith was a woman who turned heads. A lot of people would have noted that he had driven her into town, gone with her into the courthouse, and then left with her, not to mention the fact that she was yelling at him. Well, there was nothing he could do about it now. Given the same set of circumstances he'd been faced with today, he'd do the same thing again.

Faith jammed the two ends of the seat belt buckle together. "I know you didn't have anything to do with the cat, or either of the notes," she said, anger seething in her voice. "But you aren't above using it to your own advantage, are you? You've wanted me gone from day one, and it sticks in your craw that you can't make me do what you want."

He gave her a hooded, dangerous look as he negotiated the traffic in the square. "Don't believe that for a minute," he said quietly. "I could have you gone in half an hour if I wanted. I decided against it."

"Really?" she drawled, infusing the word with disbelief. "Why pull your punches?"

"For two reasons. One is that you didn't deserve what happened twelve years ago, and I wasn't inclined to treat you that way again." He took his gaze from the street long enough to sweep it down her body, lingering briefly on her breasts and thighs. "You know what the second reason is."

The truth of that simmered between them, just below boiling point. He wanted her. She had known that . . . oh, almost from the first, certainly since that incendiary kiss in New Orleans. But he wanted her on his terms; he wanted to set her up in a little house somewhere away from Prescott, completely out of the parish, so his liaison with her wouldn't upset his family. Those circumstances would be perfect for him, because he would be accomplishing both his goals with one fell swoop.

"I won't let you hide me away as if I'm something shameful," she said, her eyes hot and bitter as she stared fixedly out the windshield. "If you can't associate with me out in the open, then stay the hell away from me."

He slammed his fist against the steering wheel. "Goddamn it, Faith! That cat wasn't from the Welcome Wagon. I'm thinking of your safety! Yes, it would please the hell out of me if you moved to another town. My mother drives me crazy, but that doesn't mean I want to hurt her. Am I supposed to apologize for loving her, despite everything? You know how to roll with the punches, but she doesn't. I'm a greedy bastard; I want to do what's best for her, and have you, too. If you moved, we could have a damn satisfying relationship, and I wouldn't have to worry that some maniac is stalking you!"

"Then don't. Let me do the worrying."

He made a sound of muffled anger and frustration. "You won't budge an inch, will you?"

Again, she had to fight the urge to tell him that she had reasons for staying right where she was, reasons that went beyond their personal entanglement. The mood he was in, he wouldn't believe her anyway.

They were out of town now, and there was very little traffic on the road. Soon he turned off on the secondary road that led to her house. She had never really noticed before how isolated her house was, at least not from the viewpoint of her own vulnerability. She had enjoyed the peace and quiet, the sense of space. *Damn* the unknown, unseen enemy, for destroying her pleasure in at last coming home.

She didn't speak again until he turned in to her driveway. It was late afternoon, and the setting sun bathed the little house in a golden glow. In only a short while she had settled in here, surrounded by her own things, her own walls, covered by her own roof. Leave here? She couldn't imagine it.

"Answer something for me," she said, one hand on the door handle. "I don't want to have an affair with you, no matter where I live. Does that lessen your concern for my safety?"

He stopped her, wrapping his fingers around her wrist and holding her in the car. His eyes were black with anger, but he didn't answer the insulting question, merely replied to the statement. "I can change your mind," he said softly. "We both know it."

She opened the door and he let her go, content that he'd had the last word. He often did, she thought. He had a knack for pushing the conversation further than she wanted it to go, so that her only recourse was silence.

She was aware of him sitting in the driveway, watching until she was safely in the house. He was right, damn him. He *could* change her mind, with little or no effort. Her statement had been a bluff, but not a lie. She didn't *want* to have an affair with him, but that didn't mean she would be able to resist him. If he had insisted on coming in with her now, after one kiss she would probably let him lead her straight into the bedroom. Afterward was when the regret would begin.

"Gray, what in hell were you thinking of?" Alex asked irritably. "Driving around town with her, arguing with her in front of the courthouse. My God, half the town saw you, and the other half heard about it within the hour."

Monica's head came up, and she turned stricken eyes on Gray. He felt like throttling Alex for bringing up the subject in front of her.

"I was trying to convince her to leave," he replied shortly, and even without looking directly at her, he could see the tension ease in Monica's body. "Someone's playing nasty tricks on her. Today a dead cat was left in her mailbox."

"A dead cat?" Alex made a face. "That's disgusting. But why was she in your car?"

"She called me when she found it—"

"Why call you?" Monica demanded resentfully.

"Because." Gray knew his answer was blunt and uncommunicative, but he didn't care. "I called Mike, and he came out to her house. He wanted both of us to go to the courthouse for fingerprinting—" Monica gave a sharp cry "—and Faith was still shaky, so I drove her there."

"Why did you have to be fingerprinted?" Monica asked, incensed. "Did she accuse you of doing it?"

"No, but I handled the box. If Mike didn't know which fingerprints were ours, he couldn't tell if there were any belonging to the son of a bitch who left the box."

Monica chewed on her lip. "Did he find anything?"

"I don't know. When she was finished filing a report, I drove her home."

"Is she going to move?" Alex asked.

"Hell, no." Gray shoved an agitated hand through his hair. "She turned stubborn about it." Turned stubborn, nothing. She'd been born stubborn. He pushed away from the desk and got to his feet. "I'm going out."

"Now?" Monica asked, startled. "Where?"

"Just out." He was as restless and fractious as a stallion who could scent a mare in season, but couldn't get to her. His blood was throbbing through his veins, urging him to action, any action. He felt as if there should be a violent thunderstorm brewing, but the weather was calm, and the lack of thunder frustrated him. "I don't know what time I'll be back. We'll get to those papers tomorrow, Alex."

Baffled, worried, Monica watched him stalk out of the room. She chewed her lip some more. It sounded as if Gray was getting increasingly involved with the Devlin woman. She couldn't understand how he could do it, after all the misery her family had caused. And Michael had been out to her house! Monica didn't want him anywhere around Faith Devlin; those Devlin women were like spiders, spinning sticky little webs that trapped the men unwary enough to wander into their vicinity.

Alex shook his head, his own eyes worried. "I'll go say good night to your mother," he said, and went upstairs. Noelle had retired to her own sitting room not long after dinner, pleading fatigue, but the truth was that she was simply more comfortable upstairs.

He stayed up there for half an hour. Monica was still sitting in the study when she heard him coming down the stairs, his step slower than when he had gone up. He came to the door and paused, looking at her. Monica's head came up and she stared at him, stricken. His hand went to the light switch. Monica froze in dread, her breath clogging in her lungs, as he turned out the light.

"My dear," he said, and she knew the words were spoken to the woman upstairs.

Faith prowled the house, unable to interest herself in either reading or television. Despite her insistence on staying, she was more disturbed than she wanted to admit. She had to force herself to go into the kitchen, the memory of that box on the table was so strong. It was a relief to see the table bare, to find that the association faded as she made herself a skimpy meal. Skimpy or not, she could only eat half of it.

She called Renee again. She knew it was too soon, but some faint, long-buried instinct made her reach out to Mama, not so much in search of comfort but because there was a link between them beyond kinship: the Rouillard men.

To her relief, Renee answered. If her grandmother had answered, Faith knew that Renee never would have come to the phone.

"Mama," she said, and was disconcerted to hear her voice shake a little. "I need help."

There was silence on the other end of the line, then Renee said warily, "What's wrong?" Motherly concern wasn't a natural response for her.

"Someone left a dead cat in my mailbox, and I've gotten a couple of threatening notes, telling me to stop asking questions or I'll end up like the cat. I don't know who's doing it—"

"What kind of questions?"

Faith hesitated, afraid Renee would hang up on her. "About Guy," she admitted.

"Damn it, Faith!" Renee yelled. "I told you not to be nosing around, but would you listen? No, you have to stir shit up, and now the stink's gettin' too bad for you. You're going to get yourself killed if you don't shut up!"

"Someone killed Guy, didn't they? You know who did it. That's why you left."

Renee's breathing sounded over the line, harsh and rapid. "Stay out of it," she begged. "I can't tell, I promised never to tell. He has my bracelet. He said he'd blame the killing on me if I ever told, he said he'd put the bracelet where it would look like Guy and me had had a fight, and I'd killed him."

After the weeks of suspicion, of sifting through old rumors and continually coming to dead ends, to suddenly hear the truth was startling. It took Faith a moment to recover from the shock, to absorb it.

"You loved Guy," she said, her own conviction ringing in her voice. "You couldn't have killed him."

Renee began to cry. It wasn't noisy sobs, designed to gain sympathy. Her tears were betrayed by the sudden thickness in her voice. "He's the only man I ever did love," she said, and Faith knew that whether or not Renee really had loved Guy, she believed she had, and that was enough.

"What happened, Mama?"

"I can't tell—"

"Mama, please." Desperately Faith searched her mind for a reason that would mean something to Renee. It would take a lot to overcome her mother's basic self-interest, and in this case, Faith couldn't really blame her for looking out after number one. The only thing that had ever been greater than Renee's self-absorption had been her greed . . . "Mama, as far as everyone is concerned, Guy is still alive somewhere. He hasn't been declared dead, so that means his will hasn't been read."

Renee sniffed, but the word "will" caught her interest. "So what?"

"So if he left anything to you, it would be in his will. You could have had a lot of money coming to you all these years."

"He always said he'd take care of me." A whining note of self-pity entered Renee's voice. She took a deep breath, as if to calm herself, and Faith could almost hear the decision being made.

"We met at the summerhouse, as usual," Renee said. "We'd already . . . you know. Done it. Anyway, we were lyin' in the dark talkin' when he drove up. We didn't know who it was, and Guy jumped up and grabbed his pants, afraid it might be one of his kids. He didn't never worry about his wife none, because he knew she wouldn't care.

"They went out to the boathouse to talk. I could hear them yellin', so I put on my clothes and went down there. Guy opened the door and came out just as I got there. He stopped and looked back, and I'll never forget, he said, 'I've made up my mind.' That's when he was shot, right in the head. He fell on the grass, there in front of the boathouse. I was on my knees beside him, yellin' and cryin', but he was dead when he hit the ground. He never even twitched."

"Was it Gray?" Faith asked, agony in her tone. It couldn't be. Not Gray. But she had to ask. "Did Gray kill his daddy?"

"Gray?" A startled note sounded through the tears. "No, not Gray. He wasn't there."

Not Gray. Thank you, God. *Not Gray.* No matter how she had told herself that he couldn't have done it, there must have been a hidden reservoir of doubt, because she felt a sudden relief, a lightening of spirit.

"Mama—Mama, no one would believe you shot Guy. Why didn't you go to the sheriff?"

"Are you kiddin'?" Renee gave a sharp laugh, which ended in a sob. "People in that town would believe anything about me. Most of 'em would've been glad to see me arrested even if they knew for certain I was innocent. Besides, he had it all figured out—"

"But you didn't even have a gun!"

"He was goin' to kill me, too! He said he'd put the gun in my mouth and make me pull the trigger, his hand over mine, if I didn't promise to leave and never come back, and never say nothing about it to anybody. He's strong, Faithie, strong enough to do it. I tried to fight him and he hit me, I couldn't get away—"

"Why *didn't* he kill you, then?" Faith asked, trying to make sense of why a murderer would deliberately let a witness go.

Renee couldn't answer for a moment, she was crying too hard. Finally she gulped, and regained shaky control of her voice. "He—he didn't mean to kill Guy, he was just so damn mad, he said. He didn't want to have to kill me too. He told me to go away, and he t-took my bracelet. He said if I ever came back, he could make it look like I'd killed Guy, and I'd get the death sentence. He can do it, you don't know him!" Her voice rose shrilly on the last sentence, and she dissolved once more into wrenching sobs.

Faith felt her own eyes burning. For the first time, she felt pity for her mother. Poor Renee, without education, influence, or friends, with all her wild living and lack of responsibility, had been a prime target for anyone who wanted to make her a scapegoat. She had seen the one man she cared for, the man she was depending on to make her life easy, shot to death, and then been threatened with having his death blamed on her. No, the killer had gauged her well; there was no way Renee would have gone to the sheriff. She would have believed everything he said, probably with good reason.

"It's all right, Mama," she said gently. "It's all right."

"You—you won't say anything? This has to be our secret, or he'll have me arrested, I know he will—"

"I won't let anyone arrest you, I promise. Do you know what he did with the body?"

Renee hiccuped, caught by surprise. "His body?" she asked vaguely. "I guess he must have buried it somewhere."

That was possible, but would the killer have wasted time digging a grave, a grave that might be noticed, with the lake right there? Weight the body, and the problem of disposal was solved.

"What kind of gun did he use? Did you see it?"

"I don't know anything about guns. It was a pistol, is all I can tell you."

"Was it a revolver, like the ones used in Westerns, with the round chamber that the bullets fit into, or was it the kind with the clip in the handle?"

"Clip in the handle," Renee said after a moment's thought.

An automatic. That meant the shell casing had been ejected, somewhere inside the boathouse. The killer had had a body to dispose of, and a witness to terrify into fleeing. Had he thought about the casing, gone back to pick it up?

What were the chances that a shell casing would still be there after twelve years? Almost none. But the place had fallen into disuse after Guy's disappearance, so it was likely only the minimum upkeep had gone into the boathouse. The casing could have landed in the boat, or even in the water, to be lost forever.

It could also have landed in a corner, or behind something. Stranger things had happened.

"Don't say anything," Renee begged. "Please don't say anything. You never should have moved back there, Faithie; now he's after you too. Leave before you get hurt, you don't know him—"

"I might. Who is he, Mama? Maybe I can do something—"

Renee hung up the phone, the connection breaking in the middle of a sob. Faith slowly replaced her own receiver. She had learned so much tonight, and still not enough. The most important thing was that Gray was innocent. The most frustrating thing was that she still had no idea who was guilty.

The killer was a "he." That eliminated Andrea Wallice and Yolanda Foster, even if Faith hadn't already decided they likely weren't guilty. Supposedly Lowell Foster hadn't known about his wife's affair with Guy until afterward, but the way gossip moved through the town like fat through a goose, it was possible some self-righteous busybody had taken it upon himself to enlighten the wronged husband. Never mind that the wronged husband had been screwing around with his secretary; that was different. So Lowell had to remain on her list.

Who would have been arguing with Guy that night, and why? A business associate, upset at some financial wheeling and dealing? The way Guy got around, an enraged husband was more likely. Who else had he been sleeping with that summer?

Faith couldn't find the answer to those questions tonight. She could, however, see for herself whether or not a stray shell casing was still lying overlooked in the boathouse.

She glanced at the clock. It was nine-thirty. If she was

going to do it, night would be the best time, with much less chance of running into Gray and a much better chance of avoiding him if she did.

Faith wasn't one to tarry once she'd made a decision, though this time she paused long enough to put on sturdier shoes. She grabbed a flashlight on her way out the door.

She started to drive right to the summerhouse, on the private road, but changed her mind at the last minute. Someone might see her turn onto the road and notify the Rouillards, which she definitely didn't want. And if the god of misfortune smiled on her twice, and someone was at the summerhouse, she didn't want her headlights to give advance warning.

So she drove instead to the same place she had parked before, even though it meant walking a mile through the woods at night. It wasn't a problem for her. She had never been afraid of the dark, or of snakes and the other denizens of the forest, though she did pick up a stick to be on the safe side, if she did come upon a snake before the shy creature could slide away.

The woods at night were noisy, filled with rustles as the nocturnal animals went about their business. Possums and raccoons clambered in the trees, owls hooted, frogs croaked, insects zinged, night birds called, and crickets chirped frenetically. The breeze added its own whisper to the cacophony, the pine trees swaying gently. Faith took her time, making certain she didn't wander off track; when she came to the little creek, in exactly the same place she had always crossed, she smiled at the accuracy of her old instincts. She paused to shine the light around the creek to make certain no water moccasins were enjoying a swim, then stepped onto the flat rock in the middle of the water and from there onto the other bank. From here, it was only a couple of hundred yards to the summerhouse.

Five minutes later she stopped at the edge of the clearing, taking stock before she left the cover of the trees. The house was dark and silent. She listened, but heard only the normal night sounds. The lake murmured, slapping against the dock pilings, its glassy surface rippling occasionally with a breeze and disturbing the reflection of the three-quarter moon. Night-feeding fish added their own ripples and the occasional quiet splash to the subtle commotion.

Faith walked down the slight slope to the house, her steps soundless.

She didn't know what she would do if the boathouse was locked, which, of course, it probably was, though the house had been open the other day when she'd been here. But Gray had also been here; he could have unlocked the house, gone inside to make certain nothing had been vandalized.

If she were a truly adventurous type, she thought wryly, she could swim under the wall of the boathouse and come up in the boat slip. To hell with locked doors.

Not bloody likely.

Nighttime underwater swimming wasn't her cup of tea. The thought of stripping down to her underwear and sliding beneath the surface of that dark water was enough to make her shiver. If the boathouse had been closed all these years, it was probably inhabited by mice, snakes, squirrels, maybe a raccoon or two, all of which would be startled by a visitor suddenly popping up from the water. No, she would much rather give any boathouse occupants sufficient warning to skedaddle, by jiggling door locks or maybe breaking windows, if the boathouse had a window. She had never noticed.

The boathouse loomed over the shiny black water, the white walls ghostly in the moonlight. As Faith crossed the graveled drive, she flicked the flashlight beam across the front of the wide doors, and stifled a groan of disappointment. A thick, shiny padlock was looped through both hasps, securing the doors with stainless steel. She might have jimmied or broken a normal door lock, but she couldn't do anything with that big padlock. Her only recourse now was a window.

There wasn't one on the side facing the dock, only smooth blank wall. She walked around to the other side, and stared with mixed feelings at the window that sat like a black eye in a pale face. The good news was that it *was* a window, with breakable glass. The bad news was that solid ground ended about a foot shy of being directly underneath it. The window was also high enough that it would be difficult for her to hoist herself through; not impossible, not if she set her mind to it, but definitely difficult.

A very warm, very solid hand closed over her bare arm and whirled her around, bringing her against a hard, muscled body. "I told you what I'd do if I caught you here again," Gray said softly.

～ Sixteen ～

He carried her onto the porch, where the screens would protect them from the mosquitoes and other biting insects. Frightened almost out of her wits by his abrupt appearance, a panic that wasn't much relieved by recognition, Faith could do no more than cling to his shoulders as he lifted her in his arms and carried her swiftly across the grass, to the house.

She was submerged almost at once by a dark tide of desire, sucking her below the level of reason or will. Protest wasn't an option; the needs of her body, so long suppressed, surged to the forefront and pushed thought aside. She was shaking by the time he released her legs and let her body slide down, all along the front of his, the sweet friction almost painfully arousing. It was time. Dear God, it was past time. She wanted him with a blind, ferocious need that could no longer be delayed, and she clung to him, her body pliant, willing.

He backed her up against one of the square columns supporting the porch, pinning her against the wood. Despite the bright moonlight, it was dark there on the porch, dark and warm, scented with the perfumes of summer and his own hot, musky smell. His breathing was fast and urgent as he leaned heavily against her, pushing himself into the yielding softness of her body. He thrust his fingers into her hair, holding her skull cradled between his big, powerful hands, holding her head still for the deep thrust of his tongue into her mouth. He was fully aroused, his erection as hard as marble, straining against her belly.

Faith whimpered into his mouth, squirming hungrily against him, trying to lift herself enough so that she could cradle that thick ridge in the yielding notch between her legs. She was aching and empty, so empty, growing moist with the need to have him there.

His shirt was hanging open. The flesh where her fingernails dug into his shoulders was covered by cloth, but his chest was bare. She could feel his skin, slick with sweat, and the roughness of curly hair. Her breasts grew taut, her nipples rising hard and tight, throbbing with the need to be touched.

He tore his mouth away from hers, gasping for air, his chest working like bellows with each breath. Faith licked her bruised lips, tasting him on them, and tugged on the back of his neck to bring him back down to her. He obliged at once, his mouth hard and biting, the primal force of it exciting her beyond what she had ever known before.

He cupped both of her breasts, roughly kneading them, and the relief was so acute that she made a small keening sound of both pleasure and want, but in only seconds that wasn't enough. He knew her need, or perhaps his own was the same, for he jerked at the front of her blouse and sent buttons flying, the small popping sounds loud in the bubble of silence that surrounded them. With one hand he released the front clasp of her bra and shoved the cups aside, baring the firm rise of her breasts to his hungry, demanding mouth. He wrapped one arm under her bottom and lifted her, his open mouth sliding down her chest, a damp path marking where his lips had been. A taut nipple popped into his mouth and he sucked hard at it, making her breast prickle with a sharp sensation that had her arching against him as if to throw him off. He responded by holding her tighter, gripping her bottom and grinding his erection into the soft notch between her legs. The blatant sexuality of his movements let loose the firestorm of her response, and helplessly she felt herself sliding down the dark, slippery tunnel toward climax.

She fought it; she didn't want this wild fever to end so soon. She shrank back against the wood, trying to pull her hips away from that hard ridge. She couldn't; his arm around her bottom kept her molded to him, allowing her so little movement that she couldn't even close her legs. A heavy coil tightened in her loins, the tension pulling tighter and tighter—

He set her on her feet again and jerked at her skirt, pulling it to her waist. Faith leaned weakly against the column, her senses whirling with the speed and violence with which this was happening. Dimly she thought of that time she had watched him making love, so slowly and tenderly, his smoky voice soothing and cajoling, crooning love words. She had thought it would be like that, but instead she was caught like Dorothy in a whirlwind, being hurled dizzily into uncharted territory. They were going at each other like animals, unable to slow down or inject any tenderness into the act, and she didn't care. The urgency was too strong, too immediate.

He wound his left hand in her skirt, holding it up and to the side, while with his right one he stripped her panties down. The night air washed over her naked buttocks, making her feel excruciatingly exposed, and she quivered in his grasp. He forced the panties down to her knees, then lifted one booted foot and set his toe in the crotch of the garment, pushing it down the rest of the way. She heard fabric separate with a faint sibilant protest, then the cloth fell around her feet and he lifted her out of the ruins of her underwear.

He braced her against the column, pulling her thighs wide and pushing himself between them. Faith's head fell back; she heard her own panting breath as she waited in agonized anticipation for the hard thrust that would fill her emptiness, ease the deep ache of desire. His hand worked frenziedly between their bodies, fumbling with his belt, tearing at the fastening of his jeans, and the brush of his knuckles against her moist, yearning flesh was enough to make her cry out with longing. He managed to open the zipper and his straining flesh sprang free, pushing upward into the folds between her legs.

"I want to fuck you," he muttered indistinctly, the sound low and harsh as he hoisted her a bit, adjusting her position. "Let me in. *Now.*" His hand was still between their bodies, his fingers moving with sure knowledge over her slick flesh. He found her soft, damp opening and sank one finger deep into her, drawing the moisture out to prepare her for his entry. Faith shuddered, her arms wrapping tight around his head as that long finger rasped exquisitely sensitive tissues and set off subterranean explosions of pleasure. Her inner muscles eagerly clasped the intruding finger, tightening, subtly caressing, and Gray swore with savage arousal. Unable to wait any longer, he withdrew his finger and guided the broad head of his penis into place.

Faith went still, frozen by the enormous pressure between her legs as he began pushing into her. The fever of desire faded, banished by alarm. In a flash of clarity she remembered Lindsey Partain's startled, panicked cry at his entry, and now she knew why. Then all thoughts fled, her mind focused only on the massively thick shaft that each short, powerful thrust of his hips forced deeper into her body. He grunted at the difficulty of penetration, his entire body taut and straining.

She writhed in his arms like a worm caught on a fishing hook, sharp little cries of distress breaking from her throat. Gray stopped, sweat dripping off his face to trace tiny paths down the slope of her bare breasts. Desperately he fought for control, the effort tearing at his guts.

"Shhh, shhh," he whispered, his lips pressed against the delicate curve of her jaw. The sound was a mere rustle of reassurance, wafted away in the night breeze. "It's all right, baby. You can handle it. Just be still now, and let me get it in. I won't hurt you, I'll be real slow and easy." As he spoke he began rocking his hips back and forth, slight movements that coaxed her taut muscles to relax, allowing the next forward rock to slide him deeper into the hot, wet, incredibly tight clasp of her. She moaned, shuddering in his arms. He felt her body arch convulsively, in an instinctive effort to accept and adjust to him; he tried to control the movement, but he was too late. The sharp, twisting movement impaled her on his rigid shaft, seating him to the hilt, and the hot gloving of her body made him feel as if his entire body was exploding.

Shock reverberated through her. She sagged weakly in his arms, her head falling back like a daisy on a broken stem. His hard-won control splintered. His hips jackhammered, driving in and out of her. She hung there, supported only by his driving body and the wooden column at her back. For a measureless length of time her senses narrowed to the thudding of her heart and the hard pounding of his body into hers, relentlessly battering. She clenched her hands on his shirt, twisting fistfuls of the fabric as she tried to endure, tossed helplessly about in the violent upheaval of his lust.

Then he stopped, a growl rough in his throat, as her physical and mental withdrawal registered through the demanding throb of his body. "No," he said with furious frustration. "I won't let you pull back from me. Come for me, baby. Let me feel it."

Faith tried to speak, to say anything. *I can't do it,* she thought, but no words would form on her lips. Climax, which had shimmered so maddeningly near a short while ago, now seemed totally out of reach. She felt painfully stretched, impaled, beyond pleasure.

But he adjusted his position, hooking his arms under her thighs and holding them wider apart, the weight of his torso pinning her to the column. She felt herself open completely, unable to either control or react to his thrusts. He briefly freed one hand, reaching down to find the small sexual bud at the top of her sex, using his finger and thumb to open the protective fold and expose it. He adjusted his position again, moving deep into her so that he pressed hard against the little nub, and then he began again to thrust.

Lightning speared through her body, gathering between her legs. She had no defense against the rush of sensation, ruthlessly intensified with every inward thrust. He had known exactly what he was doing, inexorably forcing her toward orgasm. In seconds she was moaning with the return of desire; in less than a minute the fury was upon her, and she screamed with the force of her release, her body arching and shuddering in his restraining arms. It went on and on, so strong that she knew nothing else, reduced to a completely physical being.

Her spasms had barely slowed when his began, and he bucked heavily under the lash of it, his head thrown back and his neck corded as he shook and pulsed. A deep, harsh groan rumbled up from his chest, repeated again and again in rhythm with his pumping hips.

The aftermath was silent, punctuated only by the rapid harshness of their breathing and the occasional, involuntary little moan or grunt as laggard nerve endings twitched in the remnants of pleasure. Faith was dazed, her head drooping forward to lie against his shoulder. He sagged heavily in her arms, the column supporting them both. Where naked flesh touched, sweat glued them together. Their clothes were damp and twisted. She felt as numb as if she had just been through a battle.

His breathing slowed and he gathered himself, as if every movement was an effort. His heart was thudding against her breast, each beat slow and heavy. He withdrew carefully from her body, holding her steady when she tensed, for even with the slickness of his climax easing the way, her swollen tissues released him with almost as much difficulty as she had accepted him.

Gray was stunned, rocked to the foundation by the intensity of what had just occurred. That wasn't sex. He'd had sex before, more times than he could count. Sex was a pleasure, sometimes gentle, sometimes raunchy; an appetite, persistent but easily satisfied. What he'd just had with Faith was as powerful and unstoppable as an avalanche, a fire that left him scorched and already needing to feel the flame again. He could feel her lithe, tender body trembling in his arms, and he wanted to lie down with her, comfort her, and then thrust himself deep into her again. He wanted it with a violence that twisted in his guts. Because he didn't trust himself not to do it, he let his arms drop from around her.

Shaken, only one thought came to his mind. "My God," he said, his voice still harsh from his wrenching climax. "If fucking Renee was like that, I understand why Dad couldn't stay away from her."

Faith froze, the delicious heat of their mating turning cold under the bite of his words. She didn't respond to his insulting crudeness, though it had been effective. If he had set out to make her feel cheap, he had succeeded admirably. Humiliation and misery pooled in her stomach, forcing her to clench her teeth against a sudden rise of nausea. She had felt as if her heart were leaving her body, but to him it had been—what? A measure of revenge? Renee was beyond his reach, so take it out on her daughter?

She didn't look at him as she fumbled her clothing back into order. Her bra was twisted, but she finally managed to secure the clasp. There were no buttons left on her blouse, so she tied the shirttail into a knot at her waist. She bent to pick up her panties, intending to put them on, but they were ripped beyond wearing. Color burned in her face, but thankfully the darkness hid that bloom of shame from him.

Silently she slipped the ruined, flimsy underwear into the pocket of her skirt and turned away, walking with as much dignity as possible, under the circumstances. It wasn't much. How could a woman have any dignity when she had just been taken, standing up, with all the grace and tenderness of a sailor just off a six-month cruise nailing a whore in an alley? Her legs trembled like noodles, her loins ached from the battering, and, even worse, his semen was wet between her thighs.

She opened the screen door and wobbled down the steps. The flashlight lay where she had dropped it, the beam illuminating blades of grass and the darting insects attracted by the light. She retrieved it, and collided with him as she straightened. He moved like a ghost, she thought; she hadn't heard him leave the porch. She stepped around him, and he caught her arm, dragging her to a halt.

"Where the hell do you think you're going?"

"Back to my car."

He snorted. "If I wouldn't let you walk back alone during the daytime, you can sure as hell bet you won't do it at night."

She could feel an angry tension in him, but she was too

exhausted and sick to worry about it. Gently she disengaged her arm, still not looking at him. "I grew up roaming these woods. I don't need an escort."

"Get in the car," he said, that soft, steely edge in his voice that said he'd made his decision and wasn't going to change it. "I'll take you back."

Car? Bewildered, Faith looked around. Until now, she hadn't had time to wonder how he'd gotten to the summer-house. She saw the Jaguar now, parked by the side of the house rather than in the drive. As always, she had approached from the other side, so she hadn't seen it. What evil genie had prompted him to park there, instead of in the drive? If she had seen the car, she never would have left the safety of the woods.

He was propelling her toward the car, and Faith didn't waste her time arguing. She simply wanted to get away from him, and the fastest way to do that was to give in and get it over with.

He opened the car door and urged her inside with a hand on the small of her back. Faith sat down, sighing shakily at the relief of being off her trembling legs. He walked around and slid under the steering wheel, his powerful hands sure and competent as he started the motor and put the transmission into gear. "Are you parked the same place you were before?" he asked, that muted anger humming through his tone.

"Yes," she murmured, then lapsed into silence. Maintaining that silence seemed to be both the safest and easiest thing to do, so she concentrated on staring at the dark trees sliding past the car window.

The road looped around the lake, entered the highway, and then he had to take another turn onto the rutted track that had once led to her home. Getting there didn't take much less time than if she had walked, but for all the tension, she was grateful she hadn't had to put her shaky limbs to the test. She probably would have stumbled over every root and rock in her path.

The Jaguar purred around a curve and her car came into view. She felt for her keys, and her searching fingers patted an empty pocket. Panic twisted her stomach. "I've lost my keys," she said thinly. Of course she had. Her skirt had practically been over her head. It would have been a miracle if the keys had stayed in her pocket.

"Here." A small, jangling heap landed in her lap. "I picked them up."

Her cold hand closed over the keys as Gray stopped the Jaguar beside her car, and she had her door open before he could let out the clutch and turn off the ignition. She stumbled out, ignoring his demand to wait, and frantically sorted through the keys in her hand, looking for the one to open the car door. She found it, and turned it in the lock. Gray was out of the car, coming around the front of it toward her. She jerked open the door and slid inside.

He said, "Faith," but she jammed the key into the ignition and started the engine, then pulled the gear lever down and started moving with the door still open. She leaned out and slammed it, wrenching it away from Gray's hands, and left him standing as she reversed too rapidly down the track until she reached a spot wide enough for her to turn around.

Gray stood in the middle of the road, watching her headlights veer crazily as she maneuvered the car, followed by the red dots of her taillights disappearing. His hands were knotted into fists, tight with the effort it took not to get in his car and chase her down. She was too shaky, drawn so tight, any more pressure could make her shatter. If he chased her, she was likely to drive headlong into a tree.

He turned back to the car, cursing viciously under his breath. If he could reach his own ass, he'd have kicked it. God, of all the stupid, boneheaded, downright *cruel* things to say! The irony of it wasn't lost on him. He had smooth-talked more women than he could remember, and none of them had meant a hill of beans to him. But with Faith, who tied his guts in knots, he managed to say exactly the worst thing possible. She had immediately withdrawn into herself, all of that wonderful fire reduced to ash, her face as smooth and blank as a doll's. He had seen that expression once before, on another night he'd never forget, and he hoped to God he never saw it again.

The tumultuous events of the day had left him more than

a little shaken himself. First there was finding that damn mangled cat on Faith's table, then the frustration of trying to convince her that she could be in danger, damn it, and it would be in her own best interest if she moved away from Prescott. Telling her that was like talking to a fence post, except the fence post at least wouldn't argue back. She just got that stubborn look, her chin went in the air, and she dug those dainty heels in deeper than the Grand Canyon. Then Alex had gotten huffy about Faith being in the car with him, as if she were contaminated somehow, damn it, and Monica had looked as if he'd slapped her in the face with a fish.

He'd driven out to the lake for complete solitude, and he'd been sitting on the porch with his back against the wall, watching the moonlight on the water and sorting through the day's irritants, when Faith had drifted by, as silently as a ghost. He'd stared, not trusting his eyes, fighting the surge of fury that she'd evidently walked through the woods at night, because she sure as hell hadn't driven there. She'd headed straight to the boathouse, the beam of her flashlight flickering over it. What in *hell* was she looking for? This was twice he'd caught her prowling around.

And then the lust had hit him, washing away everything else. He'd warned her, and the fact that she was here meant she was willing to pay the price.

He wanted to believe he could have stopped if she'd said no, but he was glad he hadn't been put to the test. She hadn't said no, she hadn't said anything. Instead she had squirmed against him as if she were trying to get inside his skin, and the top of his head had damn near come off. She had been sweet and hot, her body arching into his touch, her mouth tender and wild. At that moment, nothing and no one could have kept him off of her, and he was still shaking from the results.

He had called her a Puritan, and been right on target. He shook his head, still trying to come to grips with what he'd learned about her tonight. Faith Devlin Hardy, the daughter of a drunk and a whore, didn't drink, didn't smoke, and didn't screw around. He'd had virgins who weren't as tight. She had probably been a virgin when she'd married, and Gray was abruptly certain that he was the only man she'd been with since her husband had died. For all the searing sensuality with which she responded to him, she was a bit of a prude. Not judgmental of others, but certainly holding herself to strict standards.

It was because of her parents, of course. Growing up the way she had, Faith was determined that she would never be like them.

That was fine with him, as long as she didn't try to retrench and keep herself from him. He had a feeling that was exactly what she would do, and no way in hell was he going to let her get away with it.

Don't think about it. Don't think about him.

Faith woke early from a restless sleep, her eyes heavy, feeling as tired as when she had gone to bed. She had shut thoughts of Gray from her mind last night, ignoring the lingering throb from his use of her body, even blanking him out while she showered away the evidence of that use. But for all her will, her subconscious had betrayed her, admitting him into her dreams so that she had awakened to find herself reaching for him, her flesh trembling with eager need.

For four years, the needs of her body had been so firmly repressed as to be nonexistent, but she had no control where Gray was concerned. She might as well admit it. Last night he had ruthlessly aroused her, forcing her to a completion that had eluded her, and now her body wanted more. It didn't seem to matter that she was sore and stiff, or that he had battered her mind with hurtful words; physically, she wanted him. She wanted more of that violent, shattering pleasure. She hadn't known it could be like that, and the discovery left her both stunned and humiliated.

He had treated her like a whore. He had seduced Lindsey Partain with patience and tender care, and Faith had seen it, so she knew the difference. He had murmured French love words to Lindsey, and raw Anglo-Saxon sex words to herself. Evidently only his social equals rated consideration. Her soul writhed with shame, but her body was already craving more of that rough treatment. Maybe he'd been right in the way he'd treated her. Maybe her heritage had only been dormant all these years, and was now coming to life.

He wouldn't leave her alone. She knew that as well as she knew her own name. He had tried to get her to move away from Prescott so they could be together, but perhaps the opposite tack would be more effective. She would try, but she wouldn't be able to avoid him completely, and she didn't know how many more encounters with him her self-esteem could take.

She still had to find out who had killed Guy. Not so much for herself now, but for Gray. Guy's family deserved to know that he hadn't run out on them. She hadn't been able to get into the boathouse, and she needed to do that. She needed to check with Detective Ambrose and see if he had found Mr. Pleasant. She needed to ask more questions, prod a killer into action, for only if he moved would she be able to see him.

❧ Seventeen ❧

The telephone drove her crazy that day. Faith thought about unplugging the damn thing, but reminded herself that she still had a business to run. She didn't have a separate line for the fax, so the phone had to stay in operation. She did let the answering machine screen her calls. Unfortunately, most of them were from Gray.

His tone in the first message had been both exasperated and soothing. "I wanted to see you today, but I had to go to New Orleans first thing this morning. I'm there now, and it looks like I won't get back until late tonight." Well, that was a relief, she thought. Now she wouldn't be on edge, afraid he would show up on her front porch at any moment.

The message continued, his voice sliding into a deeper, more intimate tone. "We need to talk, baby. Do you want me to come by tonight when I get home? I'll call you back later."

"No!" Faith shouted at the phone as he hung up and the answering machine clicked off.

It was about half an hour later when realization dawned on her. Gray was in New Orleans. She wasn't anxious to return to the summerhouse, but at least if she went now, she knew she would be safe from detection. This might be the best chance she'd ever get, and she wouldn't even have to walk through the woods.

If she broke out the window, Gray would immediately suspect she had done it, since he had caught her slipping around the boathouse the night before. Besides, climbing through the window would be difficult without a ladder, and she didn't own one. But it wasn't night now, and she was a good swimmer. What had been unthinkable the night before was very doable under a bright morning sun.

The phone was ringing when she left the house with her supplies in hand. Not normally prepared for this kind of adventure, she made do. She had changed into her old swimsuit, and covered it with slacks and a blouse. In a bag she carried two towels and her flashlight, which she might need for searching dark corners. The flashlight wasn't waterproof, so she had sealed it in a Ziploc plastic bag. For her safety, she also carried the longest butcher knife from the kitchen. She didn't know what use she would have for it—she hoped she wouldn't be close enough to an angry snake that she had to stab it—but carrying it made her feel better, so she did.

She was almost gleeful as she drove out to the summer-house. Twice before she had tried to search the place, and twice Gray had caught her. The third time was the charm.

When she reached the lake, she resolutely refused to look at the summerhouse, but she couldn't entirely escape the memories of what had transpired there on the porch. How could she, when she felt the soreness between her legs with each step she took? But she also felt a faint throb of desire, and she hated herself for it.

Hurriedly she undressed, and beat on the door to the boathouse to roust any inhabitants. She didn't hear any scurrying, or the plop of anything into the water, so perhaps the place was clear. Nevertheless, she beat on the door again, and rattled the chain for good measure. Satisfied that she had done all she could in that regard, she walked out onto the dock until she was even with the garage door that sealed the boathouse on the lake side.

Gray and Monica and their friends had swum here often

during the summers; Faith had sneaked into the water for a swim on more than one occasion herself, but never when anyone else was present. She wasn't afraid of being in the water alone, and she knew how deep it was around the dock. Clutching the plastic-enclosed flashlight in one hand, she entered the water with a shallow dive, and surfaced with a gasp at the coldness. By July and August, the water would be pleasantly warm, but this was the end of May and it still held some of the winter chill. She swam briefly back and forth, acclimatizing herself to both the water and the activity, and in a moment the temperature felt much better.

It would be dark under the boathouse. Fumbling through the plastic, she switched on the flashlight, then didn't give herself any more time to think. Taking a deep breath, she dove beneath the edge of the door.

Visiblity was poor, even with the flashlight, and beneath the boathouse it was almost stygian. Above her was a rectangle of light, thankfully unoccupied by a boat, which would have made climbing out more difficult. Faith kicked for the light, and her head popped out of the water almost before she realized she had broken the surface. She reached out and grasped the edge of the boat slip to steady herself, and placed the flashlight on a solid surface. Only then did she brush her hair out of her face so she could clearly see her surroundings.

The interior of the boathouse was dim and mostly empty. She hauled herself out of the water and stood dripping, looking around and letting her eyes grow accustomed to the dimness. Once the boathouse had been littered with air mattresses and inner tubes, with life jackets festooned on wall hooks. The ski boat had rocked gently against the padded edges of the slip, and cases of marine oil had been stacked in one corner. All of that was gone. The boathouse had been emptied and cleaned; all it held now was a lawn mower, of the push variety, a yard rake, and a worn broom. There was no chance a single shell casing would have remained in place for twelve years.

Knowing it was useless, she looked anyway. She shone the flashlight into every corner, got down on her hands and knees and looked from that angle. Nothing.

Well, it had been a long shot anyway, she consoled herself. She had tried, and had enjoyed a nice morning swim.

She dove back into the water and under the door, surfacing into bright sunlight. This time there were no surprises waiting for her. Uneventfully she climbed onto the dock and stripped off the wet swimsuit, then toweled dry and dressed, having also had the foresight to bring along dry underwear. Except for her wet hair, she looked perfectly normal as she drove back to her house.

The answering machine held two more messages from Gray.

"Where are you, baby? Are you sleeping late, and have the phone turned off? I'll call back."

She buried her face in her hands. The machine beeped, and played another message. "You can't put it off forever. You have to talk to me sooner or later. Pick up the phone, baby."

She went to shower the lake water out of her hair. She heard the phone ringing even with the water running, and tried to ignore the sensation of being hounded. It wasn't easy. The calls continued all day long, each message becoming more and more irritated. He stopped cajoling, and started demanding.

"Faith, damn it, pick up the phone! If you think I'm going to let you ignore me—" He hung up without finishing the threat.

In between calls from Gray, she placed one to New Orleans, but Detective Ambrose wasn't available. She left a message for him, and waited for him to return her call.

It was late afternoon before he did so. She snatched up the receiver as soon as she heard the detective's voice. "This is Faith Hardy, Detective. Have you found Mr. Pleasant yet?"

"Nothing, Mrs. Hardy. I'm sorry. His car hasn't been found, either." His voice gentled. "Frankly, it doesn't look good. He doesn't fit the profile of someone who would disappear voluntarily; he had nothing to run from, and nothing to run to. He could have lost control of his car, had a heart attack, gone to sleep . . . If the car left the road and went into a bayou or river . . ." He let the sentence trail off, but Faith didn't need it spelled out. He thought a fisherman would eventually find Mr. Pleasant.

"Will you let me know?" she whispered, blinking back tears.

"Yes, ma'am, just as soon as I hear anything."

He wouldn't hear anything, though. Faith replaced the receiver in its cradle. Guy Rouillard had been murdered. It wasn't just a theory now; her mother had witnessed it. Mr. Pleasant had been asking pointed questions about Guy's disappearance. Would the murderer just have sat tight, figuring there was no evidence to be found, or would the fact that Mr. Pleasant was an investigator make him nervous? Nervous enough to commit another murder, perhaps?

That sweet little man was dead, and it was her fault.

No sooner had the thought registered than she rejected it. No, it wasn't her fault, it was the fault of the murderer. She wasn't willing to absolve him of one iota of blame.

Finding proof of Guy's murder would be extremely difficult, after twelve years. Mr. Pleasant had been missing less than two weeks. It would be smarter to concentrate on finding Mr. Pleasant. The evidence wouldn't be destroyed by time.

If she had killed someone, where would she hide the body? In Guy's case, the most likely answer was the lake. At the time of the murder, the boat had been right there. What would have been easier than to take him out to the deepest part of the lake, weight his body, and push him overboard? Such a convenient means had been lacking in Mr. Pleasant's case. For one thing, he probably hadn't been at the lake, and for another, there was no boat. So where would the killer try to dispose of the body?

Someplace where he wasn't likely to be seen. There were plenty of woods around for a hasty burial. Every so often, hunters would stumble across a body that had lain hidden for months, even years. But the killer had already successfully concealed one murder, so wouldn't he be likely to use the same method to dispose of a second body? If she thought so, and she did, then the Rouillard private lake was the place to search.

She couldn't do it by herself. She was willing to tackle

almost any job, but she had sense enough to know when she needed help. The lake would need to be dragged. That required boats, people, equipment. The sheriff could order it done, but she would have to convince him there was cause, and that the lake was the place to look. She couldn't do that without telling what she knew about Guy.

And she couldn't tell what she knew about Guy without first telling Gray. She couldn't let him find out from someone else, couldn't let his family be dragged into this mess without warning. Despite the hurt that still compressed her chest, despite the fact that she was too ashamed of herself to face him, she would somehow have to bring herself to tell him his father had been murdered, and she didn't know if she could do it.

Right on cue, the telephone rang. Faith closed her eyes.

"Goddamn it, Faith!" The muted fury in his voice came through loud and clear. "If you don't pick up the phone and tell me you're all right, I'm calling Mike McFane to come out there—"

She grabbed the receiver. "I'm all right!" she yelled, and slammed it back down. The *persistence* of the man!

The phone rang again, after just enough time for him to have redialed the number. "All right," he said when the machine answered, his voice under control now, though the anger still seethed in every word. "I shouldn't have said what I did. I was an asshole, and I'm sorry."

"I'm sorry you're an asshole, too," Faith muttered at the phone.

"You can kick my ass or slap my face tomorrow, whichever you want," he continued. "But don't think you're going to avoid me forever, because I'm not about to let it happen."

The line clicked as he hung up, and she sent up a hopeful prayer that he would stop calling now.

The phone rang again. She groaned. The machine picked up.

"I didn't wear a rubber last night," he calmly informed her.

"I noticed," she said sarcastically.

"I'd bet my ass you aren't using any kind of birth control, either," he said. "Think about it." The line clicked off again.

"You *fiend!*" Faith shrieked, her face turning red with rage. Think about it! How was she supposed to think about anything else, now that he'd so kindly brought the matter to her attention?

She stomped around the house, angry at both Gray and herself. They had no excuse; they weren't irresponsible teenagers, operating on hormones instead of brains—but that was exactly how they had acted. How could they have been so careless? She should have thought of the possibility of pregnancy before, but she had been so upset and miserable that consequences hadn't occurred to her.

Well, they were occurring now, with a vengeance. As if she didn't already have enough to worry about!

She was so panicked that it was half an hour before she thought to consult the calendar and count days. When she did, she sagged with relief. Her period was due to start in a week, and she had always been very regular. Nothing was certain, but the odds were on her side.

The next morning there was another note. Faith had been careful to keep her car locked since the first one, so this one was secured under the windshield wiper. She noticed it when she glanced out the window, and went out to investigate. When she saw what it was, she didn't touch it. She didn't want to know what it said. It had evidently been there all night, because the paper was wet with dew, the ink smeared.

She hadn't heard anything last night, even though she had slept restlessly once again. At least it was just a note, rather than another mutilated animal.

She was still in her pajamas, having just finished breakfast. Leaving the note where it was, she returned to the house. Within fifteen minutes she had dressed, put on her makeup, brushed her hair, and was on the way out the door.

She unlocked the car door and dropped her purse into the seat. Being careful not to tear the soggy paper, she lifted the windshield wiper and retrieved the note, holding one corner between thumb and forefinger. Then she got in the car and drove straight to the courthouse.

She parked in front of the square and, holding the note exactly the way she had before, marched up the three long, shallow steps. There was an information desk stationed just inside the doors, and she paused to ask a blue-haired little woman exactly where the sheriff's office was located.

"Just down this hall, dear, and to the left." The little woman pointed to her own left, and Faith obediently turned.

The smell of the courthouse was surprisingly pleasant, settling her jangled nerves a bit. It was composed of paper and ink, cleaning compounds, the ever-changing mix of people, and the cool gray scent of the marble floors and halls. The courthouse had been built fifty or sixty years before, when buildings had individual character. It had, of course, been "updated" several times over the years, with fluorescent lights replacing the original incandescent ones, so the clerks could have headaches to go along with the cheaper lighting costs. Window air-conditioning units were attached like barnacles to the building, growing randomly from office windows. In some places, though, particularly the hallways, ceiling fans still whirled lazily through the workday, keeping the air moving and fresh.

She reached the end of the hallway and turned left, to find another hallway stretching before her. Five doors down she came to an open set of double doors, with SHER DEPAR stenciled on the left half and IFF'S TMENT on the right, so that they made whole words only if the doors were closed. Inside was a long room with a high counter running the length of it; behind the counter were several desks, the dispatch radio, and two offices, one of which was slightly bigger than the other. The biggest office had Sheriff McFane's name on the door, which was half-open, but Faith couldn't see into the office from where she was standing. Photographs of past sheriffs hung on the wall, the extent of the parish's efforts at decoration. It wasn't a cheerful effect.

A middle-aged woman in a brown deputy's uniform looked up as Faith approached the counter. "What can I do for you?"

"I want to speak with Sheriff McFane, please."

The deputy peered over her reading glasses at Faith, obviously recognizing her from her visit the day before yesterday. All she said, though, was, "What's your name?"

"Faith Hardy."

"Let me see."

She went into Sheriff McFane's office with only a perfunctory knock, and Faith heard the murmur of voices. The deputy came out, said, "Come through there," and indicated a half door at the end of the counter. She hit a buzzer located under the counter, and the door clicked open.

Sheriff McFane came to the door of his office to greet her. "Good morning, Mrs. Hardy. How're you doin' today?"

For answer, Faith held up the note. "I got another one."

The good humor faded from his face, and he was instantly serious. "I don't like this at all," he murmured, plucking an evidence envelope from a desk and holding it open for Faith to drop in the note. She released it with the air of one disposing of smelly trash. "What does it say?"

"I haven't read it. It was under my windshield wiper this morning when I got up. I've only touched one corner, so I wouldn't smear any fingerprints, assuming any are left. The paper's wet," she explained.

"Dew. That means it had been on your windshield for several hours. Actually, we have several good prints already, from the other note and the box. The problem is, we won't be able to find a match unless the note writer has been fingerprinted before." He ushered her into his office and dumped the note out onto his desk blotter.

"Since you haven't read it yet, let's see what it says." He opened the lap drawer of his desk and pawed through the contents, finally coming up with eyebrow tweezers. Using the tweezers and the tip of a pen, he carefully unfolded the damp paper. Faith angled her head to read the block letters:

YOU'RE NOT WANTED HERE LEAVE BEFORE YOU GET HURT

"Same person," Sheriff McFane said. "No punctuation."

"A deliberate signature?"

"Maybe, but could be it's just a departure from his usual style, sort of camouflage." He frowned at her. "Mrs. Hardy

—Faith—Gray and I both told you the other day, living out there all by yourself could be dangerous."

"I'm not going to move," she said, repeating a sentence she must have said twenty times when she had been here to fill out the report on the dead cat.

"Then how about getting yourself a dog? It doesn't have to be a guard dog, just one that will set up a racket if it hears anything outside."

Surprised, she stared at him. A dog. She'd never had a pet of any kind, so that option simply hadn't occurred to her. "Why, I think I will. Thank you, Sheriff. That's a good idea."

"Good. Get one as soon as possible. Stop by the pound and pick out a young, healthy one. A half-grown youngster would be good, still young enough to take to you real quick, but old enough that it can bark, not just make puppy yaps." He looked down at the note on his desk. "About all I can do right now is have my deputies drive by your house a couple of times each shift. We just don't have much to go on."

"And a few notes and a dead cat aren't exactly the crime of the century."

He gave her a quick grin, full of Huckleberry Finn charm. "Can't even get 'im for cruelty to animals. If it makes you feel any better, the cat wasn't tortured. It was a road kill. Somebody just scooped it up, is all. It makes *me* feel a little better about the danger of the situation. A real psycho would have enjoyed killing a cat."

It did make her feel better. The memory of that mangled little corpse had made her feel sick every time it came to mind. The cat was still just as dead, but at least if it had been hit by a car, it had probably died instantly. She couldn't bear to think that it had suffered.

She left the sheriff's department and retraced her path. Halfway down the long corridor, she saw a tall, powerfully built man with long, dark hair stop to speak to the little blue-haired lady.

Faith's heart almost stopped. Without missing a step she whipped around to go back toward the sheriff's department, panicked at the thought of facing him again after the rawness of their last meeting. It was a purely instinctive reaction; her mind knew she needed to talk to him, but her body fled.

She heard the low rumble of his voice, recognizable anywhere, and speeded her steps. As she reached the end of the hallway and turned the corner, she glanced back and saw him striding rapidly toward her, his long legs shrinking the distance between them at an alarming rate. His dark eyes were locked on her.

She whisked around the corner, and the women's rest room was right there, on the left. She saw the sign and darted inside, then pushed the door closed and stood with one hand pressed to her chest in an effort to calm the thudding of her heart. She glanced around. She was alone in the tiny, two-stall facility, and she waited, frozen, for the sound of his footsteps passing by.

The door swung abruptly inward, forcing her to jump back to avoid being hit. Gray filled the doorway, big and muscular and threatening, a dark scowl on his face. His eyes glittered like black ice.

Faith tried to back away, but she bumped against the wash-area counter. There was very little room for maneuvering in the tiny rest room. "You can't come in here!"

He stepped forward and shut the door. "Are you sure about that?"

She took a deep breath, reaching for calmness. "Someone will come in."

"Maybe." He moved closer, so close that only inches separated them and she had to tilt her head back to see him. "Maybe not. You chose the place, I didn't."

"I didn't choose anything," she snapped. "I was trying to avoid you—"

"I noticed," he said dryly. "What are you doing here?"

There was no reason not to tell him. "I found another note on my car this morning. I brought it to Sheriff McFane."

His scowl grew darker. "Damn it, Faith—"

"He told me to get a dog," she said, interrupting the sermon. "I was just on my way to the pound."

"That's a good idea. Don't bother with the pound,

though; I'll get one for you. Why didn't you answer the phone yesterday?"

"I didn't want to talk to you." She glared up at him. "I'll get my own dog, thank you. And I'm not pregnant."

His dark brows arched. "How do you know? Did you start your period?"

"No, but it isn't the right time of the month."

He snorted. "Honey, I'm Catholic. I know a lot of kids who got their start at the wrong time of the month."

"Maybe you do, but you can take my word on this." As she spoke, she tried to slide sideways.

Gray put his hands on her waist, trapping her. "For God's sake, stand still," he said irritably. "You're always trying to run away. What do you think I'm going to do to you?"

"The same thing you did the last time I saw you," she retorted, then blushed. As much as she had dreaded meeting him again, now that it had happened, she felt the usual rush of excitement. No matter what, she could never be matter-of-fact about being with him, whether in battle or anything else. Gray wasn't a man who elicited boredom in the people around him. He was too big, too vital, too overwhelmingly male and sexual. Even as a child she had responded to his presence, and now that she was a woman, the effect he had on her was painfully magnified. She would try not to let *him* know it, but she couldn't lie to herself. Already her body was tightening, growing warm and moist with response. It was instinctive, and totally separate from the dictates of her mind.

His brows lowered over those midnight eyes, which began to glitter. "You liked it," he said softly, dangerously. "Don't try to pretend you weren't willing. I felt every little ripple, baby."

Faith felt the color intensify in her cheeks, and not just from embarrassment. If only he hadn't touched her, if only he weren't so close that she could smell him, hot and musky and deliciously male. "No," she said just as softly. "I wasn't saying that." She paused, gathering herself for the lie of her life. "I just don't want to do it again. It was a mistake, and—"

"You're lying." His gaze was on her breasts. Slowly his

273

eyes lifted, and his expression changed again, tightening with lust. "Your nipples are puckered," he whispered, "and I haven't even kissed you yet."

Her breath caught. She didn't have to look down to see if he was telling the truth; she could feel the heavy tightness of her breasts, feel her nipples rasping against the lace that covered them. Warmth was gathering in her body, seeping down to pool in her loins. She stared helplessly at him.

Color darkened his high cheekbones, and his breathing deepened. "Faith," he murmured.

The tension was like a cord between them, thrumming with awareness. She felt as if the cord were being reeled in, inexorably pulling them together. Panicked, she flattened her hands on his chest and pushed, with a total lack of results. "We can't," she said weakly. "Not here, for God's sake!"

He wasn't listening. His eyes were fastened on her mouth. He said, "What?" in an absent tone as his hands tightened on her waist and pulled her against him. She moaned aloud at the feel of his hard, vital body pressed all along her. He bent his head to kiss her, and she automatically lifted her mouth. His lips were soft, his mouth hot. Response thrilled through her, as irresistible as the tide, and her hands stopped pushing against him to clench fistfuls of his shirt. He urged her even closer, and slanted his head to deepen the kiss, his tongue thrusting into her mouth. She made a little "hmmm" of delight and sucked at it, curling her own tongue upward to stroke his.

He shuddered as if struck, and cupped her buttocks to lift her hard against his thick erection. The heat of desire exploded into a wildfire, melding them together. He tore his mouth free and groaned, "Jesus," as he jerked up her skirt and roughly shoved her panties down her thighs.

The sink counter was cold against her bare buttocks, and she blinked at the shock, surfacing a bit from the dark tide. "Wait," she blurted.

"I can't." His voice was rough, shaky. He gripped her hips with one arm as he bent to strip her panties completely off. Before she could react, he straightened and hoisted her onto the counter. Pushing her thighs apart, he moved between them, then began jerking frenziedly at the zipper of his fly. He grunted as he freed his erection, and then guided himself to her. Faith dug her nails into his heavy shoulders as she felt the heat of his naked flesh pressing against her soft folds, burrowing between them, searching for the opening to her body. He found it, and she moaned at the pressure as that heavy invasion began. He pushed into her, stretching her almost unbearably. She was still a little sore from the first time, and he felt even more massive than before.

Then he was in her to the hilt, and he paused, resting his damp forehead against hers. "God, you're tight as a fist," he gasped. She was trembling violently, and he gathered her closer, stroking her back, comforting her. After a moment he moved experimentally, restrained little thrusts that set off spasms of painfully intense pleasure and made both of them shudder wildly.

"Just putting it in you makes me ready to come." His voice was thick, his breath warm in her ear. He thrust a little harder, a little faster. She felt the thick ridge of his penis head moving back and forth inside her, and her inner muscles clamped down in frantic pleasure. She moaned again, digging her nails into him in an effort to control that wild rush. He cursed, the words low and shaky with delight. Putting his hand on her bare bottom, he pulled her to the edge of the counter, positioning her so that every thrust ground him against her exposed, straining little sexual nub. It was what he had done before, and she had no more defense against it than she'd had the first time.

He began thrusting heavily into her, pounding toward orgasm. She felt on fire, arching helplessly to meet his hips, the ecstatic tension in her loins coiling violently, out of control, her body taken over by and intent on this swelling, ungovernable pleasure.

The door creaked as it began to open.

Gray moved like lightning, slapping his left palm against the door and slamming it shut before it had opened more than a fraction of an inch. "Hey!" a woman squawked indignantly from the other side.

"This one's occupied," he said hoarsely, not missing a beat with his plunging hips. "Go somewhere else." Faith couldn't say anything. Her eyes widened with alarm, but all she could do was look helplessly up at him.

Gray's lips drew back over his teeth and his head dropped forward as he began hammering faster. His face was flushed, satisfaction only a few moments away.

Faith shuddered wildly as the coil of tension suddenly released and the fierce, pulsing flood of sensation swept through her. Shivering and pushing hard against him, she buried her face against his chest and bit his shirt to muffle her gasping cries.

He kept his hand flat against the door, gripping her bottom with his right hand to anchor himself. He shoved hard into her, twice, three times, again, then bucked violently. His head fell back and a harsh, guttural cry rumbled up from his chest.

There was an insistent banging on the door. "What are you doing in there?" the woman said in shrill, grating tones. "That's the lady's room! You aren't supposed to be in there!"

Slowly Gray's head came up. The expression in his eyes was indescribable, as if he couldn't believe what was happening. He took a deep breath, and exploded. "Goddamn it, woman!" he roared with furious indignation. "Can't you tell I'm *busy?*"

Faith dissolved into laughter.

❦ Eighteen ❧

Faith had never been more embarrassed in her life. When she got home, she dashed into the house and locked all the doors, as if that would do any good. She had no clear memory of the drive home, but she could recall in excruciating detail every step she had made through the courthouse, with her face flaming and her thighs sticking together, and every curious look had made her want to cringe. She hadn't, though; she had walked out with her chin in the air and an "I dare you to say anything" look on her face. The bluff must have worked, because no one had stopped her.

She had jumped off the counter as soon as Gray released her, and locked herself in one of the stalls. Uncontrollable giggles shook her as she tried to tidy herself. The arrival of her panties, tossed over the top of the stall, sent her into absolute whoops. "Would you shut up?" she heard Gray mutter fiercely, and she all but collapsed in hysterics. He said something else, but she didn't understand him, and a moment later the door squeaked as he left. It swung open immediately, and a pair of navy pumps took up residence in the stall next to Faith. The owner of the pumps was also the owner of the shrill voice, and she was extremely indignant.

"I ought to tell the sheriff," she said huffily, loud enough that Faith could hear her over the sound of her own giggles.

"Carryin' on in the ladies' rest room! No telling who might have walked in, maybe a mother with her little kids, and just imagine children seein' something like that. It's sinful and disgusting, the way people don't have no shame any-more—"

The tirade was delivered to the accompaniment of a steady stream of urine splashing into the toilet bowl. Evidently part of the lady's wrath was due to the fact that she had been in desperate need of a bathroom. Trying to control her giggles, Faith took advantage of the woman's preoccupation and dashed out of the stall. Once in the hallway, she tried to assume a normal air, and walked quickly to hcr car. Gray hadn't been anywhere in sight, but then she hadn't exactly looked for him. Probably he'd ducked into the men's room.

Faith sank down in a kitchen chair and covered her face with her hands, groaning with mortification. What was wrong with her, that she couldn't manage to say no to him even in a public place? *The courthouse rest room!* Even Renee had used more discretion than that.

The telephone rang, but she didn't move to answer it. The machine in the office picked up, and she heard Gray's deep voice, but was too far away to understand what he was saying. He hung up, and a few minutes later the phone rang again. This time, however, Faith recognized Margot's voice. She knew she should pick up, but she didn't. She simply couldn't carry on a normal conversation; her nerves were still jangling, and she was physically shaking from the aftereffects of an adrenaline rush. She didn't understand how risk junkies got addicted, because the crash was making her sick.

When she thought her knees would support her, she got up and headed for the bathroom. What she needed right now, more than anything, was a shower.

Gray shook his head in disbelief at himself as he drove to Faith's house. He was sure she was there, even though she hadn't answered the phone. He couldn't believe what they'd done, or the force of the attraction that had made it irresistible. He hadn't done anything *that* stupid even as a teenager, and God knows he'd been wild as a buck.

He snorted with suppressed laughter. That damned old biddy! Faith had jumped up and hidden in a stall, laughing like a maniac, and he'd been left there with one hand on the door to keep it shut, and his pants down around his knees. Quickly he'd shifted position, moving to stand with his back against the door while he pulled up his pants. Faith's panties had been lying on the floor, so he'd scooped them up and tossed them over the stall, and she'd shrieked all the louder despite his order to be quiet. The old bitch outside wasn't going away; she kept beating on the door, getting louder and louder. Between her and Faith, he was almost deafened.

Finally he told Faith he'd meet her out front, but he wasn't certain she'd heard him, the way she was whooping hysterically. There was nothing to do but brazen it out. After glancing down to make certain everything was zipped and fastened, he opened the door and stepped out, glaring down at a plump, red-faced woman who was all but squirming with indignation. She sputtered furiously at him, but Gray cut her off. "The men's room was full," he snapped. "What did you expect me to do, piss in the hallway?" Then he stalked into the men's room, which was right next door, and leaned against the wall until his shoulders stopped shaking with silent laughter, because the old biddy had snapped right back, "Then what *did* you piss in, the sink?"

Oh, Jesus. He began laughing helplessly again. He knew the old biddy, at least by sight. She worked in the tax assessor's office. The tale that he'd been fooling around with some hussy in the women's rest room would be all over the courthouse by lunch, and all over the town by tomorrow morning.

His grin faded. Faith would be mortified.

She probably was anyway. She hadn't waited for him out front, but had probably driven home with all possible speed, and barricaded herself in the house. His little Puritan would be sick with embarrassment.

He sighed with relief when he saw her car in the driveway. He pulled in, but didn't stop behind her car. Instead he steered his car around to the backyard, and circled behind the open tool shed where she kept her lawn mower. Honeysuckle vines grew over the shed and part of the way up a steel cable bracing a power pole, forming a nice screen to hide the car. He nosed the Jaguar forward until the hood was just touching the honeysuckle, then got out, checking in both directions. The road wasn't visible in either direction, so that meant the car wasn't visible from the road. He felt like an idiot, but he hoped Faith appreciated the concern for her reputation.

He went to the kitchen door and rapped on it, waiting impatiently. She didn't open it, and he knocked again. "Faith, open the door."

Faith halted on the other side of the door, her hand hovering at the curtain. She had just been about to twitch it aside and see who was pounding on her kitchen door. She had almost jumped out of her skin at the sounds of a car pulling into her driveway and behind the house. She was relieved that it was Gray, but of all the people she didn't think she could face right now, he headed the list.

"Go away," she said.

The doorknob rattled. "Faith." Her name was spoken softly, calmly. "Open the door, baby."

"Why?"

"We have things to talk over."

Undoubtedly, but she didn't want to do it. She wanted to be a coward about the whole thing, and hide until she was over the embarrassment. "Maybe tomorrow," she hedged.

"Now." There it was, that gentle, inflexible note that said her door would be kicked open within the next ten seconds if she didn't open it herself. Helpless and resentful, she unlocked the door.

He stepped inside and immediately turned the lock again, his gaze never leaving her. She had just gotten out of the shower, and hadn't had time to dress before she heard the car pulling in. She had grabbed her thin robe from the back of the bathroom door, and put it on. There was nothing seductive about the robe; it was plain, white cotton, belted at the waist. But she was acutely aware that, beneath it, she was damp and bare. She clutched the lapels together over her breasts. "What do you want to talk about?"

An incredibly gentle smile spread over his face as he looked down at her. "Later," he said, and swept her up in his arms.

Two hours later, they lay sweaty and exhausted amid the tangled sheets on her bed. The noon sun forced its way through the closed slats of the blinds, throwing thin lines of white across the floor. A gentle breeze from the ceiling fan wafted across her bare flesh, raising tiny goose bumps. Her body was so acutely sensitive that she imagined she could feel each fine, downy hair lifting at the slight chill. Her heart was beating in slow, heavy thumps, her veins and arteries pulsing with each beat. Gray lay sprawled on his back, his eyes closed and his chest heaving, while she was curled against his side with her head pillowed on his shoulder.

It was a long time before she felt as if she could move. Her limbs were heavy and limp, utterly boneless. In those two hours he had taken her three times, with as much ferocity as if the time in the courthouse hadn't happened. And as demanding and immediate as his hunger had been, her response had matched it. She had clung to him, her nails digging into his back, her hips lifting eagerly to meet each thrust, and it seemed as if her fire had only fed his own. She didn't know how many times she had reached satisfaction; this last time had felt like one long swell that crested, then refused to subside, so that she had been awash in sensation, drunk with pleasure.

As his breathing slowed, Gray stirred beside her and tried to lift his head, only to let it fall back with a groan. "Oh, God. I can't move."

"Then don't," she muttered, opening her eyes a slit.

A couple of minutes later, he tried again. With a great deal of effort he raised his head and slowly surveyed the tangle of their nude bodies lying amid the wreckage of the bed. His gaze settled on his penis, lying soft on his thighs. "You damn fool," he barked. "This time, *stay down!*"

The whimsy startled her, and she began giggling helplessly. She buried her face against his shoulder, her entire body shaking.

Gray let his head drop back to the pillow, and cuddled her closer. "Easy for you to laugh," he grumbled. "The damn thing's trying to kill me. It never has had much stopping sense, but this is ridiculous. It must think I'm still sixteen."

"It can't think," she pointed out, her giggles increasing.

"You're telling me. You can reason with something that thinks." Her giggles escalated even more, and he tickled her in revenge. "Stop laughing," he ordered, though a smile teased his mouth. "Do you know what it's like to have a prominent body part that won't listen to either common sense or orders?"

"Well, no, but I know what it's like to be in the vicinity of one."

He chuckled and lazily rubbed his hand across his chest. "Do you know why men name their cocks?"

"No, why?" she asked, trying to stifle her laughter.

"So most of the major decisions in their lives won't be made by a total stranger."

They shook with laughter, and Faith grabbed a corner of the sheet to dry her eyes. She had never seen this playful, bawdy side of Gray before, and she was charmed down to her toes.

He heaved himself up on his elbow, holding her head cradled in the crook of his arm as he smiled down at her. "It's all your fault, anyway," he told her, smoothing a tangle of dark red hair away from her face. His hand continued in a slow stroke down her throat, over the delicate sweep of her collarbone, to close over her breast.

"Mine?" she asked indignantly.

"Sure." Gently he cupped her breast, lifting it. He lightly rasped the pad of his thumb over the puffy pink swell of her nipple, and watched in fascination as it immediately puckered and turned red. "Your nipples are like raspberries," he marveled, and leaned down to take that particular raspberry into his mouth, circling it with his tongue, rolling it back and forth.

Faith quivered in his arms, alarmed by the immediate swell of desire. She didn't think she could stand it again. "I can't," she moaned, but he noticed that her other nipple had also puckered.

He drew back and admired his work, the red nipple glistening wetly. "That's good," he said absently, "because I sure as hell can't." Faith's breasts were pale, with the sheen of satin, and her skin so translucent and fine that the blue tracery of veins seemed just under the surface. They were firm and full and upright, and he couldn't keep his hands off of them. Hell, he couldn't keep his hands off of her, period. "Just think how pretty these will be, when they're full of milk."

She slapped his shoulder. "I told you, I'm not pregnant!"

"You don't know that," he teased.

"Yes, I do know that."

"Your timing could be off."

"My timing is never off."

"This once it could be."

She glared at him, then returned to what he'd said before. "How is it my fault?"

"It must be," he said reasonably. "Every time you're near, I get hard."

"I'm not doing anything. It has to be your fault."

"You're breathing. Evidently that's enough." He collapsed back on the bed and pulled her so she was lying half on him. His free hand smoothed over her slender back, and down to stroke the round curves of her bottom. "Part of it's the way you smell, like honey and cinnamon, all sweet and spicy at the same time."

Her head lifted and she stared at him, startled. "I've always loved the way you smell," she confessed. "Even when I was a little kid. I thought you were the best smell in the world, but I've never been able to exactly describe it."

"So you've had a crush on me since you were little?" he asked, pleased.

To hide her expression, she tucked her head back into its resting place in the hollow of his shoulder, and inhaled the delicious male scent she had just mentioned. "No," she said softly. "It wasn't a crush."

He grunted and settled himself more comfortably, pulling her thigh up to ride across his hips. She felt his penis twitch warningly against the soft inside of her leg, then subside. "I used to worry about you," he murmured, his voice becoming sleepy. "Running around alone in the woods the way you did."

She was silent a moment. "How often did you see me?"

"A couple of times."

"I saw you," she said, gathering her courage.

"In the woods?"

"At the summerhouse. With Lindsey Partain. I watched through the window."

His eyes shot open. "Why, you little sneak!" he said, and swatted her bottom, hard. "I guess you got an eyeful."

"I sure did," she agreed, rubbing her bottom indignantly. She retaliated by twisting her fingers in his chest hair and pulling.

He yelped and rubbed his chest. "Ouch!"

"Revenge is sweet," she said. "And prompt."

"I'll remember that," he said ruefully, squinting down at his chest. "Damn, there's a bald patch there."

"There is not."

She rubbed her cheek against him, her eyes closing as she luxuriated in the feel of him, so warm and solid and vital. She had been in paradise from the moment he carried her to bed. Lying here like this with him, so relaxed, all hostility gone and desire thoroughly sated, was more than she had ever dared hope for in her life. None of their problems were solved and the hostility would undoubtedly return, but for right now, this moment, she was happy.

So happy, in fact, that there was only a little hurt mixed in with the curiosity when she said, "You made love to Lindsey in French."

His eyes had closed drowsily, but they popped open again. "What?"

"I heard you. You made love to her in French. Lots of love words and compliments."

Gray was too experienced not to notice how she felt about that, and immediately discerned the reason. He gave her a disbelieving look, then put his head back on the pillow and shouted with laughter. Faith's lower lip trembled and she tried to turn away, but his arms tightened and he held her right where she was.

"Oh, Jesus," he said, wheezing with the effort it took to control himself. He wiped his eyes with the back of his hand. "You little innocent. I'm fluent in French, but it isn't my first language." It was plain by the mortified expression in those green eyes that she didn't understand, so he explained. "Baby, if I can still think clearly enough to speak French, then I'm not totally involved in what I'm doing. It may sound pretty, but it doesn't mean anything. Men are different from women; the more excited we are, the more like cavemen we sound. I could barely speak English with you, much less French. As I remember, my vocabulary deteriorated to a few short, explicit words, 'fuck' being the most prominent."

To his amazement, she blushed, and he smiled at this further evidence of her charming prudery. "Go to sleep," he said gently. "Lindsey didn't even rate a replay."

God only knew why she found that reassuring, but she did. She went to sleep as easily as a child, exhausted by the events of the morning, and woke to make love again. He was more leisurely this time, and, with a positively wicked gleam in his dark eyes, whispered French love words to her. Then he had to grab her hands to protect his chest hairs, roaring with laughter at her indignation. That was how they passed the afternoon, sleeping, making love, and murmuring drowsily to each other afterward. If the lovemaking was wildly exciting, it was in the pillow talk that a deeper kind of intimacy was forged, a quiet sharing of secrets and thoughts, a linking together of their pasts.

"Tell me about the foster home you were in," he said once, and was relieved when she smiled.

"The Greshams. They gave me the first real home I'd ever known. I still keep in touch with them."

"How did you wind up in a foster home?"

"Pa took off not long after . . . after that night," she said, faltering a little. "Russ, my oldest brother, wasn't far behind him. Nicky tried to earn enough to feed us, I'll say that for him, but he was relieved when the social services people found us. We were in Beaumont at the time. Jodie was put in one foster home, and Scottie and I in another. It wasn't easy to find someone who would take Scottie, too, but the Greshams agreed if I would take care of him. As if I would leave him behind," she said softly.

"What happened to him?"

"He died the next January. At least he was happy, the last six months of his life. After we moved in, the Greshams were wonderful to him. They bought him toys, played with him. He had so much fun at Christmas, but he faded fast after that. I sat up with him," she said in a quiet voice, her eyes liquid with tears as she stared down the years. "I held his hand while he died." She brushed her hand across her eyes. "I used to wonder if Guy was his father."

He'd never thought of that. He stared at her, disturbed both by the idea that his father might have sired other children, and by the horrifying thought that he might have thrown his little brother out into the dirt.

Faith groped for his hand. "I don't think he was," she said, compelled to comfort him. "Your father wouldn't have left one of his children to live the way we did. If Scottie had been his, he'd have taken care of him. There's no telling who Scottie's daddy was; I doubt it was Pa."

Gray blinked, his own eyes shiny with tears. "Yes," he said hoarsely. "He'd have taken care of him."

Later, he asked, "What happened to the rest of your family?"

"I don't know. I think Jodie's living around Jackson, but I haven't seen her since she turned eighteen. I don't have any idea what happened to Pa and the boys." She carefully didn't mention Renee.

So her family, such as it was, had been shattered by his actions. He held her tight, as if he could shield her from the pain of the past.

"I hated Dad, for a while," he admitted. "God, when I found out he'd left—he was our rock, not Mother. It hurt so much, I couldn't stand it."

Faith bit her lip, thinking of what she had to tell him, and soon.

"Monica tried to kill herself," he said abruptly. "She cut

her wrists right after I told her Dad was gone. She almost bled to death before I could get her to a hospital. When I came to the shack that night, I'd just left the hospital in Baton Rouge."

He was trying to explain his rage, she realized, why he'd done what he had. She kissed his shoulder, forgiveness in the gesture. Actually, she had forgiven him long ago, understanding the pain and sense of betrayal he must have been feeling.

He stared up at the ceiling fan. "Mother withdrew completely. She stopped talking, even stopped feeding herself. She didn't come out of her room for two years. She's the most self-centered person I've ever known," he said with brutal honesty, "but I don't ever want to see her that way again."

And that was why he was so adamant that neither Monica nor his mother be upset by anything Faith said or did. She had experienced some of his overprotectiveness herself. In some ways, he was like a feudal lord in Prescott, his influence touching almost every aspect of parish life, and like a feudal lord, he took his responsibilities seriously.

He rolled on top of her, entering her with a gentle insistence that nevertheless made her catch her breath, for she was sore from all the other times. He braced himself on his elbows and cradled her head in his hands. "That night is a link between us," he whispered. "Ugly as it was, we share the memories. And it wasn't all ugly. I wanted you that night, Faith." He began moving slowly inside her, his eyes darkening with the slow build of passion. "You were only fourteen, but I wanted you. And when I saw you again, in the motel, it was as if the twelve years apart didn't exist, because I still wanted you."

Then he began to smile. "Do you want me to say it in French?" he asked.

When she woke the next time, she lay quietly and watched him sleeping. His black lashes were dark smudges on his cheekbones, and black beard stubbled his lower jaw. His lips were softly parted as he slept, his powerful body relaxed. The beauty of him shook her. With his long hair tousled around his shoulders, he looked like a pirate taking his rest in a lady's bed after a long day of ship-boardings and sword fights. The tiny diamond in his left ear didn't do anything to detract from the image.

She was too sore to possibly make love again, she thought, but still his body drew her. He was wonderfully made, all long bones and hard muscle. One arm dangled off the side of the bed, but his other hand lay relaxed on his chest. He had big hands, his fingers lean and well shaped, but his little finger was as thick as her thumb. She thought of those hands on her body and shivered with delight.

She leaned over him, delicately inhaling the warm scent of his skin, rising off him on waves of heat. This was *Gray*. The realization stunned her anew. He was actually here. She could touch him, kiss him, do all the things she had spent most of her life only dreaming about.

His flesh drew her like a lodestone, making her breath come a little faster, and her skin flush. There were no restraints on her natural sensuality now, and the freedom to touch him, and be touched by him, was intoxicating. She laid her hand on his thigh, feeling hard muscle under the roughness of hair, then slipped her fingertips, in a dreamy, sensual sampling, down to where the flesh was smooth and hairless, trailing her fingertips across it. His scrotum hung low, his testicles like two small eggs in their soft sac. She turned her hand and cupped it, feeling it cool and heavy in her palm. He stirred restlessly, his legs falling apart, but he didn't wake. He was a wonderfully male animal, and, for the moment at least, totally hers.

She leaned over him even closer, letting the tips of her breasts drag through the crisp, curly hair on his chest, and sucked in a quick breath at the sharp tingle of sensation that drew her nipples erect.

His eyelids fluttered and opened. "Ummm," he said, a low hum of pleasure, and automatically reached up to circle her with his arms.

She nuzzled her face against his throat and slid all the way onto him, her entire body squirming sinuously as she rubbed herself over him, feline in her enjoyment. "You feel so good," she whispered, nipping his earlobe, then licking it. "All three of the H factors."

"What are the H factors?" he asked. "Or do I want to know?"

"Hot, hard, and hairy."

He chuckled, and stretched languidly beneath her. It was a startling sensation, like being on a lumpy raft tossed about by the ocean. She hung on to his shoulders to keep from falling off.

His hair brushed her fingers, and when he had settled, she thrust her hand into the black mass of it. It was thick and silky, with just a hint of curl. Most women would have killed to have hair like that. "Why do you wear your hair long?" she asked, picking up another strand and pulling it around to tickle his nose with the end of it. "And why the earring? That's pretty dashing for a man who sits on several corporate boards."

He obligingly made a face, then began to laugh. "Promise not to tell?"

"Promise—unless you say someone scared you with a picture of Sinéad O'Connor; I'd have to tell that."

His white teeth flashed as he gave her a faintly embarrassed grin. "It's almost as bad. I'm afraid of hair clippers."

She was so astonished that she slipped off his chest. "Hair clippers?" she echoed. This six foot four, over-two-hundred-pound pirate was afraid of *hair clippers?*

"I don't like the noise," he explained, turning onto his side and curling one arm under his head. His eyes were smiling. "Gives me the willies. I can remember when I was four or five years old, howling my head off as Dad tried to hold me still for old Herbert Dumas to give me a haircut. Evidently holding me down made Dad feel like a traitor, so he started trying to bribe me to be good, but I just couldn't do it. I'd hear that first *bzzz* and nearly jump out of my skin. By the time I was ten, we had negotiated our way to scissor cuts. The older I get, the further apart the hair trims are. As for the earring—" He laughed out loud. "It's sort of camouflage. Wearing the earring makes it look as if my hair is long on purpose. A style, rather than a phobia."

"Who trims your hair?" she asked, too fascinated to laugh. She was still trying to deal with the image of a grown man avoiding barbershops the way some people avoided the dentist.

"Sometimes I do. Sometimes I'll get it trimmed when I'm in New Orleans. There's a salon there with a standing rule not to turn on any hair clippers while I'm there. Why? Do you want to take over the job?" He laid his hand on the side of her neck, his thumb brushing her earlobe. He was smiling, but she sensed he was serious.

"You'd trust me to cut your hair?"

"Of course. Wouldn't you trust me to cut yours?"

Her reply was swift. "Not in this lifetime. But I'd let you shave my legs."

"It's a deal!" was his reply, just as swift, as he grabbed for her.

It was almost twilight the next time he stirred awake, and groaned as he rubbed his hand over his face. "I'm starving," he announced in a rumbling voice. "Damn, I need to call home and let someone know where I am."

Faith rolled onto her back, cautiously stretching. Though she had spent most of the day in bed, she was as tired as if she had been up all night. Being in bed with Gray Rouillard was not restful. It was a lot of fun, it was wonderfully exciting, but restful, it wasn't.

Now that he had mentioned it, she realized how hungry she was. The idea of lunch hadn't occurred to either of them, and breakfast had been many hours ago. Food was just what she needed.

He sat up on the side of the bed, giving her a wonderful view of his buttocks. She reached out and stroked them as he picked up the phone, and he tossed a quick grin over his shoulder. "Feel free," he invited, punching in his own number.

His back was just as marvelous as his front, she thought dreamily. Thick with muscle, bisected by the deep groove of his spine, tapering from those wide shoulders down to a taut waist.

"Hi," he said into the phone. "Tell Delfina I won't be home for dinner."

Faith heard the indistinct murmur of a voice, evidently asking where he was, because he calmly replied, "I'm at Faith's house."

The voice was still indistinct, but considerably more agitated. She watched his back muscles tense and immediately felt uncomfortable, as if she was eavesdropping. She had to get away, she thought distractedly. She couldn't bear to listen to him make an excuse for his presence here. She sat up and swung her legs off the bed, wincing at the unexpected stiffness of her back and legs.

"Monie," Gray said patiently, and sighed. "We have to talk. I'll be home in the morning—no, not before. In the morning. If anything important comes up, call me here."

Slowly Faith stood up, straightening with difficulty. Every muscle in her body seemed to be protesting. Her legs were ridiculously weak, her thigh muscles trembling. She desperately wanted to leave the room, but nothing was cooperating. She took one hobbling step, wincing with pain, then another.

"I said, we'll talk tomorrow." His voice was firm. He looked over his shoulder at Faith, started to glance away, then his attention focused on her like a laser beam. "'Bye," he said absently to Monica, hanging up and cutting her off in midprotest. Then he was on his feet, coming around the end of the bed to where Faith wobbled.

"Poor baby," he crooned. "Muscles sore?"

She scowled at him.

"I know just the thing," he promised, stripping the top sheet from the bed and shaking it out.

"So do I. A hot shower."

"Later." He wrapped the sheet around her and picked her up. "Just be quiet and enjoy."

"Enjoy what?"

"Being quiet, what else?" he replied maddeningly, and she couldn't even hit him, because her arms were wrapped up in the sheet.

She found out soon enough. He carried her into the

kitchen and carefully laid her on the table, unwrapping the sheet to spread it out beneath her. "I had some great ideas about this table the first time I saw it," he said, with more than a little satisfaction.

Startled, she said, "What are you doing?" She had been naked in his arms for hours, but somehow, lying naked on top of her kitchen table made her feel unbearably exposed, as if she were a human sacrifice lying on a stone altar.

"Massage," he said. "Stay there." He left the room, leaving her lying there. The hard surface was uncomfortable, but the promise of a massage kept her in place. He returned to the kitchen with a bottle of baby oil and a washcloth in his hands. "On your stomach," he ordered. He turned on the hot water in the sink and let it run until steam began to rise, then filled a bowl and dropped the bottle of oil into it.

Stiffly she obeyed. He hadn't turned on any lights and the kitchen was deeply shadowed, twilight only a few moments away. The air conditioning was on, and though she had been perfectly comfortable in the bedroom, the cold of the table seeped through the sheet and chilled her. She shivered, wishing he would hurry.

"Close your eyes and relax," he said quietly. "Go to sleep if you want."

Her sore muscles were adjusting to the hardness of the table, allowing her to relax fractionally. She closed her eyes and concentrated on the sounds of what he was doing. She could hear water splashing, and sighed in anticipation of feeling that warm oil being rubbed into her skin.

His voice was low and soothing, little more than a murmur. "I'm going to wash you, so you'll be more comfortable," he said, just before she felt a wet, very warm washcloth between her legs. The heat felt wonderful on her sore, swollen flesh. He was incredibly gentle, but just as thorough as he cleaned away the evidence of his lovemaking. He took the cloth away, and she heard water running again. "It's going to be cold this time," he warned, and the cold pad of the washcloth was pressed between her legs. He repeated the compress several times, soothing the ache. Then he reached for the oil.

He began at her shoulders, his powerful fingers digging deep into her muscles. She automatically tightened in resistance, then relaxed as the strength and tension seemed to flow out of her. The heated oil made his hands slide over her skin, leaving it slick and fragrant. He worked down each arm, even massaging her hands, and between her fingers. And everywhere his hands went, they left behind loosened tendons, limp muscles, and total contentment. Faith purred her pleasure as he returned to her back, starting at her waist and moving his hands upward in long, powerful sweeps that compressed her rib cage and made her groan aloud with each stroke. He relentlessly searched out every stiff muscle, and kneaded it until it was pliant beneath his hands.

Her legs were next. He kneaded her hamstring muscles, her calves, her Achilles tendons, the bottoms of her feet. He rotated her ankles back and forth, pressing his thumbs hard into her arches, and a startlingly sexual pleasure made her toes curl.

"Oh!" she said involuntarily.

"Like that, do you?" he asked, his voice soft and muted in the growing darkness of the room. He did it again, and she moaned in response.

He moved back up her legs, spreading them apart and massaging the stretched, sore tendons on the upper insides of her thighs. Her moan this time was of pain, and she gripped the sides of the table. He murmured reassuringly, moving his attention to her buttocks. She relaxed again, closing her eyes. She was feeling pleasantly warm now, and not just from the oil; his stroking hands were having another effect entirely. Desire was curling lazily, heating her blood, totally without urgency.

"On your back, now," he said, and helped her to roll over. He looked with interest at her peaked nipples, and smiled.

His big, oil-slick hands covered her breasts, gentle there, smoothing the oil into nipples sore from vigorous sucking and the rasp of his stubbled face. "Your skin's as delicate as a baby's," he observed. "I'll need to shave twice a day."

Faith didn't reply, too caught up in what he was doing.

By the time he was finished with her stomach and thighs, she was in an agony of anticipation, her body arching under his hands. The room was almost completely dark now, the lavender shadows of twilight giving way to the night. He paused to turn on the light over the sink, isolating them in a small glow.

The sore muscles on the insides of her thighs received more attention, and this time he didn't relent until her groans had turned to purrs. His oily fingers slipped higher then, gently stroking and probing, and she shook with delight.

"Gray." Her voice was smoky, drugged with desire. She reached out for him. "Please."

"No, baby, you're too sore for another round," he whispered. "I'll take care of you."

He dragged her to the end of the table, sheet and all, the fabric slipping easily over the smooth surface. "What—?" Faith began, then fell back with a moan as he draped her thighs over his shoulders. Gently he opened the swollen folds between her legs, and she felt his warm breath wash over her. She barely had time to catch her breath before his tongue delved into her painfully sensitive flesh with a lightning bolt of sheer sensation that made her cry out. He was very tender, and very thorough, reducing her to quivering, screaming ecstasy within minutes.

Afterward, he carried her into the bathroom. She stood sleepily in the shower with him, her arms around his waist and her head on his chest. A lot of the soreness was gone, but now her muscles felt like mush.

When the hot water began to go, he lifted his cheek from the top of her head. "Food," he murmured.

Reluctantly she released him and let him turn off the water. She sleeked her wet hair back from her face, and looked up at him with diamonds of water clinging to her lashes. He seemed so ruthless and strong, but he was very human, with desires and fears and quirks, and she loved him all the more deeply for those qualities. Just for a while, though, she would have wished he were more impervious, because she couldn't put off much longer telling him about his father.

The least she could do was feed him first.

He wolfed down two ham and tomato sandwiches, then

took his time on the third while she polished off one. Afterward, they remade the bed with fresh sheets, and he flopped down with a sigh of exhaustion. The sprawl of his arms and legs took up most of the room, but she crawled into one of the niches and burrowed her damp head into its accustomed place on his shoulder. She put her arms around him, holding him tight as if she could shield him from the pain.

"I have to tell you something," she said quietly.

✑ Nineteen ✑

Monica cried for a long time after Gray hung up, her arms folded on top of his desk and her head resting on them. Hot, salty tears dripped onto the polished surface and she rubbed them away with her sleeve, not wanting to mar the finish of his desk. She had never felt more lost and confused, even when Daddy had left.

Nothing was working out right. She hadn't managed to tell Alex she wouldn't let him screw her anymore; when he had come down from Mama's room the other night and stood in the doorway, staring at her, her heart had stopped. She had tried to get the words out, but her throat had been too dry, and then he had been bending over her and it was too late. She squirmed with shame every time she thought about it. How *could* she have let him touch her? She was going to marry Michael. She felt dirty, felt as if she were dirtying *him* by going into his arms after having been with Alex. And she still hadn't told Gray that Michael had asked her to marry him, much less telling Mama that she was even dating him. She had been so careful to keep her life under control after the stupid stunt with her wrists, but now it all seemed to be spiraling away again.

Gray was with Faith Devlin. Another man she loved and depended on had been seduced away by one of those whores. How could he do that, Gray, of all people? Monica rocked back and forth, hugging herself and moaning with pain as tears streamed down her cheeks. He was spending the night with her, uncaring of what people might say, of the gossip that would eventually reach Mama no matter how hard they tried to keep it from her. Family hadn't mattered to Daddy when he was in bed with Renee Devlin, and now it looked as if Gray was following in his footsteps with Renee's daughter. Just give them sex, and they didn't care who they hurt.

Monica sobbed until her eyes were sore and almost swollen together, until her chest ached with the effort of breathing. Then, finally, a sort of terrible calm came over her.

She opened Gray's desk drawer and stared at the revolver he kept there. The Devlin bitch hadn't paid any attention to the warnings Monica had given her, so it was time to stop being subtle. In her furious hurt, it didn't matter that Gray was with Faith; it might do him good to be shaken up, she thought, reaching for the pistol. This time, *she* was ridding the parish of a Devlin.

"What is it?" Gray asked, stretching to turn off the lamp. In the sudden darkness, he cradled Faith against him. "You sound serious."

"I am." She blinked back the sudden burn of tears. "I've put off telling you this because I—I can't bear to hurt you. And I—I want you to know something else, first." She gasped for breath, and seized her courage with both hands. "I love you," she said in a low voice, aching with tenderness. "I've always loved you, even when I was a little girl. I lived for glimpses of you, and the chance to hear your voice. Nothing has ever changed that, not what happened that night, not the twelve years when I was gone."

His arms tightened and his lips parted, but she laid her fingers on his mouth, stopping the words. "No, don't say anything," she begged. "Let me finish." If she didn't get it all said in a hurry, she might lose her nerve.

"Gray, your father didn't run away with Mama." She felt his body tense, and she hugged him closer. "I know where

Mama is, and he isn't with her. He never was. He's dead," she said as gently as possible. The hot tears leaked out of her eyes to slowly trickle down her cheeks. "Someone killed him that night. Mama saw who did it, and was scared he'd kill her too, so she ran."

"Stop it," Gray said harshly. He pulled her arms away from him and gave her a hard little shake. "I don't know if this is your lie or Renee's, but I got a letter from him that was postmarked the next day, in Baton Rouge. If he was killed the night before, then a dead man wrote it."

"A letter?" she asked, stunned. Of all the things she'd thought he might say, this wasn't one of the possibilities. "From your father? Are you sure?"

"Of course I'm sure."

"It was in his handwriting?"

"It was typed," he said, his annoyance rapidly escalating into anger. He sat up and swung his legs out of bed. "The signature was his, though."

Faith flung herself at him, wrapping her arms around his shoulders to hold him, though she was well aware he could have shaken her off as if she were no more than a pesky mosquito. Desperately she said, "What did the letter say?"

"What does it matter, goddamn it?" He caught her wrists, trying to free himself without hurting her. She clung all the harder, pressing her body against him.

"It matters!" She was weeping now, her tears hot and wet on his back.

He muttered another curse, but sat still. Despite how furious he was with her for even bringing up the subject, much less trying to convince him of such a ridiculous lie, she was crying, and he had to fight the urge to drag her around onto his lap and comfort her. Roughly he said, "It was a letter of proxy. Just that, no explanation. Without it, we likely would have lost almost everything we owned."

His chest expanded as he took a deep breath. "If it hadn't been for that letter, I'd have tried to find him. But he didn't even say he was sorry, didn't say good-bye. It was as if he was taking care of a minor detail he'd forgotten."

"Maybe someone else wrote it," Faith said, aching with the pain he must have felt then. "Maybe the murderer did.

Gray, I swear, Mama said she saw him get shot! They were out at the summerhouse that night when someone drove up. She said that Guy and the other man went into the boathouse and she heard them arguing—"

He erupted off the bed, breaking free of her grasp. He whirled around to catch her arms and pin her to the mattress. "That's why you were sneaking around the place," he said incredulously, and reached out to turn on the lamp so he could see her face. He glared down at her, his eyes burning like coals. He shook her again. "You little witch! That's why you've been asking all those questions about Dad! You think he was murdered and *you've been trying to find out who killed him!*"

He had seldom in his life been more furious; his hands shook with the effort of controlling himself. He didn't believe his father had been murdered, but it was obvious that Faith did, and the foolhardy woman had been trying to find a murderer all by herself. If there really had been a murder, she would have been putting herself at enormous risk. He was torn between snatching her up in his arms to kiss her and turning her over his knee. Both choices held enormous attraction.

While he was still trying to decide, she said, "I knew I likely wouldn't find anything, but I searched the boathouse for a shell casing—"

"Wait a minute." He rubbed his hand over his face, trying to get a handle on this latest confession. "When did you search the boathouse?"

"Yesterday morning."

"It's kept padlocked. Have you added breaking and entering to your repertoire?"

"I swam underneath the door and came up in the boat slip."

Gray closed his eyes and counted to ten. Then he did it again. His hands twitched, and he balled them into fists. Finally he opened his eyes, staring down at her in appalled disbelief. Foolhardy wasn't the word for her. She was too intrepid for her own safety, much less his sanity. The net beneath the boathouse, designed to keep out unwelcome guests of the reptile variety, had come loose over the years and he hadn't had it repaired, but it was still there. She could so easily have become entangled in it and drowned. He would have lost her forever. Clammy sweat formed on his brow.

"I didn't find anything," she said, eyeing him uneasily. "But I'm making someone nervous. Why do you think I got those threatening notes?"

It was like being punched in the stomach. He hung there, his mind reeling. Then his knees sagged, and he sat down heavily on the bed. "My God," he said blankly, as horrified realization began to form.

"I hired a private detective," she said, reaching for him again, desperately needing to touch him. She pressed close, and this time his arms came up to wrap around her, hauling her against his chest. "Mr. Pleasant. He searched credit card records, Social Security records, tax files—there was no trace of Guy after that night. Gray, there was no reason for Guy to walk away from you and Monica, or from all that money! He wouldn't have left you for Mama; why should he? It didn't make sense that he would disappear like that, unless he was dead. Mr. Pleasant thought he must be, too, and he was going to ask some questions in town." A sob rose in her chest. "Now he's disappeared, too, and I'm afraid the same person killed him!"

"Oh, God," Gray said, his voice tight. "Faith—don't say anything else. Be quiet for a minute. Please."

She pressed her face into his chest and obeyed. Despite everything, his arms were around her, and she began to hope. He rocked her gently back and forth, comforting himself as well as her.

"Alex sent the letter," he finally said, his voice muffled in her hair. "I should have guessed. He was the only other person who knew Dad hadn't left a letter of proxy, and he knew what a mess we were in without it, if Dad didn't come back, so he didn't take the chance. He was almost as upset as I was, and he said the same thing you did: What *reason* did Dad have for running away with Renee? He already had her, and Mother turned a blind eye to his affairs, so he wouldn't have . . . He's dead. He's really dead." He choked, and his chest heaved beneath her cheek.

Faith held him tight, guiding him down onto the bed. He clutched at her, his hands desperate. "Turn . . . turn off the light," he said, and she did, understanding how a strong man could need darkness for his tears.

He shook in her arms, his wet face buried against her breasts as harsh sobs tore up from his chest. She cried with him, stroking his head, his back and shoulders, not speaking but offering him the comfort of her body, of not being alone. Without the intimacy of the day they had just passed binding them together, she doubted he would have allowed her to see him so vulnerable. But they were linked, as he had said, their lives inextricably woven together by the past, and cemented by the long hours of intense pleasure.

Something he had said jarred, but the significance of it escaped her. She pushed it aside, for the moment intent only on holding him.

Gradually he calmed, but his desperate grip on her didn't relax. She smoothed his hair back from his damp face, her fingers gentle.

"All these years," he said in a hushed, choked voice. "I've hated him, and cursed him . . . and missed him . . . and all the time he's been dead."

Something else needed to be said, something hurtful. "Have the lake dragged," she suggested, and felt him flinch. He had swum in that lake, fished in it.

There were other things to talk about, decisions to make, but his head was heavy on her breast and she sensed his utter exhaustion. Her own fatigue, mental and physical, was dragging her down. "Go to sleep," she whispered, stroking his temple. "We'll talk in the morning."

She must have dozed, but for all her tiredness, something kept dragging her back to semiconsciousness. She shifted restlessly, feeling Gray's heavy weight against her. What was it he had said? Something about the letter of proxy . . .

His body was like a furnace, pouring off heat in waves. Sweat dewed her body, despite the efforts of the ceiling fan. She didn't open her eyes, but her brow furrowed as she tried to bring the thought into focus. The letter of proxy . . . Why would Alex have sent a bogus letter of proxy so quickly, when no reasonable person would expect Guy to completely walk away from his family and business? Surely he had expected Guy to get in touch . . .

Unless he had known that it was impossible.

Alex.

Her eyes flew open, and she stared in confusion at the strange red glow that suffused the room. The heat was more intense, and the air was acrid, burning her eyes and nose. Realization exploded in her head.

"Gray!" She screamed his name, shaking him hard. "Get up! *The house is on fire!"*

Monica stopped the car where she had both times before, pulling off the road onto a pasture access, out of sight of the house. She wore dark clothes and soft-soled dark shoes, for moving quietly without being seen. It was so easy to sneak up to the house on foot, leave her messages, and depart undetected. Leaving the package had required more planning, since it had been daylight, but Faith had simplified things by not being at home. It had just been a matter of slipping the package into the mailbox and driving away.

She got out of the car, pistol in hand, and stepped into the dark road. There wasn't much traffic on this road even during the daytime, and if a car did come along, she would be able to both see and hear it in plenty of time to hide. In the meantime, the road was the easiest walking, and left no footprints.

There was a strange reddish glow in the night sky, just visible above the trees. Monica stared at it, puzzled. It was a few seconds before she realized what it was, and her eyes widened with alarm. The house was on fire, and Gray was there! Her throat closing on a moan of terror, she began to run.

Gray rolled off the bed and dragged her with him, down onto the floor where it was easier to breathe, though the acrid smoke still burned her throat and lungs with every breath. He grabbed her robe from the chair and thrust it at her. "Crawl into the hall, then put this on," he ordered, "and some shoes." He snagged his pants and shoes, jerking them on with three fast motions. "I'll be right behind you."

She obeyed, glancing back several times to make certain he was there. Coughing violently, she pulled the robe around her.

Once in the hallway, they could see flames licking outside the bathroom window, too. Gray ignored it, crawling into the bathroom and snatching towels from the rack. By some miracle, there was still water pressure, and he soaked the towels in the sink. He was coughing and gagging as he tossed one sodden towel at her. "Put it over your face," he said hoarsely.

She did, holding the dripping material over her mouth and nose with one hand and crawling as best she could. The towel helped, and she breathed a bit easier.

The fire seemed to surround them, the wicked orange flames dancing every way they turned. The thick smoke filling the house reflected the glow, so that it seemed to come from all directions. How could it have spread so fast, so completely engulfing the house? The cackle of licking flame had become a roar as it grew stronger, consuming more and more of her home. The heat seared her skin, and sparks showered down like thousands of tiny glowing knives, pricking where they landed. The boards beneath her hands felt as if they were breathing, growing hotter and hotter, and she knew that soon the floor would combust. If they weren't out before then, they would die.

Gray could feel the same thing. Faith wasn't moving fast enough; her robe tangled around her legs, slowing her. Roughly he shouldered her aside so he could move in front of her. He gripped the collar of her robe and used it to pull her along, all but dragging her, forcing her to a faster pace. He could feel the floor getting hotter and hotter beneath them, and knew they had only a minute at most to get out, or it would be too late. He strained his eyes to see through the swirling smoke, and the relative darkness at the front of the house gave him a glimmer of hope. "The front door!" he roared, trying to make himself heard above the din of the inferno. "It isn't burning yet!"

Her house was so small, but the front door seemed so far away. Faith's lungs ached and burned, desperately pumping for air, but the fire was consuming all of the precious oxygen. Her sight dimmed, and she felt the world sliding sideways. The wood floor scraped her knees as Gray dragged her, and the pain roused her to greater effort. Gathering herself, she forced her muscles to keep moving as she silently repeated a litany of desperation: *Don't stop, don't stop, if you stop Gray will too, don't stop.* Terror for his safety, above all, kept her moving.

Abruptly he staggered to his feet and hauled her upright, holding her clasped tightly to him. She stared dimly up at his beloved, smoke-blackened face. "Get ready!" he bellowed, and used his towel to cover the heated doorknob as he jerked the door open.

He ducked as flames licked in with a deep, whooshing sound, then just as quickly subsided. Picking Faith up, he tucked her under his arm as if she were a football, and ran through the burning portal.

His speed carried them off the porch, and they pitched into the empty darkness. Gray twisted in midair, trying to put his body between Faith and the ground, but he only partially succeeded and they sprawled on the grass with a bone-jarring impact. He heard her soft, gasping cry, but they were still dangerously close to the house and he couldn't take the time to see if she was injured. He caught her under the arms and began pulling her. "Move! Get away from the house!"

"No," someone said hoarsely, with horror in the tone. The crackle and roar of the flames almost drowned out the words. "Gray, *what are you doing here?*"

Gray straightened slowly, pulling Faith up with him and automatically tucking her behind him. They were caught between two dangers, the fire at the back and the rifle in the hands of the man who had been his honorary uncle, and lifelong friend and advisor.

"No," Alex moaned, his eyes white-edged with panic. He shook his head in denial of Gray's presence. "I thought she was alone! I swear, Gray, I would never have put you in danger—"

The heat on Gray's naked back was intense, scorching his skin. Deliberately he moved forward, never taking his eyes away from Alex but desperate to get Faith away from that heat. He stopped as fits of coughing racked him. He could hear Faith coughing and gasping, and he kept a hard grasp on her arm, forcing her to stay shielded behind him.

Several ugly suspicions were crowding his mind, and all of them made him sick. When he could talk, he straightened and wiped his streaming eyes with a grimy hand. "You're the one who's been sending those notes, aren't you?" he rasped, his voice so raw as to be almost unrecognizable. "And the cat—"

"No," Alex denied, his voice filled with ludicrous indignation, under the circumstances. "I wouldn't do something like that."

"But you would set fire to a house and try to kill an innocent woman?" Gray asked coldly, the harshness of his voice making the words even more jarring.

"I hoped she would leave," Alex replied in a frighteningly reasonable tone. "But nothing you did made her leave, and neither did the notes. I didn't know what else to do. I couldn't let her keep asking questions, and upsetting Noelle."

Gray gave a rasping crack of laughter. "You didn't care whether or not Mother was upset," he snapped. "You were afraid she'd find out what happened to Dad!"

"That's not true!" Alex said furiously. "I've always loved her! You know that!"

"Did you love her so much that you shot my father so you could have her?"

Gray bellowed the accusation at him, so infuriated by the danger to Faith and the realization that Alex had killed his father that it was all he could do to keep from leaping at Alex and strangling him with his bare hands. The only thing that held him back was the knowledge that, if he failed, Faith would die.

They still stood dangerously close to the burning house, the hellish light enveloping them in a red circle beyond which nothing else existed. Alex's face twisted with pain. "I didn't mean to!" he screamed. "I just wanted to stop him—he was going to divorce Noelle! The humiliation would have killed her! I tried to make him see reason, but he was determined. My God, how could any man prefer that slut over your mother? I think he was crazy, he had to be."

The irony of Alex calling Guy crazy wasn't lost on Gray. Then, to his horror, Faith wrenched loose from his grasp and stepped out from the protection of his body. "So you shot him," she said, her own voice so raspy, he could barely hear her over the roar of the hungry flames. "And told my mother that you'd say she'd done it if she ever said anything. There wasn't any doubt who would be believed in this town, was there?"

Alex glared at her with such hatred and fury that the rifle trembled in his hands, and Gray reached out to pull her close. He wasn't afraid for himself; Alex's horror at having endangered him had been genuine. But Faith—oh, God, even now, Alex still intended to kill her. Gray could see it written plainly in his eyes.

"I didn't mind your moving back," Alex told her. "You didn't have anything to do with what happened. But you wouldn't keep your mouth shut, you kept asking questions, and you hired that old bastard to stick his nose into things—"

"Did you kill him, too?" she interrupted, her face twisting with rage. *"Did you?"*

"I had to, you stupid bitch!" Alex howled, beside himself with fury. "He got too close . . . he asked me if Noelle had had any affairs . . . She wasn't like that—"

"Did you dump his body in the lake, the way you did Guy's?" Faith spat, her entire body quivering. But it wasn't fear Gray felt running through her, it was absolute fury, a mirror of his own, and he had a sudden nightmare vision of her going for Alex herself. There wasn't much Faith wouldn't dare, when she had made up her mind to do it. She had deliberately tried to stir up a killer and bring him out into the open, even though she'd known she was putting herself at risk.

Her plan had worked like a dream, he thought viciously. Now if he could just keep her from getting killed. Holding her with bruising force, he jerked her behind him again, trusting that Alex wouldn't shoot through him to get to her.

She immediately began twisting, fighting to get away from him.

Alex stared at them as they struggled, Faith trying to get away from Gray so he wouldn't be hurt, and Gray desperately trying to hold her close for the same reason. Alex's handsome face twisted. "Let her go! She isn't worth it, Gray. I'll take care of her, and everything can go on the way it was. She's only a Devlin; no one will care. She's ruined everything! Guy was my best friend, damn it! I loved him! But he was dead . . . I had to do something."

"You could have turned yourself in," Gray pointed out, trying to keep a reasonable tone in his voice as he finally wrapped his arms around Faith and crushed her in his embrace. If he could lull Alex, then get close enough to knock the barrel of the rifle upward . . . He was much stronger than the older man, he could subdue him. "If it was an accident, you wouldn't have—"

"Oh, please. I *am* a lawyer, Gray. The charge would have been involuntary manslaughter, not murder, but I still would have done time." Alex shook his head. "Noelle would never have spoken to me again . . . she wouldn't associate with someone who had been in jail. I'm sorry, but it has to be this way." Lifting the rifle, Alex sighted along the barrel, and Gray knew he was going to fire.

He shoved Faith away, and charged Alex. He saw the rifle barrel track to the side, following Faith, and he plowed into Alex with more force than he had ever used playing football. The sharp crack of rifle fire split the night, and the hot casing hit his cheek as it ejected. He caught the rifle, shoving it upward as they hit the ground, but the impact broke his grip. With surprising speed Alex rolled away, springing to his feet and grabbing the rifle again. Gray got to his feet and began advancing on Alex. He didn't dare glance at where Faith lay, couldn't bear to see . . . The thought of losing her clawed at his gut with unbearable pain. Terror and rage combined in his chest, and Alex's death was written on his stark features as he moved forward.

"Don't," he pleaded, backing away a few steps. "Gray, don't make me shoot you, too—"

"You *bastard!*"

The shriek came out of nowhere. Blinded by the fierce glare of the fire, Gray couldn't see anything at first. Then Monica materialized out of the night, dressed head to toe in dark clothing that had cut down her visibility. His sister's face was dead white, her dark eyes wild.

"You bastard!" she shrieked again, advancing on Alex like a Fury. The firelight gleamed on the barrel of the revolver in her hand. "All these years . . . you've been screwing me . . . pretending I was Mama . . . and you *killed my father!*"

Maybe Alex saw her intention to fire in Monica's eyes. Maybe he was simply startled by her appearance, her screaming attack. For whatever reason, he swung the rifle around toward her. Gray leaped for him again, a roar of protest on his lips, knowing he couldn't reach him in time any more than he'd been able to a moment before.

Monica closed her eyes and fired.

∾ Twenty ∾

"The bastard," Monica kept whispering in a drained, lifeless voice. "The bastard."

Faith sat in a county patrol car with Monica, holding her when she cried, letting her talk as she would. The door on her side of the car had been left open, while the one on Monica's side had been closed; a subtle splitting of hairs on the part of the parish law enforcement. Monica didn't seem to care that the door beside her didn't have any inside handles. She was in shock, shivering occasionally despite the heat of the night, added to that from the fire, and Sheriff McFane himself had carefully spread a blanket over her.

Faith stared out the open door, feeling more than a little numb herself. It had all happened so quickly . . . The house was gutted, a total loss. Alex had poured gasoline all around the house and tossed a match to it, intending that she be trapped inside with no clear way out. Had she somehow managed to get out, he had been waiting with a rifle. It would have been assumed that she'd been killed by whoever had been sending her the notes, and since he was innocent of that, he'd felt safe. But Gray had hidden his car behind the shed, and in the darkness Alex hadn't seen it. When Gray had come stumbling out of the burning house, Alex's careful

309

plans had been shattered. He had been shocked by Gray's presence—Gray, whom he loved like a son. All they could do now was guess what Alex would have done, faced with that dilemma.

Her car, sitting so close to the house, was also a total loss. Without the key to crank the engine and pull it away, she had watched as a section of wall fell on it and set it afire. Gray's Jaguar had been pulled away from the shed and now sat safely on the side of the road. The shed still stood, though. She stared at it through the smoke. Maybe she could sleep there, she thought with ghoulish humor.

Her small yard swarmed with people. The sheriff and his deputies, the volunteer firefighters, the fire medics, the coroner, the sightseers. God knows what so many people had been doing out that time of night, but an inordinate number of them had evidently followed all the flashing lights.

She watched Gray's tall body, silhouetted against the dying blaze. He was talking to Sheriff McFane, a few yards away from Alex Chelette's covered body. He was shirtless, his long hair flying around his bare shoulders, and even from here she could hear him coughing.

Her own throat felt like fire, and she could feel the stinging of several burns, on her hands and arms, her back, her legs. It hurt to cough, which didn't stop her lungs from periodically trying to clear themselves, but all in all she felt lucky to be alive and in relatively good health.

"I'm sorry," Monica said abruptly. She was staring straight ahead. "I sent the notes . . . I just wanted to scare you into leaving. I never would have—I'm sorry."

Stunned, Faith sat back, then immediately straightened her sore back away from the seat. She started to say, "That's all right," then changed her mind. It wasn't all right. She had been frightened, and sickened. She had known there was a killer out there. Monica hadn't known, but that didn't excuse her. She hadn't killed the cat, but that didn't excuse her either. So Faith said nothing, leaving Monica to find her own absolution.

Faith watched as a medic approached Gray and tried to get him to sit down, tried to put an oxygen mask on him.

Gray shook him off, gesturing angrily, and pointed him toward Faith.

"I'm going to tell them," Monica said, still in that expressionless voice. "Gray and Michael. About the notes, and the cat. I won't be arrested for shooting Alex . . . but I don't deserve to go unpunished."

Faith didn't have time to respond. The medic brought his equipment over to the patrol car, and squatted in the open door. His penlight flashed in her eyes, making her blink. He took her pulse, checked the burns on her hands and arms, tried to put the oxygen mask on her. She pulled away. "Tell him," she said, indicating Gray, "that I will when he does."

The medic stared at her, then gave a little grin. "Yes, ma'am," he said, and jauntily returned to his first reluctant patient.

Faith watched as he repeated what she'd said to Gray. Gray wheeled around to glare at her. She shrugged. Annoyed and frustrated, he grabbed the oxygen mask and with ill grace clapped it over his nose and mouth. He immediately began coughing again.

Because she had promised, she had to submit to treatment when it came her turn again. The medics agreed that her lung function was good, meaning that her smoke inhalation wasn't critical. Her burns were mostly first-degree, with a few second-degree blisters on her back, and they wanted her to see Dr. Bogarde. Gray was in much the same shape. Both of them were extremely lucky.

Except he had lost a friend, and she had lost every possession except the robe on her back and the shoes on her feet. And an open shed, a lawn mower, and two rakes, she reminded herself. She had insurance on both the house and car, but it would take time to replace everything. Her tired mind began trying to catalogue all the things she would have to do: have her credit cards replaced, get new checks, buy new clothes, get a car, find a place to live, have her mail rerouted to somewhere.

So many things to do, and she was so tired that she felt incapable of accomplishing a single one. At least nothing was irreplaceable, except for the few photographs she'd had of Kyle. There were no other family mementos.

Alex's body was eventually taken away. Monica stared at it being loaded in the hearse, for transport to the parish morgue. Because he had died by violent means, there would be an autopsy. "For seven years he used me," she whispered. "He pretended I was Mama." She shuddered. "How do I tell Michael?" she asked bleakly.

"Who's Michael?"

Monica gave her a puzzled look. "The sheriff. Michael McFane. He's asked me to marry him."

Faith sighed. The tangle just kept getting worse. "You don't," she said, and touched Monica's arm. "Put it behind you. Don't hurt Michael by telling him. It won't make you hurt any less, and it'll give Alex just one more victim. Pick up from here and go on."

Monica didn't reply, to either agree or disagree, but Faith hoped she took her advice. She had picked herself up enough times to know the value of going on.

Eventually both she and Gray were taken to Dr. Bogarde's clinic and put in separate examining rooms. The dapper little doctor checked Gray first; Faith could hear them talking through the thin walls. Then he came bustling into the tiny room where she sat uncomfortably on the table. He cleaned and dressed her burns and checked her breathing, then gazed at her with a sympathetic eye.

"Do you have a place to sleep?"

Faith gave him a rueful smile and shook her head.

"Then why don't you stay here? You look out on your feet. There's a rollaway bed that we use sometimes, and you're welcome to it. I can give you a set of scrubs to wear—don't tell, but I sneaked them from the hospital in Baton Rouge." His eyes twinkled at her. "A few hours' sleep will do wonders for you. My nurses get here at eight-thirty, and then you can call your insurance agent, buy clothes, handle all those things. Trust me, you'll feel a lot more capable after you've had some sleep."

"Thank you," she said sincerely, accepting his offer. The difficulties of being virtually naked, without transportation, cash, or credit cards, were almost more than she could deal with at the moment. In the morning she could have Margot wire her some money, and she would begin the process of picking herself up again, but for tonight she simply couldn't cope.

Dr. Bogarde left, and in a few minutes Gray came in. His torso and face were still streaked with black smoke, but the doctor had cleaned some patches and applied bandages, giving him the look of a large calico cat. Figuring she looked much the same, and not wanting to look in a mirror to verify it, she smiled at him.

His tired face moved into an answering smile. "Dr. Bogarde said you're okay, but I wanted to see for myself."

"I'm fine, just tired."

He nodded, then simply put his arms around her and folded her against him, sighing deeply as he absorbed her nearness. Until he had seen that she was okay, merely stunned from her fall when he'd shoved her, he had lived in a hell of fear. The events of the night were still catching up with him; part of him felt numb, while another part was still aching with almost inexpressible grief. It didn't matter that his father had been dead for twelve years; he had just learned of his death, so the pain was fresh. If anything had happened to Faith, too—

"Come home with me," he said, pressing his lips to her temple and smelling the smoke in her hair. He didn't care.

Shocked, she drew back and stared at him. "I can't do that," she blurted.

"Why not?"

"Your mother . . . No."

"Leave Mother to me," he said. "She won't like it—"

"That's an understatement if I've ever heard one!" Faith shook her head. "You can't spring me on her at a time like this. Everything that's happened tonight will be enough of a shock at one time. Dr. Bogarde offered to let me sleep here tonight, and I accepted."

"Forget it," he growled. He hated to admit she was right, but he could see that she wasn't going to budge. "If you won't come home with me, then I'll take you to the motel."

"I don't have any money or credit card—"

He set her away from him, and temper sparked in his dark

eyes. "Damn it, Faith, did you think I'd charge you for the room?"

"I'm sorry," she apologized. "I'm used to paying my way, so I just didn't think." A motel room *would* be more comfortable, and more private.

He sighed, and reached out to cup her cheek. The anger died out of his eyes. It was amazing how flowers could grow in the damnedest places, but the Devlin weed patch had sprouted quite a wildflower in Faith. "Come on," he said, helping her down from the examination table. "Let's tell Dr. Bogarde you're going with me."

Ten minutes later, he drove up to the motel office and wearily unfolded his long length from the Jaguar. There was still a lot to be done this hellish night. Uncaring how he looked, he went inside and got a key, returning in less than a minute to escort her to room number eleven. He unlocked the door, turned on the light, and stepped aside to let her enter. Tiredly Faith moved past him, and looked longingly at the bed. She would love to just lie down and sleep, but couldn't bear the thought of getting the sheets filthy with soot.

Gray followed her inside, closed the door, and pulled her to him. She laid her head on his chest, shutting her eyes as she reveled in the feel of him, so hard and strong and vital. Death had been so close . . .

His fingers gently encircled one of her wrists, and he lifted her sooty fingers to his lips, then folded his hand around hers. "We start dragging the lake tomorrow," he said abruptly.

She rubbed her cheek against his hand, aching for him. "I'm sorry," she said gently.

He took a deep breath. "There's a lot to be done. I don't know when I'll have a free minute."

"I understand. I have a lot to do myself. All of the insurance claims, things like that." It would have been nice if they could have leaned on each other during the coming ordeals, but necessity was pulling them in different directions. Because the dragging of the lake would be done under law enforcement authority, access to the process would be limited; she knew that without having to have it explained.

Gray would be there, but no other civilians not directly involved in the dragging operation would be allowed.

"I don't want to leave you," he murmured, and indeed he seemed incapable of making himself move, despite everything else that had to be done before this long night was over.

"You have to. My problems are mostly paperwork and shopping; I can take care of them. You have more serious problems."

He tilted her head up with his fingers, dark eyes boring into hers. "We'll talk when this is over," he said, the promise somehow sounding ominous. He kissed her, the pressure of his mouth warm and hard. "Call if you need me."

"All right."

He kissed her again, and she sensed his reluctance. She stroked his hair in comfort. "I don't want to go," he confessed, resting his forehead against hers. "Twelve years ago I had to tell Mother that Dad had left her for another woman. Now I have to tell her that he was murdered, instead. The hell of it is, I know this won't upset her as much as the first did."

"You're not responsible for what she feels or doesn't feel," Faith replied, touching her thumb to his lower lip. "You and Monica loved him, so he won't be unmourned."

"Monica." Gray's mouth tightened, and his eyes turned flinty. "She confessed what she did, about the notes and the cat. Michael's all torn up about it. She broke several laws with that little caper."

"Let things settle down before you do anything," Faith advised. "Family's family, after all. You don't want to do anything rash and cause a breach. Remember, she's been through a lot, too." Her own family was scattered to the four winds, and her life was littered with loss, so she knew what she was saying. She saw the swift acknowledgment of that reflected in Gray's eyes.

A huge yawn overtook her, and her head dropped against his shoulder. "That's my last piece of advice for the night," she said, and yawned again.

He kissed her forehead and eased her away from him. He had to force himself to leave her, but he knew if he didn't do it now, he'd collapse on the bed with her. "Get some sleep, baby. Call if you need me."

She had one friend in town, Faith realized over the next few days. Whether Halley Johnson had learned from town gossip where Faith was staying and volunteered her own services, or Gray had called her and asked her to help, Faith didn't know and didn't ask. Halley knocked on the motel room door at ten o'clock the next morning, and put herself at Faith's service.

Faith had already called Margot and arranged for money to be wired to her, but she still needed some means of getting to the bank to get the money. She also needed, quite desperately, to do some shopping, and she didn't know if any of the stores in town would sell anything to her. The situation between herself and Gray had altered drastically, but no one in town knew it.

"First things first," Halley announced, when Faith said she had to go to the bank. She looked Faith over with a critical eye as she carefully walked out to get into Halley's car. The burns weren't all that uncomfortable, but Faith felt as if she'd been hit by a truck, probably the result of the two bone-jarring collisions she'd had with the ground. "I'll take you to my house," Halley said. "Feel free to use my makeup, do your hair, pamper yourself a little. And while you're doing that, if you'll tell me your sizes, I'll do some quick shopping for you. Nothing fancy," she said, holding up her hand when Faith opened her mouth to protest. "Just underwear, a pair of slacks and a shirt, so you can get out of that robe. You can pay me back when you pick up your money."

With it put to her like that, Faith couldn't refuse. "Thanks," she said, smiling at Halley. "I was wondering if I'd be able to buy clothes in town."

"You will," Halley said with complete assurance, "or I'll call Gray Rouillard myself, and tell him to straighten out his mess. Besides, the whole town's buzzing with the news that his daddy didn't really run off with your mama, that you figured he'd been killed and came back to town to try to prove it. We're all just flabbergasted about Mr. Chelette. Imagine getting in an argument with his best friend and accidentally killing him, and trying to hide it all of these years! It must have driven him crazy, for him to burn down your house like that. Is it true he tried to shoot you, too, and Monica Rouillard managed to shoot first?"

"Something like that," Faith said faintly, wondering what the official version was. She didn't want to contradict whatever was being told. As far as she knew, only she, Gray, and Monica knew about Monica's unwilling seven-year affair with Alex.

Halley dropped her at her house, and Faith enjoyed another long, soaking shower, shampooing her hair twice with strawberry-scented shampoo before the stench of smoke was completely gone. She took Halley at her word and indulged in moisturizer from head to foot, after which she began to feel almost human again. She used a minimal amount of makeup, just enough to put a bit of color in her face, and blow-dried her hair. By the time she was finished, Halley was back with her packages, which blessedly included a new toothbrush.

The clothes were simple, cotton panties and bra, and a lightweight knit pants and tunic outfit. Just having underwear again was wonderful. She had been acutely aware of being naked beneath the robe and scrubs. Halley had a good eye for color; the knit outfit she'd selected was a flattering pale pink. A carroty redhead couldn't have worn the color, but Faith's hair was a dark, almost wine-colored red, and the knowledge that she looked good in the pink perked up her spirits.

Halley stayed with her most of the day, driving her where she needed to go: the bank, first and foremost. Having a thousand dollars in cash did wonders for her sense of security, and the first thing she did was reimburse Halley for her clothes. Next visit was to the insurance office, which thankfully was one-stop shopping, because the same company insured both house and car. Faith had recovered enough to be amused by the sympathetic, almost deferential treatment she received in the insurance office; the line between celebrity and notoriety was a very thin one, but evidently she was now on the celebrity side.

As the morning wore on, she was grateful for her new

status. Because she was totally without identification, the insurance agent had to step in and verify everything before she could get replacement credit cards, credit card companies not being inclined to blithely send out cards to everyone who called. New cards were being expressed to her in care of the insurance agent, and would be there the next day. The insurance company also took care of a rental car for her, and one would be there that afternoon.

Next was shopping, and Faith needed so much that her mind boggled at the enormity of it. Even when she'd been run out of the parish, she hadn't lost all her possessions, meager as they'd been. This time she was starting from scratch, but this time she also had resources.

Efficient Halley suggested they make a list, and that helped Faith get her thoughts organized. Suitcase, purse, wallet; shampoo, soap, deodorant, toothpaste, tampons; makeup and perfume; razor, brush, comb, hair dryer, travel iron; underwear, hosiery, shoes, clothing. "My God," Faith said, staring at the list, which kept getting longer and longer. "This will cost a fortune."

"Only because you're buying it all at one time. Everything on there is something you would have bought anyway, eventually. What would you leave off, anyway? The makeup?"

"Get real," Faith said, and they laughed. It was her first laugh of the day, and it felt good.

They descended on the local Wal-Mart, and filled two carts. Even keeping her purchases to a minimum of the necessities, she was accumulating major stuff. None of the shoes fit, however, which meant another stop. Halley was so cheerful about the entire process, though, that Faith found herself enjoying the expedition. She had never participated in that rite of American girlhood, shopping with friends, and this was a new experience for her.

Halley unwittingly echoed her thoughts. "Wow, this is fun! I haven't done this in a coon's age. We need to do it again—under different circumstances, of course."

The total tally put a sizeable dent in her cash fund. That accomplished, Faith realized she was exhausted, and an observant Halley drove her back to the motel.

Gray called her that night, and he sounded as exhausted as she still felt. "How are you, baby?" he asked. "Did you get everything done today?"

"I'm fine," she said. "Functional, at least." She had taken a two-hour nap, but it hadn't helped much. "The insurance company is handling the details with the rental car and credit card companies, so everything is working out. Halley took me shopping, so I have clothes now."

"Damn."

She ignored that comment, but a smile flirted with her mouth. "How do *you* feel?"

"As if I'm three days older than dirt."

She hesitated, not certain if she wanted to hear the answer to her next question. "Have you found anything yet?"

"Not yet." His voice was strained.

"How's Monica?"

He sighed. "I don't know. She just sits with her head down. She and Mike will have to work this out themselves; I can't run interference for her on this."

"Take care of yourself," she said, tenderness vibrant in her tone.

"You, too," he said softly.

As soon as he hung up, Faith called Renee. She felt guilty for not having thought of it sooner, knowing how upset Renee had been.

Her grandmother answered the phone. When Faith asked for Renee, the old woman said in a fretful voice, "Guess she's gone. Took her clothes and lit out, night before last. I ain't heard from her."

Faith's heart sank. Renee had probably panicked after confessing what had happened at the summerhouse, and now she was running again, for no reason.

"If you hear from her, Granny, there's something I want you to tell her. It's important. The man who killed Guy Rouillard is dead. She doesn't have to be afraid anymore."

Her grandmother was silent a moment. "So that's why she was so jumpy," she finally said. "Well, maybe she'll call. She left some stuff, so she might come back for it. I'll tell her, if she does."

* * *

Mr. Pleasant's car was pulled from the lake the next afternoon. Mr. Pleasant was in it.

Probably on Gray's orders, a deputy came to the motel to tell Faith. The young man was uncomfortable and respectful, twisting his hat in his hands. He couldn't say how Mr. Pleasant had died, but the body was being taken to the parish morgue, where he would lie in the same room with his killer. Faith had to bite back an instinctive protest, knowing it would be useless.

After the deputy left, she sat down on the bed and had a good cry, then called Detective Ambrose. Poor Mr. Pleasant didn't have any remaining family, but the detective promised to find out what he could about any arrangements Mr. Pleasant might have made for his own funeral, given the state of his health. There was red tape to go through, of course, since his death was a homicide, but with his killer already dead, gathering forensic evidence for a trial wasn't an issue.

Guy Rouillard's Cadillac was found the next morning, not far from where Mr. Pleasant's car had been found. The long skeleton in the backseat was the only earthly remains of Gray's father. Alex Chelette's method of disposal had been simple: put them in their cars, prop a brick on the accelerator, and put the car in gear. Sheriff McFane was the one who had thought about finding the cars, and there were only three places on the lake where the water was deep enough to hide a car, and it was possible to get a car there. With their search locations narrowed down, it hadn't taken them long to find the bodies.

Faith didn't get to talk to Gray, but information flew around the town, and she knew he was ruthlessly using his influence to get Guy's remains released as soon as possible, for a funeral twelve years delayed. Noelle Rouillard appeared in town for the first time since her husband's disappearance, looking tragic and unbelievably beautiful in a black dress. Gray's cynical assessment of his mother's reaction had been on target; being a widow was far preferable to being abandoned. Now that everyone knew her husband had *not* left her for the town whore, she could hold her head up again.

The funeral was held four days after Guy's remains were found. Though she knew people would whisper about her presence, Faith bought a black dress and attended the service, sitting on a back pew beside Halley and her family. Gray didn't see her there at the church, but later, after the funeral procession had transported Guy's body to the burial site, his dark gaze was drawn by the sunlight on her flaming hair.

He was standing with a supporting arm around Monica. Sheriff McFane was on her other side, so Faith supposed the engagement was still on. Noelle was bearing up with the sympathetic support of all her old friends, the ones she had refused to see for a dozen years. Faith was some ten yards away, separated from him by a group of people, but their eyes met and she knew he was thinking about what she had said. Guy was sincerely mourned by his children; what Noelle felt didn't matter.

She stared at him, drinking him in with her eyes. He looked tired, but composed. His mane of hair was pulled back and secured at the back of his neck, and he wore a beautifully fitted, double-breasted black Italian suit. Sweat gleamed on his forehead in the noonday heat.

She made no move to go to him, and he didn't gesture her closer. What was between them was private, not for public display at his father's funeral. He knew he had her support, for he had cried out his grief in her arms. It was enough that she was there.

It was as they were leaving the grave site that Faith saw Yolanda Foster, standing by herself; Lowell was nowhere in evidence. Yolanda had been crying, but now her eyes were dry as she stared at the grave, an open look of heartbreak on her face. Then she gathered herself and turned away, and Faith felt all the pieces of the puzzle click into place.

It had never made sense that Guy would leave everything for Renee, not after all the years they'd been having an affair. Alex had said that Guy had been planning to divorce Noelle, and that had made more sense, but abruptly Faith knew that it wasn't Renee Guy had been planning to marry. After all his years of tomcatting around, Guy Rouillard had fallen in love that summer, with the mayor's wife. He had protected Yolanda's reputation, not even telling his best friend about her. Gossip about them had leaked out, or Ed Morgan wouldn't have known, but their affair hadn't been common knowledge. It was even possible Renee had told Ed that Guy was seeing the mayor's wife.

Yolanda and Guy had made secret plans. And now, after all these years, she knew that her lover hadn't deserted her. Guy was sincerely mourned by someone other than his children, after all.

It was late that night before all of the sympathizers ran out of excuses to stay any longer, and Gray had a private moment with his family. He sipped his Scotch as he studied Noelle, who was infinitely more cheerful now after burying her husband than she had been during the twelve years he'd been missing. He needed Faith, he thought. He wanted to be with her. Seeing her at the cemetery had made the hunger even sharper. Sexual hunger, emotional hunger, mental hunger. He simply wanted her, in all the ways possible. He remembered the way his heart had swelled in his chest when she'd told him she loved him, remembered the moment of blinding joy. Like a fool, he hadn't yet told her that he loved her, too, but that was an oversight he intended to rectify as soon as they could be alone.

Right now, he had something to say to his mother and sister.

"I'm getting married," he said calmly.

Two startled pairs of eyes looked back at him. He saw Monica's dismay, saw it quickly change to acceptance, and she gave him a tiny nod.

"Really, dear?" Noelle murmured. "I'm sorry, I haven't been keeping current with your social life. Is it someone from New Orleans?"

"No, it's Faith Devlin."

Calmly Noelle set her glass of wine aside. "Your joke is in extremely bad taste, Grayson."

"It isn't a joke. I'm marrying her as soon as it can be arranged."

"I forbid it!" she snapped.

"You can't forbid anything, Mother."

Though he said it calmly, Noelle reacted as if he'd slapped her. She rose to her feet, holding herself as erect as a queen. "We'll see about that. Your father may have associated with trash, but at least he never brought it home and expected *me* to associate with it!"

"That's enough," he said, his tone soft and dangerous.

"On the contrary, if you lower yourself to marry that slut, you'll find it's just beginning. I'll make her life here so miserable—"

"No, you won't," he interrupted, slamming his glass down so that the Scotch sloshed over the rim. "Let me make your position plain, Mother. I know what's in Dad's will. He left you enough money to keep you in style, but he left everything else to Monica and me. If you behave yourself, and treat my wife with every courtesy, you may continue to live here. But make no mistake, the first time you upset her, I'll escort you out the door myself. Is that clear?"

Noelle shrank back, her face pale, her eyes livid as she stared at her son. "Monica," she said, her voice abruptly frail. "Help me to my room, darling. Men are so uncivilized . . ."

"Put a sock in it, Mother," Monica said tiredly.

"I beg your pardon." The words were freezing.

Monica visibly braced herself. She was as pale as Noelle, but she didn't back down. "I'm sorry, I shouldn't have said that. But Gray deserves to be happy. If you don't want to come to his wedding, fine, but I'll be there with bells on. And while we're on the subject, I'm getting married, too. To Michael McFane."

"Who?" Noelle asked, her face blank.

"The sheriff."

Disdain curled Noelle's lip. "The sheriff! Really, dear, he's—"

"Perfect for me," Monica finished firmly. She looked both scared and exhilarated at finally having stood up to Noelle. "If you want to come to my wedding, I'll be pleased, but you can't stop me from marrying him. And, Mother—I think you'll be happier if you move to New Orleans."

"Good idea," Gray said, and winked at his sister.

* * *

The next morning, Faith drove down to New Orleans for Mr. Pleasant's funeral. She had hoped Gray would call her, but understood why he hadn't. She had pestered Sheriff McFane mercilessly about doing what he could to get Mr. Pleasant's body released, and he had told her that Gray was embroiled in the process of having Guy's will probated, using his influence to hurry the process. The legal difficulties of a forged letter of proxy, under which he had been governing their financial holdings all these years, were mostly negated since Guy's will had left everything to Gray and Monica anyway, but there were still problems to handle.

Margot flew down to New Orleans to be with Faith, somehow discerning over the telephone that she was more upset about Mr. Pleasant than she had let on. The brief funeral service was attended by only a handful of people: some neighbors, herself and Margot, the little blue-haired lady from Houston H. Manges's law office. To her surprise, Detective Ambrose came by, wearing what looked like the same fatigued suit. He patted Faith's hand, as if she were Mr. Pleasant's family, and all the while his cynical cop's eyes never left Margot's face.

Too tired to drive home, Faith got a hotel room for the night. Margot decided to stay overnight too—no surprise there—and went out with Detective Ambrose.

"I don't sleep with men on the first date," Margot said the next morning, chattering nervously. "I mean, I just don't. It's too dangerous, and tacky besides." She couldn't sit still as they ate their breakfast at the room service cart in Faith's room; she fidgeted with her napkin, her silverware, her clothes. Her gaze flitted around the hotel room; hers was connecting, and virtually identical, but she seemed to find everything of immense interest. "I may be old-fashioned, but I think sex should wait at least until there's a commitment, and waiting until marriage would be even better. Women risk too much by sleeping with men who aren't their husbands—"

"So was he any good?" Faith interrupted, sipping her coffee.

Margot clapped her hand to her chest and rolled her eyes dramatically. "Oh my Gawd, was he!" She jumped up and began to pace the room. "I couldn't *believe* what was happening, I just don't *do* that, but that man had made up his mind and it was like being on a roller coaster, there was just no way to get off. Well, that's not exactly what I mean. About getting off, that is, because I did—" She stopped and turned dark red. Faith almost choked on her coffee, she was laughing so hard.

"He wants to see me tonight, but I told him I have a flight back to Dallas, and he should call me at home if he wants to see me again." Margot looked anxious. "Do you think there's any way I can slow this down and get back on the right track?"

"Maybe," Faith said, but she had seen Margot in love before, and doubted anything could slow her down.

They spent the morning shopping, replenishing Faith's wardrobe from the chic New Orleans boutiques. She left the city about two o'clock, giving Margot both the privacy and time for another meeting with Detective Ambrose.

She arrived back at the motel, her temporary home, at four. Reuben waved to her, and came out to help her carry in her purchases. Then, hungry from the exertion, she drove downtown to Halley's café.

She chatted with Halley for a while, then ordered the chicken salad sandwich that had become her usual supper. She was sitting in a booth with her back to the door, and her sandwich had just been placed in front of her, when she heard the door crash open behind her, and an abrupt silence fell over the café.

Startled, she looked up and found an enraged Gray Rouillard towering over her. Reuben must have called him, she thought absently. His black hair was loose, tangled around his shoulders. "Where the *hell,*" he barked, "have you been?"

"New Orleans," she replied in a mild tone, though she was acutely aware of the breathless interest of everyone in the café.

"Would it be asking too much of you to let me know where you're going to be?" he snapped.

"I went to Mr. Pleasant's funeral," she said.

He slid into the booth opposite her, some of the fury

fading from his face. Beneath the table, his long legs clasped hers, and he reached across to take both her hands in his. "I was scared sh—spitless," he confessed, quickly adjusting his first word choice to something more socially acceptable. "You hadn't checked out, but Reuben saw you put a suitcase in the car. I even had him open your room to see if any of your things were still there."

"I wouldn't have left town without telling you," she said, secretly amused that he thought she might have left town at all.

"You'd better not," he muttered. His hands tightened on hers. "Look," he began, and stopped. "Ah, hell, I know this isn't the best place to do it, but I've still got tons of paperwork to wade through and I don't know how long it'll be before I see daylight. Will you marry me?"

He had succeeded in surprising her. He had gone beyond surprising her. She sat back, stunned into speechlessness. Gray wanted to *marry* her? She hadn't dared let herself even think of it. With their tangled pasts . . . the thorny situation with his mother and sister . . . well, it just hadn't seemed to be an option.

Evidently he took her reaction as rejection, and his dark brows drew together. Being Gray, he immediately took ruthless measures to get what he wanted. "You have to marry me," he said, loudly enough that everyone in the café could hear him. "That's my baby girl you're carrying. She'll need a daddy, and you need a husband."

Faith gasped, her eyes rounding with horror. "You *fiend,*" she shrieked, scrambling out of the booth. She wasn't pregnant and she knew it, her period having arrived right on time, three days before. She had a confused, dizzying impression of a room full of avid faces, staring at her, and Gray wore a ruthlessly satisfied look on his face as he smiled at her, enjoying her sputtering, incoherent fury. Maybe he saw something in her eyes, a split second of warning, but it wasn't enough. Her hand shot out for her glass of iced tea and she dashed it full in his face. "I am *not* pregnant!" she yelled.

Gray climbed out of the booth, wiping tea from his eyes

with Faith's napkin. "Maybe not now, but if you want to be, we'd better get married."

"Marry him," Halley advised, leaning over the counter. She was grinning hugely. "And make his life hell. He deserves it, after this stunt."

"Yeah," he said positively. "I deserve it."

Faith stared up at him. "But—what about your mother?" she asked helplessly.

He shrugged. "What about her?" Faith opened her mouth to yell at him again, and he grinned, holding up his hand. "I told her and Monica that I intended to marry you. Mother went into her acute disapproval syndrome, but Monica told her, literally, to put a sock in it. Funniest thing I've ever seen. Well, except for one." His eyes glittered at her, outrageously reminding her of the courthouse. "Monica gives us her best wishes; she and Michael are getting married next week. She strongly suggested to Mother that she move to New Orleans, which she's always liked better than Prescott, anyway. So, baby, I'm going to be rattling around in that big house all by myself, and I need my own personal redhead to keep me company."

He meant it. Faith swallowed, once again unable to speak. Gray's head tilted as he smiled down at her, dark eyes full of desire and tenderness. "There's something else I've been meaning to tell you," he murmured. "I love you, baby. I should have told you sooner, but things started happening."

She thought of hitting him. She thought of snatching someone else's tea to toss in his face. Instead she said, "Yes." He held out his arms, and she walked into them, to the accompanying spatter of applause from the café patrons.

No one combines the thrill of attraction with jolting suspense the way Linda Howard has in her acclaimed bestsellers. Now, two of her classic novels are brought together to savor all over again—or discover for the first time—in a collection that burns with the heat of desire . . . and the mysteries of the night.

"The incomparable Linda Howard brings high-voltage power and hard-edged sensuality to this emotional roller coaster of a novel, which is sure to keep readers riveted until the final nail-biting conclusion. They don't get much better than this."

—*Romantic Times*

ABOUT THE AUTHOR

LINDA HOWARD is the *New York Times* bestselling author of *Kill and Tell, Son of the Morning, Shades of Twilight, After the Night, Dream Man, Heart of Fire, The Touch of Fire, Angel Creek,* and *A Lady of the West.* Her newest novel, *Now You See Her,* is currently available in hardcover from Pocket Books. Her many awards include the Silver Pen from *Affaire de Coeur* and the *Romantic Times* Reviewer's Choice Award for Best Sensual Romance.

LINDA HOWARD

NIGHT MOVES

Dream Man

After the Night

POCKET BOOKS
New York London Toronto Sydney Tokyo Singapore

This book consists of works of fiction. Names, characters, places and incidents are products of the author's imagination or are used fictitiously. Any resemblance to actual events or locales or persons, living or dead, is entirely coincidental.

POCKET BOOKS, a division of Simon & Schuster Inc.
1230 Avenue of the Americas, New York, NY 10020

Dream Man copyright © 1994 by Linda Howington
After the Night copyright © 1995 by Linda Howington

All rights reserved, including the right to reproduce
this book or portions thereof in any form whatsoever.
For information address Pocket Books, 1230 Avenue
of the Americas, New York, NY 10020

ISBN: 0-671-02747-6

First Pocket Books trade paperback printing October 1998

10 9 8 7 6 5 4 3 2 1

POCKET and colophon are registered trademarks
of Simon & Schuster Inc.

Cover art: *Dream Man* by Alan Ayers, *After the Night* by Brian Bailey

Printed in the U.S.A.

These titles were previously published individually.

DREAM MAN

Marlie Keen was trying to lead a quiet, ordinary life. She thought the clairvoyance that allowed her to witness crimes as they happened had been destroyed in the nightmare of her past. Then one night it returned with a vengeance, and she desperately needed to find someone to make it stop.

Detective Dane Hollister of the Orlando police department had never met anyone like Marlie. He had doubts about her clairvoyance, but there was no doubt how much he desired her. Her soft, sweet scent set his blood afire, and he wanted to wrap her in his arms and chase the sadness from her eyes. To Marlie, Dane was all heat and hard muscle, and he made her body come alive as it never had before. But not even she could foresee where their passion would lead: a hungry quest for the elusive, dreamy ecstasies of love   and a dangerous journey into the twisted mind of a madman who would threaten their happiness and their lives. . . .

This is dedicated to Joyce, Liz, Marilyn, Beverly, Cheri, and Kathy, for their encouragement and participation. To Gary, for taking care of me all those long months when I could barely walk. To Robin, for the pep talks. To Claire, for her patience. To Iris and Catherine and Fayrene and Kay, for the support. Thanks, guys.

1

It was eleven-thirty when Marlie Keen left the Cinemaplex with the rest of the Friday night moviegoers. The movie had been a good one, a lighthearted romp that had made her laugh aloud several times and left her in a cheerful mood. As she walked briskly to her car, she thought she could tell which movie people had seen by how they were acting now. It wasn't that difficult; the couples who were holding hands, or even exchanging kisses in the parking lot, had obviously seen the sexy romance. The aggressive bunch of teenage boys had seen the latest martial arts thriller. The well-dressed young professionals who were in earnest discussions had seen the latest *Thelma and Louise* imitation. Marlie was glad she had chosen the comedy.

It was as she was driving home on the brightly lit expressway that it hit her: She felt good. The best she had felt in years. Six years, to be precise.

In startled retrospect, she realized that she had been at peace for several months now, but she had been so caught up in the sedative routine of the life she had built here that she

hadn't noticed. For a long time she had simply existed, going through the motions, but time had done its slow work and eventually she had healed, like an amputee recovering from the loss of a limb and learning to cope, then to enjoy life again. Her loss had been mental rather than physical, and unlike an amputee, she had prayed through dark, endless nights that she never recover that part of herself. At some point in the past six years, she had stopped living in dread that the knowing would return, and simply gotten on with her life.

She liked being normal. She liked being able to go to movies the way normal people did, liked being able to sit in a crowd; she hadn't been able to do that before. Several years ago, when she had realized it was actually possible, she had turned into a movie junkie for a while, visually gorging on the films that she thought were safe. For a long time any degree of violence was unbearable, but for the past couple of years she had been able to watch the occasional thriller, though they weren't her favorite type. To her surprise, she hadn't yet been able to watch any sex scenes; she would have thought that violence would have been immeasurably more difficult for her to handle, maybe even impossible, but instead it was the portrayal of intimacy that gave her problems. Dr. Ewell had been fond of saying that no one should ever lay bets on the human psyche, and she was amused to find he was right. The violence in her life had been traumatic, devastating, while the sex had been merely unpleasant, but it was the "love" scenes that still had her squeezing her eyes shut until it was over.

She exited off the expressway onto a four-lane street, and of course was caught by the traffic light at the bottom of the exit ramp. The radio was tuned to an easy-listening station and she inhaled deeply, feeling the slow music and the lingering lightheartedness of the movie combine in a delicious, physical sense of contentment—

—*the knife flashed down, gleaming dully. A sodden,*

muffled THUNK! as it struck. The blade rose again, dripping red—

Marlie jerked back, an unconscious physical denial of the horribly real image that had just flashed in her mind. "No," she moaned softly to herself. She could hear her own breathing, sharp and gasping.

"No," she said again, though she already knew the protest was useless. Her hands were clenched on the steering wheel, white-knuckled, and even that wasn't enough to stop the trembling that started at her feet and went all the way up. Dimly she watched her hands start shaking as the spasms intensified.

—Black, gloating pleasure. Triumph. Contempt—

It was happening again. Dear God, *it was coming back!* She had thought herself free, but she wasn't. The knowing was coming closer, growing, looming, and she knew from experience that soon it would overwhelm her. Clumsily, her coordination already deteriorating, she steered the car to the right, so she wouldn't block the exit ramp. A car horn blared as she wavered too close to the vehicle beside her, but the noise was distant, muted. Her vision was fading. Desperately she braked to a stop and shoved the gear lever into park, hoping that she had managed to get completely out of traffic, but then the nightmare image was back, hitting her full strength like a beacon that had brushed by her in search before homing in.

Her hands fell limply into her lap. She sat in the car staring straight ahead, her eyes unblinking, unseeing, everything focused inward.

Her breathing became harsher. Rough sounds began to form in her throat, but she didn't hear them. Her right hand lifted slowly from her lap and formed itself into a fist, as if she were gripping something. The fist twitched violently, three times, in a rigidly restrained stabbing motion. Then she was quiet again, her face as still and blank as a statue's, her gaze fixed and empty.

3

It was the sharp rapping on the window beside Marlie that brought her back. Confused and exhausted, for a terrifying moment she had no idea who she was, or where, or what was happening. An unearthly blue light was flashing in her eyes. She turned a dazed, uncomprehending look at the man who was bent over, peering into the window as he tapped on it with something shiny. She didn't know him, didn't know anything. He was a stranger, and he was trying to get into her car. Panic was sharp and acrid in her mouth.

Then identity, blessed identity, returned with a rush and brought reality with it. The shiny thing the man was using to rap against the glass transformed itself into a flashlight. A glint on his chest became recognizable as a badge, and he, frown and commanding voice and all, was a policeman. His patrol car, Mars lights flashing, was parked at an angle in front of hers.

The images of horror were still too close, too frighteningly real. She knew she had to block it out or she wouldn't be able to function at all, and she needed to get control of herself. Some vague danger was threatening, some memory that danced close to the surface but wouldn't quite crystalize. Desperately she pushed away the fog of confusion and fumbled to roll down the window, fighting for the strength to complete even that small act. The exhaustion was bone-deep, paralyzing, muscles turned to mush.

Warm, humid air poured through the open window. The officer flashed the light beam around the interior of her car. "What's the problem here, ma'am?"

She felt cotton-brained, thought processes dulled, but even so she knew better than to blurt out the truth. That would immediately get her hauled in on suspicion of being under the influence of some kind of drug, probably a hallucinogen. Yes, that was it; that was the vague danger she had sensed. A night in jail, for a normal person, would be bad enough; for her, under these circumstances, it could be catastrophic.

She had no idea how much time had passed, but she knew that she must look pale and drained. "Ah . . . I'm sorry," she said. Even her voice was shaky. Desperately she sought for a believable explanation. "I—I'm an epileptic. I began to feel dizzy and pulled over. I think I must have had a slight seizure."

The flashlight beam sought her face, played across her features. "Please step out of the car, ma'am."

The trembling was back; she didn't know if her legs would hold her. But she got out, holding to the open door for support. The blue lights stabbed her eyes, and she turned her head away from the brightness as she stood there pinned in the glare, a human aspen, visibly quaking.

"May I see your driver's license?"

Her limbs were leaden. It was an effort to retrieve her purse, and she dropped it immediately, the contents spilling half in the car, half on the ground. Innocuous contents, thank God; not even an aspirin bottle or pack of cigarettes. She was still afraid to take over-the-counter medications, even after six years, because the mental effects could be so unpredictable.

By concentrating fiercely, holding the crippling fatigue at bay, she managed to pick up her wallet and get out her license. The policeman silently examined it, then returned it to her. "Do you need help?" he finally asked.

"No, I'm feeling better now, e-except for the sh-shakes," she said. Her teeth were chattering from reaction. "I don't live far. I'll be able to make it home."

"Would you like for me to follow you, make sure you get there okay?"

"Yes, please," she said gratefully. She was willing to tell any number of lies to keep from being taken to a hospital, but that didn't mean she had lost her common sense. She was incredibly tired, the aftermath worse than she remembered. And there was still the nightmare image—knowing or memory, she couldn't tell—to be dealt with, but she

pushed it out of her mind. She couldn't let herself think about it; right now she had to concentrate only on the tasks at hand, which were remaining coherent, upright, and functional, at least until she could get home.

The policeman helped her pick up her belongings, and in a few moments she was behind the wheel again, edging back onto the pavement, driving with excruciating care because every movement was such an effort. Twice she caught herself as her eyes were closing, the darkness of unconsciousness inexorably closing in.

Then she was home, turning in to the driveway. She managed to get out of the car and wave at the officer. She leaned against the car, watching him drive away, and only when he turned the corner did she set herself to the task of getting inside the house. To safety.

With weak, shaking, uncooperative hands she looped the strap of her purse around her neck, so she wouldn't drop it. After pausing for a moment to gather strength, she launched herself away from the car in the direction of the front porch. As a launch, it was spectacularly lacking in power. She staggered like a drunk, her steps wavering, her vision fading. Every movement became more and more difficult as the fatigue grew like a living thing, overwhelming her muscles and taking them from her control. She reached the two steps leading up to the porch and stopped there, swaying slowly back and forth, her blurred gaze fixed on those two steps that normally required no effort at all. She tried to lift her foot enough to take the first step, but nothing happened. She simply couldn't do it. Iron weights were dragging around her ankles, holding her back.

She began to shiver, another familiar reaction from before, in that other life. She knew she had only a few minutes to get inside before she completely collapsed.

She dropped heavily to her knees, feeling the resulting pain as only a dull, distant sensation. She could hear her own harsh, strained breathing, echoing hollowly. Slowly,

torturously, she dragged herself up the steps, fighting for each inch, fighting to keep the darkness at bay.

She reached the front door. Keys. She needed the keys to get in.

She couldn't think. The black fog in her brain was paralyzing. She couldn't remember what she had done with her keys. In her purse? Still in the car? Or had she dropped them? There was no way she could retrace her steps, no way she could remain conscious much longer. She began fumbling in her purse, hoping to find the key ring. She should be able to recognize it by touch; it was one of those stretchy bracelet things, the type that could be slid onto the wrist. She could feel metal, but it eluded her grasp.

Bracelet . . . She had slipped the keys onto her wrist. It was a habit so ingrained that she seldom even thought about it. The shaking was worse; she pulled the key ring off her wrist but couldn't manage to fit the key into the lock. She couldn't see, the blackness almost complete now. Desperately she tried again, locating the lock purely by touch, concentrating with her last fierce vestige of strength on the herculean task of guiding the key into the lock . . . Got it! Panting, she turned the key until she felt the click. There. Unlocked.

She mustn't forget the keys, mustn't leave them in the lock. She slid the bracelet back onto her wrist as she twisted the doorknob and the door swung open, away from her. She had been leaning on the door, and with that support suddenly gone she sprawled in the doorway, half in and half out of the house.

Just a little more, she silently urged herself, and struggled to her hands and knees again. *Get in far enough to close the door. That's all.*

It wasn't really crawling now. She dragged herself in, whimpering with the effort, but she didn't hear the noise. The door. She had to close the door. Only then could she give herself over to the blackness.

Her arm waved feebly, but the door was out of reach. She sent a command to her leg and somehow it obeyed, slowly lifting, kicking—a very weak kick. But the door swung gently shut.

And then the darkness overwhelmed her.

She lay motionless on the floor as the clock ticked away the hours. The gray dawn light penetrated the room. The passing morning was marked by the path of sunlight, shining through a window, as it moved down the wall and across the floor to finally fall on her face. Only then did she move in a restless attempt to escape the heat, and the deep stupor changed into a more normal sleep.

It was late afternoon when she began to rouse. The floor wasn't the most comfortable of sleeping places; each shift of position brought a protest from her stiff muscles, nudging her toward consciousness. Other physical complaints gradually made themselves felt, a full bladder protesting the most insistently. She was also very thirsty.

She struggled to her hands and knees, her head hanging low like a marathon runner at the end of the race. Her knees hurt. She gasped at the sharp, puzzling pain. What was wrong with her knees? And why was she on the floor?

Dazedly she looked around, recognizing her own safe, familiar house, the cozy surroundings of the small living room. Something was tangled around her, hampering her efforts to stand—she fought the twisted straps and finally hurled the thing away from her, then frowned because it looked familiar, too. Her purse. But why had her purse straps been around her neck?

It didn't matter. She was tired, so tired. Even her bones felt hollow.

She used a nearby chair to steady herself and slowly got to her feet. Something was wrong with her coordination; she stumbled and lurched like a drunk on the way to a common destination: the john. She found the comparison faintly humorous.

After she had taken care of her most pressing need, she ran a glass of water and gulped greedily, spilling it down her chin in the process. She didn't care. She couldn't remember ever being so thirsty before. Or so tired. This was the worst it had ever been, even worse than six years ago when—

She froze, and her suddenly terrified gaze sought her own reflection in the mirror. The woman who stared back at her had her face, but it wasn't the soothingly ordinary face she had become accustomed to. It was the face from before, from six years in the past, from a life that she had thought, hoped, was finished forever.

She was pale, her skin taut with strain. Dark circles lay under her eyes, dulling the blue to a muddy shade. Her dark brown hair, normally so tidy, hung around her face in a mass of tangles. She looked older than her twenty-eight years, her expression that of someone who has seen too much, lived through too much.

She remembered the stark, bloody vision, the storm of dark, violent emotion that had taken control of her mind, that had left her empty and exhausted, just as the visions always had. She had thought they had ended, but she had been wrong. Dr. Ewell had been wrong. They were back.

Or she had had a flashback. The possibility was even more frightening, for she never wanted to relive that again. But it suddenly seemed likely, for why else would she have seen that flashing knife blade, dripping scarlet as it slashed and hacked—

"Stop it," she said aloud, still staring at herself in the mirror. "Just stop it."

Her mind was still sluggish, still grappling with what had happened, with the aftereffects of the long stupor. Evidently the results of a flashback were the same as if she had had a true vision. If the mind thought it was real, then the stress on the body was just as strong.

She thought about calling Dr. Ewell, but a gap of six years lay between them and she didn't want to bridge it. Once she

had relied on him for almost everything, and though he had always supported her, protected her, she had become accustomed to taking care of herself. Independence suited her. After the encompassing, almost suffocating care of the first twenty-two years of her life, the solitude and self-reliance of the last six had been especially sweet. She would handle the flashbacks by herself.

2

T HE DOORBELL RANG. DETECTIVE DANE HOLLISTER OPENED
one eye, glanced at the clock, then closed it again with a
muttered curse. It was seven o'clock on a Saturday morning,
his first weekend off in a month, and some idiot was leaning
on his doorbell. Maybe whoever it was would go away.

The bell rang again, and was followed by two hammering
knocks on the door. Muttering again, Dane threw aside the
tangled sheet and swung naked out of bed. He grabbed the
wrinkled pants he had discarded the night before and jerked
them on, zipping but not fastening. Out of habit, a habit so
ingrained that he never even thought about it, he picked up
his 9mm Beretta from the bedside table. He never answered
the door unarmed. For that matter, he didn't even collect his
mail unarmed. His last girlfriend, whose tenure had been
brief because she couldn't handle a cop's erratic hours, had
said caustically that he was the only man she knew who
carried a weapon into the bathroom with him.

She hadn't had much of a sense of humor, so Dane had
refrained from making a smart-ass remark about male

11

weapons. Except for missing the sex, it had been a relief when she had called it quits.

He lifted one slat of the blinds to peer out, and with another curse he clicked the locks and opened the door. His friend and partner, Alejandro Trammell, stood on the small porch. Trammell lifted elegant black brows as he studied Dane's wrinkled cotton slacks. "Nice jammies," Trammell said.

"Do you know what the hell time it is?" Dane barked.

Trammell consulted his wristwatch, a wafer-thin Piaget. "Seven oh two. Why?" He strolled inside. Dane slammed the door with a resounding bang.

Trammell halted, belatedly asking, "Do you have company?"

Dane ran his hand through his hair, then rubbed his face, hearing the rasp of beard against his callused palm. "No, I'm alone." He yawned, then surveyed his partner. Trammell was perfectly groomed, as usual, but his eyes were dark-circled.

Dane yawned again. "Is this a very late night, or an early morning?"

"A little bit of both. It was just a bad night, couldn't sleep. I thought I'd come over for coffee and breakfast."

"Generous of you, to share your insomnia with me," Dane muttered, but he was already on his way to the kitchen. He had his own share of bad nights, so he understood the need for company. Trammell had never turned him away on those occasions. "I'll put on the coffee, then you're on your own while I shower and shave."

"Forget it," Trammell said. "I'll put on the coffee. I want to be able to drink it."

Dane didn't argue. He could drink his own coffee, but so far no one else could. He didn't much care for the taste of it himself, but since the caffeine kick was what he was after, the taste was secondary.

He left Trammell to the coffee and sleepily returned to the

bedroom, where he stripped off his pants, leaving them in their original location on the floor. Ten minutes in the shower, leaning with one hand propped on the tile while the water beat down on his head, made waking up seem possible; shaving made it seem desirable, but it took a nick on his jaw to convince him. Muttering again, he dabbed at the blood. He had a theory that any day that started with a shaving nick was shit from start to finish. Unfortunately, on any given day his face was likely to sport a small cut. He didn't deal well with shaving. Trammell had once lazily advised him to switch to an electric shaver, but he hated the idea of letting a razor get the best of him, so he kept at it, shedding his blood on the altar of stubbornness.

Dressing, at least, was easy. Dane simply put on whatever came to hand first. Because he sometimes forgot to put on a tie, he always kept one in his car; it might clash with whatever he was wearing, but he figured a tie was a tie, and it was the spirit rather than the style that mattered. The chief wanted detectives to wear ties, so Dane wore a tie. Trammell sometimes looked horrified, but Trammell was a clothes-horse who tended toward Italian silk suits, so Dane didn't take it to heart.

If any other cop had dressed the way Trammell did, or drove a car like Trammell's, Internal Affairs would have been all over him like stink on shit, which was an appropriate way to describe IA. But Trammell was independently wealthy, having inherited a nice little bundle from his Cuban mother as well as several successful concerns from his father, a New England businessman who had fallen in love while on a vacation in Miami and remained in Florida for the rest of his life. Trammell's house had cost a cool million, easy, and he never made any effort to tone down his way of living. His partner was such an enigmatic son of a bitch that Dane couldn't decide if Trammell lived as luxuri-ously as he did simply because he liked the life-style and had the means, or if he did it to piss off the bastards in IA. Dane suspected the latter. He approved.

He and Trammell were opposites in a lot of ways. Trammell was whipcord-lean, and as aloof as a cat. No matter what the circumstances, he always looked elegant and cultured, his clothes hanging perfectly. He liked— actually *liked*—opera and ballet. Dane was the exact opposite: he could wear the most expensive silk suit made, perfectly tailored to fit his muscled, athletic frame, and he would still look subtly unkempt. He liked sports and country music. If they had been vehicles, Trammell would have been a Jaguar, while Dane would have been a pickup truck. Four-wheel drive.

On the other hand, Dane thought as he wandered back out to the kitchen, nature had balanced itself out in their faces, in a kind of backwards way. In person, Trammell was smoothly handsome, but in photographs his face took on a sinister cast. Dane figured his own face would frighten children and small animals, assuming there was any difference between the two, but the camera loved him. All those angles, Trammell had explained. Trammell was a camera buff and took a lot of photos; he was never without his camera. Dane, being his partner and constantly in his company, was naturally in a lot of the photos. On film, the brutal lines of high, prominent cheekbones, the deep-set eyes and cleft chin, all became brooding and intriguing instead of merely brutish. Even the broken nose somehow looked right in a photograph. In person, he looked grim, his face battered, his eyes a cop's eyes, watchful and too old.

Dane got himself a cup of coffee and sat down at the table. Trammell was still cooking, and whatever it was smelled good.

"What's for breakfast?" he asked.

"Whole wheat waffles with fresh strawberries."

Dane snorted. "There's never been any whole wheat flour in *my* house."

"I know. That's why I brought it with me."

Healthy stuff. Dane didn't mind. He could be pretty damn affable when someone else was doing the cooking. When

they were working they mostly lived on junk, whatever was fast and easy, so he didn't mind balancing it with low-fat, nutritious shit whenever they had the time. Hell, he'd even learned to like sprouts. They tasted like green peanuts, fresh out of the ground and not quite developed, with the hulls still soft. He'd eaten a lot of green peanuts when he was a kid, preferring them over the fully formed ones that had to be shelled.

"So what kept you awake last night?" he asked Trammell. "Anything in particular?"

"No, just one of those nights when a weird dream starts every time you doze off."

It was funny how the dreams came and went. All cops had dreams, but he and Trammell had gone through a rough patch a few years back, just after the shootout; the dreams had come every night for a while. Most cops went through their entire careers without ever firing their weapons on the job, but Dane and Trammell hadn't been that lucky.

They had been trying to find a suspect for questioning in a shooting and had been led, by the suspect's pissed-off girlfriend, right into the middle of a big-time drug operation, operated by none other than the suspect himself. That was usually the way the bad guys went down; they weren't caught by sharp detective work most of the time, but by someone dropping the dime on them.

That particular time, instead of bailing out any available window and disappearing down rat holes, the bad guys had come up with lead flying. Dane and Trammell had hit the floor, diving into another room, and for five of the longest minutes in history they had been cornered in that room. By the time backup had arrived, in the form of every cop in the vicinity, uniformed and otherwise, who had heard Dane's radio call of "officer under fire," three of the bad guys and the girlfriend were down. The girl and one of the men were dead. A slug had ricocheted, splintered, and part of it had hit Dane in the back, just missing his spine. It had still packed enough punch that it had broken a rib and torn a

hole in his right lung. Things had gotten a little fuzzy there, but the one clear memory he had was of Trammell kneeling beside him and cussing a blue streak while he tried to stop the bleeding. Three days in intensive care, fifteen days total in the hospital, nine weeks before he'd been able to return to the job. Yeah, they'd both had a lot of bad dreams for a while after that.

Just as Trammell served up the waffles, the phone rang. Dane stretched to pick up the receiver, and at the same time Trammell's beeper went off. "Shit!" they both said, staring at each other.

"It's Saturday, damn it!" Dane barked into the receiver. "We're off today."

He listened while he watched Trammell hurriedly gulp a cup of coffee, then sighed. "Yeah, okay. Trammell's here. We're on our way."

"What canceled our day off?" Trammell wanted to know as they went out the door.

"Stroud and Keegan are already working another scene. Worley called in sick this morning. Freddie's in the dentist's office with an abscessed tooth." Things happened; no sense getting hot about it. "I'll drive."

"So where are we going?"

Dane gave him the address as they got into his car, and Trammell wrote it down. "A man called in and said his wife was hurt. An EMT was dispatched, but a patrol officer got there first. He took one look and canceled the EMT, and called Homicide instead."

It took them about ten minutes to reach the address, but there was no mistaking the house. The street was almost blocked with patrol cars, a paramedics van, and various other official-capacity vehicles. Uniformed officers stood around on the small lawn, while neighbors gathered in small bunches, some of the onlookers still in their nightclothes. Dane automatically studied the onlookers, looking for something that didn't fit, someone who didn't seem to

belong or who was maybe just a little bit too interested. It was amazing how often a murderer would hang around.

He shrugged into a navy jacket and grabbed the spare tie out of the backseat, loosely knotting it around his neck. Somehow, he noticed, Trammell had managed to impeccably tie his own tie in the car. He looked again. Damn, he didn't believe it! The dapper bastard had chosen a double-breasted Italian suit to wear *on his day off!* He'd simply slipped into the suit jacket as they'd left the house.

Sometimes he worried about Trammell.

They showed their badges to the policeman at the door, and he stood aside to let them enter.

"Sheeit," Dane said in an undertone as he got a good look.

"And all the other bodily excretions," Trammell replied in the same disbelieving tone.

Murder scenes were nothing new. After a while, cops reached the point where violent crimes were pretty routine, in their own way. Stabbings and shootings were a dime a dozen. If anyone had asked him half an hour earlier, Dane would have said that he and Trammell had been detectives long enough that, for the most part, they were unshockable.

But this was different.

Blood was everywhere. It was splattered on the walls, on the floor, even on the ceiling. He could see into the kitchen, and the bloody path wound from there through the living room, then into a small hallway and out of sight. He tried to imagine the kind of struggle that would have sprayed blood so extensively.

Dane turned to the uniformed policeman who was guarding the door. "Have the crime lab guys showed up yet?"

"Not yet."

"Shit," he said again. The longer it took the crime lab, or forensics, team to arrive, the more the crime scene would be compromised. Some disturbance was unavoidable, unless the forensics boys were the ones to discover the victim and

immediately secured the area. But forensics wasn't here, and the house was crowded with both uniformed and plainclothes policemen, milling around and inevitably muddying the evidential waters.

"Don't let anybody else in except for Ivan's guys," he told the officer. Ivan Schaffer was head of the crime lab team. He was going to be really pissed off about this.

"Lieutenant Bonness is on the way."

"You can let him in, too," Dane replied, his mouth quirking.

The house was middle-class, nothing out of the ordinary. The living room was furnished with a couch and matching chair, the required coffee table and matching lamp tables of genuine wood veneer, while a big brown recliner had the best spot in front of the television. The recliner was occupied now by a dazed-looking man in his late forties or early fifties, probably the victim's husband. He was giving monosyllabic answers to the questions put to him by another uniformed officer.

The victim was in the bedroom. Dane and Trammell forced their way through the crowd and into the small room. The photographer had already arrived and was doing his job, but for once was noticeably lacking in his usual nonchalance.

The nude woman lay jammed in the cramped space between the bedside table and the wall. She had been stabbed repeatedly—*hacked* was a better description. She had tried to run, and when she had been cornered in the bedroom she had tried to fight, as evidenced by the deep defensive wounds on her arms. She had been nearly decapitated, her breasts mutilated by the sheer number of wounds, and all of her fingers had been severed. Dane looked around the room, but he didn't see the missing digits. The bed was still neatly made, though splattered with blood.

"Has the weapon been found?" Dane asked.

A patrolman nodded. "It was right beside the body. A

Ginsu knife from the kitchen. She had a whole set. It looks like they really do what the ads say; I think I'll get my wife some."

Another patrolman snorted. "I'd rethink that idea if I was you, Scanlon."

Dane ignored the black humor, which all cops used to help them handle the ugliness they saw on a daily basis. "What about her fingers?"

"Nope. No sign of 'em."

Trammell sighed. "I think we'd better go talk to the husband."

It was a fact that most homicides, except for the random gang drive-bys, were committed by someone who knew the victim: a friend, a neighbor, co-worker, or relative. When the victim was a woman, the usual list of suspects was narrowed down even more, because the murderer was almost invariably her husband or boyfriend. A lot of times, the murderer was the one who "discovered" the body and reported the crime.

They went back to the living room, and Dane caught the eye of the officer who was talking to the husband. The officer came over to them.

"Has he said anything?" Dane asked.

The officer shook his head. "Most of the time he won't answer the questions. He did say that his wife's name is Nadine, and his name is Vinick, Ansel Vinick. They've lived here twenty-three years. Beyond that, he ain't talking."

"Is he the one who called it in?"

"Yeah."

"Okay. We'll take it now."

He and Trammell went over to Mr. Vinick. Dane sat down on the couch, and Trammell moved the other chair closer before sitting down, effectively sandwiching Mr. Vinick between them.

"Mr. Vinick, I'm Detective Hollister and this is Detective Trammell. We'd like to talk to you, ask you a few questions."

19

Mr. Vinick was staring at the floor. His big hands hung loosely over the padded arms of the recliner. "Sure," he said dully.

"Are you the one who found your wife?"

He didn't answer, just continued to stare at the floor.

Trammell stepped in. "Mr. Vinick, I know it's tough, but we need your cooperation. Are you the person who called the police?"

Slowly he shook his head. "I didn't call no police. I called 911."

"What time did you call?" Dane asked. The time would be on record, but liars often tripped themselves up on the simplest details. Right now, Vinick was a suspect by virtue of being married to the victim.

"Dunno," Vinick muttered. He took a deep breath and seemed to make an effort to concentrate. "Seven-thirty or thereabouts, I guess." He rubbed his face with a trembling hand. "I got off work at seven. It takes about twenty, twenty-five minutes to drive home."

Dane caught Trammell's glance. They had seen enough death to know that Mrs. Vinick had been dead for several hours, not half an hour or so. The medical examiner would establish the time of death, and if Mr. Vinick had been at work during that time, if witnesses could reliably state that he hadn't left, then they'd have to start looking at other possibilities. Maybe she'd had a boyfriend; maybe someone had been keeping Mr. Vinick's bed warm for him while he worked third shift.

"Where do you work?"

There was no answer. Dane tried again. "Mr. Vinick, where do you work?"

Vinick stirred and named a local trucking company.

"Do you normally work third shift?"

"Yeah. I work on the dock, loading and unloading trailers. Most freight comes in at night, see, for delivery during the day."

"What time did you leave to go to work last night?"

"Usual time. Around ten."

They were on a roll, finally getting some answers. "Do you punch a time card?" Trammell asked.

"Yeah."

"Do you punch in as soon as you get there, or wait until time for your shift to start?"

"As soon as I get there. The shift starts at ten-thirty. We have half an hour to eat, and get off at seven."

"Do you have to clock in and out for lunch?"

"Yeah."

It looked like Mr. Vinick's night would be pretty much accounted for. They would check out everything he'd told them, of course, but that wouldn't be any problem.

"Did you notice anything unusual this morning?" Dane asked. "Before you came in the house, I mean."

"No. Well, the door was locked. Nadine usually gets up and unlocks it for me, then starts cooking breakfast."

"Do you usually come in the front door or the back door?"

"Back."

"What did you see when you opened the door?"

Mr. Vinick's chin trembled. "Nothing, at first. The shades were pulled and the lights weren't on. It was dark. I figured Nadine had overslept."

"What did you do?"

"Turned on the light in the kitchen."

"What did you see then?"

Mr. Vinick swallowed. He opened his mouth but couldn't speak. He put his hand to his eyes. "B-Blood," he managed. "All—all over the place. Except—it looked like ketchup, at first. I thought she'd dropped a bottle of ketchup and broken it, the way it was splattered. Then—then I knew what it was. It scared me. I thought she must have cut herself, real bad. I yelled her name and ran to the bedroom, looking for her." He stopped, unable to carry the tale any further. He began

to shake, and didn't notice when Dane and Trammell got up and stepped away, leaving him alone with his grief and horror.

Ivan Schaffer and an assistant arrived with their bags and disappeared into the bedroom to gather what evidence they could salvage from the carnage. Lieutenant Gordon Bonness arrived practically on their heels. He skidded to a stop just inside the door, his expression one of shock. "Holy shit," he muttered.

"That seems to be the concensus," Trammell said in an aside to Dane as they joined the lieutenant.

Bonness wasn't a bad sort, even if he was from California and could come up with some pretty weird ideas on things. He was as fair as possible in the way he ran the unit, which Dane considered a pretty good recommendation, and he was tolerant of the different quirks and work habits of the detectives under him.

"What have you got so far?" Bonness asked.

"We have a lady who was hacked to pieces, and a husband who was at work. We'll check out his alibi, but my gut says he's in the clear," Dane answered.

Bonness sighed. "Maybe a boyfriend?"

"We haven't gotten that far yet."

"Okay. Let's move fast on this one. Jesus, look at these walls."

They went into the bedroom, and the lieutenant blanched. "Holy shit," he said again. "This is sick!"

Dane gave him a thoughtful look, and his stomach tightened. A feeling of dread went up his spine. Sick. Yeah, this was sick. And he was suddenly a lot more worried than he had been before.

He squatted beside Ivan as the tall, lanky man painstakingly searched for fibers, hair, anything that could be analyzed into giving up its secrets. "Found anything?"

"Won't know until I get it to the lab." Ivan looked around. "It would help if we could find her fingers. Maybe there'd be some skin under the nails. I've got people going through the

trash in the neighborhood. No garbage disposal here, so that's out."

"Was she raped?"

"Don't know. There's no obvious semen."

Dane's feeling of dread was growing stronger. What had seemed like a fairly simple, if gruesome, murder was getting complicated. His gut feeling was seldom wrong, and he had alarm signals going off like an entire brass section.

He followed the gory trail back to its beginning, in the kitchen. Trammell came with him, and they both stood in the small, homey room, looking around. Nadine Vinick had evidently liked to cook; the kitchen was more modern than the rest of the house, with gleaming appliances, a small cooking island, and a variety of shiny but well-used pots and pans hanging over the island. A butcher's block stood at one end of the counter, and a set of Ginsu knives, with one knife missing, was arranged in a rack on top of the butcher's block.

"How did the son of a bitch get in?" Dane muttered. "Has anyone even looked for signs of forced entry, or did they just play the odds that the husband was the one who did her?"

Trammell had worked with him long enough to read him. "You getting a feeling about this?"

"Yeah. A bad one."

"You don't think maybe she had a boyfriend?"

Dane shrugged. "Maybe, maybe not. It was just something the lieutenant said, about this being sick. It is. And that makes me real uneasy. Come on, let's see if we can figure out how he got in."

It didn't take long. There was a small cut at the bottom of the screen on the window in the spare bedroom. The screen was in place but unfastened, and the latch on the window was open, not that it would have kept out even a determined ten-year-old. "I'll get Ivan," Trammell said. "Maybe he can lift a print, or find a couple of stray threads."

Dane's gut feeling was getting worse. A forced entry put a different slant on the situation, indicating a stranger. This

didn't feel like a burglary that had escalated into violence when the intruder had been suddenly confronted by Mrs. Vinick. The ordinary burglar would have been more likely to run, and even if he had attacked, it would have been quick. The attack on Mrs. Vinick had been both vicious and prolonged. *Sick.*

He walked back into the kitchen. Had the first confrontation taken place here, or had Mrs. Vinick seen the intruder and tried to run out the back door, getting as far as the kitchen before he caught her? Dane stared at the appliances as if they could tell tales. A small frown knit his brows and he went over to the automatic coffee maker, the kind that was installed under the upper cabinets so it didn't take up counter space. The carafe held about five cups of coffee. Using the backs of his fingers, he touched the glass. It was cold. The coffee maker was the kind with the automatic switch that turned off the warming plate after two hours. A coffee mug, filled almost to the rim with coffee, sat on the counter. It didn't look as if it had been touched since the coffee had been poured into it. He stuck his finger into the dark liquid. Cold.

He pulled a pair of surgical gloves out of his pocket and put them on. Carefully touching only the wooden rim of the cabinet doors rather than the metal handles, he began opening them. The second door revealed a canister of decaffeinated coffee. Mrs. Vinick could drink it late at night without worrying about her sleep being disturbed.

She had made a pot of coffee and she had been in here, in the kitchen. She had just poured the first cup and replaced the carafe on the warming plate. The door from the living room was behind her and to the right. Dane went through the motions as if he had just poured the coffee himself, standing where she would have stood. According to the placement of the cup on the counter, she would have been standing slightly to the left of the coffee maker. That was when she had seen the intruder, just as she had set the carafe in place. The coffee maker had a dark, shiny surface, almost

mirrorlike, behind the hands of the built-in clock. Dane bent his knees, trying to lower himself to Mrs. Vinick's general height. The open doorway was reflected in the surface of the coffee maker.

She had never even picked up her cup of fresh coffee. She had seen the intruder's reflection and turned, perhaps thinking, in that first moment, that her husband had forgotten something and returned home to get it. By the time she had realized her mistake, he had been on her.

She probably hadn't been standing naked in her kitchen, though Dane had been a cop long enough to know that anything was possible. It was just another gut feeling. But she had been naked when the killer had finished with her, and probably naked when he had started.

The odds were that she had been raped at knife point, right here in the kitchen. The lack of obvious semen didn't mean anything; after so many hours, and with the struggle that had gone on, it would take a medical examiner to make a judgment. And a lot of times, rapists didn't climax anyway. Orgasm wasn't the point of rape.

After the rape, he had started work with the knife. Until then, she had been terrified but hoping, probably, that when he was finished he would just go away. When he started cutting her, she had known that he intended to kill her and she had started fighting for her life. She had escaped from him, or maybe he had let her escape, like a cat toying with a mouse, letting her think she had gotten away before easily catching her again. How many times had he played his sick little game before finally cornering her in the bedroom?

What had she been wearing? Had the killer taken her clothing with him as a souvenir or trophy?

"What?" Trammell asked quietly from the doorway, his dark eyes intent as he watched his partner.

Dane looked up. "Where are her clothes?" he asked. "What was she wearing?"

"Maybe Mr. Vinick knows." Trammell disappeared, and returned in less than a minute. "She had already changed

into her nightgown when he left for work. He said it was white, with little blue things on it."

They began looking for the missing garment. It was startlingly easy to find. Trammell opened the folding doors that hid the washer and dryer, and there it was, neatly placed on top of the pile of clothing in the laundry basket that sat on top of the dryer. The garment was splattered with blood, but certainly not soaked. No, she hadn't been wearing it when the knife attack had begun. Probably it had been lying on the floor, thrown aside, and the blood had splattered on it later.

Dane stared at it. "After raping and killing her, the son of a bitch put her nightgown in the laundry?"

"Rape?" Trammell queried.

"Bet on it."

"I didn't touch the handle. Maybe Ivan can get a print; he came up empty in the second bedroom."

Dane had another gut feeling, one he liked even less than the others. "I'm afraid we're going to come up empty all the way around," he said bleakly.

3

I‍T HADN'T BEEN A FLASHBACK.

She knew because she had been having real flashbacks all day, frightening resurgent memories that swept over her, overwhelmed her, and left her limp and exhausted when her own reality returned.

Marlie knew the details of her own particular nightmare, was as familiar with them as she was with her face; the details that had been flashing in her brain all day were new, different. When she had awoken from her stupor the afternoon before, she had been able to remember little more than the image of the slashing knife, and she had still been so tired that she had barely been able to function. She had gone to bed early and slept deeply, dreamlessly, until almost dawn when the details began to surface.

The bouts of memory had happened all day long; she would barely recover from one when another, vivid and horrible, would surge into her consciousness. It had never happened this way before; the visions had always been overwhelming and exhausting, yes, but she had always been

able to immediately recall them. These ongoing *attacks* left her bewildered, and helpless from fatigue. Several times she had been tempted to call Dr. Ewell and tell him about this frightening new development, but something in her had held back.

A woman had been murdered. It had been real. God help her, the knowing had returned, but it was different, and she didn't know what to do. The vision had been strong, stronger than any she'd ever had before, but she didn't know who the victim was and couldn't tell where it had happened. Always before she had had at least an inkling, had grasped some clues to identity and location, but not this time. She felt disoriented, her mind reaching out but unable to find the signal, like a compass needle spinning in search of a magnetic pole that wasn't there.

She had seen the murder happen over and over in her mind, and each time more details had surfaced, as if a wind were blowing away layers of fog. And each time she roused from a replay of the vision, more exhausted than before, she had been more horrified.

She was seeing it through *his* eyes.

It had been *his* mind that had caught hers, the mental force of *his* rage that had blasted through six years of blank, blessed nothingness and jolted her, once again, into extrasensory awareness. Not that he had targeted her; he hadn't. The enormous surge of mental energy had been aimless, without design; he hadn't known what he was doing. Normal people never imagined that there were people like her out there, people with minds so sensitive that they could pick up the electrical signals of thought, read the lingering energy patterns of long-ago events, even divine the forming patterns of things that hadn't yet happened. Not that this man was normal in any sense other than his lack of extrasensorial sensitivity, but Marlie had long ago made the distinction to herself: Normal people were those who didn't know. She had the knowing, and it had forever set her apart,

until six years ago when she had been caught in a nightmare that still haunted her. Traumatized, that part of her brain had shut down. For six years she had lived as a normal person, and she had enjoyed it. She wanted that life to continue. She had slowly, over the years, let herself come to believe that the knowing would never return. She had been wrong. Perhaps it had taken this long for her mind to heal, but the visions were back, stronger and more exhausting than ever before.

And seen through the eyes of a murderer.

Part of her still hoped . . . what? That it hadn't been real, after all? That she was losing her mind? Would she really rather be delusional than accept that the visions had returned, that her safe, normal life had come to an end?

She had looked through the Sunday paper but hadn't been able to concentrate; the memory flashes had been too frequent, too strong. She hadn't found any mention of a murder that had triggered a response. Maybe it had been there and she had simply overlooked it; she didn't know. Maybe it hadn't happened anywhere nearby, but by some freak chance she had happened to catch the killer's mental signals. If the woman had lived in some other town, say in Tampa or Daytona, Orlando's papers wouldn't carry it. Marlie would never know the woman's identity or location.

Part of her was a coward. She didn't *want* to know, didn't want to become part of that life again. She had built something safe and solid here in Orlando, something that would be destroyed if she became involved again. She knew exactly what would happen: the disbelief, followed by derision. Then, when people were forced to accept the truth, they would become suspicious and afraid. They would be willing to use her talent, but they wouldn't want to be friends. People would avoid her; little kids would daringly peek in her windows and run, screaming, if she looked back. The older kids would call her "the witch." Inevitably some religious fanatic would start muttering about "the work of

the devil," and sporadic picket lines would spring up in front of her house. No, she would have to be a fool to get involved in that again.

But she couldn't stop wondering about the woman. There was an aching need to at least know her name. When someone died, at least her name should be known, a tiny link with immortality that said: This person was here. This person existed. Without a name, there was only a blank.

So now, still shaking with fatigue, she turned on the television and waited, in a daze, for the local news to come on. She almost dozed several times, but shook herself awake. "It's probably nothing," she mumbled aloud. "You're just losing it, that's all." Strange comfort, but there it was. Everyone's private fears were different, and she would rather be crazy than right.

The television screen flickered as the talking heads segued into another story, this time devoting an entire minute to an in-depth look at the effect of crack and gangs on inner-city neighborhoods. Marlie blinked, suddenly terrified that the visual images would overwhelm her with mental ones, as had happened in the past when she had picked up on the emotions of the people she had watched. Nothing happened. Her mind remained blank. After a minute she relaxed, sighing with relief. Nothing was there, no bleak feelings of despair and hopelessness. She began to feel a little more cheerful; if she couldn't receive those images and emotions the way she had in the past, maybe she *was* just going a little crazy.

She continued watching, and became a little drowsy again. She felt herself begin to give in to the fatigue, effortlessly sliding into a light doze even though she tried to remind herself to stay awake for the rest of the newscast—

—". . . NADINE VINICK . . ."

Marlie jerked violently as the name blared both inside and outside of her head, her inner awareness amplifying the name just spoken by the television announcer. She struggled to an upright position on the couch, unaware of having

slumped over as she dozed. Her heart pounded frantically against her ribs and she heard her own panicked breathing, fast and shallow, as she stared at the screen.

"The Orlando police aren't releasing any information about the stabbing murder of Mrs. Vinick, as the slaying is still under investigation."

A photo of the victim was flashed on the screen. Nadine Vinick. That was the woman Marlie had seen in the vision. She had never heard the name before, but there was a strong sense of recognition, too strong to ignore. Just hearing the name spoken on television had been like a bullhorn sounding in her head.

So it was true, it was real. All of it.

The knowing was back.

And it would tear her life apart again if she did anything about it.

On Monday morning Dane stared at the stark photographs of the murder scene, examining each minute detail over and over as he allowed his thoughts free range, hoping that some crucial, previously unnoticed item would slip into focus, something that would give them a direction, any direction. They had nothing to go on, damn it, absolutely nothing. A neighbor across the street had heard a dog bark around eleven, she thought, but it had stopped and she hadn't thought anything else about it until they had questioned her. Mr. Vinick had definitely been at work; he had been helping another dockman unload a trailer, his time completely accounted for. The medical examiner couldn't give an exact time of death, because unless there was a witness, such a thing was impossible, and the time frame unfortunately included the half hour before Mr. Vinick had gone to work. Dane still went with his gut feeling: Vinick hadn't done it. According to his co-workers, Mr. Vinick had been completely normal when he had arrived at work, joking around. It would have taken a real monster, which Mr. Vinick had never given any indication of being, to have

butchered his wife, coolly cleaned up and changed clothes, then gone to work as usual without any vestige of nervousness.

They had no semen, though the medical examiner said that vaginal bruising indicated Mrs. Vinick had been violently penetrated. They had no fibers alien to the house, except for what the Orlando Police Department had brought in themselves. They had no hair samples, pubic or otherwise. They had no fingerprints. And they hadn't found Nadine Vinick's fingers.

"We don't have shit," he muttered, tossing the photographs onto his desk.

Trammell grunted in agreement. They were both tired; they had scarcely stopped in the forty-eight hours since they had first entered the Vinick home. And with every passing hour, the chances of finding Mrs. Vinick's murderer diminished. Crimes were either solved fast, or they tended not to be solved at all. "Look at the rundown of their garbage."

He handed the itemized list over to Dane, who glanced down it. Typical garbage: food waste, empty milk cartons and cereal boxes, an assortment of uninteresting junk mail, plastic shopping bags from a couple of stores, used coffee filters, a pizza box with two remaining slices of pizza, soiled paper towels, an old shopping list, last week's *TV Guide,* a couple of scribbled phone numbers, a voided check made out to the telephone company, various empty spray cans, about a week's worth of newspapers—evidently the Vinicks hadn't been into recycling. Nothing that was out of place or unusual.

"What about the phone numbers?" he asked.

"I just called both of them." Trammell leaned back in his chair and propped his Italian-leather-clad feet on the desk. "One is the pizza delivery joint, the other is their cable company."

Dane grunted. He leaned back in his chair and propped his own feet on the desk. Dan Post instead of Gucci, and scuffed at that. What the hell. He and Trammell eyed each

other across their four feet and two desks. Sometimes they did their best brainwork in this position.

"Pizza delivery would involve a stranger coming to the house, and there's a fifty-fifty chance the cable company would send out a repairman."

Trammell's lean, dark face was thoughtful. "Even if a repairman had gone out to the house, it wouldn't have been at night."

"And it would probably be too much to hope that Mrs. Vinick ordered a pizza that late at night, to pig out all by herself. The analysis of her stomach contents . . ." Dane stretched out his right arm and sifted through the scattered papers on his desk, finally plucking the one he wanted out of the mess. "Here it is. Doc says that she hadn't eaten anything for at least four or five hours. No pizza. So the pizza in the trash was from earlier, at least lunch. Maybe a day or two." For all the tantalizing possibilities, in his experience it never had been a pizza deliverer.

"We can find out from Mr. Vinick exactly when they ordered the pizza."

"And the cable company can tell us if they had to send a repairman out to the Vinick's house."

"So we have definitely one, and possibly two, strangers who have been to the house. A pizza delivery boy would have been kept outside, but he could still have seen her. A repairman might actually have been in the house."

"Women chat to repairmen," Dane said, eyes narrowed as he followed the line of reasoning. "Maybe she asked him to please be quiet, since her husband worked third shift and was asleep in the bedroom. The guy says, yeah, he used to work third, too, and it was rough. Where does her husband work? And she tells him, even throws in what time hubby leaves, when he gets home. Why should she worry? After all, would the cable company have hired him if he hadn't been an upstanding citizen? Women don't think anything about letting a repairman in and spilling their guts to him while he's working."

"Okay." Trammell got a pad and propped it on his legs. "One: We check with Mr. Vinick on when the pizza was actually delivered, and maybe a description of the delivery boy."

"Delivery person. It could've been a girl. So could a cable repairman."

"Repairperson," Trammell corrected. "Possible. If not, then we get a name from the pizza place and go from there. Two: Do the same with the cable company."

Dane felt better. At least they were working, had come up with a direction in which to start looking.

His phone rang. It was the intercom line. He punched the button and lifted the receiver. "Hollister."

"Dane," Lieutenant Bonness said. "You and Trammell come to my office."

"On our way." He hung up the phone. "LT wants to see us."

Trammell swung his feet down and stood. "What have you done now?" he complained.

Dane shrugged. "Nothing that I know of." He certainly wasn't the movie image of a rogue cop, but he did have a certain knack of stepping on toes and pissing off people. It happened. He just didn't have much patience with bullshitters.

The lieutenant's office had two big interior windows; they saw the woman with the lieutenant, sitting with her back to the door. "Who is she?" Dane murmured, and Trammell shook his head. Dane rapped once on the glass, and Lieutenant Bonness gestured them inside. "Come on in, and close the door," he said.

As soon as they were inside he said, "Marlie Keen, this is Detective Hollister and Detective Trammell. They're in charge of the Vinick case. Miss Keen has some interesting information."

Trammell took a seat on the other side of the lieutenant's desk, away from Miss Keen. Dane leaned against the wall on her other side, out of her direct line of vision but where he

could still see her face. She had barely glanced at either him or Trammell; nor was she looking at the lieutenant. Instead she seemed to be concentrating on the blinds that shaded the outside windows.

A short silence fell as she seemed to be bracing herself. Dane eyed her curiously. She was so tense, he could almost see her muscles tighten. There was something vaguely intriguing about her, something that kept him looking at her. She wasn't a beauty, though she was even-featured and certainly not hard on the eyes, but she sure didn't do anything to attract attention. She wore plain black flats, a narrow black denim skirt that came down to midcalf, and a sleeveless white blouse. She had nice, clean-looking dark hair, but it had been pulled back into one of those severe French twists. About thirty years old, he guessed, his policeman's eye making an automatic assessment. Hard to tell with her sitting down, but probably average height, maybe a little less. A little slimmer than he liked, about a hundred and twenty pounds; he preferred a woman to be soft rather than bony.

Her hands were tightly clenched in her lap. He found himself watching them: slim, fine-boned hands, free of any jewelry, and a dead giveaway to her tension even if he hadn't already noticed that her posture was stiff rather than still.

"I'm psychic," she said baldly. He barely kept himself from snorting in derision. His eyes met Trammell's in a lightning-quick glance of shared thought: *Another one of the lieutenant's weird California ideas!*

"Last Friday night I was driving home from a late movie," she continued in a flat little monotone that didn't diminish the low, raspy quality of her voice. A smoker's voice, he thought, except he'd bet the farm that she didn't smoke. Uptight types like her seldom went in for the easy vices. "It was about eleven-thirty when I left the theater. I had just left the expressway when I began to have a vision of a murder that was taking place. The . . . visions are overwhelming. I managed to pull off the street."

She paused, as if reluctant to continue, and Dane watched her hands twist together until they were bloodless. She took a deep breath.

"I see it through his eyes," she said tonelessly. "He climbed in through a window."

Dane stiffened, his attention shifting to her face. He didn't have to look at Trammell to know that his partner's attention had sharpened, too.

The recitation continued in a slow, evenly spaced cadence that felt oddly hypnotic. Her eyes were wide and unfocused, as if she were looking inward. "It's dark in the room. He waits there until she's alone. He can hear her in the kitchen, talking to her husband. The husband leaves. He waits until the husband's car has pulled out of the driveway, then he opens the door and starts the stalk. He feels like a hunter after game.

"But she's easy prey. She's in the kitchen, just pouring a cup of coffee. He pulls a knife from the set that's sitting there, waiting for him. She hears him and turns. She says, 'Ansel?' but then she sees him and opens her mouth to scream.

"He's too close. He's already on her, his hand over her mouth, the knife at her throat."

Marlie Keen stopped talking. Dane kept his concentration on her face. She was pale now, he noticed, colorless except for the full bloom of her lips. He could feel the hair on the back of his neck lifting in response to that eerie present tense she was using when she spoke, as if the murder were happening right now.

"Go on," the lieutenant urged.

It was a moment before she resumed, and her tone was even flatter than before, as if she could thus distance herself from the words. "He makes her take off her nightgown. She's crying, begging him not to hurt her. He likes that. He wants her to beg him. He wants her to think that she'll be okay if she just does as he says. It's more fun that way, when she realizes—"

She interrupted herself, leaving the sentence unfinished. After another moment she resumed. "He uses a condom. She's grateful for that. She tells him thank you. He's easy with her, almost gentle. She starts to relax, even though she's still crying, because he isn't hurting her and she thinks he'll just leave when he's finished. He knows how the stupid bitches think.

"When he's through, he helps her to her feet. He holds her hand. He bends down and kisses her cheek. She just stands there, until she feels the knife. He keeps the first cut shallow, enough to let her know what's going to happen, so he can see the look in her eyes when she panics, but the cut shouldn't be so bad that it slows down the chase. There wouldn't be any fun in that.

"She panics; she screams and tries to run, and the rage in him is let loose. He's held it in check all this time, toying with her, enjoying her fear and humiliation, allowing her to hope, but now he can let it out. Now he can do what he came for. This is what he likes best, the complete terror he can see in her eyes, the feeling of invincibility. He can do anything he wants to her. He has total power over her, and he revels in it. He is her god; her life or death is *his* choice now, *his* decision. But it's death, of course, because that's what he enjoys most.

"She's fighting, but the pain and loss of blood have slowed her down. She makes it into the bedroom and falls down. He's disappointed; he wanted the fight to go on longer. It makes him angry that she's so weak. He bends over to slice her throat, to finish it, and the bitch turns on him. She's been faking it. She hits at him. He'd meant to make it quick, but now he'll show her, she should never have tried to trick him. The rage is like a hot red balloon, swelling up and filling him. He slashes at her over and over, until he's tired. No, not tired. He's too powerful to be tired. Bored. It was over too soon; she's learned her lesson. She hadn't been as much fun as he'd hoped."

Silence fell. After a few seconds, Dane realized that she

was finished. She still sat stiffly in the chair, her gaze locked on the window blinds.

Lieutenant Bonness seemed disappointed by Dane and Trammell's lack of reaction. "Well?" he demanded impatiently.

"Well, what?" Dane straightened away from the wall. Rage had slowly built inside him as he had listened to the flat, emotionless recital, but it was a cold, controlled anger. He didn't know what the bitch's motive was in coming here, but there was one thing he knew for certain, and he didn't have to be any sort of mindreader to figure it out: She had been there. Maybe she herself had murdered Mrs. Vinick, maybe not, but she had been in that house when it had happened. At the very least she was an accomplice, and if she thought she could waltz in here with that bullshit story and get a lot of media attention while she jerked them around, she had tangled with the wrong guy.

"What do you think?" Bonness snapped, irritated that he had to ask.

Dane shrugged. "A psychic? Get real, LT. That's the biggest load of bullshit I've ever heard."

Marlie Keen stirred, slowly unknotting her hands as if the movement were difficult. Just as slowly she turned her head and looked at Dane for the first time. Despite his icy rage, his stomach muscles contracted abruptly in reaction. *No wonder Bonness had been taken in!* Her eyes were the deep, dark, fathomless blue of the ocean, the kind of eyes a man could look into and forget what he'd been saying. There was something exotic about them, other than the richness of color: a sort of otherworldliness that he couldn't quite grasp. The expression in them, however, was easy to read, and Dane knew beyond a doubt that he hadn't exactly overwhelmed her with his charm.

She stood and faced him, squaring off with him as if they were two adversaries in the old West about to draw down on each other. Her face had gone calm and curiously remote. "I've told you what happened," she said in a clear, deliber-

ate voice. "You can believe it or not; it doesn't make any difference to me."

"It should," he replied just as deliberately.

She didn't ask why, though he paused for her to do just that. Instead her mouth twitched into a tiny, humorless smile. "I realize that I just became your prime suspect," she murmured. "So why don't I save your time and mine by telling you that my address is 2411 Hazelwood, and my telephone number is 555-9909."

"You know the routine," he said with sarcastic admiration. "I'm not surprised." He moved a step closer to her, close enough that she had to look up to maintain eye contact, close enough to intrude into her space and subtly threaten her. "Or maybe you're just reading my mind, since you're psychic." He put an unflattering emphasis on the last word. "Maybe you can tell me what comes next, unless you need a crystal ball to tell you what I'm thinking."

"Oh, that doesn't take a mind reader, but then you aren't very original." She paused, then gave him that little smile again. "I have no intention of leaving town." She wasn't backing down, and his stomach muscles knotted again. At first glance she had looked like a drab, a nonentity afraid of making herself more attractive in any way, but the first look into her eyes had forcibly changed that opinion. The woman facing him didn't lack self-confidence, and she wasn't the least bit intimidated by him even though he was almost a foot taller. Something else stole into his awareness. Damn, he could smell her, a sweet, soft scent that had nothing to do with perfume and everything to do with female flesh. His involuntary reaction made him even angrier.

"See that you don't." His voice was low and harsh. "Is there anything else you see in your crystal ball, anything you want to tell me?"

"Of course," she purred, and the sudden glint in her blue eyes told him that he'd walked right into that one. "Go to hell, Detective."

4

DAMMIT, HOLLISTER!" BONNESS GLARED AT HIM. "DID YOU have to be such an asshole? The woman came in here trying to help, for Chrissake! She told us some amazing stuff—"

"Amazing, my ass," Dane interrupted, still aware of the fury boiling up inside, though now at least half of it was directed at himself. "If she didn't do it herself, then she was there when it was done. She did it, or she's an accomplice, and she's daring us to catch her by feeding us this loony psychic story."

"She knew details that no one but the killer, or killers, could have known," Trammell said tersely. "Hell, we've all heard the kind of crap those so-called psychics describe in their so-called visions. 'I'm getting an impression of the letter *C,*'" he mimicked. "'It's something to do with the letter *C*. And it's wet . . . Yes, yes, I'm definitely getting the impression of wetness. The body is close to water.'"

"Which narrows it down to the whole fucking state," Dane finished. "That wasn't a psychic vision she described;

it was an eyewitness account. The lady was there when it happened, and she just placed herself at the top of my list."

"She couldn't have done it," Bonness protested weakly, his disappointment plain.

"Not alone," Dane agreed. "She wouldn't have been strong enough."

"We definitely should check this lady out," Trammell said.

The lieutenant sighed. "I know you think it was a goofy idea, but psychics have really helped in some cases I've been involved in."

Dane snorted. "As far as I can tell, a psychic is just a psychotic with a couple of letters missing."

"All right, all right." Bonness still looked unhappy, but he flapped his hand at them in dismissal. "See what you can find out about her."

Trammell was right behind him as they walked back to their desks. "What the hell's the matter with you?" he muttered to Dane's back.

"Whaddaya mean? You think I should have pretended to believe her?"

"No, I mean you had a hard-on the size of a goddamn nightstick, and you were standing so close, you were about to poke her in the belly with it," Trammell snapped.

Dane turned and glared at his partner, but he couldn't think of any excuse to give. He didn't know what had happened, only that from the minute she had turned those dark blue eyes on him, he'd had a boner so hard a cat couldn't scratch it. He was still twitching. "Hell, I don't know," he finally said.

"If you're that horny, partner, you'd better get the itch scratched before you get around her again. Either the lady's very familiar with a knife, or she hangs out with someone who is. I wouldn't want any of *my* body parts sticking out to draw her attention."

"Stop worrying about my sex life," Dane advised grimly. "We need to find out all we can about Marlie Keen."

It had never made her angry before. Marlie was used to mingled disbelief and derision, but she had always felt an almost desperate need to *make* people believe, to convince them that she could help, that her claims were true. She felt no such need where Detective Hollister was concerned. She didn't give a damn what that Neanderthal thought, assuming he was capable of such an advanced mental process.

Maybe it was because she had dreaded going to the police so much, with the full knowledge of how this could disrupt her carefully built life. Maybe it was simply that *she* had changed. But when he had been so insultingly dismissive, she had felt nothing but anger. She certainly wasn't about to stay there and plead with him to believe her. She was already late to work, damn it, and though she had called in, she resented it that she had gone to so much trouble for nothing. She had put herself through the ordeal of recounting what she had seen, and that big jerk had called it bullshit!

Her movements were jerky as she negotiated the heavy traffic, and with sheer force of will she made herself calm down before she caused an accident. She had dealt with jerks before, many times. He was nothing new, except for the way he had moved so close to her, trying to intimidate her with his brute size. She had had to steel herself to face him, to allow him that close. He had used his masculinity as a weapon, knowing that any woman would feel threatened by a strange man looming over her like that, especially a man who looked as if he were hewn out of wood and ate nails for breakfast. In any good cop/bad cop routine, his looks would automatically make him the bad cop. No one in his right mind would expect leniency or consideration from that man.

She had almost panicked when he had moved so close. In her mind, she could still feel the heat his body had generated, overpowering the small space that had been between

42

them. Furiously she wondered if he would have done that if she had been a man; her instinct said no. That was a tactic that men used only on women, the threat of touching. Odd that something so simple, so basic, could also be so frightening.

She shuddered. She couldn't have borne it if he *had* touched her. She would have bolted like a total coward.

As late as she was, it was difficult to find a parking space at the bank where she worked. She had to circle the lot three times before a departing customer left an open slot that she managed to get to before someone else did. Then she sat in the car for several minutes, taking deep breaths and trying to achieve some sense of calm. She stared at the bank building, finding comfort in its solidity. Her job was such a nice, safe, passionless one, in accounting. She had chosen it deliberately, when she had moved here. Numbers didn't bombard her with thoughts and feelings, didn't ask for anything from her. Their qualities never varied; a zero was always a zero. All she had to do was align them into columns, feed them into a computer, keep track of their credits and debits. Numbers were always neat, never messy like human beings were.

And it felt good to support herself, even though she knew she didn't have to. The small house she had made into a home had been bought outright for her, when she had decided that she wanted to live in Florida, on the opposite end of the country from Washington. Dr. Ewell would have arranged for her to receive a check each month, had she wanted; she hadn't, preferring to finally stand alone, without all the support systems of the Association. Even now, all she had to do was pick up the telephone and tell Dr. Ewell that she needed help, and it would be provided. Though it hadn't been his fault, hadn't been anyone's fault, Dr. Ewell was still dealing with his guilt over what had happened six years ago.

She sighed. She was paid by the hour; every minute she sat there was being deducted from her paycheck. Resolutely she

pushed Detective Hollister out of her mind and got out of the car.

"Hey, doll, found anything interesting yet?" Detective Fredericka Brown, who answered only to "Freddie," patted Dane on the head as she passed behind his chair. She was a tall, lanky, endearingly plain woman, with a habitually cheerful and amused expression that invited smiles. It was tough for a woman to be a cop in general, and a detective in particular, but Freddie had fit right in. She was blissfully married to a high school football coach, size huge, who looked as if he would tear limb from limb anyone who caused his Freddie the least upset. Freddie tended to treat all of the other detectives as if they were the teenage boys on her husband's team, with a disconcerting blend of light flirtation and motherliness.

Dane scowled at her. "This should have been your case. We had the weekend off, damn it."

"Sorry," she said blithely, giving Trammell a smile of greeting when he looked up from the telephone that had been welded to his ear for most of the morning.

"How's the tooth?" Dane asked.

"Better. I'm up to my eyeteeth in antibiotics and painkillers, no pun intended. It was an abscess, so now I'm having a root canal."

"Tough." The sympathy was sincere.

"I'll live, but Worley's doing all the driving while I have to take this stuff." Worley was her partner. "Anything we can do to help, any leads we can run down? We have our own cases, but from what I've heard, the scene Saturday morning was straight out of a horror movie."

"It wasn't pretty." An understatement if he'd ever made one. Freddie patted him again, this time on the shoulder, and went about her business. Dane turned back to his.

Detective work was mostly boring; it involved a lot of talking on the telephone, going through papers, or going out to talk to people face-to-face. Dane had spent the last few

hours involved in the first two activities. Usually Trammell handled this part of the job better than he did, being more patient, but this time he had set himself to it with grim determination. What had happened to Nadine Vinick should never happen to anyone, but it really pissed him off that Marlie Keen had all but rubbed his nose in her knowledge of it.

"Got anything yet?" Trammell asked, frustration plain in his voice as he hung up the telephone. "I came up empty on both the pizza delivery and the cable company. The entire street had trouble with the cable, and it was repaired on the line, over a block away. It wasn't necessary to enter any residence. And the pizza was delivered by a sixteen-year-old girl. Mr. Vinick is the one who paid her, anyway. Dead end."

"Nothing here, either," Dane muttered. "Yet." Marlie Keen had never been arrested, had never even had a parking ticket, as far as he could find. He didn't let that discourage him. Maybe "Marlie Keen" was an alias. If so, he'd eventually turn up that information. People could be tracked through Social Security numbers, tax returns, any number of means. He knew where she worked and what kind of car she drove. He'd already sent out various requests, such as for a record of calls she'd made and received; by the time he was finished, he'd even know her bra size.

He bet he could make a damn good guess at that right now: 34C. At first he would have guessed no more than a B cup, but that nunnish white blouse had been deceiving. He had noticed a tantalizing roundness—

Damn it! He had to stop thinking about sex, at least in connection with her. Every time he remembered that eerie, macabre tale she'd spun, he almost choked with rage. Nadine Vinick had endured unutterable hell before she'd died, and Marlie Keen, if that was her real name, was trying to turn it into a sideshow. He wouldn't be surprised to get a call from the local media, asking if there was any truth to the rumor that the OPD was working with a psychic to find the

murderer. If Marlie Keen wanted publicity, for whatever sick reason, her next move would be to notify the media herself.

Her gall still astounded him. He totally discounted that psychic shit; the only way she could have known the things she'd known was to have been there. He didn't know if the murder had been played out exactly as she'd said, but the pertinent details of it had been dead on the money. The only way she would have had the nerve to bring herself to their attention was if she knew there was no evidence to link her to the crime. The murderer had been excruciatingly careful; forensics hadn't turned up even the tiniest shred of alien material. Therefore, she had done it for the thrill of thumbing her nose at the police department, flaunting the details before them and knowing they couldn't pin anything on her.

She hadn't handled the knife herself; he was fairly certain of that. So the actual murderer was someone she knew, someone she was close to. A brother, maybe, or a boyfriend. Someone close enough to share torture and murder. He thought of her in bed with the bastard who had carved up Mrs. Vinick, and his stomach twisted.

She had made a mistake, taunting him with her knowledge. She was the thread that would lead him to the murderer, and he wouldn't let go until he reached the end.

He stood up and reached for his jacket. "Let's go," he said to Trammell.

"Any place in particular?"

"To talk to Ms. Keen's neighbors. Find out if she has a boyfriend."

She didn't. The neighbors on the left, retirees from Ohio, were certain of that. Bill and Lou, as they introduced themselves, described Marlie as quiet, friendly, and always accommodating about collecting their newspaper and mail whenever they visited their daughter back in Massillon, and feeding their cat. Not many neighbors were so friendly.

"Have you noticed anyone coming or going from the house? Does she have many visitors?"

"Not that I've seen, though of course, we don't just sit and watch Marlie's house," Lou said with all the indignant righteousness of someone who did just that. "No, I don't think I've ever noticed any visitors over there. Have you, Bill?"

Bill scratched his jaw. "Don't think so. She's just about the perfect neighbor, you know. Always speaks when we see her, don't have her nose in the air like some. Keeps her yard neat, too."

Dane frowned as he scribbled in the small notebook that every policeman carried. "Not *any* visitors?" he stressed. "Ever?"

Lou and Bill looked at each other and shrugged helplessly, shaking their heads.

"No family? Brothers, sisters?"

More head shaking.

"Girlfriends?" he growled.

"No," Lou repeated a bit testily. "No one. She even takes care of the yard work herself, instead of hiring a neighborhood boy. I've never seen anyone over there except for the mailman."

Dead end. He was frankly puzzled by it. He glanced at Trammell and saw the small frown that said his partner was just as buffaloed. Men could be loners, but women seldom were. He tried another tack. "Does she go out much?"

"Not often, no. She sees an occasional movie, I think. I can't believe she's in any sort of trouble. Why, when Bill broke his leg two years ago, she'd stay with him whenever I had to go out." Lou glared at him. Dane noticed that she was saving it all for him, rather than including Trammell in her bad graces.

He flipped his notebook shut. "Thanks for your help." Some help.

The neighbors on the right had basically the same com-

ments, except the lady of the house had two squalling rug rats hanging on her legs and couldn't be expected to pay a lot of attention to the comings and goings next door. No, she'd never seen anyone visiting Marlie.

They went back to the car and got in, both sitting in silence and staring at 2411 Hazelwood. It was a neat, solid little bungalow, typical of houses built in the fifties, though it had been spruced up with a cool, sand-colored paint and enlivened with the kind of touches women put on their nests, the trim done in what he thought of as ice cream colors, which only women and gays knew the names for. The front porch was decorated with a couple of ferns and some pinkish flowers, all in pots hanging from hooks. So what had they just found out? That their most likely suspect sounded like some kind of nun?

"That big thud we just heard was us, hitting a blank wall," Trammell finally said.

Dane scowled, but there was no denying it. He felt frustrated and angry, but underlying it was a certain . . . relief? Damn, what was wrong with him? He was feeling relieved because a murder case was turning into one big headache, and he couldn't come up with anything on the best lead they'd had?

"She had to have been there," he said. "She knew too much."

Trammell shrugged. "There's another possibility."

"Like what?"

"Maybe she's psychic," he suggested lightly.

"Give me a break."

"Then you explain it some other way. I can't. I've been thinking about it, and nothing that we've been able to find out about her even hints that she'd be involved in something like this. Weird as it sounds, maybe there's something to it."

"Yeah. And maybe aliens are going to land on the White House lawn."

"Face it, buddy. That neighbor lady is the type who peeps out the window every time a pizza delivery car goes down

the street. If Marlie Keen went out, or had anyone over, you can bet it would have been noticed."

"We still haven't checked out her friends at work, who she has lunch with."

"Yeah, well, let me know how it goes. I for one know how to recognize a dead end when I see one."

5

SHE SAW HIM IMMEDIATELY WHEN SHE LEFT THE BANK. HE WAS alone in his car, just sitting there, watching for her. The late afternoon sunshine glinted off the windshield and prevented her from clearly seeing his face, but she knew it was him. Detective Hollister. Though she could really only discern the width of those heavy shoulders and the shape of his head, some primal sense of self-preservation, an alertness to danger, recognized him.

He didn't get out of the car, didn't call to her. Just watched her.

Marlie strode to her car, stonily refusing to react to his presence. When she pulled out of the parking lot, he pulled out right behind her.

He stayed there, tight on her rear bumper, as she threaded her way through the normal afternoon traffic. If he thought he could rattle her with this juvenile game, he was in for a surprise; her nerves had been tested in circumstances far more dire than this, and she had survived.

She had errands to run, things she would have done over the weekend if she hadn't been overwhelmed by that nightmare vision. She didn't let his presence stop her; if he wanted to see what she did after work, he was in for a real thrill. She stopped at the cleaners, leaving a few soiled garments, picking up the clean ones. Next stop was the library, where she returned two books. Then she went to the neighborhood grocery store. At every stop, he parked as close to her as possible, twice right beside her, and imperturbably waited until she returned. When she came out of the grocery store, he watched as she wheeled the cart, loaded with four bags, to the back of her car. She put her foot on the cart to keep it from rolling while she unlocked the trunk.

He was out of the car and standing beside her almost before the sound of the car door slamming could alert her. Her head jerked up and he was there, as big and grim as a thunderstorm. His eyes were hidden by a pair of very dark sunglasses. Sunglasses had always made her vaguely uneasy. As before, his physical presence was as forceful as a blow. She had to restrain herself from automatically stepping back. "What do you want?" she asked in a cool, flat voice.

He reached out one big hand and effortlessly lifted a grocery bag from the cart into the trunk. "Just helping you with the groceries."

"I've managed all my life without you, Detective, so I can manage now."

"It's no problem." The smile he gave her was both humorless and mocking. He stowed the remaining three bags in the trunk beside the first one. "Don't bother saying thank you."

Marlie shrugged. "Okay." Turning away, she unlocked the door and slid behind the wheel. The parking space in front of her was empty, meaning she didn't have to back out; she pulled out through the space in front, leaving him to park the cart or do whatever he wished with it. She wasn't in the mood to be gracious. She was tired, depressed, and angry.

Worse than that, she was frightened. Not of Detective Hollister, as unpleasant as he was. Her fears were much deeper than that.

She was afraid of the monster who had butchered Nadine Vinick.

And she was afraid of herself.

By the time she stopped at the second traffic light after leaving the grocery store parking lot, he was right behind her again. The man really had a talent for getting around in traffic.

The sight of her house wasn't as enticing as it usually was. She was wryly certain that its sanctuary was going to be violated by a big, grim man who seemed to have taken an immediate dislike to her. She was used to skepticism from people, but not actual dislike; his attitude wounded her a little, though she was surprised at herself for feeling that way. Detective Hollister wasn't anything to her, so it had to be merely that it was human nature to want others to think well of oneself.

Just as she had expected, he pulled into her driveway before she had time to cut the ignition off. He got out of the car and took off the sunglasses, tucking them into his shirt pocket. No matter how uneasy sunglasses made her, she suddenly wished he had left them on, because his hazel green eyes, caught by the last rays of the sinking sun, were hard and frighteningly intense.

"What now?" she asked. "Or did you come all this way to help me carry in my groceries?"

"You said you could manage them without my help," he pointed out. "I thought we'd have a little talk."

Someone came out next door. She looked up and saw her neighbor, Lou, standing on the porch and staring curiously at them. Marlie waved and called out a hello. Beside her, Detective Hollister also waved.

"Nice to see you again," he called.

Marlie sternly controlled her temper. Of course he had already been out questioning her neighbors; she wouldn't

have expected him to do otherwise. He had made it plain this morning that he was very suspicious of her.

Despite what he had said, when she opened the trunk he plucked all four bags of groceries out, clutching two in each hand. "After you," he said politely.

She shrugged; if he was willing to carry her groceries, she was willing to let him. She unlocked the front door and held it open for him, then followed him inside and directed him back to the kitchen, where he placed the bags on the table.

"Thank you," she said.

"Why say thank you now, when you didn't before?"

She lifted her brows. "You told me not to." She began putting the groceries away. "What's on your mind, Detective?"

"Murder."

The circumstances of Nadine Vinick's death weren't something she could be flippant about. Strain tightened her face as she said simply, "Mine, too." Her eyes were wide and haunted.

He leaned against the cabinet, eyeing her thoughtfully as she moved about the kitchen, bending to stow this item here, stretching to put another on a top shelf. He hadn't missed the strain in her expression.

He looked around. He liked the kitchen, which was a rather unsettling thought; whatever he had expected the interior of her house to be like, this soothing coziness wasn't it. His own kitchen was strictly utilitarian; Trammell's was the latest in high tech, totally intimidating. Marlie Keen's kitchen was comforting. Rows of herbs in small pots grew in a rack in the window over the sink, giving the air a fresh scent. The tile under his feet was a creamy white, with patterns of soft blues and greens. The open shutters over the windows were painted the same soft blue. A white ceiling fan was positioned over the table.

"Did you find out anything interesting about me today?" she asked, keeping her back turned to him as she placed canned goods on a shelf.

He didn't reply, just broodingly watched her. He wasn't about to keep her informed of his progress, or lack of it.

"Let me tell you," she offered lightly. "Today you found that I've never been arrested, never had a traffic ticket, and that to the best of my neighbors' knowledge, I don't date or have anyone over. I pay my bills on time, don't use credit cards, and don't have any books overdue at the library, though I would have if I hadn't returned those today."

"Why don't you tell me again about Friday night," he said. His tone was sharp. She had neatly outlined his day, and he didn't like it. The anger that had simmered in him all day was under control, but just barely. The lady definitely put his back up.

He could see her shoulders tense. "What part didn't you understand?"

"I'd like to hear it all. Humor me. Just start at the beginning."

She turned around, and she was as pale as she had been that morning, when she had related the story for the first time. Her hands, he noticed, were knotted into fists at her sides.

"Does it bother you to talk about it?" he asked coolly. He hoped it did. If her conscience was bothering her, maybe she'd spill her guts. It had happened before, though usually it was sheer stupidity and a perverted sort of pride that led the perp into confession.

"Of course. Doesn't it bother you to hear about it?"

"Seeing it was a lot worse."

"I know," she murmured, and for a moment the expression in her eyes was unguarded. There was pain in those dark blue depths, and anger, but most of all he saw a desolation that punched him square in the chest.

He had to clench his own hands, to prevent himself from reaching out to support her. Suddenly she looked so frail, as if she might faint. And maybe she was just a damn good actress, he grimly reminded himself, pushing away the

unwanted and uncharacteristic concern for a suspect. "Tell me about Friday night," he said. "What did you say you were doing?"

"I went to a movie, the nine-o'clock one."

"Where?"

She told him the name of the cinemaplex.

"What movie did you see?"

She told him that, too, then said, "Wait—I may still have the ticket stub. I usually put it in my pocket. I haven't done laundry since then, so it should still be there." She walked swiftly out of the room; he didn't follow but listened intently, tracing her movements through the house so she wouldn't be able to slip out without his knowledge, if that had been her intention. Of course, he had her car blocked in the driveway, and he didn't think she would try to run away. Why should she, when she was so certain he didn't have anything on her? The hell of it was, she was right.

She came back in only a minute and gave him the ticket stub, being careful not to touch him as she let the small piece of paper drop into his hand. Then she swiftly retreated a few steps; his mouth twisted as he noticed the move. She could hardly make it more plain that she didn't like being close to him. He looked down at the ticket stub in his hand; it was computer-generated, with the name of the movie, the date, and the time printed on it. It proved that she had bought a ticket; it didn't prove that she had actually watched the movie. He hadn't seen it himself, so he couldn't ask her any pertinent questions about it.

"What time did you leave the movie?"

"When it was over. About eleven-thirty." Marlie stood tensely beside the table.

"Coming home, what route did you drive?"

She told him, even the exit numbers.

"And where were you when you had this so-called vision?"

Her lips tightened, but she kept her composure, and her

voice was steady. "As I told you this morning, I had just left the expressway. The visions have always been very . . . draining, so I pulled off to the side."

"Draining? How?"

"I lost consciousness," she said flatly.

His eyebrows rose. "You lost consciousness," he repeated, disbelief so plain in his tone that her palm itched with the urge to slap him. "You mean you fainted from the stress?"

"Not exactly."

"What, *exactly?*"

She shrugged helplessly. "I'm taken over by the vision. I can't see anything else, I don't hear anything else, I don't know anything else."

"I see. So you sat there in your car until the vision ended, then calmly drove home and went to bed. If you're so certain that you're psychic, Miss Keen, why did you wait over two days before telling the police? Why didn't you call it in immediately? We might have been able to catch the guy still in the neighborhood, or maybe even in the house, if you'd called."

Marlie's face lost its last tinge of color under the lash of that deep, sarcastic voice. There was no way she could explain what had happened six years before, why some of the details had confused her until she wasn't certain if she'd had a flashback or if the knowing had returned. She couldn't expose herself to this man like that, strip her psyche naked to let him see all of her fears, her vulnerabilities. Instead she focused on the one thing he'd said that she could refute.

"N-No," she stammered, hating the unsteadiness of her voice. She took a deep breath to banish that hint of weakness. "I didn't just drive home. A patrolman noticed my car and stopped to see if there was any trouble. I don't remember anything except the vision from the time I pulled over until he knocked on my window and brought me out of it. I was pretty shaky, and I told him that I was an epileptic and must have had a mild seizure. He was a little suspicious

and made me get out of the car, but finally he let me go, and followed me home to make certain I got here okay."

Dane didn't straighten away from the cabinet, but acute attention was in every line of his big body. "What time was this?"

"I don't know."

"Estimate. You left the movie at eleven-thirty; about what time did the vision start?"

"Eleven-forty, eleven forty-five. I'm not certain."

"So what time did you get home? How long did the vision last?"

"I don't know!" she shouted, whirling away from him. "I barely made it home; I collapsed afterward and didn't wake up until late Saturday afternoon."

Dane studied her rigid back. She was shaking, a very faint but visible tremor. He should have been glad that he had her rattled, but instead he had this crazy urge to comfort her.

"I'll be in touch," he said abruptly, and left before he gave in to that urge. Damn it, what was it about her? He was very aware of the heaviness in his loins, and knew that if she had looked, there was no way she could have missed it. Thank God, she seemed to want to look anywhere but at him. He'd heard of cops who got turned on by danger, but he'd never been one of them. What in hell was the matter with him?

As he got into his car he admitted that he never should have come here, at least not without Trammell. Ostensibly they had called it a day, but he hadn't been able to. Instead he'd waited for her in the parking lot where she worked, then followed her home. Stupid move; what if she called the lieutenant and complained that he was harassing her? The LT had given them the go-ahead to investigate her, but Dane knew he'd been out of bounds this afternoon.

At least she'd given him something interesting to check out. If a patrolman had stopped to investigate a suspicious vehicle, it wouldn't be difficult to verify. He had the location and date, and he knew it was on third shift. Piece of cake.

He went back to the office and started making phone calls. It took him an hour to get the name of the patrolman in question, Jim Ewan, a six-year street veteran. When he called Officer Ewan's home, there was no answer.

He waited another hour, calling Officer Ewan four more times, without results. He checked his watch; it was almost eight o'clock, and he was hungry. He supposed he could get up early in the morning and catch Officer Ewan as he was coming off his shift, but he'd never been very good at waiting when he wanted something. What the hell; Ewan would be reporting in to work in less than three hours, so Dane figured he might as well get something to eat, then come back and talk to the officer tonight. Whatever he found out, it would give him the night to think about it.

He drove home and slapped together a couple of sandwiches, then checked his messages while he munched and caught up on the scores of the new baseball season. He was still pissed at the San Francisco Giants, and wanted anyone but them to win.

Baseball couldn't hold his attention, and his thoughts kept slipping back to Marlie Keen, to deep blue eyes that held more shadows than a graveyard. Whatever scheme she was running, she wasn't entirely comfortable with it; she became visibly upset every time she talked about Friday night. Not even an Oscar-winning actress could make herself go as white as chalk, the way Marlie had been this afternoon.

He remembered how her slender frame had been shaking, and the urge welled up again to put his arms around her, cradle her close to him and tell her everything would be all right. What was with this crazy protectiveness? He accepted his natural male instinct to take care of a woman; he was bigger and stronger, so why shouldn't he put himself between a woman and any danger that might threaten her? Why shouldn't he guard her when she went up or down stairs, always ready to catch her if those treacherous high heels women wore caused her to trip? Why shouldn't he do

any grunt work for her when he could, schedule permitting? When he'd been a patrolman, investigating car accidents, he had always gone first to check on any woman or child involved, without even thinking about it. But damn it, his protectiveness had never before extended to someone he suspected of murder.

He was a cop; she was a suspect. He couldn't allow himself to touch her in any way, except those necessary in his job. Cuddling her wasn't included on that list.

But he wanted to. Damn, he wanted to. He wanted to let her rest her head on his shoulder, he wanted to stroke her cheek, her neck, then let his hand drop lower to investigate her breasts, the curve of her belly, the soft notch between her legs.

He surged to his feet, cursing to himself. He'd seen her for the first time that morning, and hadn't been able to stop thinking about her since. That good old physical chemistry had sure blindsided him with this one.

He checked the time: nine-fifteen. Hell, he might as well go down to the station and wait for Officer Ewan. At least the usual bullshit going on would keep him from thinking about her so much. He paced restlessly for a moment, then got his car keys and put the plan into action.

As he had hoped, Officer Ewan came in early, as a lot of policemen did, so he would have plenty of time to change clothes and drink coffee, kind of settle into routine before the shift began. Jim Ewan was average in almost every way: average height, average weight, average features. His eyes, though, were the alert, cynical eyes of a cop, someone used to seeing everything and expecting anything.

He remembered the incident Friday night very clearly.

"It was a little spooky," he said, thinking about it. "She was just sitting there, like a statue. Her eyes were open and fixed; at first I thought I had a stiff. I turned on the flashlight, but couldn't see anything suspicious in the car, and I could tell then that she was breathing. I rapped on the window with the flash, but it took her a while to come around."

Dane felt an uneasy tingle up his spine. "Had she fainted, maybe?"

Officer Ewan shrugged. "Only people I've ever seen with their eyes fixed like that were stiffs or crazies. The eyes close when it's just a faint."

"So what happened then?"

"It was like she was real confused, and she looked scared at first. She had trouble moving, like someone coming out of anesthesia. But then she managed to get the window rolled down, and she said that she was an epileptic and must have had a seizure. I asked her to get out of the car, and she did. She was shaky, trembling all over. I couldn't smell any alcohol, and she didn't seem to be on anything; I'd already called in her plate number, and it had checked out okay, so there wasn't any reason to hold her. Like I said, she was pretty wobbly, so I followed her home to make sure she made it."

"What time was this?" Dane asked.

"Let's see. I can check my paperwork for that night to give you the exact time, if you need it, but I think it was a little after midnight, maybe twelve-fifteen."

"Thanks," Dane said. "You've helped a lot."

"My pleasure."

He drove back home, mulling over everything Officer Ewan had said. For such a brief meeting, it had given him a lot of information.

For one thing, Marlie Keen had been on the opposite side of town from the Vinick residence at about the same time Nadine Vinick was being murdered.

Officer Ewan's observations pretty much verified what Marlie had told him about how the "vision" affected her.

So what did he have now? Logically he could no longer consider her a suspect, and something inside loosened with relief. She hadn't been there; she had an alibi. There was nothing to connect her to the murder . . . except her own words. She had *seen* the murder happen. There was no other way. But how?

She knew something, something she hadn't told him. Something that put those shadows in her eyes. He was going to find out what she was hiding, find out exactly how she was tied to this murder. The only alternative was that she really was psychic, and he couldn't buy that. Not yet. Maybe not ever, but . . . not yet.

6

He could feel the anger burning in him as the woman marched away, and he sternly controlled it, as he controlled everything. Now wasn't the time to let his anger show; it would be inappropriate. Everything in its own time. He looked down at the complaint form the woman had filled out and smiled as he read her name: Jacqueline Sheets, 3311 Cypress Terrace. The guarantee of retribution gave him a certain peace. Then, taking care that his body blocked Annette's view of what he was doing, he slipped the complaint form into his pocket to be disposed of later. Only a stupid person would leave it lying about, perhaps for some busybody to look at and remember later, and Carroll Janes did not consider himself stupid. Quite the opposite, in fact. He prided himself on taking care of every little detail.

"I don't know how you can be so calm when people talk to you like that, Mr. Janes," Annette muttered behind him. "I wanted to punch her in the face."

His expression was perfectly calm. "Oh, someday she'll get hers," he said. He liked Annette; she had to put up with

the same things he did, and she was always sympathetic when someone gave him a hard time. Most people were acceptably courteous, but there were always those few who needed to be taught a lesson. Annette, however, was unfailingly polite, calling him Mister. He appreciated her perception. She was a homely little thing, short and dark and plain, but generally amiable. She didn't irritate him as so many other women did, with their silly airs and pettishness.

Carroll Janes carried himself in an erect, military posture. He had often thought he would have been perfectly suited for the military—as an officer, of course. He would have been at the top of his class in any of the academies, had he been able to attend. Unfortunately, he hadn't had the connections necessary to get into any of the military academies; connections were imperative, and those who lacked them were shut out. It was how the upper class kept their ranks closed. Joining the military as an enlisted man was unthinkable; he had likewise rejected both ROTC and OCS as being a poor second to the academies. Instead of the distinguished military career he should have had, he was stuck in this degrading job handling customer complaints in a ritzy department store, but that didn't mean he would let his personal standards slide.

He was five foot ten, but his erect carriage often fooled people into thinking he was taller. And he was generally considered a nice-looking man, he thought: in good shape, thanks to twice-weekly visits to a gym; thick, curly blond hair; even features. He enjoyed dressing well, and was always meticulous in his grooming. Attention to detail meant the difference between success and failure. He never let himself forget that.

He wondered what Annette would say if she discovered the power he kept concealed, under perfect control until it was time to be unleashed. But no one suspected, least of all Annette. Fooling them all so completely gave him immense satisfaction; the cops were so stupid, so utterly outclassed! He was patient enough to wait until Annette took her

afternoon break before going to the computer to see if Jacqueline Sheets had a charge account with the store; to his delight, she did. It was always so much easier when he had this initial access to information. He wasn't interested in her payment record, however. The information from each customer's credit request form was at the top of each file, and that information included the spouse's name and occupation. Jacqueline Sheets was divorced. He clucked his tongue. What a pity, she couldn't maintain a relationship.

Of course, that didn't mean she lived alone. She might have children, or a live-in boyfriend, or a lesbian roommate. She might live with her mother. Any of those scenarios would make his task more difficult, but by no means impossible. He almost hoped such a complication would develop, for it was a truer test of his nerve and intelligence. It was unusual to have another transgressor so soon after the last one; he was a bit curious to see if he would be sharper, like an athlete intensifying his training, or if the opposite would be true. He hoped he would be even stronger and faster, his mind clearer, the surge of power more intense.

When he left work, he could already feel the anticipation humming in him. He ignored the pleasurable sensation and followed his normal routine, for of course, he couldn't allow it to strengthen now; it wasn't time. The pleasure would be all the more intense for having waited, once he let it go. So he drove to his apartment, read the newspaper, popped a microwave dinner into the oven. While it was heating, he set the table: place mat, napkin, everything just as it should be. Just because he lived alone was no reason to let his standards slide.

Only after it was fully dark outside did he allow himself to get out his map of the Orlando area and locate Cypress Terrace, marking the route from his apartment with a yellow highlighter, carefully memorizing the turns. It was closer than he'd expected, no more than fifteen minutes by car. Convenient.

Then he went for a pleasant, leisurely drive, enjoying the

mild spring weather. This first reconnaissance was little more than a drive-by, to locate the house and fix it in his mind. He'd also notice a few other details, such as how close the other houses were, if there were a lot of pets in the neighborhood, how many children seemed to be around. If there was a fence around the yard, how many cars were parked in the driveway, or if there was a garage. Little things like that. Details. Later he would find out more, much more, discovering more on each trip until the final reconnaissance, when he would go inside the house itself, learn the layout of the rooms. He would let the pleasure begin building then, for there was something delicious about wandering through her house when she wasn't there, touching her things, looking in her closets and bathroom cabinet. He would already be inside her, and she wouldn't even know it. It would lack only the finale.

He drove past 3311 Cypress Terrace; there was a narrow, one-slot carport instead of a garage, and a five-year-old Pontiac occupied the space. There were no other cars, no bicycles, no skateboards, nothing to indicate kids. Only one light was on in the house, indicating that there was either only one person there, or everyone was in one room. Usually it was the former.

He circled the block and drove by a second time; twice was all he allotted himself on one trip. If anyone was watching, which wasn't likely, the second pass would be attributed to someone lost, while a third pass would be suspicious. The second time he noted the fence that ran down the left side of the house, on the opposite side of the carport. Good. A fence was nice concealment. The right side was more open than he liked it, but all in all the situation was very nice. Very nice indeed. Everything was falling into place.

Marlie had been curled up on the couch, reading a book that was only mildly interesting and slowly feeling herself relax. She had felt the strain all day long, wondering if

Detective Hollister would be waiting in the parking lot when she left work as he had been the day before. She wasn't certain she could handle another of those hostile confrontations with him, but at the same time she felt curiously cast adrift when she walked out of the bank and he wasn't there. It was like waiting for the other shoe to drop, only it never did.

She leaned her head against the back of the couch and closed her eyes. His face formed behind her eyelids: the rough planes, the broken nose, the hazel green of those deep-set eyes. Not the face of a sophisticate; even if the features had been more even, the expression in those eyes would always set him apart. They were the piercing eyes of a predator, always watching. She rather thought that the people of Orlando could count themselves lucky that he had come down on the side of the law, making criminals his natural prey instead of themselves. Now, added to the force of his own nature, was the look that all cops had: that all-encompassing cynicism, the cool distance, the wall that those in law enforcement erected between themselves and those they served.

She had known a lot of cops, had seen it in all of them. Cops relaxed only with their own kind, with others who had seen the same things, done the same things. None of them went home and told their spouses about the meanness and depravity that they saw every day. What a great topic that would have been over dinner! Cops had a high divorce rate. The stress was incredible.

Cops had never known how to take her. At first, of course, they had all thought of her as a joke. After she had proved herself, though, they had all become very uneasy around her, because her psychic insight had included them. Only a cop understood another cop: That was a given. But *she* had felt their emotions, their anger and fear and disgust. They couldn't erect that wall against her, and they had felt vulnerable.

Then, six years ago, she had had to learn how to read people's emotions the way everyone else did, by picking up subtle clues of body language and voice tone, by reading expressions. She had been like a baby learning how to talk, because she had never before had to rely on visual clues. For a while she hadn't wanted to learn, all she had wanted was to be left alone in the blessed silence. But total isolation wasn't human nature; even hermits usually took up with animals. Instinctively, once she had felt safe, she had begun to watch people and read them. It was difficult to read Detective Hollister, though. Her mouth quirked with wry humor. Maybe she had such a hard time reading him because she could barely stand to look at him. It wasn't that he was repulsive, because for all his rough features, he wasn't, but rather because he was so intense. He made her uncomfortable, glaring at her the way he did, battering at her until he forced her to pull up memories she would rather forget.

She wasn't afraid of him; no matter how much he might try, he couldn't tie her to Nadine Vinick's murder, because there was no tie. He couldn't find evidence that didn't exist. The uneasiness she felt—

Marlie froze, her eyes flying open and focusing on nothing as she mentally searched the feeling that had crept over her. It wasn't a vision, or anything else that overwhelming. But she definitely sensed a vague, cold malevolence, a threat.

She got jerkily to her feet and began pacing as she tried to order her thoughts. What was happening? Was the knowing truly returning, or was she experiencing a perfectly normal reaction to a lot of stress?

She had been thinking of Hollister, and all of a sudden she had felt uneasy and threatened. Easy enough to understand that, if Hollister was the source of the threat. Most people would think so, but Marlie analyzed the feeling again and couldn't find any fear of Hollister in any way connected with his investigation.

The malevolence slapped at her, growing stronger. Marlie

gagged on a sudden rise of nausea. Something was happening. God, something was happening. What? Was it connected with Hollister? Was he in danger?

She lurched to a halt, her fists clenched. Maybe she should call him, see if he was all right. But what should she say? Nothing. She didn't have to say anything. If he answered the phone, then he was obviously all right. She could just hang up.

Childish trick. This unformed threat was sickening. She broke out in a sweat, torn with indecision, and all of a sudden the old instincts took over. Blindly she reached out with her mind, searching for Hollister, trying to pinpoint that nebulous cloud of evil. It was like groping in fog; she couldn't focus on anything.

Groaning, she sank down on the couch again. What had she expected? She hadn't been able to do that for six years, and even before, it hadn't been easy. Just because she had had one freak vision, and felt this vague threat, she thought all of the old skills had come back? She hoped they never would, damn it! But just now she needed them, needed something to calm this panic she felt.

But if he was unconscious—she banished the word *dead* before it could form—then she wouldn't be able to pick up his mental signals. Feeling even more frantic, she summoned up an image of his partner, Alex Trammell. She hadn't paid much attention to him, but she was observant enough to be able to recall his face. She closed her eyes, concentrating, hearing her own harsh, fast breathing as she tried to find one particular person. *Think!* she fiercely commanded herself. Think of Trammell.

It was no use. Nothing.

Swearing under her breath, she grabbed the phone book and ran her finger down the *H*s until she found the Hollisters. Why were there so damn many of them? Ah, there it was. Dane Hollister. She picked up the receiver and punched in the number before she could talk herself out of this.

And suddenly she knew that he was all right.

It wasn't like before. She hadn't tuned in to his emotions; there was no mental barrage. She just knew. She had a mental picture of him sitting barefoot and bare-chested in front of the television, watching a baseball game and sipping on a beer. He muttered a curse as he reached for the telephone—

—"Yeah."

Marlie jumped. The word had sounded in her ear just as she had pictured him in her mind, speaking. "Ah . . . uh. Sorry," she stammered, and dropped the receiver clattering into the cradle. She stared at the phone, so stunned she didn't know what to do. She had heard the definite sounds of a baseball game in the background.

Dane shrugged with mild irritation and hung up the telephone. He had missed an out in the game, just in that short time when he'd taken his attention off the screen. He settled back down with a grunt, his bare feet propped on the coffee table and crossed at the ankle. This was the most comfortable he'd been in a while: no shirt, no shoes, the beer in his hand so cold that it made his mouth tingle to drink it.

The caller had been a woman. He knew it instinctively, even though the voice had been low and unusually husky. A smoker's voice.

He thought of Marlie Keen. Her voice had that little rasp; just hearing it gave him a hard-on every time. Reflexively he looked down at his lap. Bingo.

He reached for the phone.

"Did you just call?" he demanded tersely, after a quick call to local Information.

"I . . . yes. I'm sorry."

"Any reason for it?"

He could hear her breathing over the line, the sounds fast and shallow. Something had upset her. "I was worried," she finally admitted.

"Worried? About what?"

"I thought you might be in some sort of trouble. I was wrong. I'm sorry," she said again.

"You were wrong," he repeated, with exaggerated disbelief. "Imagine that."

She slammed the receiver down in his ear. He winced, angrily started to punch the redial button, but hung up instead. Instead of being sarcastic, he should have tried to find out more about what had her so upset; maybe Nadine Vinick was weighing on her conscience. Maybe she'd been about to spill the beans; Officer Ewan had cleared her, though she didn't know that yet, but he'd still bet money that she knew the perp's identity. Now, because of his own big mouth, he had blown the chance to find out, because she sure as hell wasn't going to talk to him now.

Then he realized that neither of them had identified themselves. She had known who he was, just as he had known who she was.

And she had been right about one thing, damn it. He *was* in trouble. He looked down at his lap again. Big trouble.

Temptation gnawed at him. He slammed the beer down onto the table so hard that foam sloshed out of the can. Then, cussing at his own stupidity, he picked up the receiver and hit the redial.

"What?" she snapped, answering before the first ring had even completed.

"What's going on? Talk to me."

"What would you like me to say?" she asked sweetly.

"How about the real reason why you called."

"I *told* you. I thought something was wrong."

"What gave you that idea?" Try as he might, he couldn't keep the skepticism out of his tone.

She took a deep, steadying breath. "Look. I had an uneasy feeling about you and I was worried. I was wrong."

"What made you think it had anything to do with me?"

Dead silence. He waited, but she didn't say anything. It was such a complete silence, without even the sound of her breathing, that alarm chilled his spine. "Are you all right?"

he asked sharply. "Marlie?" Silence. "Come on, babe, talk to me, or I'm on my way over there."

"No!" Her voice sounded strangled. "No—don't come over."

"Are you okay?"

"Yes. Yes, I'm fine. I just . . . thought of something else."

"Such as?"

"Maybe it wasn't connected with you. Maybe it was someone else. I have to think about this. Good-bye."

"Don't hang up," he warned. "Goddamn it, Marlie, don't hang up—shit!" The dial tone buzzed in his ear. He slammed the phone down and surged to his feet. He'd go over there, check it out—

—And find what? He sincerely doubted she'd open the door to him. Nor did he have a reason, because Officer Ewan had cleared her. That had eaten at him all day; unless something else turned up, and things were looking damn hopeless in that respect, he had no reason to talk to her again. And solving Nadine Vinick's murder seemed more and more unlikely. It pissed him royally that it looked as if the case would be a real mystery, a stranger-to-stranger killing, the kind that was almost never resolved. Mrs. Vinick deserved better than that.

And he didn't want never to see Marlie Keen again. If she wasn't involved in the case, and officially he had to accept that, then he'd have to arrange something else. He didn't like what he was feeling, but it was too damn strong to ignore.

Marlie paced, alternately swearing and wiping away tears. Damn Hollister! He made her so angry, she could have cheerfully taken a swing at him, had he been there right then. But Hollister was the least of her problems. The knowing was definitely coming back, maybe a little altered from before. Maybe she wasn't as empathic as she had been; maybe there was a bit more clairvoyance. How else could she have known that Hollister was watching a baseball

game? How else could she have anticipated his answer right down to the second? That had never happened before.

She had been thinking about him, unwillingly, but he had definitely been on her mind when the uneasiness, the sense of danger, had swept over her. She had automatically thought it had something to do with him, but it hadn't; he had just been so strongly in her mind that she hadn't realized the two weren't connected. That meant she had two problems; no, three. One: Her extrasensorial skills were coming back, in fits and starts. She didn't want them to, but they were, and she'd have to deal with it. She pushed that acknowledgment away, because though this problem would have the biggest effect on her life, the others were more immediate.

Two: Detective Hollister was going to be a big complication. He already was. He made her angrier than anyone else she'd ever met, and he did it without even trying. He was a big Neanderthal, sarcastic and skeptical, and she could feel his own anger blazing at her. He was so intense that she almost yielded to the impulse to hide her face every time she saw him. He burned with the sort of fierce masculinity that made women turn and go all google-eyed when they watched him. Marlie knew she didn't have much experience with men, but that didn't mean she was stupid, either. Her reactions to him were too intense, out of all proportion. The last thing she needed right now was a sexual attraction to handle, especially when nothing could come of it. Groaning, she realized that Hollister felt the same reluctant attraction. He had called her "babe." Probably the only thing that had held him back was his suspicion of her, and that couldn't last in the absence of evidence. Men like him didn't hesitate when they wanted a woman; once he admitted that she had nothing to do with Nadine Vinick's murder, she would have to fend him off.

Which brought her to problem number three, the one so distressing that she had put off thinking about it: The evil she had felt, which had made her so uneasy, had the

same . . . texture, or personality, as the force she had felt the night Nadine Vinick had been murdered. It was the same man. He was still out there, and his evil was focusing on someone else. It was unformed as yet; she had caught only an echo of it. But he was going to act again, and she was the only hope the police had, and his intended victim had, to stop him in time.

She had nothing to go on. No face, no name. Eventually, though, she would be able to focus on him, stay with him, and he would make some mistake that would tell her his identity.

She would have to work with the police, and that meant working with Hollister. She had no doubt it would be an uncomfortable, difficult situation, but she had no choice. She was caught up in this and had no way of getting out.

7

MARLIE HAD JUST FINISHED DRESSING THE NEXT MORNING
when the heavy knock at the front door made her jump, then
frown with both annoyance and alarm. She had no doubt
who was pounding on her door at seven-twenty in the
morning, and it didn't take any special skills to figure it out.

The best way to deal with him, though, was to not let him
know that she reacted to him in any way. He would see her
anger as a weakness, and heaven help her if he should get
even a hint of the unwilling attraction she felt. He was too
aggressive to let either circumstance pass by.

She wasn't about to invite him in. She had to get to work,
and she had no intention of letting him make her late. She
got her purse and had her keys in hand as she marched to the
front door. When she opened it, he was standing almost in
her face, leaning with one muscular arm braced against the
frame and the other one raised to pound on her door again.
The closeness of his body made her catch her breath, a
reaction she hid by stepping out and turning to close the
door behind her. Unfortunately, he didn't move back, and

she fetched up solidly against him, all heat and hard muscle. She was practically in his arms; all he had to do was close them around her, and she would be caught.

Grimly she concentrated on locking the door, trying to ignore the situation. The brief look she had had at his face told her that he was ill tempered this morning, but now she sensed an alarming male edginess beneath the temper. He was as fractious as a stallion scenting a mare in season.

The mental image was unfortunate, and so apt that her heart began beating wildly. With her back turned to him as she wrestled with the stubborn lock, she was suddenly acutely aware of the press of his body against her buttocks. An unmistakable ridge had formed, thick and hard, blatant in intent.

The lock finally clicked into place. She stood motionless, frozen with indecision. If she moved, she would be rubbing against him; if she didn't move, he might take it as an invitation. She closed her eyes against the insidious temptation to simply turn and face him, giving him silent permission by giving him access. Only the certainty that it wouldn't work, that she would freeze under the onslaught of a six-year-old horror, kept her from giving in. She couldn't go through that again.

She forced her voice to work. "What do you want, Detective?" Then she could have bit her tongue. Bad choice of words, under the circumstances. With his erection insistently nudging her, what he wanted was obvious.

For two seconds he didn't answer. She felt the lift of his chest as he slowly inhaled; then, thankfully, blessedly, he moved back a step. "I'm not here as a detective. I just came to see if you're all right."

The heavy sexual tension eased with the small distance between them, making her feel as if she had been freed from shackles. The relief made her light-headed, a reaction she countered with action. "I'm fine," she said briskly, and went down the steps before he could stop her. Oh, damn. His car was blocking hers in the driveway. She stopped, and her

self-control had returned enough that she hesitated only briefly before turning to face him. "I have to leave or I'll be late to work."

He glanced at his wristwatch. "It's a fifteen-minute drive. You have plenty of time."

"I like to leave early, in case of trouble."

The explanation didn't budge him. His heavy-lidded hazel eyes moved over her, their expression shielded. "Anything else scare you last night?"

"I wasn't scared."

"Couldn't prove it by me."

"I wasn't scared," she repeated, this time with her teeth clenched. His obstinance was already fraying her temper. She needed to get away from him, *now.*

"Sure you were. And you're scared now." His gaze raked over her again. "Though not for the same reason," he said softly. This time when his eyelids lifted, she saw the predatory gleam of male awareness.

Marlie stiffened, a chill of apprehension touching her. He might not be psychic himself, but his male instincts were acute. It would be more difficult to evade him than she'd thought, for he sensed the response she couldn't quite mask. He came down the steps toward her, and she swiftly retreated to her car. She jerked the door open and slid behind it, using it as a barricade against him.

He regarded her over the open door, his eyes sharp now, piercingly intent. "Calm down," he murmured. "Don't get in such a snit."

She glared at him, agitated almost beyond endurance. If he didn't leave soon, she was going to lose control and say something she knew she would regret. She clutched at the door for support, her knuckles white with the effort. "Move your car, Detective. And unless you have a warrant, don't come to my house again."

Great going, Hollister. Dane felt violent as he swore at himself. He glared down at his desk, ignoring the noise

76

around him of overlapping voices and the incessant ringing of the telephones. He was raw with frustration, both sexual and professional. There were no leads in the Vinick case, no evidence. The investigation was going nowhere, and it looked as if his interest in Marlie Keen was rapidly headed in the same direction.

What else had he expected? That she wouldn't notice his erection jammed against her ass? The wonder was that she hadn't started screaming.

He should have moved back immediately when she had stepped out of the house, but he hadn't. The first accidental touch of her body had frozen him in place, all of his senses painfully focused on the contact. It had felt so good that he had barely been able to tolerate it, but at the same time it hadn't been enough. He had wanted more. He had wanted to strip her naked, to thrust inside her. He had wanted to feel her legs wrapped around his hips, wanted to feel her quivering beneath him as she came. He wanted to dominate her, smash her resistance, bend her so thoroughly to his will that he could take her whenever he wanted . . . and he wanted to protect her from everything and everyone else. That was why he had been on her front porch this morning. He hadn't been able to rest all night, almost certain something had frightened her but totally certain that she wouldn't welcome his concern if he'd called her again. When morning came, he hadn't been able to resist. He'd had to see for himself that she was all right.

So what had he done? Alienated her even further. He had mishandled her from the very beginning, and he still had no idea what he was supposed to do about her. Officer Ewan had cleared her of being at the scene of Nadine Vinick's murder, but she obviously knew something about it, and had come to the police with it. So what was she, a suspect or a witness? Logic said the former, some uneasy instinct said the latter, and his dick frankly didn't give a damn.

"You're in a piss-poor mood," Trammell commented

lazily, all tipped back in his chair and watching Dane's expression.

He grunted. There was no denying it.

"Talked to Marlie lately?"

Annoyed, Dane shot him a glance. "This morning," he said briefly.

"And?"

"And nothing."

"Nothing? Then why did you call her?"

"I didn't." Restlessly Dane twirled a pencil. "I went over there."

"Oh, ho. Keeping secrets from your partner, huh?"

"No secrets to keep."

"So why did you go over there?"

Damn, all this interrogation was making him feel twitchy. Dane had a brief moment of sympathy for the suspects he and Trammell had questioned for hours. A very brief moment. "No reason," he replied, blatantly stonewalling and not giving a damn if Trammell knew it.

"No reason, huh?" Trammell was having fun. His dark eyes were gleeful. He had never thought he'd see the day when his good buddy Dane would be so antsy over a woman, and he intended to enjoy every minute of it. Dane *never* had woman trouble; they had always cared about him far more than he cared for them, which gave him a tremendous advantage in his relationships. He'd never mistreated a woman, but at the same time their influence on him had been very slight. If they didn't like his irregular hours, tough. If he had to miss a date, so what? He'd never given anything of himself beyond the physical to a woman, because the job had always come first. Dane was a damn good cop, one of the best. But he'd pretty much sailed unscathed through the rough seas of romance, unlike the rest of them who wrestled with the conflicts between job and relationships, so it was nice to see him squirming now.

Trammell prodded the beast again. "What did she say?"

Dane scowled, and darted another irritated look at his partner. "Why are you so curious?"

Trammell spread his hands, feigning innocence. "I thought we were working on this case together."

"It didn't have anything to do with the case."

"Then why were you over there?"

"Just checking on her."

Trammell couldn't hold back a chuckle, and the telephone rang while he was still laughing.

Dane picked up the receiver. "Detective Hollister," he barked.

"Finally turned up some stuff on the Keen woman you asked about," a laconic voice said in Dane's ear. "Interesting. Damn interesting."

Dane had stiffened at the first mention of Marlie's name, his entire body alert. "Yeah? Like what?"

"I'll let you read it for yourself, pal. I'm faxing it to you. Didn't know you went in for that kind of shit. Nice-looking woman, though."

"Yeah," he said automatically. "Thanks, Baden. I owe you one."

"I'm marking that down in my little book," Baden said cheerfully. "See ya."

Dane hung up the phone to find Trammell watching him with sharp interest, all amusement gone. "What's up?"

"Baden's faxing me some information on Marlie Keen."

"No kidding." Trammell's eyebrows lifted. "I didn't think anything would turn up on her."

"Well, it has." The fax machine in the corner began to hum and spit out paper. Dane got up and went over to it, his face grim. He wasn't sure he wanted to see this. Two days ago he would have loved to get his hands on some information about Marlie, but not now. Ever since she had called him the night before, he had stopped even trying to deny the effect she had on him. He wanted her, damn it. And he wanted her to be innocent. He wanted there to be some

explanation of the things she had told them on Monday. Trammell came over to stand beside him, his dark gaze inscrutable as he watched Dane.

The first sheet came out. It was a photocopy of a newspaper article. Quickly he scanned the headline: TEENAGE PSYCHIC FINDS MISSING CHILD.

Trammell whistled, the single note almost soundless.

Page after page followed. They all had a common theme: Marlie Keen's psychic abilities. Some of the articles seemed to be from psychology magazines, or were papers on parapsychology. Several grainy photographs were printed, showing a younger, almost childish-looking Marlie. Most of them were newspaper articles, reporting how "noted psychic" Marlie Keen had worked with police to solve various cases. The articles were all from the Northwest, he noted. Oregon and Washington mostly, though there were a couple in Idaho, one in northern California, one in Nevada.

Sometimes she was described as a "youthful clairvoyant," once as "lovely," twice as "extraordinary." It was a common theme in the articles that the local police forces had been, at the beginning, both skeptical and derisive of her talents, until she had done exactly what she had said she could do. Usually it was to find a missing person, though on a couple of occasions she had helped find kidnappers. Several times it was mentioned that, when not involved in a case, Miss Keen lived in Boulder, Colorado, at the Institute of Parapsychology. A Dr. Sterling Ewell, a professor of parapsychology at the Institute, was quoted several times.

Trammell was standing right beside him, reading each sheet as he did. They were both silent. Even though they had been forewarned, by Marlie herself, reading about it in black and white was unsettling.

Then one stark headline jumped out at them: KILLER ATTACKS PSYCHIC. Dane grabbed the sheet, holding it taut as it was printed, and they began reading as it emerged from the machine.

There had been a series of child kidnappings in a remote

area of Washington; one child had been found dead, two others were still missing. Marlie had been brought in by the local sheriff, with whom she had worked before in another town, to help find the children. Just before she had arrived, another child had disappeared. A big article about her had been printed in the paper the same day.

That night Arno Gleen had kidnapped Marlie from her motel room and taken her to the same place he had taken the most recent missing child, a five-year-old boy. He had been seen, though, and the sheriff alerted. It was a small town; they were able to identify Gleen and track him down. But the little boy was already dead when they got there, and though they were in time to save Marlie's life, she had been severely beaten.

Her condition, "poor," was reported in a subsequent article. Then there was nothing else. Absolutely nothing. Dane checked the date on the last article. A little over six years ago. For six years Marlie Keen had literally disappeared from the public eye. Why had she relocated to Florida? As soon as he had the thought, he pictured a map in his mind and knew why. Florida was as far from Washington as she could get and still stay in the country. But why, after six years of anonymity and a completely normal life, had she walked into the lieutenant's office and told them about Nadine Vinick's murder?

"It couldn't have been easy," Trammell murmured, his thoughts obviously following the same path. "To have involved herself after what happened the last time."

Dane ran his hand through his hair. Part of him was elated, the last doubt demolished. There was an explanation for her knowledge. If he still couldn't quite believe, at least now he had to suspend his disbelief. There was no longer any reason at all for him to stay away from her; he could go after her the way his body had wanted right from the beginning. But another part of him, perversely, didn't want to accept what he had read. Half of it was the sheer unlikelihood of it, for it went against the grain with someone

so solidly grounded in reality and facts. The other half was alarm. Shit, what if it was for real? He didn't want anyone reading his mind, though after a moment's reflection he had to admit that it would be convenient if a woman could tell how he felt and he wouldn't have to talk about it.

But it was more than that. He was a cop. He had seen things, heard things, done things, that he didn't want to have as common knowledge between him and his woman. It was something only another cop would understand. The job marked them, forever set them apart from civilians. Some cases would go with him to the grave, living in his mind. Some victims' faces, he would always see.

He didn't want anyone invading the privacy of his mind. Not even Marlie. His nightmares were his own.

He gathered up the sheets. "I'm going to check on some of this," he said. "Talk to this Dr. Ewell, find out about the past six years."

Trammell looked a little strange, a kind of amusement vying with sympathy. Dane scowled at him. Sometimes having a partner was like living with a psychic, you got to know each other so well. Trammell was sadistic enough, damn him, to enjoy seeing Dane squirm over a woman.

"What's so damn funny?" he growled.

Trammell shrugged. "It looks like we'll be working with her, and I was just picturing you trying to get on her good side, after the way you two hit it off. Or didn't hit it off, I should say."

Dane went back to his desk and got on the horn. Wryly he remembered when he had put in for detective. He had pictured a lot of fieldwork, fitting obscure pieces of evidence together like Sherlock Holmes. Instead, he had spent a lot of hours on the phone, and he'd found out that a detective was only as good as his snitches. A smart detective cultivated a lot of contacts on the street, lowlifes who were willing to drop a dime on someone else. Too bad he hadn't had any snitches in Nadine Vinick's neighborhood.

A call to Information got him the number for the Institute

of Parapsychology in Boulder. Less than a minute later he was being connected to Dr. Sterling Ewell.

"Dr. Ewell, this is Detective Dane Hollister, Orlando Police Department."

"Yes?"

Dane frowned slightly. There had been a wealth of caution in that one word. "I'd like to ask you some questions about Marlie Keen. She used to be affiliated with the Institute."

"I'm sorry, Detective," the professor said coolly. "I don't give out any information over the telephone about my colleagues."

"Ms. Keen isn't in any trouble—"

"I never thought she was."

"I simply need some background information on her."

"As I said, Detective, I'm sorry. I have no way of knowing if you are who you say you are. Tabloid reporters have often tried to get information by claiming to be with various police departments."

"Call the Orlando Police Department," Dane said tersely. "Ask for me."

"No. If you want any information about Ms. Keen, you'll have to apply for it in person. With the proper identification, of course. Good-bye, Detective."

The receiver clicked in his ear, and Dane hung up with a curse. Trammell said, "No luck?"

"He wouldn't talk to me."

"Any reason why?"

"He said he doesn't give out information over the phone. If I want to know anything about Marlie, I have to go to Boulder and talk to him in person."

Trammell shrugged. "So what's the big deal? Go to Boulder."

Dane gave him an irritated look. "The LT is going to be tickled that she's really a psychic, but there's no way he'll authorize a plane ticket just for a background check on someone who isn't a suspect."

83

"You won't know until you try."

Ten minutes later, he had the answer he'd expected. Bonness was indeed elated that his hunch about Marlie had turned out to be accurate, and he even gloated a bit that he must have a touch of psychic ability himself. Dane barely managed to restrain himself from rolling his eyes at that. But no way could the lieutenant justify the cost of sending Dane to Colorado to check out something that didn't really need checking out. They already had all the verification they needed, didn't they? He dismissed the six missing years as being unimportant. The budget was tight, and they needed all the resources they had to be used tracking down criminals, not snooping into the private lives of people who weren't doing anything wrong.

But those six years were important to Dane. "Do you have any objection if I take off tomorrow and go on my own?"

Bonness looked startled. "You mean pay your own way?"

"That's exactly what I mean."

"Well, no, I don't guess there's any problem, except that you're in the middle of a murder investigation."

"This is related. And the investigation isn't going anywhere. We have no evidence, no motive, no suspects."

Bonness sighed. "Take off, then. But just tomorrow. I want you back here by Friday morning."

"No problem."

Dane returned to his desk and told Trammell what was happening, then got on the phone again. He had to call three airlines before he found an available flight. After booking his ticket, he called Professor Ewell again and tersely informed him when he would be arriving.

Dane felt naked without the Beretta, but since he wasn't traveling in any official capacity, he reluctantly left it at home. He couldn't make himself travel without any weapon, though; he carried a pocketknife that was only a little larger than normal, with nothing else about its appearance that

was out of the ordinary, but which had a single blade made from an alloy stronger than steel. The knife also had perfect balance, a requisite for a throwing knife. Throwing a blade was an arcane little skill he had taught himself, on the theory that it might come in handy someday. The knife wasn't the equal of a pistol, but it was better than nothing.

He was a nervous flier. It wasn't the flying itself that got to him, but the strain of being trapped in a small space with so many strangers. He couldn't leave old habits behind, couldn't draw a boundary between on-duty and off-duty. He was the same man regardless. That meant he automatically watched everyone, subconsciously noting any erratic behavior, studying appearance, constantly evaluating the situation. The situation was boring, but that didn't mean he could stop. Just as sure as he let his guard down, something bad would happen; it was an unwritten law.

He had taken the earliest flight out. Because of the two-hour time difference between Orlando and Colorado, he arrived in Denver well before lunch. He had no luggage, so all he had to do was go to the car-rental desk and lease a car for the day. Boulder was about twenty-five miles to the northwest, interstate all the way.

Once in Boulder, he stopped to look up the address of the Institute and ask for directions. With one thing and another, it was twelve-thirty when he drove up to the Institute. There were no fences, no gates; his policeman's eye noted that the security measures were skimpy, at best. There was an alarm wired to the door, but nothing any third-rate burglar couldn't disarm. INSTITUTE OF PARAPSYCHOLOGY was neatly painted in large block letters on the double glass doors. He pushed the doors open and noted that there was no tone to signal his entrance. It looked as if anyone could walk in off the street.

About twenty feet up the hallway was an office on the left, the door open. Dane approached it and stood for a moment in the doorway, silently observing a neat, middle-aged

woman in front of a computer, typing a letter while she concentrated on what she was hearing through the headset plugged into her ears. Dane cleared his throat, and she glanced up, a smile breaking like sunshine. "Oh, hi. Have you been waiting long?"

"No, I just have walked up." She had a very cheerful face, and he found himself smiling back at her. This place seemed to be as short on formality as it was on security. "I'm Dane Hollister, Orlando PD. I'm here to see Professor Sterling Ewell."

"I'll give him a call to let him know you're here. He was expecting you, so he brought his lunch today instead of going out."

The artlessness of that reply made him smile again. Her brown eyes twinkled at him. "He's my husband," she confided. "I can deflate his dignity if I want to, not that he gives a hoot." She picked up a phone and punched two numbers. "Sterling, Detective Hollister is here. Okay."

She hung up the phone. "Go on back to his office. I would take you myself, but I'm swamped today. Take the next corridor to the right, and his is the office on the right at the very end of the hall."

"Thanks," he said, winking at her as he left. To his amusement, she winked back.

Professor Ewell was a tall, barrel-chested man with thick white hair and a lined face that wore his years with grace. Like his wife, he seemed a very cheerful man, and he wasn't very big on formality either. He was wearing an ancient pair of chinos and a faded chambray shirt, and his feet were clad in scuffed boots. Dane immediately felt a sense of kinship, for the professor evidently ranked clothing fairly low on his list of priorities. His blue eyes were bright with intelligence and humor, but he regarded Dane very sharply for a long minute before some hitherto unnoticed suspicion faded away.

With a jolt, Dane understood. "All of that about tabloid

reporters was bullshit," he said. "You're . . ." He paused, unwilling to accuse the professor of being something he didn't really believe in.

"Psychic," Professor Ewell supplied benignly. He waved a large hand at a comfortable-looking chair. "Sit down, sit down." When Dane had complied, he resumed his own seat. "Not very much," he said. "Nothing like some of the people I work with. But my one small talent is that I'm very good at reading people when I meet them in person. Because of that, I don't give out any information over the telephone. My long-distance instincts are deplorable." He smiled ruefully.

"No reading minds, or anything like that?"

The professor chuckled. "No, you can relax. Telepathy definitely isn't one of my talents, as my wife will gladly tell you. Now, tell me about Marlie. How is she?"

"I'd hoped you would give *me* information about her," Dane said dryly.

"You haven't asked anything yet," the professor pointed out. "I have."

Dane was torn between impatience and humor. There was something in the good doctor that reminded him very much of an impudent six-year-old. He let humor get the upper edge, and gave in to the professor's air of expectancy. "I don't know what I can tell you. I'm not her favorite person," he admitted, rubbing his jaw. "When I saw her yesterday morning, she told me not to set foot on her property again unless I had a warrant."

The professor sighed blissfully. "That's Marlie. I was afraid the trauma might have permanently damaged her. She can be very patient, when she wants, but sometimes she can be a bit testy, too."

"Tell me about it," Dane muttered, then latched on to what had just been said. "This trauma you mentioned; was it when Gleen kidnapped her?"

"Yes. It was horrible. Marlie was in a catatonic state for a week, and didn't speak for almost two months. Everyone

thought, including her, that she had lost all of her psychic abilities." Bright blue eyes studied Dane. "I assume, from your interest in her, that those abilities have returned."

"Maybe." Dane didn't want to commit himself to anything.

"Ah, I see. Skepticism. But you're intrigued enough by what she told you to take a flight to see me. It's okay, Detective; skepticism is not only expected, it's healthy. I'd worry about you if you automatically believed everything you're told. For one thing, you'd be terrible in your job."

Dane firmly returned the conversation to the subject. "About the kidnapping. There was a newspaper article saying that she'd been beaten." Ruthlessly he kept himself from imagining details; he'd seen too many results from beatings, and didn't want to picture Marlie in that condition. "There's been nothing else about her since then. Are you saying the injuries were so severe—"

"No, not that at all," Professor Ewell interrupted. "I don't mean to downplay the severity of her injuries, but she was fully recovered from them well before she started talking again. In this case, it was the mental trauma that did her the greatest harm."

"What happened, exactly?"

The professor looked thoughtful. "How much do you know about parapsychology?"

"I know how to spell it."

"I see. From that, I take it that most of your information about it is gleaned from television shows and fortune-tellers in county fairs."

"Just about."

"Well, discard all of what you think you know. I've always thought that the basis of it was very simple: electrical energy. Every action and every thought uses electrical energy. This energy is detectable. Some people are sensitive to bee stings; others are sensitive to energy. There are degrees of sensitivity, with some people being only mildly sensitive and a very few being ultrasensitive. I don't see why

the issue has to be confused with hocus-pocus, though of course, there are charlatans who wouldn't know psychic ability if it bit them on the ass—" The professor broke off, and gave Dane a sheepish look. "Sorry. My wife says I get carried away."

She was right, too. Dane smiled. "I understand. Now, about Marlie—"

"Marlie is exceptional. Most people have some extrasensory ability, and call it hunches, gut instinct, mother's intuition, whatever they're comfortable with. Their degree of ability is mild. Some are a bit sharper than that. A few others are even more sensitive, to a degree that can be tested. And then there are the rare ones, like Marlie. She's the most sensitive receptor I've ever seen. To give you a comparison, most people are biplanes, some few are Cessnas, and Marlie is a high-performance fighter jet."

"You've tested her, of course?"

"My God, Marlie's been tested almost continuously since she was four years old! She could be fractious even then," he said fondly.

"What exactly are her—er, talents?"

"Mainly, she's an empath."

"A what?"

"Empath. She's empathic. She feels others' emotions, so much so that an ordinary drive on a crowded street could make her scream with frustration. All those feelings bombarding her, from all directions. She described it once as a blend of screams and static, at high volume. The biggest problem she had was controlling it, blocking it out so she could function normally."

"You said mainly. What else does she do?"

"You said that as if she's a trick pony," the professor observed, his tone disapproving.

"No offense meant. I won't lie and tell you that I'm buying all of this, but I'm interested." And that was an understatement if he'd ever made one.

"You'll come around," Professor Ewell predicted with a

certain amount of malicious satisfaction. "All of you do, once you've been around Marlie any length of time."

"Who is 'all of you'?"

"Policemen. You're the world's most cynical people, but eventually you won't be able to deny what she can do. Back to your question: She's also a bit clairvoyant, though certainly not to the same degree that she's empathic. She has to concentrate to block her empathic abilities, something she had never quite managed to completely do, while she has to concentrate to *use* her clairvoyance."

"You mean she predicts that things will happen?"

"No, that's precognitive."

Dane rubbed his forehead, feeling a headache come on. "I don't think I have all of this straight. I've always thought a clairvoyant is someone with a crystal ball, predicting the future."

Professor Ewell laughed. "No, that's a charlatan."

"Gotcha. Okay, an empathic person is someone who receives and feels the emotions of other people."

The professor nodded. "A clairvoyant senses distant objects, and is aware of events in distant places. A precognitive is someone who knows of events in the future. A telekinetic is someone who can move physical objects with the force of their minds."

"Spoon benders."

"Mostly charlatans." The spoon benders were dismissed with a wave. "I won't say that one or two don't have telekinetic talent, but for the most part it's just showmanship. None of the extrasensory abilities can be neatly categorized, because capability varies from person to person, just like reading ability."

"And Marlie's particular blend of talents made her good at finding people?"

"Mmmm. Extraordinary. Her empathy was so strong that, when she focused on one particular person, she would . . . well, she called them 'visions,' but I've observed her during the events, and I would use a stronger word than that.

A vision is something that can be easily interrupted. It was as if her mind would leave, though of course, it didn't. But she would be totally taken over by the event, so completely in empathy with the subject that she was aware of nothing else. Terribly draining for her, of course. She would virtually collapse afterward. But while she was linked, she would observe enough about the surroundings to pinpoint the location, and she always managed to fight off the exhaustion long enough to pass the details along to the local law enforcement officers."

"What else happened with Arno Gleen?"

Professor Ewell's face changed, his expression that of mingled pain and hatred. "Gleen was a monster. A pedophile, a sadist, a murderer. Little boys were his favorite. He would kidnap them, take them to a remote place, abuse them for a day or two, then kill them. Unfortunately, there are no secrets in a small town, and when the sheriff called Marlie for help, the news was all over town before sundown. The next day there was a prominent article in the local newspaper about her, mentioning her successes and when she would arrive. Gleen was waiting. As soon as he caught her alone, he grabbed her."

"But if she's as empathic as you say she is, why didn't she sense him?"

"By that time, she had learned how to block, and she automatically did it whenever she was in a town. It was the only way she could function. And there are some people who naturally block their own transmissions; maybe Gleen was one of them. Maybe he was simply a sociopath, and didn't feel anything for her to pick up. She's never said. In fact, she's never discussed it at all."

Dane was beginning to get an ugly feeling, one that was all too likely. "Did he rape her?" His voice was low and harsh.

The professor shook his head. "He couldn't."

Dane exhaled, his eyes closing briefly.

"But he tried." The professor looked down at his hands, his mouth tight. "He took her to where he had his latest

victim stashed. The little boy had been horribly abused. Gleen had him tied to a bed. I believe the child was about five years old. Gleen dumped Marlie on the floor, stripped her, and tried to rape her. She wasn't a little boy, though, so he couldn't achieve the necessary erection. Every time he failed, he would hit her, working himself into a greater rage. Maybe he thought inflicting pain would arouse him enough. But it didn't, and in a frenzy he turned on the child. He stabbed the little boy to death in front of her. There were twenty-seven puncture wounds in the child's face, chest, and abdomen. And all the while Marlie was linked with the child. She felt him die."

8

Dane felt as if he had been scraped raw on the inside. He didn't have to imagine what Marlie had gone through. He was a cop; he had seen too much to ever have to rely on his imagination to supply details. He knew what beatings really were. He knew what stabbings looked like. He knew how much blood there was, how it spread and spread and got all over everything, even your dreams. He knew how the little boy had sobbed and screamed, had seen in other children's faces his terror and despair, his pain, his utter helplessness.

Marlie had endured that. And when she had had the vision of Nadine Vinick's murder, what had it cost her to see those images again? The similarity was sickening.

At some point during the visit with Professor Ewell, his healthy cynicism had gone south. The germ of possibility had been planted. He didn't like it, but despite himself, he accepted that Marlie had "seen" Mrs. Vinick die. Maybe it was a one-shot deal. According to the professor, after Marlie had recovered from her injuries and the emotional trauma she had suffered, she had had no extrasensory abilities at all.

For the first time in her life, she had been able to live normally. It was something she had always wanted to be able to do, but the price had been horrendous. Even after six years, she was still paying it. Now Dane knew why there were no boyfriends.

It made him all the more determined that *he* would change that situation.

Objectively he could be a little amused at the range of conflicts that were clouding his mind and tangling his guts. He'd always been able to hold himself a little apart, unaffected by most of the worries that gnawed at other cops. Subjectively he wasn't enjoying it worth a damn. He didn't believe in paranormal stuff, had always laughed at those who did. Now he found himself not only halfway believing, but trying to figure out how he could use Marlie to find Mrs. Vinick's murderer.

That last thought tied another knot in his intestines. He wanted to protect her; he didn't want her involved with another murderer in any capacity. But he was a cop, and his job was to use whatever source he could to solve a crime, especially one as brutal as this. The bastard didn't need to be walking around, loose among the unsuspecting public. And despite the primal male instinct that told him to keep Marlie away from it, he knew that, if possible, he would use her. He would do everything he could to keep her safe, but the greatest need was to find this guy and put him away. Unless he was a certified wacko, the savagery of the murder was such that he was almost certain to be given the death penalty . . . but first he had to be caught.

Another conflict was with his own male wariness. No man he knew gladly embraced the turmoil and restrictions of an emotional relationship with a woman, and he was no exception. He liked his life; he liked not being tied down to any one woman. He didn't want to have to account for his time to anyone, didn't want to have to consider someone else when making plans for what he wanted to do. But now there was Marlie, and damn it if he didn't feel as if he'd been

cornered. He'd been attracted to a lot of women before, but not like this. This was a fever, a gnawing need that never left him. It had been only four days since he'd walked into Bonness's office and seen her for the first time, and she hadn't been out of his mind since. The more he learned about her, the more involved he became. The hell of it was, *she* certainly wasn't doing anything to get him involved; he was doing it all on his own, and having to fight her every inch of the way.

She had totally avoided men, romantically and sexually speaking, since Gleen had almost destroyed her. Dane tried to tell himself to back off, to give her both time and space in order to come to trust him, but he knew it wasn't going to happen. He'd never been the type to sit and wait. He was going to make her his, and pretty damn soon, too. She would understandably be afraid of sex. He, and no one else, was going to teach her that it could be pleasurable, too. He'd never been jealous before in his life, but now he felt almost violent with it. Not jealous of Gleen, God knows, but of every other man out there who would take one look and get lost in Marlie's bottomless blue eyes. He wanted the right to pull her possessively against his side and glare a warning at any bastard who dared look too long at her.

Trammell would gloat at the irony of it. Dane had never had any trouble separating his love life from his work, because his work had always taken precedence. Now here he was, obsessed with a woman who was his best link with a killer.

It was nine-thirty when his plane landed. He was tired, having been up since before dawn, not to mention having flown most of the way across the country and back. He checked in with Trammell from a pay phone in the airport, told him he'd see him in the morning and tell him every-thing then.

After hanging up, he stood there for a minute, thinking. He was tired, his clothes were tired, he was grumpy. He should go home and get some sleep, think things over. He

knew what he should do, but damn if he'd do it. He wanted to see Marlie. He might not like the complications, but he couldn't wait to get entangled with them, like a moth rushing giddily toward a flame.

Marlie jerked the door open on his fifth knock. She stood squarely in the doorway, her posture plainly denying him admittance. "It's ten-thirty, Detective," she said coldly. "Unless you have that warrant, get off of my porch."

"Sure," Dane replied easily, and stepped forward. She wasn't prepared for the maneuver, automatically moving back to give him room before she caught herself. She tried to recover, grabbing for the door, but it was too late; he was already over the threshold.

He didn't take his eyes off her as he shut the door behind him. She was wearing a pair of cutoffs, droopy socks, and a flimsy old T-shirt that draped over her braless breasts as faithfully as her own skin. Very pretty breasts, he noticed, making no effort to hide the direction of his gaze. High and pointed, with small dark nipples peaking the fabric. His mouth went dry and his loins tightened, the same reaction he had every time he was in her company. He was beginning to expect it, anticipate it, enjoy it.

The casualness of her clothing jolted him, making him acutely aware of the prim facade she normally projected. Behind that facade was a woman whose natural sensuality took his breath, and made him realize how successfully she had managed to hide it. He wanted to shake his head at the waste and at the same time thank God that, evidently, no other man had seen through her defenses.

She had more layers than an onion, and she was determined to keep them hidden beneath that prickly shield she had developed. The blistering glare she was giving him should have shriveled his skin. Instinctively he knew that her hostility was because of her vulnerability; she was naturally angry at his previous suspiciousness and less than

gentle questioning, but most of her dismay was caused by the fact that he was seeing her like this, without the armor of her bland disguise.

Patience wouldn't work with her. She was too used to hiding, to protecting herself. He was going to have to break down her defenses, force her to let him get close to her. His blood surged hotly as he decided how to do it.

Deliberately he let his gaze roam over her. Her glossy dark hair was hanging loose on her shoulders. He liked that. Her bare legs . . . He felt another jolt of lust. Damn, her legs were great. And her breasts were so tempting that his mouth began to water, until he was all but drooling. He wasn't going to try to hide his attraction another minute; it was time to start getting her accustomed to it.

Marlie flushed angrily as he continued to stare at her breasts. She crossed her arms over them in a half-belligerent, half-defensive gesture. "If you don't have a good reason for this, I'm going to file a complaint about you," she warned.

His gaze flicked upward. "I've been to Boulder," he said abruptly. "I just got back an hour ago." He paused, watching for any flicker of expression. She didn't give much away, but he was learning to read her eyes. She hadn't quite learned how to shield the expression in them. "I talked with Dr. Ewell."

Her pupils dilated wildly, and there was no disguising her dismay. She stood stiffly, glaring at him. "So?"

He moved closer to her, so close that he knew she could feel his heat, close enough to intimidate her with his size. It was a deliberate tactic, one he had used before in interrogation, but there was a big difference this time in his own attitude. Talking to her was still important, but underlying it was the powerful sexual need to make her aware of him as a male. The closeness of his body shocked her; he saw her waver, saw the sudden color in her cheeks, saw the alarmed flicker of her eyes. She didn't allow herself to retreat, but she

went very still, her nostrils flaring delicately as the hot scent of his skin reached her.

Her own feminine scent wrapped subtly about him, drawing him even closer. It was a clean, soapy odor that told him she wasn't long from her bath, mingled with the warm sweetness of woman. He wanted to lean down and nuzzle her neck, to follow that faint scent to its source, investigate all the intriguing places where it might linger.

Later. It was too soon for that.

"So the good doctor had a lot of interesting things to say," he murmured. He began to slowly circle her, letting his body brush hers, the light touches tingling through his nerves like electricity. Stallion circling mare, getting her accustomed to his touch, his smell. Gentling her. "It seems you're some kind of miracle of ESP, if you believe in that kind of stuff."

Her lips tightened. She had herself under control again, not even glancing at him as he continued to circle her, ignoring the fleeting contact of his arm, or his chest, the graze of his thigh. "You don't, of course."

"Nope," he said blithely. It wasn't a complete lie, but he wasn't about to tell her he was at least halfway convinced. He'd get a lot more reaction out of her if she was angry, and reaction was exactly what he wanted. "Unless you can prove it to me. Why don't you give it a try? Come on, Marlie, read my mind or something." Slowly, slowly, around and around. Never letting her completely escape his touch, his heat.

"I can't. There has to be something *in* your mind."

"Nice shot, but it doesn't prove anything." He kept his voice low, almost crooning. "Make me believe it."

"I don't do parlor tricks," she snapped, goaded. She was drawing more and more taut, the force of his nearness wearing on her nerves.

"Not even to prove yourself innocent of murder?" He pushed her even further. "This isn't a party, babe, in case you haven't noticed."

Her head whipped around, dark hair flying, and she gave him the full force of her glare, blue eyes narrowing like a cat's. "I suppose I *could* change you into a toad," she said speculatively, then shrugged. "But someone has already beaten me to it."

He gave a bark of laughter, startling her. "You've seen too many of the old 'Bewitched' shows; that's witchcraft, not ESP."

The slow circling finally got to her. Abruptly she bolted, toward the kitchen. He let her go, following closely behind her. "Coffee," he said blandly. "Good idea."

She hadn't planned on making coffee, of course. She had simply been fleeing. But she seized gratefully on something to do, as he had known she would. She was rattled, and fighting it every inch of the way. He was beginning to realize how important control was to her. Too bad he couldn't let her keep it.

She opened a cabinet door and took down a canister of coffee. Her hands were visibly shaking. Then she halted, her back to him as she carefully set the canister down on the countertop. "I don't read minds," she blurted. "I'm not telepathic."

"Aren't you?" That wasn't what Dr. Ewell had said, exactly. He felt a tinge of triumph. Finally she was starting to talk to him, rather than resisting him. He wanted to put his arms around her and hold her close, shelter her from the trauma of her own memories, but it was too soon. She was physically aware of him now, but she was still frightened, still hostile.

"Not—not a classic telepath." She looked down at the coffee. He could see that her hands were still shaking.

"So what are you?"

So what are you? Marlie heard the question echo in her mind. *Freak,* some people might say. *Charlatan* was the word others would use. Detective Hollister hadn't been that

99

polite. He'd called her a fake, and possibly an accomplice to murder. It was ridiculous, of course. Even he would have had to give up on that idea by now, faced with a complete lack of evidence, opportunity, and motive. But he'd checked her out, he'd actually gone to Boulder and talked to Dr. Ewell. He knew about her now. He might not believe, but at least now he was asking instead of simply accusing. But how much did he know? Dr. Ewell could teach discretion to a diplomat, when he so chose; how much would he have told a stranger, even if that stranger was a cop? Marlie hoped desperately that he didn't know it all, because then he would ask her about it, and she didn't think she could bear to bring it all up now. She felt oddly vulnerable and exposed, her nerve endings raw. *He* had done that to her, forcing his big body so close to her that his heat had seared her skin, deliberately brushing against her, blatantly staring at her breasts.

She didn't want to be even more aware of him than she had already been. She was safe in her solitude.

"What are you?" he repeated calmly.

She turned to face him, her movements slow and deliberate. She squared her shoulders as if bracing herself for an ordeal. "I'm a clairvoyant empath. Or I was." Suddenly confused, she rubbed her forehead. "I suppose I still am."

"But you have read minds before."

"Maybe. Not exactly." It was difficult to describe being so linked with someone that you could interpret his thoughts through his emotions. Sometimes the link was so strong that it happened.

Choosing his words carefully, he said, "According to Dr. Ewell, you were the most sensitive receptor he's ever known."

She gave him a harassed look. "Receptor's as good a word as any. I pick up—I *used* to pick up things. Emotions, energy from actions. Thoughts, too, sometimes, but usually it was emotion rather than actual thoughts. The static was unbelievable."

"That's why you joined Dr. Ewell's study, for the peace of controlled surroundings."

She bit her lip. "Yes. I couldn't drive down a street, shop in a mall, go to a movie. It was like a thousand voices screaming at me at once. Most people don't make any effort to shield themselves, they just blast everything out like a shotgun, spewing their emotions in all directions."

"You didn't live at the Institute, though."

"No, I had a little place outside of Boulder. It was peaceful."

"I know about what happened six years ago."

The brusque statement was like being hit between the eyes. She reeled from the force of the blow, staggering back against the cabinet. He moved, coming toward her with that lethal, catlike grace so unusual in such a big man. Dazed, appalled, she held out a hand to ward him off. With ludicrous ease he brushed it aside and instead pulled her into his arms.

The shock of his hard body against hers was stunning. He was incredibly hot, burning her even through their layers of clothing. His muscled arms were as unyielding as steel bands; they forced her closer, until her thighs were against his, until her breasts were flattened against the hard ridges of his stomach muscles. She felt weak, disoriented, and automatically clutched his biceps in an effort to steady herself.

"Don't be scared," he murmured, bending his head down to hers. His warm breath tickled her ear as he gently nuzzled the side of her neck. He licked the small hollow beneath her ear and the sensation, as tender as a mother's kiss, made her begin to tremble. "I won't let anything like that happen to you again. I know you're skittish with men now, babe, but I'll take care of you. I'm going to take *real* good care of you."

She pulled her head back so she could look at him. Her eyes were huge, and edged with panic. "What are you talking about?" she cried thinly. She was afraid, scared by the way things had so suddenly gotten out of her control, afraid of the proximity of his big body. She didn't want this,

didn't want to have to deal with the memories and unpleasantness. For whatever reason, he had decided not to ignore the wildfire of attraction that they had both been fighting, and moved with bewildering speed to change their situation. There was nothing of the detective in him now; he was purely a man, his hazel eyes glittering with sexual intent.

He pressed his mouth to her temple. "In bed, babe. When we make love."

She stiffened, pushing against his heavy shoulders as hard as she could. He didn't budge at all. "No, I don't want that. Let me go!"

"Hush," he said firmly, gathering her even closer. "I'm just holding you, Marlie. That's all. I've wanted to hold you since I first set eyes on you Monday morning."

"There has to be some sort of rule against a detective making a pass at a suspect," she blurted, searching for any weapon at all. "If you think I won't report you—"

"You're not a suspect," he interrupted. His mouth quirked. "Maybe I should have told you sooner, but the officer who saw you Friday night gave you a pretty good alibi, since you couldn't have been in two places at once."

She went still, her attention focusing on what he had just said. Her gaze locked on his. Uncomfortably he realized that there was something oddly compelling about her eyes. "When did you talk to him?"

The even tone of her voice didn't fool him. He winced inwardly. "Um . . . Tuesday night." He should have lied. He shouldn't have brought it up in the first place, at least not right now. He should have—

She bit him. He had been halfway expecting her to take a swing at him. He had to admit that he might deserve one, and he was willing to absorb a shot if it would make her feel better. Besides, the way he was holding her, he knew she wouldn't be able to put much power behind it. Evidently she realized that, too, because she simply leaned forward and sank her teeth into his chest.

"Ouch!" he bellowed, startled by the sharp pain. She hung on like a bulldog, and the pain caused by his involuntary movement quickly convinced him to stand still. "Shit! Turn loose!"

She did, and regarded him with baleful satisfaction as he hastily stepped back and rubbed his chest. A wet spot on his shirt marked where she had bitten.

Gingerly he unbuttoned his shirt and took a look, expecting to see blood. It didn't make him feel a lot better to discover that, though the indentations of her sharp little teeth were plain in his hide, there wasn't even much bruising. "The professor said you were testy," he muttered. "But he didn't mention the cannibalism."

"Serves you right," she said. "You've been hounding me for two days when you *knew* I'd been telling you the truth."

He looked a little sheepish, and continued to rub his chest. "I had to have some excuse."

"To do what?"

"See you."

"That's supposed to endear you to me?" she asked caustically, turning away to pick up the canister of coffee and return it to the cabinet. "I'm not making coffee. You can leave now."

"Will you have dinner with me tomorrow night?"

"No."

He folded his arms. "Then I'm not leaving."

She slapped the countertop in frustration and whirled to face him. "Can't you take a hint? *I don't want this.* Whatever you're offering, I don't want it."

"That's a lie."

Those hazel eyes were glittering again, this time with stubbornness. She had already noted that trait in him. It felt as if she had a bull in her kitchen, and couldn't budge him.

"You feel it the same way I do," he continued relentlessly. "You're attracted to me, and it scares the hell out of you, because of Gleen."

Her face closed up. "I don't want to talk about Gleen."

"That's understandable, but I'm not going to let you hold him between us. The bastard's dead; he can't ever hurt you again. There's too much pleasure in life to turn your back on it."

"And you're just the man who can show me what I'm missing, right?" she asked with heavy sarcasm.

"Bet on it, babe."

She crossed her arms and leaned back against the cabinet, holding herself away from him. "I've always hated being called babe or baby," she observed.

"Fine. I'll call you whatever you like."

"I don't want you to call me anything. Can't you get it through your thick head, Detective? There can't be anything between us, full stop, period."

He grinned suddenly, and her heart gave a thump at the miracle it worked on his harsh features. "There already is something between us. Can you think of anyone else who makes you as angry as I do?"

"Not right offhand," she admitted.

"See? I've been the same way. Since I saw you Monday morning, I've been in a hell of a mood, mad at you for being a suspect, mad at myself for being so attracted to you in spite of it."

"Maybe we just intensely dislike each other," she suggested.

"I don't think so." He glanced swiftly downward. "There's evidence to the contrary."

Marlie fiercely controlled the impulse to let her own gaze drift downward. After what she had felt yesterday morning on the porch, she was fairly certain what she would see. Despite herself, she was charmed by his air of slight bemusement at his body's response, and it took all of her willpower not to let it show. It just wouldn't do. He was going to be difficult enough to discourage as it was, without letting him see how very much she wished things could be different. She had always longed for a normal relationship,

but she had always been set apart, first by her own talents, then by Gleen.

"It won't work," she said aloud.

He looked downward again. "You think so? I dunno," he said doubtfully, "it looks like it will work pretty well to me."

Startled, she laughed aloud, and quickly clapped her hand over her mouth to stifle the sound. He grinned at her again, making her heart do acrobatics even as she tried to control herself. He was far more dangerous than she had feared; he could make her laugh.

"I can't," she said, sobering quickly. Her voice was soft, with an undertone of regret that she couldn't hide. "Gleen—"

With two long steps he reached her, closing his hands on her waist. The humor fled his face as if it had never existed. "Gleen is dead. The only way he can hurt you anymore is if you let him."

"Do you think it's that easy?"

"Hell, no, I don't think it's easy. I'm a cop, remember. I've seen what rape victims go through."

"I wasn't—"

"Technically raped? I know. But he tried, and beat the hell out of you because he couldn't. Your reaction probably isn't any different than if he had been able to penetrate."

She laughed again, but this time the sound was harsh, tearing. "It's a little different. I wish he *had* raped me! I lie awake at night and know that if he'd been able to get an erection, maybe if I hadn't fought him so hard, that little boy would still be alive! But he got more and more frenzied, and I kept struggling, and all of a sudden he left me and attacked the little boy." She was silent for a minute. "His name was Dustin," she said. "His parents called him Dusty."

Dane's hands tightened convulsively on her waist, then relaxed. "It wasn't your fault; no one can predict what a madman will do. But that's a bad thing to have to deal with," he said quietly. His chest was tight with suppressed emotion. Gently he smoothed her hair, then slid his fingers

under the warm, silky weight to cup her head in his big hand. "Have you ever told anyone everything that happened that night?"

She shook her head. "Not everything. Not the details. It was too . . . ugly."

"Have you ever told anyone else what you just told me?"

"No." She looked up, confusion in her eyes. "I don't know why I did."

"Because there's something between us, and you can't deny it any more than I can. We aren't comfortable with each other yet, but one day it will be okay. I can wait. And I can wait until you're ready to make love, too."

Frustrated at his stubbornness, at her inability to convince him, she shook her head. She didn't know whether to laugh or scream. "You're so damn sure of yourself."

"Trust me," he murmured. His hard fingers massaged her skull, relieving tension she hadn't even been aware of. "You'll think about it now, and the more you think about it, the more used to the idea you'll get. Then you'll start getting curious, wondering about how we would be together. You've done a good job putting your life back together, but you're too smart not to know that until you can trust a man in bed again, you're still letting Gleen have a hold over you. The next step is obvious. And I can promise you one thing: If anyone gets in bed with you, it's going to be me."

Before she could think of a response to that supremely self-confident statement, he took her by the hand and led her back into the living room. His palm was callused, his fingers hard and warm. His touch was consciously gentle, that of a man who was very aware of his own strength and was careful not to squeeze. There was something beguiling about his hand linked with hers, a subtle asking for, and reassurance of, trust. She felt oddly safe with him, though not safe *from* him.

"Let's sit down," he said, urging her toward the couch. Belatedly she tried to detour to a chair, but he tugged her to the couch and pulled her down beside him. He kept her

hand folded in his as he settled back with a sigh of relief, stretching his long, muscular legs out before him. "Airplane seats aren't made for anyone over five and a half feet tall. I still feel cramped."

"Why don't you go home," she said tiredly. "It's late."

"Because we still need to talk."

She shook her head and tried to tug her hand free. It was a useless effort. "We don't have anything to talk about."

"I've got some more questions about what you saw Friday night."

She stiffened. She couldn't help it; every time she was reminded of that evil, something inside her froze. "I've already told you everything. Tomorrow's a workday, and I'd like to get some sleep."

"Just a few minutes," he coaxed, smiling at her. That little crook of his mouth caused another disruption in her cardiac rhythm, and she quickly looked away. Whoever would have thought that such a roughhewn face could produce such a charming smile? He shouldn't be allowed to do anything except frown, for her own protection.

"I kept thinking about it on the plane," he said, taking her silence for acquiescence. "You aren't a suspect, you're a witness. In fact, you're the only witness we have. We have no leads, no evidence, no idea who we're looking for. Two earlier possibilities turned out to be dead ends. I'm not saying I buy into this paranormal stuff, but I'm willing to investigate any leads you can give me. For instance, can you give me a description of the guy?"

She shook her head, ignoring the dismissive way he said "this paranormal stuff."

"Nothing at all? C'mon. You described the murder scene down to the smallest detail."

"But I saw it from *his* eyes. I saw . . . everything else. Not him."

"Did you see his hands?"

A memory swam into focus, that of a hand reaching for a knife, holding the knife, slashing—

"Yes." The word was a whisper of sound.

"Good." Her eyes had gone slightly unfocused. Dane made his voice as soothing as he could, not wanting to startle her. "What color was his skin? Light or dark?"

"I don't know."

"Think, Marlie."

"I don't know! He was wearing gloves. Surgical gloves. And he had long sleeves." She paused, looking inward again. "His clothes were dark."

"He didn't pull off the gloves even when he raped her?"

"No."

"Okay, then let's work on his height. We know how tall Mrs. Vinick was; how tall was he in comparison?"

Marlie silently marveled at how his cop's brain worked; she hadn't thought of height at all. Her head tilted in concentration as she tried to focus the mental images.

"When he first grabs her, in the kitchen, he holds her close, with one hand over her mouth and the other holding the knife." Marlie lifted her hands into the positions she described, pantomiming the action. "The hand over her mouth is . . . like this. Even with his shoulder."

"So that's the level of her mouth. That puts him around six feet. We can't know how long his neck is—he may be an inch shorter or taller—but at least that's something. What about his voice? Do you remember anything about it?"

She closed her eyes. "Nothing that stands out. It was just a man's voice, not particularly deep or high." His actual voice hadn't mattered; it had been overwhelmed by the raging violence, the hatred, of his emotions.

"How about an accent? Can you distinguish an accent?"

"Not southern," she said promptly, opening her eyes. "Big deal. This is Orlando; half the population, including me, is from somewhere else."

"Can you narrow it down any more than that? There are a lot of distinctive accents: New York, Boston, Ohio, Chicago, Minnesota, the western accents."

She was shaking her head even as he rattled them off.

"Nothing that I can pin down. He didn't actually *say* that much, or maybe I didn't pick it up."

"Then let's move on to something else. Did you get an impression of his body?"

Utter revulsion crossed her face.

"I mean his weight," Dane said hastily. "Was he thin, average, or heavy?"

She gave him a dirty look. "Average, I think. And strong. Very strong. Maybe it was anger, or the adrenaline, but she was helpless against him. He gloated about it. He loved it."

She leaned back, suddenly very tired, and discovered that sometime during their conversation he had draped his arm behind her, so that when she sat back she was all but in his arms. She bolted forward, only to find that heavy arm around her shoulders and herself being urged back once more, and his face was very close to hers.

"Shhh, don't panic," he murmured in a dark, soft voice. "You're still holding my hand, and the other one's behind you. You're okay."

She glared at him. "I am *not* holding your hand," she snapped. "You're holding mine!"

"Minor detail. I'm going to kiss you, Marlie—"

"I'll bite you again," she swiftly warned.

He shrugged. "I always have had more guts than sense," he said, and very gently brushed her mouth with his.

It was only a fleeting contact, lighter than a whisper, but laden with a tantalizing hint of his taste. Her pulse leaped again, but he was drawing back before the expected fear could materialize. A tiny frown drew her brows together.

He released her hand, finally, and cupped her chin in his palm. The rough pad of his thumb traced the fullness of her lower lip, his gaze focused on the movement.

"Any bad thoughts?" he asked. His voice was even darker, softer.

"No." Her response was a whisper.

"In that case . . ."

This time his mouth lingered. He wasn't holding her; she

didn't feel constrained, but was somehow helpless to move away. His lips were firm and warm, but tender in their pressure even as they moved, and shaped her own lips to accommodate him. Marlie closed both hands around his thick wrist, and her eyes fluttered shut.

The gentle pleasure of the kiss made her dizzy. She hadn't expected such tender consideration from him, or the flood of sensation that rushed through her. She made a little sound of confusion, and he lifted his head immediately.

"Are you okay?"

"Y-Yes," she stammered, her eyes blinking open.

"Good." He bent his head to her again, and resumed the kiss. His tongue slipped into her mouth, not thrusting deep but inviting her to taste him. Marlie didn't know what to do; what was happening was so opposite to what she had expected that she couldn't think. The most stunning fact was that she wasn't afraid. This was nothing like—no, she wouldn't even think his name. The shimmering pleasure she was feeling was too precious to destroy.

Hesitantly, trusting a long-unused instinct, she accepted the invitation and sucked lightly at his tongue. Instantly a shudder ran through his big body, astonishing her. She did it again, and he groaned aloud, a deep sound that reverberated through his chest. Delight in this newfound sensual power shyly bloomed inside her.

He suddenly released her mouth and sat back. His skin was flushed, and pulled taut across his cheekbones. "That's enough. That's almost too much. I'm going to leave now, before I try to push you too far."

She blinked at him, her eyes languorous and dazed, as if she wasn't quite certain what had happened. He wasn't too sure himself. He hadn't been that turned on by a simple kiss since he'd been fifteen, and lost his virginity under the stadium bleachers with a seventeen-year-old cheerleader.

He forced himself to stand up before he made a big mistake and changed his mind about leaving. He had kissed her; that wasn't enough for him, but it was probably as much

as she could stand. All in all, he was extremely pleased with the evening.

"I'll call you tomorrow," he said as he walked to the door. She followed him, the awareness rushing back into her eyes. He winked at her. "Your sexy voice turns me on even over the telephone."

Like a light blinking off, all of the softness vanished from her expression. "I'm glad you like it," she said flatly. "I screamed so much when Gleen was butchering the little boy that my voice broke. It hasn't been the same since then."

9

HE WAS SO ALIVE THAT IT WAS ALMOST PAINFUL. CARROLL Janes could feel the anticipation pooling in him, the power gathering, until it felt as if he should be glowing. He was always amazed that people couldn't *see* the power, but then most people really were extraordinarily stupid.

It would be tonight. It was unusual that only a week had passed since the one last Friday, but this was so *easy,* there was no point in putting it off. And it was pleasant, this buildup of power almost as soon as the glow had faded from before. Of course, he couldn't count on this occurring every week; the really rude ones didn't happen all that often. And he normally liked to draw it out much longer, maybe even as long as a month, but that was because there were almost always difficulties to be overcome, complications to solve. Jacqueline Sheets had none. She lived alone, and her routine was suffocating in its rigidity. No, there was no reason to wait.

It was odd that it was almost always women who were rude, though there had been a man once or twice whom he

had been obliged to punish. He didn't like it when it was a man. It wasn't that a man's strength made it more difficult; he was contemptuous of that concept. He was strong enough to handle almost anyone, and religiously worked out to maintain that strength. Men simply didn't offer the pleasure, the opportunity for prolonged teasing while the power built. Men were almost boring. And of course, he wasn't queer, so at least half the fun was missing. No way would he screw a man. If he was sometimes a bit more lenient with a man's rudeness—well, it was *his* decision to make, after all, not anyone else's. If he preferred women, that was no one's business but his own.

He hummed all day, causing Annette to remark that he was certainly in a good mood. "You must have big plans for the weekend," she said, and he heard the unconscious note of jealousy in her voice. He liked that. Of course, he had been aware that Annette yearned for him, for all the good it would do her. She simply wasn't his type.

"A hot date," he replied, not caring if she heard the quivering anticipation in the words. It might liven up her fantasies.

He thought of Jacqueline Sheets waiting for him. He had been inside her house, and could picture the scene exactly. He knew where she sat while watching television—which was about all she did. He knew how her bedroom looked, what she wore to sleep in: utilitarian pajamas. He hadn't been surprised. He preferred nightgowns, but pajama bottoms weren't a problem. She would pull them off for him; they all did, with a blade shining in their faces.

He had checked out the kitchen. Her knives had been in disappointing shape, with dulled edges barely capable of slicing a banana. She was obviously not a very good cook, or her knives would have been in better condition. He had selected a filleting knife and carried it home, where he had spent the past two nights painstakingly putting a razor edge on the blade. He hated having to work with inferior tools.

He could barely wait for the night, when the ritual would

begin, as his father had taught him. When you are rude, you are punished.

Dane had called Marlie at seven that morning, just to say hello and ask if she'd slept well, and the irritation in her voice had made him chuckle. She was still resisting him mentally, but physically it had gone much better than he had ever hoped. He had kissed her, and she not only hadn't been afraid, she had enjoyed it. Considering her background, that was a giant stride forward.

He grinned like an idiot all the way to work. He had kissed her! So what if it had been a kiss that would make the average teenage stud roll his eyes in boredom? What did teenage studs know? They weren't interested in anything but squeezing breasts and a few quick thrusts. He was old enough, thank God, to know that the slower it was, the better it was. He might be crazy with frustration by the time Marlie came to him, but after last night he had no doubt that it would happen. He was dizzy with delight, anticipation fizzing in him like champagne bubbles.

Trammell was already there when Dane walked in, his dark eyes sleepy as he leaned back in his chair and watched Dane approach. People moved around them, talking and swearing; telephones rang incessantly, the fax machine and photocopier hummed almost without pause. A typical day, but Dane didn't feel typical. He was still smiling as he went to the coffee machine and poured two cups of coffee. He sipped one as he returned to his desk, and gave Trammell the other. "You look like you need it. Bad night?"

"Thanks." Trammell cautiously tasted it, eyeing Dane over the rim. "It was a long night, but not a bad one. Well? Did you find out anything interesting yesterday?"

"Quite a bit. For one thing, let's say I'm not as skeptical as I was before."

Trammell rolled his eyes. "What about Marlie? What's she been doing for six years?"

"Trying to recover," Dane said briefly. "Arno Gleen beat

her, tried to rape her, and when he couldn't, he killed the kid in front of her. According to Dr. Ewell, the trauma of it severely damaged, maybe even destroyed, her paranormal abilities. Evidently this vision about the Vinick murder is the first psychic tickle she's had since then."

"So the psychic stuff is coming back to her?"

Dane shrugged. "Who knows. Nothing else has happened." *Thank God.* "I talked to her last night, asked a few more questions about what she saw in the vision, and she remembered a couple of details."

"Like what?"

"The guy is about six feet tall, he's in very good shape, and he isn't from the South."

Trammell snorted. "That really narrows it down for us."

"It beats what we had before."

"Agreed. Anything beats nothing. That's assuming we accept a psychic's vision for leads, because a court sure as hell won't accept her as evidence."

"What choice do we have? There *is* nothing else. This guy didn't leave a clue. I'll take any lead I can get, and worry about proof when we find him."

"Actually," Trammell said slowly, "we've already talked to someone who fits that description."

"Yeah, I know. Ansel Vinick. He's as strong as a bull, and even though he's lived in Florida for over twenty years, he still has a midwestern accent." He hadn't been surprised; very few people who weren't raised in the South ever managed to get the accent right. The movie and television industries never had. "But my gut says he didn't do it."

"He had opportunity."

"But no motive. No boyfriend, no insurance. Nothing."

"Maybe an argument that got out of hand?"

"The medical examiner didn't find any bruises on her that would indicate blows. She wasn't just killed, she was slaughtered."

"The textbooks say that when there are that many stab wounds, the killer was really pissed at the victim. And that if

he spends a lot of time doing it, he probably lives in the neighborhood. You know the numbers as well as I do: Eighty percent of the time, when a woman's killed, it's her husband or boyfriend who does her in. And a lot of the time, the killer is the one who calls the police when he 'discovers' the body. Vinick fits into all of the categories."

"Except for the first one. If they were arguing, no one knows anything about it. The neighbors didn't hear anything, they always seemed to get along fine, and Vinick didn't act unusual in any way at work that night. And she was raped, but there wasn't any semen. Marlie says the perp wore a rubber; why would Vinick bother? She was his wife, for Pete's sake. Finding his semen in her wouldn't be incriminating. What really bothers me," he said, thinking hard, "is her fingers. Why chop off her fingers? We haven't found them. There wasn't any reason to cut off her fingers, unless—"

"—she scratched him," Trammell finished, dark eyes shining intently. "She scratched him, and he knew about DNA profiling. He cut off her fingers so forensics couldn't get a skin sample from under her nails."

"Vinick was wearing a short-sleeved shirt that morning," Dane recalled. "Do you remember any scratches?"

"No. It's possible he could have had some on his chest or upper arms, but the hands and lower arms are the most likely location."

"Don't forget the cut screen in the bedroom. If Vinick had done it himself, to make it look like a forced entry, wouldn't he have made it more obvious? He didn't strike me as a subtle type of guy, anyway. And everything that Marlie told us dovetailed with what we found at the scene. It wasn't Vinick."

"Wait a minute," Trammell said. "Marlie didn't mention the fingers, did she?"

Dane thought about it, then shook his head. "No, and it doesn't seem like the kind of detail anyone would forget."

The omission troubled him, and he made a mental note to ask her about it that night.

"All the same, I'd feel better if we talked to Vinick again," Trammell insisted.

Dane shrugged. "It's all right with me, I just feel like it's wasted time."

Trammell tried several times that day to get in touch with Mr. Vinick, between the hundred other things they had to do, but there was no answer. He called the trucking company where Mr. Vinick worked, and was told that he had been off all week, and all things considered, they really didn't expect him to return to work for at least another week.

"The funeral was yesterday," Dane said. "Maybe he's staying with friends. Hell, of course he isn't staying in the house. Forensics is finished with the scene, but would you want to sleep there?"

Trammell grimaced. "Guess not. But how are we going to get in touch with him?"

"Ask one of the neighbors. They'll know."

It was late afternoon when they pulled up in front of the Vinick house. It had a closed, unoccupied look. The yellow crime scene tape had been removed, but the house still looked set apart, made forever different from its neighbors by the violence that had happened within. A car was parked in the driveway, and Dane recognized it as the one that had been sitting there last Saturday morning. "He's here."

They knocked on the front door. There was no answer, no sound of movement inside the house. Trammell went around to the back door, with the same results. All of the curtains were pulled, so they couldn't see in any of the windows.

Both doors were locked. They banged again, identifying themselves. Nothing.

Dane walked next door. A woman came out on the porch at his knock.

"I'm Detective Hollister," he said, flipping his ID wallet

open. "Have you seen Mr. Vinick? His car is here, but we can't get anyone to the door."

She frowned, and pushed her hair out of her eyes. "No, I haven't seen him since the funeral. I went to it; just about everyone on the street did. She was such a nice lady. I don't know when he parked his car in the driveway. It wasn't there late yesterday afternoon, but was when I got up this morning."

"You haven't seen anyone over there at all?"

"No. Of course, I haven't been here all day, but no one has been there that I've seen."

"Thanks." Dane nodded in good-bye and walked back to the Vinick house. "I don't like it," he said, after telling Trammell what the neighbor had said. "How do you feel about forced entry?"

"I think we'd better," Trammell said soberly. "If we're wrong, we'll grovel and apologize and pay for the damages."

They went around back. The top half of the kitchen door was small, diamond-shaped panes of glass. Dane pulled out the Beretta and used the butt to knock out the corner pane closest to the doorknob. He was always surprised at how hard it was to actually break out a window. Shattered glass tinkled on the tile floor inside. Carefully wrapping his hand in a handkerchief, he reached inside and unlocked the door.

The house was hot, and foul with the odor of death that had been closed up inside it. The silence was almost physical.

Dane unwrapped the handkerchief from his hand and held it over his nose. "Shit," he muttered, then raised his voice. "Mr. Vinick? Detectives Hollister and Trammell."

Nothing.

The smell seeped through the cloth. It wasn't the cloying, sickeningly sweet odor of decayed flesh, but a pungent smell of human waste underlaid with the metallic scent of blood, both old and new. Dane's stomach knotted. He cursed again, quietly, and stepped inside.

The living room was empty; he had expected it to be. The walls were still splattered with Mrs. Vinick's blood, the stains turned brown.

Mr. Vinick was in the bedroom.

It hadn't been cleaned, either. Chalk still outlined the position of her body, there in the corner. Mr. Vinick lay beside the outline. There was a small pistol lying close by his head.

He hadn't taken any chances with botching the job. Anyone who jams the barrel into his mouth is serious about the attempt.

"Ah, shit," Trammell said tiredly. "I'll call it in."

Dane squatted by the body, being careful not to touch anything. Nothing he could see indicated that it was anything but a suicide, but it was habit not to disturb a scene.

He looked around, and saw a sheet of paper lying on the bed. The sheets had been stripped off, leaving only the bare mattress, and the white paper wasn't immediately noticeable against the white ticking. He could read what it said without bending down.

I don't have any family now, with Nadine gone, so I don't guess it matters much. I just don't want to go on. He had dated and signed it, even noted the time. Eleven-thirty P.M., just about the same time of night his wife had been murdered.

Dane rubbed the back of his neck, his mouth set in a grim line. Damn, this was tough. The guy had buried his wife, then returned to where she had been murdered and put a bullet in his head.

Trammell came back into the room and stood beside Dane, reading the note himself. "Was it guilt or depression?"

"Who the hell knows?"

"Shit," Trammell said. There was just something about this house of death that reduced comment to that crude, simple word. It was sad.

By the time the scene had been secured, the body taken away, and the paperwork dealt with, it was almost nine o'clock. Dane thought about calling Marlie, but decided against it. He wasn't in a good mood, and didn't feel up to any romancing. Trammell had had a date, but he was as surly as Dane, and called to cancel. Instead they went to the cops' favorite bar and slugged back a couple of beers. A lot of cops had a drink or two, or three, before they went home. It was the easiest way to wind down, and an opportunity to dump all the tension on people who knew exactly what they were talking about, before they went home to the spouse and kiddies and pretended everything was sweetness and light.

"If he *was* the perp, we'll never find out now," Trammell grunted, licking foam off his upper lip.

Dane had always liked it about Trammell that the man drank beer, instead of some hoity-toity wine. He could accept the Italian suits and silk shirts, the Gucci loafers, but he would have had a hard time connecting with a wine drinker. He didn't know why Trammell had suddenly decided that Ansel Vinick was their best bet as a suspect, but they all got maggots in their heads from time to time. "I don't think he did it. I think the poor sad son of a bitch just couldn't face living after finding his wife like that."

"I wasn't convinced he did it," Trammell denied grumpily. "I just wanted to make sure he didn't get away because we were too busy looking for phantoms."

Dane finished his beer. "Well, innocent or guilty, he didn't get away. You want another one?"

Trammell considered the level of beer in his glass. "No, this will do it." He paused, still frowning at the amber liquid. "Say, Dane . . ."

His voice trailed off, and Dane lifted his brows, waiting inquisitively. "Yeah, what?"

"These gut feelings you get. Your instincts are usually right on, and everyone knows it. Have you ever thought . . . you aren't a lot different from Marlie?"

If Dane hadn't already finished his beer, he'd have spewed it all over the table. He choked, and his outraged "What?" was just a wheeze of sound.

"Just think about it." Trammell warmed to his subject, leaning forward to prop his elbows on the table. "We all get hunches, we all go with our guts. Most of the time we don't need to, because the perp is sitting there singing like a good little birdie, but every so often we get a mystery. So how are our hunches different from what Marlie does?"

"That's a crock. Hunches are just the subconscious noticing something that consciously we haven't thought about yet."

"That's pretty much what a psychic does, isn't it?"

Dane gave him a sour look. "I think two beers is maybe one over your limit. We get hunches because of evidence we can see, and circumstances we can think about. Hell, a psychic doesn't have to be anywhere around or know anything about the situation, they just pick up these vibes, or whatever."

Trammell rubbed his head, disturbing his hair. Dane began to feel vaguely concerned; maybe two beers *was* too much for Trammell. God knows he'd never seen Trammell with so much as one hair out of place, except for that time when they'd gotten in a shootout and Dane had caught a bullet, but those were extenuating circumstances.

"I can't make up my mind what to believe," Trammell muttered. "Logic and the law of averages says that Ansel Vinick was the most likely suspect. But Marlie knew everything, except about the fingers, and how did she know unless she's for real? If she's for real, then Vinick was innocent and we're back to square one." He picked up the glass and drained it, then set it on the table with a thunk.

"That's exactly where we are. Square one. I'm beginning to feel stupid, because we sure as hell aren't accomplishing anything."

"No evidence, no witnesses, no motive. Know what?"

Trammell's lean, faunlike face was so funereal that Dane had to bite the inside of his cheek to keep from grinning. "No, what?"

"I don't metabolize alcohol very well," his dapper partner announced with grave dignity.

"No!" Dane clapped his hands to his face. "I never would have guessed." Privately he thought that anyone who could still say "metabolize" without tripping over the syllables was in damn good shape.

"I'm usually more careful than this. I . . . sip."

"You're a world-class sipper."

"Thank you. But it's probably a good thing that you're driving."

"I think so. Are you ready to go home now?"

"Any time you are. You won't have to put me to bed or anything like that, but I wouldn't want to drive."

"I wouldn't want you to drive, either, buddy. C'mon, let's go."

Trammell was steady on his feet, but he was humming under his breath, and Dane almost laughed again. Humming "My Darling Clementine" didn't fit with the image. "Will you have a hangover?" he asked curiously. A hangover from two beers would be hilarious.

"Never have," Trammell said. They were outside, and he inhaled a deep breath of smoke-free air. "This doesn't happen very often. Not since college."

"That's good."

"You won't tell anyone, will you?"

"Naw. I promise." It would be tempting, but he'd keep it to himself. Though most embarrassing things were fair game, this was something Trammell couldn't help, and the guys would rag him unmercifully for the rest of his life. On the other hand, it was nice to have something he could hold over Trammell's head occasionally. He whistled cheerfully as they got in the car, his good mood restored.

* * *

The ritual was comforting. He liked for everything to happen in exactly the same order every time, because *he* commanded it. He didn't do it often enough for it to be routine—that would weaken the power of it—but there was reassurance in the sameness of preparation. Knowing that these very preparations would make it impossible for the police to ever catch him gave him a sense of gleeful power. They caught only stupid people who made stupid mistakes, and he had never made a mistake. Not one.

Anticipation for the coming night kept rising in him, but he kept it firmly under control. He wanted to concentrate on the preparations.

First the hairpiece of blond curls came off. It was a very good hairpiece; he had paid an outrageous amount for it, but it had been worth every penny. No one had ever discovered that it was a full wig. Not only was blond his natural coloring, which meant the color wasn't jarring, but the style of blond curls was something that people remembered. It was very recognizable.

There was nothing wrong with his own hair, he thought, examining his temples for any telltale sign of a retreating hairline. But it would be stupid to let a stray hair give the police a means of identifying him. He carefully shaved his head, taking his time about it, though there was only stubble because the last time had been so recent.

He loved shaving, the wetness, the slick feel of the shaving gel, the glide of the razor over his flesh. It was almost like sex.

His beard was next. It wouldn't be gentlemanly to scratch her with a rough chin. Then his chest. He had a neat diamond of chest hair, and he was rather proud of its thickness, but it had to go.

Then his legs and arms. Slick. No wonder women shaved their legs. It really felt marvelous.

Finally, his crotch. No curlies left behind to be combed out, examined, gloated over. He was extremely careful in

this area, for even a tiny nick could leave an unnoticed stain of blood behind. That simply wouldn't do. And of course, he always wore a condom, so there was no semen left behind. He even had a contingency plan in case the condom broke; so far, he hadn't had to use the plan.

Some men, he'd read, couldn't be identified by their semen; they were called "nonsecreters," and about one man in five was like that. It would have been nice to know if he was in that twenty percent, but he could hardly go to a lab and ask to have his semen classified as secreter or nonsecreter. He didn't mind wearing the condom; he didn't want his sperm inside the transgressors anyway.

Next were his clothes. Leather. No fabric fibers to be left behind, nothing to give them a clue. He kept his leathers carefully stored in a cardboard box, away from everything else. He had a vinyl seat cover that he put over his car seat, and the floorboard was covered with vinyl mats. He was always very careful not to let his feet touch anything but the mat, so his boots wouldn't pick up any fibers from the carpet. Detail. Attention to detail was everything. There was no way the police could identify him, because he left nothing behind except the object of the lesson.

Detective Hollister hadn't called, though Marlie had expected him to, or even shown up unannounced as he had a tendency to do. She had been on edge, afraid he *would* call or come by, then irritable with him for not doing so. Either way, he had managed to ruin her quiet evening at home.

She had toyed with the idea of going to a movie, partly to stymie Hollister if he did call, but had rejected the idea. She couldn't forget what had happened last Friday night. Had it only been a week? It seemed like a month. Perhaps next week she would go to a movie, but not tonight.

She went to bed earlier than normal, before ten, not even staying up to watch the late news. She was tired; the week of tension had taken a toll on her. It was a relief to close her eyes and know that she didn't have to go to work in the

morning, that she could stay in bed as long as she wanted. She relaxed into the mattress, feeling her muscles go limp and her mind ease into sleep . . .

—He moved silently through the house. The television was blaring, masking his presence. He stood in the doorway for a moment, watching the woman who sat with her back to him while she watched an old movie, and contempt filled him. She was so easy. He walked forward, taking his time, enjoying the suspense. The flickering light from the television glinted on the slim, curved blade of the knife in his hand—

A grunting, animal sound tore from deep in her chest as Marlie tried to scream, tried to send a desperate warning through her closed throat. God, oh God. She whimpered, fighting the covers as she tried to throw herself out of bed. The vision was so real that she expected to see him coming at her out of the darkness, silver blade gleaming.

—He stood right behind her, looking down at her. The stupid bitch had no idea he was there. He liked that. Maybe he'd just stand here until the end of the movie, and all the time she'd never know—

She scrambled out of bed and fell, caught by the sheet tangled around her legs. She fought her way free of the sheet and stumbled to her feet, lurching wildly from side to side as she staggered for the door. Panic blinded her, froze her brain—no, it was dark, the lights were off. She careened into the wall, and the hard impact steadied her, somehow. She groped for the light switch, but it wasn't there.

—This was boring. Smiling, he reached out to touch her neck—

Marlie stumbled into another wall, a wall that wasn't supposed to be there. She stood there, trembling, totally disoriented. Where was she?

Headlights from a passing car briefly illuminated the room. The living room. How had she gotten in here? She remembered trying to get to the bedroom door, but not reaching it. But at least now she knew where a light was.

She almost knocked the lamp over as she fumbled with

the switch, and the sudden bright flare of light momentarily blinded her. The phone. The phone was right there, on the table.

His number. What was his number, damn it? She couldn't remember, couldn't think—the redial button. Had she called anyone since that night? She didn't know, didn't care. It would reach someone. She lifted the receiver, banging it painfully against her temple as she tried to hold it in place with a violently trembling hand, and punched what she hoped was the redial button. Her vision was blurring, and she wasn't certain.

The first ring buzzed in her ear. She closed her eyes, fighting to remain within herself.

The second ring. Hurry. Please, hurry hurry hurry.

The third ring cut off in midbuzz, and a deep, sleepy, grouchy voice said, "Hollister."

"D-Dane." Her voice was thin, wavering out of control.

"Marlie?" All sleepiness was gone. "Marlie, what's wrong?"

She tried to speak and couldn't; her throat was too tight. She took deep, gulping breaths.

"Marlie, goddammit, say something!" He was yelling at her now.

It was coming. She couldn't fight it off any longer. The trembling was convulsive, the light fading as her vision went. She made a desperate effort, screaming, and her voice was only a whisper. "He's . . . doing it . . . again."

10

HE COULDN'T GET HER TO SAY ANYTHING ELSE, THOUGH THE line was still open. Dane scrambled into his clothes and shoved his sockless feet into running shoes. He grabbed his shoulder holster, with the Beretta in it, but didn't take the time to slip it on. Barely a minute after answering the telephone, he was on his way out the door.

His heart was slamming painfully against his ribs. What had she said? Her last sentence had been so faint, he could barely hear; something about doing it again.

It didn't matter what she had said. Her panic had reached through the phone line to him, as real as if he could see it. She was in trouble, serious trouble.

It was raining lightly, just enough to slick the streets and make him keep the wipers on. He couldn't drive as fast as he wanted, but he was still going too fast for the road conditions. The sense of urgency kept his foot on the accelerator. He merely slowed down for stop signs, and halted at red lights only until there was a break in traffic.

An accident on the expressway forced him to cut across

the median, backtrack, and take another route, wasting valuable time. Almost twenty minutes had passed when he pulled into Marlie's driveway. Her car was in its customary place, and a light was on in the living room. He didn't bother with the two shallow steps, but leaped onto the porch with a single bound and knocked on the door.

"Marlie? It's Dane. Open up."

The silence inside was absolute, as complete as it had been that afternoon at the Vinick house, as if no living creature were inside. Dane's blood chilled, and his voice was hoarse as he called her again, banging on the door with his fist.

There were no windowpanes in this door to break, and he didn't take the time to go around back and check out the kitchen door. He backed up and lashed out with his foot. Four kicks broke the lock and splintered the frame, and the door flew open to crash against the wall. He knew he should take his time, not rush in without knowing the situation, but fear was greater than caution and he hurled himself through the opening, the Beretta in his hand.

"Marlie!"

She was just sitting there on the couch, in a pool of light from the lamp, like a statue in a niche. Her eyes were open, fixed and unseeing. She was utterly still, utterly white, and for an agonized moment he stopped breathing. The pain was like a fist, clenched around his heart.

Then he remembered what Officer Ewan had said, that at first he had thought she was dead, and he started breathing again, managed to move, though the fear hadn't released its icy hold on him. He laid the pistol aside and knelt on the floor in front of the couch, picked up one of her hands from her lap and held it against his chest while he put two fingers on her fragile wrist, pressing and finding the reassuring throb of her pulse. It was slow but steady. Her skin was cool, but the warmth of life lay just under the surface chill.

"Marlie," he said again, much calmer now. There was still no response.

Carefully he looked her over, then examined the surroundings. There was no sign of struggle, and no injuries that he could see. She seemed fine, physically.

The phone receiver was lying beside her on the couch, a beeping noise coming from it. He picked it up and replaced it in the cradle.

He swallowed as he realized what must have happened. She had had another vision, might even still be locked in it. What was it this time? Another murder? God knows, with drugs and street gangs, it was a wonder she didn't spend most of her time in a catatonic state. Did she ever pick up on the good stuff, on happy times, on people playing with their kids or groaning at a dumb joke? How could she function, if she was overloaded with all the shit in people's lives?

She was wearing only a thin tank top and panties, and her legs felt chilled to his touch. He got up and closed the ruined door, then went into her bedroom in search of a blanket. The small room, like every other room he'd seen in her house, was cozy and soothing. She had made the house her retreat, her barricade against the world. He stood in the middle of it and looked around, getting to know her in little ways. The covers on the double bed were twisted and half on the floor; she had evidently been in bed when the vision had started, and the condition of the covers was a measure of her agitation.

There was a crocheted throw lying across a rocking chair. He picked it up and returned to the living room, where he draped it over her, tucking the folds around her bare arms and legs. As far as he could tell, she hadn't moved even a centimeter, except for the barely perceptible rise and fall of her chest as she breathed.

He didn't know what else to do, except wait. He went into the kitchen and put on a pot of coffee; she might not need it when she came out of this, but he sure as hell did.

He sat on the couch beside her, watching her. Her expression was as blank and empty as that of the statue she had reminded him of earlier. There was no awareness in her;

her eyes were open, but she was either unconscious or . . . gone, somehow.

He studied her oblivious face. Seen in profile, there was an otherworldly purity to her features that he hadn't noticed before. When she was awake, the sharpness of her tongue and the cool intelligence in those bottomless blue eyes took most of his attention. Most, but not all. If she had been awake, he sure wouldn't have put a cover over her half-naked body. He looked at the tender curve of her lips, remembering how they had felt, how she had tasted. Her shape was all feminine daintiness, soft, lithe curves that made his entire body feel hot, and his skin too tight.

Ten minutes had ticked by. The mechanical thumping and spitting in the kitchen had stopped, indicating that the coffee had finished brewing.

He fetched a cup of coffee, then resumed his seat beside Marlie and placed the cup on the lamp table. Very gently he lifted her, and settled her on his lap.

"Marlie. Can you wake up now? Come on, honey, wake up." He stroked her face, then grasped her shoulder and shook her.

She made a little sound, not quite a whimper, and her lashes fluttered.

"Come back to me, Marlie. It's Dane. Wake up and tell me what happened." Her head lolled against his shoulder. He cradled her with his supporting arm and rubbed his free hand over her upper arm and shoulder, feeling the cool, sleek skin under his hard palm. He shook her again, but not hard, only enough to jar her. Her eyes were closed now, which seemed to him at least more natural, as if she were sleeping.

"Marlie!" He made his voice sharp. "Wake up and talk to me, damn it!"

She moaned and tried to push away from him, but her hand fell heavily to her lap as if she couldn't quite control it. She drew several jerky breaths, and her lashes lifted, then closed again, the effort beyond her.

"Marlie, look at me." He deliberately said her name, calling her from the far reaches of darkness, back toward the light.

Someone was insistently calling her name. Marlie's exhausted mind latched on to the familiarity, like a drowning person desperately clutching at a life ring. It gave her a center, a sense of identity in the swirling fog of nightmare. The voice was far away at first, but then came closer and closer, until it was right over her head. Reality seeped back, though there was something very *un*real about it. It felt as if she was lying against someone, as if arms were around her, and the sensation was so alien that it confused her. She didn't allow people to hold her; the mental intrusion, strengthened by physical contact, was just too disrupting. But someone *had* held her, a dim memory insisted. Oh, yes. Dane. Gently bullying, stubborn, refusing to listen to her . . . Of course. Dane.

She forced her heavy eyelids to lift, and found herself staring at that roughhewn face, the hazel eyes dark with worry. His heart thumped steadily against her, a comforting rhythm that made her want to curl against him. The heat of his big body was under her, around her, chasing away the bone-deep chill. Why was she so cold?

Hazily she looked around. She was in her living room. But why was Dane here, and why was she on his lap? Why was she so tired? She had expected him to call, but he hadn't, and she had gone to bed—

She had called him. She stiffened, memory returning in a flood of awful details that she would have given anything not to recall. Her exhausted mind struggled to cope.

"Dane." She clutched his shirt, fingers twisting in the material.

"It's all right," he murmured, smoothing back her hair. "I'm here. You had another vision, didn't you? What was it about this time? Just take your time, settle down. Do you want some coffee? Will that help?"

He was holding a cup of coffee to her lips, and she sipped

it, hoping the caffeine would buy her a few extra minutes. She had to get her thoughts ordered, tell him as much as she could, but the coffee was the worst she had ever tasted, and with a grimace she turned her head away when he tried to get her to drink again.

"He did it again," she said, the words slurred a little.

"Who did?" he asked absently, trying to get her to drink a little more coffee. She turned her head away from the cup.

"Him. He killed another woman tonight." The trembling had started again, shaking her from the inside out.

He tensed. She could feel his muscles coiling beneath her. "The same one who killed Nadine Vinick?" he asked carefully.

"Yes. I knew he was out there, looking . . . I felt him, just a hint, the night I called you." She forced the words out in a tumble, trying to get it all said.

"That's what scared you?"

She nodded, her head barely moving in the hollow of his shoulder.

Holding her securely against him, Dane picked up the telephone and called central dispatch. He identified himself and said, "Has a stabbing murder of a woman been called in?"

"No, it's been pretty quiet for a Friday night. Guess the rain's put a damper on things. You know something we don't?"

"Maybe, maybe not. Listen, if there is anything like that, give me a call on the pager. Night or day, no matter what."

"You got it."

He hung up and looked down at Marlie. "Nothing's been called in."

She was still gripping his shirt, and her eyes had taken on that faraway look they had had Monday morning, when she had recited a horror tale in a flat, emotionless voice. The trembling in her slight body had increased; he held her with both arms, trying to cushion her against the shock waves he could feel rippling through her.

"She has red hair," she said in that small, ghostly voice. "She's very pretty. She's watching television, some old movie. She doesn't know he's there. He walks up behind her and stands there, looking down. He's amused; how long will it be before she senses his presence? Too long. She's a stupid cow, and he's getting bored. He touches her neck, with his left hand, then slaps it over her mouth before she can scream. He loves that first moment of terror. The knife is in his right hand. He holds it to her throat."

"Are you sure it's the same one?" Dane asked. He desperately wanted her to say that she wasn't certain.

"Yes. The movie is still on; it masks the noise. He makes her take off her pajamas and lie down on the floor. Couches are too cramped; he doesn't like couches. He uses a condom. She doesn't deserve his sperm. Slow and easy, slow and easy . . . let her relax, not be so afraid. Don't hurt her, not yet, not yet."

Dane anchored her to him, holding her so tight he expected her to protest, but she didn't, all of her attention on her litany of terror. Chills rippled up his spine, and the hair on the back of his neck stood up. Oh, God.

"He's finished. He's on his knees beside her. She's looking up at him, eyes wide and scared, but hoping. That's good, that's real good. He smiles at her, and her stupid mouth quivers, but she smiles too. She's afraid not to, she thinks he's crazy. Too stupid to live. He's bored; this isn't as much fun as the last one. Maybe he can liven her up. He sticks her a little and she squeals like a pig, and the race is on. Around and around the mulberry bush."

"Jesus God," Dane said, his voice hoarse. "Marlie, stop it. That's enough."

She blinked and refocused on him, and the expression in her eyes made him want to cry. The pallor of exhaustion lay over her face like a clay mask.

"You have to catch him," she said in a drugged voice.

"I know. I will, honey. I promise."

She turned her face in to his shoulder and closed her eyes.

Her body went limp in his arms. He looked down at her as she began breathing in a slow, heavy rhythm that signaled deep sleep. As quickly as that, she had slipped into unconsciousness. He wasn't alarmed. After seeing her as she had been when he'd first arrived, this looked downright normal.

He sat there for several minutes, his face grim as he considered the ugly ramifications. Finally he got to his feet, with Marlie still in his arms, and carried her into the bedroom, where he carefully placed her on the bed. She didn't move when he pulled the throw away and re-covered her with the sheet.

He refilled the cup with hot coffee, then resumed his seat and thought about what had happened tonight. He didn't like any of it.

He glanced at the clock; it was after midnight. He called Trammell anyway.

The receiver was fumbled upward on the other end and he heard a very feminine "Hello?" at the same time as Trammell was saying, "Don't answer that!" Evidently two beers hadn't incapacitated him *too* much, and evidently the canceled date had been rescheduled.

Then Trammell got the phone away from his lady friend. "Yeah?"

Dane wasn't in the mood to tease him. "Marlie had another vision tonight," he said without preamble. "The same guy. She says he did another one."

Trammell was silent for a shocked two seconds as the ramifications of it hit him, too. "Where?" he asked.

"Nothing's been called in yet."

More silence. Then he said, "This will prove one way or the other if she's for real."

"Yeah. She was in pretty bad shape. I'm at her house, if you need me. Dispatch is going to call if anything's reported."

"Okay. If she's right . . . shit!"

Yeah, shit. Dane sat there drinking coffee, brooding. If Marlie was right, and the same guy who had murdered

Nadine Vinick had done another woman, in the same way, they had big-time trouble. As bad as he had wanted the bastard, he thought he had been looking for a one-timer, he had hoped it was someone who had known Mrs. Vinick. He had thought it had been personal, though he hadn't been able to find anything to indicate what that would have been. Multiple stab wounds usually meant someone was really pissed at the victim.

But another victim, killed with the same MO, meant they had a psychopath in Orlando. A serial killer. Someone without conscience, someone who acted only according to his own weird rules. Worse, it looked as if he was an intelligent serial killer, taking pains to leave no evidence behind. Serial killers were a real bitch to catch under any circumstances, and a smart one was almost impossible. Look at how long Bundy had killed before he'd finally made a mistake.

He couldn't do anything but wait. He couldn't investigate a murder that hadn't been reported, a body that hadn't been found. Until a victim turned up, all he had was a vision by a burned-out, trauma-damaged psychic. He believed her, though; his gut believed her, and that was frightening in itself. A cold corner of logic in his brain was still saying "wait and see," but logic couldn't dissipate the knot in his stomach.

He knew the terminology. Escalating sexual serial killer. He tried to remember if there had been any unsolved stabbing murders in Orlando before Nadine Vinick, but none came to mind, at least none that resembled it. Either the guy had just recently started murdering his victims, or he had moved in from another city. If a killer moved around, kept the murders spread out over different jurisdictions, cops might never figure out that it was the work of a serial killer because they wouldn't have the other murders to compare the method to.

If Mrs. Vinick was his first victim, then to have killed again so soon the guy had to have gone totally out of control,

and they would soon have a bloodbath in the city. An escalating killer started out slow; there might be months between his victims. Then the killings would start getting closer and closer together, because that was the only way he could get his rocks off, and he wanted it more and more often. Only a week between victims signaled an incipient rampage.

And he couldn't do anything except wait.

When would the body, if there was a body, most likely be discovered? Maybe the husband worked third shift, like Mr. Vinick. Maybe that was the common denominator, that the husband was gone nights. If so, the discovery would be in the morning, say from six until eight. But if the lady lived alone, it could be a couple of days or longer before anyone missed her enough to check on her. Hell, he'd seen cases where people had been dead for *weeks* before anyone noticed.

Wait.

He looked at the clock again. Five after two. The coffee was gone, and he drank so much of the stuff that it only worked as long as he was pouring it in. He was tired; his eyelids felt like sandpaper.

He looked at Marlie's couch, and snorted in dismissal. He was six two, and the couch was five feet. He'd never been into masochism.

He peeked into the one room in the little house that he hadn't seen, wondering if it was a spare bedroom. It wasn't. This was where she stored odd pieces of furniture, luggage, boxes of books. It wasn't as cluttered as the main rooms in his home usually were.

The only bed in the place was the one Marlie was sleeping in. He supposed he could go home, but he didn't want to leave her alone. The lock on her door was ruined. He didn't know how long she would sleep, but he intended to be there when she woke.

He hesitated for only the barest second, wondering what she would say if she woke up with him in bed beside her, but

then he shrugged and went into her bedroom. As far as he could tell, she hadn't moved at all.

He stripped down to his shorts, tossing his clothes over the rocking chair, and placed the pistol on the bedside table. His pager went right beside the pistol. There was only the one table, and Marlie was lying on that side of the bed. Dane scooted her over, then without even a twinge of conscience, slid in beside her and turned off the lamp.

It felt good. Contentment spread through him, a warm antidote to the worry of the last few hours. As big as he was, the double bed felt cramped to him, but even that had its good points because Marlie was so close to him. He put his arms around her, holding her cradled to him with her head in the hollow of his shoulder. Her slight body felt soft and fragile, and her breath moved across his chest with the lightest of touches.

He would be willing to lie awake for the rest of his life, if he could protect her from what she had gone through tonight. She had told him, Officer Ewan had told him, the professor had told him, but until he had seen it with his own eyes, he simply hadn't realized how traumatic it was for her, how it hurt her, how much it cost her.

What a price she had paid! He knew the toll it took on the human spirit to see so much ugliness, day in and day out. Some cops handled it better than others, but they all paid, and they had only normal sensitivities. What must it have been like for her, feeling everything, all the pain and rage and hate? Losing her empathic ability must have been like being rescued from torture. Now that it was evidently coming back, how must she feel? Trapped? Desperate?

Desire pulsed in his loins; he couldn't be around her and not want her. But stronger than desire was the need to hold her close and protect her, from the horrors within as well as those without.

He slept until eight, and woke instantly aware that the pager hadn't beeped at him during the night. Neither had

Marlie stirred. She lay limply against his side, her very stillness a gauge of her exhaustion. How long did this stupor normally last?

He showered, figuring she wouldn't mind the use of her bathroom and towels. Then he shaved, using her razor and swearing when he nicked himself. Then he went into the kitchen and put on another pot of coffee. He was beginning to feel as comfortable in Marlie's house as he was in his own. While he was waiting for the coffee to brew, he measured the ruined front door for a replacement. He had just finished that when the phone rang.

"Heard anything?" Trammell asked.

"Nothing."

"What does Marlie say?"

"She hasn't said anything. She's been asleep almost since she came out of the vision last night. She managed to tell me what she'd seen, then passed out."

"I thought about this for hours last night. If it's a serial killer . . ."

"We've got trouble."

"Should we tell Bonness what we think?"

"We'd better. After all, he believed Marlie before either of us did. We can't do anything until the murder is verified, but we should keep him informed."

"We're going to feel like fools if no one's found."

"I hope so," Dane said grimly. "I honest to God hope I feel like the biggest fool walking. That would be a hell of a lot better than the alternative."

Trammell sighed. "I'll talk to Bonness," he volunteered. "How long are you going to be at Marlie's?"

"I don't know. At least until she's capable of functioning on her own. All weekend, the way it looks."

"Wipes her out, huh?"

"You don't know the half of it." A thought occurred to him. "And while you're out and around today, I need you to get a door for me. Marlie's isn't very secure."

* * *

138

The voice pulled insistently at her, refusing to let her rest. It was a very patient voice, though relentless. On the far fringes of consciousness she knew that it was familiar, but she couldn't quite recognize it. She was tired, so tired; she just wanted to sleep, to forget. The voice had pulled her from oblivion before. Why didn't it leave her alone? Fretfully she resisted the disturbance, trying to find the comfort of nothingness again.

"Marlie. Come on, Marlie. Wake up."

It wasn't going to stop. She tried to turn away from the noise, but something was holding her down.

"That's right, honey. Open your eyes."

Surrender seemed easier; she didn't have the energy to fight. Her eyelids felt like stone, but she forced them open, and frowned in confusion at the man who was sitting on the bed beside her. His arms were braced on either side of her, holding the sheet tight; that was what was preventing her from moving.

"There you are," he said softly. "Hi, honey. I was getting worried."

She couldn't think; everything was fuzzy. Why was Dane holding her trapped like this? Her confusion must have been on her face, because he smiled and lifted one hand to smooth her tangled hair back from her face. "Everything's okay. But you've been asleep for a long time, and I didn't know if it was normal or not, so I decided to try to wake you up. It took some doing," he added wryly.

"What . . . ? Why are you here?" she mumbled, trying to sit up. He sat back, releasing the sheet, and she struggled into an upright position. It took so much effort that she ached. What was wrong? Had she been sick? The flu, maybe; her bones ached so, that could be the explanation. But why was Dane here?

"If I had to make a guess," he said, his voice pitched to a soothing rumble, "I'd say your need for the john has to be critical. Can you make it there?"

When he mentioned it, she realized that he was exactly

right. She nodded and clumsily pushed the sheet away. He stood so she could swing her legs off the bed. She didn't have many clothes on, she thought weakly as she sat on the edge looking down at her bare limbs, but she just didn't have the strength to care.

She tried to stand and sank heavily back onto the mattress. Dane bent and lifted her easily in his arms. Her head drooped into the curve of his shoulder and neck, and the position seemed so comfortable that she let it stay there.

She heard the hum of the air conditioner. The air was cold on her bare skin, and the radiant heat of his big body was heavenly as he carried her . . . somewhere. She closed her eyes.

"No you don't," he scolded, putting her on her feet. Her heavy eyelids opened and she saw that she was in her own bathroom. "Make an effort, honey. Now, can you manage by yourself or do you want me to stay in here with you?"

She wasn't so tired that she couldn't give him a "get real" look, and he chuckled. "I'm fine," she said, though she heard the fretful weakness in her own voice. She ignored it. She would manage; she always had.

"Okay, but I'll be right outside the door. Sing out if you need me."

She stood swaying in the small room after he had left, staring longingly at the bathtub and wondering if she could stand upright long enough to take a shower. It would be so embarrassing if Dane had to help her, handling her naked body as if she were a helpless infant.

First things first, though. She was very thirsty, but there was a more pressing concern. When that was taken care of, she gulped two glasses of water, then stood with the cool glass pressed against her forehead. Her mind was still so foggy, every thought such an effort. She needed to remember something, she felt the urgency, but couldn't concentrate long enough to bring it to mind. All she wanted to do was sleep. Blessed sleep. She didn't want to remember.

She really wanted that shower a lot.

Finally the simplest thing to do was to turn on the water and step under it, clothes and all, so that's what she did. She deliberately left the water not quite lukewarm, knowing that it would wake her up, not wanting to but accepting the necessity. She stood under the cool spray, her face turned up to catch the full blast, and let the fog dissipate. Let memory return. Let the water overcome and wash away the hot salty tears, the way a flood overcomes and obliterates a trickle.

Until it wasn't enough and she buried her face in her hands, sobs shaking her body.

"Marlie . . . ?" The worried, impatient tone changed at once, became quiet and steady. "I know, honey. I know it's bad. But you're not alone now. I'll take care of you."

The water was turned off, and his strong hands were on her, helping her out of the tub. She stood dripping on the mat, her eyes still closed while tears tracked down her cheeks.

"You're soaked," he said, still in that soothing, rock-steady tone. "Let's get these clothes off—"

"No," she managed, the word strangled.

"You can't keep them on."

"I'll do it."

"Are you sure?"

She nodded.

"Okay. Just open your eyes for me, honey, and tell me that you can manage, and I'll get some dry clothes for you and leave you to it. But I want to see those eyes before I do."

She swallowed, and took two deep breaths to control the tears. When she thought she could handle it, she forced herself to open her eyes and look up at him. "I can do it."

His gaze was piercing as he studied her, then he gave a short nod. "I'll get your clothes. Tell me what you want."

She tried to think, but nothing came to mind. "I don't care. Anything."

"Anything," left to his decision, was a pair of panties and her cotton robe. While he waited outside, she stripped off her wet clothes, clumsily dried herself, then dressed in what

he had provided. She was rubbing her wet hair with a towel when he decided she had had enough time, and opened the door again.

"Here, I'll do it," he said, taking the towel from her and putting down the lid on the toilet for her to sit down. She did, and he carefully blotted all the excess water from her hair, then took the comb and smoothed out all the tangles. She sat there like a child, letting him minister to her, and the small attentions gave her a comfort she'd never had before. Numbly she realized that what he'd said was true: She wasn't alone this time. Dane was with her. He had been there last night, and he was still there, taking care of her, lending her his strength when she had none.

"What time is it?" she finally asked. Mundane thing, but the small and unimportant were the anchors of life, the constants that held one steady.

"Almost one. You need to eat; come on in the kitchen and I'll put on a pot of fresh coffee, then fix breakfast for you."

She remembered his coffee. She gave him an appalled look. "I can do the coffee."

He accepted the rejection of his coffee with good grace, being used to it. She was coming out of it; she could say anything she wanted about his coffee. She was more alert, though her face was utterly colorless, except for the shadows under her eyes, and tight with strain. He put his arm around her waist to support her as they slowly made their way to the kitchen.

She leaned against the cabinet while she made coffee, then sat and watched Dane competently assemble a meal of toast, bacon, and a scrambled egg. She ate a couple of bites of egg and bacon, and one slice of toast. Dane ate the rest.

When she crumpled, without a word he scooped her onto his lap and held her while she cried.

11

Trammell arrived about four that afternoon, driving a pickup truck he had borrowed, with the replacement door in the truck bed. Dane paused for a moment to savor the incongruity of Trammell driving a truck, then went out to help him unload the door. "Whose truck is it?" he asked.

"Freddie's husband's." They each grabbed one side of the door and slid it off the bed. They didn't have to ask if anything had been reported; if it had, they both would have heard. Next door, Lou came out on her porch to watch them with open and suspicious interest. Dane took the time to wave to her. She waved back, but frowned disapprovingly. No doubt she had looked out her window first thing this morning and seen his car in Marlie's driveway; he had undoubtedly besmirched Marlie's spotless reputation.

"New lady friend?" he inquired delicately as they carried the door to the porch.

"Um, no." Trammell was being unusually reticent, and Dane was instantly suspicious. It wasn't that Trammell was the kind of guy who regaled the squad room with play-by-

play details of a hot night, but he was usually forthcoming enough to at least give the lady a name.

"I thought the date was called off."

Trammell cleared his throat. "She came over anyway."

"Anything I should know about?"

"No. Maybe. But not yet."

Dane didn't get to be such a good detective by being stupid. He wondered why Trammell would feel it necessary to protect a woman's identity, and only two possibilities presented themselves. One: The lady was married. Trammell wasn't a poacher, though; married women were off limits to him. Two: The lady was a cop. That made sense; it fit. Immediately he began running through names and faces, trying to match them to the voice he'd heard last night. Everything clicked into place like three cherries in a slot machine. Ash blond hair sternly subdued to fit under her patrolman's cap, a rather austere face, quiet brown eyes. Not beautiful, but deep. She wouldn't enjoy being the butt of the raucous gossip that squad rooms specialized in, and she wasn't the kind of woman to be trifled with. "Grace Roeg," he said.

"Goddammit!" Trammell dropped his end of the door to the porch with a thump, and glared at him.

Dane set his end down with less force. "I'm good," he said, shrugging. "What can I say?"

"Nothing. Make sure you say absolutely nothing."

"No problem, but you're really getting in deep with me. That's two secrets I have to keep."

"God. All right. If you feel the need to blab about something, if you just can't stand the pressure, then tell them about the beer. I can live with that. But keep Grace out of it."

"Like I said, no problem. I like her; she's a good cop. I'd spill the beans on *you,* but I wouldn't upset *her* for anything. Watch yourself, though, pal. You could be asking for major trouble. You outrank her."

"There's no question of sexual harassment."

"Maybe not to you, maybe not to her, but the paper pushers may not look at it that way." Though the concern was a legitimate one, Dane was enjoying himself immensely. Trammell was glaring at him, black eyes as hot as coals. It was nice to get back at him, after the way he'd silently laughed at Dane's predicament with Marlie. "How long has it been going on?" Not long, he'd bet. He'd have noticed it before now.

"A couple of days," Trammell said grumpily.

"Moving a little fast there, partner."

Trammell started to say something, shut his mouth, then mumbled, *"I'm* not."

Dane started laughing at the helplessness in Trammell's tone. He knew exactly how it felt. "Another good man bites the dust."

"No! It's not that serious."

"Keep telling yourself that, buddy. It might keep you from panicking on the way to the church."

"Damn it, it isn't like that. It's—"

"Just an affair?" Dane inquired with lifted brows. "A good time in bed? It doesn't mean anything?"

Trammell looked hunted. "No, it's . . . ah, shit. But no wedding bells. I don't want to get married. I have no intention of getting married."

"Okay, I believe you. But it'll hurt my feelings if I'm not your best man." Smiling at Trammell's frustrated curse, Dane went inside to get a screwdriver, and Trammell followed him. Marlie was lying curled on the couch, asleep. Dane paused to look down at her and tuck the light coverlet around her feet. She looked small and pale, utterly defenseless as her mind recovered from the devastating exhaustion.

Trammell was watching Dane's face rather than looking at Marlie. "You have it bad yourself, partner," he said softly.

"Yeah," Dane murmured. "I do." So bad he was never going to recover.

"I thought it was just a case of the hots, but it's more than that."

"Afraid so."

"Wedding bells for you?"

"Maybe." He smiled crookedly. "I'm still not her favorite person, so I'll have to work on that. And we have a killer to catch."

He continued on into the kitchen, where he went through the cabinet drawers in search of a screwdriver. All kitchens, in his experience, contained a junk drawer, and that was the most likely place to find a screwdriver since he couldn't imagine Marlie having an actual toolbox. *Her* junk drawer, bless her neat little heart, was more organized than his flatware, and lying there in its own clear plastic holder was a set of screwdrivers. He could picture her carefully selecting the appropriate tool, using it, then sliding it back into its place in the holder, never getting them out of the order they'd been in when she'd bought them. He took the entire pack, and the small hammer lying there.

She woke as he used the hammer to tap the pin out of the second hinge, sitting up on the sofa and pushing the heavy curtain of her hair out of her face. Her eyes were heavy-lidded, her expression still showing the remoteness of mingled fatigue and shock. Dane gave her an assessing glance and decided to let her have a moment to herself. She sat quietly, watching with only mild interest as they removed the damaged door and replaced it with the new one.

It wasn't until they were finished that she said bemusedly, "Why did you change my door?"

"The other one was damaged," Dane explained briefly as he gathered up the tools.

"Damaged?" She frowned. "How?"

"I kicked it in last night."

She sat very still, slowly reconstructing the memories, putting details into place. "After I called you?"

"Yes."

There was another pause. "I'm sorry," she finally said. "I didn't intend to worry you."

"Worry" wasn't quite how Dane would have described it. He had been in a gut-twisting panic.

"Do you remember my partner, Alex Trammell?"

"Yes. Hello, Detective. Thank you for helping replace my door."

"My pleasure." Trammell's voice was more gentle than usual. It was obvious that Marlie was still struggling to get things together.

"Have you heard anything yet?" she asked.

He and Trammell exchanged a quick look. "No," he finally said.

A faraway look drifted into her eyes. "She's just lying there. Her family doesn't know, her friends don't know. They're going about their routine, happy and oblivious, and she's lying there waiting to be found. Why doesn't someone call or go by, just to check on her?"

Dane felt uncomfortable, and Trammell did, too, restlessly shifting position. They were more objective about bodies, especially bodies that might not even exist. They saw so many of them that they were hardened, for the most part thinking of the bodies as victims but not as individuals. The possibility of another murder victim had them both worried, because of the implication of a serial killer on the loose in Orlando. For Marlie, however, it was personal. She didn't have that inner wall to protect her.

"There's nothing we can do," he said. "Unless you can give us a name or a location, we have nothing to go on, nowhere to look. If it happened, someone will eventually find her. All we can do is wait."

Her smile was bitter, and not really a smile. "It happened. It's never *not* happened."

He sat down beside her. Trammell took a chair. "Can you think of any details, something you didn't tell me last night? Not about the killing, but about the location. Could you see anything that might give us a clue? Is it a house or an apartment?"

"A house," she said instantly.

"A nice-looking house, or a slum?"

"Very neat, good furnishings. One of those larger-screen televisions, on a pedestal." She frowned, rubbing her forehead as if she had a headache. Dane waited. "Cypress."

"Cypress? There's a cypress tree out front, a park with cypress trees, what?"

"I don't know. I didn't really see it. He just *thought* it."

"That's a big help," Dane muttered.

"What did you expect?" she snapped. "That he'd think, 'Now I'm breaking into this house at so-and-so number on so-and-so street, where I'm going to rape and kill Jane Doe?' *Nobody* thinks like that, everything's more automatic and subconscious. And I'm not telepathic anyway."

"Then how did you pick up on a cypress tree?"

"I don't know. It was just an impression. This guy is an unbelievably strong broadcaster," she said, trying to explain. "He's like a superpowerful radio station, overriding all the other signals."

"Can you pick him up now?" Trammell interjected, his eyes bright with interest.

"I can't pick up *any*thing now. I'm too tired. And he probably isn't broadcasting."

"Explain," Dane said briefly.

She glanced at him, then away. His attention was focused on her so intently that she almost couldn't bear it, because the lure of it was so strong and she was afraid to give in.

"His mental intensity builds as he gets closer and closer to the kill. Probably he can't maintain that level of rage for very long; he couldn't function at anything approaching normality if he did. So the only time his mental energy is strong enough for me to read is right before and during the kill, when he's at his peak. I lose him shortly after that; I don't even know how he leaves the scene."

"That explains the fingers," Dane said to Trammell, who nodded.

"Fingers?"

"Did Mrs. Vinick scratch him at any time?" Dane asked, ignoring her puzzled question.

Her eyes went blank again as she turned inward. "I'm not certain. She tried to fight, clawing at him. It's possible, but I don't think he noticed if she did."

Until afterward, Dane thought. That was why Marlie didn't know anything about Mrs. Vinick's fingers. The killer had been very calm and deliberate when he'd done it, because he hadn't noticed the scratches until his killing frenzy had cooled. That her fingers had been cut off was one of the details that hadn't been released to the press, and he didn't intend to tell Marlie about it. She had enough to bear, enough gory details to fill a thousand nightmares; he wasn't going to add to it.

"You said that you picked up a hint of him the other night."

"It wasn't a clear image; it wasn't an image at all. It was just a feeling of evil, a sense of threat. He was probably stalking her," she said, her voice trailing away as she realized that was exactly what he'd been doing. He had controlled the rage, but the hatred and contempt had leaked through, and she had felt it.

She was becoming very tired again, and her eyelids drooped. She wanted to curl up and sleep. She wanted him to leave her alone. She wanted to lose herself in the sanctuary of his arms. She wanted everything and nothing, and she was too tired to make up her mind.

But then Dane's hands were on her, strong and sure, turning her so that she was lying down, and the light blanket was arranged over her again. "Sleep," he said, his deep voice immensely reassuring. "I'll be here."

She took one slow, deep breath, and settled into oblivion.

Trammell's lean, dark face was somber as he watched her. "She's helpless," he said. "Is it like this every time?"

"Yeah. She's recovered some now. It was a lot worse last night, and earlier today."

"Then I hope the killer never finds out about her; she's

completely vulnerable to him. If his mental energy is so strong it can block hers even from a distance, think what it would do to her if *she* were the one he was after. He'd be right on her, and she wouldn't be able to protect herself in any way."

"He won't get the chance to get to her," Dane said, and in the grimness of his voice there was a promise. No matter what, he'd keep Marlie safe. "Have you talked to Bonness?"

"He wasn't thrilled with the possibility that there could be a serial killer, so he said to play it close to the vest and not mention it to anyone else until, and if, we find out there really was another murder. But he was also as thrilled as a kid at the idea of working with Marlie, because after all, it was *his* idea. I swear to God, sometimes I wonder if there isn't some weirdo juice in the water in California."

"Don't laugh," Dane advised. "Right now we're pretty involved in it ourselves."

"Yeah, but we aren't jumping up and down with joy over it."

"Bonness is a good guy; a little weird, but okay. I've seen worse."

"Haven't we all." It was a statement, not a question.

Dane's gaze wandered over Marlie's sleeping face, and his brows drew together in a frown. "Cypress," he said.

Trammell read him immediately. "You've thought of something."

"Maybe. That's all she said. Cypress. Not cypress *tree*. That was just an association I made."

"Cypress. Cypress," Trammell muttered. They looked at each other, two minds racing madly down the same track. "Maybe it's the—"

"Address," Dane finished, already on his feet. "I'll get the map." Like all cops, he had a city map in his car.

A minute later they were both bent over the map, open on the kitchen table. Dane ran down the alphabetical list of streets. "Shit! Don't developers ever think of any other word

to use? Cypress Avenue, Cypress Drive, Cypress Lane, Cypress Row, Cypress Terrace, Cypress Trail—"

"It's worse than that," Trammell said, scanning the other listings. "Look at this. Old Cypress Boulevard. Bent Cypress Road. And isn't there an apartment complex called Cypress Hills?"

"Yeah." Dane folded the map in disgust. "There's no telling how many streets have cypress in the name. That's a dead end. We can't go door to door on every one of them, checking for bodies. What would we do if no one answered the door? Break in?"

Trammell shrugged. "You've done it twice in less than twenty-four hours."

"Yeah, well, there were extenuating circumstances."

"You're right, though. We're stuck. We may be fairly certain Marlie's for real, but Bonness wouldn't authorize that kind of search. People would be calling the mayor at home, screaming that Orlando wasn't a police state and we had no right to come into their homes like that. And they'd be right. We can't do that."

"So we're back to waiting."

"Looks like it."

There was no point in fretting over something they couldn't change. Dane allowed himself a moment of frustration, then changed the subject. "Would you mind going over to my place and getting some clothes for me? And my shaving kit. I had to use Marlie's razor this morning."

"I noticed," Trammell said, eyeing the nick on Dane's jaw. "Sure, no problem." He checked his watch. "I have time. I have a date tonight, but I'll be close to a phone."

"Grace?" Dane asked slyly.

Trammell scowled. "Yes, I'm seeing Grace. What about it?"

"Nothing, just asking."

"Then stop grinning like a jackass."

He left and was back within the hour with Dane's clothes

and shaving kit. "Your wardrobe is severely limited," he groused, dumping the clothes on a chair. He glanced down at Marlie, who was still asleep. "Maybe she can do something about it."

"Maybe," Dane said. "What's wrong with my clothes?" he asked innocently. If anything was certain to send Trammell into a tirade, it was that question.

"What's *right* with them?" Trammell snorted. "You have mostly jeans, very old ones. You have one suit, and it looks as if you got it from the Salvation Army store. Assorted slacks and sport coats, none of which really go together, and the most disgusting collection of ties I've ever seen. Did you actually *buy* this stuff? You paid good money for it?"

"Well, yeah. Nobody gives stuff away, you know."

"They should have paid you to take it off their hands!"

Dane hid his grin as he picked up the clothes and carried them into Marlie's bedroom, where he hung them in her closet, her very neat closet. His haphazardly hung garments looked out of place there, but he stood back and admired the sight for a minute. He liked the idea of his clothes in her closet, or her clothes in his closet. He thought about that possibility for a minute. He'd have to clean out his closet before she could, or would, put anything of hers in it.

Trammell left, and Dane watched television for a while. He couldn't find a baseball game, so he settled for a basketball playoff game. He kept the volume low, and Marlie slept undisturbed.

He'd been on a lot of stakeouts, spent a lot of time just waiting. In stakeouts, boredom and the need to piss were the two biggest problems. This reminded him of a stakeout, because the waiting seemed interminable, but the quality was different. They weren't waiting to catch a criminal, or to prevent a crime. The crime had already been done, they just didn't know where or to whom. They were waiting for a victim to surface, waiting for suspicion and worry to send someone to a quiet house somewhere in the city, to check on

a friend, neighbor, or relative. Then the waiting would be over.

"You're thinking about it, aren't you?"

Marlie's voice startled him. Dane jerked his head around to look at her; she was sitting up again, her somber eyes on him. He realized that he had been staring sightlessly at the television for some time, because it was almost eight o'clock.

"It isn't something you put out of your mind," he said.

"No, it isn't." For her more than anyone else.

He got up and turned off the television. "How about calling out for a pizza? Are you hungry?"

She thought about it. "A little."

"Good, because I'm starving. What do you like? The works?"

"That's fine." She yawned. "You call it in, and I'll go take a shower while we're waiting. Maybe it will wake me up."

"Take your clothes off this time," he advised, and she smiled a little.

"I will."

The water felt good, washing away the mental cobwebs and cleansing her of the sensation of having been tainted, dirtied somehow by the evilness she had witnessed. She was tempted to linger under the cool spray, but thinking of the pizza, forced herself to briskly shower and shampoo. After blow-drying her hair to a semblance of order, she thought about clothes, but settled for the light robe Dane had selected for her.

She left the bathroom and halted, staring at her unmade bed. If she had been more alert, she would have noticed it sooner. The fact that her bed was unmade was unusual enough, but what riveted her to the spot was the sight of twin indentations in the pillows, where two people had slept. Awareness roared through her like a brushfire. Dane had slept with her, in her bed.

She had docilely accepted his presence all day, knowing

that she had talked to him the night before but never wondering about his location during the lost hours. Now she knew. He had been right there, in bed with her.

A wave of sensual heat overcame her and she closed her eyes, shuddering at the deliciousness of it. Her heart pounded, her breasts tightened, and a flooding, loosening sensation in her loins made her knees go weak. Lust. She was astounded as its presence, at its power. Instead of being outraged that he had taken advantage of the situation, she was aroused by the thought of him sleeping beside her.

He had been so gentle in his care of her that day, that iron strength and fierceness controlled so that she had felt only the protection he offered. He had combed her hair, fed her, held her while she cried, and most of all, he had given her the comfort of his presence. She hadn't been alone this time, though somehow she always had been before, even while she had still been with the Institute. Dr. Ewell and the others had always maintained a distance from her; mental privacy had been so difficult for her to attain that they had gone out of their way to let her recover in her own way, at her own pace. Until now, she hadn't realized how lonely and terrifying that had been.

Dane knocked briefly on the door and opened it without waiting for an answer. "Pizza's here."

As always, the impact of his presence was like a blow. He was so big and rugged, exuding a male vitality that made her shiver. For the first time she began to think that it might be possible, that Arno Gleen's legacy of terror was losing its power over her. Gleen had been a sick, sadistic bastard. Dane was pure, hard-edged male, too intense and grim for life around him to ever be entirely comfortable, but a woman would always feel safe with him, in bed and out.

His eyes narrowed. "Are you all right?" He reached her in two long strides, his arm sliding around her waist and pulling her into the support of his body.

"Yes," she said, not thinking about it, and slipped her hand around the back of his neck.

He didn't hesitate, didn't give her time to think about it. She wasn't certain she was extending an invitation, but he accepted it before she could decide. This time there was no careful restraint; he set his mouth over hers with open hunger, a hunger so intense and greedy that it stunned her. He caught her chin with his free hand and held her, then moved his tongue deep inside her mouth, touching her own tongue in blatant demand. She sagged against him, both frightened and tempted, and he gathered her in against his hard frame. His erection pushed against her belly. She had never been wanted before like that, so swiftly and violently. She had no experience of men like Dane Hollister, or of how he could make her feel.

But contact with that potent body was suddenly all she wanted. She put both arms around his neck, moving against him, trying to get closer. He was bruising her with the force of his kisses, and she wanted more. Her loins were tight and achingly empty, growing moist with yearning.

He put his hand on her breast, and her breath locked in her throat. His thumb rubbed over and around her nipple; at first it was a curious sensation, like a slight pricking of pins, then it suddenly intensified and pure sensation zinged from the nipple to her loins. She moaned aloud, frightened by the way her own body had so swiftly gone beyond her control.

Dane lifted his head. There was a hard, predatory expression on his face, the faint cruelty of arousal, and his lips were wet from their kisses. His hand remained on her breast, with only the very thin cotton of the robe between them. His breath was coming too fast, and she could feel the hard pounding of his heart against her. "Bed, or pizza?" he asked. His voice was so guttural, she could barely hear him. "If it's pizza, you'd better say so *now.*"

She wanted to say "bed," she wanted it so much. She had never felt desire before, and the lure of it was almost irresistible. She wanted to forget the reason he was there, the murders she had seen, and simply give herself over to the

physical. She had never been able to do that before, and maybe couldn't now, but for the first time it seemed possible.

"P-Pizza," she managed, and closed her eyes as she fought for control. Sick dismay filled her at her own cowardice.

She could feel him bracing himself, and he took a deep breath. "Pizza it is, then." Slowly he released her and stepped back. A huge, obvious ridge in his pants told her how difficult it had been for him to stop. Most men wouldn't even have made the offer.

He gave her a wry, crooked smile that lit his rough features. "I guess I was going too fast for you, honey. I'm sorry. It's just that I have a hair trigger where you're concerned, and I'm not talking about firearms."

Marlie stared at him, a lump in her throat and a huge knot in her chest. She felt dizzy with shock and realization. Oh, God. She had been attracted to him from the first, had recognized it and fought it, but with that smile she slipped helplessly over the edge. She had loved, but she had never been in love before, and the power of it made her actually feel faint. Swaying, she put out her hand in search of support, and he was there, solid and vital and so hot that she almost melted. His arm was around her, and her head lay against his chest.

"Shhh, it's okay," he crooned. "I didn't mean to scare you. I'm sorry."

"No," she managed to croak, alarmed that he thought he had reminded her of Gleen. He hadn't; she had been expecting it, but it simply hadn't happened. She had always assumed that sexual fear would be a constant in her life, and now that it hadn't materialized, she felt oddly adrift and off balance. "It isn't you. I was just dizzy for a minute." Somehow she formed a smile, and it was a real one for all its shakiness. "Maybe your kisses are more potent than you thought."

"You think so?" His voice rumbled under her ear. "We'll have to experiment, won't we? After the pizza."

He walked her into the living room and guided her to the couch. "Just sit; I'll get the drinks. Do you want a plate?"

"Well . . . yes. Of course."

He chuckled. "It must be a woman thing."

"I prefer a napkin, too," she said politely. "As opposed to licking my fingers."

He winked at her. "I'll be glad to lick your fingers."

She shivered in response and sat, dazed and quiescent, while he puttered around in the kitchen. He seemed to know his way around in her house. How had this happened? She was bewildered by the speed and force of it. In less than twenty-four hours he had taken over; he had spent the night with her, apparently moved in with her, and with a grin made her fall in love with him. He was a one-man SWAT team, overwhelming her defenses without effort.

He was back in a few minutes with the iced soft drinks, a plate and fork for her, and a couple of napkins. He sat beside her on the sofa, turned on the television to a sports channel, and gave a grunt of satisfaction when a baseball game filled the screen. He served her a slice of pizza, got one for himself, and settled back with obvious enjoyment. Marlie blinked at him. This was what she'd gotten herself into? She didn't know whether to laugh or cry. In the end she simply concentrated on the pizza, sitting curled beside him on the sofa, bemused that she was so content to just be close to him and watch his face as he watched the game.

Sometimes his size overwhelmed her and sometimes she was comforted by it, but this was the first time she had had the opportunity to simply sit and study him. He was definitely a big man, even bigger than she had thought, at least six two and over two hundred pounds. The feet parked on her coffee table had to be size twelves, or larger. His shoulders were so wide, he took up almost half the couch; his arms were thick and hard, sinewy with ropy layers of muscle. His chest, she knew, was rock-hard, and so was his abdomen. His long legs, stretched out before him, looked like tree trunks.

His hair was darker than hers, almost black. She eyed the blade of a nose and the brutally carved cheekbones, and wondered if there was any American Indian in his heritage. He had a heavy beard; evidently he had shaved that morning, since there was a fresh-looking nick, but already the black stubble had darkened his jaw.

He leaned forward to get another slice of pizza, and her gaze fell on his hands. Like everything else about him, they were big, easily twice the size of her own. But they weren't thick hams; though powerful, they were lean and well shaped, with short, clean nails. She felt safe with those hands on her; not safe from *him,* but from everything else. She didn't want to be safe from him. She had lost her heart about fifteen minutes ago, and she was still reeling from the shock of it.

He was a cop, a man who made his living in violence. He didn't commit the violence, as a rule, but he had to clean up after it, he was constantly surrounded by it. Close by his right hand was a big automatic pistol. At some point during the day she had become aware of it, and now she realized that it was never far from his side. A shoulder holster was slung across the back of the couch, beside him.

There was a scar across the back of his right hand. She caught a glimpse of it when he reached for a third slice of pizza, and recognition congealed in her. "That scar on your hand," she said. "How did you get it? It looks like a knife wound."

He turned his hand to look at it, then shrugged and gave his attention back to the television. "It is. A close encounter of the punk kind, when I was still working patrol."

"It looks bad."

"It wasn't any fun, but it wasn't serious. It was a shallow cut, didn't slice through any tendons. A few stitches and I was as good as new."

"Gleen cut me," she said. She didn't know why she said it; she hadn't meant to.

His head snapped around, all affability gone as if it had

never been, and the expression in those hazel eyes was scary. "What?" he asked softly, putting down the slice of pizza. His thumb moved on the remote control, and the television screen went blank. "The professor didn't say anything about that."

She set the plate aside and drew her knees tighter to her chest. "They weren't serious cuts, just little slices. He was playing with me, trying to break me down with pain and fear. He got off on that; it was what he needed. And he wasn't trying to kill me, at least not then. He wanted to keep me alive so he could play with me. He would have killed me later, of course, if the sheriff hadn't gotten there."

"Let me see." The words were a soft growl and he was already reaching for her, uncurling her, his hands opening the robe. Marlie struggled briefly for control of the robe, but then he had it open, spreading it wide as he looked down at her, naked except for thin, brief panties.

The scars, six years old, weren't disfiguring. They would, given time, probably fade completely. She had never fretted about them, because they were so unimportant compared to everything else, and she had never been vain anyway. They were just small, silvery lines, five of them: one on the inner curve of her right breast, the rest on her abdomen. There would have been more, but Gleen had swiftly lost control when the gambit hadn't worked, degenerating to the crude force of his fists to elicit the response he had wanted.

She quivered, a hot blush staining her cheeks as Dane slowly examined her. She was acutely aware of her bareness, in a way she never had been before. His mouth was a grim line as he traced the line on her breast with his fingertip, the touch as light as a breath. Her nipple tightened, though he wasn't even touching it. She heard her own ragged breathing as he slowly touched every scar. He was shaking, too, and suddenly she realized that it was with pure fury, at a man forever beyond his reach.

She put her hand on his hair, threading her fingers into the warm thickness of it. "They aren't important," she said,

forgetting her embarrassment. "Of everything that he did, those little cuts amounted to the least."

"It isn't the cuts." His voice was thick with rage as he pulled her into his arms, cradling her head against his shoulder. "It's knowing what you went through, how terrified you were. You didn't *know* that he wasn't going to kill you."

"No, I expected to die. In some ways, that would have been easier."

12

SOMEHOW SHE WAS BEING HELD ON HIS LAP, HER ROBE STILL open and his hand inside it, but instead of threatened, Marlie felt utterly safe, his warmth and strength surrounding her like a citadel. It was a delicious sensation, one she had never been able to enjoy before. She wanted to sink into him, revel in this new freedom, for that's what it was, an entirely new vista opened up to her. But Dane wanted information, chapter and verse, and Detective Hollister was very good at getting his way. She could have resisted bullying, but not the waiting silence in which he held himself, a silence in which she could feel his tension. The tension wouldn't ease until he knew, and so she told him, the ugly details, the guilt that she had held inside for years.

Her head was lying on his shoulder, her face turned in to the muscled wall of his chest. Somehow it was easier that way, as if she could neither see nor be seen.

"He had knocked me out," she began. "When I came to I was naked, lying flat on my back on the floor, with my hands tied to some kind of pipe, maybe an old radiator. Gleen was

naked, too, sitting astride my hips with the knife in his hand, smiling and waiting for me to wake up. Dusty was tied to a cot about five feet away, watching the whole thing. He was such a pretty little boy." Her voice was soft and distant as she remembered. "Auburn curls all over his head, and big, round blue eyes. He was so scared. He cried the whole time."

Dane looked down at his big hand lying on her belly, almost completely spanning her. The thought of Gleen seeing her like this, and using a knife on this slender, womanly soft body, was so obscene that he barely stifled the growl that began rumbling up from his chest. She seemed to have forgotten that she was all but naked now, her mind lost in the past, but Dane was very aware of it. Even in his rage, he looked at those soft, round breasts with their tender pink nipples, and felt the desire burning low in his belly. He controlled it, forcing it aside so he could hold her, and listen to her. Had anyone ever held her, given her comfort? He thought not, and that added to his anger.

"I don't know why I did it," she continued, her head lying trustingly in the hollow of his shoulder. "But something in me refused—I couldn't give in to him. I would rather have died than give him what he wanted. He wanted me to beg, but I wouldn't. He wanted me to be afraid, and I was, but I didn't let him see it. I laughed at him. Oh God, I *laughed.* He cut me, and I yelled at him that he was a pitiful excuse for a man. He pulled my legs apart and tried to put it in me." She hesitated uncomfortably. "You know—*it,* not the knife."

"I know what 'it' is," he growled.

She buried her face deeper into the curve of his neck. "He couldn't, and I laughed at him. I made fun of him, I told him what a miserable little worm he had, and what a miserable little worm he was. He was wild with it, I could feel how out of control he was, all that hate and fury pouring out, but I just kept pushing. I could feel Dusty, too, so terrified, reaching out for me, begging me not to let the bad man hurt him again.

"So I kept laughing at Gleen, and kicking at him as much as I could. Somehow I managed to kick him between the legs, not really hard because my foot slipped off his thigh, but he . . . lost it. It was like he exploded, somehow. One second he was on me and the next he was on Dusty, and Dusty was screaming. I still hear him scream. I could feel him, the absolute terror, the agony. It was like a black wave, all over me, all through my brain, and I was screaming too. I screamed and screamed and screamed. Blood was everywhere . . ." She paused, and after an interminable silence that lasted only a few seconds, said simply, "I don't remember anything else. Dusty died, and I died with him."

Dane knew what had happened after that; the professor had told him. Her screams had pinpointed Gleen's location to the sheriff and his men, and they had killed Gleen before he could turn his murderous fury on Marlie. But they hadn't been in time to save Dusty, and in a way they hadn't been in time for Marlie either. As linked to Dusty as she had been, his death had been her death, too, and it was a miracle she had survived the shock.

He smoothed her hair behind her ear, and stroked her cheek. "But you came back," he said with controlled ferocity.

"Eventually. It was a long time before I felt anything, any kind of emotion. Before, I had felt everything, everyone clsc's cmotions, and after that I couldn't even feel my own. I didn't have any."

"You healed, Marlie. It's been a long time, but he didn't win. He couldn't break you."

"He came damn close," she said. She quietly rested against him for a minute. "If I hadn't pushed him, if I'd given him what he wanted, probably Dusty would still be alive."

Dane snorted. "Yeah, it'd be nice if we were all omnipotent." He wasn't going to waste his time babying the natural guilt she felt. He jostled her a little, forcing her to look up at him. "I'm glad you're here," he said deliberately.

She managed a fragile smile. "So am I. And sometimes that seems like the most callous thing of all, that I'm glad to be alive. I wasn't thinking beyond the moment when I was laughing at Gleen; the only thing I knew was that I absolutely couldn't bear for him to rape me. The thought of him being inside me was so revolting that I was willing to push him into killing me, rather than tolerate his touch. Of all the things that gave me nightmares, sex was the worst. I can watch some violence on television or in movies, but I still can't watch a sex scene. I can't think of it as love. I remember Gleen's face, the smell of his breath, the way saliva sprayed when he screamed at me. I remember the feel of him against me, between my legs, and I still want to gag." She took a deep breath. "Not that sex was ever good for me anyway," she said honestly.

"How so?" His voice was undemanding, and his touch almost absent as he stroked her hair back from her temple, but his hazel eyes were intense.

She had never talked about the difficulty she'd had with sex, but somehow, lying cradled in his protective arms, with the rest of the world held at bay, she could. She felt oddly dreamy, caught in a combination of fatigue and the aftermath of stress, as if nothing else were quite real. "It was awful. Mentally, I couldn't bear it. I had to work so hard to build a shield, to protect myself from everything," she explained. "It was the only way I could function, and the shield was at best only a partial protection. All my life I wanted to be *normal*. I wanted to love someone, I wanted a relationship, I wanted what normal people had. I didn't want to be alone. I wanted intimacy to be wonderful, but it wasn't. Being intimate, physically, just blew away my mental shields. I couldn't block out anything. The mental interference was enormous; all I could feel was *his* emotions, blotting out any physical enjoyment I might have felt. It wasn't very flattering, either." Her mouth quirked. "He wasn't overcome by fondness for me; all he wanted was sex.

And he was feeling proud of himself for daring to have sex with a weirdo psychic."

"The son of a bitch," Dane said softly.

She lifted one shoulder in a small shrug. "I *was* weird. I still am."

"Hell, no wonder you're skittish about sex. All you've ever seen is the ugly side of it; you've never had any romantic illusions, have you? You know about scoring, and about rape. You must think men are scum."

"No," she denied. "When you know what other people are feeling, the way I did, you know that couldn't be so. There are selfish, mean-spirited women just like there are nasty men. But when it came to sex, I couldn't close my mind and just feel. It wouldn't have been any different if I'd been madly in love with a wonderful guy who loved me just as much; I couldn't have enjoyed sex with all that mental static going on.

"I think I had accepted that I couldn't have any sort of romantic relationship," she continued. "I liked being alone, in my little cabin in the mountains. Dr. Ewell thought that moving into the cabin was good for me, a move toward normalizing my life. And it was; it was great. I worked with him on experiments and documentation, and occasionally helped find missing people, though the effort involved was such a strain that—well, you know what it's like. Once upon a time, before Gleen, I could direct the knowing. I could lock on to someone specific, and go into a vision. I can't control it at all now."

"Do you want it to be like before?"

"I never wanted to have another vision in my life," she murmured. "But if I don't have any choice about it, then yes, I'd like to be able to control them. This—this is like being ambushed." She was getting drowsy again, and her eyelids drooped.

"But except for the two visions, you haven't had any other episodes?"

She thought of the first night she had called him, and known what he was doing, what he would say, even as he answered the telephone. "There was one flash of clairvoyance, but it wasn't related to the murders, and hasn't happened again. It was just a second or two. I don't think of the visions as clairvoyant episodes; they're . . . different, more strongly grounded in emotion. Anyway—no. Nothing else."

"Good."

There was a wealth of dark satisfaction in his voice, a satisfaction she couldn't quite decipher. Then his warm hand covered her breast, and she knew, with an instinct that had nothing to do with her psychic abilities, and everything to do with being a woman. No longer sleepy, she tilted her head back on his arm to look at him.

"It seems to me that now is the perfect time to show you some of the pleasure of sex," Dane murmured. Those hazel eyes were blazingly intent, and deeply green. "You can't feel my emotions, so that takes care of one problem. If you were afraid of me, you wouldn't have been lying almost naked on my lap for half an hour, which takes care of the other problem. All you have to do is lie there and let me make you feel good."

She quivered, her gaze locked with his. Was now the time? Until Dane, she hadn't felt desire. Sex had been an experiment, a hope, and ultimately, a disappointment. She wasn't afraid of him, but rather that she would fail again. Loving him was still so new, so startling, that she didn't want to tarnish it. It was cowardly, but she would prefer to never try, and retain the frail hope that it might have been possible, than to try and fail. Might-have-been was a poor comfort, but better than nothing.

"I don't know," she said nervously. "What if—"

"Stop worrying about it," he interrupted. "Just lie back, close your eyes, and leave everything to me."

Easier said than done. Still she stared up at him with worried eyes, unable to decide yes or no. Too much had

happened to her for her to be able to make that move. She hated herself for being so weak, and tears began welling.

Dane gave her approximately two seconds, then settled the issue himself. He stroked down her body and beneath the waistband of her panties, tucking his hand into the notch between her thighs. Marlie cried out in surprise, automatically grabbing his wrist. Her thighs clamped tight around his hand. Her eyes were huge, eclipsing her wan face. But even as they stared at each other, hectic color warmed her cheeks.

"Do you trust me?" he asked in a calm voice, as if it weren't taking every bit of self-control he had to keep from rolling her beneath him and sinking into her, finding blessed relief for his throbbing erection.

She chewed her lower lip, and he almost groaned aloud at the provocation. "Well, yes."

"Then relax your legs. I'm not going to hurt you. As a matter of fact, I guarantee that you'll like it."

She managed a wobbly smile. "Guarantee, huh?"

"Absolutely." He bent his head and brushed a gentle kiss across her mouth.

Marlie quivered, caught on the twin prongs of cowardice. She was afraid to try and fail, and afraid that if she didn't trust him now, she might never have another chance. In the end, the second fear proved stronger. No matter what, she wanted to know what it was like to cradle Dane within her body, to feel his incredible strength as he drove into her, to give *him* pleasure if nothing else. He was determined to bring her to pleasure first, she knew, but she also knew that afterward it would be his turn. She wasn't agreeing to just heavy petting, but to the complete sex act.

She drew a deep, shaky breath. "Okay. As long as I have your personal guarantee."

"I'll put it in writing and have it notarized," he promised, and kissed her again.

She couldn't control the fine tremors that shook her entire body, but she took another deep breath and slowly parted

her thighs. He gently stroked the soft, closed folds, and Marlie released her death grip on his wrist. "Easy now," he whispered, then deftly opened her and penetrated her with one long finger.

She stiffened in his arms, her thighs locking together again in an effort to control his invading hand. It was useless, because there was nothing she could do to stop the slow probe of his finger inside her. Shock made her dizzy. Oh, God.

She wasn't dry, but she was far from being ready for penetration. The friction made his finger seem as big as a penis. She struggled briefly to contain the chaos of her rioting nerve endings, then collapsed against his chest in surrender.

"There, that's good," he crooned, and pushed another finger into her. Her hips arched, then subsided. She felt stretched, invaded, her body no longer under her control. Some dormant, primal instinct was stirring into life. Her inner muscles contracted gently in adjustment, and Dane's entire body shivered.

His voice was hoarse. "This is the most that I'm going to do to you, at least right now. You can relax because it's already happened. Am I hurting you?"

Yes. No. She hadn't realized it could feel like this. She was a little delirious with shock and pleasure, and shook her head, her hair cascading over his chest. She was stunned that her body was capable of such intense sensation.

"Then close your eyes, honey. Close your eyes and feel. Don't think, just feel."

Helplessly, she did. With her eyes shut, her concentration centered on her body and what was happening to it. Color swirled behind her eyelids. Heat surged through her, followed rapidly by a chill that wasn't really a chill, but rather a ripple of almost painful delight. Her skin felt too tight, too sensitive. Her nipples puckered and hardened, standing firmly upright.

His fingers reached deep inside her, rasping her delicate

inner tissues. Helplessly she arched her hips again, taking his touch deeper within. Her thighs fell open, giving him easier access. Her heart was thundering, and she felt as if she might fly apart. She clutched his shirt, her fingers digging into the flesh beneath as she tried to anchor herself against the storm that was buffeting her.

She heard him say something, but there was a roaring in her ears and she couldn't quite make out the words. The words weren't important; she could hear the fierce tenderness in his tone, and that was what she needed. His fingers slipped out of her, and she made a soft sound of distress, her hips rolling toward him. Swiftly he stripped her panties off and returned his hand to her body. This time she willingly parted her thighs, and felt the eager dampness between them. The intrusion, when it came, was exquisite relief, yet the relief lasted only a moment. The slow thrust of his fingers elicited a deep, powerful hunger, so that his touch wasn't an easing, but a need. Then his rough thumb searched upward in her soft folds and pressed on the small, tautly swelling nub at the top of her sex. Pure fire exploded through her nerves, and she gave a strained cry as she curled toward him.

He held her tightly against him, subduing her sensual struggles. He was talking to her, the words low and hoarse in her ear, encouraging her to greater heights while his strength kept her safely grounded. He continued to circle and rub with his thumb, tormenting the little nubbin, each touch making the fire burn hotter. A pulse began throbbing between her legs, beating in a rhythm she had never felt before. Passion was a brand, searing her flesh with its invisible mark.

"D-Dane!" It was a wail almost of anguish. He tilted her head back and set his mouth on hers, his tongue repeating the invasive movements of his fingers, the pressure hard and rough. She reveled in it, reaching up to cling to his heavy shoulders, offering her mouth more fully to him.

It built quickly, sensation spiraling into a tighter and

tighter coil, and suddenly it was too much. Her entire body clenched, then surged wildly as her climax rolled through her in waves. She shook in uncontrollable spasms, feeling as if she were flying apart. He held her close, letting her know that she wasn't alone in the tempest. She cried out in a thin, hoarse voice, and he muffled the cries with his own mouth.

The crest of sensation subsided, though small shock waves continued to ripple through her loins. She went limp, her face buried against his chest while she gasped for breath. He shifted her, then his muscles tensed beneath her and he got to his feet, holding her firmly in his arms. She gripped his shirt as he carried her swiftly into the bedroom and placed her on the bed. Her robe was hanging on her shoulders, and he pulled it completely away, then stood and began stripping off his own clothes.

He hadn't turned on the light, but the door was open, and light from the living room spilled across the bed. Marlie lay without moving, enveloped in a lassitude so complete that she thought she might never move again. In that quiet state of subconsciousness, with her physical senses so acute and her mental processes barely functioning, she could feel every slow, heavy beat of her heart as it moved blood through her veins. Her pulse throbbed in the tender places of her body.

With an effort, she lifted her heavy eyelids and watched him undress. His urgency was an almost palpable force, his movements swift and violent. In only seconds, his powerful form was bare. He crawled over her, his hard thighs pushing between hers and forcing them wide, then settled his heavy weight on her.

There was a wonderful stillness, a silence, both without and within. With incredible joy, and some trepidation, she felt the hardness of his genitals against the yielding softness of her own. He braced himself on one arm and reached between them with his other hand, guiding his shaft as he tensed his buttocks and slowly began pushing into her.

Marlie's breath tangled in her throat, and she felt herself

drowning in sensation again. She had felt stretched by his fingers probing her, but his thick sex filled her to the point of distress. Though she was damp, her delicate inner tissues were swollen by his previous attentions; her sheath was ultrasensitive, tightening convulsively on him as he inexorably thrust himself to the hilt. She gave a soft, panicked sound of discomfort that verged on real pain.

Dane paused, holding himself deep within her. His powerful body was shaking. "Are you okay?" His voice was hoarse, and barely audible.

She couldn't think what to say. She wasn't having any empathic interference; her attention was wholly focused on her body. But physically she wasn't certain she could bear it when he started thrusting. He was so big, and the slightest movement rasped along her inner nerve endings; the sensation hovered between ecstasy and pain. Her mind was a blank, and she couldn't find the words to give him the reassurance he wanted.

He was a man, not a saint. His male flesh was throbbing inside her. He held himself rigidly still for a tense moment while he waited for her answer, but when none came his control shattered. A rough sound burst from his throat and he began thrusting with heavy power, reaching deep into her. The impact shook her entire body. Now she knew her answer, and clung fiercely to him as his hips hammered. The sharp slap of their bodies coming together mingled with his harsh breathing, and her own soft moans.

She had wanted Dane, and she had wanted this. Tightly she shut her eyes, savoring every moment. She loved his roughness, the savagery of his hunger. She loved the helpless groans that escaped him, the heat and sweat as his body coiled and struck. She had always felt apart, an oddity, but with Dane she was simply, and purely, a woman. Nothing interfered with the moment; they were male and female, mating with fierce and uncomplicated passion. She wished it could go on forever.

It didn't, though. It couldn't, given the urgency of his

need. All too soon his rhythm quickened, and he reared back, pounding into her with heavy force. He pushed her legs high, lifting her ankles onto his shoulders. Gasping, she felt him getting even bigger and harder inside her. He gave a harsh cry, one last thrust, and began shuddering convulsively.

When he had stopped shaking, when the last small quake had rippled through him, she opened her arms, and he weakly let himself sink into them. His heavy weight crushed her into the mattress, but she was too tired to care. His heartbeat thudded slowly against her breast. His dark head, wet with sweat, rested beside hers on the pillow. His face was turned toward her, and his warm breath washed over her neck.

She stroked his back, loving the feel of his heated skin beneath her palms. He was becoming heavier as he drifted into sleep, but she didn't care. She was limp with utter contentment. Only heaven could be better than this, lying in the aftermath of lovemaking, the man she loved sleeping cradled in her body and her arms. She wanted time to stand still in a place where evil couldn't intrude.

It intruded with a sudden shrill beeping.

Dane reacted instantly, withdrawing from her and sitting up in the same fluid motion. He turned on the lamp and silenced his beeper, briefly glancing at the digital readout. Marlie lay frozen. Without a word he picked up the phone and punched in a number, holding the receiver cradled between his head and shoulder while he began putting on his rumpled clothes. "This is Hollister," he said tersely. He listened for a moment, then said, "I'll be there in ten minutes. Have you called Trammell? Never mind, I'll do it. Radio back to the patrol officer and tell him to make damn certain the scene is secured."

He depressed the button and got another dial tone. While he called the second number, Marlie got out of bed and fumbled for her robe. It was twisted, one of the arms turned inside out. Her hands were shaking, but she managed to

straighten the garment and wrap herself in it, pulling the belt tight. Dane sat down on the side of the bed and began putting on his shoes.

"We have a victim," he said quietly into the phone. "I'll meet you there." He didn't glance at Marlie. "It's 3311 Cypress Terrace."

Cypress. Her stomach knotted into a cold lump. She had known, but this dispelled the last faint doubt.

He hung up the phone and went into the living room, shrugging into his shirt as he walked. Marlie followed him, as silent as a ghost, and stood in the doorway watching as he slipped into his shoulder holster. He tucked the big pistol into place under his left arm.

She didn't approach him, and he didn't come to her. He paused by the front door and looked back at her. "Are you all right?" he asked, but there was remoteness in his eyes and his voice, his mind already on the job awaiting him.

"Sure," she said, burying the terror and pain and loneliness deep inside her. She couldn't allow her weakness to delay him.

"I'll be back when I can," he said, and left.

She stood until the sound of his car had died away, then steadily went to the front door and locked it. Next she cleaned up the remains of their pizza, and washed the few dishes that were dirty. When she went back into the living room, she saw her panties in the corner of the couch and picked them up, wadding them in her hand.

She was very tired, but sleep seemed impossible. The delight of the night had been destroyed by a return of horror. She couldn't allow herself to think of either right now. She sat down on the couch and quietly watched the minutes of the night tick away, as she held her own vigil.

13

LIGHTNING FLASHED IN THE DISTANCE, REVEALING THE UNDER-belly of low, purplish black clouds. It would rain again before morning. Dane drove automatically, clearing his mind of everything. He couldn't let himself think about Nadine Vinick, or the expectation might lead him to see similarities that weren't there. He couldn't think about Marlie, or his concentration would be completely shot. He tried not to anticipate anything about the scene he was about to see, tried not to remember how Marlie had described it. Again, he didn't want to prejudice himself. He had to see everything clearly.

It was still early enough that traffic was fairly heavy. Anxious to reach the exit, he tucked up too close behind a semitrailer. One of the retreads on the rig chose that moment to come apart, throwing up a big road gator that slapped into the front of his car. Cursing, he backed off to a safer distance, but the distraction helped, pulled his mind away from everything he was trying not to think about.

It took a little longer than ten minutes to reach 3311 Cypress Terrace. The street was cluttered with the usual assortment of official vehicles and sightseers. Dane got out of the car, studying the bystanders with acute interest, looking for one who seemed familiar. If the same guy had done both women, he might have been at the Vinick scene, too. Nothing; not one of the gawkers triggered a memory.

Cypress Terrace was in a slightly more upscale neighborhood than the Vinicks had lived in. The houses weren't bigger, but they were about ten years newer. There was a small, attached carport, and that was where the knot of uniforms had gathered, though one patrolman was guarding the front door, and he hoped another one was at the back.

Freddie Brown and her partner, Worley, were the detectives on call that weekend, and they were already there. Freddie detached herself from the group of patrolmen as soon as she saw him. "Hi, doll," she said, tucking her hand inside his arm and drawing him to a standstill. "There's no hurry. Talk to me for a minute."

If it had been anyone but Freddie, Dane would have shrugged him off. But it was Freddie, and this was her crime scene. She wouldn't have taken him to the side without a good reason. He looked down at her and lifted an eyebrow in question.

"Word is that you asked to be notified of any female stabbing fatality," she said.

He gave a brief nod, hoping she wasn't irritated about him horning in on one of her cases.

She patted his arm, reassuring him. "I figured you wouldn't have done that without a damn good reason, so I've held the scene for you. We'll consider it a birthday present."

"Held the scene?" he repeated, stunned. "You mean no one has gone in?"

"That's what I mean. The patrolman who found the body deserves a medal. He backed out as soon as he saw her,

didn't touch anything except the doorknob, and secured the area. It's probably the most pristine crime scene you'll ever get. Ivan's on the way."

"We'll wait for him," Dane decided. "Thanks, Freddie. How did a patrolman happen to find the body?"

She flipped to her notes. "The victim's name is Jacqueline Sheets, divorced, no children. Her ex-husband lives in Minnesota. She worked at one of the bigger law firms as a legal secretary, very good at her work. She had made plans to meet a friend for dinner, one of the other legal secretaries. When she didn't show, the friend tried to call, but there was no answer. Evidently Sheets was normally very punctual, and had recently had some medical problems, so the friend was concerned. She drove over here to check. Sheets's car is in the carport, there's a light on, and the television is blaring, but she can't get anyone to the door. She went to a neighbor's house and called 911. Patrol Officers Charles Marbach and Perry Palmer were nearby and got here before the emergency crew. They beat on the doors and couldn't get any response. Officer Marbach forced the lock on the front door, saw the victim immediately when he opened it, and stepped right back out." She closed the notebook. "The friend's name is Elizabeth Cline. She's sitting down in the carport. She caught a glimpse of the body and she's pretty rattled."

Another car added itself to the congestion. Dane glanced at it and identified Trammell. Freddie did the same, and looked back at Dane with a wry look. "Now, how about you tell me what's going on?"

"We want to look for similarities to the Vinick case," he said quietly. "We think it might be the same perp."

Her eyes widened, and a look of horror came over her freckled face as the implications hit home. "Oh, shit," she breathed. "It's even the same day of the week."

"Don't think I haven't noticed." He could just see the headlines about the Saturday Slasher. He wondered what sensational name the newspapers would apply if the time of

death was put before midnight, making it a Friday murder. The Friday Fucker?

Trammell joined them, resplendent in oatmeal linen slacks and a sky blue silk shirt. His hair was perfectly combed, his exotic face freshly shaved, and there wasn't a wrinkle in sight. Dane wondered how in the name of God he did it.

He brought Trammell up to date on what had happened so far. Freddie asked, "Do you want to question the friend?"

Dane shook his head. "This is your show. All we want is to see the scene."

"You don't have to wait for Ivan, you know."

"I know. I'd just like for him to get it as clean as possible."

"At a guess, I'd say he's never going to get one any cleaner." She patted both of them in that motherly way she had, and returned to the group in the carport.

"It's a house," Trammell said unnecessarily. "No cypress trees, but the address is Cypress Terrace. We were on the right track. It's going to be interesting to see if the television is one of the big-screen models, on a pedestal."

Dane put his hands in his pockets. "Do we really have any doubt?"

"I don't."

"I don't either. Damn it."

"I called the lieutenant. He should be here any time."

Ivan Schaffer arrived, in the crime scene van. He unfolded his long, lanky body from behind the steering wheel as Dane and Trammell walked to meet him.

Ivan wasn't in a good mood. He scowled at both of them. "I don't know why I had to personally handle this one. I have good people on duty. Why did Freddie insist that I be here?"

Evidently Freddie had sensed something unusual all the way around, bless her. Dane wondered if her husband would break his nose if he kissed her. "This one's special," he told Ivan, helping him unload his kits and equipment. "For one thing, the scene's untouched. You're the first person in."

Ivan halted. "You're shitting me." His eyes began to gleam. "That doesn't happen."

"It's happening this time. Don't expect it again in your lifetime."

"What do I look like, an optimist? Okay, what's the second thing?"

Trammell was coolly studying all the murmuring bystanders. "The second thing is, we think it was done by the same guy who did Nadine Vinick."

"Ah, jeez." Ivan sighed and shook his head. "God, I wish you hadn't told me that. That's big trouble, but I guess you already know that."

"We'd thought about it. Is this all your stuff?"

"Yeah, that's it. Okay, let's see what we have."

Dane called Officer Marbach to go in with them. A patrolman who had done that good a job deserved to be included. Marbach was young, not long out of training, and was pale under his tan. But he was steady as he detailed his actions for them, even telling them the body's approximate distance from the front door.

"Can the body be seen from the street when we open the door?" Freddie asked, she and Worley having joined them.

Marbach shook his head. "There's a little entry, with the living room to the right. I had taken one step in before I saw her."

"Okay. Ivan, it's your show."

Ivan opened the door and went in. The rest of them followed, but stopped in the small entry hall and shut the door behind them. The television, tuned to an all-movie channel, was currently showing a Fred-and-Ginger. It was too loud, as if Jacqueline Sheets had been a little hard of hearing. Either that, or the sound had been turned up to drown out her screams. Ivan punched the power button and the screen went to black, filling the room with blessed silence. Dane and Trammell, standing in the entry, looked at the television. It was a thirty-five-incher, very modern and sleek, set on a pedestal.

None of them said anything. Ivan silently began his collection ritual.

From their viewpoint, only the upper half of the body was visible. She was nude, and her torso looked as if it had been savaged by a wild animal. The pattern of blood completely circled the couch, splattering over walls and carpet, and Dane remembered the odd phrase Marlie had used: *around and around the mulberry bush.* But it hadn't been a bush, it had been the couch. Why had she used those words? Had they been something the killer had said, or thought? Had the bastard been *amused* by Jacqueline Sheets's fight for her life?

The door opened behind them and Lieutenant Bonness came in. He looked at the gore and turned white. "Oh, Jesus." The first scene had been more gruesome, but they had looked at it as a onetime deal, unconnected to anything else. This time, however, they knew better. Now they were looking at it as the work of a madman who would do this again and again, murdering innocent women and devastating the lives of their families and friends, until they could stop him. And they knew that the odds weren't in their favor; serial killers were notoriously difficult to apprehend.

But this time, Dane thought grimly, they had something the killer couldn't have anticipated. They had Marlie.

Worley said, "Dane, you and Trammell have a look around. You know what you're looking for."

"That's why you and Freddie should do it," Trammell said. His thoughts had run the same as Dane's, but then they almost always did. "Just tell us what you find, and then we'll have a look ourselves."

Worley nodded. He and Freddie briskly began their methodical search of the house. Ivan summoned the fingerprint team, and they began dusting every hard surface with black powder. Soon the house was crowded with people, most of them standing about, some of them actually working. Eventually Jacqueline Sheets's body was bagged and removed. Dane could hear the clamor of reporters' voices

outside, see the glare of television lights. They wouldn't be able to keep the lid on it much longer, but he thought nothing much would be made of a second stabbing within a week. If there was a third one, though, no reporter worth his or her salt would let it pass as coincidence. Even if there were no similarities in the cases, there would be enough interest to warrant a "special segment," whatever the hell that was.

Bonness took Dane and Trammell aside. "If it looks like the same guy did it—"

"He did," Dane said.

"Everything's just the way Marlie described it," Trammell added. "Even the type of television set."

"Any way she could have had any prior knowledge? I know, I know," Bonness said, holding up his hands. "I was the one who originally thought she could help us, and you guys were the ones who thought she was an accessory, but this is a question that needs to be asked."

"No," Dane said. "We established that there was no way she could have been at the crime scene of the first murder, and I was with her last night. She called me when the vision started, and I drove straight to her house."

"Okay. I want to see everyone in my office tomorrow morning at ten. We'll go over what we have, anything new that Ivan's found, set up a task force. I'll notify the chief, and he can decide when and how much to tell city hall."

"I hope he holds off," Dane said. "Information leaks out of city hall like it's a damn sieve."

Bonness looked unhappy. "This isn't something he can keep to himself. It would cost him his job if the media break the story and he hasn't kept the head honchos informed."

"Then ask him if he can give us a couple of days, at least. Both of the murders have been on Friday night or early Saturday morning, so if the pattern holds, the guy won't hit again for almost another week. The longer we can work without him knowing that we're on to him, the better chance we have of catching him."

"I'll talk to him," was all Bonness would promise. Dane really hadn't expected any more than that.

Worley and Freddie joined them. "The murder weapon was a kitchen knife, probably belonging to the victim," Worley reported. "It matches others in the kitchen. He entered through the window in the guest bedroom, by cutting the screen."

"It rained last night," Dane said. "Any footprints beneath the window?"

Freddie shook her head. "Nothing. He was very careful."

"Or he got in before it started raining, and waited in the bedroom," Trammell suggested.

The idea made Freddie blanch. "God, that gives me the queasies, thinking of him in the house with her for hours, and her not knowing it."

"What about afterward?" Officer Marbach asked. He blushed a little when they all turned to look at him. "I mean, it should have been raining when he left. Wouldn't he have been likely to leave footprints then?"

"Only if he exited the same way he entered," Dane said. "And there was no reason for him to. All he had to do was walk out the door, making him much less conspicuous if anyone happened to see him, which I doubt. The sidewalk and driveway are concrete; no prints."

"She was evidently wearing pajamas at the time of the attack," Freddie continued, looking at her notes. "We found a pair with blood on them, dropped into the laundry basket. We're having the blood typed to make sure it's the victim's."

"How about a husband or boyfriend?" Bonness asked.

"Nope. According to her friend outside, there's an ex-husband who lives in Minnesota, but they've been divorced for twenty years, and it's been almost that long since Sheets had any contact with him. No current boyfriend, either. Okay, guys, level with me: Does this sound like the same guy did both women?"

"Afraid so," Dane replied. "Did Sheets frequent bars, gyms, anything where she'd be in contact with a lot of men?"

"I don't know. We hadn't gotten that far in questioning the friend when you guys got here. Why don't you talk to her while we finish up in here? We're all going to be pooling our notes, anyway," Worley suggested. From his tone, he would have been glad to hand the entire investigation over to Dane and Trammell.

A low wall of cement blocks, two high, enclosed the carport on the open side. Elizabeth Cline was sitting on the wall, huddled in on herself, staring numbly at the crowd of policemen milling around. She was a tall, sleek blonde, with her hair cut short in a feathery cap, and long earrings that dangled almost to her shoulders. Despite the earrings, she wasn't togged out in party clothes; she was wearing sandals, yellow leggings, and a long white tunic with a gaudy yellow and purple parrot on the front. She wore several rings, Dane noticed, but none of them was a wedding band.

He sat down beside her on the block wall, and Trammell, more aloof as always, leaned against Sheets's car a couple of feet away.

"Are you Elizabeth Cline?" Dane asked, just to make certain.

She gave him a vaguely startled look, as if she hadn't noticed him sitting beside her. "Yes. Who are you?"

"Detective Hollister." He indicated Trammell. "And Detective Trammell."

"It's nice to meet you," she said politely, then a horrified look edged into her eyes. "Oh, God, how can I say that? It *isn't* nice to meet you. It's because of Jackie that you're here—"

"Yes, ma'am, it is. I'm sorry, I know it was a shock for you. Would you mind answering a few more questions for us?"

"I've already talked to those other two detectives."

"I know, ma'am. But we thought of a couple of other things, and anything you can tell us will help us find her killer."

She inhaled shakily. She was shivering, and hugging her

arms. It was a warm, muggy night, but shock was getting to her. Dane wasn't wearing a jacket to put around her, so he asked a patrolman standing nearby to get a blanket. A few minutes later a blanket was produced, and he put it about her shoulders.

"Thanks," she said, huddling gratefully into the folds.

"You're welcome." His instincts were to put his arm around her and comfort her, but he felt constrained and settled for patting her on the back. The only woman he could hold now was Marlie; somehow, in taking her, he had forever set himself apart from other women. He was uneasily aware of the change but pushed it beneath his consciousness, to be considered later when he had the time.

"You told Detective Brown that Ms. Sheets didn't have a current boyfriend. Had she recently broken up with someone, or maybe had a casual date or two?"

She shook her head. "No."

"No one? Any steady boyfriends at all since her divorce?"

Elizabeth gathered herself enough to lift her head and give him a shaky, wintry smile. "Sure." The one word was bitter. "She had a twelve-year affair with one of the attorneys in the firm. He told her they'd be married when he divorced his wife, but the time wasn't right while he was building his career. Then the time was right, he got his divorce, and promptly married a twenty-three-year-old trophy wife. Jackie was devastated, but she'd been with the firm for a long time and couldn't afford to start over. He wanted to continue the affair, but Jackie broke it off, very quietly. At least he didn't try to get her fired, but I don't guess there was any reason for it. Their affair wasn't a secret; everyone in the office knew about it."

"When was this?"

"Let's see. About four years ago, I guess."

"Who has she dated since then?"

"I don't know that she's dated at all. Maybe once or twice, right after the affair ended, but I know she hasn't gone out with anyone for at least a year. She started having health

problems, and she didn't feel well enough for the dating scene. We would eat dinner out every week or so; it helped keep her spirits up."

"What kind of health problems?"

"Several things. She had really bad endometriosis, and about a year ago finally had a hysterectomy. A stomach ulcer, high blood pressure. Nothing life-threatening, but everything seemed to hit at once, and it made her depressed. Lately she'd fainted a couple of times. That was why I was so worried when she didn't show up at the restaurant on time."

They had hit a dead end on ex-boyfriends, but Dane hadn't really expected anything different. He was just covering all the bases. "Had she mentioned anyone she'd met recently? Did she get into an argument with anyone, or had she mentioned anyone following her?"

Elizabeth shook her head. "No, Jackie was very even-tempered, got along with everyone. She didn't even lose her temper when David married his little bimbo. Actually, the closest she came to getting angry recently was when a new silk blouse came apart at the seams the first time she washed it. Jackie loved clothes, and was very particular about them."

"Did she go any place regularly, where she might have met someone?"

"Not unless it was the grocery store."

"Everyone has a routine," Dane insisted gently. They had to discover how the killer picked his victims. Nadine Vinick and Jackie Sheets had had something in common, something that had brought them to the killer's attention. They had lived in different neighborhoods, so it had to be something else, and putting his finger on that something else was vital. "Did she have her hair done regularly, go to the library, anything like that?"

"Jackie had beautiful red hair. She got it trimmed every few weeks, at a little salon close to the office. The Hairport. The stylist's name is Kathy, I think. Maybe Kathleen, or Katherine. Something like that. The library? No, Jackie

wasn't much of a reader. She loved movies; she rented a lot of movies."

"Where did she rent them?"

"At the supermarket. She said they have a nice video selection, and it saved making an extra stop."

"Which supermarket did she shop at?"

"Phillips, about a mile from here."

A neighborhood market, not one where Nadine Vinick would have shopped. But Dane made notes of everything; they wouldn't know exactly what they had until they had compared every detail with the Vinick case.

"What about you?" he asked. "Are you married?"

"Widowed. Seven years ago. Jackie helped me through a rough time, and that's when we became close friends. We were friendly before that, you know, working in the same office for as long as we had, but that's when I really got to know her. She was—she was a really great friend." Tears slipped down Elizabeth's cheeks.

Dane patted her some more, aware of and ignoring Trammell's enigmatic gaze. Trammell hadn't spoken once, leaving all the questioning to him. Occasionally he did that, when for some reason he decided Dane would have better luck getting answers.

"I'm sorry," Elizabeth said, still weeping. "I know I haven't been able to help."

"But you did," Dane assured her. "You helped us eliminate several things, so we know where to concentrate and won't waste our time on dead ends." Basically it was a lie; all they had was dead ends. But she needed all the comfort she could get, lie or not.

"Do I need to come down to the station or anything? Funny," she said, wiping her eyes and trying a pathetic smile. "I know how law works on the finished end, the courthouse end, but nothing about the raw stages."

"No, there's no need for you to come to the station," he said, soothing her. "Does Detective Brown have your address and phone number?"

"I think so. Yes, I remember telling her."

"Then I don't see why you can't go home, if you like. Do you want me to have someone drive you? Or call someone, a friend or relative, to stay with you tonight?"

She looked around vaguely. "I can't leave my car here."

"If you want someone to drive you, I'll get a patrolman to drive your car and another one to follow, to bring him back. Okay?"

But she didn't seem able to make a decision, still too stunned and devastated to think clearly. Dane made the decision for her, getting her to her feet, calling a patrolman over and arranging for her to be taken home, giving instructions for her to call a friend or neighbor to stay with her that night. She nodded as docilely as a child taking homework instructions.

"I have a niece nearby," she said. "I'll call her." And she looked at him as if asking for his permission to call the niece instead of a friend. He patted her and told her that was fine, and sent her off with the patrolman, who had taken his cue from Dane and treated her as gently as he would a lost child.

When Dane turned around, Trammell was still looking as enigmatic as a cat.

"What?" he demanded testily.

Trammell raised his eyebrows. "I didn't say anything."

"You're thinking something, though. You've got that shit-eating smirk on your face."

"Why would anyone smirk while they eat shit?" Trammell asked rhetorically.

He loved the man like a brother, but honest to God, sometimes Dane felt like messing up that pretty face. But when Trammell was in one of his moods, nothing could pry information out of him. Dane thought about giving him a couple of beers to loosen his tongue, then decided to leave well enough alone. He'd save the beer for special occasions.

There was nothing left to do but assist Freddie and Worley in tying up the loose ends: make certain the trash had been sacked up, to be gone through later; search the house for

personal papers such as a diary, telephone and address books, life insurance policies. In death, Jackie Sheets would lose all of her privacy. They would go through her closets and her cabinets, in search of that one snippet of coincidence and fate that linked her to Nadine Vinick. Whatever the two women had had in common was the key to the killer. If poor Ansel Vinick hadn't killed himself, he could have helped them pinpoint the crucial link, and maybe found a reason for living in helping to find his wife's killer. In Dane's opinion, the bumper sticker "Shit happens" should have the word "frequently" tacked on to the end of it.

Ivan had taken his meager findings back to the lab to begin analyzing them; the medical examiner's office had Jackie Sheets's body, though there was little to be added other than the approximate time of death. They could have saved the ME the time and trouble; Dane knew the time of death, because Marlie had called him.

Worry had settled new lines in the lieutenant's face as he glumly surveyed the outline on the floor where Sheets had lain. "Everyone be in my office at ten tomorrow morning," he said. "For now, go home and get some sleep."

Dane glanced at his watch. It was almost one, and he was suddenly aware that he hadn't had much sleep the night before.

"Are you going back to Marlie's?" Trammell asked.

He wanted to; God, did he want to. "No, I won't disturb her," he said. "She'll be asleep."

"You think so?"

He remembered the way she had looked when he'd left, that haunted expression back in her drawn face. He hadn't even kissed her, he realized. His mind had already been on the murder scene, and he had totally blocked Marlie out. He had just made love to her, had gotten off her warm body to answer the beeper's summons, and he had walked out without kissing her. "Damn," he said tiredly.

Trammell said, "See you in the morning," and got in his

car. Grace Roeg would probably still be waiting, Dane thought. She was a cop, too; she would understand that he had had to leave suddenly. But Marlie wasn't a cop; she was a woman who had been too solitary her entire life, a woman who had borne enough pain for ten lifetimes. She was strong, incredibly so; she hadn't cracked, but she wore the scars, both physically and mentally. It had taken guts for her to let him make love to her, and what had he done? Their first time, and he had turned it into a slam-bam; he hadn't even said "thank you."

If he could have reached it, he'd have kicked his own ass.

She wouldn't be asleep; she would be sitting on the couch, still and quiet, waiting for his return. He couldn't protect her by keeping her in the dark, because she knew more than he did. She was an eyewitness, inside the killer, watching through his eyes as he gleefully hacked and slashed.

Dane drove quickly, the streets much emptier now. It began raining, the slow-moving storm finally reaching the city. He felt as if it were a replay of Friday night, when he had hurried through the wet streets to reach Marlie.

As he had expected, there was a light on in the living room when he pulled into the driveway and killed the motor. Before he could get out of the car, she had opened the front door and was standing there, silhouetted against the light, waiting for him.

She was still wearing the thin robe, and he could see the outline of her body through the fabric. He ran through the rain and leaped up the two shallow steps onto the porch. She didn't say anything, just stepped back to let him in. She didn't have to ask what they had found, because she knew.

She was tired, her face wan, her eyes dark-circled. In those eyes was a weariness that went far beyond the physical, and the subtle air of distance had settled around her again.

He meant to offer comfort, if she would accept it. He meant to take care of her, give her the healing unconsciousness of sleep. She could relax, knowing that she was secure.

He meant to hold her all night long, offering her the primitive animal comfort of his closeness.

That was what he meant to do. But as they silently faced each other, with the rain pattering outside in rhythm to his suddenly racing heart, he forgot about all the noble things he meant to do. He had claimed her only a few hours before, making her his in the physical possession of mating, but they had been interrupted. The act had been completed, but the seal of the flesh hadn't been. True intimacy wasn't found in penetration and climax, but in the quiet time afterward, in the small ways that two lives meshed. He had left that undone, and his instincts were too primal and sure for him to ignore it.

He shut the door and locked it, without once looking away from her. Then, without haste, he picked her up and carried her into the bedroom, pausing on the way to turn off the lamp.

There were no angry recriminations from her, no reluctance. She lay quietly where he had placed her on the bed, waiting while he impatiently threw off his clothes. He removed the robe from her for the second time that night. Her naked body gleamed dimly in the darkness; he felt the delicious softness of her beneath him, felt her thighs opening to embrace him. He held her head between his palms and kissed her with slow hunger as he probed, found the moist yielding of her entrance, and pushed within. The heat and tightness of her enfolded him, making his shaft throb so violently that he groaned into her mouth.

"Make me forget," she pleaded, whispering in broken desperation. He forced his way in to the hilt, holding her as she arched beneath him in an effort to accommodate her body to his size and force. She made a hot little whimpering sound, and her tight nipples stabbed against his chest.

He could give her only the forgetfulness of passion, fill her senses with his body, and the pleasure he could give her. He couldn't make the night go away, but he could turn the

darkness into their own private sanctuary. He could rein in his own unruly passion and make certain she was with him this time, and afterward, lying in the warm silence, he could hold her so that, all through the night, she could feel his warmth and the steady beat of his heart and know that she wasn't alone.

14

Marlie stirred and came abruptly awake, startled by the realization that there was someone in the bed with her. She knew who he was, recalled everything, but still there was that first jarring moment when consciousness adjusted to reality. He had slept with her the night before last, too, but she hadn't been aware of it. This was the first time that she had awakened with a very hard, very warm man lying close beside her, one heavy arm thrown across her waist and anchoring her to the bed. It was a good thing he was holding her, she reflected, since he took up most of the space, and she might well have fallen off if he hadn't held her pinned.

She turned her head to look at him, enchanted by the novelty of having a naked man in her bed, of having *Dane* naked in her bed. She savored the moment, a small, quiet oasis of happiness.

The soft morning light, filtered through a light rain, gleamed on the curve of his shoulder. She lightly cupped her hand on the ball of the joint, feeling the cool resilience of his

flesh, the relaxed power of the muscle beneath her palm. He stirred at her touch, tucking her more closely into the curve of his body before lapsing with a grunt back into his morning dreams.

He radiated heat like the healthy animal he was, despite the surface coolness of his skin. She felt as warm and cozy as if the bedcovers were tucked around her, rather than lying in a tangled heap on the floor.

In all her life, she had never been physically demonstrative because the mental barriers had always gotten in the way. But the psychic damage she had suffered at Gleen's hands had demolished those barriers, and last night Dane had forcefully shown her, several times, that now she could give herself over to the physical.

She felt tremulous with joy at this new world he had opened up, a world she had thought permanently closed to her. She loved him, and he had claimed her body, and given her his own. She had always been alone in the darkness, but not last night, and she had understood what he had been saying with his body, his hunger. There was death, yes, but life marched hand in hand with it. There was evil out there, but between the two of them there had been pleasure, a basic and joyful celebration of life and flesh. She had always protected herself from the world, set apart from birth by her own abilities, while he had reveled in and dominated the hot, pulsing currents. He was fierce and vital in his intensity, meeting life on its own terms and coming out the victor. Last night, with Dane, she had broken free of her self-imposed restrictions.

And now this big bruiser was lying totally, blissfully naked in her bed. She had the freedom of his powerful body, to explore and excite as she wished. She felt like a child at an amusement park, an adventurer opening the sealed door to a room of treasure. There was so much to see and do, and she quivered with excitement at the possibilities. To totally give in to the needs of her body, to find out exactly what those needs *were*—she almost couldn't bear it.

She smoothed her hand over his chest, delighting in the roughness of the thick, curly hair under her palm. Beneath the hair was a rock-solid layer of muscle, hard and warm. She found his nipples, flat brown circles with tiny points in the middle, points that hardened when she touched them. Fascinated, she rubbed her fingertip over one of the little points and watched chills roughen his skin.

A deep rumble in his chest made her look up. He was awake, the hazel eyes heavy-lidded and sleepy. Down below, his sex twitched and stretched, prodding her in the stomach. "Like what you see?" His early morning voice was like distant thunder, rough and barely audible.

"Very much." Her own voice was raspier than usual, too.

He rolled over onto his back, spreading his arms and legs wide. "Then take a good look."

The temptation was irresistible. Though they had made love several times, it had been in the dark. She hadn't been able to see her lover's body, only to feel him. Now that he had given her permission, there was no way she could deny her fascination. She got to her knees, unconscious and unheeding of her own nudity, intent on exploring this new and wondrous territory.

She put both hands on his chest and circled his nipples with her thumbs, watching in delight as they hardened again. She looked up at him, eyes luminous with discovery. "You like that, too."

He swallowed. He was breathing roughly, his deep chest expanding with the force of it. "Yeah. A lot."

His heart almost stopped at the luminous smile of discovery she gave him.

She turned her attention back to him, leaning down and circling a nipple with her tongue, then gently sucking at it. He stifled a groan as a shudder racked through him. She moved her attention to the other nipple, giving it the same tender treatment while her hands slipped around his rib cage, molding the shape and feel of him, learning the textures of his skin.

Dane sucked in his breath, digging his fingers into the mattress as he tried to control himself. Oh, God, he wanted to touch her so much, he could barely stand it. He had never felt anything as excruciatingly gentle, as exquisitely painful, as her slow exploration of his body, and he had the feeling that it was going to get much worse.

She ran her hands up to the tufts of hair under his arms, enjoying the silkiness that seemed so incongruous on so tough a man. His skin, in those hidden, protected areas, was as sleek as her own.

The crisp mat of hair on his chest narrowed to a thin line that ran down the center of his belly, circled his tight navel, then flared again at his loins. She followed the line of hair with one finger, down, down, until her hand brushed his straining erection. She paused, then turned her hand and curled her fingers around him. He gave a shaky groan, and his legs shifted restlessly, then he was still again. Marlie lifted her other hand and held him between her palms, examining him with absorbed fascination. She was entranced by the contrasts, the coolness that contained intense heat, the soft skin lying over iron hardness. He was very thick, and pulsing with arousal. She thought of taking that thickness into her body, and grew excited; she could hear herself breathing, in soft, rapid pants. Her blood was singing through her veins and she felt too warm, her skin too tight.

The sheer masculinity of him was beautiful. She cupped his heavy testicles in her hands, very gently, and his powerful body arched. He shook from head to toe. "Lord have mercy," he said in a strangled tone.

"The Lord?" she asked softly. "Or me?" The sense of her own feminine power over him was heady.

"You. Or both. I don't care."

Her secret places were damp and swollen, throbbing with need. Sex, even last night with Dane, had always been something that had been done *to* her. She wanted, needed, to be in control this time of her own body, and his. She wanted to give pleasure as well as seek it. She wanted the

warm sexual confidence of a woman who had no fears, no restraints. She was tired of boundaries.

With a sigh like a soft spring breeze she mounted him, straddling his hips and holding his shaft steady as she positioned it and slowly sank down. She was sore; she bit her lip at the discomfort of her tender flesh stretching to admit him. But there was also the wonder of feeling that warmth and hardness probing deeper inside her as she slowly took him, and lingered over the taking, inch by slow inch. The sensation was so exquisite that she lifted herself almost completely off him and began again. And again.

Dane's fists knotted in the sheets, and sweat popped out on his forehead. She was only taking about half of him before sliding upward again, and he thought he was going to go howling mad for sure. He didn't dare touch her, because if he did, he would lose control. This was her show, all the way. Her face was solemn, dreamy, absorbed as she explored the pleasure she could take from his body. She was concentrating on nothing except her physical sensations as she slid up and down on him, but he didn't feel left out. Watching her learn about her own sensuality was as much a turn-on as anything in his life had been, and the way she was doing it was killing him with pleasure.

Marlie closed her eyes against the almost overwhelming surge of passion and pleasure. All that she had learned the night before was as nothing compared to this; now her body knew the sublime ecstasy awaiting, and enjoyed as well every inch of the path leading up to it. She fought against the need to rush to the finish. She wanted to savor every delicious explosion of sensation deep inside her as she lifted herself from him, feeling the drag of his sex on her acutely sensitive tissues, followed by that indescribable moment of deepening penetration as she took him again. She moaned aloud, sensing the approach of climax drawing inexorably nearer. *Not yet,* she thought dimly. She was enjoying this too much. There was no hurry.

Dane writhed on the sheet. Oh, God, if she didn't hurry,

he was going to die. The shallow way she was riding him was working the swollen head of his shaft with almost ceaseless pressure. A harsh groan tore from his chest. He wanted to thrust, deep, needed to thrust more than he had ever needed anything, but he refused to let himself do so. There would be times when his needs would take precedence. This time, however, was Marlie's. He shivered with the intensity of the pleasure. He thought his heart was going to explode; he knew for damn sure his cock was.

She was very wet now, and her rhythm had become faster. The fitted sheet came loose as he pulled at it. He arched, his body so rigid that his weight was supported only on his heels and his shoulders. A mist swam in front of his eyes.

"Marlie." The word was guttural, his voice almost unrecognizable. Despite himself, he was pleading. "Deeper . . . please. Deeper. Take . . . the rest . . . of it."

If she heard him, she didn't respond. She was lost in her own sensual whirlpool, unheeding of everything else. Her hands were braced on his chest, her eyes were closed. Her hips rocked. A breathless sob broke from her lips, and with a convulsive shudder she went down into the swirling depths, her entire body given over to the pleasure racking it.

The rhythmic tightening of her inner muscles on him blasted the last shred of his control to smithereens. With a harsh, explosive growl he released his death grip on the sheet and grabbed her surging hips, forcing her downward as his own hips slammed upward, pushing his full length into her. He came with the first stroke, his orgasm bursting from him in a powerful stream as he convulsed beneath her, clamping her to him with ruthless, implacable hands, until it was over for both of them and she lay limply on his chest. Their heartbeats pounded together, shaking them from within.

He felt as if he would never have the strength to move again. She felt as if she were warm wax, melted and poured over him. Neither of them could bear to separate their bodies.

He trailed his hand up the slender length of her spine,

feeling the way she was put together. He didn't know how many women he had made love to in his lifetime, but he did know that the way he had felt then was nothing compared to how he felt now. There had been no other woman like Marlie; everything about her was new. He had never before been so fascinated by the details of a woman's body, soft and fragrantly feminine. He had never before concentrated so intensely on a woman, so that he saw every flicker of expression and read every nuance of emotion. From the very beginning he had been aware of her slightest move, his body and senses attuned to her. He couldn't even remember the name of his last lover; there was only Marlie.

But as much as he wanted to spend the rest of the day right where he was, the red digital numbers of the clock beside the bed continued to chronicle the silent, relentless stream of time. It was eight-fifteen. He had to shower and shave, eat breakfast, and be downtown at ten.

"I have to go," he murmured.

She didn't lift her head from his chest. He continued to stroke her spine. "Where?"

"To the station. We have a meeting with the lieutenant at ten."

She didn't tense, but he felt the stillness that came over her. "About last night?"

"Yeah. It was him, all right."

"I know." She paused. "What happens now?"

"We put together all the details we have from both cases, try to find what the victims had in common. Set up a task force to concentrate on this guy. Maybe call in the FBI."

She said steadily, "If you need me to go over it again, I will."

He knew what that offer could cost her, and he knew she had already braced herself to pay it. She would be met with ridicule, disbelief, and suspicion; that was what she had gotten from him, even though he had been so attracted to her, he could barely think straight. She knew what she was letting herself in for, and was willing to do it anyway.

He squeezed her. "I don't want to put you through that."

"But you will if you have to."

"Yes."

To his relief, her feelings weren't hurt. She accepted the necessity. He smoothed her hair. "There's something I need to tell you," he said reluctantly. "I don't want you to read about it in the papers, or see it on the news."

She waited, knowing that it was going to be bad. Dane wished that he didn't have to tell her, but he'd put it off as long as possible. Yesterday she hadn't been in any shape to watch the news, but today was a different story. He didn't want her to be alone when she found out.

"Ansel Vinick killed himself Friday night."

The breath she had been holding leaked out in a sigh. So much pain, she thought sadly.

"That's three," she said. "In one week, he's killed three people."

"We'll catch him," Dane assured her, though they both knew it was far from a sure thing. He looked at the clock again. Eight-twenty.

He rolled with her until he was on top, then gently disconnected their bodies. "Want to shower with me?"

She looked at the clock, too. "No, I'll cook breakfast. It'll be ready when you're finished."

"Okay. Thanks, honey."

Amused at how quickly he had accepted her offer to cook for him, she dressed and went into the kitchen. She usually ate simply, cereal and fruit, but a man his size would probably need more than that. She put on a pot of coffee, then hauled out her seldom-used waffle iron. While it was heating she stirred up the batter from a package mix. How much would he eat? She couldn't finish one, but suspected he could put two or even three away with no trouble.

She could hear the shower running, hear him whistling. The coffee maker was hissing and popping in the manner peculiar to coffee makers. She was cooking his breakfast. The domesticity of it stunned her, and her arms dropped to

her sides. She had never cooked breakfast, cooked *any* meal, for another person in her life.

For six years she had worked to build a safe, secure, ordinary, and solitary life. In one week, though, her life had been totally changed, and she was still struggling to find her balance. Safe, secure, and ordinary had gone by the wayside; now, evidently, her solitude was also gone. It wasn't something she had chafed against; she had enjoyed being able to do things at her own pace, to sit up all night reading if she chose, to eat whatever she desired at the moment. Before Gleen, she had very much wanted a relationship, marriage, children. After Gleen, however, she had wanted only to be left in peace.

Instead, there was a man in her shower. Not just any man, but Dane Hollister: grim, rough, frighteningly intense, a police detective who never went anywhere unarmed—and who was the most generous man she'd ever met. He gave of himself in a way she'd never expected, given the hostility of their first few encounters. He had come to her without hesitation, after her despairing cry for help on Friday night, and since then she had seen only tenderness in him. She had been attracted to him before, but had fallen in love with him because of his unhesitating generosity. She had needed him, so he had been there. It was as simple as that.

She heard the shower cut off, then water running in the basin as he shaved. She finished the preparations for breakfast: a dusting of powdered sugar on the waffles, fresh strawberries, and syrup that she had heated in the micro-wave. She was pouring the coffee when he came into the kitchen. He wore only a pair of pants, and she went weak in the knees at the sight of that broad, muscular chest. His hair was damp and his face was freshly scraped, with two small nicks decorating his jaw. She inhaled deeply, drawing in his moist, soapy, slightly musky male scent.

He smiled when he saw the meal awaiting him. "Waffles," he said appreciatively. "I was expecting cereal."

She laughed. "That's what I usually eat."

"I usually grab a doughnut, or a fast-food biscuit." He sat down and began eating with obvious relish.

She clicked her tongue reprovingly. "All that fat and cholesterol."

"That's what Trammell says."

"How long have you been partners?" She hadn't been around Trammell much, but she had liked him. He reminded her of a panther, sleek and exotic, with the same kind of supple, dangerous strength.

"Nine years. We were on patrol together before we made detective, which we did at the same time." Dane set to work on the waffles with obvious zeal.

"That's longer than a lot of marriages last."

He grinned. "Yeah, but if I'd had to sleep with him, it wouldn't have lasted a day."

"Have you ever been married?" She bit her lip as soon as the question was out. Her own privacy had been at such a premium for most of her life that she seldom asked any personal question. "Never mind. Forget I asked."

"Why?" He shrugged. "I don't care if you ask. I've never been married, never been engaged." He cleared his throat, evidently feeling that called for some explanation. "But I'm heterosexual."

"I noticed," she said dryly.

He grinned, his hazel gaze moving warmly over her. "For the record, I'm thirty-four. My folks live in Fort Lauderdale, and I have three brothers and two sisters, all of whom are married and have contributed to the population growth. Between the five of them, I have eighteen nieces and nephews, ranging in age from two to nineteen. When we all get together for holidays, it's a zoo. All of them live in Florida, though we're scattered all over the state. There are also the uncles and aunts and cousins, but we won't go into them." He watched her carefully as he outlined his large family, knowing that someone who had lived as Marlie had might find even the thought of all those relatives alarming. He had never before wanted to include any of his women

200

friends in his private life, but everything was different with her. He hadn't yet decided *how* it was different, but he accepted that it *was*.

Marlie tried to imagine that kind of extended family, but couldn't. She had always been forced to keep relationships of any kind at a minimum, and though in the past six years that limitation hadn't been necessary, still she had clung to it, reluctant to let herself be vulnerable in any way.

"My mother died in a fire when I was three," she said. "Lightning struck our house. I don't remember anything about it except this loud crack, louder than anything you can imagine, and even the air seemed to dissolve. A white light blotted out everything. A neighbor got me out of the house, and I was only slightly burned. My mother was in the part of the house that took the direct hit."

"Thunderstorms must make you nervous," he commented.

"They should, but they don't. I've never been frightened of them, not even immediately afterwards." She had had all of her waffle that she wanted, so she laid her fork down and picked up her coffee cup. "Lightning does some funny things. Dr. Ewell theorized that the enormous jolt of electricity somehow altered or enhanced my normal mental processes, making me more sensitive to the electrical energy given off by others. I was supposedly normal before, but afterward I became difficult, easily upset."

"Maybe because you'd lost your mother."

"Maybe. Who knows? I could have had the ability before, but simply wasn't old enough to make myself understood. From what I was told, my mother was a quiet, serene sort of person, so maybe her presence kept me calm. At any rate, my father had a difficult time trying to raise me. The more frustrated and angry he became, the more I felt it. I had no idea of how to block him out. We were both very unhappy people.

"I was the area weirdo. When I started school I didn't make any friends, but that was okay with me because it was

just too exhausting. Then I found some toddler who had
wandered off, and it was in the newspapers, and Dr. Ewell
came to talk to my father. I went to the Institute to be tested,
liked the peace and quiet of it, and stayed. My father and I
were both relieved."

"Where is he now?" Dane asked.

"Dead. He visited me regularly for a while, but it was
uncomfortable for both of us. The visits became further and
further apart. He remarried when I was fourteen, I think,
and moved to South Dakota. I met his wife only once. She
was nice enough, but very uneasy with me. She had two
children from her first marriage, but she and Dad didn't
have any. He died of a massive stroke when I was twenty."

"No other relatives?"

"A few aunts and uncles, and some cousins I've never
met."

She had essentially been alone since she'd been a child, he
thought. No snuggling, no hugging. No giggling sleep-overs
with friends during her teen years. He wondered if she had
ever really *been* a child, if she had ever played. Probably not.
There was something very adult about Marlie, a mental
maturity that went far beyond her years. But despite her
unorthodox childhood and, by necessity, very austere life-
style, she was amazingly normal. Almost any eccentricity
could have been justified by her upbringing, but she didn't
have any oddball habits or quirks.

Unless he counted picking up the thought waves of a serial
killer.

He looked at the clock, and took one last sip of coffee. "I
have to go, honey. This was great. What are we having for
supper?"

Caught between amusement, hope, and absolute terror
that he evidently planned to stay with her again, all she
could do was start laughing. "You've just finished breakfast," she said between giggles.

He pinched her chin. "Even in the *Rubaiyat,* old Omar
listed food first."

"I thought the wine came first."

"Tells us a lot about him, doesn't it?" He winked at her and went into the bedroom to finish dressing, and Marlie began clearing the table. She felt giddy. He was coming back that night.

She wondered how he usually conducted his affairs. Was he satisfied with spending a night together every now and then, maybe just the weekends? Or would he come by every night, spend time with her, make love, and then go home to his own house? She didn't know what to expect. There was a very satisfied air about him that led her to think he was very pleased with the personal outcome of the weekend, but perhaps that was just sexual satiation. She wasn't experienced enough to tell the difference, assuming there was one. Despite his kindness, his tenderness, even his passion, despite the fact that she had fallen headlong in love with him, she was aware that she really didn't know him.

He was shrugging into his shoulder holster as he came out of the bedroom. "I forgot that I don't have a jacket here," he said, frowning. "I'll have to stop by my house to get one, so I have to run." He bent down to kiss her. "'Bye, honey. I don't know how long this will take."

She put her hands on his chest and lifted herself on tiptoe for another kiss. "I have to do my grocery shopping, if you want anything at all to eat. If I'm not here, that's where I'll be."

He put his arms around her and pulled her close, forcing her hips against his. His mouth settled on hers for a kiss so hard and hungry that she went limp in his arms, shivering with delight. His hands sought her breasts, and rubbed between her legs. He forced her back against the cabinets and swiftly lifted her up onto them, pushing his hips between her spread thighs. She clung to his heavy shoulders, feeling the leather of the holster beneath her palms.

He tore his mouth away with a groan. "God Almighty. We can't do this. I don't have time." Sweat glistened on his forehead, and his eyes had that heavy-lidded, intent look

that nearly made her beg him to stay. But she of all people knew the price of duty, and she forced herself to release him.

"Go," she said. "Now."

He stepped back, wincing as he reached down to adjust himself. "I'll be back as soon as I can, but it may take several hours. Do you have an extra house key?"

"Yes, of course."

"Let me have it."

No hesitation or uncertainty for *him,* she thought as she jumped off the countertop and hurried to her purse. She gave him the extra key, and he slipped it onto his key ring. He started to reach for her, for another kiss, but caught himself in time. "Later," he said, winking at her, and headed for the door.

When he was gone, Marlie collapsed on the couch and tried to take stock of her life. She was wary, even frightened, of what was happening, but nothing on earth could have stopped her from plunging into the experience. For the first time in her life, she was in love, and it was wonderful.

To Dane's surprise, the chief of police was present at the meeting. Rodger Champlin, tall, white-haired, and stooped from too many years behind a desk, was nevertheless a career policeman who had come up through the ranks, and he had over forty years of service under his belt. He was a sly old dog who had managed to stay abreast of the flood of new technologies involved in police work, rather than stubbornly clinging to the outmoded ways he had learned in his youth.

Bonness's cramped office wasn't big enough to hold everyone, so they went into a conference room and closed the door. Ivan was there, his lined face and bloodshot eyes evidence that he had been up all night. All the detectives were there, most of them obviously puzzled by this Sunday morning meeting, especially one that involved the chief.

Bonness was drinking coffee as if it were all that kept him going. From the looks of him, he hadn't slept much, if at all,

and the hand holding the coffee cup trembled slightly from caffeine overload.

Everyone got his own cup of coffee and settled into his chosen seat. Dane decided to stand, and propped himself against the wall.

Bonness looked down at the sheaf of papers on the table before him, and sighed. He was obviously reluctant to begin, as if officially putting it in words would make it more real.

"People, we have a big problem," he said. "We only have two cases to compare, but the similarities are so overwhelming that we're pretty certain we have a serial murderer operating in Orlando."

Dead silence filled the room as the detectives exchanged glances.

"We were alerted to the possibility," he said, without going into specifics, "which is why we're able to get on it so fast." He passed some of the papers to the detective seated to his right, Mac Stroud. "Take one and pass it down. These are the files on Nadine Vinick and Jacqueline Sheets. Read both of them carefully. Mrs. Vinick was murdered a week ago Friday, Ms. Sheets was killed this past Friday night."

"So what do we have?" Mac asked.

Bonness looked at Ivan Schaffer. "Nothing," Ivan said flatly. "Not a damn thing. No fingerprints; he wears gloves. No semen, though vaginal bruising in both women indicates that they were raped. He either wears a condom or uses a foreign object. I haven't found any stray hairs, either. No footprints, no fibers from his clothing, no witnesses. We have nothing."

"Let me understand this," Chief Champlin said. His eyes flashed at the group. "I'm supposed to tell the mayor that there's a serial killer working in the city, and we don't have a shred of evidence on him? That even if, by some miracle, we managed to get our hands on him, we couldn't tie him to the crimes?"

"That's about it," Ivan said.

"How can you be so sure it's the same guy? There have

only been two murders, and stabbing deaths aren't that unusual—"

"Two stabbing deaths with absolutely no evidence left behind?" Dane interrupted. "Both of them occurred on a Friday night, at roughly the same hour. Both of the murders were done with a knife from the victim's kitchen, and both times the weapon was left behind. It's the same guy." He didn't mention Marlie, and he was betting that Bonness wouldn't, either. She would have to be brought into it sooner or later, but he wanted it to be later, when it was the right time and everything was under his control.

"Any connection between the two victims?" Mac asked.

Dane looked at Freddie and Worley, who had handled the paperwork on Jackie Sheets. Freddie shook her head. "There are still several people we need to talk to, but so far we haven't found any connection at all. They didn't look alike, they didn't live in the same neighborhood. Mrs. Vinick was a housewife, Ms. Sheets was a legal secretary. They didn't frequent the same places. As far as we've been able to find out, they never met."

"We can get a list from the telephone company of the calls made from both residences, and compare them. Maybe we'll get lucky and they have some numbers in common," Trammell said. "And there's the always interesting contents of the trash."

"And we need to get copies of their canceled checks from the banks." Dane wrote a note to himself. "Also copies of their charges on any credit cards. There's a link. There's always a link."

"I want to hold off on telling the mayor for a day or so," the chief said, glaring at all of them. "Until you can come up with a little concrete evidence so I won't feel as big of a fool as I do right now."

"The total lack of forensic evidence is a characteristic in itself," Dane pointed out. "I think we should take it to the FBI for analysis."

As he had expected, the chief's face took on a sour

expression. "Goddamn Feds," he snapped. "Are you saying you aren't good enough to handle it yourself, Hollister?"

Dane shrugged. All cops were jealous of their jurisdiction, and nobody, especially the old-timers, liked bringing the Bureau in on anything. Inevitably the federal boys got all the credit. "The Investigative Support Unit specializes in this, and I'd say we need all the help we can get. I don't have to prove that my dick's bigger than theirs."

"That's easy for you to say," Freddie remarked dryly. "But what about me?"

"What about the rest of us?" Worley countered in a plaintive tone.

The room erupted into laughter and a few coarse remarks. Bonness flushed at the lack of decorum, but couldn't keep himself from grinning. Dane winked at Freddie, and she winked back.

"If all of you are through comparing inches—or lack of them," the chief said, raising his voice, "maybe we can get back to the business at hand. Okay, maybe we take it to the FBI. But not until I say so, and not until I've talked to the mayor. Is that understood? Exhaust all the other avenues first."

"We can't afford to wait too long. Another Friday is only five days away."

"I know what day of the week it is," the chief snapped. "I'll talk to him Tuesday afternoon, and that's the absolute soonest I'll do it. That means, people, that you have two days to come up with something, so I suggest you all get to work."

15

THERE WASN'T A HELLUVA LOT THAT COULD BE DONE ON A Sunday. A call to the Hairport, where Jackie Sheets had regularly gotten her hair cut, didn't even get an answering machine but instead rang endlessly. No banks were open. The telephone company, however, was on duty and protecting the public's right to reach out and touch whomever they wanted twenty-four hours a day, seven days a week. Someone was *always* there, so Dane started the process of getting a listing of all the calls made from the Sheets residence.

Bonness organized a task force, choosing Dane, Trammell, Freddie, and Worley, since the four of them were already working on the two known cases. All of their other ongoing cases were parceled out to the other detectives, who were warned to tie up as many loose ends as they could, as fast as they could, because they would all probably be brought in on the task force soon.

What with one thing and another, it was after four when Dane and Trammell were finally able to leave the building.

Dane squinted up at the bright sky before slipping on his sunglasses. After the morning rain, the day had turned into a scorcher, with the rainfall only adding to the humidity as the heat turned the moisture to steam.

"How's Grace?" he asked.

Trammell was annoyed. "You sound as if you expect us to elope at any moment, and, old buddy, it ain't going to happen." He paused. "Grace is fine."

"Still at your place?"

Trammell checked his watch. "No."

Dane chuckled. "Not quite yet, huh? Maybe en route? You made a call right before we left; now, who could it have been to?"

"Fuck you," Trammell said mildly. "Where are *you* going?"

"Home. To my place."

Black eyebrows lifted inquiringly.

"To pick up more clothes," he enlarged, with some satisfaction.

"Why don't you just pack a suitcase and move in?"

"I would, but I still have to go by the house every day to get my mail, so that wouldn't be saving me any trouble. Most of my clothes will end up at her house eventually."

"All of your other girlfriends have moved in with you," Trammell pointed out.

"Marlie's different. She feels safe in her house; she won't willingly leave it." Besides, he didn't like the idea of Marlie moving into his own house. As Trammell had pointed out, several women over the years had taken up temporary residence there. He had liked and enjoyed them at the time, but in the end they hadn't been very important to him, certainly not as important or interesting as his job. Marlie *was* different; she didn't belong in that company of ultimately forgettable women.

Thinking of his house made him restless. It had always suited him before, but then, he had never been picky.

Suddenly he wanted to change things around. "My place needs some work done on it," he decided abruptly. "This would be a good time to have it done."

"What kind of work?"

"Maintenance stuff. New paint, the floors refinished. The bathroom needs complete renovation."

"I see." Trammell's dark eyes began to gleam. This was something he'd been itching to do for years. "How about new furniture while you're at it? That stuff you're using is about twenty years old."

"The place belonged to my grandparents. When they left it to me, the furniture came with it."

"It shows. How about it? New furniture, too?"

Dane considered it. Unlike most cops, and not counting Trammell, his bank account was healthy. He was single and had cheap tastes in food, clothes, and cars. He had inherited the house from his grandparents, so he didn't have a mortgage payment every month. He actually lived on half of his income, so the other half had been accumulating in the bank for years. Several times he'd thought about buying a boat, but when would he have time to use it? No other money-using schemes had come to mind. The house *did* need redecorating. He would like to take Marlie there occasionally, though he really couldn't imagine her living there with him, and he wanted the place to look nice for her. Unfortunately, now it looked exactly like what it was: a bachelor's home. And a bachelor who didn't pay much attention to his surroundings, at that. He wasn't the kind of slob who left food and empty beer cans everywhere, but he wasn't great on dusting or replacing things, either.

"Okay," he said. "New furniture, too."

Trammell rubbed his hands together. "I'll get started tomorrow."

Warily Dane eyed his friend. "Whaddaya mean, *you'll* get started? You're going to be busy. I'll arrange for the painters and floor refinishers, and pick out some new furniture next weekend."

"That's not quite how it's going to be, old buddy. We've already agreed that your taste in everything except women is atrocious. You have great taste in women. Just leave the rest to me."

"Hell, no! I know you. You'll put one of those little rugs that costs a fortune on the living room floor, and I'll be afraid to even walk on it. My bank account isn't yours, *old buddy.*"

"I'll take that into consideration. And no dhurrie rugs. Unlike you, I have excellent taste. It'll be a place you can be comfortable in, but it'll look a hell of a lot better. Marlie will like it," he added slyly.

Dane scowled at him, and Trammell clapped him on the shoulder. "Just relax and enjoy it."

"That sounds like I'm going to get fucked."

"I can do it for about ten thousand. How does that sound?"

"Like a damn expensive fuck. How about five?"

Trammell snorted. "Only if you want to sleep on a futon and sit on a bean bag."

Ten thousand. It was a lot of money. But Trammell was right, the self-satisfied bastard: He did have good taste. The house needed renovating, and he wanted it fresh and clean for Marlie, even if she never actually lived there. None of those other women had left much of an imprint, but he wanted even the hint of them gone. "How are you going to find time to do it?" he asked grudgingly.

"Ever hear of the telephone? It's no problem. I'll have stuff delivered, drop by to take a look at it, and if I don't like it, the store will pick it up again."

"You've been rich for too long. You need to come out of the stratosphere and live like regular folks for a change."

"Conspicuous consumers like me create jobs and keep the economy growing. It's time you did your part."

"I agreed, damn it."

"Then stop complaining about it." Trammell checked his

watch again. "Gotta go. If you have an extra house key, bring it to me in the morning."

"Sure," Dane said, wondering if his house would be recognizable as the same residence when Trammell got through with it. Still, it accomplished two things at once: The place *did* need some work, and it gave him a perfect excuse to completely move in with Marlie during the renovation. He was whistling as he got in his car.

An hour and a half later, Marlie went still with shock as she stood in the doorway and watched him unload suitcases and boxes from his car.

"What's all that?" she asked faintly. Silly question; she could see very clearly what it was. The question she really wanted to ask was "Why?" but she figured she knew the answer to that, too. Dane might enjoy very much the physical side of their relationship, but she couldn't let herself forget that, no matter what, he was always a cop. What better way to keep an eye on her than to move right in? That way he would know immediately if she had another vision.

"My stuff. My house is being renovated, and I have to clear out for a couple of weeks." He stopped on the porch, watching her intently. "I apologize for not asking, but it was a sudden decision to have the work done."

"I see." She managed an ironic smile. "Moving in is a good way to stay on top of the situation, I guess. Figuratively as well as literally."

Very carefully he set the box down on the porch. His expression was both cool and blank. "What does that mean, exactly?"

She shrugged. "Can you honestly say that moving in with me has nothing to do with the murders, with this entire situation?"

"No," he said bluntly. It was the truth. He couldn't. Marlie was his best chance of catching the bastard, but it wasn't just that. He had seen how the visions affected her,

the physical and mental price she paid. For both of those reasons, in addition to the fact that he was violently attracted to her, he wanted to stay close to her.

She stood silently for a moment, considering the situation. They had become lovers, but her instinct was to take things slowly. Circumstances had decreed otherwise, throwing them together in a pressure cooker. Even though she would like to put the brakes on now, feel her way through this strange new relationship, those same circumstances were still aligned against her. He was, first and foremost, a cop, and she was his direct link to a killer. Until the murderer was caught, she couldn't expect Dane to stray far from her side. She would simply have to remember that the main reason he was there was his job; it was a sure bet that he didn't practically force his way in to live with every woman with whom he had gone to bed.

She stepped aside. "Just so we understand each other. Come on in."

Trammell gave a long, low whistle when Dane walked in the next morning, and everyone in the squad room turned to look. Never mind that there was a serial killer on the loose; cops were never too busy to harass one of their own. Freddie clutched her heart and pretended to swoon. Bonness, who had been standing beside Keegan's desk, was totally deadpan as he asked, "May we help you, sir?"

"You sure can," Dane replied good-naturedly as he dropped into his chair. "All you smart-asses can apologize for the crap you've given me for years about how I dressed."

"He said it in the past tense," Trammell noted, turning his eyes upward. "Please, God, let it stay that way."

Dane smiled at him. "Want to go for a couple of beers after work?" he asked silkily. Trammell picked up the hint and subsided, but still with an unholy gleam of amusement in his dark eyes.

"Take *me*, take *me!*" Freddie cried, waving her hand exuberantly.

"Yeah, sure, and get my legs broken?"

She shrugged. *"I* don't mind."

"Gee, thanks. I'm overwhelmed by your concern."

Bonness left Keegan's desk to perch on Dane's. "What caused the transformation?" he asked. "Were you mugged by a fashion designer on the way to work?"

Dane grinned, knowing that his answer would make Bonness choke. It wasn't something he could keep to himself, so he decided to have a little fun. "Marlie doesn't like wrinkles," he explained calmly.

Bonness looked blank. "Marlie?" Obviously he could think of only one Marlie and just as obviously he couldn't get the connection.

"Marlie Keen. You know, the psychic."

"I know who she is," Bonness said, still confused. "What does she have to do with it?"

"She doesn't like wrinkles," Dane explained again, as deadpan as Bonness had been. He could hear Trammell snickering, but didn't dare glance that way.

Poor Bonness was slow that day. "So she goes around the city zapping them out?" he demanded with heavy sarcasm.

"No." Dane smiled, a slow, very satisfied smile. "She ironed them out. At least, she ironed the shirt. She made me iron the slacks myself, because she said I had to learn."

Bonness gaped at him. Trammell was making choking sounds as he tried to keep from laughing aloud. "You—you mean . . . Marlie . . . that is, you and Marlie—"

"Marlie and I are what?"

"Um . . . dating?"

"Dating?" Dane pretended to think. "No, I wouldn't say that."

"Then what would you say?"

He gave a negligent shrug. "It's simple. When I got dressed this morning, she said that no way was I leaving the house looking like that, so she hauled out her iron and ironing board and made me take off my clothes. When I put them back on, they looked like this." He wondered why a

crisply ironed shirt, neatly knotted tie, and slacks with a razor-edge crease were such a big deal, not just to Marlie but to everyone else. Not that he minded; he just hadn't cared before. He didn't care about his clothes now, but Marlie did, so therefore he would make more of an effort. Simple.

Bonness was literally sputtering, his eyes bugging out. "But you only met a week ago. You ridiculed her, accused her of being an accomplice to murder. She hated your guts on sight."

"We changed our minds," Dane said. "If you need me, you can reach me at her house."

"Shit. You're kidding me. I thought she had better taste than that."

Dane smiled peacefully. "She does. She's already improving me." And he would let her do it. If she wanted him to wear Italian loafers like Trammell's, he'd do it. If she wanted him to shave twice a day, he'd do that too. If she wanted him to stand on his head for an hour every morning, he would happily put his butt in the air. When he had returned the afternoon before, with his clothing, it had been plain that the thought of living with him made her uneasy. He knew he should have lied to her about his motives, but damn it, his interest in her *was* two-pronged. He couldn't just forget about the murders and assure her that her involvement never entered his mind. Hell, her involvement never *left* his mind.

After this was over, he would devote all of his attention to her, but right now he couldn't, and she knew it. Right away he had sensed a slight distance that hadn't been there when he'd left. She kept rebuilding that damn wall of reserve, as if she couldn't quite trust herself to let go, or trust him to catch her if she did. He would let her reform him from the ground up if it would make her feel more secure with him.

Marlie was a solitary creature who didn't easily share either her space or her time. He had carefully spent the evening not crowding her too much, but all the same establishing a tone of normalcy to his presence. They had

done very ordinary things—cooked dinner, cleaned the kitchen, watched television—just as if they had been together for months instead of one stressful weekend. It had worked; she had relaxed more and more as the evening wore on. And when they had gone to bed and he had begun making love to her, the reserve had completely vanished. He didn't know if it was permanently gone; probably not. But he would deal with each reappearance as it happened, and in the meantime insinuate himself ever more deeply into the everyday fabric of her life. Besides, he had enjoyed it when she had made several acerbic remarks about his clothes. She had been too subdued and vulnerable for the past two days, and he had been delighted to see her return to her normal, sharp-tongued spirits.

Still shaking his head at Marlie's evident loss of common sense, Bonness gestured for Freddie and Worley to come over. When everyone was grouped together, they decided their course of action for the day. Freddie and Worley were going to talk to the people Jackie Sheets had worked with, including Liz Cline again, for she would be calmer now and might remember something else. They arranged to get copies of the canceled checks of both victims. Dane and Trammell went to the Hairport to talk to Jackie Sheets's hair stylist.

The Hairport was situated in a small, renovated house. There was none of the pink neon and purple-and-black decor so beloved by the trendier salons where all the clients came out looking as if they'd stuck their finger into a light socket. But there were real ferns (Dane knew because Trammell stuck his finger into the dirt to check), and comfortable waiting chairs, as well as a truly impressive selection of magazines, stacked in rickety towers on every available flat surface. There were several women in the salon, in various stages of tonsorial improvement. A sharp chemical smell hung in the air, with an undertone of hairspray and nail polish.

The Kathy who cut Ms. Sheets's hair was Kathleen McCrory, who looked as Irish as her name. She had sandy red hair that feathered around her face, a very fair complexion, and round blue eyes that widened even more when Dane and Trammell introduced themselves. She led them back to the tiny break room the stylists used, poured them each a cup of coffee, and offered them their choice of any of the varied snacks piled on the small table. They accepted the coffee, but turned down the Bugles and Twinkies.

Kathleen was a cheerful, self-confident young woman. Trammell began to ask her about Jackie Sheets, and Dane settled back to enjoy his coffee, which was pretty good. He watched Kathleen lightly flirt with Trammell, and his partner lightly flirt in return, all the while asking questions. Kathleen did stop flirting when he told her that Jackie Sheets had been killed, and her big blue eyes slowly filled with tears. She looked back and forth between Dane and Trammell, as if wanting one of them to say it was a joke. Her lips began trembling. "I—I haven't watched the news this weekend," she said, and swallowed hard. "My boyfriend and I went to Daytona."

Dane reached across the small table and covered her hand with his. She clutched his fingers, and clung tightly to him until she had fought off the tears. She gave him a small, watery, apologetic smile as she began groping for a tissue to wipe her eyes.

Yes, she had cut Jackie's hair about every three weeks. Jackie had gorgeous hair, thick and silky, with a lot of body. She could do anything she wanted with it. Trammell gently interrupted the hair analysis to get her back on track. No, Jackie hadn't mentioned seeing anyone for quite a while now. No, Kathleen couldn't remember anyone named Vinick.

Did she have any male customers? Sure. There were quite a few. Had Jackie spoken to any of them, gotten acquainted? Not that Kathleen could remember.

Another dead end, Dane thought. He was getting damn tired of them.

Tuesday was more of the same dead ends. A comparison of canceled checks and credit card receipts revealed that the Vinicks and Jackie Sheets had shopped at some of the same department stores, which told them exactly nothing. Dane imagined that almost everyone in Orlando had been in at least one of those stores at one time or another. Still, it was the only link they had come up with, so he doggedly pursued it, comparing dates to see if maybe they had been in any store at the same time.

Jackie Sheets had had several department store credit cards, but Nadine Vinick hadn't had any, usually paying for her purchases by check or charging the expense to their one credit card, a MasterCard, when she didn't have the ready funds. But Mrs. Vinick had been very frugal, and had used the card only twice in the past year. Mostly the Vinicks had operated in a pay-as-you-go household, while Jackie Sheets had regularly made charges on her cards and paid in monthly installments, always living slightly above her means. Most of her purchases had been clothes, from the best stores in the city.

Their life-styles had been different. The Vinicks had been blue-collar, and Nadine's greatest interest had been cooking. Jackie Sheets had been white-collar, a woman who had loved clothes and made an effort to always look her best. But somewhere, somehow, the two women, as different as they were, had had the bad luck to attract the attention of the same man. But *where,* and *how?*

Chief Champlin had clearly hoped they would come up with something; his disappointment that afternoon wasn't pleasant. But he was also a cop, and he had looked at the files. The same man had done both women. The very lack of forensic evidence was as much an indicator as if they had found the same fingerprints at both scenes. This was a smart bastard, and they needed help.

"All right," he said. "Call the Bureau. I'll tell the mayor."

Bonness made the call, and briefly explained the situation. The local Bureau guys knew big stuff when they heard it, and said they would like to go over the files immediately.

"Hollister and Trammell, get the files and go," Bonness said.

Dane saw Trammell check his watch, a sure sign that he had something else to do. "Why not send someone from each case?" he suggested. "They may have questions about Jackie Sheets that Trammell and I can't answer."

"Okay," Bonness agreed. "Freddie? Worley? Which one of you wants to go?"

Worley grimaced. He clearly wanted to go, but he, too, checked his watch. "It's my mother-in-law's birthday. If I'm late for the party, my wife won't speak to me for a year."

"I'm free," Freddie said. "Which one of you guys is going?"

"I am," Dane said, and Trammell flashed him a grateful smile.

FBI Agent Dennis Lowery was waiting for them. Lowery had that Ichabod Crane look to him: thin, long-legged, stoop-shouldered, his clothes always flapping about him as if they were too large. His eyes were deep-set, his nose was beaky. But he was a calm, intelligent man who was more diplomatic than some when it came to dealing with local law enforcement agencies. Dane had dealt with him before, and liked him well enough.

A second agent, Sam DiLeonardo, was a young fart barely out of training, all spit and polish. Dane wasn't as inclined to like him, because he looked like the type who would insist on going by the book even when everything was falling apart around him, but the kid redeemed himself by taking one look at Freddie and immediately falling in lust. He went absolutely still, his eyes widening a little as he stared at her. A slight blush darkened his cheeks. Freddie was always kind and could be very ladylike when she chose, so she pretended

not to notice the kid's fascination. Dane and Lowery exchanged wry glances as they sat down at a long conference table.

"So what do you have?" Lowery asked, pulling a legal pad toward him and uncapping a pen.

Freddie gave copies of the files to both agents, who silently leafed through them. DiLeonardo forgot his preoccupation with the plain but remarkably fetching Detective Freddie Brown, his expression turning grim as he stared at the stark photos of the bodies, in both color and black and white.

"He probably stalks them before acting," Dane said. "He knows if they're alone or not. In both cases, we think it's possible that he was in the house for some time before they knew it, hiding out in the spare bedroom. In the Vinick case, he was probably waiting for her husband to go to work. With Jackie Sheets, we don't know why he waited."

"Maybe for the neighbors to go to bed," DiLeonardo said absently, still studying the notes.

"They would be less likely to hear anything if they were still up, with the television on. At any rate, none of the neighbors heard any screams."

Lowery's face was impassive as he looked at the photos. "You'd think, the way these women were butchered, that they would have been screaming bloody murder, but a lot of times it doesn't work that way. He chased them, didn't he? They were terrified, breathless, already traumatized by being raped. It's difficult to scream, really scream, under those conditions. The throat tightens up, restricts sound. Probably they didn't make all that much noise."

He tossed the files onto the table and rubbed his jaw. "Just two cases? That doesn't give us much to work on, but I agree, it looks like the same guy. What's the link?"

"We haven't been able to find one," Dane said. "Not looks, life-style, friends, neighborhood, anything. We compared canceled checks and credit card receipts, and except for shopping at some of the same department stores, which

applies to everyone else in town, their paths never crossed. They never met each other."

"They did something to attract this guy's attention, though. Did they both buy something from the same store within, say, the last month?"

"Not that we can find. It's hard to say, because the Vinicks evidently paid cash for a lot of things." Dane wasn't irritated by Lowery's questions, though some people would have been, taking it as a suggestion that the local cops hadn't done a good job. The same questions were bound to come up over and over again, as different people grappled with the problem. There had been a lot of times when he had doggedly gone over the same file time and again, until something clicked and he saw a detail that had been there all along, but just hadn't registered.

"I'll get this up to Quantico," Lowery said. "Two murders in a week isn't a good sign. If he's escalating that fast, he's out of control."

"I'm hoping it was unusual for him to kill two so close together. Maybe Jackie Sheets was an easy opportunity that he couldn't resist."

"Maybe. But if he liked it, he won't wait long before doing it again."

"Oh, he likes it," Dane said bitterly. "He takes his time, plays with them. The son of a bitch loves his work."

16

CARROLL JANES WAS SULKY. HE HAD BEEN IN A SOUR MOOD since last Friday night. Jacqueline Sheets hadn't been as much fun as he had anticipated. The big rush of power he had expected just hadn't materialized. She had been pathetic, just whining and scrambling in circles, rather than making it interesting. And there hadn't been much press coverage about it either, which really disappointed him. Part of the fun—as it turned out, *most* of the fun—of this last one had been knowing that the cops would go crazy, with two incidences so similar, so close together, and absolutely no clues with which they could work. But evidently the cops were more stupid than he had thought, which took even more of the fun out of it. Where was the challenge? Not that they could catch him, but he had thought they would at least have *noticed*.

He wasn't sure what had interfered with his pleasure. Maybe Sheets had just been too soon after the last one. He hadn't been in the proper state of anticipation, hadn't

drawn out the stalking over several weeks while the tension drew tighter and tighter, until he was at fever pitch, all of his senses almost painfully acute, all of his power focused.

Of course, he would have to try another one to make certain. He hated to waste himself on a disappointment, but it was the only way he could find out. If the next one was as boring, he would know to spend more time on the process and wouldn't let the apparent ease of a job sucker him into moving too fast, and cheating himself of his pleasure.

Every day at work he waited and watched for the slightest transgression. Which unhappy customer was going to have to pay? After all, to make it a fair test, he would have to act as soon as possible.

Marlie felt edgy, restless from an inner tension that just wouldn't let up. She couldn't pin down any one reason for it, because there were so many candidates from which to choose. The biggest reason, of course, was dread of the coming weekend. She couldn't explain to anyone, not even Dane, how she felt after touching the killer's thoughts during those bloody moments. She didn't just feel dirty, she felt permanently contaminated by his evil, as if her soul would never be free of the ugliness. More than she had ever wanted anything in her life, she wanted to run, to get far away so she wouldn't know when he killed again. That relief, unfortunately, was the one thing she couldn't allow herself, or then she would be truly contaminated by her own cravenness. She had to stay, had to stick it out, for the sake of the two women who had already died, for the others she didn't know about, for little Dusty . . . for herself.

Then there was Dane. She loved him, but having him around all the time was still disconcerting. She had spent so many years alone that it sometimes startled her to turn around and bump into him. Suddenly there was twice the amount of laundry to do, three times as much food to prepare, schedules to adjust since there was only one

bathroom, and very little room in bed. Her life had been totally in control, and now everything had changed.

He knew, of course. Those sharp hazel eyes saw everything, though she struggled to hide how unsettled she was. He didn't just dump all the chores in her lap, as a lot of men would have done; he was accustomed to doing his own laundry and didn't hesitate to wash a load of clothes. The safe limits of his cooking were heating the contents of cans or slapping a sandwich together, so she did all of the cooking, and he took over the cleanup chores. He did what he could to ease the transition for her, but at the same time he refused to back off and give her more space. He was there; she had to accustom herself to him. She was happy to do so, to have this time with him no matter what his motivation, but it was still unnerving.

She couldn't escape the coming weekend, couldn't distract herself. Would the killer strike again? The thought of some other innocent woman being butchered, of herself being sucked into the sickening, evil morass of the killer's mind, was almost more than she could bear. She tried not to think of it, but it was like being tracked by a mad dog and trying not to think about that, either. With every tick of the clock, the weekend loomed closer, and there was nothing she could do to avoid it. She tried to brace herself to endure, instead, because she was Dane's only link to the killer. Sooner or later, he would give her a clue to his identity. All she had to do was wait, and endure his killing frenzies without going mad herself.

By Thursday, she was so tense that she couldn't eat the Chinese food Dane had brought for dinner, and she loved Chinese. Her throat was tight, and when she swallowed, the food seemed to form a lump halfway down her esophagus. She didn't have an appetite anyway, so finally she stopped even making an effort.

As usual, Dane hadn't missed a trick, though he was making impressive inroads on the food. "Worried?" he asked.

224

"How can I not be? The last two weekends haven't been a picnic."

"Are you picking up anything from him?" Dane asked the question casually, but the interest behind it was intense.

"I'm uneasy, but it's *my* feelings, not his." She rubbed her hands over her arms. "How long will it take the FBI to get a profile on him?"

"I don't know. We only had two cases, so that may make it harder for them. But they may be able to match the MO to other cases that have been brought to their attention, and that will help."

"Do you think he's killed before?" she asked tensely, looking out the back door. She could see Bill trimming the shrubbery at the rear of his lot. Her neighbors lived such nice, ordinary lives; she envied them the boredom of their security.

"Probably. He's too good at it to be a beginner. It's likely that he moves around, to keep any one area from becoming too hot for him."

"So he's moved here recently?"

"I'd say so."

"Isn't there any way you can check on recent arrivals? Wouldn't the post office have a record? Or maybe you could get a list of new customers from the utility companies."

"Do you know how many people move to central Florida every year?" he asked. "It would take a helluva lot of time. Still, it's an idea."

"You could eliminate all the women, which would cut the list in half."

"And still leave us with a cast of thousands." He stood and began clearing the table. "I'll talk to Bonness about it."

She knotted her hands together and stared at him. "Do any of the others know about me?"

"You mean, any of the other detectives?"

"Yes."

"Just Bonness, Trammell, and me. Why?"

"I've been worried about it."

"Again, why?"

"They would talk." Restlessly she got up and helped him clear the table.

"So?"

"That kind of talk would get to the media. You know how it is."

"So far, the media doesn't even know about the killer. I'm surprised, because once we told the mayor, I expected it to be blasted on the six-o'clock news that there's a serial killer loose in Orlando. No one in city hall can keep a secret. It'll leak out any day, though." He began washing their few dishes, and watched her as she paced the kitchen. "Have you had a rough time with the media before?"

She shot him an incredulous look. "Are you kidding?"

"What happened?"

"Which time?" she asked caustically. "The reporters are bad enough, every time a story breaks, with the phone ringing incessantly, and cameras and microphones pushed in my face every time I open the door. But the reporters aren't the worst of it. They're just the cause. The worst comes after they've done their stories, when the death threats start, and the crackpot evangelists hold prayer meetings in front of my house to drive out Satan, because I obviously do the devil's work. If it got out this time, I'd probably lose my job. I've never been in these circumstances before, because the Institute always supported me. But can you imagine a *bank* tolerating that kind of publicity? A weirdo psychic working in their accounting department! Some of their customers would close out their accounts, afraid I would pry into their business."

"Wonder what they have to hide," Dane said, his eyes speculative.

"Nothing, probably. Some people are paranoid enough that they think the 'authorities,' whoever that may be, watch everyone and check everything. They won't fill out their census papers because they think the information will be turned over to the IRS."

"How do you know?" he asked, sliding the question in as smooth as silk. She glanced at him to find those hazel eyes glittering with amusement.

She choked on a spurt of laughter as she realized where he had led her. "Because I used to be able to read them! *Used* to, Hollister. I can't do it anymore."

"Are you sure? Have you tried?"

"Yes, smarty, I've tried."

"When?"

"Last week. I tried to pick *him* up, but couldn't. I tried to find you. I tried to find Trammell. Nothing. I did finally see you, very briefly, but I couldn't read anything from you."

"You saw me." He didn't look pleased at the idea. "What was I doing?"

"Watching a ball game and answering the telephone," she snapped. "It was when I called you the first time. If I hadn't been so worried and frightened, I doubt if I could have seen you. That never was my strength, anyway."

He rinsed the dishes and stacked them in the drainer, then dried his hands. "But that was before we became involved. Now, maybe you could do it any time you wanted."

"Maybe. I don't know. I haven't tried again."

He turned around and propped against the sink, his arms crossed as he studied her. Marlie stood her ground, but she wasn't certain what against. He looked grim, and bigger than usual. He had removed his jacket when he'd gotten home with the cartons of takeout Chinese, but still wore his shoulder holster. A chill went through her. He had been with her for a week now, and in that short length of time she had become accustomed to his protectiveness, even to being cosseted. But a week *was* a very short time, and before that they had been adversaries.

In a flash she realized what the problem was. He wanted her, but he didn't trust her. How could he? He didn't know her well enough. Wasn't that a big part of *her* problem, too? They had been propelled together without having time to get to know each other. He was a cop; distrust and suspicion

were his stock in trade. He had made love to her, moved in with her, thinking that she had lost most of her psychic abilities. He didn't at all like the idea that she could check up on him without his knowledge. He wanted to keep himself private, except for the parts he chose to share with her.

It hurt, but she couldn't blame him. She had spent a lot of effort in trying to secure privacy for herself, so she couldn't decry the same instinct in him.

"Do you want me to apologize for being what I am?" she asked steadily. "Or put my hand on a Bible and swear a sacred oath that I'll never again try to reach you?"

"You don't know that you can, except in an emergency."

She shrugged. "I won't try it even then, if you don't want me to."

"I don't like being spied on," he said, his gaze never leaving hers.

"Then I won't do it."

He shoved his hand through his hair. "Damn it," he said under his breath. "Does it work the other way around? The other time, you were worried about me. But what if you're the one in trouble? Can you call me, psychically?"

"I can place the call, Detective," she said sardonically. "But if you don't have a receiver, you can't get the signals. But I wouldn't, anyway."

"Why not?" He didn't like that. She could see his temper rising.

"That boundary you just drew. If you don't want me to cross it for my convenience, I'll be damned if I'll cross it for yours."

"Shit! I don't believe this." He closed his eyes and pinched the narrow bridge of his nose. "We're arguing about something that doesn't exist. If you can't contact me anyway, what the hell difference does it make that you wouldn't even try?"

"You tell me. You're the one with the problem about it." She turned around and headed for the living room. She had

taken maybe three steps when a hard arm passed around her waist from behind and drew her back against him. She didn't try to struggle free, but neither did she relax and let him take her weight. She stood stock still, waiting. He had an erection; she could feel it pressing against her bottom. She wasn't surprised, because in the week they had been together, it seemed as if he had been hard most of the time.

"We aren't going to get this settled, are we?" His breath was warm against her temple.

"I don't see how."

"Then let's forget about it for now. Want to go for a ride?"

"Where to?"

"My place. I'm curious about what Trammell is doing to it."

She turned her head to stare incredulously at him. "You mean you don't know?"

"Nope. He told me to stay away until he's finished."

"For heaven's sake, why? It's your house."

"He said that I know as much about decorating as I know about clothes."

"In that case, I understand completely," she said wryly.

"Smart-ass. Do you want to go or not?"

"Sure." She had to admit to being curious about his house. She knew that it would be a mess while the renovation work was in progress, but houses were very personal things. Since she couldn't read Dane psychically, she had to pick up clues about him any way she could.

The drive to Dane's house took her mind off the uneasy feeling that had been her constant companion. Dismissing their quarrel for now, because there was nothing they could do about it, she prepared to enjoy prowling through his house.

Though it was late, almost seven, and long past the time when the workers would have gone home, there was another car in the driveway, and lights were on in the house. "Uh-oh," Dane said. "Caught in the act. Trammell's here."

"You don't have to stop," Marlie pointed out.

He smiled. "And miss the fun?" Deftly he pulled in behind Trammell's car.

They had barely gotten out of the car when Trammell appeared in the doorway. "I told you to stay away," he called.

"So arrest me. I've been good for four days. How long did you think it would last?"

"Three," Trammell said, stepping aside to let them in.

A tall, slim woman came forward to greet them. "Grace," Dane said, pleasure evident in his voice as he hugged her. "Marlie, this is Grace Roeg, a patrol officer with the city. Grace, Marlie Keen."

"Hello," Grace said in a slow, grave voice. Marlie swiftly evaluated her, and liked what she saw. There was something stately about Grace Roeg, and her deep brown eyes reflected the inner stillness of an unshakable serenity.

"Well, go ahead, look around," Trammell said irritably.

Dane looked around at the empty room, all the while keeping his arm around Grace. "Where's my stuff?"

"In storage," Trammell growled, forcefully removing his arm from Grace's shoulders. He glanced sharply at Marlie, as if instructing her to take Dane into custody and control him. She put an innocent look on her face, amused by watching the elegant Trammell descend to the primitive levels of jealousy.

Grace said, "Don't mind him. We're getting married, and he's still in shock." She extended her left hand to show them an exquisite marquise diamond, about three carats worth.

"I am not." Trammell turned a violent look on Dane. "Don't start."

Dane was grinning. "Start what? I'm glad for you. Congratulations, buddy. Grace is way too good for you. When are you going to do the deed?"

"About six months," Grace answered comfortably. "I thought a nice, long engagement would give him time to get used to the idea. Things have happened pretty fast, so we

don't want to rush into anything and maybe make a mistake."

"I don't need time," her intended said, looking haunted. "It was my idea, wasn't it?"

"Of course it was, darling," she soothed, tucking her arm through his. "But it will take that long to plan the wedding. Now, why don't you show Dane what you're doing to his house?"

"Is it going to be a big wedding?" Marlie asked.

"Big enough," Trammell said, and turned an evil smile on Dane. "You'll have to wear a tuxedo."

"I'm tough," Dane replied, concealing his instant dread. "It might damage me, but it won't kill me. For you, old buddy, anything."

Trammell scowled, as if he had been hoping for more of a reaction, but turned and led the way through the empty rooms. Dane was frankly amazed at what had been accomplished in just four days. His grandmother had loved wallpaper, and every room in the house had sported a different pattern. The wallpaper was gone now, and in its place was fresh stucco, painted a soothing, mellow white. All of the interior doorways had been reframed into arches.

"It would look better if the exterior doors and the windows were arches," Trammell said, "but changing them would cost a lot more money than you want to spend. The floor refinishers start tomorrow."

Dane skidded to a halt, gaping at the hull of what had been his bathroom. "You've gutted it," he blurted.

"Yeah. I hadn't planned to do it, but the plumbing was fifty years old. It'll cost you probably another thousand."

"Damn it, the next time you feel the urge to spend another thousand or so of my money, ask me first!"

"If I'd asked, you'd have said no," Trammell replied calmly. "Wait until I'm finished, and you'll agree that it was worth the money."

"It had better be," Dane muttered. He sensed Trammell's

amusement, and knew his partner was getting back at him for being so gleeful about the impending marriage. He didn't mind, much. He was glad Trammell had found someone as wonderful as Grace, though he understood exactly his partner's sense of panic, as if his life had suddenly rocketed out of control.

He had felt that way himself since meeting Marlie. Things had happened too fast. Trammell and Grace had decided to get married, then set the date far enough in the future to give themselves time to settle down and be certain of their feelings. Dane hadn't mentioned marriage or even love to Marlie, preferring to give himself the time *before* the commitment. Maybe what he felt for her wouldn't last. It sure felt permanent, but maybe it wasn't; time would tell. In the meantime, they were together, and in the end that was really all that mattered. He woke up with her every morning and went to bed with her every night. As long as he had that, he could wait for the rest.

He wasn't certain how Marlie felt, either. There was passion, liking, companionship . . . maybe love. Who could tell? She had been under considerable stress from the first. When everything was settled down, then they would be able to tell more about their relationship. For the first time he considered marriage a possibility, and that in itself was a huge step for him.

It would all have to wait, though. There was a killer to catch, a plan to put into action, and he had to protect Marlie while he did it. And if he had learned anything about Marlie in the time he had been with her, it was that she wasn't going to like his plan worth a damn.

17

Lowery called first thing Monday morning, asking them to come over immediately. He had just returned from Quantico with the character profile.

The day was hot and clear and sticky, with the temperature already in the mid-eighties, predicted to reach the high nineties, and the humidity there already. Dane hadn't slept well the entire weekend, probably because Marlie hadn't. She had been restless, able to doze for only short periods before jerking awake. The strain of the weekend, waiting for a vision of murder to appear, had left her pale and withdrawn, with dark circles of fatigue under her eyes. He had spent long hours cuddling her, letting her know that she wasn't alone even if he couldn't prevent the vision, if it came. It hadn't.

How much more of this could she take? She was under so much stress, both physically and emotionally, that he was afraid for her. A lot of people would have broken under the strain, years ago. She hadn't, which was a testimony to her strength; Marlie wasn't a delicate flower, wilting at any

hardship. Despite the finely drawn lines of her too thin body, she was remarkably sturdy. But even an oak tree could be felled, and he was worried.

Trammell was showing strain, too, probably from terror of his impending nuptials. He and Dane barely spoke on the way over to the Bureau, each of them absorbed in his own worries.

Freddie and Worley were already there, as was Bonness. DiLeonardo was present, with that besotted look on his face again as he maneuvered around the conference table for a seat next to Freddie.

Lowery was freshly shaved but was more rumpled than usual, making Dane think that he had truly just arrived from Virginia, on the early-bird flight.

"The ISU really worked on this," he said quietly. "You're to be congratulated on noticing the pattern so quickly, but catching this guy isn't going to be easy. He's the worst kind of killer, the Bundy type. He's as cold as ice; he's intelligent, resourceful, and totally without a shred of guilt.

"I have a list of similar murders: slashings, no suspects, no evidence. It's possible some of them were done by the same guy. Some of them are impossible, because they took place at roughly the same time on opposite sides of the country as some of the other murders, but there's no way of telling which one to eliminate.

"The murders started approximately ten years ago. ISU puts his age in the early to mid-thirties. Most serial killers start killing in their early twenties. But ten years of success-ful killings means he's going to be very hard to apprehend; he's experienced, he has learned from his mistakes and perfected his crime. He knows what he's doing. He has studied forensics and police procedure, and he's very care-ful to leave no identifiable evidence behind."

"Could he have been a cop?" Bonness asked. "Maybe in the military?"

"Not likely," Lowery replied. "He wouldn't deal well with authority of any type, so it isn't feasible that he would have

been able to complete any type of military or police training. He wouldn't even have been accepted as a candidate.

"He's white; all of the victims have been white, and serial killers seldom cross racial boundaries. He's athletic, very strong. He's an organized killer, very confident, and that's the worst kind. An unorganized killer is messy, makes mistakes, has no clear plan. This guy has everything planned, down to the last detail. He doesn't knock the victims out or tie them; he's confident that he can control the situation, and so far, he has. The weapon he uses is a knife from the victim's kitchen, which he leaves at the scene. Since there are no fingerprints, the weapon can't be connected to him. He takes no trophies. ISU thinks he stalks the victims, possibly for weeks beforehand; he enters the house when no one is home, becomes familiar with it. He's very patient.

"He rapes, but doesn't use restraints, and that's a slight aberration. Some women will fight even with a knife at their throat. For some reason, his victims haven't."

Because he soothes them, at first, Dane thought violently. He made them think that they wouldn't be hurt if they just didn't fight. He was gentle, and he used a rubber. They were paralyzed by the unexpectedness of being attacked in their own homes, and in that first terror, they believed him. But those were details Marlie had given him, so he kept quiet.

"He doesn't blindfold the victims," Lowcry continued, "doesn't keep the corpses. Again, those are traits of the organized killer. It was surprising that he cut off Mrs. Vinick's fingers, because mutilation isn't one of the traits—"

"We think she scratched him," Dane interrupted.

Lowery sighed. "If so, that's even more evidence of his intelligence. He couldn't risk his skin samples being found under her fingernails. A brutal but effective solution. He doesn't panic. He thinks on his feet, and isn't a slave to a rigid plan.

"He likely holds down a full-time job, is outwardly

normal. The other murders were all done at roughly the same time for each area. In one area, the murders were committed in the daytime, meaning he was either unemployed or working nights somewhere. I suspect he was working, because there's nothing about this man that would attract attention. He's methodical, predatory, and has this down to a science. His car will be several years old, nothing flashy, the kind of car you would see hundreds of in any neighborhood. Middle-class all the way. He could walk into police headquarters and no one would think anything about it, except to ask how they could help him.

"There is the danger that he's escalating. Until now, he has kept himself under control, spacing out the murders. Killing on two successive weekends could mean that he is beginning to need the thrill of the hunt more often. I know there haven't been any slashing murders reported this weekend, but it's possible the victim simply hasn't been found."

A quick look passed between Dane, Trammell, and Bonness. They knew there hadn't been another murder, because Marlie hadn't had a vision.

"Identification at this point is impossible," Lowery said. "Unless he makes a mistake and leaves some evidence behind to link him to the crime, he'll have to be caught in the act."

It was a grim group that returned to headquarters, though Lowery hadn't told them much that they hadn't already known. The killer was a smart son of a bitch, and ordinarily they wouldn't have had a prayer of catching him. Dane was silent, thinking of Marlie. She was their secret weapon; she would be the one who caught him.

It broke on the news that afternoon. Dane was surprised that the leak had taken that long; for something to remain a secret at city hall for a week was almost unheard-of, particularly something that dramatic. It was the headline story for all the local television and radio news; he caught it on the radio while he was driving home.

"A source in city hall has confirmed that police believe a serial killer is stalking women in the Orlando area," the announcer intoned solemnly. The plummy voice continued, "Two recent murders appear to have been committed by the same man. Two weeks ago, Nadine Vinick was murdered in her home, and a week later Jacqueline Sheets was found murdered in *her* home. Chief of Police Rodger Champlin refuses to comment on the cases or say if they have any suspects. He does urge women in the city to take precautions for their safety—"

He snapped off the radio, infuriated by the knowledge that the killer was getting a real rush from this. He had expected the news to break, was prepared for it, but knowing that the bastard was laughing and soaking up all the attention was still hard to take.

Marlie was sitting curled on the couch when he got home. The television was on, though the news program had advanced to the weather portion. He tossed his jacket across a chair and sat down beside her, then lifted her onto his lap. They sat silently, watching the meteorologist point to this high-pressure system and that low one, make sweeping movements of his hand to indicate their projected movement, and finally make his prediction: hot and muggy, the way it had been all day, with the ever-present possibility of thunderstorms.

"Anything interesting happen today?" she asked.

"The local FBI gave us the character profile they had worked up; this guy has probably been moving around the country for the last ten years, leaving a string of victims behind, and nobody has a clue what he looks like, or a shred of evidence that connects to him." He hugged her to him. "But we're working on getting a list of new accounts from the utility companies. It's a long shot, but it's something."

She had changed into shorts and a T-shirt when she had gotten home from work, and he stroked his hand appreciatively over her bare thighs. "What about you? Anything interesting happen in the accounting department?"

She snorted. "Get real. The most exciting part of the day was when a man called, irate because he had been charged an overdraft fee on a bad check when he had been a customer of the bank for years."

"Bet that got the old ticker revved up."

"I almost fainted from the stress of it all." Marlie sighed and climbed from his lap. "I'd better see what's in the kitchen if we're going to eat tonight."

"Want me to go out for something?" he offered.

"No, I'm not in the mood for takeout. I'll think of something. Why don't you just sit here and read the newspaper? You look as if you need to unwind a little."

He definitely agreed with that assessment, and went into the bedroom to change out of his sticky, wrinkled clothes. Marlie poked around in the refrigerator and cabinets before deciding on chicken stir-fry. She was glad Dane had gone along with her suggestion, because she needed more time by herself. He was so intuitive that he would soon figure out that something more than the situation was upsetting her, and she didn't want to be around him until she had herself more under control.

She hadn't been paying much attention today when the head of accounting had been talking to the irate customer, trying to explain and soothe without backing down, but suddenly she had been overwhelmed by frustration and anger. Startled, she had automatically looked around for the source, and only then realized what had happened. She was picking up the department head's emotions.

She had quietly panicked, sitting frozen in her chair and trying to shut out the flow of emotion. To her surprise, it had stopped as abruptly as it had started, though the conversation behind her had continued.

She didn't know if she had succeeded in blocking it, or if her ability to read people was merely sputtering to life again. Either way, Dane wouldn't like it.

She knew that he viewed the visions differently, that he didn't see them as a threat to his privacy. But if her ability to

read people returned in full force, she didn't know if Dane would be able to accept it. He hadn't liked being the target of clairvoyance, which was not, and never had been, her major talent. If he knew that she could read him at will . . . he would probably leave, even though she had promised that she wouldn't invade his privacy. She had to face that likelihood. Dane cared for her, but she doubted that he cared enough to stay under those circumstances. It wasn't anything new; people had always been uncomfortable around her.

The decision not to tell him had been easily made. She didn't know what was happening: if her abilities would return in full force, if she would recover only a portion of her former capability, or if she would be even stronger. She hoped it wasn't the last possibility, for if her empathic powers returned stronger than before, she would have to move into an underground bunker to find any peace. It was a certainty that Dane wouldn't share that bunker with her.

She felt as if she were living in limbo with him. There had been none of the customary courtship stages, no getting to know each other. They had been thrown together in a crisis, had first been adversaries, then, abruptly, lovers. They had never had a discussion about their relationship, whatever it was. He had simply moved in, and she had no idea what to expect. After the killer was caught, would he simply return to his own house with a blithe "See you around" or—or what? If circumstances had been normal, the logical step, the one she had expected, would have been for him to spend a few nights each week with her.

She needed emotional security. She could bear anything if she had a solid foundation to fall back on, but she wasn't certain she had that with Dane.

It was silly, considering that she was living and sleeping with the man, but somehow she couldn't bring herself to ask him outright what his intentions were. She admitted to herself that she was frankly afraid of hearing the answer. Dane wasn't a man who would prevaricate; he would

bluntly tell her the truth, and she wasn't ready for that. Later. Everything had to wait. After this was all over, then she would be able to handle anything he said, even if it was exactly what she didn't want to hear.

She had fallen in love with him, but she didn't fool herself that she knew all about the kind of man he was. For all their physical intimacy, he kept a large part of himself private, safely secluded behind an iron wall. Sometimes he watched her with a silent, intent speculation that was almost frightening, because she couldn't read any desire in his eyes during those times.

What was he thinking? More important, what was he planning?

The media were relentless. The phones in headquarters rang endlessly. Reporters camped outside the chief's office, outside the mayor's office, outside police headquarters. Both uniformed and plainclothes officers began taking evasive action when entering or leaving the building, going to extraordinary lengths to avoid the hassle.

Even worse than the media were the crank calls that began pouring in. Hundreds of people in Orlando suddenly recalled suspicious persons skulking around Dumpsters and storefronts. People with grudges found revenge by phoning in anonymous tips, accusing the person they disliked of being the killer. Every night officers investigated panicked calls of a prowler in the house, but most times it was nothing. Several mothers-in-law turned in their daughters' despicable husbands, certain that the lazy bastards were guilty of all manner of unspeakable crimes. The hell of it was, all of it had to be investigated. No matter how wild an allegation, it had to be checked. The uniformed officers were run ragged, worn down by the sizzling heat and neverending demands on their time.

Chief Champlin held a news conference, hoping to ease some of the intense media pressure. He explained that there wasn't a lot of information he could give them, because of

the ongoing investigations. But logic was a useless weapon; it didn't satisfy the voracious appetite for facts, for stories, for airtime and column space. It didn't sell newspapers or jack up the ratings numbers. The reporters wanted juicy, gory, frightening details, and were frustrated when none were forthcoming.

Carroll Janes watched the news programs and read the newspapers, and smiled with satisfaction. The police couldn't give the media much information because they didn't have much. The stupid saps were overmatched, just as all the others had been. He was too smart for them to catch—ever.

18

ALL IN ALL, CARROLL JANES WAS PLEASED WITH THE FRENZY. Just two punishments, and look how he had taken over as top story. Of course, he would have to take back his insulting thoughts about the Orlando PD; they weren't as stupid as he had feared. Though the second punishment *had* been rather obvious, a lot of departments wouldn't have made the connection between the two, for after all, he had left the fingers intact on the second one. It had irritated him when the Vinick bitch had scratched him and he had been obligated to go to the extra trouble of removing her fingers and disposing of them, but at least fingers were small and easy to get rid of. Dogs had no trouble with them at all, and the tiny bones, if any remained, were unidentifiable.

There was no way the cops could catch him, but at least they *knew* about him; it added an extra fillip to the process. It was nice to be appreciated, rather like the difference between an actor performing in an empty theater and one performing before an awestruck, standing-room-only

crowd. He enjoyed the details so much more, knowing that the police would be amazed at his intelligence, his inventiveness, his absolute perfection, even while they cursed it. How gratifying it was to know one's opponents were properly respectful of one's talents.

He had been frustrated in his attempt to find another transgressor, for experimental purposes, but Janes considered himself a patient man. What would be, would be. It would be cheating to rush things; it would take away from the power of the moment. He had been more content since the news had broken, for of course, it was always exhilarating to read about oneself, to be the topic of conversation on everyone's lips. Even Annette, at work, had talked of little else. She had told him about all the elaborate precautions she was taking, as if he would ever be challenged by her, the little sow. But it amused him to commiserate with her, to feed her fear and drive her to even more ridiculous safety measures. She refused to even walk to her car by herself, as if he had ever dragged anyone off the streets. How pedestrian that was—he chuckled at his own wit—when the real challenge was to take them in their own homes, where they felt safest.

Annette was at lunch on Wednesday when a tall, buxom brunette sailed up to the counter, her face tight with anger. "I want to speak to someone about the service in this store," she snapped.

Janes gave her his best smile. "May I be of assistance, ma'am?"

The crux of the problem was that she was on her lunch hour and had stood for fifteen minutes in the clothing department trying to get someone to exchange a blouse for her. She still hadn't been waited on, and now she wouldn't have time to eat lunch. Janes controlled a thrill of anticipation as she ranted on, fury in every line of her body.

"I'll call the clothing department and make certain you're taken care of immediately," he said. "Your name is . . . ?"

"Farley," she said. "Joyce Farley."

He glanced at her hands. No wedding ring. "Do you have an account with us, Miss Farley?"

"That's *Ms.* Farley," she snapped. "What difference does that make? Does a customer have to have a charge account before this store is interested in her?"

"Not at all," he said politely. It was simply easier to get vital information if she was in the computer bank. She was one of those prickly, man-hating feminists. The anticipation grew stronger; he would enjoy punishing her. He slid a form toward her. "If you don't mind, would you fill out this complaint form? We like to follow through on all complaints, and make certain the customer is satisfied with our action."

"I really don't have time for this. I'm going to be late back to work already."

"Then just your name and address will do. I'll pencil in the details myself."

Hastily she scribbled her name and address at the top of the form while he phoned the clothing department and spoke with the head clerk. He smiled again as he hung up. "Mrs. Washburn will be waiting personally to make the exchange."

"This shouldn't have been necessary."

"I completely agree." He slid the form off the top of the counter.

She turned to go, took a step, then abruptly stopped and turned back. "I'm sorry," she said. "I have a terrible headache and I'm angry, but I shouldn't have taken it out on you. It wasn't your fault, and you've done everything you can to help me. I apologize for being so nasty to you."

He was so taken aback that it was a moment before he could say, "Think nothing of it. I'm glad I could be of service." Conventional reply, one that was mouthed thousands of times a day by thousands of bored salespeople, because it would mean their jobs if they said what they

really wanted to say. Ms. Farley gave him a brief, hesitant smile and walked away.

Janes stared after her, fury rising in him. Viciously he crumpled the complaint form and threw it in the trash. How dare she apologize! She had ruined everything. That wasn't the point. Punishment was the point. He felt cheated, as if a ripe prize had been dangled in front of him and then snatched away. He had already begun to feel the flow of vitality, and known the hunger to let his power have free rein. Now he was left with nothing! He should kill the bitch anyway, to teach her that she couldn't act any way she wanted and then escape the consequences by whining an apology.

No. Rules were rules. He had to obey them; it would ruin everything if he didn't. There were certain criteria to be met, standards to be upheld. If he couldn't maintain those standards, then he would *deserve* to be caught. No matter how much he wanted to discipline her, he had to save himself for the true lessons.

Marlie sat very still at her desk, trying to control her trembling. Thank God it was lunchtime, and almost everyone had gone out to eat. She had brought her lunch and a book, intending to spend a quiet hour reading. She had been happily engrossed in the book, absently munching an apple, when a dark sense of mingled anger and anticipation had filled her. It hadn't been as overwhelming as a full vision, but she had recognized the source. There was no mistaking the cold evilness at the core. And then, suddenly, the anger had intensified, but the anticipation was gone, and she sensed disappointment instead.

She had come to know him. His mental force hadn't been strong enough for her to "see" the events, but she knew without seeing. He had selected his next victim, and something had happened to deprive him of his sadistic pleasure.

He was out there. And he was hunting.

* * *

"He's looking for someone," she told Dane that night. She prowled restlessly around the room. "I felt him today."

He put aside the newspaper he had been reading—which was full of slightly hysterical and mostly erroneous stories about the Orlando Slasher—and focused the full intensity of his attention on her. Even the planes of his face hardened; she had grown accustomed to that roughhewn face, seeing it through the eyes of love, but abruptly she perceived him again as she had seen him the first time they had met: Dane Hollister the cop, the Dane Hollister who was dangerous.

"What happened?" he asked, a bite in his tone. *"When* did it happen? Why didn't you call me?"

She shot him a brief glance and resumed her aimless pacing. "What could you have done?"

The answer was "nothing," and she saw he didn't like that. "It was during my lunch, about twelve-thirty. All of a sudden he was there. I could feel his anger, but he was excited, too, like a kid anticipating a treat. He had picked her out, I know he had. Then something happened, I don't know what, but she got away and he was disappointed."

"And then?"

"Nothing. I couldn't feel him anymore."

He was watching her closely. "But you can tell when he's choosing his victim?"

She shrugged. "I did this time."

"Anything else? Could you tell anything about the victim?"

"No."

"The slightest detail would help—"

"I told you, no!" she suddenly shouted, wheeling toward the bedroom. "Don't you think I've tried?"

He moved like a tiger pouncing, springing up from the couch and catching her before she could reach the bedroom and close the door between them. He wrapped his arms around her from behind, pulling her tightly against him. Now he could feel the slight tremors running through her,

the shaking that hadn't completely left her since lunch. "I'm sorry," he murmured, rubbing his rough chin against her temple. "I know how hard this is for you. Are you okay?"

She hesitated, then reluctantly admitted, "I'm a little spooked."

He rocked her back and forth for a minute, letting her absorb the security of his presence. She had been living with the stress for almost a month now, and it had to be much worse for her than for him. She needed a break. He brushed her hair back from her face, thinking hard. "Want to go see a movie?"

"That was your solution last time," she said tautly. "Going somewhere."

"Did it work?"

Involuntarily she relaxed a little. She was so tired; it felt good to lean on him. "You know it did."

"Then let's go to a movie. Isn't there something you'd like to see?"

"I don't know." She was hesitant. "I haven't been to a movie since the first murder."

"Then it's time. I haven't seen a movie in a couple of years. What interests you?"

"I don't know what's playing." She turned to face him, and managed a smile. "I'd rather just go for a drive, I think."

He was relieved to feel the tension easing out of her. He would have preferred to take her to bed, but knew she was too tense to enjoy it. "Then that's what we'll do," he said.

The twilight air was thick and heavy when they left the house, the heat lingering even though the sun had gone down, and thunder rumbled dully in the distance. Dane rolled down his window, hit the interstate highway, and turned the car's nose toward the Gulf Coast, straight into the approaching storm. The cloud bank loomed overhead like a great beast, streaks of lightning darting across its purplish black underbelly.

The air blasting in through the open window became

cooler, almost cold, and carried with it the sweet, dusty scent of rain. Marlie sat silently beside him, her eyes on the storm. The first raindrops splatted on his windshield. He had time to roll up his window and turn on the wipers, and then they were plunging headlong into the torrent sweeping toward them.

He had to slow down to almost a crawl, while the thunder boomed around them and lightning cracked. Other, more prudent drivers pulled off the highway completely, seeking shelter under overpasses or simply getting out of traffic. A few daring souls continued into the heart of the storm, as darkness crashed down and the puny efforts of headlights could illuminate only a short distance in front of them.

Marlie was motionless. The fierceness of the storm emptied her, sucked out all sense of self and filled her instead with its own raw power. She knew she should have been afraid of electrical storms, but she wasn't. The magnificence of it filled her with awe, and the energy unleashed somehow replenished her.

Dane always drove with his interior lights extinguished, and the car was a dark cave. He didn't speak, and neither did she. She felt no need for words. She was safe and dry while the fury thrashed around them, battering the car with sheets of rain and gusts of wind that rocked it from side to side. Dane held it steady, his powerful forearms rippling with muscles as he fought to counteract the storm's fury. Marlie didn't feel even a second of uneasiness; she was safe and she knew it.

Eventually they drove out of the storm, leaving it flashing and rumbling sulkily in the distance. It continued to rain, but it was a light, steady, ordinary rain. They rolled their windows down a couple of inches and let the sweet air flow around them.

He looped around on the next exit and headed back toward Orlando, this time chasing the storm.

She leaned her head back. The storm had intensified

everything; she had never felt quite like this before. Her heartbeat was slow and heavy, a silent drum; her body felt heavy and ripe, pulsing with life. She wanted him, wanted his hardness and passion inside her. She could feel him beside her, taut with sexual awareness. His eyes were on the road, but his attention was focused on her; she knew that he was acutely aware of every movement she made, of the slight rustling of her breathing, the warm, faint scent of her body.

"Dane," she said. The one word vibrated in the darkness.

He was sweating; she could see the sheen on his face whenever they met an oncoming vehicle. Heat was rolling off him in waves. Excitement coiled in her belly; he was almost out of control, in a way she hadn't experienced before. Always before, even the first time, no matter how aroused he was, he had managed to hold himself back until she had been satisfied. He had wanted her before they had left the house, and the primal fury of the storm had only fed his hunger, just as it had awakened hers.

She wanted to ask him if he loved her, but the words wouldn't come. He was with her here and now, and if sexual attraction was all he felt, she would find out all too soon. Since the present was all the time she was guaranteed, she decided to stop fretting and make the most of it. Wasn't that what life was about anyway? Hadn't she learned anything from all the pain, her own and others, she had experienced? No one made it through life without suffering. The trick was to make the most of the present, and enjoy the gifts of life as they were offered.

She reached out and gently trailed one finger along the crease between thigh and groin, feeling his muscles harden beneath her touch. His erection was like iron, pushing against the constraint of his pants. She stroked her finger up and down the length of it.

His breath hissed out between his teeth. "Stop teasing me."

"I'm not teasing," she murmured, almost purring the words. "I'm very serious." She delved her hand between his legs, and he groaned as involuntarily he shifted them apart. The car slowed, then he gathered himself and increased speed again.

"I can't stop now," he said with stifled violence. "There's too much traffic."

"See any interesting motels?" she asked, her tone absent as she concentrated on unbuckling his belt.

He shuddered, sucking in his breath to give her hands more room. He wanted her to stop, but at the same time he was helpless against the pleasure. "I don't have any rubbers with me." Except for their first night together, he had used a condom every time they made love. That first night, he hadn't been able to think of anything except getting inside her. Privately he had been shocked at his own carelessness, which had never happened before, and since then had made damn sure it hadn't happened again.

The solution of stopping at a drugstore occurred to her, but she dismissed it. She didn't want the distraction, and he wasn't in any shape to go shopping. "You'd better drive faster," she said, just as she eased down his zipper and worked her hand inside his pants to close her fingers around his naked shaft.

A rough moan burst out of him. She savored the sound of it, just as she savored the feel of him throbbing in her hand. She knew that a few quick, hard pumps would finish it for him, so she deliberately kept her touch light, slow, and lingering. His face was set in taut lines as she snuggled closer and kissed the underside of his jaw. Her breasts were pressed against his muscled arm, and she could feel the fine tremor shaking it.

"You're going to pay for this," he warned.

She bit his earlobe. "Sounds interesting. Got any ideas?"

He had several, but none that could be enacted in the car. He only hoped he wasn't stopped for speeding, because he

didn't think there was any way in hell he could get his pants fastened. She continued to gently caress him, keeping him achingly hard. "Are you having fun?" His lungs were constricted, preventing him from speaking above a growl.

"Oodles." Her tongue dipped briefly into his ear, and he shivered convulsively. "I'm not ready to stop, either. You just keep on driving."

He did. He drove as he had never driven before, with a desperate concentration that still wasn't enough to block out what she was doing to him. A rough laugh escaped his throat. "You little witch, you're enjoying this."

She gave him a slow, satisfied smile. "Of course I am. You usually drive *me* crazy. How does it feel to be on the receiving end?"

"Like I'm going to die," he gasped.

She looked around and pinpointed their location. "We'll be home in another five minutes. You can hold out that long, can't you?" She continued caressing him, using every bit of knowledge she had about his body to enflame him further. She licked him very delicately.

He gasped again, his body going rigid. "Maybe."

By the time they got home he was wild, his hips surging upward with every lingering stroke of her hand. He literally dragged her out of the car and into the house, where they stumbled into the bedroom, tearing and pulling at each other's clothes. They were still half-clothed when they fell onto the bed. Dane managed to delay until he got a condom on, then he flipped her onto her stomach, kneed her legs apart, and drove into her with battering force.

Marlie dug her fingers into the bedcovers, her body shuddering under the force of his thrusts. She was as excited as if she had been the one so deliciously tormented. She lifted her buttocks, wriggling against him to take him deeper, though that didn't seem possible. He groaned with every thrust, wild, guttural sounds that hung in the darkness of the night. And then his entire body tensed and he shoved

violently into her and held himself there, shuddering, hoarsely crying out his satisfaction as his climax shook him to the core.

Afterward he eased down to lie half beside her and half on her, his movements blind and uncoordinated, his big body trembling. His chest heaved as he struggled to get enough oxygen, and she could feel the force of his heartbeats thudding through his body. "Oh, God," he wheezed. "That damn near killed me."

"Really?" she murmured. "I thought you enjoyed it. But if you didn't like it, I won't do it again—"

He thrust his hand into her hair and turned her head so he could stop the words with a hard, forceful kiss. "I'll try to bear up under the strain."

"My hero," she said, nipping at his lower lip, then returning for a deeper kiss.

A bass purr rumbled in his chest. He turned her in his arms and lifted himself to loom over her. "Now, lady, let's see about you."

He took care of that very well, leaving her exhausted, limp, and satiated. Afterward they lay together in the darkness, listening to the rain. She absently played with the curly hair on his chest. After a while she yawned and said, "Did you close the car door?"

He went still, thinking very hard. Then he said, "Oh, hell," and heaved himself out of bed. She lay there giggling while he pulled on his pants and stumbled through the dark house. She heard the front door open, then close again a couple of seconds later. In another minute he came back into the bedroom. "Yes, I did, smart-ass," he rumbled.

"Well, I didn't remember."

He chuckled. "I didn't either." He shucked his pants and crawled back into bed. He yawned as he gathered her close to him again, tucking her protectively into his embrace. "When this is over," he murmured into her hair, "we're both going to need a vacation. Which do you like, the mountains or the beach?"

Her heart gave a little skip of happiness. It was the first time he had said anything about a mutual future, even if it was something as casual as planning a vacation. "This is Florida," she replied. "We can go to the beach anytime."

"Mountains it is, then. We'll rent a cabin with a hot tub, get naked, unwind, and shock the squirrels."

"It's a deal."

The phone rang, and Dane stretched out his arm to get it. "Hollister," he said lazily. Lying against him as she was, Marlie felt him tense. He sat up and swung his feet to the floor. "Okay, okay, I'll be there in about fifteen minutes. Try to keep the media from driving everyone into hysterics."

He hung up the phone and turned on the lamp. "There's been another slashing murder," he said, hastily pulling on his clothes.

Marlie sat up, fear consuming her as she remembered earlier in the day when she had felt the killer searching for another victim. She and Dane had gone for that drive out of town; had they been so far away that she wouldn't have been able to pick up the killer's energy? Had he acted, after all, and somehow she hadn't felt him?

19

WHAT'S THE VICTIM'S NAME?" DANE ASKED, LOOKING AT THE body as the police photographer snapped pictures from different angles.

It was a typical murder scene, if there was such a thing. The place was working like a beehive, and most of the people weren't doing a damn thing except standing around. The house was crawling with policemen, and the neighborhood was crawling with reporters, who ignored the light rain in favor of getting comments from anyone who would talk to them. Bonness was there, Trammell was there, Freddie and Worley were there—hell, it looked as if every detective on the squad was there—and the chief was reportedly on the way. The fingerprint guys were dusting their black powder over everything, the forensic evidence people were vacuuming—it was a zoo.

"Felicia Alden," Freddie said. "Her husband, Gene, found her. He's a sales rep for a pharmaceutical firm and had been away on business."

"And he just happened to come home right after his wife

was murdered," Dane said wearily. They all looked at one another. They had seen the other scenes, and this was nothing like them, except for the fact that a woman had died from knife wounds. For one thing, the victim was still clothed, and she was lying on the bed as if she had been arranged there. There was no indication of sexual attack.

Dane sighed with relief. Marlie hadn't failed; they all knew, and it was just a matter of proving it, that Gene Alden had probably murdered his wife and tried to set it up so that it looked like one of the serial murders. Alden had likely thought that, since the media had reported there was no evidence left behind, he would be safe when investigation turned up only forensic material that could be linked to him; after all, he *lived* there.

"Take him in for questioning, and find out about any life insurance policies he had on her," Bonness said. "Or maybe if he caught her fooling around. I'll try to calm the reporters down, but I can't say much until we actually charge the guy, so they won't believe me." He looked depressed at the thought of facing the horde of shouting reporters.

"At least we'll be able to do something about this one," Freddie said.

Trammell walked over to join Dane, and they went outside. Reporters were mobbing Bonness, shouting questions at him. He was trying to talk, but they kept interrupting him. "I guess Marlie didn't have a vision with this one," Trammell said.

"Not even a glimmer, but it was scary anyway; it wasn't a vision, but this afternoon she sort of locked on to him. He had picked out his next victim, but something happened and he lost her."

Trammell whistled. "How's Marlie?"

"On edge. It's wearing her down."

"No wonder. I wish there was some way to make it easier for her."

"I'll make damn sure she's okay," Dane said grimly. "By the way, how's the work going on my house?"

"The floors are almost finished, and the furniture will be delivered this weekend. You can move back in on Monday, if you want."

Dane snorted as he got in his car. "Get real, buddy."

Trammell laughed. "Yeah, that's what I thought. See you in the morning."

As Dane had expected, Marlie was still awake when he got there. "It wasn't him," he said, and watched the tension ease out of her face. She looked very small, curled up in a corner of the couch with her robe pulled tightly around her. "Probably the woman's husband did it, and tried to make it look like the other murders." He held out his hand to her. "Come on, honey, let's go back to bed."

Janes carefully controlled his elation Friday afternoon as he watched the indignant customer stalk away. Annette was there, so it wouldn't do to let even a hint of his emotions show. At last! He was going to savor this one; too much time had passed, three weeks, for him to accurately compare it with the last one. Besides, he had concluded that it was the haste of the last punishment that had ruined it for him. He would do this one the way it should be done, with slow and careful planning, letting the anticipation build. He needed at least a week to do it properly.

He checked the calendar, though of course, he didn't need to. It was just a part of his incredible precision. Yes, the earliest possible date would be next Friday night. The weekends were the best because those were his off days, and he could sleep late the next day. Let the media hoopla, satisfying as it was, die down a bit. The frenzy had nothing to feed on, though there had been that silly burst of hysteria the other night when some salesman had offed his wife and tried to blame it on him. It hadn't worked, of course; the stupid bastard hadn't had the same attention to detail. The cops had immediately seen through him. The television reports had sounded a tad disappointed.

Yes, this one would be good, maybe the best yet. The

woman had been a complete bitch, the kind he had always despised on sight: lean, tanned, brittle, overloaded with jewelry of questionable taste. She flaunted her money. She might have a security system, or even guard dogs. The possibility was intriguing. It would be a real test of his genius, if she did. He disregarded the probability of a husband; that had never stopped him before.

He looked down at the name she had scribbled, repeating it in his mind, savoring the syllables. Marilyn Elrod. Anticipation was already flooding his body with energy. Marilyn Elrod. He hummed a few bars of a song, substituting her name. Mar-uh-lynn, O Mar-uh-lynn, ta dum de dum something. It was played before the Preakness race. The joke was, she didn't know she should be running.

Friday night, Marlie asked him how work was coming along on his house. Dane lied without hesitation. "It's almost finished," he said. "There's been a delay on the furniture Trammell ordered."

The furniture was in place, and everything looked great, but he had no intention of moving out of Marlie's house until the killer was caught. Another weekend had come and gone without a murder. A few sarcastic reporters were beginning to ask if the police were *certain* there was a serial killer, or had they just been spooked by a similarity between the murders of Nadine Vinick and Jackie Sheets?

"Feel anything today?" he asked.

She shook her head. "Nothing concrete. Just kind of uneasy." And when she had been driving home, she had passed a young couple so engrossed with each other that they had been passionately kissing there on the sidewalk. She had been in that automatic state that takes over when driving, her guard down, and suddenly she had been reading the young man. Again, it had been such a shock that she had immediately shut down, withdrawing from the emotional contact. She had had the wry thought that she hoped they would find somewhere private soon, given the intensity of

the young man's arousal, or she wouldn't be the only one shocked.

Then the realization dawned that twice now she had been able to control the contact, to break it off. Even before, at the height of her abilities, she hadn't been able to do that. She had learned how to partially shield herself, but had never managed complete protection. Okay, so the initial contact had slipped in, when she had been relaxed; she had still been able to immediately sever the connection.

She hadn't wanted the return of her abilities, but suddenly she was filled with a sense of triumph, and contentment. Gleen hadn't won, after all. The healing process had taken a long time, but in the end, she was the victor. She had emerged from the trauma even stronger than before, better able to control the gift that had been given her. She had even, with Dane, gotten past the physical terror and learned the joy of sexual pleasure. She couldn't have done it two years ago, even a year ago, but her healing had finally progressed to the point that she had won.

"Is he hunting?" Dane asked.

"Who knows? Like I said, it wasn't anything concrete. Maybe it's just that I dread tonight so much."

"Maybe I can do something about that," he said in a slow, deep tone. He was leaning against the cabinets while she threw together a quick meal, getting in her way as usual. She looked at him and went weak in the knees. He looked so thoroughly male that every cell in her body responded. Dane was always slightly rough-edged, even when his clothes were freshly ironed, but even more so now with his shirt wrinkled, his dark hair disheveled, and his jaw showing both the mark of this morning's assault with a razor and the need for another shave. As always, he still wore his shoulder holster, the butt of the big pistol sticking out under his armpit; he was so accustomed to being armed that he no longer noticed it. Those sharp hazel eyes were greener than usual, and held a predatory gleam as he watched her.

"Maybe you can," she agreed, her own voice huskier than usual. Maybe, nothing; she was certain of it. His sexual power over her was so strong that the only thing that kept her from panicking was the knowledge that, when she chose, she could drive him just as crazy. She might have doubts about his emotional involvement, but there was no mistaking his physical response. All she had to do was brush against him, or give him a certain look, or even do nothing, and he would get aroused.

It sometimes startled her, for she was certainly not a sex kitten by any stretch of the imagination. She had always deliberately dressed to downplay her femininity, because she had never wanted to attract attention of any kind. None of that mattered with Dane; it was as if he never saw the clothes, but looked straight through to the woman. She still dressed the same, out of habit and convenience—after all, the clothes were *there*—but now, a bit surprised at herself, she realized that she didn't feel the need to continue the camouflage. Things had changed. She didn't have to hide herself away to protect her mental privacy, nor did she have to worry about the sickening intrusion of sexual advances. Dane intruded with sexual advances quite often, and there wasn't anything the least sickening about them.

She was stronger. Her abilities had changed. She had healed, and was in control. She felt another little jolt as she truly realized, for the first time, that she was no longer at the mercy of her own mental powers.

She could dress any way she wanted. She could buy the trim, stylish clothes she had always admired, or even something downright sexy.

"What are you thinking?" Dane asked uneasily. "You've been staring at me like I'm Tweetie Bird, and you're a hungry cat."

She let her gaze drop lower, and delicately licked her lips.

His face changed. He straightened away from the cabinet, every muscle in his powerful body growing taut. Then he

reached out and deliberately turned off the stove. She raised her eyebrows at him. "This may take a while," he explained, his eyes heavy-lidded as he pulled her close.

Nothing happened that weekend, though Marlie couldn't shake the uneasy anticipation. She was beginning to think she would feel that way until the man was caught. But she managed the tension better than she had the weekend before, perhaps because of her newfound confidence. She tested her control when she stood talking to Lou for a while on Saturday, deliberately opening herself up; she immediately read her neighbor's emotions, and when she decided to stop, the flow was blocked. It was like opening a door and closing it again. She could do it!

It wasn't an entirely satisfying experience, however; she found that Lou was extremely disapproving of the situation next door, with that man, even if he was a police officer, just blatantly moving in. Lou felt it set a bad example. Marlie wondered who she was setting a bad example *for,* since she was the youngest person in the neighborhood anyway. Most of her neighbors were retirees.

It didn't help when Dane chose that moment to come out on the front porch, wearing only a pair of disreputable jeans. Because they had spent a lazy day around the house, he hadn't shaved. He looked big, rough, slightly dangerous, and wholly masculine, with his powerful chest bare. "Hi, Lou," he called. "Sorry to interrupt. Honey, do you know where I put my gun oil?"

"You didn't," she replied. "You left it out. *I* put it in the kitchen, second drawer from the right."

He flashed a grin at her. "Sorry." Then he disappeared back into the house.

Lou's face was stiff, her eyes wide as she stared at the spot where he had stood. Marlie shifted uncomfortably. This was one time she definitely didn't want to open that door and feel what Lou was feeling.

Then Lou exhaled in a long sigh. "Holy cow," she said.

Her cheeks looked a little flushed. She gave Marlie a slightly embarrassed look. "I may be old-fashioned," she admitted, "but I'm a long way from blind."

Marlie entered the kitchen a few minutes later to find Dane calmly reassembling his pistol. There was no way he could have cleaned the weapon in the time that had elapsed. "You did that deliberately," she accused, keeping her voice level with an effort. Lou had still been a little giddy when she had gone inside.

He grinned, not pausing in his brisk, practiced actions. "I like ruffling her feathers," he admitted. "I thought about unsnapping my jeans, but I decided against it. Overkill."

"It's a good thing. You might not have made it back into the house unscathed, if you had."

"Really pissed her off, huh?"

"Not exactly."

He glanced up, his expression quizzical. Marlie smiled sweetly at him. "Lou fell in lust with your manly form, big boy."

After a startled moment, he began laughing. He was too heavy for her to budge his chair, so she shoved the table away and planted her hands on his shoulders as she straddled the chair and sat down on his lap. His laughter stopped, that familiar tenseness hardening his features. "I know how she feels," Marlie whispered, nuzzling his jaw. Her heart pounded at the scent of him, all hot, musky male mingled with the sharp odor of gun oil. She moved slowly against the ridge in his jeans.

"Wait." His protest was feeble. "I have oil on my hands."

"So? I'm washable," she murmured, and that was all he needed to hear.

The weekend was wonderful. She ignored the frisson of alarm that was always there, never quite allowing her nerves to settle down, and enjoyed what she had. There were no visions, no false alarms of copycat murders. She suggested going over to his house to see how everything looked, but he was in a lazy mood and didn't seem interested. They

watched television and read. They tried out recipes . . . or rather, Marlie tried them out, while Dane kept her company and sampled the results. And they made love, often. It was exactly the type of life Marlie had always wanted, and always thought impossible.

By Monday, with nothing happening over the weekend, the press reports were scathing. The Orlando PD had overreacted, like Chicken Little squawking about the sky falling. One columnist suggested that not only had they made fools of themselves on the basis of two similar murders, but the hoopla might even have triggered the copycat murder of Felicia Alden.

"They forget," Dane said sarcastically, "that the department isn't responsible for all the publicity; the media did that. We've been trying to keep everything as low-key and under wraps as possible."

Marlie gave him a troubled look. "But now, with them calling it a false alarm, people will stop being as careful. It's giving him a greater opportunity of success."

"Tell that to the press. All they'll give you is the smart-ass answer that they don't make the news, they just report it."

"If reporting was all they did, that would be fine. But they angle it, they slant it, they 'interpret' it."

He saw how truly upset she was; he was pissed off, but the press reports bothered Marlie on a deeper level. He remembered that her experiences with the media generally weren't pleasant, and he swiftly changed the subject.

Janes was pleased with what he had accomplished over the weekend. He had made several casual trips by the Elrod house, and been delighted by what he had discovered so far. The house was large and upscale, set in the middle of a big lot with an excess of landscaping that would provide plenty of cover. Six-foot-high fences marked the boundary lines of almost every lot in the neighborhood, which further restricted any nosy neighbor's observation.

He hadn't seen Mr. Elrod, though the city directory listed

one. Was he out of town? It was a concern that had been laughably easy to answer, though the answer had come from an unexpected source. Marilyn Elrod had conveniently left the house not five minutes before her mail was delivered, and Janes had simply used the opportunity to collect the mail and go through it. Some of the usual assortment of junk mail had been addressed to a Mr. James Elrod, confirming his existence. A more interesting envelope bore the imprint of an Orlando law firm. Janes didn't hesitate to open it, and what he read greatly pleased him. It seemed Mr. and Mrs. Elrod were currently embroiled in divorce proceedings, and Mr. Elrod had recently moved out. What a pity.

He kept the letter, since it had been opened, and shoved the remainder of the mail back into the box. A quick look around the house revealed that there was no dog—if there had been, it would have been barking like mad by then—but there was an alarm system. Not particularly sophisticated, he saw, but a problem. Still, every system had a weakness, and he had no doubt that he would be able to find a means of entry. All in good time, though, all in good time. He wouldn't make the mistake of hurrying as he had the last time.

"We're being made to look like fools," Chief Champlin growled. He wasn't in a good mood. The mayor had raked him over the coals for jumping the gun and driving old women all over the city into hysteria. Not only that, the bad publicity had cost the city money. Orlando relied heavily on the tourist trade, with visitors from all over the world coming to the Mouse House. The rate of occupancy at the local motels and hotels had fallen off since the news had broken.

"I can't believe this," Bonness said plaintively. "Everyone is bitching because someone *hasn't* been murdered!"

"There were just two murders. Granted, the details were eerie in their similarity—"

"The FBI agrees that it's the same man," Dane broke in.

"We didn't go out on a limb in this, Chief. He's out there. With the Bureau's help, we think we've identified at least seventeen other killings that he's done."

"So maybe he left the city when the news broke!" the chief snapped.

Dane shook his head. "We think he's still here."

"On the basis of what information?"

"Marlie," he wanted to say, but he didn't. He contented himself with replying, "He never left an area so soon before. We're going with his established pattern."

"The mayor wants to know, and so do I, just what you're doing with your time. If there is no evidence, just what in hell are you doing?"

Dane's face had taken on a stony look. Trammell saw the signs of an incipient loss of temper and stepped in. "We've received lists of names from the utility companies on new customers for the past year, and we're working our way down the list, investigating all the men on it. With the profile the FBI gave us, we'll be able to narrow it down to a few possibilities."

Chief Champlin was from the old school. He didn't like Trammell's slick sophistication, his money, his snappy clothes, or his exotic looks. He did, however, respect the political ties that Trammell had in the city, courtesy of that same money. He growled a reply along the lines of "They'd better come up with something soon, or else," and left Bonness's office.

Bonness sighed and pulled out a handkerchief to blot his forehead. "Shit. Anything on those names we're running?"

"Nothing that sets off any alarms, but we still have a lot of names to go."

"Okay. Let me know the minute you hear bells."

"Will do."

"Son of a bitch," Dane said between his teeth as they returned to their desks.

"Calm down, partner. He doesn't know what we know,

because we can't tell him about Marlie. I don't think he'd understand."

"Bonness was right." Cold fury was still in Dane's voice and eyes. "These bastards won't be satisfied until another woman is killed."

Janes made good use of his time at night. He found a secure place to leave his car, he checked out the situation with the neighbor's dogs. There were two, but one of them tended to bark at everything, and the other, across the street, would join him. The barking usually elicited no more than a few irritable "Shut ups."

Marilyn Elrod was a party girl. She was out hitting the bars almost every night, which may have been the reason Mr. Elrod was no longer living there. So far, though, she hadn't brought anyone home with her. Her active night life gave him plenty of opportunity to make sure things were perfect.

Her night life also gave him a means of getting into the house. Thick shrubbery grew all along the house, right up to the garage. She had a habit of backing into the garage, so she could just drive right out whenever she left; since she was facing ahead, it was child's play for him to slip from his hiding place in the shrubbery into the garage, before the automatic door closed. She never looked back.

The door leading from the garage into the utility room wasn't wired into the security system, though the door from outside into the garage was. It was locked, but locks weren't a problem for him. It was another skill he had taught himself, with the aid of a mail-order locksmithing course that he had taken under an alias, just as a precaution. Another little detail he had foreseen and taken care of.

The first time he entered the house he had simply walked around and familiarized himself with it. He kept himself calm, not letting anticipation trick him into acting before he was really ready, as he had the last time.

The second time, he explored more. He opened her closets and went through her clothes, deciding that her taste seemed frozen in the eighties singles-bar style. She spent a fortune on makeup, he noticed, prowling through her bathroom vanity.

He satisfied himself that there were no guns in the house. Guns could be a big problem.

Then, humming to himself, he explored the kitchen. She wasn't much on cooking; the refrigerator held mostly microwave stuff. But she had catered to the fashion of having a large rack of butcher's knives standing on the shiny black countertop, something he had counted on. Since she cooked so little, it wasn't likely that she would miss a knife. He examined each knife, *tsk*ing at the dulled edges on the stainless steel blades. Most women no longer had any pride in the domestic skills, which he deplored. If she had kept her knives in good condition, he wouldn't have to take the slight but admitted risk of removing one of them so he could put a proper edge on it.

All in all, he severely disapproved of Marilyn Elrod.

"Come to the house for dinner with Grace and me tonight," Trammell said on Friday.

Dane leaned back in his chair. He was so sick of the damn lists on his desk that he wanted to cram them all into the trash. He never would have believed that so many people had moved into the Orlando area in the past year. What really pissed him off was that they weren't turning up a damn thing. He was glad the weekend had come, though he and Trammell were on call.

"It's Friday," he reminded Trammell.

"So? You have to eat on Fridays the same as any other day, don't you?"

"Marlie gets pretty tense on Fridays."

"Then it will do her good to take her mind off things. If she has a vision, she can have it just as well at my house as at hers."

"Okay, let me call her."

Marlie advanced the same arguments that he had, and he gave her the same answers Trammell had given him. She really didn't need much convincing, because she had spent the week dreading the approaching weekend. Dinner with Trammell and Grace would be a welcome distraction.

She had spent a few of her lunch hours shopping this past week, and for the first time wore one of her new outfits that evening. Trammell had said to dress casually, and she did, but the slim, white cotton pants and sleeveless white vest were very fetching, if she did say so herself. Dane shared the opinion. When she came out of the bedroom, his gaze settled on her bare shoulders and the deep vee of the neckline. "Are you wearing a bra?" he asked in a strained voice.

She looked down at herself. "Why?"

"I just want to know. Are you?"

"Can you see anything?" she asked, returning to the bedroom to examine herself in the mirror.

Dane followed. "Damn it, Marlie, are you wearing a bra or aren't you?"

"Do I need one?"

"I'll find out for myself," he said in frustration, reaching for her.

She slipped away, giving him a roguish smile. "Down, boy. You'll have to wait until later to find out. We're going to be late if we don't leave right now."

"I haven't seen that outfit before," he said as he followed her out the door.

"It's new. I bought it this week."

He studied her back, trying to decide if he could make out the outline of a bra beneath the white vest that bared a disconcerting amount of her. It wasn't that it was indecent, just that he wasn't used to seeing her dress like that. He liked the hell out of it, but he didn't want anyone else to appreciate the view.

Trammell's house was large and airy, with sleek furnish-

ings in light, soft colors that opened up the rooms even more. His taste, Marlie admitted, was wonderful. There was a sense of space, serenity, and coolness, enhanced by lush indoor plants and overhead fans gently stirring the air.

Dinner was relaxed, with a lot of joking and teasing. Marlie asked Trammell when Dane's house would be finished, and he lied without turning a hair. More delays, he said solemnly.

Grace told Marlie all about the wedding plans she was making, and how lucky it was that they had planned on a long engagement because she would need all the time to plan a large, formal wedding. Trammell broke out in a slight sweat as he listened to the discussion, but the look of wild panic was gone; he was adjusting to the idea of marriage in connection with himself.

A series of thunderstorms, normal during the hot summer nights, popped up and entertained them with dramatic flashes of lightning and booms of thunder. After dinner, Trammell took several photographs of them all, and that led him into showing the thick albums of shots he had taken over the years.

Dane figured prominently in a good many of them, and Marlie studied his face with interest. He looked different, somehow, in the stark black-and-white photos Trammell had taken. Seeing her interest, Trammell settled beside her to tell her all about every shot.

It was earlier than usual when Marilyn Elrod arrived home, but the passing storms had knocked out the electricity at the bar, and the patrons had been politely but firmly invited to leave. She was also tipsier than usual, and when the garage door didn't lift, she pressed the button on the opener again. Still nothing happened.

"Damn it," she muttered, pointing the opener directly at the doors and holding her thumb on the button. Nothing. She threw it onto the car seat beside her. "Stupid batteries."

She tottered in her high heels up the walk to the front

door, then stood weaving as she tried to remember the code for the security alarm. She only had a few seconds after unlocking the door, she didn't remember how long, to punch in the code and prevent the alarm from sounding. She hated that damn alarm, so shrill it hurt her eardrums. The security system had been James's idea, not hers. Men and their gadgets.

It took her a minute to notice that the little red light above the lock wasn't shining. Damn, was everything in the house malfunctioning?

Then she laughed softly to herself. Of course! The electricity was off here, too. She should have noticed how dark the neighborhood was.

She fumbled the key into the lock and opened it, stumbling a bit over the threshold as she went inside. Damn, it was dark as a tomb! How was she supposed to see?

Candles, she thought. She had candles. She had bought an assortment of incense candles, thinking of the sexy atmosphere they would make when she brought a lover home. There hadn't been any lovers yet, but she was prepared just in case. James had probably had some flashlights around, but she didn't know where they were. It was likely he had taken them with him, the bastard. He wouldn't want his little dolly to be caught in the dark.

But where had she put them? The kitchen? That didn't seem like the right place to put incense candles.

On the other hand, that's where the matches were, and maybe she had put them there. She slipped out of her heels as she felt her way through the dark house to the kitchen. She found the matches first and struck one, relieved by the small flare of light. Three of them burned down before she located the incense candles.

She lit one immediately, to give herself light. Well, this was a fine end to a boring evening, she thought in disgust. She might as well go to bed, since she couldn't even watch television.

She carried the sack of candles in one hand and the

lighted candle in the other as she went upstairs, only stumbling once. "Oops," she whispered. "Have to be careful. I'm carrying fire." The thought made her giggle.

In her bedroom, which she had changed completely after James had left—she had burned all the sheets the bastard had slept on—she lit the candles one by one and set them on her dresser, so she could see the effect when they were reflected in the mirror. Yeah, she thought. Pretty damn sexy. The thick aroma of incense rose, and she coughed a little. Maybe she should go for unscented candles.

She began to undress, leaving her clothes were they fell. The incense grew stronger, and she coughed again.

She halted, her head tilted a little to the side. Had she heard something? She waited, but the house remained silent. Too silent, she thought. Yeah, that was the problem. She was accustomed to hearing the quiet hum of the refrigerator, the clocks, the ceiling fans. Without them, she was too aware of the sounds outside.

When she was naked, she pulled on a robe and belted it loosely at her waist. She was suddenly too sleepy to do the complete cleansing cream routine, so she simply wet a washcloth in the dark bathroom and scrubbed it over her face, then dropped it in the basin.

She yawned as she went back into the bedroom. The candle flames flickered, sending up sickening waves of incense. She leaned over to blow them out, and a face appeared in the mirror.

She whirled around, a scream lodging in her throat.

"Hellooo," the man said softly.

20

THE ALBUM WENT SKIDDING ACROSS THE FLOOR, STARTLING everyone. Marlie was on her feet, swaying, her face utterly white. Her pupils were so constricted that only tiny black dots remained, the intense blue of the irises dominating her stricken face.

"Dane," she said. Her voice was thin and almost soundless.

"Oh, hell." He lunged out of his chair and caught her weight against him as her knees began to buckle.

"What's wrong?" Grace cried in alarm.

Both Dane and Trammell ignored her, their attention focused on Marlie. She was breathing in heavy, jerky gasps, her eyes wide and fixed as she stared at something they couldn't see.

"Dane?" she said again, pleading despair in her voice. Her hands clutched his shirt, twisting the fabric.

Dane gently eased her down onto the couch. "I'm here, baby," he said, hoping she could hear him. "Is it happening

again?" She didn't answer. He shook her insistently. "Marlie!"

The jerky breaths roughened into dry sobs. "He's looking at me," she said in a voice that was no longer hers.

Dane couldn't get her to respond again. She sat motionless, her breathing evening out until it was barely perceptible. Her eyes were open and unseeing, unblinking.

"Shit," Trammell said softly, crouched beside Dane. "When I said she could have a vision here as well as at home, I was joking."

"Alex," Grace said in a very clear, determined voice. "What is going on?" Her lack of understanding proved that Trammell had been his usual closemouthed self, not telling even Grace about Marlie's abilities.

Dane didn't take his worried gaze off Marlie's face. She was beyond his reach and he didn't like it, didn't like knowing that she was going through hell and there was nothing he could do. The waiting was over.

"Alex." Grace sounded as if she were about to resort to violence.

"Go ahead," Dane murmured absently to Trammell. "You might as well tell her."

"Tell me what? What's wrong with Marlie?"

Trammell stood up and put his hand on Grace's arm. "Marlie's psychic," he explained softly. "She has visions of the murders while they're happening."

"Psychic?" Grace glared at him. "I'm warning you, Alex Trammell—"

"It's true," Dane said. Violently he wished that it weren't. "She's having a vision now. Another murder is happening right now."

"If this is a joke—"

"It isn't," he said flatly.

"Don't tell anyone," Trammell instructed. "Other than the three of us, and Lieutenant Bonness, no one else knows."

She looked uneasily at Marlie. "How long does this last?"

Dane checked his watch. It was 10:36, earlier than the other two murders had happened. "I don't know. Half an hour, maybe." The last time, when Jackie Sheets was killed, it had taken him longer than that to bring her out of it. Somewhere in the city, at this very moment, another woman was dying a horrible death; Marlie was gone from him until it was finished.

At 10:54, her right hand twitched convulsively several times, in an abbreviated stabbing motion. Both Dane and Trammell understood the significance of the small movement. Sweat rolled down Dane's face despite the chill of the air conditioning. He caught her hand and held it, hoping that the contact would comfort her on some unconscious level. Trammell paced restlessly, his dark eyes hooded and dangerous.

"Make some coffee," Dane murmured. "Or tea. She'll need it." Grace moved toward the kitchen, but Trammell waved her back to her seat and went to do it himself.

At eleven, Dane sat down beside her and eased her against his shoulder. Her arms felt icy to his touch. He shook her gently. "Marlie? Can you come back to me now, honey?"

Her eyes didn't even flicker.

He waited a couple of minutes and shook her again, calling her name. He saw some small movement in her eyelids.

He began stroking her hands and arms, trying to rub some warmth back into her skin. "Wake up and talk to me, honey. Come on, pull out of it."

Slowly her eyes began to close, and she drooped in his arms as the rigidity began to leave her muscles. He shook her again, not wanting her to slide into that deep, unconscious sleep. "You have to talk to me, Marlie. You can't go to sleep yet."

With visible effort she lifted her eyelids and looked at him. She was dazed, incomprehension in her eyes. Panic

edged into the blue depths as she fought for consciousness, for her sense of self. It was another moment before recognition flared, followed closely by horror and anguish.

"Shhh, shhh," he whispered, holding her close. "I'm here, baby." He could feel the tremor that started in her legs and worked upward, becoming stronger and more violent with every passing second. He reached out, and Trammell put the coffee cup in his hand. Carefully he held it to Marlie's trembling lips, forcing her to sip. She was gray now, as the shock worsened.

"Please," she begged, her voice shaking and barely audible. "Let me lie down."

"Not yet. Drink some more coffee." He wanted to carry her to bed and let her sleep, while he held her close against the terrors of the night, but ruthlessly he pushed that impulse away. He had to get the details before he could allow her to rest.

"Tell me about it," he demanded, putting force in his voice. "Tell me what you saw."

She closed her eyes, trying to pull away from him.

"Damn it, Marlie!" He wasn't gentle when he shook her this time. "Tell me!"

Her mouth trembled wildly, and tears seeped out from under her lashes. "It's dark," she said. She took a deep breath and let it out with a shuddering sigh. She opened her eyes. "The electricity is out. The storm knocked it out."

That flat, expressionless tone entered her voice, as she let herself sink into the horror again. She stared straight ahead, and Dane braced himself. "She came home earlier than expected. She's drunk. She puts some candles on the dresser, lights them. Incense candles, in little glass holders. They stink. She takes off her clothes, puts on a robe. Nice of her; saves him some trouble. She goes into the bathroom and washes her face. When she comes out, he's waiting for her."

"Dear God," Grace said quietly, as the horror of what she was hearing, of what Marlie had endured, began to come home to her.

"He comes up behind her when she bends down to blow out the stinking candles. She sees him, turns around. She doesn't scream; they almost never do. He's already too close, the knife already at her throat. Even though she's drunk, the stupid bitch, he can see that she knows what's happening. Good. There's no point in punishment if they don't understand the lesson.

"He makes her take off the robe. She's too skinny; he can see her ribs. He doesn't like that. She's terrified. She doesn't argue when he tells her to lie down. Not on the bed—the floor. He prefers the floor. He's gentle with her, but he can see in her eyes that she knows who he is, knows his power. That's nice, but it takes away the element of surprise.

"Afterward, he helps her to her feet. He kisses her cheek, strokes her hair. He pulls on her hair a little to make her tilt her head back, and she looks up at him. Please, she says, begging already. No pride. They never have any pride. He smiles at her, and watches her eyes as she feels the first sting of the blade. Then he lets her go, so the race can start."

Trammell swung away, muttering a curse.

Marlie wasn't looking at any of them, wasn't seeing any of them. "She doesn't run. She just looks at him. He cuts her again. Says, *Run bitch.* She doesn't. She swings at him, hits him in the face. Then she's all over him, hitting, kicking, screaming at him. He's furious; this isn't the way he wanted it to work. Stupid bitch. If that's the way she wants it, he'll give it to her. He slices deep, again and again, to get it over with. He hates her. She was stupid, she ruined it for him. It was supposed to be a race, like the Preakness. Maryland, O Maryland." Marlie sang the last little bit.

"She's down. His arm is tired. She isn't even grunting now when the knife goes in. He gets up . . ." Her voice suddenly wavered. Dane felt her jerk, then begin to tremble again.

"What?" he asked softly.

Her face was colorless, her eyes stark. "He looked in the mirror," she said. When Dane merely stared at her, puzzled,

she said it again. "He looked in the mirror! He saw himself—and *I* saw him!"

"Jesus Christ." Every hair on his body stood upright, and a chill chased down his spine. Trammell and Grace were utterly silent, their attention riveted on her.

"He's completely bald," she whispered. "He shaves his head. A square jawline. H-His eyes are a little too small, a little too close together."

Dane couldn't contain himself. He was on his feet, his powerful body tense and ready for action. "We'll get a police artist in," he said. "He'll work with you on the sketch, and then we'll get it to all the television stations and newspapers in the area." It was their first break, and it was a huge one. "Call Bonness," he told Trammell. "Fill him in on what's happened. We need to find the woman, too, one way or another. Marlie, what did she look like—" He turned back to her, and broke off in midsentence. Her head had fallen back against the couch and her eyes were closed, her hands lying limply in her lap.

"Ah, honey," he said softly. She had given in to the debilitating exhaustion. For a moment he had forgotten the physical price she paid in this. He wanted to kick himself. Immediately he pushed all other concerns aside; others could take care of the details in finding the victim, but only he could take care of Marlie. "You handle everything," he told Trammell as he bent over her to lift her in his arms. "I'm taking her home."

"You can both stay here," Trammell said, but Dane shook his head.

"She's confused when she first wakes up, and it takes her a while to get her bearings again. It'll be easier for her if she's in her own home."

"How long will it be before she'll be able to talk to an artist? Bonness will want to know."

"Noon, at the very earliest. More likely two or three in the afternoon."

"He won't like waiting that long."

"He'll have to." With Trammell and Grace flanking him, and cradling Marlie gently in his arms, he carried her to the car. Trammell opened the door for him, and he placed her on the seat, let the back down into a reclining position, and buckled her seat belt.

"Do you need me?" Grace asked. She eyed Marlie's pale, unconscious face worriedly. "I'll be glad to sit up with her."

"I can handle it. She'll sleep for at least twelve hours."

"Well, all right. Call me if you need me."

"I will," he said, and kissed her cheek. "Thanks for the offer, though."

Marlie didn't move during the drive through the misty, foggy night. Having seen it before, he wasn't as worried as he had been the first time, but on the other hand, now he knew how exhausted she would be, and how long it would take her to recover. This had to be the last one. He couldn't let her go through this time and again. As soon as they got a police sketch ready and to the media, he would put his plan into action.

He had barely gotten Marlie home and placed her on the bed before the phone began ringing. Irritably he snatched it up. "Hollister."

It was Bonness. "We can't wait until tomorrow to get started on that sketch. This is information that needs to be in newspapers tomorrow."

"It'll have to wait," Dane said harshly. "She can't do it now."

"She *has* to."

"She can't," he snapped. "This isn't a choice she has, or that you have. She's unconscious with exhaustion, and it takes hours for her to recover."

"Maybe a doctor can give her adrenaline or something, to snap her out of it—"

Dane ground his teeth together to control a flare of fury. "I'll break anyone's arm who comes near her with a needle," he said, his voice hard and crisp.

Bonness paused, taken aback more by the warning implic-

it in his tone than the actual words. The words were bad enough, but the tone was deadly. Nevertheless, he tried again. "Damn it, Hollister, you need to get your priorities straight—"

"They're as straight as they're going to get," Dane interrupted again. "No one is touching her. I'm turning off the phone here, so she won't be disturbed. If you need me, call the beeper number, but don't waste my time trying to change my mind. Talk to Trammell if you have any doubts about her condition."

"I already have," Bonness said reluctantly.

"Then why the hell did you call?"

"I thought maybe there was something we could do—"

"I've already pushed her as far as possible, to get what information we did. This hit her harder than the last time, harder and faster. Just leave her alone and let her sleep. I promise that I'll call as soon as she wakes up."

"Well, all right." Bonness was still reluctant. "But the chief is going to be pissed. Obviously, for us to have a sketch, there has to be a witness. He's going to want to know who and how."

"You can keep it quiet about the sketch until we actually have one. Until then, just say that a street informant gave us the word on another murder."

"That's a good idea. Okay. But when he finds out—"

"Blame it on me," Dane said impatiently. "I can take the heat. But make it damn plain that if anyone gets to her, he'll have to go through me."

"I'll do that."

Hanging up the phone, Dane first cut off the ringer, then turned his attention back to Marlie. She lay limply where he had placed her, her chest barely moving. She had lost weight during these past few weeks, he realized, and she hadn't had a lot to spare. When this was over, he was definitely taking her away on that vacation he had promised her, someplace quiet and serene, with nothing to do but eat, sleep, and make love.

Gently he removed her clothes and placed her, naked, between the sheets. Since he had moved in, she hadn't worn anything to bed anyway. He checked the time: fifteen after midnight. Time for him to be in bed, too. He doubted he would sleep for quite a while yet, but at least he could hold her. He threw off his own clothes and got into bed beside her, then gathered her thin, silky body against his sheltering warmth. The faint, sweet scent of her skin soothed him. He buried his face against the thick swath of straight, dark hair. "Sleep, baby," he whispered. "I'll take care of you."

He began trying to rouse her at eleven the next morning, but she was totally unresponsive. His beeper had been driving him crazy all morning. Bonness had called every half hour. Trammell had called twice. Grace had called three times, demanding to know if there was anything she could do, if he needed her to spell him so he could rest.

Trammell had hit on the idea of having the television and radio stations broadcast the information that there had been another murder, but that so far no victim had been found, and asking that people check on their neighbors and call their relatives to account for everyone. It was a tactic likely to drive some people into hysterics if a family member was unreachable for any reason, and Chief Champlin had gone through the roof when he heard it on the radio. The mayor was apoplectic. Didn't they realize the risk they were running with lawsuits? He envisioned thousands of people suing over emotional distress. Bonness covered his ass by blaming it all on Trammell, even though he had given his approval. When the chief called him, screaming in fury, Trammell coolly pointed out that the tactic had precedence, that during natural disasters and emergencies, such as heat alerts, people were often urged to check on their friends and relatives. That calmed the chief down somewhat, but he still wasn't happy.

All over the city, telephones and doorbells rang.

Carroll Janes, indulging in a lazy morning in bed, was

puzzled when he turned on the television at noon and heard the news. If the cops hadn't found the victim, how did they know there was one? He wasn't alarmed, though; he was almost certain no one had seen him, even at a distance, but even if someone had, he couldn't be identified. He yawned and turned off the television set. Let them look.

By twelve-thirty, Dane had gotten Marlie roused enough to visit the bathroom and drink some water, but she had gone to sleep again as soon as he helped her back into bed.

At 12:55, his beeper went off again. The number displayed was Trammell's. Impatiently Dane dialed it.

"We found her," Trammell said, his voice cool and expressionless. "Her name is Marilyn Elrod. Her estranged husband heard the bulletin and called from his girlfriend's house to check up on her. When he didn't get an answer, he drove over. Her car was in the driveway, and she always put it in the garage, so that bothered him right away. He still had keys to the house and let himself in, and found her upstairs in her bedroom."

"Marilyn," Dane said. "Not Maryland. Marilyn."

"Yeah. Look, do you want Grace to come over and stay with Marlie so you can go to the scene?"

He didn't like leaving Marlie, but it was his job, his weekend on call. "Send her over," he said gruffly.

"She's on her way," Trammell said. "I gave her directions. She should be there in five minutes or less."

"You think you're smart, don't you?"

"I just know you, pal."

Grace proved that she drove faster than Trammell by knocking on the door right then. Her normally serene face was troubled when Dane let her in. "How is she?" she asked immediately.

"Still sleeping. I managed to rouse her for a few minutes about half an hour ago, but she was still too groggy to think. She conked out again as soon as I got her back to bed." As he talked, Dane was slipping into his shoulder holster and putting on his jacket.

"I'm on second shift tonight," Grace said, following him to the door. "I brought my uniform so I can stay until the last possible minute, but I can't stay much past two-thirty. I know it isn't enough time," she said apologetically.

Dane swore under his breath, but didn't see anything else he could do. "It's okay. She'll be more alert next time. Let her sleep until two, then *make* her respond to you. Tell her where I am, and that I'll be back as soon as possible."

Grace nodded in understanding. As he started down the steps, she said hesitantly, "Dane? Um . . . I was wondering. That is . . . Marlie . . . Can she . . . ? Oh, damn," she said in frustration. "I don't know how to say this."

Dane turned back. It was unusual for Grace to lose her composure. He saw how uncomfortable she looked, and took a guess. "Can she read your mind?"

Grace bit her lip. "Alex said you were good at doing that yourself," she muttered. "But . . . yes. Can she read my mind?"

"She says she doesn't." Let Grace see if she could find any more reassurance in that than he did. "And I didn't read your mind. It was a lucky guess, because the idea makes *me* uncomfortable too."

Grace nodded, understanding completely. Dane went to his car, and she stepped back inside, closing the door against the heat.

She followed his instructions and at two began shaking Marlie and talking to her. To Grace's relief, Marlie blinked her eyes open after only a minute. "Grace?" she asked, the word as blurred as if she had been drinking.

Grace sighed with relief. "Yes, it's me. I've made some fresh coffee. Would you like some?"

Marlie swallowed, trying to push aside the thick fog in her brain so she could think. "Yes," she finally said.

"I'll get it. Don't go back to sleep."

"I won't." It was difficult. Marlie fought it, struggling to understand. Grace was here . . . Where was Dane? Had something happened to him? Sudden panic dissipated the

fog even more, and she managed to sit up. She was nude under the sheet; she clutched the bedcovers to her, looking around, trying to gather some clue about what was going on.

Grace returned with a cup only half-full of coffee, making it easier for Marlie to hold without spilling any. "Where's Dane?" she blurted, her eyes dark with distress. "Has something happened to him?"

"No, of course not!" Seeing her distress, Grace sat down on the bed and patted her arm. "Dane's fine. He left just an hour ago."

"Left?" Confused, Marlie closed her eyes. Behind her lids flashed a nightmare image, surrounded with what seemed like a hundred candles, reflected in a darkened mirror. She caught her breath as part of her memory returned. "What day is this?"

"Saturday," Grace replied.

"Then it was just last night that it happened." She inhaled deeply, shoring up her fragile control, and opened her eyes.

"The victim's been found. Dane's at the scene now." Grace knew, from talking to Trammell, that the scene was exactly as Marlie had described it. If she hadn't been there herself last night, and listened to Marlie talking, she would never have thought it possible. Being an eyewitness, however, tended to make one a believer. "He didn't want to leave you alone, so I came over."

"Thank you," Marlie said. "I'm so foggy when I first wake up that it's easier if someone is here to explain things." She had always gotten through it alone until Dane, but still, it was nice to have someone there.

"I can't stay much longer. I'm on second shift," Grace explained. "Will you be okay by yourself?"

"I'll probably go back to sleep." Marlie sipped the coffee. "Does Trammell mind that you work nights?"

"Of course. If I were on first shift and he worked nights, I wouldn't like it either," Grace said, her eyes twinkling. "However, being an intelligent man, he hasn't made the

mistake of demanding that I quit work or try to arrange my hours around his."

"He's doing better. We mentioned the word 'marriage' several times last night, and you couldn't see the white around his eyes."

Grace considered the matter. "His eyes did look rather like those of a panicked horse, didn't they?" she said judiciously. "I keep reminding him that it was his idea, and he can change his mind any time he wants. Then he thinks that I must not be sold on the idea myself, so he tries to convince me it's the right thing to do and convinces himself instead."

"Dane may have to prop him up at the altar."

"I expect he'll be steadier by then. I hope so, anyway. It's just that it happened so fast between us. Things were out of control from the first time we went out together. Alex likes to be in control, so it's driving him crazy."

Tactfully Grace didn't ask about Marlie's relationship with Dane, and Marlie was grateful. There was nothing settled between them, no hint of permanence despite their living together, and she was too tired to try to explain. She liked Grace a lot, but she had never had the comfort of a confidante, nor had she grown up spending long hours giggling with other girls her age while they dissected every detail of their lives. Until Dane, she hadn't really spent a lot of time just talking with anyone.

"Do you want to shower while I'm here?" Grace asked. "That will clear out a few of the cobwebs. Trammell said that they'll want you to work with a police sketch artist as soon as possible, to get the killer's description out."

Marlie shoved aside the memory of his face. She couldn't let herself dwell on it right now. "I'd love a shower. I'll hurry, so you won't be late."

Grace left her alone, and Marlie got out of bed. She felt stiff and uncoordinated, her muscles weak. She had made an effort with Grace, but things still hadn't quite clicked back

into their proper places for her. She would have to make an even greater effort to concentrate, later on, so the sketch would be accurate.

She kept the shower brief, and as cold as she could stand it. After dressing and drinking more coffee, she felt more in control. Grace was reluctant to leave, but Marlie shooed her on her way, then forced herself to walk around rather than lying down as she wanted.

How long would Dane be gone? Would he immediately take her to headquarters, so they could get started on the sketch? She paced until she was dragging, then stretched out on the couch. Sleep came almost immediately, but right before the dark curtain dropped, she had one last, very clear thought:

How long would it be before she no longer saw that face every time she closed her eyes?

21

THE SKETCH ARTIST WAS A SHORT, PLUMP REDHEAD NAMED
Esther. Esther had small, quick, ink-stained fingers, shrewd
eyes, and a voice like Tinkerbell's. Her age could have been
anywhere between thirty and fifty; her hair was liberally
salted, but her skin was smooth and fresh. Like most artists,
she wore whatever was at hand. In this case, it was a pair of
cutoff sweatpants, one of her husband's shirts, and sneakers
but no socks.

With a cup of coffee in her hand to sustain her, Marlie sat
beside Esther and worked through the details of the killer's
appearance. It was a painstaking chore, involving endless
variations of eyebrows and noses, size of eyes, width and
thickness of lips, slant of jaw, jut of chin. She could close her
eyes and picture the face, but duplicating it on paper wasn't
easy.

Dane didn't interrupt but was always close by, frequently
refilling Marlie's coffee cup. It had been close to six when he
had gotten home and roused her from the couch, where
she had been sleeping. Though he had been solicitous of her,

his mood had been grim as he drove her to police headquarters.

"The bridge of the nose should be higher," Marlie said thoughtfully, examining the latest effort. She'd done work with police artists so many times in the past, she knew what they needed from her. "And his eyes were a bit closer together."

With a few deft strokes of her pencil, Esther made the changes. "Is this better?"

"Better, but still not quite right. It's the eyes. They're small, hard, and close together. Sort of deep-set, with a straight browridge."

"Sounds like an ugly son of a bitch to me," Esther drawled, making more minute adjustments.

Marlie frowned. She was very tired, but forced herself to concentrate. "No, he really wasn't, not physically. I suppose he could have been called attractive, even with a bald head."

"Bundy was a handsome devil, but he wasn't anyone's dream man. Just shows that you can't tell by looks."

Marlie leaned forward. This time Esther's corrections had brought the sketch closer to the face in her memory. "That's good. Make the forehead a little wider, and taper the skull more. His head wasn't that round."

"More like Kojak, huh?" Deft pencil strokes changed the shape of the head.

"Stop. That's good." Seeing the face on paper made her feel a little queasy. "It's him."

Dane came over to stand behind Marlie and look at the finished sketch, staring hard at it. So that was the bastard. Now he had a face. Now he would be hunted.

"Thanks, Esther," he said.

"Any time."

Marlie stood and stretched, vaguely surprised at how stiff she felt. Trammell, who had been waiting patiently in the background, came forward to stand beside Dane and examine the sketch. "I'll get this circulated," he said. "Take Marlie home and put her to bed before she collapses."

"I'm okay," she said, but the flesh around her eyes was dark with fatigue, and her face was drawn.

Dane didn't argue. "I'll call later tonight," he said, putting his arm around Marlie and urging her toward the door. Once they were in the car, she tried to stay awake, but her eyes drifted shut before they had reached the second traffic light.

As he had the night before, Dane carried her inside, put her on the bed, and efficiently stripped her. "Good night, honey," he whispered, bending over to kiss her.

She put her arms around his neck and clung. "Hold me tonight," she said.

"I will. Go to sleep now. You'll feel better in the morning."

She was in his arms when she awoke the next morning. Seeing her eyes open, Dane turned her to her back and moved on top of her, pushing her thighs apart and settling himself between them. Gently he penetrated, and rocked them both to climax.

His lovemaking made her feel alive again, pushed the ugliness into the background. They lay together for a long time, each finding comfort in the other's embrace. Finally she said, "Tell me about her."

Dane kissed her temple, and held her closer as if his nearness would keep the horror at bay. "Her name was Marilyn Elrod," he said. "Recently separated from her husband, but he was concerned enough to check on her, and went to the house when he couldn't get her on the phone. He seems pretty broken up about it now, when it's too late."

"Marilyn," she said, making the connection. "Not Maryland, then. Marilyn."

"The storm had knocked out the electricity in the neighborhood. She lit candles on her dressing table. Everything else was the way you saw it."

"She fought him?"

"Looks like it. Her knuckles were bruised. Pity she didn't

manage to scratch his face; that would have given us an identifying mark." Though it probably would have gotten her fingers cut off like Nadine Vinick's, but he had never told Marlie that little detail. If she didn't see it in the vision, he certainly wasn't going to add to her burden of knowledge.

"Won't his face be marked? Maybe she cut his lip. Was there any blood other than hers?"

"Not that we've been able to identify," he said carefully. He tried not to think about the savage butchery, the vast amount of blood that soaked the room. Finding a few alien drops of blood wouldn't have been feasible; it would have taken pure dumb, blind luck, and luck hadn't been their best friend so far. If it hadn't been for Marlie, they wouldn't have a clue even now.

"But there should be a bruise, or a fat lip."

"That was Friday night. A cut lip heals quickly, and isn't all that noticeable anyway. A bruise can be minimized with ice, and covered with makeup. This is a smart guy. He'll know all the tricks."

"But you'll catch him anyway."

"Yes," Dane said grimly. "I will."

Carroll Janes stared at the Sunday morning newspaper in infuriated disbelief. The police sketch was eerily accurate, though of course, it showed him completely bald rather than with thick blond curls. He crushed the paper and threw it aside. For the first time, he felt a twinge of alarm, and that made him even angrier. The police weren't supposed to get this close to him! Oh, they wouldn't catch him, but they shouldn't even know this much. Who had seen him? He would have sworn he had been unobserved. Had that stupid bitch had a security camera somewhere? He couldn't believe it, for if she had, it would have shown him the first two times he had entered the house, unless, of course, she had been so stupid that she never checked the tape. The police would have, even if she hadn't. No, there hadn't been a camera. He would have discovered it, had there been.

How had this happened? What had gone wrong?

He took comfort in the fact that, as usual, he hadn't left any forensic evidence behind. No hair, no skin, no fingerprints, no footprints. The knife belonged to the victim, and had been left at the scene. He had taken no trophies, nothing that could link him to the scene. He was safe.

But someone had seen him. He had slipped up—totally unacceptable—and someone had seen him. To atone for his error, he would have to correct it. He would have to find this person, and eliminate him—or her.

"Will you go with me over to the Elrod house?" Dane asked.

Marlie stared at him, so stunned for a moment that she couldn't believe what he'd asked. To actually go into the house . . . Her mind reeled away from the idea. It was bad enough to see it in her mind; to walk into that blood-soaked room was more than she thought she could bear.

Dane's mouth set in a hard line as he saw her sudden loss of color. He clasped her shoulders so she couldn't turn away. "I know what I'm asking," he said harshly. "I know how much it will cost you. I wouldn't ask if I didn't need your help. We're all stumbling around in the dark here, and you're the only light we have. It's a long shot, but maybe, if you were at the actual scene, you'd be able to pick up more about him."

The last scene she'd been at had been when Dusty had been murdered, when she had lain helplessly and watched as Gleen butchered a terrified, equally helpless little boy. She had lived with the memories ever since; it wasn't fair of Dane to ask her to add to those memories. He knew what she'd been through, but he hadn't lived it, so he didn't know the torment as intimately as she did.

She stared up into those fiercely determined hazel eyes, feeling the force of his will batter at her. She could withstand him, she thought dimly. It was much more difficult to withstand the silent entreaties of Nadine Vinick, of Jackie

Sheets, of Marilyn Elrod. She could see all of them, their shades crying out for justice.

Why hadn't she been able to get into *their* minds, instead of his? He had to select them in some manner; maybe one or all of them had known his name. But instead it was his mental energy that had reached out and tapped into hers, forcing her to feel his evil. But she had once before been in the victim's mind, had felt Dusty's death, and it had nearly killed her too. What would it have done to her to have mentally endured that pain and terror again?

"Marlie?" Dane shook her lightly, forcing her to focus on him.

She squared her shoulders, bracing herself. She couldn't turn her back on this now any more than she could have at the beginning. "All right," she said steadily. "I'll go with you."

Once she had agreed, he didn't waste any time. Within five minutes they were on their way. It was just after noon; churches had let out, and children were swarming as they drove through the upscale neighborhood where the Elrods had lived. She sat silently, her eyes on her hands as she tried to prepare herself. She didn't know what to expect; maybe nothing, maybe she would relive the vision, maybe she really would sense something new.

And maybe she would look in the mirror and come face-to-face with a killer.

She knew him, knew that he killed without remorse. He enjoyed it. He gloated over his victims' pain and terror. He wore a human form, but he was a depraved monster who would keep killing until someone stopped him.

Dane pulled into a driveway. The house was sealed with yellow crime scene tape. Though it had been twenty-four hours since the body had been found, neighbors stood in small knots pointing and gawking, rehashing the few details they had gleaned from television and newspaper reports, and adding new gory ones from the multitude of rumors that raced through the neighborhood.

"We think he entered through the garage, when she went out early in the evening," Dane said, keeping a firm hand on Marlie's elbow as they went up the walk to the front door. He held up the crime scene tape for them to duck under. "Because the power was off when she got home, the electric garage door opener wouldn't work. She left the car in the driveway and entered through the front door. The alarm system didn't work, either, because of the power outage, but it wouldn't have helped in any case: It wasn't connected to the door from the garage into the house. People can make some of the dumbest decisions, for the dumbest reasons. Mr. Elrod said that particular door wasn't connected so they would have a way of entering without having to fool with the alarm code. They might as well have put a sign on it saying 'Criminals Enter Here.'"

He talked steadily as he unlocked the front door and ushered her inside. The alarm system had been turned off, because there had been so many people coming and going the day before.

Marlie took a deep breath. The house looked deceptively normal, except for the black powder dusting every slick surface. It had been a very nice, upscale home at one time. She wondered if anyone would ever live here again, if Mr. Elrod would be able to sleep in this house, or be able to sell it if he couldn't. Perhaps it could be unloaded on some unsuspecting snowbird newly migrated from the North. In her opinion, it should be razed.

She looked around at the spacious, open, high-ceilinged rooms. There was a sense of airy coolness; it must have been a wonderful place to live. The downstairs floors were either polished hardwood or designer tile. She wandered silently through the rooms, trying to force herself to relax and let her mind open, but she couldn't lock out the dread of going upstairs. She didn't want to, but knew that she would have to.

Maybe if they waited another day; she wasn't fully recovered from the vision. Maybe that was why she couldn't open

the mental door that would allow the impressions to enter. She glanced at Dane, then abandoned the suggestion that had been on her tongue. He hadn't been following her every step, but remained in the doorway of each room while she prowled it. His face was grim, his expression shuttered as she had never seen it before. There was something curiously remote about him, as if he had shut himself off from any appeal she might make.

"Anything?" he asked, seeing her look at him.

She shook her head.

He didn't push her. He didn't urge her to try harder. He didn't try to hurry her, or tell her to go upstairs to the scene. He was just there, waiting, implacable.

But when she put her hand on the railing and her foot on that first step of the staircase, he caught her arm. His gaze bored into hers, an expression she couldn't quite read flickering in his eyes. "Are you all right?"

"Yes." She took a deep breath. "I'm not enjoying this, but I'll make it."

"Just remember," he muttered. "I'm not enjoying it either."

She looked at him questioningly. "I never thought you were."

Then she went upstairs. He was right behind her, his tread silent, his presence as solid as a wall.

Where had the killer waited for Marilyn to come home? Her vision hadn't quite picked up on that; it had begun when he had begun trailing her through the dark house. Maybe, when the electricity had gone off, he had left his hiding place and made himself comfortable where he could see if anyone drove up. She stopped in the hallway and closed her eyes, concentrating, trying to read any leftover energy. Cautiously she opened that mental door, and a buzz of static assaulted her. She slammed the door shut and opened her eyes. She had gotten an impression of many people, of much activity; too many people had been here since the murder, blurring the image.

The door at the end of the hall stood open. That was Marilyn's bedroom. Marlie walked steadily toward it, and once more Dane caught her arm. "I've changed my mind," he said abruptly. "You don't need to go in there."

"Marilyn Elrod didn't need to die, either," she replied. "Neither did Nadine Vinick or Jackie Sheets, or any of the other women he killed before moving here." She gave him a wintry smile and tugged her arm free. "Besides, I've already been in there, remember? I was there when it happened."

Four quick steps carried her into the room. She stopped. She couldn't go any farther without stepping on dark brown bloodstains. There was no way to avoid them; the blood was spattered all over the carpet, the walls, the bed, though the largest stain by far was the huge one beside the bed, where Marilyn Elrod's life had finally ended. But she had fought him all over this room, and left her own blood as her witness. About ten incense candles in their tiny glass pots still sat on the dresser; it was in that mirror that Marlie had seen the killer, looking at him through his own eyes.

She had to open that mental door again, to perhaps glean some other snippet of information. Marilyn deserved that she at least try.

"Don't talk to me for a minute, okay?" she said to Dane, her voice soft, almost soundless. "I want to think."

Maybe the energy was in layers, with the most recent on top. She closed her eyes, picturing the layers, giving them different colors so she could more easily tell them apart. She had to block out that top layer, the one peopled with detectives, uniformed officers, photographers, forensic squads, the multitude who had swarmed the house after Marilyn's death. They had been trying to help, but they got in the way. Mr. Elrod had been here, too, adding another level of energy.

She assigned blue to the policemen and related others, and red to Mr. Elrod. The killer's color was black, the density evil and thick, resisting any penetration of light.

Marilyn . . . Marilyn's color would be a pure, translucent white.

She formed the picture in her mind, seeing the layers, concentrating on them so all else was forgotten. She existed only inside herself, pulling inward so her ability wouldn't be diluted. Very delicately she peeled off the blue layer and put it to the side. Next came the red layer, very thin because Mr. Elrod hadn't contributed much, harder to handle. It, too, went to the side.

Only black and white were left, but the layers were so entwined that she didn't know if she could separate them. Killer and victim, locked together in a life-and-death struggle. Marilyn had lost that fight.

Very clearly she saw that if she tried to pull the layers apart, she might damage them, damage the information they held. She would have to leave them as they were.

Now was the time to open the door. She mentally stepped into the layers, like stepping into a mist, wrapping the energies around her. She let them surround her, soak into her pores. And then she opened the door.

The blast of evil was suffocating, but nothing she hadn't felt before. She forced herself not to retreat from it, to examine it, while fighting to keep it from overwhelming her as it had the first time. She couldn't let herself be sucked into reliving the murder, or the effects would be so debilitating, she wouldn't be able to continue.

The evil layer writhed around her, but bits of white kept touching her, distracting her. She pushed the contact away, intent on reading every black energy wave.

There was nothing new, no mental clue about how he had selected Marilyn as his victim. A touch of white jolted her again. There was something compelling about it, an insistence on gaining her attention.

Marlie held back. She couldn't experience Marilyn's death. She simply couldn't.

But the white layer pressed more strongly. The evil of the killer was pushed aside. Marlie saw it clearly in her mind,

and was astonished, for she hadn't done it. She looked back to the whiteness, and that break in concentration was enough to let the white energy in.

Panic squeezed her heart as sheer terror seized her. And then a sense of calm seeped in, a quiet soothing.

She stood bathed in the translucent whiteness. This wasn't the energy of Marilyn's last moments, of her terrified, pain-filled struggle for life. This was the energy of afterward, and it wasn't in the past. It was here. It was now.

There were no spoken sentences, no actual words. Marilyn wasn't suffering anymore. She seemed peaceful. But there was a sense of inconclusiveness; she was reluctant to leave. Justice had not been done, the scale was still unbalanced, and Marilyn couldn't leave until her killer no longer stalked innocent women in the night.

Don't worry, Marlie whispered in her mind. *He made a mistake. Dane will catch him now.*

Though the reassurance was welcome, it made no difference. Marilyn would linger until a resolution.

A noise tugged at Marlie's consciousness. It was irritating, but insistent. Instinctively she recognized its source, and her automatic response.

I have to go now. He's calling.

Still she was reluctant to leave that serenity. She hesitated, and felt one last touch of the white energy.

"—Marlie! Goddamn it, answer me!"

She opened her eyes to Dane's furious, worried face. He was shaking her, and her head wobbled back and forth. She squeezed her eyes shut against the dizziness. "Stop," she gasped.

He did, and hauled her into his arms. She could feel his heart pounding against his ribs like thunder, hard and frantic. He held her head pressed to his chest, and his grip was so tight that it compressed her rib cage.

"What were you doing?" he raged. "What happened? You've been standing there like a damn doll for half an hour. You wouldn't answer me, wouldn't even open your eyes!"

She put her arms around him. "I'm sorry," she whispered. "I didn't hear you. I was concentrating."

"I don't call that mere concentration, babe. You put yourself into a goddamn trance, and I don't like it. Don't you ever do that again, do you hear me?"

She had frightened him, she realized, and like all strong men, he didn't take kindly to it. In his anger he had even called her "babe," something he hadn't done since she'd told him how much she disliked it.

He bent his head down to hers, pressing his forehead against her hair. "This was a bad idea," he muttered. "Let's get the hell out of here."

But because he was a cop, when they were halfway down the stairs he reluctantly asked, "Did you pick up on anything?"

"No," she said softly. "Nothing that would help." She didn't tell him about Marilyn's presence, peaceful but resolute, patiently waiting. That had nothing to do with the investigation. It was private, between herself and Marilyn, both of them victims, in different ways, of the same evil.

Dane opened the door, and she stepped out. The bright sun glared directly into her eyes, momentarily blinding her, and she paused. She didn't see the people rushing toward her until they were right on her.

"I'm Cheri Vaughn with WVTM-TV," a young woman said. "We have learned that the Orlando Police Department is using a psychic named Marlie Keen to aid in apprehending the Orlando Slasher. Are you Marlie Keen?" Then she thrust a fat black microphone in Marlie's face.

Stunned, she stared at the lean, fashionably dressed young woman, and at the burly, shorts-clad man who stood behind her with a camera balanced on his shoulder. A van with the station's insignia blazoned on the side was parked at the curb, and the crowd of neighbors had drastically increased, drawn by the television camera. Roughly Dane shouldered in front of her. "I'm Detective Hollister," he snapped. "You're behind the police line. You have to leave—*now.*"

But the tenacious Ms. Vaughn neatly sidestepped him and once more pushed the microphone at Marlie. "Are you the psychic?"

A confusing flurry of impressions hit Marlie broadside. She couldn't read Dane; his mental shields were too strong. But Cheri Vaughn, ambitious and slightly nervous, was no match for Marlie's abilities. Marlie didn't even have to try; the truth was broadcast at her in deafening waves.

Shock hit her in the pit of her stomach, and she almost choked as the bile of betrayal rose to her throat. It was possible that someone else had leaked the news of her involvement—but no one else had. And only one person had known where she would be at this exact moment.

She felt cold, icy cold, and suddenly alone. Slowly, her face very still, she looked at Dane. He still wore that grim expression, his eyes as narrow and fierce as a hawk's as he watched her. She could barely breathe. Accusation and betrayal were in her expression as she put her hand over the microphone.

"You set me up," she said to the man she loved, the man who had used her.

22

MARLIE TURNED BACK TO THE TELEVISION REPORTER. "YES, I'm Marlie Keen," she said coldly.

"Ms. Keen, have you been working with the Orlando Police Department to help them locate the killer?"

"Yes." The one word was clipped. She could barely contain her fury, her sense of betrayal.

Dane put his hand out, as if to block the camera, but Marlie knocked it aside. Cheri Vaughn plunged ahead. "In what way have you aided them, Ms. Keen?"

"I gave them the killer's description."

"How did you know what he looked like? Did you have a psychic vision?"

Again Dane moved in front of her, his rough face furious. Marlie sidestepped. This was what he'd wanted, wasn't it? She was going to deliver, in spades. "Something like that. I know the killer the way no one else does. He's not a dream man, unless you're into nightmares," she said, borrowing Esther's words. "He's a worm, a coward who gets his jollies by attacking women—"

"That's enough!" Dane roared, pushing the camera down and grabbing Marlie's arm with his other hand, his fingers biting into her soft flesh. "You people leave this scene, *now.*"

Cheri Vaughn blinked at him, looking both frightened and elated. Marlie didn't have to guess how the reporter felt; she knew. She had come here to act a part, with the promise of some news, but she had walked into a sensational gold mine. Her stock at the station had just gone stratospheric.

Still gripping her arm, Dane hustled Marlie to the car, putting her in on the driver's side and shoving her over to make room for himself. He slammed the door and turned the key in the ignition. "What the hell were you doing?" he said from between clenched teeth.

She could feel the white heat of his rage, but she wasn't impressed. "What you wanted me to do," she replied bitterly. "Attracting the killer's attention. Wasn't that the whole point of the exercise?"

Dane thought of denying it, but realized there wasn't any point in it. She wouldn't believe any denials he could come up with, and he was so angry right now that he wasn't inclined to try. "Attract his attention, yes, not drive him into a killing rage!"

"But now you can be certain he'll come after me. He won't forgive an attack on his ego." She was facing forward, not even glancing at him as he drove.

Dane took a firm grip on his temper. He had known she wouldn't like being exposed as a psychic, but he hadn't expected her to immediately realize he had set up the entire situation, or to react by goading and taunting the killer.

"How did you know?" he asked a moment later, his voice as grim as his face. "Did you read my mind?"

"You can't get over your fear of that, can you?" she gibed. "You can relax; your head's too thick for me to get even a glimmer from you. But the reporter was a different story. She might as well have been carrying a sign. Why didn't you call her anonymously?"

"She knows me, knows my voice. Besides, I owed her a

favor for some information she got for me last year. Breaking a story would help her at the station."

"Then by all means, if it will help her, throw me to the wolves," she said, her voice flat. Now that the first shock of betrayal and exposure had passed, several likelihoods had presented themselves, none of them pleasant. She had fretted over his lack of commitment, over the way they had never even discussed their relationship, and now she knew why. For Dane, there *was* no commitment; he had simply been marking time until the killer struck again, so he could put his plan into action. He had played her perfectly, setting her up for that scene. She thought of what it had cost her to go to that house, and got even angrier.

"I haven't thrown you to the wolves!" he snapped.

"Haven't you? You've set me up as bait."

"Damn it, he's not going to get anywhere near you! Do you think I'd take a chance on something like that happening? I've arranged for a policewoman to take your place. She's already at your house. All you have to do is pack some clothes, and I'll take you to a safe house until it's over."

"No," she said, just as flatly as before.

He slammed his fist onto the steering wheel. "Don't fight me on this, Marlie. You don't have a choice."

"I'm not going to a safe house." She thought of being confined for days, perhaps weeks, with shifts of officers to guard her, and knew she couldn't tolerate it. Her nerves were already raw; that would simply be too much.

Very evenly he said, "I can take you into protective custody and lock you in a cell, if you'd prefer. I don't think you'd like it."

She whirled on him, incensed by the threat. "I don't think you would either, Hollister. I can't stop you from doing it, but I promise you that I'll make your life miserable if you do."

"For God's sake, use your common sense! You can't stay in your house. Or do you think I'd planned to actually use you as a tethered goat?"

"Why not? Why stop short of that? Using me has been your plan all along, hasn't it? Personally, I think you carried it a little far by moving in with me, but I suppose you needed to be on hand when I had another vision, so you could get the ball rolling."

His head snapped around. "Just what you are saying?"

"That if you'd bothered to *ask* me, Detective, I'd have gone along with your plan if it would help flush out the killer. I hate being exposed by the media, because this will wreck my life again, but I'd have done it. You didn't have to sacrifice your body for the cause."

Furiously he slammed on the brakes, stopping the car with a force that jerked her forward in her seat. Luckily there was no one behind them or they'd have been rear-ended. He was as infuriated as she. "Getting involved with you has nothing to do with this!"

"Doesn't it? I've been puzzled by the situation from the very beginning. Can you honestly say that you didn't have this plan in mind *before* you moved in?"

His jaw worked. "No." Damn if he'd lie.

"I didn't think so."

"Moving in wasn't part of the plan."

"It was just too much to resist, wasn't it?" she taunted.

Roughly he seized her shoulders. "You're damn right it was. I wanted you, and when I got the opportunity to move in, I took it. Or maybe you think I've been faking all those hard-ons?"

"That doesn't prove anything. I think you'd get an erection if a fly landed on you." She tried to jerk away, but he tightened his grip.

Dane took another grip on his temper; the first one hadn't lasted very long. "Our relationship has nothing to do with this. They're two totally separate things."

"If you say so," she drawled, mimicking his accent.

"Damn it, Marlie—" An angry blast of a horn interrupted him, and he darted a furious glance into the rearview mirror. Several cars were lined up behind him. He stomped

the accelerator. "We'll finish this at the house, while you pack."

"I'm not going to a safe house." The words were stony, implacable. "I'm going to work tomorrow just like always. You've probably wrecked that, too. They'll probably fire me, but I'm still going to try."

"You aren't going to be fired!"

She stared out the window. So he thought he could just use her to bait his trap, and afterward everything would return to normal? "You can pack, too."

He slanted a look at her. "What?" He couldn't stay at the safe house with her.

"I want your stuff out of my house."

For the first time, the conviction in her voice pierced his impatient anger. Marlie wasn't just upset; she was deeply, coldly furious, and she hadn't believed a word he'd said. His stomach knotted. He inhaled deeply, reaching for control. "Okay. Maybe it's for the best, for now. I'll see you as often as I can at the safe house—"

"I am not going to a safe house. Can't you understand English?"

"Maybe you don't," he said slowly. "Honey, I'm not giving you a choice in this. You can't stay in your house."

"Then I'll stay in a motel, or rent an apartment. I am not going to be locked up because of your schemes. As much as I can, I'm going to live a normal life. I'm going to work, if I have a job, and I'm going to do normal things, like laundry and shopping and going to movies. I lived like a virtual prisoner for the first twenty-two years of my life. I'll be damned if I let you lock me up again."

He thrust his hand through his hair. God Almighty, he hadn't expected her to dig in her heels like this. This was a Marlie he hadn't seen since the first week he'd known her, and somehow he had let himself forget about her temper. The woman sitting beside him was seething like a volcano, and wasn't likely to cooperate with him in anything he

suggested. He decided to shut his mouth, for now, and cut his losses.

The remainder of the drive was accomplished in silence. When they reached her house, there was a strange car in her driveway, and Trammell's sports car was parked out front. Marlie got out and went inside without looking at Dane.

Trammell and Grace were both there, as well as a young policewoman who resembled Marlie in size and general coloring. Trammell stood when Marlie entered, took one look at her face, and said, "Uh-oh."

Coming in behind her, Dane sharply drew a finger across his throat, silencing any other comments.

Marlie turned in time to see the gesture. She gave Trammell a cool look. "Were you in on it too?"

He shifted uneasily. "Not until yesterday." He had become accustomed to thinking of Marlie as someone who was vulnerable and needed protecting, but there was a look in those deep blue eyes that suddenly made him wary. Dane had told him about Gleen, but until this moment he really hadn't seen her as a woman who, tied and helpless, had nevertheless spat defiance at a crazed killer. "I take it you're unhappy."

"A mite disturbed," she said, her tone heavy with irony. "I barely lived through one attack from a maniac with a knife, so it bothers me to be set up as bait for another one."

Dane flinched. He hadn't thought of it that way. "You'll be safe," he said. "Do you think I'd have done it if there were any risk to you?"

She tilted her head, considering him. "Yes," she finally said, and went into her bedroom.

Trammell whistled through his teeth. "I sense trouble in paradise."

Grace gave Dane a dirty look. "I would think so," she said, and followed Marlie into the bedroom.

The policewoman, Beverly Beaver, sat watching them uncomfortably. "Is the stakeout canceled?"

"No," Dane answered. "You're still on. As soon as I get Marlie settled, I'll be back to help set up everything. We have time; the bit won't be on until the evening news."

Beverly said, "How are you going to keep the reporters away? The guy can't get to me if a hundred reporters and photographers are camped on the front yard."

"The television station is going to play it as a joke. The department will take a lot of heat for it, and the chief is going to say they've investigated Marlie and there isn't anything to her claims. But the killer will know the truth, and he'll come after her." He paused. "Are you sure you want to do this, Bev?"

"I'm sure. I'm closest to her in size and coloring, and I've had advanced self-defense training. I'm the best choice." Her voice was philosophical. Dane wasn't fooled; Beverly had the reputation of being a tiger. She was chomping at the bit to be in on the stakeout, even though she knew she would have to let the killer get far too close for comfort, so they would have enough on him to make the charges stick.

"Okay." He cast a harried glance toward the bedroom. "She's refusing to go to a safe house."

"We already have it set up," Trammell said.

"Tell it to her. She's agreed to leave, but she says she's going to stay in a motel, or rent an apartment. She's so mad at me that she won't go along with anything I suggest."

"I've got an idea. Maybe she'll listen to me."

"Give it a try."

Marlie looked up from the bags she was packing when Trammell sauntered lazily into the bedroom. Grace was helping, taking garments out of the closet and placing them on the bed for Marlie to fold and pack in the suitcases. Dane leaned against the doorway, his face like a thundercloud as he watched her.

"Dane says you don't want to go to a safe house," Trammell began.

"That's right."

Grace gave her a quick, concerned look. "Marlie, it's the best place for you."

"Would you like being confined, possibly for weeks? It would drive me crazy. I've done whatever I can to help, and I refuse to be punished for it."

"But it isn't punishment," Grace tried to explain. "It's to keep you safe."

"The best judge of whether or not something is punishment is the one on the receiving end," Marlie replied. "I don't mind being secluded; I even like it. But I can't bear being confined."

"A motel won't be very comfortable," Trammell said. "I have an idea. You'll still need protection, so why don't you move into Dane's house? I've finished with the renovations, and got the furniture delivered yesterday. That way you'll be more comfortable, and he'll be with you at night."

She gave him an icy glare. "That's *not* a very good suggestion."

"It's the only workable solution." Trammell countered her glare with a gentle smile. "I know it isn't ideal, but it's a compromise that will work, if you'll let it. Dane won't take you into protective custody, but I can tell you right now that the chief will order it and not blink an eye."

Frustrated fury welled up in her, almost choking her. She didn't want to stay in Dane's house, didn't want to be forced into intimacy with him. But Trammell, unfortunately, was right; the chief didn't know her, and wouldn't think twice about ordering her detained, for her own good.

"Trammell's wrong," Dane said softly, breaking into the silence. He met her angry gaze without blinking. "I *will* take you into custody. You might hate my guts for it, but I'll do it if I have to. It's better than risking your life. So, honey, it's my house or jail."

Stated like that, she accepted that she had no choice. The move was swiftly accomplished. Marlie took the time to thank Beverly for the risk she was taking, and to show her

around the house, then she was hustled out. She insisted on taking her car, so it was a caravan of three that parked at Dane's house not long afterward.

Dane had seen the completed changes Trammell had wrought in his house, and considered the money well spent. The new furniture was both comfortable and chic; his living room now felt like a patio, with the same sense of freshness and space. His bed was the one thing in the house that had been fairly new; he'd replaced his grandparents' standard double with a king-size when he inherited the house. The only reason he had endured the double bed at Marlie's these past weeks was the fact that she had been in it. For that, he had been content to have his feet hang off the end.

If he had had any hope of sharing that big bed with her now, it disappeared when she resolutely carried her clothes into the second bedroom, which had also received Trammell's sprucing up. Still he was fiercely elated. She was here; that was what mattered. She obviously wanted to make a complete break with him, but circumstances had conspired against her, and she was forced to stay with him. He would have the chance to break down that wall of anger.

Again Grace helped Marlie with her clothes. They worked quietly together for several minutes before Grace said, "You're really angry at him, aren't you?"

"Anger doesn't begin to describe it. Not only did he set me up, that was his reason from the beginning for getting involved with me."

Grace looked shocked. "That can't be so!"

"Can't it? He didn't deny planning it before he moved in with me."

"But Alex has been positively gleeful because Dane is so obviously crazy about you. Surely you know that he loves you!"

"If he does, he's never even come close to saying it. In fact, we've never discussed our relationship at all, except for sex. I'm beginning to think that's all it ever was, just sex. He

had this plan of his, and as a side benefit I happened to be acceptable in bed."

Grace thought about it. "You've never talked about your feelings at all?"

"Not one word. I called him when a vision started, he came over and took care of me, and simply never left. The next thing I knew, he was hanging up his clothes in my closet."

"I see. Even on our first date, Alex admitted that emotionally he was in deep water," Grace murmured. "And Alex is the most skittish man in the world." She thought about it some more, then pronounced: "You're right. On the evidence, you have to assume that Dane deliberately became involved with you to gain your trust, and moved in with you to stay close to the action, so to speak."

"In a nutshell, he used me."

When Grace left the bedroom, she gave Dane a frosty glare. Trammell caught his partner's eye and shrugged in amusement. Dane didn't think it was a damn bit funny. He didn't protest when they left; the sooner he and Marlie were alone, the sooner he could begin mending fences. God, what if he couldn't change her mind?

At the thought of losing her forever, he felt a cold knot of panic form in the pit of his stomach.

Marlie finally came out of the bedroom to watch the local evening news. As she had expected, she was the lead story.

"WVTM learned today that the Orlando Police Department has been using the services of a local psychic, Marlie Keen, to aid them in their search for the Orlando Slasher. WVTM reporter Cheri Vaughn talked to Ms. Keen earlier today, when she and a city detective were seen leaving the house of the latest victim, Marilyn Elrod, who lived in Wildwood Estates."

The picture switched from the studio to the tape shot earlier. Marlie watched in silence for a minute, then said,

"You played it perfectly. The way you told them to leave, and kept stepping in front of me, looked exactly as if you were trying to keep me under wraps. Do you think I came across as a publicity-hungry kook?"

"Not quite," he muttered. At least she was talking to him. He had been worried that she would give him the silent treatment for the rest of his life. No, she hadn't come across as a kook, at least not to anyone with an ounce of perception. There had been too much controlled anger in her face, too much disgust when she had described the killer.

The next scene featured Lieutenant Bonness, sweating in the heat, looking properly embarrassed. Dane had briefed him on how to play it. Bonness wasn't comfortable with what he was doing, but his discomfort fit in with what he wanted to project. Yes, Marlie Keen had contacted them. They were willing to listen to anyone who might be able to help them with the investigation. Ms. Keen's allegations hadn't panned out, though, and the Orlando PD would no longer be working with her.

Back to the studio. The evening anchors had a few pithy remarks to make about the police department wasting tax dollars chasing down wild ideas from the loony fringe. The spot ended with the information that Ms. Keen, the alleged psychic, worked in the accounting department of a local bank, and named the bank.

"There goes my job," Marlie drawled.

Dane's hand tightened on the can of beer he was holding. "I told you—"

"I know what you told me. I also know you don't know what you're talking about."

His teeth ground together. "For the last time, I didn't get involved with you just to set you up as bait."

"No? Just exactly when did you come up with this brilliant plan? And I'm not being sarcastic. It's a damn good idea. It'll probably work. But when did you think of it?"

He didn't have to think, he knew exactly when the plan

had occurred to him. Again he chose not to lie. "On the plane coming back from Denver."

Her eyebrows lifted. "You mean right before you came to my house and made a heavy-duty pass?"

"Yes," he growled.

"The timing's a mite suspicious, isn't it?"

"I wanted you before that, damn it!" he yelled. "But you were a suspect, and I couldn't get involved with you. As soon as I cleared you of all suspicion, I was knocking on your door."

She smiled. "And it was just pure luck that I could be used in this way, wasn't it? I don't mind that part of it, Dane, I really don't. What I hate is the way you used a personal relationship to set it up—though it wasn't very personal for you, was it?"

Red mist swam in front of his eyes. He was so angry that he could feel himself losing control. He got up and walked out of the house, to keep himself from doing something he would regret later.

Damn, this wasn't looking good at all. How could she doubt what they'd had together? He'd never felt like this about any other woman, and she thought it meant less than nothing to him. He walked around the yard, the lingering evening heat making him sweat. When he thought he had himself under control, he went back inside, but Marlie had gone back into the bedroom.

Probably that was for the best. Both their emotions were too raw for them to talk about this sensibly. Tomorrow, when they both had calmed down, would be better.

Carroll Janes watched the evening news telecast. So that was how they had known! A damn psychic. Whoever would have thought? That certainly wasn't something for which he could have planned.

The cops didn't seem to have much faith in her, but just looking at her had given him chills. And what she had said;

how could she have been so vicious? She had called him a worm and a coward. After a moment of hurt, he began to get angry. So he wasn't anyone's dream man, was he? What did that little bitch know?

Actually, he realized, she knew quite a lot. The cops didn't believe her—for now—but the fact was, she was a real danger to him. As no one else had, she had gotten close to him. The only way she could have seen him was in a psychic vision, and the thought made him feel maddeningly vulnerable.

It was intolerable. How ignominious it would be for his downfall to come about because of some kook psychic! The trouble was that she *wasn't* a kook. She was for real. It was the only way she could know what he looked like.

He wasn't safe as long as she lived.

The solution was obvious. The psychic would have to die.

23

J ANES CALLED IN SICK THE NEXT MORNING. MARLIE KEEN HAD been listed in the phone book, and he had looked up her address on a city map. He didn't have any time to waste; he had to get rid of her as soon as possible. And then perhaps he would think about leaving Orlando; he usually remained in an area longer than this, but the psychic bitch had loused things up for him here. They had that sketch of him. They might discount it now, but when the bitch turned up dead, they would give it a lot more credence.

He smelled setup, but he didn't dare ignore the situation. It was simply too dangerous for him. But he didn't take any chances; he switched license plates with a car belonging to an old lady in the apartment building who seldom drove anymore. He would switch them back when he returned, so that if any suspicious cop was watching the traffic on Marlie Keen's street, when they traced that tag, it would come back as belonging to a Mrs. Velma Fisher, whose car was nothing like the one that had been sporting the plate. But when they checked Mrs. Fisher's car, the license plate would be there,

convincing them that they had made an error in writing down the number.

His blond curls were snugly in place when he set out. Such an extravagant head of hair was a brilliant disguise, if he did say so himself. They were looking for a bald guy. It was an ingenious way of changing his appearance, because either way, his head was what people noticed: They would look at the blond curls, and not the face beneath it, or, if he was seen during one of his nights, they would notice the slick skull and nothing else. Simply brilliant.

He rolled down his car window and turned up the radio. That was another piece of psychological subterfuge: Cops wouldn't expect him to draw attention to himself with a loud radio. If this was a trap, they wouldn't expect him to boldly drive by, where they could get a good look at him. That was why they never had been able to catch him. He could predict their actions and reactions, but they didn't have a clue how his mind worked. After all, how could anyone without an imagination begin to understand what it was like to have one?

So he casually drove by the bitch's house, and just as casually glanced at it. There was a car in the driveway; why wasn't she working? The newscast had plainly said that she was employed at a bank. There seemed to be a lot of cars parked along the street. That chill went down his spine again. He didn't actually see anything, but he hadn't escaped for so long by being stupid; quite the opposite. This definitely felt like a setup.

He didn't risk another drive-by. He drove back to his apartment, switched the license plates again, and thought. If it was a setup, then the cops wouldn't let the bitch stay at her house. They would have her salted away somewhere they thought was safe. It would be impossible for him to locate her, much less get at her.

Or would they? The trap would look much more realistic if she appeared to be going about her normal routine.

There was only one way to check. He looked up the

telephone number of the bank where she worked and punched in the numbers. It was answered on the first ring, by a bored-sounding young woman with a breathy voice.

"Marlie Keen, in accounting, please," Janes said briskly.

"Just one moment."

Another ring, and a click. "Accounting." Another female voice.

"Marlie Keen, please."

"Hold on." He heard the woman say, in a more distant voice that indicated she had taken the receiver away from her mouth, "Marlie, line two."

Janes hung up the phone. She was at work.

He laughed to himself as he went back out to his car. What simpletons they all were, if that was the best they could do! He would follow her when she left work, though of course, if she went to her house, he would break off contact rather than take the risk of driving down her street again.

His biggest problem, he told himself, was finding some shade to park in while waiting for her to leave the bank.

He picked her out when she went to lunch; he remembered that thick dark hair and slender build. His heart pounded with excitement, then he sternly brought himself under control. He couldn't allow himself to make a mistake out of haste.

He snickered as he followed her. She wasn't much of a psychic if she couldn't tell that he was only two cars behind her. But she was still a danger to him, and that couldn't be tolerated.

She picked up lunch at a drive-through fast-food window, and returned to the bank. He had no chance to get at her. So he patiently settled down to wait once more.

She left work at four. He had carefully watched the parking lot. There hadn't been any suspicious lingerers—other than himself, of course. He hummed as he pulled out a few cars behind her, and kept about the same distance behind her.

She didn't make any stops. She drove straight to a

smallish house in an older neighborhood. He noted the address and kept on driving. He went to the library and looked up the address in the city directory; the house was listed as the residence of Dane Hollister. Janes's eyebrows shot up, and he grinned. He knew that name; it had been in the papers quite a bit lately. Detective Dane Hollister was investigating the Slasher murders. Now, wasn't that a coincidence?

The bank president hadn't done it; not even the vice president had done it. But the head of accounting had been called into a meeting with them, and this was one of those occasions when Marlie didn't need to be psychic to know what was happening. She wasn't surprised when the department head returned, looking unhappy, and asked Marlie into her office. They regretted the necessity, but their first responsibility was to their depositors, et cetera, et cetera. The bottom line was that Friday was her last day. They felt magnanimous in allowing her to stay that long.

She thought about being magnanimous in turn and quitting right then, which was obviously what they wanted, but the impulse didn't last long. She wasn't in the best of moods.

She was still angry when she drove to Dane's house, so angry that there wasn't much room for anything else. She had been angry since the moment she had realized how Dane had betrayed her, and expected to be angry for the foreseeable future.

She had been home just long enough to change into comfortable clothes when she heard a car drive up. She looked out the window expecting to see Dane, but instead watched Trammell unfold his long form from his low-slung car. She went to the door to let him in.

"Hi, sweetie." He twirled his sunglasses from one long finger and bent down to kiss her cheek.

She lifted a sardonic brow at the display of affection. "What's with the sweet talk?"

He grinned and raised his hands. "Don't shoot, I'm unarmed. I see you haven't cooled down much."

"Are you the symbolic hat through the door, to see if I attack?"

"Not exactly. Dane got delayed for a few minutes, and we don't think you should be alone."

"Thanks for the concern."

"You don't sound sincere," he teased, but his lazy dark eyes were watchful.

"I was fired today," she retorted. "I don't feel like celebrating. Out of the goodness of their hearts, I'll be allowed to finish out the week."

He snorted. "I'd have walked out on them today."

"So would I, if that hadn't been exactly what they wanted. Do you want something cold to drink?"

"Only if it isn't alcoholic."

"I can manage that. Lemonade, fruit juice, tea, or soft drink?"

"Tea."

"Coming up. Smart man, not to drink and drive."

"I don't drink much anyway. It upsets my system," he drawled. He followed her into the kitchen. "Did you get settled in last night?"

"I wouldn't go that far. I got my things put away." She took two glasses out of the cabinet, dropped ice cubes in them, and filled them up with the tea she had brewed that morning before going to work. "Lemon?"

"No, thanks. I drink my tea straight."

She chuckled as they clinked glasses.

Trammell eyed her as he sipped the cold liquid. "Are you going to forgive him?"

She shrugged. "It wasn't the media ploy that upset me as much as realizing he 'trifled with my affections,' to use an old southern phrase."

"You really think he doesn't care anything for you?"

"If he does, he's never mentioned it. What hurts is that he

deliberately cultivated my feelings for him, and then used them to manipulate me."

"He can have tunnel vision when it comes to his work," Trammell said delicately. "Let's sit down."

"Are you going to plead his case?" she asked as they took chairs at the table.

"Not really, but I know Dane better than anyone else on earth, including you, including anyone in his family. They only grew up with him; you've only slept with him. I've risked my life with him. I know him from the ground up."

"Do you think he's capable of cold-bloodedly using someone in an investigation?"

"Of course he is. He's a cop. So am I. But he's never been cold-blooded where you're concerned. How can I put this without being crude?" he mused, looking at the ceiling. "Do you remember when you came to Bonness's office, and you and Dane all but went to war right then?"

She nodded.

"Well, to put it delicately, he had a boner so hard a cat couldn't scratch it."

Marlie choked on her tea, then fell back in the chair, shrieking with laughter. Trammell stretched out his long legs, as languorous as a cat, looking pleased with himself while he waited for her to calm down.

"He's my hero," he continued lazily after a moment. He wasn't looking at her now, but a tiny, rather self-mocking smile lurked around his mouth as he stared at the ice in his glass. "I didn't join the force out of idealism or anything like that; I was bored, and it seemed like an interesting job. Dane and I were paired after the first year, and we've been together ever since. I don't believe in much, or trust much, but Dane is a rock I can rely on no matter what. Not that he's idealistic, either. He's even more cynical than I am.

"But he's got a sense of right and wrong that he's never lost touch with. All I see are shades of gray, but Dane can see the black and white. He knows that there are certain things worth fighting for, and he's willing to put himself in the

front line. He's a gallant, heroic bastard, and he's never even conscious of it. He's an old-fashioned southern good old boy, the salt of the earth. He's street-smart, woods-savvy, and sly as a fox. A real throwback. Mean, too. Damn, can he be mean! But he turns to putty where women are concerned. We used to laugh at him, when he was still on patrol and had to work an accident. If there was a woman involved, it didn't matter if she was just holding her arm and a man was lying there bleeding from a dozen places; it was as if Dane never saw the guy. He'd go straight to the woman, make certain she was all right, so tender they'd be melting at his feet within a few minutes. It would embarrass him when he realized he'd left another man lying in the street, and we were all laughing at him."

"You don't have to tell me he has a good bedside manner," she said dryly.

"No, I don't suppose I do. But I've never before seen him the way he is with you. He's always had women, and not one of them ever meant enough to him to interfere with the job. Until you. He couldn't get you off his mind. You drove him crazy; you made him so angry he couldn't think. It was the most amusing thing I've seen in a couple of years. *He* may not know he's in love with you, but trust me, he won't let you go. I know him. If you walk out that door, he'll be right behind you."

She gave him an incredulous look. "How can a man not know if he's in love? Give me a break."

"Well, it's never happened to him before."

"Had it happened to *you,* before Grace?"

He looked uncomfortable. He swallowed, hard. "Uh, no."

"Did you recognize it?"

"Let's just say that I fought it."

"But you knew it was there. *I'd* never been in love before, either, but I knew what it was."

"Dane's more hardheaded than most."

"You're telling me," she muttered. "I can't read a thing from him."

Trammell gave a shout of laughter, but quickly sobered. He gave her an uneasy look. "Can you read me?"

She smirked at him, happy to see him squirm. "I haven't tried since I regained the ability."

"How about Grace?"

"I don't intrude on my friends," she said sternly.

"Psychic's Code of Honor, huh?"

"It wouldn't be polite. I've always had to try to block people out, rather than try to receive their feelings."

They heard a car door slam outside. "There's Dane," Trammell said, and drained his glass. "Think about it, Marlie. Give the guy a break, and save our sanity. It's been dangerous to talk to the man today."

"I'll consider your view of things," she said. "But my final decision depends on him." Until ten minutes ago, she had thought that she had already made her final decision, but Trammell's explanation that Dane was hardheaded had made her pause.

Dane walked in, looking hot and irritable. His gaze settled first on Marlie, with a sort of bad-tempered yearning, then on the tea they were drinking. He prepared a glass of tea for himself and sat down with a sigh. "It's been a bitch of a day."

"Tell me about it," Marlie said sweetly. "I got fired."

He stared at her for a moment, then dropped his head to the table in despair. "Shit."

"I'm out of here," Trammell said, smiling at Marlie. "See you in the morning, partner."

Dane didn't reply. Marlie sipped her tea. Trammell let himself out.

The silence in the kitchen became thick. Marlie said, "When this is over, I think I'll move back to Colorado."

Dane lifted his head. There was a pale cast to his tanned skin, and his mouth was compressed to a thin line. "No," he said, very softly.

She leaned back and crossed her arms. "What are you

going to do, threaten me with protective custody again? I don't think you can get away with that." She pushed her chair back and got up, then carried her glass to the sink.

She had just rinsed it out and placed it in the drainer when two hard hands closed on her arms and whirled her around. She drew back as far as she could, but the cabinets halted her retreat. He leaned heavily into her, his hips grinding against hers. His face was stark.

"I won't let you go," he muttered. "Damn it, Marlie, how can you even talk about leaving when we have this between us?"

"This?" she flared, wriggling her hips and feeling him get hard. "It's just sex."

"It's more than just sex, damn it!"

"Is it? From where I stand, that's all it's ever been," she taunted him, feeling him quiver with rage and enjoying it. Something fierce and hurt inside her wanted him to feel the pain as she had.

His hazel eyes went green as his control broke. "By God, if sex is all it is, then we might as well enjoy it," he said thickly as he swooped her into his arms.

Dizzily off balance, Marlie clung to him as he strode toward the bedroom. Her heartbeat was thundering wildly, blood surging through her veins. She wanted to hit him. She wanted to bite him. She wanted to tear his clothes off and hurl herself onto him. Love and anger and lust swirled together in a volatile mixture. Maybe they couldn't communicate with words just yet, the anger was too strong, but maybe their bodies could bridge the gap. When he roughly placed her on the bed, she reached up and grabbed his shirt and tugged, pulling him down on top of her.

In fierce silence they struggled together. His hard mouth bruised hers with the force of his kisses; she bit his lower lip, making him curse, then gently sucked at it. He tore the button off her shorts in his need to get her out of her clothes. She fought with his zipper, finally got it down, and hungrily

shoved her hand down the front of his briefs. His shaft filled her hand, hard and throbbing. The head of it was already wet.

He was breathing roughly, audibly, as he stripped her panties off and in the same movement rolled on top of her, kneeing her thighs apart. He drove into her with savage need, and she cried out at the rough penetration even as she coiled her legs around him.

Supper was forgotten in the long, heated hours that followed. The heat of sunset dimmed into twilight. At first, Dane made love to her with a furious intensity that held anger and resentment at the tension he had been under. Marlie was as fierce, biting him, digging her nails into him, slamming her hips upward to take him.

They didn't talk. That first wild lovemaking didn't allow room, or thought, for words. Afterward they lay together in silent exhaustion, their bodies still linked. The bond they had just reforged felt too new, too fragile, to allow for separation just yet. They dozed, and Marlie awoke some undetermined time later when he began making love to her again.

This time he was tender, lingering over her. He kissed the bruises his fierce grip had left on her silky skin, silently apologizing. She licked the crescents her nails had made on him. He rode her for a long time, slowing down whenever he felt his climax approaching, not yet ready to release the pleasure.

Both of them were acutely aware that he wasn't wearing a condom. He supported his weight on his forearms as he moved in and out of her, their gazes locked, and the knowledge was in their eyes. When he couldn't hold off his climax any longer, when she had already convulsed twice, she gripped his buttocks and pulled him deeper into her as he let it overtake him. He shuddered and bucked with the force of his pleasure as he jetted his semen into her.

Again, it wasn't time for words. Not yet. They slept again, entwined together, and twilight became dark.

Marlie woke first. Her body ached deliciously, and she felt the hunger growing for more of what had caused the ache. Dane still slept, but when she began caressing his shaft, both he and it stirred immediately. He rolled over onto his back and closed his arms around her as she slid on top of him.

"Stay with me," he whispered, and closed his eyes in delight at the way the hot silk of her body so snugly enveloped him.

She hesitated, then felt him throb within her. "All right," she whispered in return, and gently began to move. It wasn't much, but after the ferocity of their lovemaking, she didn't doubt his sincerity. He hadn't been a cop, trying to catch a killer; he had been simply a man, wild with need for his woman. He hadn't committed himself yet, at least not with words, but the bond of the flesh had reassured her. She could wait for the rest of it.

Carroll Janes had thought it over very carefully. He had to get the bitch alone, so that meant he had to get Detective Hollister to leave.

He didn't call 911, which would give the dispatcher the telephone number he'd called from. He called police headquarters directly.

He knew himself to be a very good actor. He was proud of the frantic tone of his voice when he said, "There's been a woman killed! There's been another—it's him! I swear to God it had to be him. Blood—she's cut everywhere! Butchered! I saw him leaving, bald head just like in that sketch!"

"Slow down, slow down," the authoritative voice said. "I can't understand you. Repeat that, please."

Janes drew in deep, audible breaths. "Another woman's been killed. I saw a bald man run. She's cut all to pieces, there's blood—" He made gagging noises in the phone.

"Calm down, sir. Where are you? Can you give me an address?"

Janes rattled off an address he had looked up, on the opposite side of town. He stumbled over the street and

numbers a couple of times to make it realistic. Then he hung up and waited.

He was at a phone booth two blocks from Detective Hollister's house.

The telephone rang. Dane snatched it up. After listening a minute, he said, "I'm on my way." He rolled out of bed and began pulling on his clothes.

Marlie raised herself on her elbow. "What?"

"Another murder," he said tersely. "They think it was him."

She shook her head. "No."

He paused, remembering. "That's right. You didn't feel anything, did you?"

"Not a thing. It wasn't him." She got out of bed and began dressing, too.

He sighed. "It's probably another copycat, damn it. I'm sorry, baby."

"It isn't your fault," she said. "You're on the task force; you have to go."

He pulled her into his arms, holding her tight against him. "I don't know how long I'll be gone."

She rubbed her face against his chest, enjoying the heated scent of him. "I'll watch television and wait up for you."

He tilted her face up and leaned down to kiss her. "If you happen to go to sleep, I'll wake you up."

"It's a deal."

"We have a lot to talk about," he said, determination in his voice.

"I know. Go!"

He started toward the door, then turned back. He pulled open the top drawer of the bedside table and took out a pistol. He checked it, made certain the chamber was full and that the safety was on. "Keep this handy. Do you know how to use it?"

She nodded. She wasn't exactly experienced, but she knew how a pistol worked. After all, she had lived alone in

the mountains; it had seemed only smart to teach herself the basics.

He kissed her again. "Okay. Be careful, keep the pistol with you, and don't open the door to strangers. I'll radio in and have a patrolman over to watch the house; one should be outside within five minutes. I'll call you when I'm on the way home, so you won't shoot me by mistake."

"I said I'll wait up for you," she said, smiling.

"A man can't be too careful. Or a woman," he added sternly.

"Gotcha."

He left, and she turned on the television, settling down on the couch to run through the channels and look for something interesting.

Dane had been gone for less than five minutes when she sat bolt upright, her heart pounding. A cold chill chased over her skin, roughening it. A powerful sense of alarm filled her.

She felt the blow of recognition as an image flashed through her mind, blotting out her own thought: black-gloved hands, one of them holding wire cutters, tugging at a group of wires.

She panted, trying to draw in enough oxygen from air that suddenly seemed to suffocate. Dear God, so he was striking after all! And Dane had left. Had the call been a false alarm, to draw them away, so the killer could get at Beverly? The policewoman would be all alone.

Marlie stumbled toward the phone. A vision flashed, halting her. In her mind, she saw the wire cutters biting through plastic and wire.

And the lights went out.

24

MARLIE FROZE, BLINDED BY THE SUDDEN DARKNESS, PARA-lyzed by terror and the crashing knowledge. He wasn't after Beverly, he was after her—*and he was right outside.*

She closed her eyes, squeezing them tight, trying to hurry her night vision. She should try to get out, but by which door, front or back? Or was he at a window? Which one? *Which one?*

—Gently he cut a screen, snipping the tiny strands one by one—

Desperately she fought off the vision. Oh, God, she wouldn't let herself be swamped by the vision. She would be helpless. But she had never been able to resist one for long, never been able to block it, or control it. They rolled over her like tidal waves.

—He knew she was in there. He could *feel* her, the bitch. He could already taste the triumph, the power—

"No," Marlie moaned in a whisper. Desperately she summoned up an image of the mental door she had learned

how to open and close. All she had to do was close it, and keep him on the other side.

—He'd see how smart she was when she felt the blade biting into her—

It was washing over her in black waves. The evil was so strong, she couldn't breathe. He was so close, the power of it was crushing her. She couldn't fight him off.

—The damn lock on the window wouldn't budge. White-hot fury roared through him at this delay. Snarling, he smashed his gloved fist into the glass—

She heard the crash and tinkle of breaking glass, but the vision was roaring through her, blotting out everything else, and she couldn't tell where it was coming from. It could have been right behind her, but he was sucking all the strength out of her, and she couldn't even turn around.

Dane. Oh, God, Dane! She didn't want him to have to see this.

As soon as he got into his car, Dane radioed in and told the dispatcher to send a patrol car to his house immediately.

"Ten-four," said the dispatcher. "It'll take ten, fifteen minutes, though. It's a busy night."

"Do it faster than that," Dane said, iron in his voice.

"I'll try. Depends on when a patrolman gets free."

Dane hesitated, reluctant to leave Marlie alone for that long, but his job was to be on the crime scene, copycat or not. The detectives who had worked the other scenes had to make the call, decide if it was the same perp. He had given her his pistol, and a patrolman would be there soon. She would be okay.

He told himself that for several miles, but finally pulled to the side of the street and stopped. This didn't feel right, damn it. Something was wrong. He felt a sense of dread that had grown stronger with each passing mile and minute, but he couldn't pin down the cause.

It was a copycat killing, no doubt about that. It wasn't

unusual; they had already had one. But something was *wrong*.

He keyed the mike. "Dispatch, this is Hollister. Has a patrolman gotten to my house yet?"

"Not yet. A car is on its way."

Frustration welled in him. "Any further information on that knifing that was just called in?"

"No further—wait." Dane listened to static, then dispatch came back on the air. "That's affirmative. A squad car is on the scene, and the patrolman just radioed in. It looks like a false alarm."

Dane's sense of dread increased. His mind raced as he went through the angles. "Dispatch, was it a male or a female who called in the initial report?"

"A male."

"Shit!" He keyed the mike again. "Dispatch, contact the stakeout immediately! Verify that everything is okay. The false alarm may have been deliberate."

"Affirmative. Stand by."

Dane waited tensely in the dark car, sweat rolling down his face. Within a minute his radio crackled. "No problems at the stakeout, Dane. Everything's as quiet as a graveyard."

He shook his head. There was trouble and he knew it. But where? *Where?*

The false alarm had been deliberate, in an effort to draw off Marlie's protection. But Beverly had taken Marlie's place, and the ploy hadn't worked—

He froze, horror exploding in his brain. It had worked all too well. Marlie!

More glass shattered as he punched the window again. Desperately Marlie pictured the door, pictured the vision pressing against it, all black, loathsome evil. She pictured herself shoving against the door, forcing it shut, closing out the vision. She had to control it; she would die if she didn't. Her only chance was to control it, as she had the knowing.

She was stronger now than she had been before. She could do it.

The pistol. It had been beside her on the couch. She opened her eyes and lurched in the direction of the couch, but the vision had already sapped her strength, and her legs gave way beneath her. She fell heavily to the floor, but her outstretched hand brushed the couch, and she forced herself to her hands and knees, crawling to it and groping along the cushions for the pistol.

There it was, cold and heavy, reassuring in her hand. With wildly trembling fingers she fumbled the safety off.

—He was in. It wouldn't be long now. The knife glinted in his hand, long and lethal, the blade honed to a razor's edge—

The door! Mentally she slammed it shut once more. Keep him out. She had to keep him out.

She could hear her own breath coming in strangled sobs. Quiet. She had to be quiet. Weakly she crawled toward the corner, to put a wall at her back so he couldn't come at her from behind. The darkness in the house was almost total, with the blinds closed. She had the advantage there; she knew the house, knew where she was. He had to hunt her. She had to be very, very quiet.

Keep the door closed.

But where was he? She couldn't hear over the roaring in her ears, deafened by the thunder of her own blood racing through her veins.

She used both hands to steady the heavy pistol. Dane. Dane, who never went anywhere unarmed. *Thank you, Dane, for this chance. I love you.*

Where was he?

She closed her eyes and mentally opened the door a crack.

—Where was she, the bitch? He could turn on the flashlight, but not yet, not yet. So she thought she could hide, did she? Didn't she know how much he enjoyed the chase? Of course she did. Sweet bitch. Was she in the

bathroom? He pushed the door open. The white fixtures gleamed in the darkness like enamel ghosts. No bitch here—

She slammed the door. She could feel the pressure of his mental energy, pushing against her. She opened her eyes and forced herself to look toward the hall where the bathroom was. *Don't stare, Marlie. Don't let yourself stare. You won't see him if you do. Keep your eyes moving, don't let them fix. You'll see his movement.*

Was that him? Was that a darker shadow, coming toward her? She didn't dare open the door again, not now. If it was him, he was too close. He would be on her before she could react. But was he really there, or was it her imagination?

A bright light exploded in her face, blinding her, and a ghastly voice crooned, "Well, hellooo there."

She pulled the trigger.

Several cars converged on the house almost simultaneously. Dane had given orders for them to go in with lights flashing and siren blaring, hoping against hope that they would be in time and scare him off. He drove like a maniac, praying as he had never prayed before. He didn't care if they missed this chance to catch him. *Please, God, let them scare him off. Don't let him be in the house. Don't let him have already been and gone. God, please. Not Marlie.*

He slammed the gear into park, the car rocking violently on its springs. He was out and running before the motion stopped. The house was dark. *God, no.*

Something heavy hit Dane in the back, sending him sprawling on the ground. He rolled to his feet with a savage snarl, his fist drawn back. Trammell picked himself up, as fast as Dane, and grabbed his arm. "Get control of yourself!" Trammell roared, his face as savage as Dane's. "You won't help her by going in blind! Do it the way you know it's supposed to be done!"

Uniformed officers were swarming around the house, surrounding it. All Dane could think of was Marlie inside. He shook Trammell off and plunged at the door. It was

locked. He threw himself at it like a maddened animal, the force of his weight making it shudder in the frame. It was a solid door, reinforced with steel. The dead-bolt lock was one of the best made. It held. The hinges didn't. The screws ripped out of the wood with a tortured shriek, metal twisting.

Seeing he couldn't stop Dane, Trammell added his considerable strength to the task, and helped him wrench the door out of the frame. Hoarsely screaming Marlie's name, Dane pitched himself into the dark bowels of the house.

He stumbled over something soft and heavy, and crashed to the floor. His heart stopped beating, for a long, agonized moment that froze in time.

"Oh, God," he said, the voice not recognizable as his. "Get a light."

One of the patrol officers took his long, heavy flashlight out of his belt and thumbed the switch. The powerful beam illuminated Dane, crouched on the floor with a look of frozen horror on his face, and Trammell, who looked almost as bad. In the center of the beam sprawled a black-clad figure, the shaven skull gleaming dully. He was on his back, and his sightless eyes stared upward. The stench of blood and death was overpowering. A black pool of blood had gathered around the body.

"Dane." The almost soundless whisper raised the hairs on their arms. "Dane, I'm here."

The flashlight beam swung wildly toward the corner, and Marlie flinched from the light, closing her eyes and turning her head away. Dark wetness glistened on the white of her shirt. She still held the pistol, both hands clasped around it.

Dane couldn't manage to get to his feet. He crawled to her, his mind still unable to believe that she was alive. He cupped her cheek in a shaking hand, and smoothed her hair back from her face. "Baby. Oh, God, honey."

"He cut me," she said, as if apologizing. "I shot him, but he didn't stop. He just kept coming. So I kept shooting."

"Good," he said with barely restrained savagery. His

hands were trembling wildly, but with the utmost tenderness he lowered her to the floor. "Just lie down, honey. Let me see how bad you're hurt."

"I don't think it's serious," she said judiciously. "It's the top of my shoulder, and my left side. But it's just cuts; he didn't stab me."

He was barely holding himself together. Only the knowledge that she needed him now kept him from throwing himself on the body and tearing it to pieces. God! This was the second time in her life a madman had attacked her with a knife. How could she be so calm, when he was shaking apart?

"He cut the wiring," she was saying. Suddenly she sounded exhausted. "I'm very tired. If you don't mind, I'll tell you all about it later."

"Sure, baby." He pressed the heel of his palm over the oozing cut in her side. "Go to sleep. I'll be with you when you wake up."

She gave a little sigh, and her heavy eyelids closed. Dane was aware of the house filling with people, but he didn't look up.

"Dane." It was Trammell, kneeling beside him. "The medics are here, buddy. You need to move back so they can help her."

"I'm stopping the bleeding," he said in a hoarse voice.

"I know. It's almost stopped. She's going to be all right, partner. Everything's going to be okay." Trammell wrapped his arms around him, easing him away from Marlie. The medics moved to take his place. "We'll go to the hospital with her, but she's going to be fine. I promise."

Dane closed his eyes and let Trammell lead him away.

"I really do feel well enough to go home," Marlie said the next morning. She yawned. "It's just that I'm tired from fighting off the vision."

"And from loss of blood," Dane said. "Maybe tomorrow."

She was propped up in bed, and except for the thickness of the bandages on top of her shoulder and at her waist, it was difficult to tell there was anything wrong with her, though to Dane's critical eye she was still far too pale.

He had been at the hospital with her all night. If he lived to be a hundred and fifty, he'd never forget the absolute, bone-chilling terror of those minutes when he had realized that he had been lured away, and left Marlie unprotected. It had taken him a lifetime to get back to her, and cost him another lifetime in the effort to get into the house. The hospital had been a zoo, with cops everywhere and reporters fighting to get in to talk to Marlie, and Dane had been totally unable to cope with it. All he had been able to do, once the doctors had let him get to her again, was hold her hand and try to reassure himself that she was really all right.

Trammell had taken over; he had handled the reporters, categorically denying them access to Marlie's room but promising a news conference later in the morning. He had deflected Bonness and Chief Champlin away from Dane. He had called Grace, who had brought fresh clothes and toiletries for both Dane and Marlie. Dane had showered and shaved, but the haggard lines in his face revealed the toll the night had taken on him. If it hadn't been for Trammell, he wouldn't have made it through the night.

Trammell had been there for most of the night, too, but he had left around dawn and just returned. He was impeccably dressed, as always, though he, too, showed the signs of a sleepless night. Grace had remained with them.

Marlie pressed the button that moved the head of the bed to a more upright position. She truly did feel well enough to go home; the cuts were sore, and she had to be careful when she moved, but all in all she wasn't in any undue pain. She was alive. The heavy sense of evilness that had been pressing down on her for weeks was gone. The sun seemed brighter, the air fresher.

"I've told you everything that happened last night," she

said. "Now I want to know what you've found out this morning."

Dane smiled at her reassuringly normal tone. "Don't look at me. I haven't left this place. I don't know anything."

Grace stretched out her long legs. "Yes, Alex, spill your guts."

Trammell propped himself against the windowsill. "We found his car about two blocks away, and ran the license plate. His name was Carroll Janes; he moved here from Pittsburgh about five months ago. Pittsburgh PD have several unsolved murders that fit the bill. We searched his apartment and found a blond wig he evidently wore all the time, except when he was killing. He worked at Danworth's department store, in customer service. Evidently that's how he picked his victims. If anyone gave him a hard time— bingo."

"That was the tie," Dane murmured. "They all shopped at Danworth's. I remember Jackie Sheets's friend saying that she had been upset about a blouse that came apart, or something like that. God, it was right there in front of me. I even thought that they shopped at the same place, but that just about everyone in the city did, too."

"Don't beat yourself up over it," Marlie advised tartly. "You aren't clairvoyant, you know." After a startled second, he chuckled. He was looking better, she decided, that stark look fading as he recovered from the shock.

"Carroll Janes," Grace said. "That's a strange name for a man."

"No joke. That's why we didn't turn him up on those lists we were running. His name was crossed out because it looked like a woman's name." Trammell sounded disgusted at that oversight. "We don't have much background on him yet. We may never know what made him tick. I don't know if it even matters. A subhuman son of a bitch like that doesn't deserve to live."

Marlie saw Dane flinch. He was having a harder time handling the night's events than she was. He deeply regret-

ted that she had been touched by such ugly violence, but in an odd way she felt stronger. She wasn't elated that she had killed a man, but neither was she consumed by guilt. She had done what was necessary. If she had hesitated, she would be dead now. She had controlled the vision, and this time she had won. Carroll Janes was dead; Marilyn Elrod and Nadine Vinick and Jackie Sheets, and all of the other women he had killed, finally had their justice.

Dane picked up her hand and played with her fingers, his eyes closing as he felt again the overwhelming relief that she was all right.

Grace elbowed Trammell. "We have to go now," she said. "I have to get ready for work."

"I'll be back this afternoon," Trammell added. "Call me if you need me before then."

"Okay," Dane agreed. After they left, he walked to the door and leaned out to get the attention of the uniformed officer who stood guard there. "No visitors," he said. "Not even the mayor. No one."

"I may have trouble keeping the docs out, Hollister," the officer warned.

"Well, maybe them. But knock first." He closed the door and went back to Marlie's bedside. He stroked her face, smoothed her hair.

She reached up and touched his cheek. "I really am all right. And I'd much rather be at home than here."

He turned his head to kiss her fingers. "Just be patient, okay? If the doctor wants to watch you for another twenty-four hours, he must have a reason. Let me be certain you're okay before you leave. I need that."

There was naked emotion in his face. Dane was wide open, not bothering to guard himself. After what he had been through, he would never again try to control his feelings for her. He had almost lost her the night before; life was too short, too uncertain, to do anything but live it to the fullest.

His expression was serious as he smoothed her hair away

from her face. "We didn't finish getting things ironed out between us last night."

"No, everything got a little hectic there, didn't it?"

"Are you still mad at me?"

A little smile curved her mouth. "No."

"I swear to God I didn't string you along just to stay on top of the situation. The only thing I thought about being on top of was you."

She snorted. "Gosh, that's romantic." But the smile remained.

"I don't know how to be romantic. All I know is I want you, and I can't let you go. I've never run into this type of situation before, so I probably messed up in the way I handled it. I wanted to take my time, see how things developed. I didn't want to rush you, or put pressure on you while all of this other mess was going on. You had enough to worry about."

She bit her lip, bemused by his words. Ye gods, maybe Trammell was right; maybe Dane really was too hardheaded to know when he was in love, or that a woman would reasonably expect him to say so. She took a deep breath, conscious of how much she wanted everything to go right this time. Maybe he wasn't the only one who had been a little too cautious; maybe she needed to encourage him more.

"Is sex all you want?" she asked, tension invading her as she waited for his answer.

"Hell, no!" he said explosively. "Honey, tell me what *you* need. I can do something about it if you'll tell me, but don't leave me in the dark like this. What can I do to convince you of how I feel about you?"

She drew back in the hospital bed, giving him an incredulous look. "Convince me? Dane, you've never told me to begin with! I don't have any idea how you feel!"

It was his turn to stare incredulously. "What the hell do you mean, you don't have any idea how I feel?"

She rolled her eyes beseechingly toward the heavens.

"Lord help me, the man's as thick as a tree. How am I supposed to know if you don't tell me? I've told you time and again that I can't read you! Say it in plain English, Dane. Do you love me? That's what I need to know."

"Of course I love you!" he roared, his temper flashing.

"Then *say* so!"

"I love you, damn it!" He surged to his feet and stood over her bed, hands on hips. "What about you? Are we in this together, or am I soloing?"

She thought of punching him, but decided not to put that much strain on her stitches. She contented herself with saying, "No, you aren't soloing."

"Then *say* it!"

"I love you, damn it!" She said it just as belligerently as he had.

His chest heaved with the force of his breathing as they faced each other down in silence. Finally the tension eased out of his coiled muscles. "That's settled, then." He sat down again.

"What's settled?" she challenged.

"That I love you and you love me."

"So what do we do? Call a truce?"

He shook his head and picked up her hand again. "What we do is get married." He pressed a kiss to her fingertips. "We aren't going to wait six months, either, like some people I know. It'll probably be this weekend. No longer than a week."

Marlie's breath caught, and a luminous smile broke over her face like sunrise. "I'm sure we can manage it by this weekend," she said.

He wanted to fold her in his arms, but he was too afraid of hurting her. He looked at her, and was amazed at how calm she was. She had been stalked by a killer, had emptied a pistol into him, and she seemed so . . . peaceful. Not even getting engaged had shaken that serenity.

He began shaking, as he had several times that night. "I'm sorry," he blurted, for the fifteenth time, his expression

telling her where his thoughts had gone. "God, baby, I messed up bad. I never intended for you to be in danger. I don't know how he found you."

Her blue eyes were even more bottomless than usual. "Maybe it was meant. Maybe it was my fault that he found me. I should have gone to a safe house. Maybe, at the end, he could sense me the way I could sense him. Maybe I was the only one who had a chance against him, because I could tell where he was, what he was doing. There are too many maybes; we'll never know for certain. But I'm *okay,* Dane, in every way."

"I love you. When I thought he had you—" His voice cracked. Suddenly he couldn't stand it. With exquisite care he gathered her up in his arms and lifted her from the bed, then sat down and cradled her on his lap, his face buried in her hair.

"I know. I love you too." She didn't protest that the action jarred her shoulder, or that he was holding her too tightly for comfort. She needed that contact, the security and warmth of his embrace. She nestled against him. "Dane?"

"Hmmm?"

"There is one thing."

He raised his head. "What?"

"Are you certain you want to marry me?"

"Damn right I am. What brought this on?"

"I know how uncomfortable it makes you that I am what I am. And I can't marry you without telling you everything. I've pretty much recovered all my abilities. In fact, I'm better at it than I was before, because now I can control it."

He didn't hesitate. The only way to have Marlie was to take her as she was, psychic abilities and all. "But you can't read *me* at all, right?"

"Nope. You're the most thickheaded man I've ever seen. It's *such* a relief."

He grinned, and brushed a kiss across her temple. "It

wouldn't make any difference anyway. I'm going to marry you, no matter what."

"But I *can* check up on you," she admitted. "If you have a bad day, you won't be able to hide it from me, the way cops usually do with their wives. There won't be any tucking it away in a corner of your mind, because I'll already know what happened."

"I can live with that." Easily, he realized. At this point he could probably live with her even if she were a card-carrying swami and rode a magic carpet. "If you can handle being a cop's wife, I can be a psychic's husband. What the hell; how rough can it be?"

Epilogue

D<small>ANE ROLLED OUT OF BED, LOOKED AT</small> M<small>ARLIE,</small> <small>TURNED</small> green, and dashed for the bathroom. She propped herself up on her elbow, considering the situation with mild disbelief. "I'm the one who's pregnant," she called. "Why are you having morning sickness?"

He came out of the bathroom several minutes later, still rather pale. "One of us has to," he said. He groaned and collapsed on the bed. "I don't think I can make it in to work today."

She nudged him with her foot. "Sure you can. Just eat some dry toast and you'll feel better. You know Trammell will tease you if you don't show up."

"He already does." Dane's voice was muffled in the pillow. "The only thing that keeps him from telling everyone else is that I know something just as bad about him. We have each other in a Mexican standoff."

She threw back the covers and got out of bed. She felt wonderful. She had been queasy a little at first, but never quite to the point of throwing up, and that had soon passed.

For her, that is. Dane was still throwing up regularly, every morning, though it was just past New Year's and she was now six months along. He was paying the price for getting her pregnant immediately after their wedding.

"I wonder how you're going to handle labor and delivery," she mused aloud, giving him a wicked look.

He groaned. "I don't want to think about it."

He didn't handle it at all well. As a labor coach, he was a complete washout. From the time her pains started, he was in agony. The nurses loved him. They installed him on a cot next to her, so he could hold her hand; it seemed to give him comfort. He was pale and sweating, and every time she had a contraction, he had one too.

"This is wonderful," one older nurse said, watching him with joy. "If only all the fathers could do this. There may be justice in this world, after all."

Marlie patted his hand. She was ready for this to be over, even if the price was these steadily increasing pains that were now threatening to become very serious indeed. She felt heavy and exhausted, and the pressure in her pelvis threatened to tear her apart, but a part of her was still able to marvel at her husband. And *she* was supposed to be empathic! Dane had suffered through every month, every pain, with her; she wondered just how labor pains felt in a man.

"Oh, God, here comes another one," he groaned, gripping her hand, and sure enough, her belly began to tighten. She fell back, gasping, trying to find the crest of the pain and ride it.

"This is going to be an only child," he panted. "There won't be another one, I swear. God, when is he going to get here?"

"Soon," she answered. She could feel the deep, heavy tightening within. Their son would arrive soon.

He did, within half an hour. Dane wasn't able to be there during delivery; the doctor had been forced to give him a

sedative to ease his pain. But when Marlie woke up from an exhausted doze, he was sitting in the chair beside her bed, looking pale and exhausted himself, and he was holding the baby.

His rough face broke into a grin. "It was rough," he said, "but we did it. He's great. He's perfect. But he's still going to be an only child."